PRAISE FOR *THE STORMCALLER*

"It gallops along with scarcely a dull moment."
   Lisa Tuttle, *Times* (London)

"A fantasy with the same magnificence of conception, the same sense of looming presences whose purposes are not ours to apprehend. Fragments of old stories that stud and sometimes drive his narrative are not just there as decoration or machinery. They are there to make this world seem deeper and darker than Lloyd's gloom-ridden narrative allows."
   Time Out

"*Stormcaller*'s magical land is far from the cosy backwater we've become so used to of late. A pretty confident first novel."
   Dreamwatch

"The world that Lloyd has created seems much more real than that of most fantasy books. He has created a fantasy world that has believable politics and is inhabited by large numbers of ordinary people. . . ."
   Emerald City

THE
TWILIGHT
HERALD

ALSO BY TOM LLOYD

THE STORMCALLER

BOOK ONE OF THE TWILIGHT REIGN

THE
TWILIGHT
HERALD

BOOK TWO OF THE
TWILIGHT REIGN

TOM LLOYD

an imprint of **Prometheus Books**
Amherst, NY

Published 2009 by Pyr®, an imprint of Prometheus Books

Inquiries should be addressed to
Pyr
59 John Glenn Drive
Amherst, New York 14228–2119
VOICE: 716–691–0133, ext. 210
FAX: 716–691–0137
WWW.PYRSF.COM

13 12 11 10 09   5 4 3 2 1

Library of Congress Cataloging-in-Publication Data

Lloyd, Tom, 1979–
        The twilight herald / by Tom Lloyd.
            p. cm. — (Twilight reign ; bk. 2)
        Originally published: London : Gollancz, an imprint of the Orion Publishing Group, 2007.
        ISBN 978–1–59102–733–1 (pbk. : alk. paper)
        I. Title.

PR6112.L697T87 2009
823'.92—dc22

                                                                        2008054564

Printed in the United States on acid-free paper

Dramatis Personæ

Aftal, Voss—High Priest of Nartis in Tirah

Ajel, Lord—Yeetatchen nobleman, father of Xeliath

Alterr—Goddess of the Night Sky and Greater Moon and member of the Upper Circle of the Pantheon

Amavoq—Goddess of the Forest, patron of the Yeetatchen and member of the Upper Circle of the Pantheon

Amber—nickname of a Menin major in the Cheme Third Legion

Anarie—Goddess of Calm Glades, an Aspect of Amavoq

Ansayl, Jachen, Major—Farlan officer assigned to the rangers

Antern, Count Opess—advisor to King Emin

Aracnan—immortal wanderer of unknown origin

Aras, Count Lurip—nobleman from Scree

Aryn Bwr—battle name of the last Elven king, who led their rebellion against the Gods. His true name has been excised from history

Atro—Lord of the Farlan tribe before Lord Bahl

Azaer—a shadow

Bahl—Lord of the Farlan tribe before Lord Isak

Belarannar—God of the Earth and member of the Upper Circle of the Pantheon

Bern, Jopel—High Priest of Death in Tirah

Beyn, Ignas—member of the Brotherhood

Bohreq (The Herdfather)—Aspect of Vrest, God of Beasts

Breytech—a Chetse trader

Brohm—a thug from Scree

Burning Man, the—one of the five Aspects of Death known as the Reapers

Carel (Carelfolden), Marshal Betyn—Farlan nobleman and commander of Lord Isak's Personal Guard

Cerdin—God of Thieves

Certinse, Knight-Cardinal Horel—Commander of the Knights of the Temples, younger brother of Suzerain Tildek, Farlan by birth

Certinse, Cardinal Varn—Farlan cleric. Third son of the Tildek Suzerainty, younger brother of Suzerain Tildek, Knight-Cardinal Certinse and Duchess Lomin

Certinse, Duke Karlat—Farlan nobleman, ruler of Lomin, nephew of Suzerain Tildek

Cetarn, Shile—a Narkang mage in the employ of King Emin

Cetess, Pirlo—an artist native to Scree, one of King Emin's agents

Chalat—deposed Lord of the Chetse

Charr—deceased Lord of the Chetse, Krann to Lord Chalat

Chirialt, Dermeness—Farlan mage

Chotech, General—Chetse general of the Knights of the Temples

Coran—white-eye bodyguard of King Emin

Corci, Prior—see Jackdaw

Corlyn, the—traditional name adopted by the head of the Farlan's priest branch of the Cult of Nartis

Cytt, Lord—deceased Menin white-eye Krann

Daughters of Meqao—minor Aspects of Amavoq

Death—the Chief of the Gods

Dedev, Borl—Farlan ranger assigned to Lord Isak's Personal Guard

Derl, Major Parr—soldier from Canar Thrit, member of the Knights of the Temples

Dev, General Chate—Chetse general and Commander of the Ten Thousand

Disten, Cardinal—Farlan cleric, once a legion chaplain

Doranei, Ashin—a member of the Brotherhood

Doren, Abbot—Abbot of an island monastery and High Priest of Vellern, God of Birds

Dupres, Syen—Farlan servant, steward to Suzerain Foleh

Echat, Tachrenn Chor—Chetse legion-commander of the Ten Thousand

Echer, High Cardinal—Farlan cleric, leader of the cardinal branch of the Cult of Nartis

Ehla—the common name Lord Isak is permitted to use for the witch of Llehden

Elierl, General Brinn—deceased Farlan general, once commander of the Lomin armies

Endine, Tomal—mage in the employ of King Emin

Eperal—Aspect of Ilit

Erizol (the fire-raiser)—Shaman from an extinct tribe in the Elven Waste, now a Raylin mercenary

Erwillen (the High Hunter)—Aspect of Verllern, God of Birds, and Aspect-Guide of Abbot Doren

Farlan, Kasi—Farlan prince during the Great War, in whose image white-eyes were created and after whom the lesser moon was named

Fedei, Wisten—the Seer of Ghorent

Fernal—a Demi-God living in Llehden

Fershin, Horman—Farlan wagon-driver, father to Lord Isak

Flitter—Raylin mercenary

Foleh, Suzerain Shoqe—Farlan nobleman

Fordan, Suzerain Karad—Farlan nobleman

Galasara—Elven poet from before the Great War

Gaur, General—hybrid warrior from the Elven Waste, general of the Menin armies and advisor to Lord Styrax

Gort, General Jebehl—general of the Knights of the Temples

Grast, Deverk—former Lord of the Menin

Great Wolf, the—one of the five Aspects of Death known as the Reapers

Grepel of the Hearths—Aspect of Tsatach

Haipar the shapeshifter—Raylin mercenary of the Deneli tribe from the Elven Waste

Headsman, the—one of the five Aspects of Death known as the Reapers

Helras—Farlan monk

Herald of Death—Aspect of Death

Hobble—Farlan monk

Ial—Aspect of Ilit

Ilit—God of the Wind, patron of the Litse tribe and member of the Upper Circle of the Pantheon

Ilumene—a former member of the Brotherhood

Introl, Tila—advisor to Lord Isak

Ironskin, Tachos—Raylin mercenary of Chetse origin

Isak—Lord of the Farlan, Chosen of Nartis and Duke of Tirah

Jackdaw (Prior Corci)—former monk of Vellern

Jeil—Farlan ranger assigned to Lord Isak's Personal Guard

Jesters, the—Demi-Gods and Raylin mercenaries, sons of Death

Karkarn—God of War, patron of the Menin tribe

Kehla (of the Dawn Light)—an Aspect of Tsatach

Kelet, Sir Veyan—Farlan nobleman and Ascetite

Kels, Abbot—Farlan cleric, head of an abbey in Saroc

Keneg—Menin soldier of the Cheme Third Legion

Kenn, Shuel—Merchant from Scree and Farlan agent

Kerin, Swordmaster Orayn—Commander of the Swordmasters and Knight-Defender of Tirah

Kitar—Goddess of Harvest and Fertility, member of the Upper Circle of the Pantheon

Lady, the—Fate, Goddess of Luck

Lahk, General—Farlan white-eye, commander of the forces in Tirah

Larat—God of Magic & Manipulation, member of the Upper Circle of the Pantheon

Larim, Shotein—Menin white-eye mage, Krann to Lord Salen and Chosen of Larat

Lecha, Tachrenn Erach—Chetse legion-commander of the Ten Thousand

Leferna, Priata—member of the White Circle, leader of the uprising in Tor Milist

Legana—Farlan devotee of the Lady, employed as an assassin and spy

Lehm, Suzerain Preter—Farlan nobleman

Lehm, Countess Rais—Farlan noblewoman

Lesarl, Chief Steward Fordan—principal advisor to the Lord of the Farlan

Leshi—Farlan Ascetite soldier

Leteil, Lord—white-eye Lord of the Yeetatchen tribe and Chosen of Amavoq

Macove, Count Perel—Farlan nobleman and member of the Brethren of the Sacred Teachings

Malich, Cordein—deceased necromancer from Embere

Mariq, Shan—Farlan battle-mage

Matak Snakefang—Raylin mercenary

Mayel—a novice from Abbot Doren's monastery, native of Scree

Mehar, Lieutenant Garap—aide to General Gort of the Knights of the Temples

Meqao (Hunter of the Silent Wood)—Aspect of Amavoq

Mihn ab Netren ab Felith—failed Harlequin, now friend of Lord Isak

Mikiss, Koden—Menin army messenger

Mistress—Raylin mercenary

Mochyd, High Chaplain—Farlan cleric. High Chaplain of the Farlan, head of the Chaplain branch of the Cult of Nartis

Morghien—a drifter of Embere descent, known as the man of many spirits

Nai—manservant to Isherin Purn, the necromancer

Nartis—God of the Night, Storms and Hunters. Patron of the Farlan tribe and member of the Upper Circle of the Pantheon

Nelbove, Suzerain Atar—Farlan nobleman

Nerlos, Suzerain Jai—Farlan nobleman

Nostil, Queen Valije—Aryn Bwr's queen, first owner of the Skull of Dreams

Nostil, Prince Velere—Aryn Bwr's heir, first owner of the Skull of Ruling

Ortof-Greyl, Colonel Harn—member of the Knights of the Temples

Panro—Zhia Vukotic's manservant

Portin, Prior—Farlan cleric, prior of an abbey in Saroc

Purn, Isherin—Menin necromancer once apprenticed to Cordein Malich

Quistal, General—Centaur tribal chief and general of the Menin armies

Rojak—Minstrel originally from Embere, first among Azaer's disciples

Roqinn—Farlan white-eye cleric, High Priest of Belarannar in Tirah

Salen—Menin Lord of the Hidden Tower and Chosen of the God Larat

Saljin Man, the—daemon sent to plague the Vukotic tribe

Saroc, Suzerain Fir—Farlan nobleman and member of the Brethren of the Sacred Teachings

Sebe—member of the Brotherhood

Seliasei—minor Aspect of Vasle that now inhabits Morghien

Selsetin, Suzerain Pelan—Farlan nobleman

Shalstik—Elven oracle who predicted the return of the last king

Shandek—a criminal from Scree

Shart—Menin soldier of the Cheme Third Legion

Sheln, Brother-Captain Tanao—a member of the Brethren of the Sacred Teachings

Shinir—a Farlan Ascetite agent

Shotir—God of Healing and Forgiveness

Shyn—criminal from Scree

Siala, Mistress Fora—ruler of Helrect and Scree, member of the White Circle

Soldier, the—one of the five Aspects of Death known as the Reapers

Spider—crime-lord of Scree

Styrax, Kastan—white-eye Lord of the Menin and Chosen of Karkarn

Styrax, Kohrad—white-eye son of Lord Styrax

Styrax, Duchess Selar—white-eye mage, wife of Lord Styrax and mother of Kohrad

Tael, Sergeant-at-Arms—Farlan soldier

Teviaq—Demi-God, Raylin mercenary and daughter of Amavoq

Thonal, King Emin—King of Narkang.

Thonal, Queen Oterness—Queen of Narkang

Tildek, Suzerain Esh—Farlan nobleman. Elder brother of Knight-Cardinal Certinse; his sister, Karlat's mother, was married to the Duke of Lomin

Tiniq—Farlan ranger and brother of General Lahk

Torl, Suzerain Karn—Farlan nobleman

Tremal, Harlo—member of the Brotherhood

Triena—Goddess of Romantic Love and Fidelity, part of the linked Goddesses who together cover all the aspects of love

Tsatach—God of Fire and the Sun, patron of the Chetse tribe

Ushell—Goddess of the Mountains, Aspect of Belarannar

Vasle—God of Rivers and Inland Seas

Veck, Cardinal—Farlan cleric, second only to the High Cardinal

Veil—member of the Brotherhood

Vellern—God of Birds

Vener, Telith—General of the Knights of the Temples and ruler of Raland

Veren—first God of the Beasts, killed during the Great War

Verliq, Arasay—celebrated mage and academic, killed by Lord Styrax

Vesna, Count Evanelial—famous Farlan soldier from Anvee

Vrerr, Duke Sarole—ruler of Tor Milist

Vrest—God of Beasts

Vrill, Duke Anote—Menin white-eye general

Vukotic, Prince Koezh—ruler of the Vukotic tribe, cursed with vampirism after the Last Battle

Vukotic, Prince Vorizh—younger brother of Koezh, cursed with vampirism after the Last Battle and subsequently driven insane

Vukotic, Princess Zhia—youngest of the Vukotic family, cursed with vampirism after the Last Battle

Wither Queen, the—one of the five Aspects of Death known as the Reapers

Woren, Private Merir—soldier from Scree, member of the Knights of the Temples

Xeliath—Yeetatchen white-eye who has the Skull of Dreams fused to her hand

WHAT HAS GONE BEFORE:
THE STORMCALLER

ISAK IS A WHITE-EYE, an unnaturally strong and fast young man with a reputation for being hot-tempered and troublesome. His unpredictable and dangerous nature means he has grown up as an outcast on the wagon train where his father, Horman, works. Isak's only real friend is Carel, the captain of the guards and former soldier. When a strange mercenary called Aracnan meets them on the road and demands Isak go with him to pursue his future, Isak refuses. Aracnan instead goes ahead of them to Tirah, capital city of the Farlan tribe, and informs Lord Bahl, another white-eye, that Isak has been appointed his heir by the Gods.

Contrary to tradition, Isak has to be summoned to the palace rather than brought by Aracnan. On the way the drunken hostility of his father and the other wagon train drivers turns into outright violence and Isak is chased there, killing a man in his escape. Barely making it to the palace alive, he is taken in and fed while Lord Bahl attends to matters of state. Bahl's chief steward, Lesarl, tells him first that the traditional gifts from the Gods for every one of the Chosen are not to be handed straight to Isak and have been put somewhere safe away from Bahl also, the lure of them being thought too great for any white-eye. The gifts are Siulents and Eolis, the armour and sword of the last and greatest elven king, Aryn Bwr, and are considered the finest and most powerful mortal-made weapons ever created.

Lesarl also mentions the journal of a necromancer, Cordein Malich, who almost sparked a civil war within the Farlan. Lord Bahl had ordered him to have the journal deciphered despite its heretical nature due to his interest in a powerful artefact mentioned within: a Crystal Skull, also created by Aryn Bwr. When Isak meets Lord Bahl he faints, overwhelmed by the memory of a recurring dream in which Bahl, a man he's never met, is killed fighting an unknown knight on a distant island. When he wakes he is told of his new standing in life and given a room to sleep in. Overnight Isak dreams of their patron God, Nartis, who begins to make his newest servant even bigger and stronger than a normal man, but again things don't go exactly as they should with a mysterious light burning the elven rune, Xeliath, meaning "heart," onto his chest.

Isak is woken by Bahl and sent to begin his weapons training, but his white-eye temper flares and he ends up in a practice duel with a nobleman, Dirass Certinse, who, against all reason, tries to kill Isak. Isak reacts to that the only way a white-eye can; he kills the man. Afterwards it transpires that Certinse is a member of the tribe's most powerful family, one heavily implicated in the Malich rebellion, but Bahl is more concerned with why nothing is following a normal course in Isak's life. This fear is increased when Isak receives another gift, this time from the Goddess Fate, when his crest, a crowned dragon, is revealed to have been prepared long before Isak was even Chosen. During this time, Isak becomes close friends with his maid, Tila. However, death follows Isak when he inexplicably manages to kill a high priest of the God of Magic called to investigate why Isak has latent magical power but cannot use it.

To the southeast, the lord of the Menin tribe, Kastan Styrax, has travelled in secret to attack the city of Raland and take the Crystal Skull Lord Bahl was seeking, but Bahl has no time to do anything about it as an elven army invades the eastern Farlan lands. Bahl sends an army under Isak's command to meet the threat, at last giving Isak his weapons and introducing him to the dragon that watches over them, Genedel. The army marches off, gathering troops and noblemen along the way, including the popular hero Count Vesna, with whom he swiftly becomes friends, and Duke Certinse, the new head of the rebellious Certinse family.

Isak fares well in the battle thanks to his burgeoning strength, narrowly avoiding assassination that morning, but it is only Bahl's sudden arrival with Genedel that wins it for them. However, before Bahl's appearance, Isak loses himself in his newly found magic, going berserk on the field before passing out. He wakes a few days later to discover that the elven army was seeking the weapons he carried to fulfill a prophecy heralding Aryn Bwr's return. In the meantime, to the south, the lord of the desert-dwelling Chetse tribe, Chalat, is deposed by his Chosen heir who has been possessed by a daemon. Chalat heads north with a foreigner called Mihn, hoping to ask Lord Bahl for help. Meanwhile, far to the northeast, the mercenary Aracnan visits an old acquaintance, the immortal vampire Koezh Vukotic, to share his fears that Isak is destined to be the Saviour spoken of in the prophecy. The pair travel west to ensure they will have a hand in unfolding events.

Returning to Tirah, Isak is reunited with his friend, Carel, who is made commander of his personal guard and is sent west to Narkang by Lord Bahl, both to forge an alliance with its ruler, King Emin, and to distance him from future attempts on his life by the defeated elves. Taking Mihn, Tila, Count Vesna, and Carel with him, Isak goes as ordered, meeting a strange wanderer called Morghien on the way. Morghien says he has been sent by a white-eye girl called Xeliath to prepare Isak for a threat in his future, after which Xeliath herself visits Isak in his dreams.

Bound up in the same prophecies as Isak, Xeliath was Chosen by her patron Goddess, told she was destined to be Isak's queen, and given a Crystal Skull as a gift. When her destiny was bound to Isak's, the tangled mess of prophecy around him nearly broke her mind and damaged her both physically and mentally. Isak also begins to realise that his fears of something watching him from the shadows might not be just fancy.

Back in the south, Kastan Styrax oversees preparations to invade Chetse lands now that Chalat has fled, while he himself travels to await Lord Bahl, who he has lured away from his army. On the way he talks to the daemon he has made a bargain with to realise his plans of conquest and receives a warning from the shadow watching Isak that Styrax himself may be under threat.

Reaching Narkang, Isak learns King Emin, a longtime friend of Morghien, has unearthed a planned coup in his city. The coup in Narkang is prevented, during which they discover that the vampire Zhia Vukotic, sister of Koezh, was impersonating a conspirator to steal a Crystal Skull from the leaders. It takes a desperate move from Isak to defend King Emin's palace, but during the first stage of the battle Isak senses the death of Lord Bahl and feels the hand of Nartis descend upon him as the new Lord of the Farlan. He breaks the siege of King Emin's palace by shattering the enemy army with lightning, earning the nickname Isak Stormcaller and turning his left arm completely white as an aftereffect of the spell.

After the battle, Isak is approached by a religious order of knights, who ask that he go to a place called Llehden. On the way he meets a nameless witch who knows Xeliath. The knights give him Aryn Bwr's own Crystal Skulls, unwittingly releasing the ancient king's spirit that has been hiding within both them and Isak himself. Thanks to advice from the mysterious Morghien, Isak survives the assault and breaks that particular prophecy, leaving Aryn Bwr a prisoner in Isak's mind and the future uncertain.

PART ONE

A LINED FACE, pale against the deep shadow of the archway, looked out into the street. The ground before him was empty of people, but movement was everywhere as the deluge that was worsening by the minute turned the packed earth to spattering mud. The old man had a heavy woollen scarf wrapped over his head and tied tight under his chin so the now-sodden material framed his face. Anxiety filled his eyes as he saw only the plummeting rain churning the ground, running in rivers off the rooftops and overflowing the gutters in the middle of the street. The black feather tattoos that marked the right side of his face looked crumpled; over the decades the once-crisp lines had faded. The tumult of the rain slashing down filled the air as the old monk trembled in the darkness. He felt it crowding him, driving him back into the shadows.

"Where *are* you, Mayel?" His voice was nothing more than a shivering whisper, yet almost as he spoke a figure turned the corner and headed towards him, arms held uselessly over his head against the storm.

Mayel made straight for the archway, head hunched low, and splashed into the dark recesses of the monument that sheltered the old man. He shook himself violently, like a dog, scattering water like a fountain. "Abbot Doren," he said urgently, "I found him. He's waiting for us at an inn, just a few streets east of here." There was a flicker of triumph in his eyes that saddened the abbot. Mayel was young enough to think this was a grand adventure; that a murderer was pursuing them seemed not to have filtered through into the novice's mind.

"I have warned you," the old man said, "this is not a game: even a hint of my name could mean our deaths."

"But there's no one out here!" he protested, eyes wide in dismay. The abbot could see Mayel had not been expecting another scolding; the youth deserved praise, he knew that, but their safety was not something they could take any chances with. Their mission was too vital for that.

"Still you must be careful; you can never be sure who is around. But you've done well. Let's find ourselves somewhere warm and get a hot meal and a bed for the night. We'll find a more permanent place in the morning."

"I think my cousin will be able to help with that," Mayel said, trying to sound cheerful again, despite the storm. "He rents rooms to workmen, so I'm sure he'd give me a good price—and watch out for us." He started shivering, his saturated clothes clammy against his skin. Glancing nervously out from under the archway he saw the sky was an angry grey. It felt more like autumn than an early summer's evening, as though their pursuer swept away the joy and warmth of the season as he closed on them.

"We'll need a house, somewhere with a cellar," said the abbot. "I have work to do; I'll need complete privacy. It can't wait any longer."

"I don't understand." Mayel stared at the old man, wondering what could possibly be so important when they were fleeing for their lives.

"If Prior Corci does find out where we are, I need to be ready for him— and I need your help, not just to carry the books, but to protect me from the rest of this city."

"Do we *really* need all these books with us?" There was understandable irritation in Mayel's voice: he had been lugging around the six thick volumes for two weeks now.

"You know what they are, boy. Our order's texts are sacred. That traitor may have made me flee the monastery, but he will never force me to give up the traditions that he himself has tried to destroy. The books must not leave the presence of the abbot—that is one of the very first lessons we learn."

"Of course I know that," Mayel said, "but are you still abbot if you flee the island?"

The old man shuddered and Mayel continued hurriedly, "I mean, surely the sacred texts are there for the community, to look to for guidance. Should they not stay on the island?"

"This current situation is more complex than that," snapped the old man. "You are a novice; don't presume you are in possession of all the facts. Now, enough of your chatter. Show me to this inn where your cousin is."

Mayel opened his mouth to argue, then remembered who he was talking to and clamped it shut again. He pointed down the street, and Abbot Doren pushed past and began to make his splashing way through the puddles. His bag, which held his few possessions—two more books and a strange, pearl-inlaid box that Mayel had never seen until the night they fled—was held tight to his chest. The abbot hunched over low, his eyes on the ground, trying to protect the bag from the rain.

"You don't fool me, old man," Mayel muttered. The wail of the weather drowned his words, but if the abbot had turned round, he would have seen a coldly calculating look that had no place on the face of a novice. "There's something in that box that Jackdaw wants. He killed Brother Edin for more than madness. The prior wouldn't be following us for just a few dirty old books, so why won't you tell me what's in that box? It's got to be worth something if Jackdaw wants it so badly—enough to buy my way into my cousin's gang. If we do survive this, you'll be carrying these bloody books back to the island yourself, old man."

He scowled at the abbot's back, then hurried to catch him up, at the last moment swinging his own bag around to his chest to shelter it somewhat.

From the upper reaches of the monument where the abbot had been sheltering a soft voice spoke over the sound of the rain. "He has the Skull with him, I can feel it."

"We must sacrifice that for the greater prize. The old man is not as frail as he seems, nor as unprotected. Be content that he has done as we wanted. Now the next act of our play can begin."

"But I could kill him now." The speaker's deeply-set eyes, hooded by thick brows, glittered avariciously. He ignored the rain soaking his thick black hair and running down over the tattooed feathers on his cheek and neck as he glared down the street, but the abbot had already turned the corner.

"His God would not let you," said his companion. "Renouncing any God as you have is not done lightly, and Vellern would stop you from harming one who is first among his worshippers. Perhaps the Lord of the Birds would take the opportunity to extract a measure of revenge too." The second man wore a green minstrel's hat and tunic and hugged a flute close under his left arm. He looked only a little damp, as though the rain was reluctant to touch him. His soft brown hair was not wet enough to have darkened and his cheeks, as smooth as a young man's despite the air of age about him, remained dry. A slight smile, both knowing and scornful, curled the edges of his mouth.

"We have others who could," growled the dark-haired man. Once known as Prior Corci, now he was Jackdaw, reviled as a traitor and murderer. His new master had called him that the first time they met, no more than six months past, in one of the monastery's dank, unused cellars. He had thought it a joke, but steadily he'd found the name had spread, even amongst brothers who knew nothing of his intended treachery. Prior Corci was being steadily erased from history, as every week that passed, another man had forgotten about him. Jackdaw knew there was no going back, no escape from the choices he'd made, and only the thought of what else Azaer's power could achieve stopped him sinking into glum desperation at the loss of his former life.

Now Jackdaw blinked the rain from his eyes and squinted through the gloom at the empty street. "The old man might be strong with the Skull, but an arrow would go right through that withered neck, whether or not he was holding magic. The Hounds would be glad to tear him apart."

"He is more intelligent than that. He has taken precautions against assassination, and there are inherent dangers whenever a Skull is involved. They contain too much power for a novice to control. He already keeps his Aspect-Guide close at hand; it would be a simple thing for him to lose his grip on the magic and then we would be faced with a minor God of vast strength instead. Better to let someone else deal with the problem on our behalf. We will kill priests soon enough, that I promise you."

From a pouch, the minstrel took a peach and raised it to his lips.

His companion sniffed and then looked away in disgust. "How can you eat that? It's rotting."

"Decay happens to everything," replied the minstrel softly, eyes on the clouds above. "Corruption is inevitable. I am but its servant." He took another bite, then tossed the half-eaten fruit into the street. "No one could want that Skull more than I do, but our master has a greater plan."

"One that I am not to be party to?"

"If you have the courage to complain, do so."

"I—" Jackdaw faltered. Too late he remembered that Azaer was always close to the minstrel, lingering where the man's shadow had once been.

"You require something of me?"

Jackdaw jumped as Azaer's voice rang suddenly inside his head. Beside him the minstrel inclined his head, as though giving a slight bow.

"No, master," the former monk spluttered. He felt a hand caress his cheek, then a sharp pain caused him to yelp involuntarily. The flesh just above his jaw-line felt raw and exposed and when he touched his face, Jackdaw found blood there. Raising his hand, he saw a black feather stuck to the blood on the back of his fingers. He didn't need a looking-glass to know that part of his tattoo had gone.

"*Hush your throat, or I'll pluck more feathers out. We have a game to play here in Scree, friends to find and friends to lose. Lure them all here and let the drama unfold as it will. We take our bows when the performance is done.*"

PART TWO

I N THE HALF-LIGHT OF THE LONG CORRIDOR A SHADOW MOVED. Only the listless swish of the thin white drapes covering the tall arched windows at one end disturbed the quiet. A wrought-iron railing decorated with vine leaves separated the corridor from the open hallway below, but the heavy afternoon heat had stifled all activity within the palace; that too seemed shrouded in silence. Even the servants had found cooler corners, where they dozed wearily.

The guard sighed inwardly. The heat was oppressive enough even without the heavy leather uniform. Rivulets of sweat ran down his arms and over his scalp and prickled hot in his crotch. His head sagged, eyelids drooping as the corridor before him blurred into grey emptiness.

The shadow drifted behind him, sliding smoothly over the wall but never actually touching the soldier. Despite the gloom of the corridor, the shadow seemed insubstantial. As it hovered against the white door next to where the guard stood, the profile of a blank face showed, imprisoned within the door's border, then the shadow eased into the dark crack between door and jamb and gently disappeared into the cool shade of the room beyond.

As outside, all was still within, except for the gentle movement of drapes at the open window, through which came no more than a wisp of a breeze. A huge four-poster bed to the right of the bolted door dominated the room. Curtains of green and gold were tied at each post. The shadow ignored the bed and its occupants, who lay across the linen sheets, barely covered. It ignored the ornate basket-hilt rapier hanging on a chair-back with an axe, the blade of which was perforated by glowing red-edged runes, and moved to the far corner of the room, where a small spiral staircase took it up to a circular mezzanine no more than four yards across. A simple but elegant desk stood at the centre. Eight thin apertures cut into the stone gave a view of the room below. Hanging from the wall were eleven purple slate tablets, two feet high, each covered by a green velvet cloth embroidered with a bee with wings outspread and the name of a city. The shadow ignored the nearest and glided around the desk in the centre until it reached the cloth that bore the word "Scree." It raised a long finger that tapered into a cruel claw and began to trace through the air in front of the covered tablet. A faint scraping broke the quiet.

The shadow finished its writing and looked through a stone slit at the couple slumbering on the enormous bed. *"Come and join the performance, my friend. Yours is a starring role,"* it murmured as it twitched the cloth slightly askew.

Then the shadow spread its insubstantial fingers like an eagle's talons. As it gave a sharp twist through the air a muted crack echoed around the room. The deed done, the shadow retraced its movements, pausing momentarily at the bed where the two figures still slept, legs entangled despite the heat. One ethereal finger caressed the man's cheek before pausing over an eyelid that gave a tiny twitch.

"And what if I were to blind you now, o mighty king? Render you unable to behold this nation you love so? But I shall not; there are sights I would have you see before the end."

The heavy summer silence returned to the room as the shadow slipped towards the door and out into the twilight of the corridor, then faded into nothing.

King Emin scowled at the tablet, pulling his shirt to order and tucking it into his breeches.

"Come back to bed," purred Queen Oterness from the bed, stroking the slight bump of her belly. One sharp-eyed old countess had noticed it already and there had been a sudden surge of speculation at court that an heir to the throne might at last be on the way. The royal couple were keeping quiet for now—the pregnancy was in its early stages and the queen feared her age might cause difficulties—but in the meantime that small swelling had restored her husband's precarious affection.

"Unfortunately, I cannot," Emin muttered in reply. He didn't take his eyes off the tablet as he reached out a hand and tugged the bell-pull that hung above the desk.

"Oh, charming," muttered his queen. "My husband is too busy to entertain his wife, so he sends for his bodyguard to finish the job."

Emin's glare stopped the queen short and she pulled the sheets to cover her naked body. It was too hot for a shift, even if Coran was joining them, and she was too comfortable to leave the indentation she had shared with Emin but a minute before.

"I'm sorry, Emin, you know I didn't mean that in spite—but whatever is wrong? I've not seen you so angry in years—what's the news?"

Coran jerked open the door and hurried in before the king had time to answer his wife. The white-eye glanced at the bed and bowed his head even as his eyes followed the linen-covered curves of the queen's body. The white-eye was barely dressed himself, wearing only a long shirt tied at the waist by the sword-belt he was still in the process of buckling.

Oterness looked at the livid scars on Coran's knee, he glowered at her and hurried up the spiral staircase. He had barely reached the top stair when Emin reached out a finger and pointed to the uncovered tablet.

"Summon the Brotherhood. We ride for Scree."

Coran stared at the slate board, unspeaking, until Emin indicated they should go back downstairs. The white-eye slowly raised his knee and ran a finger over the ugly scarring there, his face darkening with fury, then followed his king.

Queen Oterness watched the two men, a shiver running down her spine as she wondered what was affecting them so.

Then Coran spoke, his voice trembling with hatred. "Ilumene," he said.

The blood drained from Oterness' face. All was explained in that one word. Before King Emin reached for his clothes he took his queen's hand and squeezed her fingers. Her other hand fell protectively to her belly, trembling. When she touched the skin below her navel Oterness could feel rough scars, and could trace a name with her fingers. The tattoo she'd put there only hid the name from sight. The scar remained.

"And where we find Ilumene, Rojak will be close at hand," Emin told her. "And they will both pay."

CHAPTER 1

AT THE PEAK OF A LONG GENTLE RISE, Isak gave a tug on his reins to bring his charger to a halt and leaned on the pommel of his saddle, surveying the ground ahead. His companions joined him on the level crest and waited quietly at his side, enjoying the view. It was well into what had been an afternoon of uninterrupted sunshine and a warm breeze drifted up off the long, empty meadow, bringing the scents of dry grass and blooming wildflowers. The undulating plain, spotted by the odd copse of trees, stretched for a dozen empty miles before reaching the dark edges of a forest. In the far distance a darker patch indicated some sort of lake.

Isak remembered the forest from when he'd travelled this way in his previous life, as an unknown and irrelevant youth on a wagon train. His life now, as the duke he had become, could not be more different. There was only one road, carpeted with pine needles, winding its way under a high canopy of massive old pines. It had felt like the last bastion of home before the Land opened up to admit everyone else, despite being well outside the Farlan border. To the right was a line of five gorse-skirted hillocks, and he remembered the sight from the other side. The regular humps had always looked too neat and, side-on, the line was like the back of some vast serpent sliding out of its burrow in the slope where they now stood.

Carel, commander of Isak's guard, the friend and mentor of his youth, had told him of the many battles that had been fought just because those hills resembled a snake, the chosen creature of their patron God Nartis; that alone had been enough for past lords in Tirah to consider this place the rightful border between nations, but they had never been able to hold it. A quirk of terrain meant this place was easily surrounded and cut off by armies approaching from the south. The watchtowers put up to warn of approaching enemies, like the castle built on the border itself, had long since been pulled down and now scarcely a trace of their position remained.

They had made good time in their urgent flight home, thanks to King Emin's royal barge, which sped them to the border where one of his black-clad agents had already secured a fast river-boat for the next leg of the trip, but suddenly Isak was in no hurry to cross into territory that was now his own. Here it was peaceful; here they had the Land to themselves. After their defeat in Narkang, the White Circle had retreated completely from the conflict in Tor Milist and the ruling duke had in turn recalled all of his forces to mop up those cut adrift. Suddenly Tor Milist's eastern border, that ran alongside the very river that had carried Isak and his party home, was quieter than at any time in the last century. Isak felt a smile creep over his face as the sun warmed his cheeks. He could hear birds, the distinctive warble of song-thrushes somewhere in the dark gorse bushes and, further off, a flock of starlings chattering as they circled in the sky.

I remember a day like this, hawking in the hills of Meyon with my sons and my cousins. The wind smelled the same as today: warm grass and wildflowers on the breeze.

Isak nodded in absentminded agreement with the voice in his head. Count Vesna caught the movement out of the corner of his eye. The handsome nobleman tilted his head up to look at Isak, then gave an almost imperceptible shiver and turned away. Isak had told his companions what happened that night in Llehden, when prophecy had invaded his life and the soul of a dead king had invaded his head. Vesna had said nothing then, and had hardly mentioned it since. Isak could tell he didn't know what to think. The implications were both terrifying and momentous, not just for Isak, but for their entire nation.

Mihn sat quietly behind Isak, watching his lord's every movement. He had accepted the situation with his usual fatalistic manner, while Carel and Tila had taken it on board quickly, momentarily stunned, then interested—they'd found their voices quickly and it had taken Isak an hour or more to calm their fears and reassure the pair that he was in no danger. It was hard for them to accept that the soul of Aryn Bwr had tried to take over his body and failed, but Isak persuaded them that Aryn Bwr's failure was his gain. If the Land expected him to act like a king, then who better to have as an advisor than the greatest king the Land had ever seen? That the dead Elf was also the Gods' greatest enemy was something of a complication, but Isak was sure he was completely under control, even if his companions had yet to be convinced.

The poppies looked like spilled blood on the ground. There were omens in the sky, and over the Land, but I failed them. I failed to see what was in front of me.

Isak ignored the voice as it fell into melancholy, determined not to let the captive spirit ruin his good mood. Unbroken summer sun was a rare thing in the Spiderweb Mountains and the Farlan cherished such days. Foreigners would joke that the Farlan would halt a war for the chance to enjoy the sun, and as Isak sat there and felt the warmth on his cheeks it sounded a perfectly sensible idea to him. The early evening sun hovered a little above the horizon, casting a golden light out over the Land, freezing it in a long moment of peace before twilight would be permitted its reign.

The last king had fragmented his own soul to escape Death's final judgment, hiding his thoughts and memories inside the Crystal Skulls he'd forged for that purpose. Now, as those memories returned to the dead king, Isak felt the echoes of Aryn Bwr's pain. He cast around, searching for something to push the Elf's dismal thoughts from his mind, but there was little to attract the attention. They were almost at the highest point in the area, but aside from the narrow dirt track they were following there was nothing but a small cairn of stones, some thirty yards away.

In the hills of Meyon I held my heir and watched him die. In the hills of Meyon I cursed the ground where Velere died.

Isak felt a wave of sadness and rage radiate through his body, and he remembered the letter he had carried to King Emin about the place called Velere's Fell. It was no longer a tale of horror on the page for him, but a glimpse of grief and fury so strong it still scarred the Land, seven thousand years later, and its echo left a sour taste in Isak's mouth. Isak sighed and scratched his cheek, waving away the inquisitive fly that was darting around his face. *Are you really going to ruin a beautiful view for me?* he wondered.

This Land is so different to the one I used to know, the voice went on, musing. *Its colour has been bleeding out over the long years. Now it is grey, and marked by the scars of my passing.* Aryn Bwr was lost in his own thoughts again; only twice since leaving Llehden had Isak actually conversed with the spirit that had taken up residence inside his head.

"That's my good mood gone," he muttered, and he slid from the saddle.

"My Lord?" Vesna enquired.

"I just need to stretch my legs for a bit," Isak said with a dismissive wave of the hand. Carel immediately gave the order for the guards to split up, as he did every time they stopped for a break, then he dismounted himself and joined his young lord. Isak forced a smile and draped an arm over the old man's shoulder. As they wandered slowly towards the cairn of stones, Isak felt his smile become genuine. Here was a strange thing: only after it had become unseemly for a man in his position had Isak ever felt the urge to hug the man he thought more of a father to him than Horman had ever been.

"You want to pray?" Carel asked in a dubious tone. He'd known Isak for most of the white-eye's life; Isak had always resented piety when it was imposed upon him.

Isak shrugged. "I should probably get into the habit one of these days, now that I'm important."

"Still, it's not something I'd expect from you," the marshal said softly, careful to keep his voice low so no one could overhear them. The soldiers were handpicked, men of the Palace Guard and completely trustworthy, but this was too astonishing a secret to entrust to anyone else.

"Nor from him," Isak reminded him with a smile. "Stop fretting like an old woman; Tila can do that perfectly well for the two of you."

"Then what is this about?" Carel said, puzzled.

Isak sighed. "It's nothing important, I just want to enjoy this view for a few minutes and clear my head. He's been finding his memories, the ones locked away in the Crystal Skulls. While part of him had been with me since I was born, there's much that has been missing for millennia, and it's not all cheering. The defeated have fewer happy memories." As he spoke, his fingers went automatically to the glassy shape now fused onto his cuirass. Having felt the vast power they contained, he'd been reluctant to test the ancient artefacts but, strangely, their presence was still comforting.

"What sort of memories?"

"Battles, the death of his son, sometimes just senseless fragments, like my dreams, and sometimes things that explain much."

"Such as?" Carel encouraged softly.

"You remember the day when this all began?"

"Aracnan?"

Anger smouldered in Isak's gut until he smothered it. "Aracnan. He killed Velere, Aryn Bwr's son and heir. I felt Aryn Bwr's hatred, which is why I wouldn't go with him—and I guess that was why Aracnan didn't come any closer; he didn't know what he was dealing with. When he reached out with his senses, I wasn't just the frightened young boy he expected."

"And if you meet him again?" Vesna, with Tila on his arm, joined Isak and Carel, both looking anxiously at the white-eye. The religious charms that were fastened to yellow ribbons and plaited into Tila's long hair tinkled gently in the breeze.

Isak scowled. "I don't have an answer to that." He looked back the way they'd come, almost as if he expected Aracnan to appear, but the trail was clear. Beehunters skimmed the ground, their crooked green wings spread stiffly as they snapped at prey he couldn't see. The slender birds would have been a good sign if he'd been truly worried about pursuit; they wouldn't hunt if there were men lying hidden in the grass. "If I meet Aracnan again I don't know what he'll do," he admitted.

"But what will you do? Will you be able to control—him—before he lashes out like he did at the High Priest of Larat?" Tila asked.

"That was different, I wasn't prepared for him then," Isak said. "Now I know exactly what danger he poses. You'll all have to just trust me that Aryn Bwr's simply not strong enough to take over now. At the Ivy Rings he had his only chance—and he failed. Prepared, I'm too strong for him—and I'm still getting stronger."

"Still?"

Isak smiled. "Perhaps not physically, but I've found there are other things that count—Gods, Carel, can you believe that it was less than a year ago I was driving your wagon and complaining that I'd never even be allowed to join the Palace Guard?" He laughed.

They reached the shrine and Isak ran his fingers over the waist-high cairn. Someone had taken great care fitting the stones together to make it concave rather than conical. It curved around an offering bowl fixed firmly into the structure so half of it was sticking out. The bowl itself was made of rough clay, plain and unfinished, but its contents showed someone valued the shrine. A carved bone comb, a worn but serviceable knife and two small copper coins; they meant nothing to Isak but they were significant enough for whatever shepherd had left them in the first place. Above the bowl was a rounded shard of slate on which had been scratched Vrest's horns symbol.

"Aye," confirmed the veteran with a grim face, "less than a year since I joked that the Gods might have a plan for you. Careless words in this life."

The silver-haired man stepped away from the shrine, hawked up noisily and spat onto the dusty ground. That act earned an admonishing look from Tila, at which Carel hung his head and, after a moment of looking sheepish, he reached into his money-pouch to find a coin for the offering bowl. Tila's reproach vanished into the glittering smile that Carel had never been able to resist. She beamed at the man as though the veteran guardsman was a five-year-old just learning right from wrong. Carel knelt in front of the shrine and said a short, silent prayer to accompany his offering. As the man bowed his head, Isak felt a touch of breeze skitter down his neck like cool breath. He turned instinctively, but there was nothing there, only the certainty in his mind that the local God of this place was close at hand.

Isak reached out with his senses as gently as he could and to his surprise saw a blurred shadowy shape, like a hawk, circling slowly above the shrine. With a start he realised how frightened the spirit was; strange, he'd expected it to keep as far from him as possible. He placed a hand on the shrine and felt a shudder run through the spirit above it. Suddenly it all made sense: the local God hadn't moved away because it couldn't bear to allow him between it and the shrine. The shrine was all it had.

"It's not been consecrated," Isak muttered.

"Eh?" Carel said. "The shrine? What about the symbol of Vrest, then?"

"I assume the shepherd who built this doesn't know much about religion. He probably built it to give thanks for finding a lost lamb or something like that, so it made sense to put the symbol there. He didn't realise a priest still needed to consecrate it."

"I will make a note of it, and we'll inform the nearest border village unmen," Vesna said.

"Don't bother," Isak replied. "It's over the border, and it won't remain peaceful in Tor Milist for long. There are too many mercenaries—any priest daring to come this way will need an armed escort, and that escort would either be the local suzerain's hurscals—and then we'll be accused of taking part in the conflict—or soldiers wearing neither crest nor colours, and they'd risk attack by anyone who sees them."

Vesna stared at him before a smile spread over his face. "Gods on high, perhaps we'll make a lord of you yet!"

Isak gave a snort and grabbed Carel by the scruff of his neck to haul him upright again. "Perhaps you will at that—and to think all I ever wanted was to join the Palace Guard. You people should learn to pay more attention when you're handing out jobs!"

The comment provoked a burst of laughter from his companions. "If you'll forgive the observation, my Lord," Vesna said, his grin widening, "you've still not passed the trials. Now I'm willing to admit you've done a few things on the battlefield some might call noteworthy, but that doesn't mean you can just walk into the Ghosts."

Isak gave a hiss of mock exasperation and thumped the count on the shoulder in response.

"I can't see Kerin agreeing to it," Carel agreed, "but I'm not going to be one to complain about unearned honours; I still don't quite believe I'm now Marshal Carelfolden, and you're still just some snotty-nosed child I took pity on a few times. Sweet Nartis, it must be more than thirteen summers since I found you snivelling in that wood, knees and elbows all scratched up—feels like last month. What'd they done to you again?"

The four of them began to walk back to the horses. Mihn stood with Mistress Daran, Tila's chaperone, holding the reins.

"They led me out to the river," Isak replied in a small voice, his smile fading somewhat, "then they pushed me down the bank and left me lost out there."

"Ah yes, nasty little buggers some of them were. Still, children don't know better and their parents didn't give 'em any reason to think what they were doing was wrong. We got them back though, didn't we?" Carel chortled.

The memory restored Isak's cheer. "Garner berries, still one of the best ideas you ever had. Never felt so happy at the smell of shit as that day!" He scratched his cheek and looked west towards Scree, where the surviving White Circle and Fysthrall troops were believed to have fled. "I think it's going to take more than garner berries to get the revenge I need nowadays."

Vesna gave a nod. Isak had put off the discussion of how he was going to respond to the White Circle's attempt to enslave him, though he had talked freely since leaving Narkang about what had happened in the abandoned temple in Llehden, and his connection with the white-eye, Xeliath. The Yee-tatchen girl was something else he didn't fully understand, and another decision Isak knew he would have to make soon. He just had to hope that those closest to him wouldn't become too nervous of the company Isak kept in his mind: the Gods' greatest enemy, and the daughter of a foreign nobleman, one of the Farlan's ancient adversaries.

"A wagon-brat shouldn't have to make this sort of decision," Isak sighed.

Tila shook her head. "Better a wagon-brat with some sort of a brain than half of those bred for the job." Her vehemence took them all by surprise, but Tila carried on regardless, "Read a history of the Litse sometime and you'll see what I'm talking about. The Farlan have remained strong because of the new blood it brings into the aristocracy. The other tribes might mock us for our rigidity in tradition, but the Litse's biggest problem has always been the fact that commoners can never amount to anything. The ruling élite has always been weak and bickering, while the armies are led by men with the right family background, not any skill at the job. You might not have the training for your title, but we'll rectify that—and at least you don't have the baggage a proud family history always brings."

"Well, that's very sweet of you to say so," Isak said with a smile.

"I mean it," Tila said, ignoring his levity. "You'll learn what you need to and Lesarl will manage the details, just as he did for Lord Bahl. The most important thing is that you have the strength to make the decisions, and your strength is one thing I'm happy to rely on."

"So I was bred for the job after all," Isak admitted after a pause. "Stronger and bigger than normal men, and unable to have children except with my own rare kind. White-eyes are born to lead, and born to lack those family ties you're talking about."

Tila nodded. "And you more than others, it appears. Since the battle in Narkang, and what happened at Llehden, you've reminded me of a line from one of the old tribal sagas, when King Deliss Farlan, father of Kasi, the first white-eye, says, 'History echoing in his footsteps.'"

"Now there's a curse," Carel muttered, the lines on his face more pronounced as he frowned.

"No it isn't," she insisted. "It's a burden, yes, but think of all you've achieved since you left the wagon train; you've only eighteen summers and already you've done things that wouldn't disgrace the heroes of myth. White-eyes were created by the Gods to fight and to lead in their names, but most will never have such a marked effect on the Land."

Isak pointed at Mihn as they approached the waiting horses. "What about him? He killed the Queen of the Fysthrall, a white-eye, and one carrying a Crystal Skull at that."

Mihn ignored the finger jabbing towards him, though his eyes took in every detail. The only non-Farlan in the group, Mihn was noticeably smaller than the other men, and his nondescript clothes and tidy manner made him easy to ignore sometimes. Only his eyes belied his unassuming appearance; they were too bright and observant, the eyes of a predator.

Isak lowered his hand as Mihn stepped forward to join them, saying, "a deed that will haunt me my entire life."

"Why?"

"You are a white-eye, and one born for great deeds; I am not of such consequence to the rest of the Land. The fate of common men who stumble into great events is never so happy."

Before any of them could contest the claim a voice called out from behind them, "Happiness is such a relative thing; it's the lack of reward that annoys me."

Isak jumped, hand closing around his sword hilt as he turned, but in the next instant he recognised the speaker and raised a hand to stop his guards closing. Morghien was looking as dishevelled as the first time they had met, and wearing that same mocking, infuriating smile. His weathered face looked as though the years had been hard on him, but Isak was one of the few who knew just how supernaturally well the man of many spirits had aged.

"You," exclaimed Carel angrily, tugging his black-iron scimitar free of the scabbard as he strode forward. Morghien didn't pull the battered axe from his belt or let the loaded pack on his back slip off his shoulders but waited beside the shrine and watched Carel come towards him, his expression unchanged.

"You're going to have to be more careful who you sneak up on next time," Carel snapped at the man. "I don't like bloody surprises 'cept on my birthday, so next time you creep up on us my boys will kick seven shades of shit out of you."

"Oh come now, is that any way to treat an ally?"

"It is nowadays," Carel said with feeling. He hadn't put his sword up. "In case you're not up with current events, surprises aren't welcome any more."

"I heard about Lord Bahl," Morghien said, no trace of emotion in voice or face. "A shame, but not much of a surprise, with hindsight. Xeliath tells me it was Lord Styrax who killed him. If that's true we have quite a problem on our hands."

"We?" echoed Isak hotly. "And which city do you rule that makes it your problem?"

"I don't care for the Lord of the Menin, and if it involves those I call allies and complicates my own plans, I consider it a problem." Morghien's eyes were fixed on Isak and he remained calm and confident—until the seconds stretched on and he became aware of Isak, slowly tapping his fingernail against the emerald set into his sword hilt. Morghien frowned, his normal self-assurance wavering slightly.

Under different circumstances Isak would have been pleased to disconcert Morghien, but there was little to be happy about here. "Your friend," he said, "the Seer of Ghorendt . . ."

"Fedei? What about Fedei?"

"We stopped there on the way back—well, we tried to. The guards made it very clear before we even reached the city walls that we were not welcome."

"Not welcome?" Morghien's face fell. "Is Fedei dead?"

"We don't know; Ghorendt is closed to outsiders. All we could discover was that it happened the day after Silvernight. As we left the river we found ourselves staring at the pointy ends of a dozen arrows, so we turned back. There was talk of the Seer being trapped behind locked doors, and every mirror in the house being broken."

As Isak spoke, Morghien's face darkened. "I know whose handiwork that is," he muttered.

"Why? Fedei didn't strike me as a major player in your games."

Morghien shook his head. "He wasn't, he's simply a warm-hearted academic with a rare skill, the ability to see the shape of future events." He broke off, then added, "Xeliath has told me something of what happened that Silvernight, of the twist in history that occurred."

"One that was in part thanks to your intervention," Isak broke in, feeling a little ashamed that he'd not remembered when Carel was threatening to kill Morghien that it had been the wanderer who had given him the key to surviving Aryn Bwr's assault. "Without you, I don't think I would have survived."

Morghien waved away the thanks as he stood in silence, frowning at the ground. After a few moments, he came to a decision. "You can tell me the rest of the story over dinner. We have more to discuss than I realised, and perhaps I can shed some light on the mystery of Ghorendt."

They continued on their way while the light was still good, following the two rangers past the small lake and on towards a spring that ran through the heart of a cluster of ash and elm trees on the periphery of the forest. They hurried past the lake out of habit; still waters were a poor omen, and only to be used as a last resort. Such places attracted all sorts of spirits. This one was little more than fifty yards wide in any direction, but being so close to a disputed border, it would undoubtedly have its share of swords and axes rusting away in its depths; tributes to the greatest of the Gods, He who had already claimed the owners of the weapons. Not every lake was a certain gateway to Death's realm, but no one wanted to linger.

The sun had sunk below the horizon before they stopped and lit fires. The warmth of the day remained as the darkness drew in, and the little group of travellers ate unhurriedly, then chatted amiably, their backs resting against tree-trunks, looking up at the comforting light of the stars and both moons.

When the soldiers started settling down for the night, Morghien stood and beckoned for Isak to follow him. The white-eye paused only to sling his sword-belt over his shoulder and indicate to Carel that he didn't want an escort.

Within a minute or two he and Morghien were walking through the trees, following the slope of the ground down until they reached a natural hollow of no great depth, no more than twenty yards across. At the bottom of the hollow was a stone lying half-buried in the earth, its surface worn flat by wind and rain and looking like a crudely carved tabletop. Isak glanced back and saw Mihn watching them from the tree line. The failed Harlequin's face, framed by shadow, was strangely comforting. He gestured for the man to return to his bed, but felt curiously pleased when Mihn ignored the order and maintained his vigil.

"This is ideal," Morghien commented, running a hand over the stone's surface.

"Ideal for what?"

"A little magic. My skills have never been remarkable, but this is a simple thing if you have the right tools."

He took out a small silver-bladed knife, battered and worn by years of use. Isak could tell it had a simple charm on it, though not what sort. Morghien scored a faint cross about a foot long on the stone's surface and connected the ends so that the cross was bound within a diamond. From the same pocket he pulled a golden chain on which was strung a set of fat, oversized coins, all made from different materials and set with gemstones.

"Gods," Isak breathed, reaching out to touch one until Morghien jerked it away, "what are those?"

"It's called an augury chain; it's used for divination. The way they fall and their position in relation to each other can reveal a surprising amount, if the caster has the experience to properly interpret what he sees." Morghien saw the sceptical look on Isak's face. "Don't look like that," he said sternly, "this isn't the random drawing of cards. Each coin is aligned to a God of the Upper Circle, blessed by a high priest of that God and thus touched by a being outside of time or the laws governing the Land. When cast by a mage, there is a pattern spread over the board that guides the fall of the coins. Trust me, this is not mere chance."

He held up a blank disc of gold, turning it over to show Isak its flip side, obsidian or polished jet. "There are two that aren't aligned to the Upper Circle: this one, the Lady's Coin, represents Chance, but in a very specific way, and the Mortal, which is usually the principal coin in a casting, since all events ultimately revolve around people."

He carefully separated out another coin on the chain as he spoke and held it out to Isak, keeping the others well away. Isak realised it was lapis lazuli, deep blue with a thin speckled line of pyrite. "This is Nartis' coin, as you can probably guess. I suggest you don't touch any of the others, as you might upset the balance." He grinned. "And here's a piece of advice for you: never trust a priest with one of these. Without the balance of alignment they're useless—worse than useless—because whatever is read that way will be horribly skewed."

"What about the cross?" Isak asked as he ran the dead white fingers of his left hand over the disc's polished surface. The snake symbol of Nartis was engraved in the centre and surrounded by an unfamiliar script Isak assumed was the huntsman's prayer. As Morghien gave an approving nod, Isak realised his magic-marked hand would probably improve Nartis' own coin.

"The cross is our board, divided into quarters: the heavens and the land above, fire and water below. I have owned this augury chain for many years now, and I know its moods well enough. The position of each coin in relation to the board and each other once the blanks have been removed should provide an answer to the question in your mind when you cast the coins."

"The blanks? Ah, only one side is engraved," Isak said, turning the Nartis coin over. "What about the Lady's Coin, though? That one's blank on both sides."

"That one is rather special," Morghien agreed. "The obsidian side indicates that a path is already taken and Fate herself cannot change a matter. Here, Fate acts as the idea of chance, or suggesting an opportunity to take. When the black side comes up on this particular chain, however, on *my* chain, I suspect it represents Azaer."

The word hung in the air between them as Isak stared down at the tiny reflection of Alterr, the greater moon, on the coin's polished surface. Though he knew little about Azaer—or the shadow, as King Emin called it—he was certain it had been watching him over the last few months. The night normally held no terrors for Isak, who had been walking the Land with only the moons for company all his life, but several times recently he'd felt an unaccountable fear, and found himself fleeing to the light. Even King Emin had been unable to tell him why the shadow did what it did. Isak did not want to be caught up in Azaer's plans.

Without wasting any further time, Morghien unhooked the clasp holding the chain closed and held the stack of coins above the board. The Mortal was on the bottom. They fell with a clatter onto the stone as the hunter's moon came out from behind a cloud to cast its tinted light over the stone board.

As Morghien leaned close over them, his hand poised to remove the blanks, a hiss escaped his lips.

Isak looked down himself, and realised that even he could read what the board was saying only too well: just inside the quarter Morghien had called the heavens lay the Mortal, almost entirely covered by the obsidian side of the Lady's Coin.

"Azaer did not want you to meet Fedei again, and so I lose another dear friend," whispered Morghien to the night, and he bowed his head in grief.

CHAPTER 2

THE NEXT DAY WAS COOLER AND OVERCAST, with wide furrowed clouds that darkened towards the horizon and threatened rain. They made for the forest road, riding mostly in silence as every member of the party listened hard for the crash of branches and drum of following hooves. Having abandoned the river, they headed directly north, skirting the borderland between Tor Milist and the lands claimed by the Farlan. Their destination now was the suzerainty of Saroc, a longer journey, but one that avoided the most obvious route home.

One glance at a map made it abundantly clear where the danger lay: on the river that took them up the border between Nerlos and the suzerainty of Tildek, seat of the inordinately powerful Certinse family. Suzerain Tildek and his nephew, the Duke of Lomin, would be overjoyed to catch Lord Isak with only small force of guards before the young heir could reach Tirah and assert his claim. Their only dilemma would be deciding between themselves as to which of them should become king.

Riding on the fringe of the group, Morghien sat awkwardly atop one of the spare horses, his eyes fixed on the lead Ghost. As there was nothing he could do for Wisten Fedei, Morghien had agreed to Isak's suggestion that he accompany them to Tirah instead. He wasn't a natural horseman, and his discomfort added to his misery as the hours crawled past.

Isak had worried that the forest was *too* quiet, but early in the afternoon, when the forest thinned to the familiar sight of groves and thickets encircled by pastureland that characterised much of Farlan territory, the Land remained deserted. Where they would expect sheep and cattle to be grazing, thus far they hadn't seen even a rabbit, and the air was empty of birdsong. Isak had spent enough time alone in the wilds to know what a quiet day sounded like; this was the silence that followed a hunting predator.

"We crossed the Longbow River two hours ago now," he said, breaking the silence. "We should have seen someone by now." Like his soldiers, Isak was riding in full armour, his helm upturned in his lap. Jeil and Borl, the rangers, were scouting ahead with Mihn; Isak didn't believe anyone could catch all three of them unawares, but still he felt better when his hand was resting on the hilt of his sword. There was something nagging at the back of his mind. He looked around again; there were few enough hiding places nearby—and yet he couldn't shake the feeling of being watched.

"Do you think we're walking into a trap?" Tila asked from behind him. Isak turned in his saddle and gave what he hoped was an encouraging smile. It didn't seem to have the desired effect; Tila twitched her nose at him and looked away.

"I hope not," he said. "I just keep getting the feeling someone's spying on us." A tremor ran down his spine like a ghostly finger and he flinched, unable to stop himself from checking around again. "Ignore me, Tila. I'm just being foolish. I'd trust our scouts over anyone else."

"Some things they can't see," Morghien said in a distant voice. He closed his eyes for the moment, an inquisitive look on his face. "Is it magic you feel?"

"I—" Isak stopped. His inexperience counted against him once more. "I don't really know enough about it to be sure."

"Isak," Carel said, an intent look on his face, "what do your instincts say? No, don't think about it—don't try magic or anything you're not so familiar with. I know you, and I trust your instincts; tell me right now: *do you think we're being watched?*"

Isak nodded. "I think we are."

"Right." Carel raised a hand to signal the halt. "Helms on, lances out. Spare mounts behind us; Tila, Mistress Daran, stay in the middle, and Morghien, stay with them, no matter what happens. The bastards must have a mage scrying for us, which means we are going to be hit, and when that happens I want you getting the women away. You're not a knight, trained in battle, so you're the one we can spare in a straight fight." He stopped for a moment, suddenly remembering protocol, and looked at Isak, gesturing at his helm. "My Lord?"

The white-eye smiled as he remembered a saying he'd heard once: *Tradition rules the Farlan, the lord just tells everyone what to do.* He pulled the blue hood from his belt and slipped it over his head, then raised the distorting mirror helm over his head. Even on a nondescript day like this the light reflected strangely off it. Isak was glad his enemies were the ones who had to look at that soulless face. "Gentlemen, your helms."

Isak's party was already diminished, with eight dead and three seriously wounded who had remained in Narkang, so the absence of the scouts was pronounced. Mihn in particular had become a comforting presence, always in Isak's shadow; in his absence Isak felt unaccountably vulnerable.

Looking around, his eyes came to rest on Carel, organising the spare horses into a train they could abandon if necessary. The old soldier wouldn't thank him for pointing it out, but it was high time he retired. Isak thought he looked too small for plate-armour now, as if the loss of youth had drained inches and more from the man. The battle in Narkang had been evidence enough; Carel was still undeniably good with a sword, but hours of combat in heavy plate was exhausting for anyone; this time the effort had nearly killed Carel. *When we get to Tirah I'll speak to Lesarl about widows with manor houses and grandchildren he could grumble about*, he thought to himself.

"Lord Isak's right; the woods are too quiet," commented Morghien as Vesna and Carel helped Tila and her chaperone pull shields onto their backs. Neither had armour, of course, but the chances were high that any ambush would be by light cavalry, and while the shields would be useless against a longbow, anything smaller might not penetrate.

"The quiet could be good for us," said the count. "There's no wind, sound will travel well, and any ambush will require more than one regiment—having seen Lord Isak in battle, any force of fewer than a hundred men would be taking quite a risk."

"Vesna, find us somewhere to defend," Isak snapped, scanning the trees ahead. He could feel movement out there somewhere, movement, and eyes on them. There was magic involved, but this was a predator and the animals of the forest had recognised it.

They broke through a line of high ash trees and moved on to clearer ground. A gentle slope ran down towards a stream which disappeared from view behind higher ground off to the left, but it was steep and thick with tangling hawthorns. Isak didn't need to be told that that was the wrong direction; they could find themselves cornered fifty yards in.

"There should be rocky ground there, where the stream comes out," Vesna said, pointing to the right. "Look at the lie of the ground: those bushes are probably hiding a sharp drop where the stream comes out. We aim for that rocky ground, and if there's no threat when we get there we move in to the trees behind and find our scouts. We must move fast. If we're caught in open ground by cavalry we don't stand a chance."

As one, the horses moved forward at a brisk trot. Isak sat high and tense in his saddle, straining to detect anything over the rattle of armour and the thud of hoofs on the hard ground. He snapped at the reins irritably, trying to hold in Toramin's impatient steps, and as he did so his arm brushed the Skull fixed in his breastplate, reminding him of the power the objects gave him. Forged by the last king of the Elves for use in the Great War, the Skulls gave access to more magic than any mortal could naturally summon. With a Crystal Skull, even the Gods of the Pantheon's Upper Circle could be killed—so he should be able to open his senses to the Land around him while he was running for cover.

Isak touched his mailed fingers to the Skull and through the enchanted silver encasing his body he felt an immediate rush of exhilaration flow through him. The power he could access now was simply terrifying—he'd been nervous about experimenting with the Skulls until he was safe in Tirah Palace, but now he didn't have a choice. He was careful to allow only a trickle of energy to leak out of the artefact and into his body, but that tiny fraction was enough. A sense of the terrain around them settled over his mind, like a silk cloak descending. The wind rippling through the fat blades of grass on the open slope made him shiver and the chill trickle of water cut sharp through his soul. He focused on the trees ahead and a noise suddenly filled his ears: hoof beats, and the clatter of metal.

"Riders ahead," he called quietly. "They're closing fast. First squad with me, battle order."

Aryn Bwr stirred hungrily in his mind, but Isak angrily crowded it out. This was Isak's fight and he didn't need anything to distract him. At his urging, Toramin leapt forward and the rest followed in two groups, one with him, the second dropping fifteen yards behind to give them space to man-oeuvre. They were closer to the river than the far tree line, and fifty yards out Isak saw what he'd been hoping for: large slabs of rock breaking up a hollow in the slope, and a jagged wall of rock and earth, leaving no more than twenty yards of ground to fight on and no space behind them to be encircled by cav-alry. Low-spreading yews were dotted all over the crest, and Isak understood why Vesna had aimed for that area in particular. Their attackers would be on horseback, and there was a good chance it wouldn't occur to cavalrymen to dismount and creep around the back any time soon.

As they reached the river and slowed to cross it, two riders burst from the trees ahead of them, riding full-tilt. One stood up in his stirrups as soon as he saw them and bellowed at the top of his voice, "Riders behind! Tildek and Lomin soldiers!"

Isak's hand tightened: the whole Certinse family. How long had they been waiting for this opportunity? They reached the cleft in the hill and Isak wheeled Toramin in a tight circle to survey where they would be making their stand. It wasn't perfect, but there were jutting stones that would prevent a full charge, and some cover at least. The two scouts, Jeil and Mihn, reached them at breakneck speed, their ponies hardly slowing as they reached the taller hunters and found gaps between them to slow and turn in. Both men looked flushed and were out of breath.

"Borl took an arrow and fell from his horse," Jeil gasped. "We saw banners from at least two different regiments of light cavalry." He was gulping air down, getting his wind back for the fight ahead as he struggled to control his words. The rangers were ruthlessly loyal, and Jeil was raging inside that he'd not been able to cut the archer's throat before he fled.

"No hurscals, no nobles, but I heard more cavalry not far away." Mihn looked rather more composed. The sudden ride had forced rare animation onto his normally stony face; he looked truly alive, instead of being a shadow of a man.

"Two regiments, and probably fifty hurscals," Vesna guessed. "Right, lances in the ground, form a spike wall. Keep the tips high so they can see what we intend. It might make them hesitate."

Isak nodded. "And I need to find those damned mages."

Harnessing the trickle of power and opening his senses again, Isak quested out, but this time with a purpose that the Skull of Hunting eagerly embraced. The pursuers had reached the tree line, three hundred yards away, but there they stopped. Going further, Isak felt more bodies and smelled the musk of horses on the wind in several distinct places. Within the last he felt some sharp pinpricks of magic and swooped in closer: *there!* Three of them, protective wards already raised, all taking no chances—Isak could taste the streams of energy surrounding them, bitter in the back of his throat, nothing he recognised, or desired contact with. A wry smile crept onto his lips; their own defences had betrayed them. In his head he heard Aryn Bwr speak with cold dispassion: *They can't sense you, kill them quickly and withdraw.*

Isak looked around as the rest of his party arrived at the cleft. In the distance he could see the spare horses milling around in fear and confusion, beginning to drift back towards their fellows.

"My Lord, I can see archers," Mihn said suddenly. Isak jerked his head round—they couldn't let archers close the gap; they had only a few bows themselves and they would never survive an exchange.

"Tila, Mistress Daran, get to the back, help hobble the horses, then find a rock to shelter behind. Mihn, tell me if they get closer."

Isak closed his eyes as everyone took up their positions. The Ghosts were on foot now, kneeling down, axes laid out before them and lances held high. No one spoke. Seeing Isak in the breach at Narkang, emulating Nartis himself in battle, had affected them all profoundly. He would never be treated with the friendly camaraderie of fellow soldiers, for they regarded him with awed devotion. They would follow his orders without question.

In the forest beyond, Isak began to delicately test the defences of the three mages until, in a very short time, he found what he was looking for. He didn't know what any of the spells surrounding them did exactly, but he could sense a gap in one, like an incomplete web. Isak reached out with his left hand, picturing the tips of his dead white fingers slipping between the threads of energy and clamping about the mage's neck. He felt rather than heard a yelp of fear as the mage's shield collapsed inwards. The revolting flavour grew in his mouth, both familiar and yet completely unknown.

Touched by Larat, that one, said Aryn Bwr, *ordained then given over to a daemon. Kill him quickly before his new master intervenes.*

The white-eye needed no further encouragement. The situation was bad enough as it was without a daemon incarnating. Tightening his hand into a fist, he felt a small snap, then let the corpse drop from his fingers.

"One dead," he announced. Isak felt rather than saw the questioning expressions behind their helms; even Carel, his oldest friend, was a little reluctant to ask what Isak was now capable of, for fear of the answer.

"Any others?" the veteran asked briskly.

"They're paying attention now; I only got one because they weren't watching for me." Isak slipped on his shield and scanned the ground ahead. Three companies of horsemen had left the cover of the trees and were intent on crossing the river to cut off any escape. They were keeping a respectful distance, perhaps uneasy even now to march on the Chosen of Nartis, but he knew that wouldn't last. Isak allowed himself a moment of pity: the soldiers and sworn bondsmen had no choice but to follow their liege into battle, even when they knew the wrong of it. He shook his head. Time enough for sympathy if he lived, and for that, he must kill as many of them as he could.

"They're just going to form up and stick us like pincushions," muttered Vesna as he watched the cavalry cross the stream. "I doubt they'll bother trying to get in behind us now they know we've got nowhere to run."

"Get the armour off the horses to give us some protection. The longer we're alive the more of them I can kill at a distance."

"There's no time for that—look, those are hurscals."

Vesna pointed to more troops leaving the trees and Isak recognised the square heraldic flags, present only when the duke or suzerain was on the field. He spotted the barbican emblem of Lomin.

"The whole festering clan is here then," Isak muttered, "but how did Duke Certinse get here so fast?"

"Doesn't matter," Vesna growled. "What we need to know is how we're going to survive this. Three companies on the left, and one, maybe two, still in the trees? Then we've got heavy cavalry, a good fifty. My Lord, we need those mages dead; we can't afford to have them keep you busy."

"I can't get to them." Isak paused, waiting for some sort of response from Aryn Bwr, but the voice in his head was silent. "I'm just going to ward them off as best I can."

"While we fight against odds of ten to one? What about what you did on the palace walls in Narkang?"

"That would kill every single one of you; I don't know whether even I would survive it. No, we need some help from somewhere." Isak's voice tailed off as a memory suddenly appeared in his head. The forest spirits in Llehden—the gentry—if they had called him friend, then perhaps other spirits of the Land would also. It might not be much of an advantage, but he'd take anything. He closed his eyes and took deep, calming breaths to get the anxious drum of his heart under control, then he opened his senses to the Land—which already felt like a seductively natural act.

The two remaining mages noticed immediately, and Isak felt them abandon the smoky ribbon of magic linking them as they scrambled to strengthen their own defences. Whatever spell they had been working on dissipated almost immediately. Instead of probing their defences further, Isak left the mages to their distraction and moved beyond them to run his fingers through the cool heavy earth and listen to the ponderous breath of the trees all around. There was a remarkable stillness shrouding the whole area, once the irritation of humans was ignored. Isak felt his heart slow and relax as his jangling fear seeped away into the black soil beneath him and disappeared. He began to quest out in all directions, nosing at stones, following a ripple dance its way down the stream, blindly weaving his way down the tunnels of rabbits and moles as the sensation of the damp earth grew around him like a protective cocoon. Only then, suffused by a sense of peace, did he notice a difference in one area, like a twisted knot of iron in a haystack. He felt it stir, only the slightest of movements, but enough to make the riverbed where it lay tremble softly.

With great care Isak approached as it stirred again, brightening and expanding, almost like a tree waking slowly into summer. There was a note of muzzy confusion before the creature shook itself to wakefulness and noticed Isak—and the water suddenly surged, a flurry of movement. He felt a shape arch up out of the water and stretch to its full height. Isak hurriedly retreated back in on himself and cut the flow of magic flowing from him, but not before he felt a pulse of pure fury radiate out from the creature.

"Bugger."

Vesna rounded on him. "Bugger? What do you mean? What in the name of Ghenna has happened now?"

"Well, it seems things could have been worse after all," Isak muttered grimly. "I think I just woke something up, and it's not happy."

Vesna opened his mouth but his retort was cut off as one of the Ghosts in the line gave a bellow.

"Piss and daemons, what's that?" The man pointed a hundred yards down the stream to where something was thrashing under the surface. Isak strained to see, but all he could make out was furious spurts of water erupting. As the taste of its anger filled the air, Isak, to his horror, recognised it.

"It reminds me—But not the same—Oh Gods, the Chalebrat, from the battle with the Elves!"

"Like a Chalebrat?" spat Mihn from Isak's left, so sudden and unexpected that the white-eye jumped at the sound. "You've just woken a Malviebrat? A water elemental? My Lord, we are the only ones near the water!"

All eyes jumped to the drifting water of the stream that ran no more than five yards to their left. Here it was calm and almost clear, about two feet deep and running smoothly over a bed of pebbles, a straight path towards the boiling chaos Isak had stirred up.

"Shit, it's coming this way!"

The churning column of water abruptly resolved into the shape of a tall figure striding down the centre of the stream, water seething and dancing furiously at its feet.

"Mihn, any ideas?"

The small man cast his eyes around desperately as the Malviebrat closed in on them. The soldiers lining up against them had stopped and all eyes were on the creature, exactly as Isak had intended. But there was no doubting the intent in its walk. "I—Perhaps a show of strength? They are creatures of magic, after all, and however much you're angered it, it must have some sense of self-preservation."

"Morghien?"

The wanderer's eyes flashed open and his features seemed to flicker for a moment until they became his usual weather-beaten face. Isak felt a moment of hope as he remembered what Mihn had called him once, the man of many spirits. One of those had been a local Goddess bound to a stream.

Morghien shook his head wearily. "Seliasei cannot reach it; the Malviebrat will not listen to her."

"A show of force?" Isak repeated.

Morghien rubbed his hand over his face to wipe away the sensation of allowing the Aspect control of his body. "Will probably not work, but it is worth a try. If you fight it, don't worry that your blade passes through it. Elementals use magic to hold their form; the more you cut through that form, the weaker it will become."

"Worth a try," Isak confirmed. He felt a wolfish grin creep onto his face as he readied himself and felt the huge reserve of energy inside the Skulls pulse with eagerness. "Cover your eyes."

Isak raised his arms, holding sword and shield up to the sky, and blistering light burst into life in an arc beyond his hands. He could feel the heat it gave off; even with his eyes almost entirely closed the light was nearly unbearable. The lashing coils of energy bucked and kicked as he fought to control them. The impact of the magic smashing into itself reverberated down into his massive shoulders. The air shuddered and screamed around him as the streams of energy within the arc writhed about each other, but after a few moments Isak felt the magic reluctantly submit to his control.

He felt as though he were rising up on the air, and all sensation other than the enormous power in his hands fell away. Isak struggled not to cry out at the overwhelming strength flowing through his body; he felt invulnerable, divine. The Malviebrat seemed to recognise his divinity too: its advance faltered, but instead of stopping, a palpable surge of rage radiated out and on it came. Isak watched the fluid motion of its limbs and it stretched out into a sprint. It looked like Siulents as it moved. The white froth of its body was tinted the faintest of blues, and it was deceptively quick with the unnatural grace of water come alive.

As the Malviebrat surged towards Isak, fists bunched and ready, he heard screams from behind him as the horses caught sight of the unearthly figure. With a thought, Isak split the weaves of magic running between his hands. The creature was not cowed, but he remembered Morghien's words. The vast energy he held would disrupt the elemental's body, even if nothing showed. Wrapping one crackling loop of magic around his shield and another around

Eolis, Isak charged forward to get clear of his own men. He readied himself to fight.

The Malviebrat swung wildly towards Isak as he came towards it. The white-eye ducked and spun around, letting momentum carry the blade into its belly and on through its body. The elemental howled as it stopped and turned, raking down with clawed hands onto Isak's raised shield. To Isak it felt like an axe had been slammed down, sending a shower of droplets into his face, blinding him for a moment. He slashed wildly upwards and felt Eolis cut something, momentarily driving the creature off. When he cleared his eyes it was on him again, but this time he was prepared, riding the blow as he cut to the knee, then reversing his blade and ripping it up into the groin, and right through to the elemental's shoulder.

Again the creature screamed, but the cuts, heavy impacts as Isak felt them, seemed to pass through and out without causing any obvious damage other than a blaze in the water of its body as Eolis cut through it. Isak gave steady ground, cutting forward again and again, until at last the elemental seemed to slow and Isak felt his chance come. With every scrap of a white-eye's unnatural speed he slashed and tore at his enemy, using his shield as a club to batter away at it, following each blow with another. The Malviebrat reeled under his furious assault and squealed like a wounded boar before bursting apart into a sudden torrent of water.

Isak stopped and looked around at the stream he was standing in. There was no sign of the elemental; the still air above seemed frozen with shock at the violence of his assault. He noticed his breathing again, ragged through his tight throat, and then the sounds of the Land once more rushed back to him. His toes twitched automatically as he felt the chill of the water invading his boots and that stirred him into action.

Turning back to his soldiers, Isak saw them staring. Most were wearing helms, but Morghien and Mihn stood with their mouths hanging open in astonishment. Isak felt a growl of annoyance as he started back towards them. Just once, it would be nice if people didn't look at him that way after a battle.

CHAPTER 3

DISTANT SHOUTS REMINDED ISAK that not all the enemy had fled: the cavalry were still formed up on each side of the stream some two hundred yards away, arrows nocked, just waiting for the order. The smaller group of knights between them were noblemen and hurscals in the dull burgundy livery of Lomin, but Isak had eyes only for the man at the centre. The scarlet wolf's head helm would have made Duke Certinse's identity obvious even without the flag of Lomin hanging limply above his head. Isak, still standing in mid-stream, allowed himself a moment to stare at one of the few men in the Land who was his peer, in both age and station.

"What are you waiting for then?" Isak said under his breath. "It's a bit late for second thoughts now."

No answer appeared, and with a flourish Isak sheathed his sword and turned his back on them. He kept his eyes fixed on Count Vesna as he returned to his comrades, keeping his pace steady. He knew he looked unconcerned, assured—the glamour of Siulents ensured that—but inside he was beginning to feel the first strains of panic. A score of men against several regiments was no battle at all, and try as he might, Isak couldn't think of any way out. To have come so far, only to be killed as he crossed the border seemed like a sick joke.

Gods, is this really it? After all those dreams? I was sure I knew who was going to kill me, but I guess that was all wrong. Perhaps Aryn Bwr was right when he said I had broken history . . . perhaps no portent will now hold true for me.

Isak couldn't help but take a quick glance around at the trees on either side. "Stop it," he muttered to himself, "there's no one there. You're being foolish. It's fear playing with you, nothing more."

"Archers coming forward at slow order," said Vesna in a neutral tone as Isak reached his guards. The white-eye nodded, not trusting himself to speak. His hand bunched into a fist as he felt a growing knot in his stomach. He'd been frightened before, many times, but this was the first time he'd had the luxury of time to savour its bitter flavour.

The absence of magic coursing through his body added to the sensation, he realised, feeling insubstantial, almost weak as his impending death reared in his mind. Everything else fled before that: here he was, armed with weapons to make a God envious—and there was no help to be found. He was outnumbered, miles from safety, and not so inexperienced that he didn't know that any magic he did use would kill him and his friends as surely as it would those they were fighting.

A flicker of anger appeared at that thought. *If I'm going to die, so is that bastard Certinse. I couldn't stand to take my last breath and see his triumphant grin. I'd rather put out my own eyes first.* He looked up at the overcast sky. The poacher's moon would have fallen behind the horizon by now. If Nartis was watching, he was obviously content to leave his Chosen to whatever fate was coming.

"More horsemen, my Lord," someone called, and a soldier pointed off to their left. A group of mounted men trotted in line at the top of the slope, following the path Isak's party had taken, anonymous against the darkness of the tall pines.

"Vesna, do you recognise them?"

Vesna craned his neck, then shook his head. "I can't tell. They're wearing a uniform I don't recognise, but they're riding hunters, and they're not knights or hurscals, not all in black like that."

"Their leader isn't," Carel said, sounding confused. "Is that—? Gods, it's a bloody chaplain leading them!"

He was right: as the party came closer they could make out the one man not in black was sporting the white robes of a legion chaplain. His hood was pushed back to display a bald head and a long grey beard hung down over his chest. As they neared, the chaplain stood up in his stirrups and called something towards the enemy cavalry, swinging his moon-glaive in a wide circle above his head and finishing his statement with a roar and a cackle of laughter.

"Bastard's a bit old to be an active chaplain," Vesna commented, "and what's he laughing about—?" He broke off abruptly, then exclaimed, "Oh Gods, of course! He's been waiting the best part of his life for this day, no wonder he's making sure he enjoys it!" He turned to Carel. "Get our men in the saddle, now—those knights are on our side but they're still outnumbered."

The men didn't wait for Carel's orders; they were already running for the horses. Isak grabbed Vesna by the arm and demanded an explanation.

"That's Cardinal Disten," the count said, his eyes shining. "He's the one who uncovered the whole bloody Malich affair. He's been after the Certinse family ever since, but he never managed to find the proof he needed to have them tried. Now they've delivered themselves to him, both Duke Certinse and Suzerain Tildek, and that's reason enough to round up the rest of the bastards."

"Who are the knights with him? That's not a cardinal's staff."

Vesna beckoned one of the soldiers to bring their horses. "Dark monks, I'd bet, my Lord. The Brethren of the Sacred Teachings themselves. Suzerain Saroc has always been known as a bit of a recluse—I think we've just found out why!"

Isak swung himself into the saddle and looked at the advancing horsemen. "I never expected to be so glad to see religious fanatics," he said as the newcomers unleashed a volley of arrows into the suddenly disordered enemy soldiers desperately turning to face the new threat. Isak grinned and drew his own sword. The dark monks didn't make the numbers even, but it was close enough for Isak. He felt the sharp hunger of magic inside his chest as Eolis glittered in the dull daylight, around the lower part of which the Skull of Hunting had wrapped itself. It looked as if the guard and a few inches of the blade had been coated in a thick layer of ice, and the weapon throbbed with barely restrained power.

"Morghien, Mihn, your weapons will do more good here, protecting Tila and Mistress Daran, than in the midst of a cavalry charge." The wanderer nodded. He was not a natural horseman and controlling his animal in the midst of battle was no easy thing. Mihn looked less impressed, but he didn't argue; his staff would be of little use against plate-armour.

"The rest of you, form line. I'd prefer them alive to put on trial, but dead will do almost as well."

The men laughed and Carel called out the first line of the Palace Guard's battle-hymn. The voices, few as they were, sang out with lusty vigour as Isak watched the enemy reel from the unexpected assault. Cardinal Disten's manic laughter echoed out and Isak gentled Toramin as he waited for the Ghosts to ready themselves.

He fixed his attention on his prey, seeing the distant Duke Certinse slapping away the hand of the knight next to him—presumably his uncle, Suzerain Tildek—and drawing his sword. Flames burst from the weapon's surface and Isak smiled and raised his own weapon in salute. The slender blade glittered in the dull light, a soft *sssshh* sounding as it cut the air.

"I'm going to have your head on a spike," Isak said softly, a promise to the wind. He gestured, and his party advanced a few yards until they were clear of the hollow and standing on firmer ground, where they stood and waited for the monks.

Wherever they came from, they were well trained and led. They swapped bows for lances quickly and neatly enough to have satisfied even that notorious disciplinarian General Lahk, and charged into the disordered cavalry, who were scattering even before the first blow had been struck. Cardinal Disten's troops didn't bother giving chase; they reordered their lines and continued on towards the knights across the stream. Duke Certinse hadn't moved; his men appeared paralysed by indecision. Even when the charge was called and Certinse levelled his sword towards Isak, still more than a few heads were turned towards the dark monks.

Vesna drew Isak's attention to the other regiment of cavalry, and both men grinned as the captain, incandescent with rage, berated his men, only to be cut off abruptly as one of them shot him and sent him tumbling to the floor.

"They've seen the sense of it," Vesna called.

"And now we finish this," Isak said, and kicked his spurs into Toramin's flanks. The massive stallion didn't need any further encouragement, slamming his enormous hooves into the ground and charging forward.

The dark monks were closer and once through the stream they crashed into the enemy's flank, forcing them to slow and turn as Isak led his own small unit to meet them head-on. The monks' impact threw the hurscals into disarray, and Toramin, moving at speed, missed the target, slamming instead into the Lomin standard-bearer's horse with such force that it threw the man from his saddle and his animal collapsed on top of him. Isak pulled Toramin away, not wanting the horse cut by a flailing leg, and hacked at the nearest hurscal, catching a hopeful swinging mace on its edge, then using Eolis to cut savagely across the knight's face, tearing through his visor as if it were made of cotton. Isak laid about himself furiously, spreading chaos through what was left of the enemy ranks as he made for the centre. He caught an axe on his shield and sheared the shaft, leaned forward to punch his shield into the man's face-plate, then moved on, not waiting to see what damage he'd done. A lance-head scraped past his belly and Isak turned to see a knight in white and yellow reach back for another stab. As Isak dropped his shield down to trap the shaft and break it on his thigh, a hurscal dressed in Lomin's red hacked at his other side. Eolis absorbed most of the force, but the axe-head spun off that unnatural blade and the spike on its reverse stabbed down into Toramin's shoulder. As the huge horse screamed and reared up, the hurscal, still clinging grimly to his battle-axe, was dragged from his saddle. Toramin stamped down on the man as Isak yanked the spike from the horse's flesh and let it fall.

A black-cowled monk pushed past them, an edged mace in each hand, and Isak took a moment to look around. He saw Count Vesna trading blows with Duke Certinse nearby, and nearer still, one of the Ghosts was savagely attacking Suzerain Tildek. In the chaos, Isak couldn't see who it was, but as he deftly worked an opening in the suzerain's defence and knocked Tildek reeling, there was no doubt the soldier outmatched the nobleman.

Isak had no time to look further as a hurscal came at him head-on. The white-eye slashed at the man's head but missed; another hurscal came in from his left and as the two attacked Isak together, words came unbidden to Isak's throat and he felt magic flow out through Eolis. The sword traced a path of blinding light that made both attackers cry out and cover their eyes. The unnatural edge did the rest.

Isak sensed rather than saw a tall knight with a swan emblazoned on his chest just as he launched a furious attack. Hacking at Isak with a gleaming broadsword, the knight forced Isak into defensive mode, warding off the blows, until Toramin, circling clockwise, managed to shove the knight's own mount off-balance and Isak was able to get a blow in himself. Eolis cut the knight's broadsword in two, then continued on down into the man's peaked helm. The knight went rigid, then flopped to the floor as Isak withdrew.

Looking around, Isak saw the enemy break and run, but beyond them was a ring of archers with bows ready. The fleeing men came to a sudden halt when a single arrow hit the lead knight with an audible *thud*. For a moment, all they could hear were the cries of the dying, then the men, broken, threw down their weapons and pulled off their helms.

"My Lord," called Vesna from somewhere behind. Isak pulled his own helm off and hung it back on his saddle as he turned to the count.

"A present, my Lord," Vesna continued, prompting laughter from those around him. Beside him, alternately scowling and grimacing with pain, was Karlat Certinse. The young duke clutched at his sword arm as blood ran freely from the elbow joint. He had no helm and his face was streaked in blood and mud, his long black hair matted.

"Get that wound bound, then his hands and mouth," Isak ordered. "I want him alive. Better to string him up in Tirah than on a field somewhere." Isak nudged his horse closer and saw a flash of fear in Certinse's eyes before hatred masked everything. Beneath the blood and mud and the purpling bruise swelling the duke's left cheek, he looked almost absurdly young. *What are you,* Isak thought, *a boy in a man's armour, playing a game you don't really understand, or the calculating traitor I'm going to hang you as? In this life, does it matter?*

Isak lifted the duke's chin with his finger and looked into his eyes. "What's more," he said quietly, "I shall hang your mother beside you, and any other member of your treacherous family that my Chief Steward takes a disliking to on the morning I sign the warrants."

The only sound that escaped Certinse's lips was a hiss of pain as a Ghost roughly removed the armour obscuring his wound and tied a tourniquet around the upper part of his arm.

Isak slipped from his horse and began to check the soldiers milling around. Those few knights who had been slow to surrender had been herded into a circle and battered to their knees. Everywhere he looked, men lay contorted in agony, screaming, or moaning softly. A pair of Ghosts appeared on either side of him as he knelt beside one of the injured on the ground, a Lomin hurscal. Isak gently pulled away the helm to reveal a man about Vesna's age, his eyes wide with fear and pain as he huffed in short sharp breaths, his hands awkwardly clasped about the broken stub of a lance protruding from his side. The bubbling rasp indicated the head of the lance was embedded in the man's lung. There was no hope for him. Taking the man's head in his massive hands, Isak ended the pain as quickly and gently as he could.

He looked around at his cream-liveried guards, their emerald dragons easy to pick out. "Carel?" he called, a flutter of anxiety in his heart. He spun around, seeking the veteran's familiar build, but his old friend was nowhere in sight. Isak stood and took a few steps forward, looking around in increasing panic.

"Here, my Lord," one of the Ghosts called, waving Isak over to where he knelt. Despite the lack of urgency in the man's voice, Isak ran the twenty yards to his side, a heavy feeling in his gut. Before he got there, he heard a familiar voice swearing, "Careful, you ham-fisted bastard!"

Isak smiled with relief as he reached Carel's side. It was the quiet ones you had to worry about. The soldier was easing off Carel's cuirass, having already cut away the arm section. There wasn't much blood; Isak guessed it might be a bad break. Crouching down, he picked up the arm section and ran his finger over the split and dented plate just above the elbow. It had been badly mangled.

"Fell off your horse, did you, old man?"

"Piss on you. It was a mace and you know it," snapped Carel in reply. He winced again as the cuirass snagged on his tunic. "Not everyone's made of iron, you shit-brained lump. Oh Gods, that hurts! Someone find me a flask of something strong."

The soldier tending his commander pulled a knife from his belt to cut away the sleeve. Carel's once-powerful arm looked white, except for the deep sickly bruise that had begun to reveal itself. Isak could see from the angle that it was a nasty break, and the colour made him think that Jeil would have his work cut out to save the arm at all.

"Gods, it doesn't look good," said the soldier, unthinkingly.

"I know that, you bastard," Carel spat. "Nartis be blessed it's my left."

"Lord Isak," called a booming voice and Isak turned to see the man Vesna had identified as Cardinal Disten advancing towards him. He was indeed dressed as the chaplain he had once been but, as he neared, Isak could see the cobalt-blue hems of his robe were faded and patched. The cardinal himself was an imposing man—several years older than Carel, Isak guessed, but standing over six feet tall, and still with a young man's bulk. His long beard and the straggly remains of his hair were completely grey and his lean, lined face bore more than a few scars. Only his eyes belied the impression of age, burning fiercely from beneath thick dark eyebrows.

"My Lord, it's an honour to meet you," Cardinal Disten said as he dropped to one knee. Isak could see the moon-glaive hooked to his belt was still dripping blood onto the torn grass.

"As it is you. But if you'll excuse me, I'm a bit busy for pleasantries right now." A groan from Carel made him turn back to the injured man.

"Isak, go and do your job. You are no surgeon, and if you think I'm going to let you touch me, then you must have been brained in the battle." Carel forced a smile that Isak returned. He touched Carel lightly on his good hand and rose.

"Well, Cardinal, it appears I do have time after all. Please, rise." He gestured over at the figure of Karlat Certinse being stripped of his armour. "And now you can at last write the final chapter of your book."

"Hah," the cardinal replied humourlessly. "It's been a long time coming, for certain, but I don't intend to stop until I'm sure I've got them all. Life will be happier when I see his mother off to face the judgment of the Gods. I'll be praying the creatures of the Dark Place find something sufficiently inventive for the lot of 'em."

To Isak's surprise there was little satisfaction in the cardinal's voice, just a grim determination. He guessed the long years pursuing Malich's followers had been his job rather than his calling. Perhaps the cardinal was just tired of dark secrets and death. Isak was already learning that too much of either could sour any man's soul.

"Would you do me the service of seeing to it? Acting with my authority to bring them all to trial?"

"I will do as I am commanded, my Lord." Cardinal Disten bowed low, then gestured to a group of men who lingered on foot behind him. "May I present Brother-Captain Sheln, and Count Macove, a major of our order."

Both men bowed low to Isak, who nodded as he inspected his newest allies. They were dressed in black studded leather and painted cuirasses and carrying their peaked Y-slit helms. Their heavy cavalry sabres were sheathed. The brother-captain was a grim, craggy-faced man of about fifty summers whose skin had an unhealthy grey pallor. There was a cold immovability about Brother-Captain Sheln that Isak was immediately wary of; there was no compassion in those eyes, and he had a sense of remorselessness, and ruthlessness—not what Isak wanted to see in the face of a religious fanatic, no matter whose side he said he was on. Isak had the impression the man was carved from stone.

Count Macove was younger, and looked like the dour expression worn by most of the dark monks didn't come so easily to him. As if to confirm Isak's first thought, Vesna approached and took the man's arm in a familiar gesture.

"I hadn't expected piety from you, Macove," Vesna exclaimed, a broad smile cracking across his face.

"Good to see you too," the man replied in equal cheer. "As for my piety, we must all grow up and take responsibility for our lives at some point—even you'll find yourself doing so one day."

Isak opened his mouth to make a comment, then closed it again. He was the Duke of Tirah now, and barrack-room banter was hardly appropriate. Instead, he looked around at the other dark monks nearby.

"Is Suzerain Saroc not with you?"

The brother-captain didn't react to his words, but Count Macove betrayed a flicker of uncertainty that made Isak press the matter.

"Come on, I could hardly expect two forces to be tramping around without at least one alerting the suzerain. Since I see no hurscals or banners, I would guess he's part of your order and just too far away to introduce himself yet. If, however, he is deliberately snubbing his new liege lord, I will have to take offence and replace him with someone a little more respectful unless he steps forward *right bloody now!*" Isak's voice had risen to a shout.

"My Lord," called a cowled figure standing twenty yards off. Revealing his face to the daylight, Suzerain Saroc marched forward to kneel before Isak, his cheeks red. The suzerain was a remarkably short man, but powerful, almost a direct opposite to the second man who stepped forward, a pace behind Saroc, and also knelt. Isak glimpsed the devices sewn over their hearts, the only signs of nobility they wore. Saroc's was a red chalice; the other man bore a white ice cobra. Isak recognised it even as the owner spoke.

"Forgive us for not coming to greet you, my Lord," said Suzerain Torl, his pale face contrasting with the black uniform when he pulled back his cowl. "It is our policy to keep those with power in the Order from having to confront their lieges as emissaries for the Brethren. Our Order does not play the great game. We have no wish to act as though we were making a show of who our members are, lest it cause complications."

Isak frowned momentarily, then reached out a hand to take the suzerain's arm in greeting.

"That's the second time you've fought by my side; if such crimes were the only ones I had to forgive, I would be a far happier man. But what are you doing here? You're a long way from your home . . ."

"I am. I was in the hills on the Danva-Foleh border on business when an associate informed me of Lord Bahl's death. As I came in search of Suzerain Saroc, one of my agents informed me that the Duke of Lomin had left with his hurscals suddenly, so we decided to keep track of them."

"A welcome decision for me—but how did you find out about Lord Bahl's death so quickly if you've come from the Danva border?"

Torl's expression was grim. "The Brethren have a number of—we'll call them *associates*—who use unorthodox methods—and in certain cases, lack sanity. These are not men we have brought into our Order, but we often find uses for them."

"That's not an explanation," Isak pointed out. The suzerain looked uncomfortable for a moment, shifting his weight from one foot to the other as he struggled to match the looming white-eye's stare.

"The College of Magic would describe him as a rogue mage, which he is, but not in an insane or impious way. His methods simply differ from other mages, and that makes him a valuable asset."

"So why did you hesitate to tell me that? It's a simple enough explanation."

Torl gave a sigh. "That may be, but how he knew of the death of Lord Bahl is not. He first saw an image after spending several hours watching sunlight filter through the branches of a yew; then again in the movement of leaves in a herb garden. To most people that sounds like he's some sort of prophet, and I wouldn't want to give you that impression of our Order."

"I'm intrigued," Isak said. "Perhaps I should meet the man—and when you bring him to Tirah Palace, I look forward to your report on your Brethren as well."

"My Lord—"

Isak quickly cut him off. "Your loyalty is not in question, but I must know what other allegiances my nobles hold. The events in Narkang and Thotel mean I cannot afford to be ignorant of anything, certainly not the activities of my subjects."

"The rumours about Thotel are true then?" Suzerain Saroc interjected before Torl could continue his objections. He was very conscious that the dark monks and the Ghosts were eyeing each other suspiciously, and neither side had yet sheathed their weapons. "Has Lord Styrax has taken the city and torn down the Temple of the Sun?"

Isak nodded. "So I've been told."

"But what about Narkang? Were you not returning to claim your inheritance because you felt Lord Bahl's death?"

"Unfortunately, it's not as simple as that. These parts may see more fighting before—"

"My Lord," the ranger Jeil broke in, "I need your help."

Isak nodded at the suzerains and returned to Carel. He crouched down beside Jeil to inspect the damaged limb. Carel was terribly pale, and sweat poured off him as he panted, almost gasping for breath.

"I can't save it," Jeil said calmly. He was too experienced to bother trying to hide the truth from Carel. "You're his best chance."

"Me? I've never done anything like this," Isak protested.

Jeil pointed at Eolis. "The marshal doesn't need a healer, not at the moment. He needs a butcher, and saving your pardon, my Lord, you're the best we have. Eolis will give the cleanest cut, and with a touch you can cauterise the wound."

Isak looked down at Carel. He could see the old man was weakening before his eyes.

"There's no other way?"

"None."

Isak looked around, but none would meet his gaze. He stood and drew Eolis. Carel couldn't stop himself howling in pain as Jeil manoeuvred the injured arm away from the body and indicated where Isak should cut. As Isak raised the slim sword, he looked at Duke Certinse, a glare of such pure venom that the duke shrank back in fear.

"On a spike," Isak growled. He slashed down.

CHAPTER 4

"**L**ORD ISAK, YOUR HEALTH." Suzerain Saroc, looking markedly different dressed up in silks and fine linens, raised his goblet for the other guests to follow. A bronze brooch bearing his chalice device was pinned to his left shoulder and he now sported his earrings of rank—though the three hoops through his left ear were not plain gold, like those worn by Count Vesna and Suzerain Torl; his were intricately carved and set with flecks of jet. To Isak's intense surprise, the deeply religious Saroc, last seen dressed in dour black, had transformed into something of a peacock once they reached his estate.

The men echoed the suzerain's words; the women, all wearing tight-wrapped dresses and feathers in their hair, *hmmm*ed agreement. It was the first time Isak had participated in a formal Farlan toast, but Tila had found a few minutes to coach him in his expected role—which largely boiled down to draining his cup whenever his name was mentioned. He still didn't grasp why only men carrying weapons were allowed to speak above a mutter, though she had pointed out one or two wearing ceremonial swords solely for that purpose.

Emptying his goblet: Isak was more than willing to do that in the name of protocol, and he did so with a flourish. He nodded graciously to each of the noblemen around the table and set his goblet down for it to be refilled— but somehow he miscalculated, and the thump as it hit the table caused the bowl of rice beside it to jump and overturn. He frowned at the table; it seemed to be closer than he'd first thought—but when he looked up, he realised there were startled faces turned his way. Perhaps that had been a little loud; suddenly he was reminded that his huge frame was oversized for this rather delicate dining hall.

A hot feeling began at the back of his neck as he felt the eyes of the room on him. With painstaking care he disentangled his fingers from the goblet and raised his hand in apology to the suzerain, who smiled back and nodded graciously as the rest of the room looked away with embarrassed expressions.

Oh damn, Isak thought, *I'm the guest of honour, I shouldn't be apologising. Didn't Tila say I couldn't do anything wrong at a meal in my honour?*

"He's going to be fine." The soft voice in his ear was accompanied by a waft of perfume. Around them, conversation sputtered back into life as the guests returned to their meals.

Isak turned to Tila and nodded glumly. The doctors were agreed on that point at least, despite it being the only one they had been able to reach a consensus on. A middle-aged monk with a hard stare, accompanied by three novices, had arrived from a nearby monastery to help tend to the wounded. He'd been friendly to the suzerain and polite to Lord Isak, of course, but his face betrayed his feelings when he saw a local woman also tending to the sick; her hair cut short to display the scars and tattoos around her neck marked the woman clearly as a witch. No one said much, but even the veteran soldiers had deferred to her opinion.

"I know he will be," Isak said, prodding the lump of pork on his plate with a knife, "but I can't seem to get the smell of burned flesh out of my mind."

Looking round at the forty or so faces in the hall, Isak saw a number still watching him with slight concern; the Countess Saroc was one who had little time for alcohol and no patience with drunks. Isak ignored her sharp eyes, which shone from her long, thin face. His natural charisma had a more dramatic effect on inanimate objects than on the Countess Saroc, but her courtesy remained faultless and her compassion for the injured unmatched; that she didn't like him was a small price to pay.

"He's too old to be leading men into battle," Isak continued, picking at his meal. It was too rich, and had set his stomach churning. Aside from the wine, he had consumed only rice and a bowl of dressed tomatoes. Popping another in his mouth, Isak licked the oil from his fingers and sighed. "I shouldn't have asked it of him."

"You're right that he's too old," agreed Tila, placing her fingers on his forearm. "You're wrong that it's your fault. The old buzzard knows his own strength better than you do, and you can't claim to be more aware of the dangers of battle than he. Let his decisions be his own."

Her hand looked like a child's against Isak's green-edged cuff. They had little time to sit together and talk as friends these days. Isak didn't resent the love that had flourished between Tila and Count Vesna, for both had become dear to him, but in his first weeks in Tirah Palace, he and Tila had spent nearly every minute of the day together.

Isak saw a fond smile appear on Tila's rosebud mouth. "And, of course, a friend should be on hand to cut one's arm off when one makes the wrong choice."

Isak resisted the urge to reach out and hug her, uncomfortably aware of the eyes on them. Instead, he stuck his tongue out at her, prompting a muted squeal of amusement, and went on the hunt for more wine.

"My Lord." Suzerain Saroc spoke as Isak filled his own goblet from the decanter in front of him, placed there by Mihn so he wouldn't have a servant hovering at his shoulder all night—the tale of the battle in Narkang had raced through the suzerain's household, and every one of the staff was surreptitiously trying to catch a glimpse of Isak's left hand that had been left as white as the tunic he wore. Isak turned towards the suzerain, his body feeling heavy and ponderous.

"Might I persuade you to rest here a few weeks before returning to Tirah? We seldom have the chance to entertain our lord down here in Saroc; your presence would be a blessing for us all."

"A good idea," Isak said with a smile. "I think Lesarl can spare me for a few weeks yet." Off past the suzerain, he saw a frown cross Vesna's face. The count was listening idly to a knight on his right, but his concentration was on Isak and the suzerain. *Old maid*, thought Isak. *He worries about everything if I've not discussed it with him already.*

"We will stay a fortnight," he went on. "I doubt Carel will be able to travel by then, but I want to see him stronger before I go. And I have a few matters that I want to attend to before I return."

"Plans, my Lord?" The suzerain's interest was piqued, especially as he saw Tila's puzzlement.

"Plans, my Lord Suzerain," Isak confirmed with a broad smile. "The tribe is run by its dukes and its suzerains, and if I am to rule, I should meet them— half of those I already knew have died in battle, and I'm planning to hang Duke Certinse in front of a crowd. Suzerain, I would like you to gather messengers ready to send out a proclamation. My advisor here will have it ready in a day or two." Isak twitched his fingers in Tila's direction—he didn't let Tila's ignorance of his plans interrupt his flow. "I intend every suzerain and duke to gather in Tirah Palace and swear fealty to me at my coronation ceremony."

A slight gasp ran around the room at that, and all attempts to pretend conversation stopped as Isak took another swig of wine and continued, "There's been too much treachery, too much plotting in recent years. I want each and every one of my most powerful nobles to swear an oath of loyalty. If they refuse, I'll know where they stand; if they look me in the eye and lie, I'll break them in half and feed them to the pigs."

Isak spoke with such vehemence that more than a few flinched. From next to Tila Isak heard Suzerain Torl clear his throat to break the silence.

"That will be a difficult undertaking, my Lord," Suzerain Torl murmured. "Some are old and infirm; many will have a long way to travel."

Isak gave a dismissive wave of the hand. "If they wish to present their apologies instead, I'll leave it up to my Chief Steward to decide who has a valid excuse . . . and who should be stripped of their title." Isak gave a dangerous grin. "I think recent events have proved that divisions remain, but that cannot continue. We will make a festival of it. Business will be done and matches made, no doubt. I'm sure most of the suzerains will have requests to present to me as well, and they will be heard, but any who consider the journey a waste of time I shall consider a wasted title. The Chetse have been conquered, the Fysthrall have returned and who knows how many new enemies we will find ourselves with come the end of the year."

Isak saw Tila tense slightly at that. *Damn,* he thought, *I didn't mean him— but you've got a point all the same. How long until the Elves discover their king is reborn? Long enough I hope; I don't want to be fighting on too many fronts all at once.*

Looking around, Isak saw worried faces, men dropping their eyes as Isak's glittering gaze swept over the tables. A handful were nodding their agreement, but most just looked shocked. It was understandable, Isak reflected. Lord Bahl had ruled for almost two hundred years, and while he had sometimes been unpredictable, the man had largely left his nobles to their own devices. Now they had an arrogant young pup who wore dark tidings like a cloak announcing two hundred years of tradition was about to change. Perhaps they were right to look nervous. He was a white-eye, after all, and wherever he went trouble tended to follow.

Isak stood, motioning the others back down as they rose with him. Hooking two fingers around the neck of the half-empty decanter, he excused himself to Suzerain Saroc and his countess. He knew he was being rude, but he didn't want to be drawn further on the subject tonight; his sour temper and too much wine might lead him to say something he didn't intend. Now he wanted a chance to hear what his advisors had to say before discussing the matter further.

Making his way out of the hall, Isak followed the corridor to the terrace that overlooked the suzerain's formal garden, apparently in the Tor Milist style. Mihn was on his heel, as normal. He crossed the terrace and felt the lush dew-kissed grass underneath his shoes and breathed in the smell of evening blooms.

The suzerain was proud of his gardens, and though the concept remained alien to Isak, who knew nothing of such things, in the warm gloom of twilight and lit by scattered paper lanterns, he had to agree that the sight before him was beautiful. Low yew hedges sectioned off the long garden, each enclosing a different style. Thin swirls of flowerbeds cut paths through the grass, blazing with the colours of summer, but it was the stillness that Isak savoured the most.

A dwarf apple tree the height of Isak's chest stood at the centre of a piece of lawn, flanked by slender stone birdbaths. Resting the decanter on the nearest, Isak fumbled in his pocket for Carel's tobacco pouch; the countess had forbidden it to the veteran. Soon, the thick smell of pipe-smoke was drifting through the slender branches of the apple tree and fading to nothing in the darkening sky. Isak inspected the snow-white skin of his hand. It hadn't changed at all since the battle in Narkang, where lightning had burned the colour from it. Not even weeks of riding with it exposed to the sun had tanned it.

"Had you planned that?" asked Mihn quietly, having checked for anyone who might overhear their conversation.

"Of course."

"Then why did Lady Tila and the count look quite so surprised?"

Isak sighed. "Because I'd not planned to announce it quite like that. Did it just sound like the ranting of a drunk?"

Mihn shook his head. "No, it was a little more eloquent. There will be serious opposition, though, even from your supporters."

"Good, that's the point." Isak jabbed the pipe towards the high roof of the hall. "Most of the Farlan legions are led by fat, contented old men. If they object to a trip to Tirah, they'll be of no use on campaign. They need waking up, Mihn, our blades have become dulled."

"What threat is it you want them to be ready for?" Mihn sounded unconcerned, but Isak could tell the man was worried by the fact they were conversing at all. He would go several days on end without speaking a word to Isak—when Mihn deemed conversation necessary, Isak knew that he'd damned well better pay attention.

"Take your pick. I don't think there's any way to tell yet, but Lord Bahl wasn't killed by accident. If Morghien and King Emin are to be believed, this is all some artifice of Azaer's—or it might be Lord Styrax, building himself an empire. And we must not give the White Circle time to regroup—they all add up to one thing: we must be prepared for war."

"You intend to punish the White Circle?"

Isak shrugged. "They brought the fight to us; what can I do except strike back?"

"There are ways to strike back that don't involve razing Scree and Helrect to the ground."

"Is that what you're worried about? My lack of proportion?" Isak took a sip of wine and screwed up his face. The wine didn't go with the bitter soldier's tobacco Carel preferred. He turned to look Mihn in the eye: the northerner's usual passivity was gone completely and he matched Isak's gaze without blinking or turning away as he normally would.

"Spreading chaos on our borders may not serve you well, not if chaos is what your enemies want. If there is another way to deal with the Circle, will you promise to consider it?"

Isak blinked. "That's the first time you've asked me for anything."

"All I ask is that you do not start the war, that you do not let yourself be goaded into fighting on the wrong front."

After a moment's pause, Isak held out his arm for Mihn to take. "All you're asking is for me to promise to act sensibly; it's a more than fair request." The smaller man bobbed his head in acknowledgement, returning to his customary reserve.

Isak stopped, hand still gripped about Mihn's forearm, and looked Mihn straight in the eye. Curiosity flickered over Mihn's face, but he had patience enough to outlast a glacier. Isak looked away briefly, then rubbed his hand over his face, as if to sober up a little more.

"You might not like what else I've decided quite so much." He could almost feel the quiet of the night, and found himself peering around at the shadows, unwilling to continue until he was sure they were not being spied on. He couldn't feel anything; it was only his muzzy brain and his innate sense of caution.

"I want you and Morghien to fetch Xeliath for me, to bring her back to Tirah. It won't be long until someone works out her part in what happened, and when that happens, she'll not live long. She knows Morghien, and you, I assume, can speak Yeetatchen. I have no one else I could ask such a thing of."

Mihn was quiet for a moment, then he bowed his head. "If she is that important to you, I will do it."

"I don't know how important she is to me," Isak said honestly. "I've only spoken to her a handful of times. All I know is that she'll be another casualty of my existence—of my twisted destiny—if I leave her to her own fate. The blood of another innocent on my hands."

He took a draw on the pipe, only to find it was out. He jabbed his thumb into the pipe bowl and hissed as he discovered the embers were hotter than he'd expected. He wiped his thumb on his tunic, leaving a smear of ash on the white fabric. "Speaking of blood on my hands, it's time to check on Carel."

Chapter 5

"XomejX? That's a long way to go for a girl you hardly know," Morghien said. "I know she's a pretty young thing—"

"She's in danger and I can hardly go myself," Isak said, raising a hand to cut Morghien off. "I need you to go because she knows you, and she can reach your mind."

"But I don't speak Yeetatchen—never been there in all my years of travelling."

"Well here's a chance to correct that oversight. As for the language problems, Mihn is going with you and I'm sure he'll manage to pick up a few words."

Isak squinted up at the old wanderer and grinned. He was stretched out on the grass in the suzerain's private garden, dressed in only a thin shirt and cropped trousers that looked more suitable for a dock worker than a duke. An eight-foot stone wall surrounded the garden, so he'd donned the shirt only when Morghien arrived—he hated displaying the scar on his chest, even to those close to him. Morghien knew the truth about his snow-white left arm, so Isak didn't worry about trying to keep that from sight.

He had declined the invitation to go hawking with the suzerain and his fellow guests, determined to spend at least one day out of the saddle. Instead, he had spent the morning lying on the grass, a cushion under his head, and a cup of apple juice to hand, enjoying the birds and butterflies swarming over the countess' flowers. A book lay unopened at his side and a grey-muzzled hunting hound, the suzerain's favourite, stretched out untidily at his feet. The dog might be too old to go hunting with its master, but it was more than willing to spend a lazy day being pampered by Isak.

Unable to summon the effort to get up properly, Isak indicated Morghien should sit. He was dressed in fresh leathers and a new shirt, a gift from the countess, whose delicate sensibilities were offended by his own filthy, tattered clothes. It was a scrubbed, shaved and nearly presentable Morghien who sat now before Isak, though the overall effect was still one of slightly dishevelled elegance. Morghien reminded the white-eye of his Chief Steward, whose fine clothes always looked untidy and rumpled, simply because he was the one wearing them. *And that's not the only similarity*, Isak thought. *Perhaps I should keep Morghien with me just to keep Lesarl off-balance when I return to Tirah.*

Morghien cupped the hound's whiskery muzzle in his hand and wiped a trace of sleep from the corner of its eye with a deft movement. "I've not visited the Yeetatchen for a reason. They don't like outsiders—they are a most inhospitable people."

"Do you think I would be more welcome?"

Morghien shrugged; there was no need to comment. Isak shifted a little to see the man's face a little better, prompting a reproachful look from the dog, now wedged against his hip. Stroking the grey fur, Isak wondered what he needed to say to persuade Morghien. Mihn had accepted the charge easily, as he accepted any order from Isak, but that was because the penance Mihn had imposed upon himself for failing in his life's calling appeared to include indulging the whims of a white-eye, no matter how ludicrous. The journey would be long, hard and dangerous—the Yeetatchen were notorious in their dislike of all outsiders, not just Farlan.

"It's not a political delegation—if Lord Leteil discovers why you're there, he'll kill you both, along with Xeliath."

"You are sure of that?"

"He's a white-eye, isn't he? Xeliath has a Crystal Skull, and if he finds out about that I can't see any other possible outcome, can you? It's not going to be easy, but I am quite sure you could think of *something* that might compensate you for the trouble."

"Rewards are no good to a dead man," snorted Morghien. He ran a hand through his own grey hair, as rough and wiry as the dog's coat.

"Don't die then!" Isak snapped back. "You've managed it thus far! I wasn't offering you gold—though that's easily given if it's all you want—I assumed you'd want some sort of a favour in return."

"You assume you have something I want," Morghien replied coolly.

"Correct. I don't know exactly what your relationship with King Emin is, but I know you've got plans for the future, and I suspect my involvement would be helpful. Just what you are up to is your own business—for the time being, at least. I'm caught up in quite enough plots as it is." He sighed. "I assume it has something to do with Azaer, so I think we would both benefit from our alliance." He felt rather than saw Morghien tense at the name.

The dog whined as Isak pulled himself to a seating position. His massive body cast a shadow that almost completely enveloped the wanderer. "Decide now whether you want my friendship or not. Emin already has, but I've yet to decide which one of you is truly in control of whatever bargain you two have going. I suspect you *were*—Emin said you met before he took over Narkang, and that happened when he was my age—but that man's too clever to still be taking anyone's orders for long. So enough of the games. I need this of you. Will you do it?" Isak spat in his hand and held it out.

After a moment of consideration, Morghien did the same and they shook on the strange bargain. Despite the warmth of day, Morghien's leathery hand felt chill to the touch.

"If we must go, let it be soon," Morghien called to Mihn, who was standing in the shade of the doorway. "Storm season on the Green Sea isn't much fun. If we have a ducal warrant from you, Lord Isak, then we can be ready to leave tomorrow."

Mihn nodded at that and walked over to join the two men. He too had stripped down to just a thin shirt and Isak could see how slender he was, all sinew and whipcord strength. It was no wonder Harlequins could hide their gender so effectively if even the men were so slim. They looked androgynous, and many thought them not even human, for their talents could appear almost supernatural. The Harlequins were trained from birth; they carried in their memories the history of all the Seven Tribes of Man, and they could mimic the speech of each of them.

"Mihn, you've been travelling for weeks," Isak said. "At least take a break before starting out again. I'm sure there's time."

Mihn shook his head. "Morghien's right. Better to leave as soon as possible. I will be ready by tomorrow morning. A ducal warrant will mean we don't need to carry much in the way of supplies, we can requisition what we need en route. Give us fresh horses and we can be off."

Isak's own heart sank at the thought of getting into the saddle again; he was astonished that Mihn was willing to just up and go, especially as he wouldn't be back in Tirah before winter paralysed the country. But it was his fault they were going in the first place; now he would have to let Mihn and Morghien do it their own way.

"You're both as stubborn as each other," he groused. "Fine, if that's how you want it, so be it. You leave tomorrow."

The return of the hawkers led to lunch, followed by an afternoon of summer games. Isak found himself as delighted with the small jokes made at his expense by normally reserved matrons as with the children who enlisted the huge white-eye in their own entertainments.

Summer was a time for relaxation for the Farlan nobility, and as the season was short, and too often occupied by campaigning, any opportunity for socialising was met with added gusto, a spirit of living Isak hadn't experienced before. He'd never even imagined people could live like this when he had been working every daylight hour with the rest of the wagon train. From the duty of the lord of the manor to present, on bended knee, a bowl of wild strawberries to any female child amongst his tenants on her birthday, to the highly juvenile Feast of Apples that made most soldiers' drinking games look sensible in comparison: the Farlan nobility took summertime amusements seriously. To his surprise, Isak loved it all.

That afternoon, he found himself kneeling on the grass with three whooping children, young relatives of the countess, balanced on his broad back. Vesna and Tila were standing close together, fingers interlocked, watching.

"Of such things are the most perfect childhood memories made," said Vesna, grinning.

"Absolutely," agreed Tila with a laugh. "Within four summers they'll be horrified when they remember clambering over Lord Isak, let alone how they bit the duke on his white-hand!" She giggled as Isak stretched out an arm so the boys could swing from it, as if it were the branch of a tree. With a roar, a little girl lunged for the arm as well, struggling to dislodge the boys. Isak could almost imagine that he was playing with Tila's children while she and the count watched on in parental approval. As he tickled the girl, provoking squeals of laughter, Isak grinned as he realised that for the next few weeks he could have a childhood of sorts, one denied to him in the past. The impositions of adulthood would return all too soon; for now, it was summer, he was surrounded by friends and the sun was shining.

Groaning, Isak swung himself into his saddle. Though the morning was a little cooler, Isak still found his new dragon-emblazoned green tunic uncomfortably warm, but he would look the part of a duke as he saw Morghien and Mihn off. As it was customary for the Saroc household to accompany those leaving for the first hour of their journey, the suzerain had decided to turn this into a visit to the nearest town.

Red oak-leaves embroidered all the way up Isak's left sleeve drew attention to the exposed skin of his hand, but he couldn't deny the overall effect. With Eolis hanging from a bright red swordbelt and scarlet leather boots, Isak looked more like a Farlan noble than he ever had before. Only the white cloak around his shoulders ruined the image a little, but they had officially proclaimed Bahl's death now, so every person in the party wore similar cloaks, embroidered with ancient symbols of mourning. The women wore white scarves, and would keep their hair covered for the fortnight of mourning.

"I must say, Countess, your seamstress has surpassed herself," commented Tila as Isak wheeled Megenn around.

"The very image of a gentleman," agreed the countess with a smile. Isak glowered at the two of them, but goodnaturedly. He had to admit it was nice to be dressed in new clothes; the months of travelling had taken a toll on their wardrobes.

"Everyone will be talking about times changing," Tila continued. "Lord Bahl's image was rather that of a hermit, and a threadbare one at that. I'm afraid it didn't serve him well."

"I hardly think people's opinion on his dress worth worrying about," Isak said. He spoke without rancour, but Tila stopped. Isak had become extremely protective of Lord Bahl since his death.

"This is your first public appearance as Lord of the Farlan," Tila said firmly. "You may not like it, but word of how you appear today will spread to the other suzerainties very quickly. They have heard only that Lord Bahl is dead. They will be reassured that you look the part, that you look like the Duke of Tirah."

"I suspect they've heard too much about me already."

"Then we have a new image to present," Tila said, still composed. "The refined, sophisticated Lord Isak, Duke of Tirah is a quite different beast to the uncivilised Suzerain Anvee!"

"The things a woman will do for a state wedding," Isak retorted, remembering Lord Bahl's parting words. He grinned at her blush. *State wedding indeed*, he thought. *Better be sooner rather than later, or there might be a little embarrassment—I'd be surprised if a virgin smiled like that!*

Before either could say more, Count Vesna ushered them all through the gates. Morghien and Mihn were already there, waiting impatiently, and as soon as they spotted Isak they swung their horses around and broke into a gentle canter. The procession took a while to catch up, but soon everyone settled in to an easy stride.

The early morning mist didn't linger for long and the air was filled with birdsong. Isak noticed the difference in the Land here, far from the mountains and dark forests a wagon-brat had considered home. The undulating ground of Saroc was mostly scrub, where the forest had given way, populated by goats and long-horned sheep, interspersed with cultivated fields neatly enclosed by drystone walls or high bramble hedges.

The hour went quickly as the warmth increased. Brief goodbyes were exchanged on the highway, under the watchful gaze of a solitary, ageing roadman whom Suzerain Saroc had greeted by name. When the time came, Isak found he didn't know what to say to Mihn, the man who had been his shadow for six months now. The words caught in his throat as he realised how much he would miss the silent presence, almost fatherly, though Mihn was only just thirty summers.

As they clasped arms, Morghien stepped away, to allow them some privacy. Isak opened his mouth, but the words wouldn't come. He released Mihn and withdrew his hand, feeling foolish and awkward.

"Don't go and get yourself killed, you hear?" he said, sounding almost angry. "I'll have things for you to do when you bring her back."

"Yes, my Lord," Mihn replied, as inscrutable as ever.

Isak shifted his weight from one foot to the other. "Well then, I suppose you should be off," he said gruffly.

"Yes, my Lord." Mihn gave a bow and turned to leave.

Ah, damn, I'm being a fool, aren't I? Isak thought suddenly. *Never had much need for goodbyes before, not to a friend.* "Mihn, wait," he said on impulse. *Right, what do I say now?* "Thank you for agreeing to go; Xeliath is really my responsibility after all. You've been as loyal a bondsman as I could have ever hoped for, as well as a friend."

A smile crept onto Mihn's usually expressionless face. "I am glad to have purpose in my life again," he said. For a moment he hesitated, off-balance himself. "I—when I was young and still with my people, weaponsmasters from the furthest clans came to watch me in a practice duel. I am—I was the best with the blades they'd ever seen. One said he thought he was watching the King of Dancers."

"The what?"

"A myth among the Harlequin, that one day we would have a king of our own, one who will end our years of service to the Seven Tribes of Man. It isn't a prophecy—even among the Harlequins we do not know its origin—but it is told to every child, down through the generations, because it is the only tale we have of our own. None of the history we relate involves the people of the clans. After that day I was treated differently, as though my destiny was assured and I carried their hopes with me.

"When I failed, the old men wept as if they had no future. I know it isn't the same for you, but I do know what it is to bear expectation. It was something I resented. I thought of it as a burden. Now I am glad I have the chance to be part of something magnificent again."

Isak didn't speak. He was transfixed by the outwelling of emotion, and by Mihn's unwarranted decision to reveal such a personal matter.

"Just remember," Mihn continued as he composed himself, "you've been blessed by the Gods. Never forget that, and never regret it." With that, he turned and walked away to his horse. He had a spring in his step, as though a weight had been lifted from him.

"I hope you remember that too," Isak said to Mihn's back, but whether he heard, Isak had no idea.

When the pair had disappeared behind a great outcrop of grass-topped granite, Suzerain Saroc led the procession in the opposite direction, eastwards, toward the town. As they travelled, the suzerain explained to Isak that the town was in fact owned by the abbey at its centre, run by the Brethren of the Sacred Teachings. His grandfather had bequeathed them land that hugged the banks of the river, but the second abbot, being a man of sharp business sense, had overseen the village's expansion and now the once-sleepy hamlet was a busy town.

As they drew closer, Isak began to note increasing numbers of fit young men in blue habits, beyond that of any normal monastery. The suzerain was a popular man, and stopped frequently to talk to the townsfolk. He introduced the most important to Isak, but most were too intimidated by the huge white-eye to do much beyond bow and mutter greetings. Even so, Isak felt the atmosphere was one of welcome more than anything else, and his fears about the Brethren began to subside—until he reminded himself that it was easy enough to put on a show for one day. He would need to hear Lesarl's opinion before he accepted it wholly at face value.

At the abbey a small party stood waiting to greet them. The men were all dressed in dark blue, as befitted monks in the service of Nartis, but on their deep cuffs were thick bands of yellow, which Isak had never seen before. The abbot looked young for his position, barely forty summers by Isak's guess, although his head was clearly bald, unlike many of his companions, who had had to resort to shaving to correctly mimic their God, Nartis.

Suzerain Saroc went through the formalities, introducing Abbot Kels and Prior Portin. There were two unnamed monks, who were standing beside a third man, dressed as a lay brother and leaning heavily on a wooden crutch, his right leg raised off the ground. The man wouldn't look at Isak, but scowled at the ground between the Duke of Tirah and Abbot Kels. There was something familiar about the man, but nothing he could put his finger on. In the distant recesses of his mind, Aryn Bwr, who had been quiet since the battle, chuckled infuriatingly. Isak tried to concentrate on what people were saying, but when the injured man did at last speak, the words escaped Isak completely.

"But of course!" exclaimed the abbot in response to whatever the man had said. "I should not have kept you here at all. My Lords, please excuse Brother Hobble, for he has just returned from the hospital with vital medicines, and as you can imagine, it is rather tiring to walk with a crutch."

Isak motioned for the man to go, which Hobble did without another word. Aryn Bwr muttered something ironic in Elvish, as the man made his way down the street.

"Brother Hobble?" Isak enquired of the abbot, who spread his hands in a gesture of helplessness.

"It is the only name he will give us. He came to us several months ago, and he has been a blessing to the abbey ever since. He's a learned and pious man who I hope will soon take his vows, but he will tell us nothing of his past, or the cause of that shattered ankle that refuses to heal properly."

"I know him," mused Vesna. "I've seen him at the palace, I think—a Swordmaster? His name escapes me, but I know I've met him."

As the memory of his first morning in the palace rose in Isak's mind, a cold chill ran down his spine and his mouth went suddenly dry. A face in the crowd as he sparred with Swordmaster Kerin; a pain in the back of his knee;

the bubbling anger as he sprawled flat on his back on the packed earth of the training ground; a savage blow as he lashed out at the man who had caught him, and the thumping connection with an ankle that was so hard it had jarred his wrist.

Isak hadn't even looked at the man, intent as he was on besting Kerin. Only afterwards had he noticed the man, face contorted by pain as he held his leg just above the shattered ankle—the ankle that still hadn't healed.

"Oh Gods."

"What is it?" Vesna asked. "Can you place him?"

Isak ignored the question and asked the abbot, "Can you not do anything for him? Have you tried to heal it with magic?"

"Of course, my Lord," the abbot replied, "we are a dual-aligned abbey, dedicated to Nartis and Shotir." He brushed the yellow cuff of his habit: Isak now realised it was the colour of the God of Healing. "Unfortunately, our best efforts—and we do have a number of talented healers here—have proved fruitless. The damage done to Hobble's ankle is no normal injury, and our magic has had no effect. I suspect Hobble believes the hurt done to him was a divine judgment, that he has something to atone for. Certainly that impression is sustained by the vigour he goes about any task he is given, but considering how selfless the man is, I cannot begin to imagine what that might be."

Isak stared down the road at the man limping through the crowds of townsfolk. "Tsatach's balls," he muttered under his breath. "An angry boy's moment of petulance, nothing more, and he takes it as a divine judgment?" Now he knew why the last king had been so amused.

"My Lord?" said the abbot anxiously, trying to catch Isak's words.

"What does he do at the hospital?"

"He is experienced at dressing wounds and spends much of his day tending to the poor folk afflicted with leprosy. He will not turn from the most menial of tasks."

"Leprosy?" Isak exclaimed, wide-eyed with alarm.

The abbot chuckled. "My Lord, calm yourself. We have tended lepers in these parts for decades; I am certain there is no risk of contagion. Brother Helras has been in charge of the hospital for ten years now, and has persisted in good health the entire time. You are quite safe."

"Did Brother Hobble know that when he volunteered for the duties?"

The abbot paused. "I'm not sure . . . perhaps. If not, it is a testament to the man's faith, no? Now, may I show you around the abbey and offer you refreshment?"

"The consequences of this life," he muttered under his breath, too softly for anyone else to hear. *He tells me to be thankful for what I have, yet every step of the way I hurt someone else. In my wake I hardly notice the futures I ruin. Oh Mihn, you've got such faith in me, but what magnificent destiny are you going to find down a road paved with broken lives?*

"My Lord?"

"Oh, yes, of course. Lead the way."

That evening, Isak found himself out in the walled garden again, staring up at the hunter's moon at its zenith. The memory of Brother Hobble, struggling with his crutch and scowling down at the ground, had haunted him all day. Clearly he had not forgiven Isak for the injury, divine retribution or no, and Isak certainly couldn't blame him for that: constant pain and the end to his life as a Swordmaster were hard things to forgive—although the latter must have been the man's own choice, knowing Swordmaster Kerin as he did. It was the heroes of war who gained Farlan titles and fame, and there were dozens of men who'd found their place in the Land through being a champion of the Ghosts.

"Contemplating the futility of existence, my Lord?"

Isak whirled around at the unknown voice, Eolis flashing from its sheath. The silver blade glowed in the moonlight as a man stepped from the shadows with a chuckle. A sword remained sheathed on his back while his hands were held out in Farlan greeting.

"With such gifts, who could lead a futile life?"

"Who are you?" Isak tried to make out the man's face. He wasn't Farlan; his lighter hair and darker complexion made him look more Western, if anything. His dress was dark, functional, reminding Isak of the King's Men of Narkang. Not quite a soldier, and more than one.

"I am Ilumene." There was a pause. The man stood with the ghost of a sardonic smile on his lips. Isak had the oddest sensation, that Ilumene was not just a King's Man, he could be King Emin's son—though of course he could not be, as he was some thirty summers old, and Queen Oterness was well noted for having failed to produce an heir . . . but this man did have every ounce of Emin's mocking arrogance.

"For a man who seems to like the sound of his own voice, you've gone suddenly quiet," Isak said. "If you don't want me to run you through, perhaps you would care to explain yourself in a little more detail?"

The edge in Isak's growling voice served only to widen Ilumene's smile. The man had two scars on his otherwise handsome face, on the left-hand side. One skirted the ridge of his eyebrow; the second was a jagged cut down the outside of his cheek.

"I am of the Brotherhood." Ilumene gave a chuckle and turned his head to the right to give Isak a better view of his scar. "But as you can see, my duties have not left me unsullied." The base of his earlobe that would have carried the Heart rune had been torn away by the cut. When Ilumene pointed at his ear, Isak saw a network of criss-crossing scars on his hands, as though the man had been dragged through a bramble bush of steel thorns.

"Strange that you didn't appear when Morghien was here."

For an instant Ilumene looked genuinely shocked. "I didn't know Morghien had been in the region. Come to think of it, I didn't know you and he were known to each other. It seems I have much to catch up on. When did he leave?"

"Today, this morning."

"I'm surprised he didn't wait then; I've not seen him for a long time. I was starting to wonder whether he could sniff us out—I can't remember how often he's stepped out from behind the only tree around on a deserted stretch of road."

Isak relaxed a little. There may have been something odd about Ilumene, but he'd not liked all of those Brothers he'd met in Narkang either—the tall, blond one with a scar all the way down the side of his face, Beyn; King Emin and Doranei were confident of his loyalty, but there was something about the man's face that Isak didn't care for. *I suspect it's just because he has a white-eye's arrogance*, he thought, being honest with himself.

As it was clear that Ilumene did know Morghien, and Isak was certain the wanderer wasn't one for casual acquaintances, he sheathed Eolis.

Ilumene stepped a yard closer so they could speak normally.

"Well, I suppose that also answers how you got past the guards," Isak commented. "I hope you didn't hurt any of them."

Ilumene gave a small smile. "One will have wounded pride when his comrades find him, but nothing more. King Emin may encourage many unsavoury traits in his men, but a love of killing is not one of them."

Though Ilumene spoke with a smile, there was an edge that left Isak with a slight frown. Most of the Brotherhood were respectful of their king to the point of reverence; Ilumene sounded like he was on more familiar terms with Emin. Maybe, Isak reflected, *it's because they're so similar.* His brief time in Narkang was enough for him to realise King Emin was not hot on excessive formality if it were not necessary.

Isak broke the brief silence. "I take it you were here for a reason?"

"There is always purpose in my master's actions."

And in your choice of words? Isak wondered. A prickle ran down his neck, but he refused to let it show. The man was playing a game, trying to unsettle Isak—but could he expect anything less of King Emin's friend?

"And that purpose is?"

Ilumene shrugged. "I was to give you a message, though I do not pretend to understand everything behind it. King Emin is secretly travelling to Scree, the Brotherhood his only guards—it was thought that you should know."

"Scree? Why? What's happened there?"

"I intend to leave tonight to find out more. The message was short; there was no space for explanations. I have heard a rumour about a monk fleeing his monastery and hiding in Scree."

"A monk? What could a monk have done to make Emin hunt him down personally?" Isak was genuinely confused. "And in Scree, no less? I'd have thought a White Circle stronghold was the last place Emin would want to go."

"Unless he considered it important enough," Ilumene corrected him. "I have the impression the king will not be the only one hunting the monk."

"What could a monk have done to attract that sort of interest—no, wait, let me think: if a monk has done something wrong, he gets assassins sent after him. If King Emin is going himself, the man would have to be a mortal enemy—or have something the king wants personally. An artefact of some kind, perhaps?"

"A reasonable assumption," Ilumene conceded, "but truly, I can tell you no more. And now, I must be on my way."

"Wait," Isak said as Ilumene turned to leave, "why did he send the message? Because he wants me not to lay siege to Scree? Or does he want me to get involved?"

"The king did not give me a reason, but I'm sure he would appreciate you pursuing a more subtle revenge than the wholesale destruction of the city if he is inside it. I cannot say if he wants you involved; if the king required your presence, I'm sure he would have summoned you."

Isak growled, disliking the implication that he was at Emin's beck and call. "Then your king might have to be more careful about what he takes for granted," he snapped.

Ilumene bowed in acquiescence and disappeared into the shadow of a laurel. Even with his remarkable hearing, Isak couldn't hear the man leave. It was as though he simply faded into the darkness.

Scree? What could possibly lure King Emin there? He looked to the south, where he fancied he saw the faintest of lights on the horizon. He had a sudden, desperate urge to know what the King of Narkang was up to.

"Home first," he reminded himself. "Everything else can wait."

CHAPTER 6

ZHIA HURRIED ACROSS INTO THE SHADE of the high-pillared porch, her thick shawl pulled low over her face to hide her from the scorching afternoon sun. Her coachman, Panro—who doubled as guard and servant, and once, on a particularly dull day in Narkang, lover—closed the coach door and climbed back up on the seat. He wouldn't bother going far; it was unlikely the Red Palace would see any more visitors during the short time Zhia intended to stay. Scree waited drowsily for evening, when the sun's ferocity would lessen; shops and stalls were shut up and even the most diligent of tradesfolk sought some shady corner or dark hallway. Zhia couldn't help smiling; the unusual summer heat had proved an unexpected bonus. In Scree everyone would be sleeping during the day, so her nocturnal life was less likely to draw notice.

Zhia paused and savoured the light breeze that greeted her through the tall panelled doors, scented with sweet roses and orange trees from somewhere within. A man dressed in a dark brown livery stood waiting for her, his head bowed. No member of the White Circle would come and greet Zhia; the custom was for visitors to be presented once they had made themselves presentable. This was particularly useful for Zhia, for any errant ray of sun would blacken and burn her skin.

"Mistress Siala has been informed of my arrival?" she asked, snapping her fingers at the liveried man. Her Fysthrall dialect and mannerisms were impeccable.

"Yes, Mistress Ostia." The man kept his head bowed as he spoke. "I am to escort you to her office immediately."

But why? thought Zhia. *She leads the White Circle now the rest of the leadership is dead, I made sure of that. Does she simply want an account of their failure? Or did she know that the Fysthrall queen carried the Skull of Paths with her? I think I was sensible to leave that in the carriage; she wouldn't think to search that, but she might well have a mage up there with her.*

The servant was waiting patiently for a reply. When she did finally jab a finger towards the inside of the palace he bowed low and moved to lead the way. As she followed him down the hall, she saw the red theme continued inside as well. Outside, the painted pillars, window frames and doors were distinctive, even arresting, especially when seen from a distance. Within, the colours looked garish and crass, and incongruous with the elegant furnishings, which were far too sophisticated for anyone local, especially the duke Siala had recently deposed. Siala was apparently from Tor Salan, but until she met the woman there was no way of telling if the sophistication was hers. Zhia hoped so; the rest of the Circle had hardly taxed her brain, and an intelligent adversary would make her stay in Scree infinitely more entertaining.

A large open staircase took her to the second floor and she looked carefully at the high windows. It wasn't often that she dared venture out during the day, but when it was necessary, she took every precaution.

Siala's study faced the head of the stairs. The door itself, flanked by blank-faced Fysthrall soldiers before whom the servant cringed, hadn't been spared the scarlet ravages of Scree's previous ruler; the faces on the four carved panels had been stained red and detailed in gold leaf. To her right, Zhia noted a pair of male functionaries sagging when they caught sight of her, apparently aware that she would be admitted ahead of them.

"Mistress Siala is just concluding a meeting," the servant at Zhia's side murmured, and at her curt nod, he fled.

The door did indeed open a heartbeat later, and to Zhia's complete astonishment a man dressed like a country minstrel strode out of the room with all the confidence of a king. Over a dirty green tunic he wore a gaudy gold chain with bejewelled coins laced through it hanging down to his navel, and a feathered hat was caught under one arm. His tanned, pinched face and narrow nose suggested southern origins. His skin was as grubby as his clothes.

Tor Salan perhaps, or Embere? Now what would Siala be doing meeting with a dirty foreign minstrel? Her train of thought stopped dead as Zhia realised the most remarkable thing about the man was that the gold chain was not costume jewellery. *Now I know all I need to about Siala,* Zhia said to herself. The minstrel had a deeply satisfied look on his face, one that might not have been there if Siala had paid enough attention to the gem-encrusted coins hanging off that chain. *But what does it tell me about this man, dressed like a vagrant musician, standing like a king and wearing a king's ransom around his neck?*

"Lady," the minstrel acknowledged, bowing with a flourish after he had taken the time to scrutinise her as carefully as she had him. The accent suggested something of the south as well, but no place she could identify.

Not "Mistress," though; he almost seems to recognise me. Could that be possible, *or has the heat just got me flustered?* "Have we met?" she snapped.

"Unfortunately not, for you are new to the city, no? But if you seek your entertainment under cover of night, I am sure your presence in Scree will be to my profit." The minstrel bowed. "Now if you will excuse me, gracious lady, I must away."

He didn't wait for permission but trotted off down the stair without a backwards glance while Zhia frowned. *Who was he? He said "under cover of night"—but did he actually recognise her?*

"You must be Ostia," declared a voice from inside the study. Zhia resumed an expression of placid innocence as she swept in to the room. Behind a desk stood a tall, slim, striking-looking woman dressed in white silk; some fifty summers of age, Zhia guessed, though her face had weathered the passing years well. To her right were two others, sitting together on a narrow chaise longue, but Zhia sensed neither was a mage and ignored them. It was the remorseless gleam in Siala's eye that had caught her attention. The woman stood perfectly still, taking in every detail of Zhia's appearance. *You don't look like a fool*, thought Zhia, a little scornfully. *You know how to deal with minor sisters like Ostia, I'm sure, but that could simply mean you're a well-born bully. What lies behind the make-up and fading beauty, anything of value?*

"I am, Mistress Siala," Zhia replied gravely, her hands clasped to her chest and head inclined slightly. Four peaked windows behind Siala spread a carpet of golden light into the room.

"Please, sit," Siala said, nodding to a chair bathed in the warm sunlight.

"If it doesn't offend you, I would prefer to stand," Zhia replied calmly. She recognised Siala's intention, to make her hot and uncomfortable as she was questioned—though the effect on a vampire would be rather more than merely uncomfortable. She stood behind the high-backed chair and arched her back theatrically. "I'm afraid all this travelling has knotted me up quite dreadfully. It would be a blessing just to be able to stand straight for a while."

Siala conceded and directed Zhia's attention to the two attendants on the chaise longue. They rose at Siala's gesture. One woman was dressed like a common soldier, but with a rapier on her hip. She had the long, pronounced features of a Deneli tribeswoman. She gave Zhia a broad smile as recognition flashed in both faces.

"May I introduce you to Haipar, who is acting as representative for a group of mercenaries we have employed."

"As a matter of fact, we've already met," Haipar said, pushing back her whitened hair. Her other hand rested on her sword hilt. Zhia ignored her; the blade was just for show. Haipar would not have been hired for her skill with a sword, but for her rather more brutal talents—and if she were representative of the mercenaries they employed, Siala had definitely bitten off more than she could chew. Zhia noted that despite being banished from her clan years ago, Haipar still brushed ash into her hair, as though trying to look as old as she actually was. It could have been a day since they last met, rather than the decade it was.

Siala arched her eyebrows. Zhia said nothing, but she shifted her weight, ready to leap for the door if Haipar gave her away. Fighting her way out of the Red Palace might be messy if some of her comrades were also around, but none were Zhia's match, even without the Skull.

"We once shared an employer," Haipar said after a moment. "Ostia was acting as political advisor, while I—Ah, I helped with certain matters of security."

"And thus I can personally testify to the efficacy of your employee's talents," Zhia said with a smile, relieved at Haipar's utter lack of loyalty. "I would have been in significant danger, had it not been for Haipar."

"Ostia flatters me; she had quite a firm grip on events, as I recall," Haipar replied, a calculating glint in her eye.

Siala watched them both, a slight smile hovering on her lip, before moving on. "The young woman next to Haipar is Legana, who has recently been persuaded to join the Circle."

Legana, a startlingly beautiful woman of Farlan origin, said nothing but offered Zhia a brief bow. She was dressed as if for a formal hunt; her light jerkin of bleached chamois leather, though detailed in mother-of-pearl, was clearly functional.

No doubt you'd wear a man's clothes if you could, Zhia thought to herself. *Dear me, Lesarl hasn't grown any more subtle with age, has he? Any fool could tell she's ideal for recruitment to the Circle—so didn't they even question it? That girl looks just a little too beautiful and a little too dangerous to be the innocent she would have us think.*

"Legana, Haipar, if you would wait outside?" Siala's voice broke into Zhia's musings. "Mistress Ostia and I have business to discuss."

Zhia felt Siala's eyes on her back as she turned to watch them leave.

"Ostia, you appear to be rather more experienced than I had realised," Siala began as the door closed. "I would not have expected you to run in the same circles as Haipar—not with her savage reputation."

Zhia restrained a smile. *Oh, if you only knew, you foolish little girl*, she thought, but said, "You know what Haipar is, then?"

"I do—or at least, I have heard stories of her kind. Considering the predicament the Sisterhood finds itself in, we are in need of such fearsome reputations."

And yet you wouldn't welcome mine. "That may be, but mercenaries like Haipar are notoriously difficult to control," Zhia said softly. "Their value on the battlefield is undeniable, but they can prove tiresome at other times." She left her comment to sink in and changed the subject. "Might I ask about the man with whom you were just meeting?"

"Who? Oh, the minstrel." Siala gave a dismissive wave. "Just the leader of some travelling players with a request."

"Just a travelling player," Zhia echoed, "yet he managed to secure a meeting with you? I'm impressed that you find time to sleep if you deal with every scrap of business yourself."

"Of course I don't, but the man had persuaded an official to request an audience on his behalf." Siala paused, her eyes becoming slightly vacant and glassy. For a moment, Zhia thought the woman had been enchanted, then she recognised it as puzzlement. "A strange one, but persuasive. Certainly suited to the stage. I found his voice quite hypnotic."

"And his request?"

"The request? Nothing important. The minstrel wanted to use condemned criminals in one of his plays to make an execution scene real."

"And your reply?" Something was troubling Zhia: she of all people had few qualms about killing, and she knew full well how best to please a mob, but the man wore an augury chain, and augury chains were not trinkets for the vain. Whether it had been a test for Siala, or something else, there was something more going on. "Did you allow it?"

"Yes. Do you disapprove?" Siala glared, daring a challenge to her authority.

"Not at all, it was mere curiosity. The man intrigued me."

"Why?"

"He wore an augury chain, not costume jewellery, but a real one," Zhia said, interested in Siala's reaction. "I would guess that no more than a hundred have been made in the last two millennia. The complexity, the materials—augury chains are incredibly expensive. That a wandering minstrel has one . . ." Zhia shrugged. "What was his name?"

"Augury chains?" Siala looked blank. "I've never heard of them. He called himself Rojak; he has rented the sunken theatre between Six Temples and the Shambles."

"Rojak?" The name meant nothing to Zhia. "If circumstances allow, perhaps I will take in a show after all."

"Well, before you do," Siala said brusquely, annoyed that she had been diverted from her intended subject, "please tell me what happened in Narkang. The few reports I've had have been patchy at best. It appears you were the only sister of any importance to survive." Her calm façade slipping, she leaned across the marble desk. "Is it certain the queen of the Fysthrall died? Were you there?"

Zhia had perfected the look of innocence thousands of years before Siala had been born. Now she knew what Siala wanted to know, and Siala's careful scrutiny would bear no fruit.

"I was not present at the queen's death, no," she began, a touch of regret in her voice. "She had assigned me as handler for the pirate Herolen Jex—she had little faith in his intelligence and thought it best to have regular updates."

Siala hid her disappointment. "And your escape from the city?"

"When the attack failed, the city was chaos. I found myself in the company of two local mercenaries and once I proved to them that I'd be useful to them alive—and problematic to kill—we fled together. I must assume we were fortunate, for I remember little beyond those frantic periods of running and hiding, and killing those in our way." She watched Siala's face as she added, "We stole some horses and my modest magic was sufficient to keep us hidden from pursuers."

"And what of the events in the jousting arena?"

"Is there much to know? They had captured the Farlan Krann and were going to bond him to the Queen's service as planned once he was awake. I cannot tell you whether they underestimated his strength, or if King Emin got a rescue party through—I do know the attack was anticipated, not the complete surprise our agents had led us to believe, so the king may well have been prepared."

Zhia watched emotions flicker in Siala's eyes and felt a moment of amusement. Scree's new ruler was obviously desperate to find out about the Crystal Skull. Possession of the Skull would doubtlessly confer complete control over the White Circle—for someone with enough strength of mind, it might even grant authority over the entire Fysthrall tribe, if she ever ventured beyond the eastern mountains to where they had been banished.

The strongest of the Fysthrall had taken part in the attack on Narkang, all those people gambled away in a desperate attempt to fulfil a prophecy, the key mistresses and warleaders lost when Lord Isak called down the wrath of Nartis. The White Circle would not recover its strength in Siala's lifetime, and those that remained this side of the mountains, already divided between cities, would soon discover they had few allies outside their strongholds. The Farlan were not known for their forgiving nature.

"Were we betrayed? Is that how he anticipated the attack?" Siala whispered.

Her thoughts were still on the Skull, but she couldn't ask more without inviting suspicion and curiosity, and Zhia was certain the existence of the Skull was not a secret she'd want to share.

"I doubt that, but King Emin is a clever and well-organised ruler," Zhia said. "Perhaps it was unwise to believe we could send an army into his city without his agents noticing."

"You accuse a dead queen of arrogance?"

"I would not presume to criticise the queen's decisions, but her advisors—Duchess Forell, for example, the senior sister, and a Narkang native: her inadequacies of intellect, information and backbone proved the difference between success and failure. I watched the battle from afar; the opportunity to take the White Palace was within their grasp. That battle should have been won."

Siala sighed and sat down in the monstrously ostentatious ivory and silver chair behind her. A seat of bone . . . Zhia recalled a rival, a thousand years before, claiming she sat on a throne of her enemy's bones. It had struck Zhia as a ridiculous thing to do, but as a tribute to his originality, she had found a craftsman to make a footstool of his remains.

"Very well, we will speak of this again later. In the meantime I have much to deal with. You have a reputation within the Circle for planning and common sense, and the Narkang débâcle has left us lacking sisters with the necessary ability to pursue the Circle's goals. More than half the Fysthrall Army this side of the Dragonspine Mountains died in Narkang, leaving us dangerously diminished, and there is no sign of reinforcements coming, especially now the tunnel under the mountains has been destroyed."

"Destroyed?" Zhia exclaimed in genuine surprise. "I had not heard that." For once she had been caught out; this piece of welcome news had completely evaded her up to now. The punishment of the Fysthrall for their part in the Great War had been banishment, and only the fortress of Tir Duria, guarded by the descendants of those Fysthrall who had remained loyal to the Gods, allowed passage from that lonely wilderness. Since crossing the mountains had become impossible, the Fysthrall, in typically dour and plodding fashion, had spent nearly two hundred years digging a tunnel. They had help from some rogue devotees of Larat, the God of Magic, among the Menin whose lands bordered the mountain range, but it was rumoured that Lord Styrax had brutally ended that arrangement.

"If we wish to regain contact before a second tunnel can be built, we must restore our own fortunes and deal with matters at this end. Without Lord Isak we cannot fulfil the prophecy and destroy Tir Duria, but before we can turn our attention to that problem, we need to concentrate on shoring up our position here." She grimaced. "Our first concern is the Farlan. Once Lord Isak arrives home, he will gather an army and invade. We have recruited as many mercenaries as we can afford, and enlisted citizens of Scree, but they are not an army and the nobles leading them are not officers. They lack discipline and organisation."

Siala looked harried now and Zhia realised that whatever she might think of the woman personally, Siala truly believed in the White Circle's cause, and she was barely holding everything together.

"That," she continued grimly, "is why I have employed Raylin mercenaries."

"They call themselves Raylin, certainly," Zhia interrupted, "but that is an affectation. The Raylin were an Elven order devoted to the perfection of martial skills; what you are employing is little more than a rabble of renegade mages and deranged psychopaths."

The distinction did not appear to bother Siala. "We need them. There are others, sniffing round the gold. Tachos Ironskin, Veren's Staff and Bane I've heard of, Mistress and the Jesters I have not. Do you know of them? Are they rabble; are they worth paying for?"

Zhia nodded. "I know them, and if you can control a group of Raylin, some are a veritable army in themselves. Think of Mistress as a superlative horse-trainer, except the horses are wyverns. The Jesters *are* worth whatever obscene price they will demand; they are bastard sons of Death himself and Demi-Gods in their own right. Veren's Staff, though, might be too much trouble: his reputation often fails to mention his intractable madness—for pity's sake, Veren died during the Great War. I'm at a loss to know how the man thinks he is inhabited by the former God of the Beasts. The same goes for Bane, whose obsession with vampires will make him impossible to trust." She smiled. "You know, I cannot remember the last time I heard of so many Raylin in the same place at once. It's rare to have more than two or three together, and yet you've gathered a dozen of the strongest in Scree."

"Whatever it signifies, it will be a blessing for us if we can forge them into an army. That is what I need you to do, Sister Ostia, organise them so that when the Farlan come we have soldiers who are trained, and know who's giving the orders. The noblemen leading them are under my control, but the troops are not battle-ready. Since you know these Raylin already, you can use that connection to influence matters. Can you do that? I have few other Sisters of the Circle I can rely on."

Zhia made a show of thinking, but this was exactly what she wanted. She had a number of enemies amongst the Raylin, but if she was in a position to influence Scree's armies, she could dictate the coming course of events.

"I can do it," she said finally. "I'm no soldier but I can organise the legions to bring this about. Do you have any competent Sisters at all I can add to my staff?"

Siala spread her hands helplessly. "Half of them have fled to Helrect, to be further from the Farlan—as though Helrect could stand if Scree fell—and of the rest, I despair. All I have is what are left of the Fysthrall, who are stretched thin enough already. The Third Army consists of our remaining Fysthrall troops' soldiers, and I need every one of those."

"What about that new girl, Legana? She doesn't look like a fool, and a pretty face is always useful to get soldiers to do what you tell them. Can I trust her?"

Again, Siala looked defeated. "I cannot say. If you want her, then take her. Can you trust her? She was working as a whore until I took control of the city and her pimp thought to make some money by selling her to us. A shame he didn't understand the principles of the Circle a little better." That put the ghost of a smile on Siala's face; the pimp had obviously found a squad of soldiers at his door, keen to explain how the Fysthrall thought women should be treated.

"Then I will take her and deliver you an army as soon as I can," Zhia said brightly.

"Good. You will find the mercenary captains based in the Dawn Barracks, where I can ensure their obedience. Recruit as many more as you can, just be sure their commanders are drawn from Scree's nobility." Siala's eyes narrowed. "There is only one ruler of Scree, so please do not forget that my agents will be keeping a careful eye on everything. And now, I have yet more city officials waiting with yet more requests. Please, send them in on your way out."

Zhia gave a slight bow and left. Outside, the men stretched and smiled with relief, then trotted obediently into Siala's room while Zhia walked to where Legana and Haipar were leaning on the banister of the stair, talking softly together. She beckoned to the pair and they followed her downstairs.

"I need somewhere private," she told them, and Haipar nodded curtly and led the way to a secluded corner on the first floor.

Once Zhia was certain they were alone, she relaxed and turned to face her new aides. "Haipar, a pleasure to see you again, and alone, too."

The Deneli tribeswoman smiled like a cat. "Erizol is outside the city, but I'm sure she'll gladly return to see you."

"Don't bother telling her; I really don't need the irritation." She stopped herself baring her teeth; Erizol the Fireraiser brought out Zhia's temper in a way that few could these days. Bane and his petty little crusade against vampires bored her, but there was something about Erizol's very personal hatred that annoyed Zhia immeasurably.

"I don't doubt it, but, ah—" Haipar cocked her head towards Legana, who was watching the exchange with a puzzled expression on her face.

Zhia smiled. "Oh, don't worry about Legana. She doesn't pose any threat; no true member of the White Circle would be here under orders from a man."

Legana stepped back, instinctively reaching for her dagger, but Zhia, moving faster than any human could, grabbed Legana's wrist in an iron grip and pulled the woman close. Legana froze, trapped in Zhia's gaze, until she blinked and let her expression soften. She released Legana's wrist and pushed her back to beside Haipar.

"Let's not get dramatic here," Zhia said calmly. "I think we might yet become allies. What are you, a devotee of the Lady?" Legana looked at Zhia and Haipar and nodded hesitantly, though she showed no fear now, only a flicker of apprehension. Zhia felt a small glow of satisfaction: Legana would indeed prove useful.

"I thought as much. Your employer is Lesarl, the Chief Steward of the Farlan, yes? When you report to your master, please tell him that one day I will instruct him in the finer points of subtlety." She smiled. "Until then, you're both my aides while I take charge of the army here and decide what I intend to do with it. Siala has just bitten off more than she can chew."

"Does this mean I'm the only genuine person here?" beamed Haipar, her accent noticeably more refined than when she was in Siala's office.

"Well, shapeshifter," Zhia snapped, "I suggest you don't spend too much time crowing about that—you've picked a poor employer this time, though I doubt you'll have heard yet."

"About the White Circle? Please Zh—Apologies, Mistress Ostia, the entire city knows of it. They attacked Narkang and almost killed King Emin." Haipar shrugged, as though the news did not interest her one bit. "But I'm a mercenary, war is my trade and I go where they can afford to pay me. If that means going up against Narkang, so be it."

"But you would prefer to be alive at the end? What Scree doesn't yet know is that the White Circle has made it clear their principal goal is to kill or capture the new Lord of the Farlan. Siala needs this army because she will soon be at war with the Farlan. Lord Isak is young and headstrong, and he now commands the largest army in the entire Land. I doubt he will be reluctant to use it."

That wiped the smile from Haipar's face. She'd been expecting the usual messy squabble, the sort of war that never quite flowers into anything too terrible but offers plenty of scope for profitable activities for her kind. Sitting across a poorly defended border from the largest army in the Land was not part of her plans. "So what are you doing here?" she asked, a scowl on her face.

"My business is my own," Zhia replied, "and I see no reason yet to discard an identity that has been useful. Things will need to be pretty desperate before I flee the White Circle, but I am quite confident that should it come to that, I would get out alive."

Haipar had seen Zhia forced into a corner before, and if the Farlan did attack the city, there was no question: Haipar would want to be allied with Zhia. Raylin had no truck with loyalty and honour; you got what you paid for, and what you paid for were unstable tempers and barely controlled skills and talents.

"So what now?"

"Now, we have work to do."

"Work?" Legana repeated, finding her voice at last. "You're going to follow Siala's orders?"

"Certainly, since that was exactly what I had hoped for. She wants me to liaise with her armies to get them trained and give her a chance against the Farlan—at the moment she has a rabble: raw recruits, mercenaries of varying talent, unblooded noblemen and Raylin of all shades. A rabble will be useless, but a rabble they will stay unless someone takes control. That means I need to find officers, ensure each regiment has *some* experienced staff, and get whatever Raylin we have onto the command staff. You Raylin can smell trouble coming. Haipar, your first duty will be to persuade the Jesters to sell me a few of their acolytes, half a dozen, if possible, for there's more than just training to do."

Haipar gave a mock curtsey. "Smelling trouble is part of our job; we are mercenaries, after all."

"I know, but it's an innate sense sometimes. You mentioned Erizol the Fireraiser; is Matak Snakefang travelling with you too? Did one of you suggest Scree for any particular reason?"

"I—" Haipar looked confused at the question. She smoothed her white-grey hair away from her tanned face. "I don't think so. We decided it was time to hit the road again, and it took us this way. We didn't know there were other Raylin here until we reached Braban, the village where I left the others. We'd been joined by Tachos Ironskin and some woman I didn't know called Flitter, and city guards tend to get over-excited when they see more than a couple of us together, so I came to speak for us all."

"The fact that so many are congregating in Scree is important, I think—your kind are as bad as white-eyes when it comes to tolerating the presence of your own. There's something in the air here, a storm brewing. I intend to find out what that is, and be ready when it comes." Her expression darkened. "When I see a wandering minstrel wearing an augury chain, it makes me think you Raylin might have got it right when you smelled trouble."

CHAPTER 7

IN THE BURNISHED LIGHT OF EVENING Lord Salen looked down over the valleys and ravines that served as streets for the great city of Thotel. At this distance the pickets and patrols that kept the conquered inhabitants under control were silent, the torches and guard-fires little more than pin-pricks of light. Salen enjoyed the sense of standing above the rest of humanity. Here, above the darkness of the streets, a trace of sunlight still remained. For a dizzying moment it felt like he stood on the peak of a moun-tain, his body light enough to float away into the abyss below.

He shook off the feeling and turned his attention back to Thotel, a city quite unlike any Menin city. The hollowed-out rock formations that the Chetse called stoneduns were massive weathered chunks of granite scattered around this deep valley like a giant's discarded toys. Wind and water had eroded the softer stone to expose these gigantic boulders, then the Chetse had chipped and scraped until the rocks were riddled with tunnels and living chambers. The mud-brick houses that surrounded them looked like worm-castings in comparison.

Each stonedun had a clan name carved into the rock, identifying it as a community, a fortress in its own right. Some clans had refused to surrender to the Menin, believing their barred gates would hold them safe through a siege . . .

Lord Salen was leaning out of an open window at the highest point of one such stonedun. The rough rock ledge felt curiously pleasant against his palms, as though the wall still resisted, long after the gates had been torn open and the inhabitants slaughtered.

A brass-bound, wax-stopped bottle hanging on a long golden chain from his neck chinked delicately against the stone and he pulled it up and slipped it into one of the many pockets of his patchwork robe. He was small for a white-eye, but he was the Chosen of Larat and Lord of the Hidden Tower, and his mind was sharper than his blade. He wore no armour and car-ried only a long dagger, but years of study had armed him with weapons few soldiers would even understand. Though the Menin were Karkarn's chosen people—the War God's own—Salen had always preferred the controlled ways of Larat to Karkarn's brutal strength. In Lord Styrax's absence, he had quietened this city with mere words. When he stirred himself to action, the very bedrock of Thotel would tremble.

"Lord Salen?" The messenger coughed uncomfortably, trying not to look too hard at the charms and amulets set into each of the brightly coloured fragments of cloth. Some made his eyes water, writhing to avoid his gaze; others, of tarnished metals, had gems that sparkled too brightly in their pitted settings. A few were impossible to make out in the gloom. Those were the one Mikiss found his eyes drawn to the most—he was glad that he couldn't discern any details.

The mage didn't move.

"My Lord, a message from Larim," Mikiss repeated.

"The maggots are quiet tonight."

"My Lord?"

"The Chetse. Don't you think they live like maggots, Mikiss? Tunnelling their way through these great stones; riddling these ancient forms with holes. There's been violence every night since we took the city, but tonight is quiet. Perhaps even maggots have primitive senses, enough to smell something in the air."

"I wouldn't know, Lord. One of the patrols killed some youths breaking curfew—one was carrying a weapon, so they were all executed, according to your standing orders."

"And the benefit of those orders is now plain to see: I am enjoying the peace it has brought to the city this evening. These people can only be cowed; a shame Styrax could not see that." The white-eye leaned over the balcony and looked directly down. Mikiss could hear the man's rings scrape on the stone as he watched a ripple run though Salen's robe, though there was no hint of any breeze.

"Ah, the message, my Lord?" Mikiss said again, trying to hide the apprehension in his voice. "Lord Larim has seen the wyvern approaching. Lord Styrax will be here very soon."

"Good. I've been waiting for him. I wonder what he's been up to; what can have taken so long." Salen's aristocratic voice was measured and calm, but Mikiss still found it sinister and shivered—he imagined a lizard would speak that way. Larat's adepts were all like that: their words were measured, whispery, their eyes were clinical and inhuman. He knew treachery was planned, and he was beginning to feel as if the foulness in the messages he'd carried over the last few weeks had seeped out to infect him with the poison of Larat's influence. A long-forgotten sense of duty, of honour, was awakening, crying for action, but he had felt Salen's gaze on him constantly over the last week and he could hardly eat or sleep with that unnatural presence sitting cold and heavy at the edges of his mind. The weight of exhaustion dragged at his heels.

"Go to Quistal; tell him to be ready to welcome our lord."

"I—" He stopped suddenly.

Salen turned around, slowly. His thin face tightened. "You have something to add?" One manicured nail tapped at the ivory hilt of his dagger, the other hand played with something in a pocket. Mikiss knew enough of the adepts of Larat to fear what was hidden more.

He couldn't bear those unblinking white eyes. He looked down at the floor and asked, "Do you wish me to find Lord Kohrad and General Gaur?" He knew the mage wouldn't want his lord's son and most loyal subject alerted, but it was as close to a protest as Mikiss could manage.

Salen didn't bother even showing his contempt. "They are out of the city with the Third Army. I am quite sure they will join Lord Styrax soon enough."

"Very good, my Lord." Mikiss fled, stumbling on the uneven floor of the stonedun's tunnels. Torches flickered weakly at each turn, barely sufficient to light the roughly hewn stone. As he descended the steep stairway to the main gate Mikiss felt a sudden breeze rush up past him, the tunnel channelling the unexpected wind. He flinched down, hands over his face, but was too slow to prevent the fine sand that lined the floor getting in his eyes. Cursing, he slowed, trying to blink the grit away.

At the ruined remains of the massive main gates, Mikiss saw a party of horsemen, one of the night patrols that kept the curfew, returning with a report for Salen's staff. A soldier stood facing away from him on the high steps below the gate. Mikiss smothered his jangling fears and walked out from the shadows, blinking furiously and tugging at his sleeve, which had snagged on the vambrace on his left arm.

The soldier on the steps gave a start at the sound of footsteps and spun around, reaching for the axe at his belt. Untangling his sleeve, Mikiss revealed the brass vambrace that had his messenger warrant inscribed in deep Menin glyphs.

Something about the soldiers puzzled him. Mikiss squinted until he was able to read the painted glyphs on one man's shoulder-plate: *Cheme 3rd Legion.* The Cheme legion? Weren't they were part of the Third Army?

"Hold it there, messenger," growled the man bearing the furled unit banner, "and where are you bound this fine evening?" The banner-man, swathed entirely in a long grey cloak, pushed back his hood to reveal bristling fur and long tusks. Mikiss froze; it was not a man at all but General Gaur. *Oh Gods.*

The air was dry and light. The soft taste of the southern plains tickled the back of his throat as he brushed past the rough stonedun walls. He noticed the forced silence: a few weeks of Salen's rule had changed the atmosphere of Thotel completely. The Chosen of Larat had done exactly as expected, performing one last act of service, however unwittingly, for the lord he had plotted against for years.

Here inside the stoneduns, Styrax could feel the pain of those slaughtered here, the entire extended family. Salen would not have noticed the voices, nor been able to sense the tears, the loss, echoing around the bloodstained tunnels. Rusty lines streaked the steps and sloping walls where blood and excrement had run down towards the deep heart of the stonedun.

He ran his stained fingernails over the rough-hewn surface. As ever, his left hand was ungloved. He almost savoured the discomfort of his damaged skin. The duel with Koezh Vukotic had left the feeling impaired in his pale and scarred hand, but it had been replaced with a less worldly sensation. He couldn't feel the evening breeze on his skin, but it *sang* when power flowed through his body. Right now, the sensation was one of needles being pushed into the back of his hand.

He could feel the currents of magic running through the city, where both Menin and Chetse mages were engaged in a variety of activities. He wondered what else was busy in the city that night, what other treachery waited in Thotel's dark streets. He thought of the daemon that had warned him of Salen's betrayal, the shadow that lingered on the edge of sight. It had spoken to him in the desert as he left his forces and went after Lord Bahl. It claimed to have nothing but contempt for its own kind, but who could tell, in truth? Was it watching him now, waiting to exploit events as they unfolded for its own purpose?

His footsteps silent, his black armour melting into the shadows, Styrax felt insubstantial, temporary, nothing but a memory when compared to the solid, immovable stone that encased him. As he reached the high chamber he stopped and waited, buoyed by the accumulating power inside him. After a while he decided the time had come. He scuffed the sole of his boot lightly on the ground.

The figure up ahead didn't move, but Styrax knew he had been heard.

After a longer pause, Salen asked, "Well, Mikiss, what do you want now?"

Styrax remained still, drawing more power into the Skull at his chest as he watched Salen's back. He wanted the man to have time to appreciate the foolishness of his treachery, to understand how he had been anticipated every step of the way, and that he had been permitted his childish delusion of supremacy—before it was *all* stripped away.

Salen's long robe of reds and yellows and blues, the seams stitched in silver and gold, moved a little in what breeze reached the tower. "Mikiss?" As he turned around, his expression of anger fell away.

Styrax smiled. His white hand burned savagely, every crease in his skin alive with sensation as the stored magic howled to be loose. He was glad of the pain; it reminded him of his mortality as much as his vast strength. He believed in the need for balance in all things—his son Kohrad was not the only person he tried to drum this into—so perhaps a demonstration would succeed where wise words had not.

"Well, Salen? You've been preparing for this moment for weeks now. Time to make your move."

The Chosen of Larat jerked into action, his hand darting into his pocket as he reached for the energy around him—and astonishment flashed across his face as he grasped nothing, the expected flow of power inexplicably absent to his touch. Instead, it was surging to the Skull fused to Styrax's armour.

"What?" Salen whispered in confusion.

Styrax saw the white-eye was still open to the absent energies in the air, but he was no longer searching for the tang of magic. The path was laid, the energies inside him screaming to be released—with a gasping shudder, he let the torrent course through his body and surge towards Salen, who rocked back on his heels, flailing wildly, as if he were being physically overcome by the raging deluge. With the Skull, Styrax had barely been able to contain the power he'd stolen; now, as he reversed the flow, his enemy screamed hideously and writhed in agony as the rampant flood of energy burned through every nerve and blood vessel in his body.

The Lord of the Hidden Tower collapsed, still convulsing, and the patchwork robe burst into pyrotechnic flames, the colours searing through Styrax's closed eyelids. He shielded his face with his hands, but still flinched as the amulets on Salen's robe exploded into bright white light.

Wind whipped across his body and Styrax jerked away as a piece of stone hit the thumbnail of his exposed hand. The night air grew suddenly close around him, pressing tight against his throat. Styrax forced his arms down by his sides and rested one hand on his sword hilt as he recognised the presence of the Gods. He would not let them see him reeling, not even if he were dying.

A profound silence fell on the chamber. Styrax opened his eyes to see just a charred pile of bones where Salen had been lying, and darkness all around. As he watched, the harsh shadows softened; Styrax imagined Death stalking back into the night, dragging Salen's scorched and pitted soul along behind him.

A sound came distantly, faint against the wind running through the city streets. Styrax listened closely, trying to identify it. For a moment he was puzzled, then he recognised Larat's hollow chuckle drifting through the night. Lord Salen's patron God was obviously amused at the irony of his Chosen's death. The white-eye grimaced. Salen's deranged indifference to life reflected his God's, and Styrax did not understand men like that, men who lived their own lives as little more than pale reflections of their God.

Styrax turned at last and moved briskly to join his guards below. He trotted down the winding steps until he reached the gate where General Gaur waited with the horses and a wretched-looking messenger. There were more deaths to come this night, more blood to spill into Thotel's ever-thirsty earth.

He drew his sword and stepped out into the pale moonlight.

CHAPTER 8

"**M**Y NAME IS MIKISS, MY LORD, Army Messenger Koden Mikiss."
He met Styrax's gaze for a brief moment, then lowered his eyes
again. His horse, surrounded by muscular cavalry horses made even more
bulky by their armour, looked fragile, and added to the picture of misery that
was the exhausted, frightened messenger.

Styrax smiled inwardly. He would surprise a man with unexpected mercy
more than once tonight.

"Come. We must ride," he said, and his party set off at a brisk canter
through the empty streets of Thotel. The looming stoneduns dotted around
the plain cast huge black shadows over the smaller buildings set in long,
wide avenues. The single cliff of the river-valley reached away to their left,
the quartz adorning ancient shrines set into the cliff-face sparkling where it
caught lamplight or moonlight.

"You have been carrying all of Salen's messages," Styrax said, turning his
attention back to Mikiss. It was not a question.

"Not all, my Lord, but many." Mikiss sounded resigned to his inevitable
fate; he had been expecting a sharp blade across the throat from the moment
he recognised the general.

"Then it is fortunate for you that I noticed an enchantment compelling you,"
Styrax said calmly, "or I would have been forced to conclude you were a traitor."

Mikiss looked up, clearly startled by the word "traitor." He cut a strange
figure, with the red-dyed skullcap that marked him out as a member of the
messenger corps and an over-large grey cloak. The brass vambrace was ceremonial; he wore no other armour.

No doubt he is a competent messenger, thought Styrax, *or Salen would not have
used him*. The harried trepidation on Mikiss' pallid face looked to be a permanent feature. Perhaps his family had bought the young man a commission as
a messenger because he'd hardly survive a week in command of a squad, let
alone a company of men. It appeared that he had not yet realised he was not
for the immediate chop.

"I'm showing clemency, man." He brushed away stammered thanks and went on. "Where is Quistal? Can I assume he's waiting for me to return to the Gate of Three Suns before making his move?"

Mikiss nodded. "His troops are camped on the Plain of Pillars and Salen's personal troops are in the sunken orchards. Where the coterie is, I don't know."

General Gaur turned towards Styrax with a questioning look; the white-eye shook his head. The two often had little need of words, for they had been something like friends for many years now.

"They are of no consequence," Styrax said out loud. "Larim should have killed them all by now. The coterie will have felt their master's death." He fell silent, thinking of the ground where they would have to fight. The Gate of Three Suns was a particularly remarkable construction. The massive stone wall was strung across a thousand yards of flat ground between a stonedun and a long rocky plateau. The three circular gates set into it served as the main passages in and out of the city. His brief inspection earlier had suggested that the wall was straightforward engineering, not magic.

The sophisticated irrigation of the sunken orchards had been his second surprise that day—this was the desert, for pity's sake. Styrax hadn't expected the Chetse to show such ingenuity, but there was no denying the enormous skill involved. He decided he was right to seek the trust of the tribe; clearly there were remarkable men within the wild, unwashed masses.

"Before we discuss matters with Quistal, we have an errand to run," Styrax announced to the unit in general.

"An errand?" echoed Kohrad. The young white-eye's voice sounded overly loud in the silent streets.

His words prompted a growled response from General Gaur. "Keep your voice down; we don't want to run into a patrol if we can help it. Salen made sure all the night patrols were his own men. We don't need word to get back to the Plain of Pillars before we're ready."

"An errand," confirmed Styrax. "Mikiss, where is General Dev being held?"

The messenger blinked in surprise. "The commander of the Lion Guard? He's at his family's stonedun, under guard. He'd been injured before the battle and couldn't be moved safely. Lord Salen wanted to make sure the general was alive for execution."

"I'm sure he did. Take us there."

"Father—" Kohrad started before Styrax raised a hand.

"No questions—have faith."

"Yes, Father."

Styrax couldn't see his son's face, which was obscured by the red-stained steel helm. It was impossible to tell if Kohrad was seething underneath; his reply had been crisp and level, but meant little. The boy was learning to hide his emotions even as his grip on sanity appeared to be weakening.

"Thank you," Styrax said. "Mikiss, is the stonedun guarded by Salen's men?"

"I believe so, my Lord."

"Right, you lead the way. We'll follow, like troops under your orders. If any of the guards work out we're hostile, you will break left and get clear. If any run once we reveal ourselves, you and your elegant horse are responsible for chasing them down. Gaur, we do this quietly and efficiently." He was watching Kohrad as he spoke and fancied he saw a slight twitch of the shoulder as his son recognised who exactly needed to be reminded.

"Now if any of you can actually remember how to ride in formation: close order, two columns, weapons hidden." The veterans accompanying Styrax all chuckled. They might be élite troops, they might not have travelled in close rank for years, but no soldier forgot their first drills. Quickly they opened up for Mikiss to reach the front, then lined up behind Styrax and Kohrad. The slither of steel indicated they were ready for the trouble to come.

"Creeping like a thief through the night," Styrax commented abruptly, "in a city I control, hiding from troops from my own army. I'd forgotten how much I enjoy this." His words faded on the light breeze. A bat darted over their heads, startling Mikiss, who shrank down in his saddle.

Styrax clapped a hand on Kohrad's armoured shoulder and smiled at the night.

Fifteen minutes later, General Dev's family stonedun came into view. It was a tall, roughly cylindrical block of granite eighty feet high, pocked with squares that indicated window holes. Lights flickered in the windows on the upper levels, but the lowest two were dark. There was a blazing fire at the gate that illuminated the guards nicely.

"Idiots," growled Gaur. "Weeks of trouble in the city and yet still they make themselves easy targets for anyone with a bow."

"Salen's best troops are waiting for us at the Gate of the Three Suns. With so many troops scattered around the city, I guess they'll have expected a quiet night here."

Kohrad's reply elicited only a curt nod; General Gaur was rigorous in his duty and would naturally expect every Menin soldier to follow the regulations, whether they were troops of the line or quartermaster clerks, on duty or off.

The gate, an oval aperture ten feet high, served as the mouth for the lion's head carved into the rock. It stood half open. A few soldiers squatted by the fire, one slowly turning a spit with the carcass of a goat speared on it. As the horsemen approached, another soldier came through the open side of the gate. He paused and peered out into the gloom, then barked at the men around the fire. They jumped up, scrambling for their weapons. Sparks scattered as someone kicked one of the logs and spread a tongue of fiery shards over the stone steps. Styrax grimaced as he heard a sound escape Kohrad's lips.

Mikiss responded by pulling back his sleeve once again and holding his arm up high. Whether they could see the brass vambrace glinting in the fire-light was hard to judge, but they all recognised the gesture. None of the soldiers drew a bow or nocked an arrow, but they did shuffle into some semblance of order, in case Mikiss turned out to be someone important.

"Who are you? What do you want?" called the man who'd spotted them first. His voice was rough, his accent Menin.

"You have a message for General Dev," murmured Styrax. Mikiss repeated the words.

"Piss on your message," the man shouted back, his hand creeping to his sword as the party continued closer. Styrax guessed he was the company lieutenant. "Lord Salen said we were to admit no one, not even Lord Styrax himself, without word from the Adepts of Larat in advance."

They were less than forty yards away. The soldiers began to drift forward instinctively; one swung an axe up onto his shoulder. Styrax could make out their uniforms now; the white tunics with multi-coloured stripes on each sleeve identified them as Guards of the Hidden Tower, Salen's personal legions. They were rightly feared: they were loyal enough to carry out any orders without question, and the Adepts of Larat put less value on human life than a troll would. Even if they were the dregs of the legion, trusted only to stand guard here while the rest fought elsewhere, they would be tough enough—for most soldiers, that was.

"I have permission. Lord Salen himself sent me with a message. I have it here in my bag." Mikiss' voice sounded uncertain, but as the horsemen closed, the guards could see clearly that he was a real army messenger.

"Leave your guards and approach."

"Leave my guards?"

"That's what I said. Stop where you are and dismount. Approach on foot."

"That's enough, I think," muttered Styrax. "Mikiss, break off."

The messenger wheeled his horse sharply to the left. For a moment the soldiers followed him with their eyes. Styrax kicked his spurs into the flanks of his horse and as he drew Kobra, startled faces flashed back to him. He saw recognition blossom in the eyes of the lieutenant. Kohrad howled at his side as they raced together into the group of men. The first man to die didn't even raise his weapon as Styrax's wide fanged blade cut down. His men were the best of the Cheme Legion; they were close on his heels, their long-handled axes hacking down at the lightly armoured infantry, moving in perfect harmony as they had a hundred times in the past.

Those with more sense fled into the stonedun, desperately trying to pull the heavy door closed behind them, but Kohrad slipped from his saddle and ran for the entrance himself. He threw his sword at the man trying to pull it shut, spearing him in a burst of yellow light, then leapt into the gap to stop the massive door on its inward swing. One man, seeing the white-eye had no sword, turned back and attacked him, but Kohrad dodged out of the way of the falling axe, then twisted back to grab the weapon, pulling the soldier off-balance.

Kohrad shoved the door open again to disentangle his foot, then snapped a kick into the man's ribs, knocking him over. A second soldier ran forward as Kohrad tugged the axe blade free and spun it upwards with a flourish to catch his attacker under the chin.

In a matter of seconds it was over and stillness returned. Styrax surveyed his troops and gave an approving nod. The Reavers were unparalleled throughout the Land, but most of them were white-eyes and they were actively encouraged to be wild. These Cheme troops were normal men—albeit many were far from *normal*—but discipline was as valuable as strength. He could trust these men to be swift and neat. Without an order spoken, they had dropped from their horses and started to drag the bodies inside. Styrax looked around and realised that Kohrad had disappeared. He opened his mouth to ask Gaur to fetch the unpredictable youth when the boy appeared again, sword drawn and dripping with blood.

"The guardroom is clear," Kohrad announced in a low, level tone. Styrax nodded briskly. His son was making a great effort to remain in control, and he wouldn't insult him by remarking on it.

"Good. Major, stay here with the men. I doubt anyone will come; if they do, deal with the matter or pull back. Gaur, Kohrad, with me."

The major nodded and unsheathed his dagger to cut the colourful robes from one of the dead men: they might as well look the part. Styrax left the man to it and swept through the door. Speed was of the essence now. The Third Army was waiting outside the city for the signal to attack. The longer they waited, the greater the likelihood that Salen's troops would discover them, losing them the element of surprise. As he moved silently up the stone steps, he heard frightened gasps. Ahead of him was a sharp turn—anyone hearing the fight outside would no doubt be waiting there to see who came up the stairs. They would be expecting an assassination, a quick death in the night for the talismanic general instead of an execution that would likely spark a riot.

Styrax checked his pace as he reached the corner, in case an axe was going to be swung blind, then shot round it. A grunt of surprise preceded a heavy spear being thrust forward. Styrax, ready, grabbed the shaft and tugged hard, pulling the youth from the shadows. Gaur, close behind as always, slammed a hairy fist into the unprotected forearm holding the spear. The youth yelped and dropped the weapon, trying to scramble back until he realised the bestial general had him by the scruff of the neck.

"You'll do," muttered Styrax. He took the boy from Gaur and gave him a shake. Startled, fearful eyes stared up at the huge white-eye as the boy froze. "You understand me?" Styrax demanded in Chetse.

The youth flinched then opened his mouth to speak. Unable to find words, he nodded hurriedly.

"That was a foolish thing to do. Lord Salen would have used it as an excuse. Lucky for you that you just tried to run me through instead of one of his men, wouldn't you say?" Styrax smelled an acrid smell rise up from the boy, who looked to be less than thirteen summers—too young to join the army, too young to have developed the muscle a Chetse warrior needed. He smiled and put the boy down, then removed his helm and let the boy see his face, instead of the unnervingly angelic aspect of Karkarn etched into the face-plate.

"I want you to do something for me, boy," he said. "Did you hear what happened at the gate?"

The boy managed a nod.

"That was us killing the men who've been guarding you. They were going to wait until dawn, and then kill the general. Are you related to General Dev?"

Again, he got a nod. In a dry rasp, the boy said, "He's my great-uncle, sir."

Styrax thought it sounded strange to hear the Chetse tongue in a high girlish voice. It sounded lighter, more poetic than he'd suspected—until now, he'd only heard it spoken by soldiers. "I thought as much. What's your name, boy?"

"Esech, sir."

"And you know who I am?"

The boy nodded, unable to say the words.

"Esech, I gave no orders for the general to be killed, nor for many of the other things Lord Salen has done in the city since I've been gone. Do you know what I do to men who don't follow orders?"

"Yes, sir."

"Good. Now tell me whether there are any more Menin in the stonedun."

"Only four, sir; two in Uncl—in the general's chamber and two at the door."

"Thank you, Esech. We're going to go and free your great-uncle now. I want to talk to him a while."

"You're—Are you going to kill him?"

"No, I'm not. You believe me, don't you?"

The boy froze, unsure, incapable of saying to this huge white-eye's face that he disbelieved the Menin lord. After a moment he lowered his eyes and nodded.

"Good. Now go back to your family's rooms and tell your family that in a few minutes the stonedun won't have any guards. That means you will be able to do what you like, but it's not going to be much fun on the streets tonight. I suggest you all stay quiet and safe. Can you do that?"

"Yes, sir."

"Then nod once more if I just keep on going up this main stair to reach the general's chambers, and go back to your rooms." Styrax watched the boy bob quickly and scramble away. He straightened and replaced his helm.

"Right, no unnecessary commotion here. Kohrad, take Gaur's crossbows and go ahead. You can see well enough to get both guards?"

Kohrad nodded and sheathed his own sword, the flames from the blade licking at the gold band on the scabbard for another heartbeat before dissipating. He accepted one of Gaur's crossbows, loaded it with ease as the general did the other, then turned and began padding softly up the steps, both crossbows levelled and ready. Styrax followed close behind, weaving a simple spell to bind the tunnel's shadows around his son.

The darkly flickering armour melted into the murky surrounds and Kohrad turned up the last corridor without hesitation. Styrax caught sight of the two drowsy, bored guards over his son's shoulder only just before Kohrad shot them, one following the other so swiftly that the second man didn't even have time to see why his companion had grunted before a bolt hit him in the throat. Styrax stepped over the corpses to the closed iron-bound door.

More sloppiness, he thought to himself as he realised the door was too thick to allow the sound to travel. *I would hope for better from my own army than this. Don't tell me they let the old man claim he'd catch a chill and allowed their numbers to be divided the night before he was damn well scheduled for execution? Haven't they even contemplated someone attempting a rescue?*

He drew a breath and hefted Kobra. The strange, fanged blade was pitch-black colour—except after it had killed, when it took on a deep red sheen. Styrax had always considered it a hateful weapon, too eager to drink the blood of those he killed. Unfortunately, that also made it the most powerful sword he'd come across, with the exception of that wielded by Koezh Vukotic, the last weapon forged by the Elf king Aryn Bwr, which was filled with the last king's grief at the assassination of his son.

Styrax could have taken that sword as he watched Koezh Vukotic's corpse putrefy and disintegrate, but it had rejected him. There was not enough loss in his soul, he suspected. After he'd touched the blade with his scarred hand, Styrax hadn't wanted it either—so much pain would eat its way into a man, and that power was not worth the high price demanded. A long time ago he had been told that he would have to take everything he had, that nothing would be given freely to the Saviour he was to become. That suited Styrax, even after he'd rejected the dubious honour. He had earned his "gifts," and bore no debt to the Gods because of them.

Kicking the door off its hinges, Styrax stormed dramatically into the room, almost colliding with the guard who had jumped up from his chair and was still fumbling for his sword. Styrax scanned the room quickly, then swung Kobra up to meet the second soldier's axe which was crashing down towards his hip. The force of his blow drove the man back and Styrax stepped away to give himself space to swing his broadsword properly, removing the man's head in a shower of blood and shattered bone. The other guard had regained his feet, but he barely had time to raise his own weapon before he found himself spitted on Styrax's sword. The magical blade pierced the centre of his cuirass and pinned him, whimpering, to the wall. Stepping close, Styrax snapped the man's neck to finish him off quickly, and left the sword jammed in the stone, feeding greedily.

He took stock of the living: two women cowered near the bed, obviously terrified, while a young unarmed Chetse soldier by the window looked almost frozen on the point of running forward. Styrax ignored them all and walked to the bedside, where an elderly man had raised himself up on his elbows. His only reaction was to raise an eyebrow at the newcomer, though the effect was somewhat spoiled by the thick grey bandage wrapped around his head.

"Ah, General Dev," Styrax said graciously. "I hear you're scheduled for execution in the morning."

"Lord Styrax." Chote Dev acknowledged his fellow soldier. "I had suspected as much—but it appears that is no longer the case."

Styrax paused and stared down at the man. "Well now, that rather depends on you," he replied gravely. He pulled up a chair and sat down beside the bed as Kohrad and Gaur arrived at the open doorway. "You are no fool, and running a guerrilla campaign at your age would be rather taxing. I think you'd enjoy an easy retirement—and I don't actually want to have to kill you and all your family in a most unpleasant fashion. It would be a tedious waste for both of us."

"What are you suggesting?" asked Dev, sounding puzzled. The ageing general was not best pleased to be at so great a disadvantage when speaking to his people's conqueror, but he was, as Styrax had gambled, a considered and cautious leader. The Menin agents in Thotel all agreed the general was one of the few men Lord Chalat had paid any attention to at all.

Styrax leaned forward. "It's simple. Your reputation precedes you, both as a warrior, and as a man of honour. To execute you is unnecessary, as well as detrimental to my position here. I have shattered the Thotel legions. Soon I will defeat those coming from the remaining free cities." The massive white-eye held up a hand as the general began to protest. "My intention has always been one of conquest, not slaughter. I have no desire to destroy the Chetse people—I am no Deverk Grast."

Styrax didn't bother concealing the scorn in his voice, and he could see the effect it had on the general. Most Menin revered Grast, despite the man's terrible acts—trying to wipe out the Litse hadn't been his only crime, just his most notable. History had many monsters, yet outside the Ring of Fire, where the Menin lived, few names were as reviled as Grast's.

"And so—?"

"And so I see no need to further insult the wounded pride of the Chetse by murdering the man who is the epitome of traditional values. I want your word that you will engineer no rebellion against me, that you will take no part in any such activities."

"And you will take my word?" wondered Dev, too surprised to hide his surprise. The look on the old man's face said the rest: *I wouldn't trust my word in your place.*

"I will. In return, you may retire to your estates outside the city in, say six months? The city needs your leadership right now."

"You want me to rule the Chetse from your pocket?" General Dev snorted. "I think I preferred Salen's conversation. At least he didn't offer false hopes." The Chetse veteran looked at the Menin soldier pinned to the wall and the beheaded man on the floor.

"I will appoint a permanent governor in due course," Styrax continued, "but I have no desire to see the city collapse into chaos because its leaders have been slaughtered. I must listen to someone among the Chetse, and better it be someone I respect."

"I'll be seen as your puppet."

"Then get something of value from it. I'm here to negotiate if you want."

"Leave the city?" the general replied quickly, prompting a laugh from Styrax.

"Perhaps not that."

"Well, I had to ask," Dev said with a sigh. "If you want me to govern this city, I need some concessions. No requisitioning of held wealth or slaves, no conscription, and a guarantee that there will be no purge of the nobility."

"No slaves beyond what would be acceptable by normal Chetse traditions," Styrax countered, "no conscription—I've never taken conscripts. If men want to join, they can, and they'll do it with the same rights and pay as any Menin. My coffers will need some refreshment, but nothing to bankrupt families or empty Chalat's treasury; it does me no good to break you. No systematic purges, of officers or nobles. I can't expect all of your countrymen to be reasonable, however, and my agents are extremely effective people. Doubtless some will die."

The general grunted. "I suppose that's reasonable. What about the Lion Guard? Salen said he would disband it."

"The Lion Guard will stay. I will, of course, take control of your armoury and disarm the men, but I realise the Lion Guard is not just a legion, to be disbanded and sent back to their homes. A Menin commander will be appointed on your retirement. Someone with sense."

"They won't stand for a Menin commander, and nor should any of the legions of the Ten Thousand have to."

Styrax called softly, "Gaur." Soft footsteps entered the room and General Dev's eyes widened at the figure approaching. "General Gaur," said Lord Styrax, "you have a new command: the Lion Guard of Thotel."

"It will be an honour," Gaur rumbled. "They were competent, at least— one of the few we met on the field."

"The few?" Dev spluttered. "It was luck and bad leadership that lost that battle. A general possessed by a daemon is a poor tactician, and his lieutenants who replaced half the army commanders were just as bad. Without that, you would have been swept away by our phalanxes and died of thirst in the desert as you ran for home."

Dev grimaced. Unable to leave his bed, he had been forced to lie there and hear of the fall of Thotel from a boy barely old enough to swing an axe. The Menin had swept across the Waste like a sudden spring storm and Lord Charr, or rather the daemon that possessed him, had rushed to meet them. In their haste the Chetse legions had been outflanked and outmanoeuvred. The core of their army, the Ten Thousand, had been severely mauled, but had managed to retreat while the rest were slaughtered on the field—and at the city gates, the Ten Thousand had found the way barred, Menin cavalry and centaurs waiting to pick off any soldiers too exhausted or thirst-crazed to have the sense to surrender.

"Perhaps we would have found you a little more challenging," Styrax agreed with a smile, "but a man makes his own luck, and so does a general."

General Dev gaped at Styrax. "That really was you behind it all?"

"You find it so hard to believe? Chalat might have been limited as a ruler, but he was no fool, and he listened to men such as you. It would have been too great a risk to try to take this city with an army brought over the Waste; only a madman would divide his forces and force-march half to meet an unknown foe."

"And in Charr you had that madman," General Dev sighed. He looked his age now, his already withered skin pallid from the weeks of being bedridden.

"Not for certain," said Styrax. "Every agent said that Charr was an idiot, the sort that gives our kind a bad name; he should never have been Chosen— but it was always a risk that he might listen to his aides and not march out. A good general makes sure of victory before he offers battle."

"But I still don't understand how you managed it."

Styrax gave a dismissive wave. "Some devotees of Larat playing with powers far beyond their control. A nasty business in all, but one that dropped a useful tool in my lap. The details—well, I think you would be safer not knowing. Now, time is rather against us so I must be leaving. I would appreciate it if you would accompany General Gaur to meet his new command staff. I'm certain you're not quite as ill as Salen believed. If he'd bothered to ask, he would have discovered that you were found on the Temples Plain, so clearly someone carried you here without killing you."

"You want me to go now?"

"Certainly." Styrax crouched down so he could speak more softly. "Take care they are courteous. The beast is a valued advisor. Any harm coming to him would do more than have me revoke the promises I have made." The white-eye gave a cold smile. "Gaur is a humourless bastard most of the time, but if you want to hear him laugh, tell him you're going to use him as a hostage when you bargain with me. Understand?"

General Dev nodded. "I do. A lord's friendship is a fickle thing."

"Then let us go. We will accompany you part of the way. The barracks overlook the sunken orchards, do they not?"

"They do."

"Excellent. I might even put on a show in your honour." Styrax stood and turned to leave, then hesitated. "Did the guards even object when you asked for the door to be closed?"

General Dev gave a throaty chuckle. "None that didn't fade before the face of an ill old man they wanted alive in the morning, although I can't say I expected you to be the one to take advantage of it!"

Styrax gave a snort and disappeared through the doorway, gesturing for Kohrad to accompany him. Gaur stepped toward the bed. With one taloned hand he gestured towards the shattered doorway. It was impossible for General Dev to make out Gaur's expression. The deep tangle of fur hid any clues.

"Come, General Dev. Our troops await us."

CHAPTER 9

THE SCREAMS OF THE DEAD soared up on thermals of violence and spilled blood. Ringed by beacons lit by the silent watching Chetse, the Menin trampled, stabbed, spitted and crushed their former comrades. Many of the attackers slipped on gore-slicked corpses and stumbled over severed limbs; the tapestry of gasps and cries was punctured by the constant clatter and crump of steel. In the borrowed light of a subjugated city, the Lord of the Menin waded through the slaughter all around him, slashing and piercing with blinding speed.

They had driven the Guards of the Hidden Tower out of the sunken orchards, their sudden thrust on two fronts sparking a panicked retreat. The stampede of confused infantry in Salen's blue and yellow livery had run as intended, into the Plain of Pillars, creating chaos in the ranks of General Quistal's centaur tribes. Swamped by their so-called allies, the centaurs milled about in confusion, wheeling and kicking at those barging past, then swinging tridents and long-bladed spears to clear themselves an avenue of escape.

From the far side of the Plain, General Gaur led the Bloodsworn, the Menin's fanatical heavy cavalry, in a thundering charge. Clad in black-iron and sporting Lord Styrax's fanged skull emblem, the dark knights had appeared like vengeful shadows to crash into the flank of Salen's traitorous troops. The beast that led them raged, going berserk as he drove deeper and deeper through the enemy.

Styrax had paused to watch his old friend arrive; even in the poor light he could see the fur around Gaur's roaring maw was matted with blood. Few had ever seen the softly spoken general this way and the knights he led hesitated briefly, then threw themselves into the attack with the abandon of men following a divine force.

Assailed on three sides, with a high stone ridge blocking their flight on the fourth, wiser heads soon realised no quarter was going to be offered. Amidst the confusion of battle, some were stirred to sense as training took over and soldiers started to form tight units working in unison. A man at the heart of the largest of these straightened up in the gloom and recognised Styrax's looming shape not twenty yards away. He pointed at their goal and the soldiers stepped forward, shields locked together against the onslaught rushing over them, like waves breaking on a stone and flowing past.

Styrax felt rather than saw the movement towards him as a unit of some thirty soldiers tramped forward. Laughter bubbled up in his throat. They thought he was vulnerable, open to a desperate and heroic last charge.

The Lord of the Menin grinned to himself and stretched out his unarmoured hand towards them. The scarred flesh looked even more shockingly white than normal, the ethereal pallor highlighted by the small cut on it that was welling as deep red as his stained fingernails.

The group quickened its pace as helms dropped low behind tall shields, but the white-eye gave them no time to consider their folly. Greedily he drank in the energies swirling over the dusty plain as a sharp prickle burned at his fingertips. He felt Kobra tremble in his other hand, resonating with the rampant power. Casting the magic forward, Styrax saw the interlocked shields crumple and collapse as a dozen men fell, leaving the others staggering. Styrax did not press his advantage, for up above he heard a voice, then others: a savage chorus of ululating shrieks piercing the air as the Reavers' mages cast their propelling spells with mechanical precision from behind the attacking main force.

The Plain of Pillars was named after the thousands of twenty-foot-high white sandstone columns erected hundreds of years before, fat columns the width of a man's outstretched arms, supporting the decorated stone lintels that divided the pillars into rows. Now the sharpened edges and deeply carved corners were proving an unexpected hazard for the plunging Reavers riding their bladed shields, though none appeared to care much. Styrax watched as one soldier, crouched low on his shield with an axe in each hand, almost gibbered with bloodthirsty delight until he clipped a pillar and was sent crashing to the ground. His shield rebounded in an explosion of sparks and buried itself into a Cheme soldier's chest, but even before his comrade was dead, the Reaver had bounded to his feet and decapitated his nearest foe.

Another of the élite white-eyes plunged down through the knot of soldiers that had been intent on taking out Styrax. His bladed shield severed two heads as it fell to earth. Its owner dismounted expertly, bringing the shield up in defence as he struck out at the nearest enemy, shattering a leg with the mace he carried. As more Reavers landed, propelled over the ranks by a cadre of mages, Styrax stepped back and watched the slaughter. His presence on the battlefield was no longer necessary—the magic-crazed monsters would not notice his lack of participation. They were there to massacre the remaining traitors, to finish the bloody work once sensible men had lost the stomach for it.

Styrax remembered his own days as a member of that wild regiment as though it had been just an opium dream. To be a Reaver was to be an animal, to revel in death and destruction, but he'd given it up when the searing flame of ambition at last overcame his baser instincts: watching the bloated figure of the man he would one day usurp in battle had broken the spell. The Lords of the Menin held greatness in their fists, yet Styrax's predecessor had been nothing more than a beast, a skilful berserker more suited to the Reavers. He had been simple-minded, blind to the value of anything beyond his baser lusts.

An echoing howl behind him intruded on Styrax's memories. He turned to see a burning figure staggering around blindly, about thirty yards away. Soldiers leapt to avoid the flames covering the man's entire body. Styrax's eyes narrowed. From the size of the figure he knew it had to be Kohrad. His son's strange armour was obviously growing in influence. Now it looked as if Kohrad had finally lost his control over it.

Styrax watched as Kohrad, impeded by one of the stone pillars, reached up to touch it. His fingers settled flat against the chill stone. Styrax heard his son snarl and saw the flames intensify, as if swelling in the fat streams of magic that flowed past him. The pillar blackened in a widening stain around Kohrad's hand and there was a loud cracking sound as the pillar started to give under the enormous pressure. Styrax began to run towards his son, his white hand reaching for the Crystal Skull at his chest. He felt the surge of magic flooding through the pillars towards them: the time had come. He had to act now, or run the risk that his son would never recover his senses, for the magic Kohrad was randomly drawing would simply burn away his mind.

This was the opportunity they had been waiting for. Styrax broke into a run. The Skull came away from his armour easily and he held it at his waist as he planned his attack. The burning figure didn't seem to notice him. "Kohrad!" Styrax roared.

His son looked up, his sword twitching, as Styrax flung the Skull named Destruction up in the air. His sword immediately forgotten, Kohrad watched the shining artefact arc up towards him, blazing in the firelight. As it neared, the light grew more intense, feeding from Kohrad's flames and drawing in power. Kohrad reached out with supplicant arms to catch the Skull he had once plucked from the Duke of Raland's plump hands, and as it fell into his embrace, he hugged it tight, pulling it to his chest so it could melt into the steel and become part of the torrent rushing through him.

He was still holding it fast when Styrax reached him. Kohrad didn't even look up as his father struck him with the pommel of his sword. The blow connected and Kohrad's head snapped back from the blow, his body rocking with the impact. For an instant the fire blazed even brighter. then the flames winked out and Kohrad crashed to the floor.

Styrax sheathed his sword. A company of Cheme troops had dropped back from the fighting and encircled their lord, leaving the rest to deal with the few remaining pockets of resistance.

"Major," he called to the leader of his bodyguard, "fetch General Gaur and a litter for my son."

The major motioned and one of his men sprinted off towards the Blood-sworn knights. Two more soldiers started gathering spears and stripping dead bodies to gather material to make a stretcher. The others fanned out and continued to keep watch.

Styrax pulled off his helm and knelt at Kohrad's side, placing a hand on the Skull that was now fused with the armour. It had already adopted the steel's blood-red colour. Kohrad was still alive. Styrax sighed in relief: he had only educated guesses where the Crystal Skulls were concerned, but this time at least, he appeared to have been right. He had needed his son to be at the point of burn-out, for only then could a combination of magic and brute force put him into this deep unconsciousness. And that was necessary for the team of surgeons and mages who were ready and waiting to remove the corrupting armour from his son's body. The Skulls were all designed to counteract the power of the Gods, and they provided a cushion of sorts against mortal blows—the Skulls didn't make men invulnerable, they just allowed a last roll of the dice against Death, the Chief of the Gods.

As Styrax crouched there, the shallow dent in Kohrad's helm twitched and distended before creeping back into shape. He watched it carefully. Kohrad had returned from a hunting trip with the armour, and Styrax had been unable to discover anything about it since then. Watching it repair the dent so quickly told Styrax it was ancient, Elven-made, but he could recall no text mentioning anything like this armour. He gave a grunt of curiosity as he gently eased the helm off Kohrad's head. His son's eyes were closed, and black hair dank with sweat stuck to his forehead. His lip was cut and a reddening graze ran over his cheek to a minor cut. There was no trace of a bruise on his temple yet, which was good—there was always the chance of bursting a vessel with a blow that hard, and few surgeons could do anything about blood leaking into the skull.

A clatter of hooves announced General Gaur's arrival. The general jumped from his horse untidily; he had never been a natural horseman, not with the legs and hooves of a goat—but right now Gaur didn't care how awkward he looked, not with the young man he loved like a son lying like a corpse.

"He lives?" he growled, almost too scared to hear the reply.

"Yes."

The two shared a moment of relief. Gaur's face bore a rare, brief smile.

"I think I hit him harder than I needed, but he's safe, I think. You have the team ready?"

"Close enough. The mages are happy with the laboratory we found in the Chetarate Stonedun and your surgeon is at the palace."

"Good. Send a messenger. He should meet us at the stonedun."

Gaur nodded, but before he could reply a voice hailed Styrax. They turned to see a party of horsemen trotting over, the white-eye mage Larim at the fore. Clearly none of them had taken part in the battle, for their robes were pristine, the discordant colours of Larat almost glowing. The major swore and snapped out an order. Soldiers immediately spread out to flank Larat's newest Chosen.

"Hold, he's no part of this," Gaur bellowed, for his men were ready to kill *anyone* in Larat's colours.

The troops froze, obedient to Gaur's every word, and the remaining few followers of Larat screamed their last in the background while Larim trotted on, apparently unconcerned.

"Say what you like about Larat's Chosen," Styrax muttered almost beneath his breath, "none of them hold a grudge. They don't have the capacity to care, not even for colleagues of twenty years."

With the mage were two guards whose uniforms echoed those Styrax had been slaughtering, looking completely terrified as they stared around at the butchered regiments. They were hauling along a pair of bruised figures, mages who had been beaten to a pulp, though Styrax recognised the pair, part of Salen's coterie, were not looking as dead as he'd ordered.

"Where are the others?" he called.

"Dead already," said Larim in a jocular voice. Styrax frowned for a moment. The Chosen of Larat was looking far too cheerful around such slaughter, even for a callous bastard who cared only about his own skin. Then

Styrax remembered Salen was dead just this hour past—Larim would still be intoxicated by the renewed blessing of the God of Magic. Considering his God's utter disregard of murder, and his amusement at Salen's death—Styrax would not forget that chuckle echoing through the streets of Thotel in a hurry—of course Larim would find the sight of his newly inherited army being slaughtered high entertainment.

"Do you see them honouring us?" Larim gestured around at the torches of the Chetse surrounding them. Atop the black bulk of the Lion Guard's barracks were more than a hundred such torches, and at least a handful could be seen in every other direction. "A ring of fire, perhaps they are welcoming us by echoing our homeland?"

"Perhaps." Styrax was in no mood to engage in foolish banter. Larim had disobeyed his orders by coming here, and Kohrad needed attention as soon as possible. Styrax reminded himself to be polite for the moment; he didn't need the distraction of another fight. "My Lord, I assume you have a good reason to be here?"

"My Lord," repeated Larim, pleased with the sound of his new honorific. The Hidden Tower was set in the remote north of the Ring of Fire, so Larim, even though Salen's Krann, had enjoyed neither lands nor actual rank before Salen's death. "My reasons are good, yes. As you ordered, I was dealing with Salen's coterie. Then something curious happened that you need to take note of."

Styrax gave an exasperated hiss. Behind Larim he could see the two Cheme soldiers returning with a rough drag-litter. Ignoring the exchange between the white-eyes, they gave perfunctory bows and hurried over to Kohrad. Styrax turned to Gaur and leaned close, so as to not be overheard. "Go ahead with Kohrad—take the regiment as escort. If this turns out to be important and I don't catch you up, don't wait. I want to know how this armour is exerting its influence over him. If we don't break the link now, either he will die, or he will wake to the armour past any chance of control, and we will never get this chance again. I do not intend for either to happen."

The general grunted in assent and together they lifted Kohrad onto the cradle while the soldiers brought over a horse to attach it to. Leather straps went around his chest and waist to hold Kohrad onto the cradle but they had to bend his knees to ensure his feet didn't drag.

His son looked suddenly frail, ashen in the weak light. Styrax remembered Kohrad as a child, an energetic sprawl of whirling limbs, storming through Crafanc's rooms with his lionhounds. His mother, Selar, was also a white-eye—they could breed only with their own kind—yet she had proved a remarkably attentive parent. It had broken Selar's heart when her cherished son effectively chose his father over her; after years of his mother's unconditional love, it was to Styrax that Kohrad had turned.

Through his childhood Kohrad had been in perpetual motion, rarely able to remain stationary. Even as an adult he would pace and gesture, brimming with childish energy and wicked humour. And now he lay there with slack lips and vacant eyes: to see Kohrad like this chilled Styrax's heart, more than any wound he'd received.

Reluctantly he lifted the drag-cradle and hooked it up to the waiting horse's saddle. Gaur gave him a nod and led the horse away, clearly intending to walk beside Kohrad all the way. Styrax took one last look and left his friend to take charge, a rare flicker of fear in his heart as he returned his attention to Larim. Whatever concerns he had, he couldn't show the ambitious young white-eye a trace of weakness. Larim might begin to think he would succeed where Salen failed.

"The young lord is badly hurt?"

"He will recover," Styrax growled in reply, glaring at Larim until the younger man shifted his gaze from Kohrad's prone form. "You had something important so show me?"

"Ah, so I did." Larim coughed and gestured to his two guards, who dragged the prisoners from their saddles. Each had his hands bound with white cord with some sort of enchantment woven into the thin rope. Styrax could just make out the glittering silver thread that held the magic. Larim took one by the arm and dragged him over to where Styrax was standing.

"I was following your orders exactly—quick simple deaths, with no experimentation or creativity. A waste of perfect subjects, in my opinion, but I understood your reasoning. Consequently, I was surprised to observe the following."

He whipped a thin dagger from his belt and slammed it into the man's chest. The man gave a high-pitched shriek and convulsed in pain. Larim frowned at the sound and jolted the man, as though to admonish him. The man gasped, then went limp, passed out from the pain and died quickly.

"Normal thus far?" commented Larim, as though conducting an experiment in front of a flock of acolytes. Styrax nodded, managing to contain his curiosity. The Chosen of Larat was doing nothing to the man. Styrax could sense no force, nor any charm that would prevent death, or even make that death notable. The only thing he suspected of Larat's Chosen was that he was enjoying the chance to provide Styrax with some instruction, and that wasn't exactly a surprise.

"But observe," Larim continued, pulling the dagger back out of his victim. A gout of blood sprayed from the corpse over the base of the pillar Kohrad had been attacking. With a fastidious sniff, Larim released the body and stepped back. The dead mage swayed and his knees buckled, limbs and neck all falling limp, but somehow he remained upright.

"You're right," said Styrax, "that is curious." He tasted the air. The Plain of Pillars was thick with the stench of death, but suddenly the odour had risen, heavy in his throat. Styrax recognised the sensation: this was necromancy, without doubt, but the source eluded him. He felt the rare sensation of being intrigued.

"Salen put some form of necromantic charm on his coterie? But no, I assume if that were the case you'd look a little less immaculate."

"You would be correct in that assumption, my Lord." Larim stepped back half a pace to give the corpse a little more room. His expression was one of calculating interest, rather than concern. Styrax again reached his senses out, to be certain this was no elaborate trap. He could feel nothing of the power that would be required normally, but there was *something* unusual. A presence of some kind? He didn't know of any daemon that could enter a corpse without some form of assistance.

"Larim?" rasped the dead mage. There was an echo to the voice, as well as the bubbling of air though a ruined windpipe.

"I'm here," was the reply, laced with a vague amusement.

"I cannot see you."

"That's because your head's hanging down at the ground."

"You wish to gauge my strength? So be it, you are but a child after all."

There was no emotion in the voice. Styrax couldn't tell whether the being was angry or amused at the game Larim was playing. Controlling the muscles was difficult for a daemon, and clearly the Chosen of Larat had broken the corpse's neck to find out how powerful a being they were dealing with.

With jerking movements the dead mage's head was forced to an upright angle, tongue lolling and eyes dead. "You have found Lord Styrax as I asked. Good."

"Aren't you going to introduce me to your friend?" Styrax enquired.

Larim turned to face Styrax. "I believe this is your friend, not mine."

Styrax felt a chill on his skin. Was he being accused of something? Had Larim proof that Styrax had made a pact with a daemon? If so, why confront him here, surrounded by Styrax's troops?

He looked at the dead mage. "Well, corpse, are you a friend of mine?"

"A friend? No. A loyal subject of course."

"Loyal subject?" Styrax narrowed his eyes, thinking frantically, then cried, "Amavoq's rage; Isherin Purn? I'd assumed you were dead—we've heard nothing from you in two years."

"I am honoured you remember me." The voice lacked any emotion, but Styrax could imagine it now, the mocking, wheedling lilt, Purn's thin lips over-forming each syllable in almost obscene pedantry. The necromancer was an unpleasant, rat-like figure, alternating wildly between ridiculous scheming and depraved experiments.

"You did your job well. I expected you to return and claim your reward. Lord Bahl would never have left himself vulnerable without your influence. I had hoped to hear just how you accomplished it."

"An artist cannot reveal too many secrets. All I will say is that it required a creative pen as much as spellcasting." The corpse paused. "I did not return because I have found myself many distractions in this part of the Land. There is so much fun to be had here."

"And yet you seek me out?"

"Ever willing to be of service to my Lord."

Styrax snorted. "When you were in my grip, perhaps. You certainly had enough sense not to challenge me. Now that you are beyond my influence, I'm not so sure." He cocked his head towards Larim. "What was it Verliq said? 'I hold no allegiance but to my art'?"

The white-eye's lip twitched in irritation. "I would not know, my Lord. You have not let us read any of his works."

Styrax gave him a bright little smile. "Ah, no, of course not. A shame, you would find them most instructive. Well, Purn? I know necromancers care little for their rulers, so tell me why you have gone to all this trouble."

"I am in Scree. It is a backward little city, typical of the Western states, caught between one powerful neighbour and another and spending all their time looking outwards for the next threat."

"So they don't worry much about people disappearing off the street from time to time. I'm sure it is paradise for you. I do already have agents however; agents who provide better information than that. Either tell me something new, or I will dismiss you in a manner you will find most uncomfortable. My son is injured so I have little time for the babbling of deranged maniacs."

"If your son is injured, then you had better be more courteous to the walkers in the dark," the corpse retorted, its jaw snapping shut, an indication of Isherin Purn's anger.

"Why? What do you know about it?" Styrax stepped forward and grabbed the corpse by its slack neck. Without any apparent effort he lifted it up with one hand and brought the dead lolling eyes level with his own. "Whatever allegiance you profess to hold, never forget my power. There is nowhere you could hide from me. There is no protector you could find to keep you safe if you made yourself my enemy. Now explain what you meant."

Returning the corpse to the ground, he stepped back and watched it jerk and spasm as Purn fought to regain control over its muscles. That close, Styrax could smell the emptied bowels, adding to the stink of corrupt magic surrounding the cadaver. Purn had grown in power since being allowed to leave Salen's tutelage at the Hidden Tower and seek out Cordein Malich. Styrax guessed that the necromancer would be unable to repeat this trick with anyone but members of the coterie he had served in, yet even so, it was impressive. And it was an illustrative point of theory—he would have to send someone to read Larim's notes when he had time to investigate it further.

"I understand," the corpse rasped eventually. "I am no threat to your son, but he walks with one foot in the dark."

"One foot in the dark? He is not as close to death as that."

"Not close to death, but walking in the dark nonetheless. He is open to the creatures of the other place. They can feel the fire raging through him. I do not know the being that fuels his fire, but it is not one that would willingly share its possessions. I do not dare investigate further else I be scorched by its vengeance."

"Kohrad is no toy to be shared," Styrax snarled. "Nor is he a possession of either God or daemon. If one seeks to claim him, it will have to fight my armies for him."

"It already has staked its claim."

Styrax hesitated. "The armour? That is what gives it power over him?"

"Ah, a suit of armour? If that is true, then you are dealing with an old one, the most ancient and cunning. Filled with malice they are—and hard to trick out of their prize. Take care how you proceed."

Styrax hesitated. He knew which inhabitant of the dark would want a hold over him: the daemon-prince he had made a bargain with many years ago. It feared his strength and scrabbled for purchase. So be it; he had always known a reckoning had to come one day. *Strange that it comes this way though, I wouldn't have expected a daemon to choose such an oblique path.*

"Was that what you came to tell me? A warning from a loyal servant?"

"No." The corpse gave a wheeze, a dribble of cloying blood emerging from the corner of its mouth. Styrax suspected Purn, back in his festering laboratory in Scree, was laughing at the notion. "To tell you there is a new air in Scree. Figures of power walk the streets, unknown songs drift on the air. It is nothing I have ever felt before, but it is more akin to the currents surging through the Dark Place than the politics of a city. Something calls to me in the night, something of incalculable power."

"You're asking for help?" Styrax's puzzlement was plain in his voice. He glanced at Larim, but the young white-eye looked just as confused. A necromancer as powerful as Purn was unlikely to ask for assistance, no matter what the task. Sharing, spoils or troubles, was not often part of the mindset.

"Scree becomes the focus of something quite remarkable, I believe. I do not know what dangers lie here, but they shift and feed off each other. Scree sees the convergence of horrors. I fear this home will soon be no home, not even for a man of culture such as I."

Styrax knew what Purn meant, but when he glanced at Larim, he didn't appear to understand; his contact with necromancers during his fifteen-year apprenticeship would have been limited. Necromancers disliked states descending into chaos. There were too many factions involved, too many mobs roaming the streets and disrupting their work. They liked their shadows still and peaceful, rather than flickering in the flames of funeral pyres.

"You lack the power to compete for whatever it is that calls to you in the night?"

"If this convergence draws more people to Scree that will certainly be true, but in fact I suspect the artefact would draw me into the games of lords and Gods, and in these troubled times that would not prove healthy. Instead, I offer to help you secure it."

"You're offering me this artefact? In exchange for what? A manor back home with your pick of the gaols? A guarantee that your activities will be unrestrained?"

"No. The pickings will be richer this side of the Waste. Every denizen of the dark knows that a storm has scattered the strands of the future far and wide. Fate lies in her chamber and weeps for what she has lost. I do not wish to be absent from such delicious chaos. The freedom you offered me is my price—as well as men to assist me here—but in Thotel, where I am not answerable to anyone but you. That—and one of the Chetse's Bloodroses for my personal use."

Styrax frowned. A necromancer offering to hand over something of such power? It hardly seemed creditable, yet Purn knew his lord well enough not to expect some foolish mistake that could put Styrax in danger, or honour an agreement where he'd been lied to. "If this artefact is as great as you claim, I agree. I will send you some men to help and they will accompany you back here."

The corpse shuddered, slumping to its knees before Purn regained his control. "I cannot hold this much longer. Who will you send? They must leave word for me at a tavern, the Lost Spur."

Styrax's thoughts began to race. Killers would be easy enough to find, but who of his staff could he send to lead them? All those men whose names came readily to his lips were men of importance, and he had few friends he could spare for such a thing. Then one appeared unbidden in his mind. Styrax pictured the terror it would cause even as he spoke, and the picture it made caused him to smile inwardly.

"Mikiss. A messenger called Koden Mikiss will lead them."

Not waiting to hear any more, Isherin Purn broke the link and the mage's corpse collapsed in a heap of stained, stinking robes. Styrax didn't move for a moment, thinking over this remarkable conversation. Of what importance was Scree? What sort of convergence could be happening there? Then Kohrad's still form returned to his memory. There were more important things to deal with this night. His skills would be required if they were going to break whatever hold the daemon had over his son. Once that was done, there was revenge to be planned.

"Major," Styrax growled. The tall soldier hurried over, his amber eyes glinting in the firelight. "Find our friend the messenger and have him waiting for when I finish with Kohrad. Do you have a few men you can trust for a trip such as this?"

"If it's as important as he said," the soldier replied with a nod towards the corpse, "I'll go myself, and take the twins with me. Any more than that will make it hard to travel quick and quiet."

Styrax gave a nod of approval. "Good. I don't want to send an army all the way up there, not yet. Find out what Purn is talking about and if you think it worthwhile, send word with what assistance you'll need to secure it. Get yourself ready, then bring the messenger to me. But first, find me a horse."

CHAPTER 10

MAYEL PRESSED HIS PALM FLAT against the door and stopped. In the gloom of the cellar stairwell, he could just make out the pitted iron ring that opened the door. He held his breath, feeling the insistent thump of his heart pounding as his ears strained to detect any sound from the house above. All was silent, but for a flutter through the house as the blustery wind rattled the shutters. A droning whistle abruptly pierced the quiet, making Mayel's heart almost leap into his throat.

Then he recognised it, and grinned in relief. "Just the wind coming through the keyhole," he muttered. "Idiot!" The lock on the kitchen door was old and broken, like everything else in this house, no matter how grand it had once been. Mayel could hardly believe anyone would let such a fine house fall into disrepair like this, letting the damp creep up the walls and seep into the floorboards until they swelled and burst like overripe fruit. The surrounding area might explain a lot for, like the house at its centre, the district was decayed, half-abandoned, home mostly to furtive figures who lingered in dark corners, hiding from the light as much as the rain. The abbot, of course, thought the area ideal. Having escaped the austere bleakness of their island monastery, Abbot Doren had sought out its cosmopolitan equivalent, much to Mayel's indignation. That the abbot had paid good silver for it only compounded the young man's irritation.

Mayel had adopted the kitchen as his own and scrubbed it clean. The abbot had the cellar room for his studies, and the rest of the house they had sealed off and left for the rats to enjoy. The abbot worked through the night, talking to himself and clattering around down there as Mayel drifted off to sleep in his makeshift bed. When the old man did sleep it was usually in a chair shaded from the afternoon sun, though his slumber was far from peaceful, his dreams plagued by fell shapes he refused to discuss . . . Mayel could see them haunting his waking hours too.

Abbot Doren was far from young, but Mayel suspected he was not as old as he appeared, despite the tired look in his eyes. Perhaps it was the dreams that aged him, perhaps it was something else. He was a mage, like most high priests, and neither magic nor Vellern were easy masters. The two together would take a lot out of any man.

Flickering light seeped through the cracks, outlining the door. Finally, Mayel turned the iron ring, and waited. *Salvation or damnation*, he wondered, slowly easing open the door. Wincing slightly at the creak of the hinges, he poked his head around the door and looked into the cellar.

The morning light was streaming down through the two grime-smeared windows facing him. The cellar had been underneath the main entrance to the house, looking up at what was, at one time, a busy street. The tall oak door that had been the grand entrance to the house was now rotten and broken, with black paint peeling from its surface like a leprous skin.

Miraculously, neither of the windows had been broken or stolen—folk avoided the house, though Mayel did not know why. Shandek insisted it wasn't haunted, and blamed the atmosphere of fear that permeated the district on a rash of recent, unsolved disappearances. Mayel hadn't been quite convinced by that, but the abandoned house was still imposing, even now, so it wouldn't be surprising if it had become the focus of suspicion. He had to admit no one was likely to store goods in a place he feared, so it was more likely Shandek had spread the rumours himself.

Mayel took a lamp down off its bracket and, stepping over sacks full of strange plants and pots of dark, glutinous liquids, took it over to the scarred table in the centre of the room. He noted the lamps were burning low. If the abbot returned from his walk early, Mayel could say he was refilling them. Mayel recognised the heavy tomes that he had personally lugged from the monastery amongst the piles of books that covered the table. He picked up one that lay open and scanned the feathery script, hoping for an indication of what the abbot was working on. It was hard to read, and even harder to make sense of. At the bottom of one page was a strange drawing, vague lines swirling about each other, that he struggled to understand. He cocked his head to one side and was frowning at the page when it came into focus: a tall figure with sword drawn, standing over a prone knight. The artist had carefully blacked out the sword's blade with ink. The caption below said *Velere's Fell*. Mayel assumed that the prone figure was Velere, the Elven prince. The archaic text appeared to be describing the feats of an immortal hero called Aracnan, and his particular devotion to his lord, though Mayel couldn't actually work out who this lord was, as his name was never mentioned. There was something about a battle in a field of wild flowers, and a shifting wall of smoke which had aided Aracnan's holy quest. That passage was worn dark, smudged by past scholars who had run their fingers along the line as they read, but Mayel could not fathom why it was important. He knew it was not from the library, but from the abbot's personal collection, and that meant the abbot himself, and maybe past abbots too, had thought that bit important.

"Don't mind that now," Mayel told himself, "you're just getting distracted. You're not here to read his books but to find that bloody box."

The room was in a chaotic state. Mayel hadn't been allowed down here since he'd dragged in the table for the abbot to work at. He continued his search, finding another valuable-looking book, bound in tarnished, silvery metal, hidden under the table. It was wrapped in waxed cloth. The cover looked as if had been inscribed by hand, but the words meant nothing to him—even in the monastery he'd not seen this language before . . . he thought it was strange that the title had been written on to such a fine book rather than embossed. He tried to open it, and found to his surprise that the cover was glued shut. There was no locking mechanism to be seen, and even turning the book over he could see nothing that would lock it shut. Mayel ran his finger down the inside edge of the hard leather cover and yelped as something sharp dug into his finger. He dropped the book back onto the table and stuck his finger in his mouth. After a moment he pulled it out again to inspect the cut. Blood still welled from a tiny incision but when he licked it clean again he realised the cut was a strange shape, almost like a tiny formal monogram of two entwined characters, V and V. Mayel, intrigued, compared it to the cover of the book. It had the same device on it, within a wreath of ivy leaves.

"Well, that's strange," Mayel muttered as he turned the book over to inspect it. Oddly, he could see nothing sharp—but when he gingerly ran a fingernail down the same spot, there was a flash of silver as if from nowhere and the same strange shape was cut into his fingernail.

"Magic," he breathed in wonder. The abbot was a skilled mage, but Mayel had no talent himself. Even holding a book bearing some small enchantment gave him a thrill that took away the sting of his bleeding finger entirely.

A scraping sound from upstairs made Mayel flinch: the kitchen door had been opened. Mayel had jammed a small stone under the door, and it was that scraping that had alerted him. He grabbed the lamp and blew out the flame and as he cast a last glance around the room, he finally spotted the box. It was open, a long red velvet scarf all that remained inside. Clearly the scarf had been protection, but whatever had been inside the lacquered box was gone now.

Mayel cursed softly, then muttered, "Well, you don't need padding for gold." With the extinguished lamp still in his hand he opened the door and started back up the stairs.

"Abbot Doren, you're back," he exclaimed, startling the old man as he appeared silently behind him.

"Yes, yes, I had an idea that I needed to note down." The abbot scowled suspiciously, but the novice had long since perfected his naïve expression for the monastery elders.

"You really should have stayed out for longer than five minutes. You need some air. You ate hardly anything last night, and you worked the whole night again." Mayel raised the extinguished lamp as though presenting evidence.

"Ah, you were changing the oil?"

"Of course, Father." His face creased into innocent puzzlement. "You said you didn't want your laboratory tidied, but you still need light to work by."

The abbot studied his young charge for a moment then scratched at his head in a distracted manner. "Very good of you." He looked unconvinced, but lack of sleep had made him a little addled. "I have an errand I need you to run," he said finally.

Mayel smiled up at the sun. It was just two hours since dawn and still cool compared to the cruel afternoon sun. The street was deserted, despite the fine morning, though he could hear the city's constant grumble all around him. He jumped at a scurrying sound from the scorched shell of a shack off to his left, feeling suddenly isolated. He could see nothing behind the shack, where bare patches of earth were interspersed with dark green clumps of grass, not even a rat or feral cat.

"Good mornin', cousin," called a voice from behind him. Mayel whirled around, a look of panic on his face, only relaxing as he recognised Shandek, who had appeared from nowhere with one of his thugs. His cousin was a burly man of thirty-three summers, with the hair and complexion of a Farlan. Mayel, who was half his age, had darker skin and fairer hair, although he'd shaved his head to get rid of the tonsure that marked him as a follower of Vellern. It felt curiously liberating to feel the breeze curl around his ears and down his nape. Shandek, however, was proud of his long, lank hair, which marked him out on the streets he ruled.

"A better morning than the previous ones that have welcomed us here," Mayel replied with a smile. Six years in the monastery had left him with a cultured voice as well as an education. Despite Shandek's wealth and influence, Mayel knew his unschooled cousin held a secret regard for those who could read and write, and he was counting on that, because the ties of blood would go only so far.

"True enough. We'd begun to wonder whether your abbot brought the dark clouds with him." Shandek stepped forward with a grin and slung his arm around Mayel's shoulder. "How goes your abbot's experiments? Have you yet learned what he's up to?"

Mayel shook his head. "He still doesn't let me in to his laboratory. He tells me it's for my own safety, but I know he's worried about trusting anyone. If Jackdaw could turn on him after years of service, anyone could."

"I still think we should just go and take it off him," rumbled Shandek's companion, a man who was wide enough to appear squat despite being almost six feet tall. "One old man won't cause me an' Shyn any problems."

Shandek reached over and gave his comrade a friendly cuff on the shoulder. "Shut it, Brohm. Even in hidin', the man's still a high priest. He'd turn you insides-out soon as you burst through the door."

"I thought they had to brew up potion to use magic? Can't see that bein' quicker than the time it takes to shove a knife in his gut."

"That just shows your ignorance, Brohm," Mayel declared. "He can draw energies out of the air—I've seen him light fires with a snap of his fingers, so unless your underclothes are made of steel, I doubt you'd get the chance to use that knife of yours. And if that didn't work, he still has an Aspect of Vellern to call upon at a moment's notice, one that will certainly take exception to you trying to hurt the abbot. His Aspect-guide is called Erwillen the High Hunter, and he has claws large enough to rip off your head and a trident to place it upon afterwards. You'd wet your drawers just to look at him in the flesh."

The larger man took a step forward, fist bunched, but Shandek stepped between them with a chuckle. "Peace, friend. Mayel, keep your bloody mouth in check until you have the muscle to back it up. Brohm in't the fool you think he is, but he *is* three times your size. Brohm, let me talk to my cousin alone. You keep an eye out for our dark man."

Brohm grunted, glaring at Mayel, then walked the few yards to the corner of the street.

"Dark man?" Mayel asked as he watched Brohm go.

"Rumours we've been hearin'; nothin' to concern a man of letters such as you. Maybe somethin' to do with the disappearances round here. Normally I'd say it's folk being fanciful, but with all the bad sorts that've turned up since the turn of the year, I'm not so sure. It may be nothin', but best you keep an eye open. Strangers walkin' these parts alone, that sort a' thing."

"I will. Thanks for the warning, cuz."

"Good. Now, what *do* you have to tell me?"

"Little. He's researching some ancient history, the Great War, among other things. I didn't get much time in there. Do you know if Jackdaw has followed us into the city?"

"Not that I've heard, but my people ain't entirely welcome in some districts, so it's hard to be sure."

"He's not hard to miss, not with his tattoos," Mayel pointed out, earning a warning look from Shandek.

"Nor is your abbot, and keepin' his presence a secret was not easy. You cost me money, boy. I don't begrudge it, not to family in need, but this abbot means nothin' to me and I'm startin' to wonder why I'm puttin' meself out so."

"It will be worthwhile, I promise. He has some sort of artefact—at the very least it will be a relic—and you can sell that to a collector without any difficulty."

"And at best?"

"At best it's some magical item. Our libraries at the monastery were extensive, and had many locked cells. Some things I think they intentionally kept away from the rest of the Land, afraid men would attack the island if they knew what was kept there." He looked at Shandek, who was still scowling. The man didn't like being kept in the dark, and Mayel could tell his patience wouldn't last long.

Finally, he nodded. "Fine then, just you don't waste my time, you hear? We've not yet discussed a price for you when you do get it. Best we get that out of the way early, since you're family. Nothin' worse than bickerin' with your blood, eh?" There was something of a smirk creeping onto Shandek's face. His cousin always liked negotiating from a position of strength.

"Well, you'll have guessed that I don't want to go back, so if it's a relic, we split the proceeds of any sale and I come to work for you. I've got clerking skills that will be useful to you."

"And if it's somethin' more?"

"Then after your costs, the money is mine."

Shandek gave a splutter of laughter and slapped him on the back.

"Wait, hear me out first," Mayel protested. "The condition will be that I use the money to buy a share—I'm not asking to be an equal partner, of course not, just to have a stake. I know you're not happy to stay another man's vassal, and this could help."

"You better be careful, talkin' like that," Shandek said softly. "Spider, he don't like to hear such talk, and he hears more than me. It could mean both our deaths if someone overheard you there, mine just because we're cousins, and he'd not trust me again after he had you killed."

"Is he really so paranoid?"

"You have to ask? Man's still a mystery to me, ten years on. Never met 'im, never even heard his real name." Shandek raised his left hand, waggling the stub of his little finger, which was covered in twisted scars. "This was a friendly reminder after I tried too hard to find that out. Other men've been killed for not gettin' the message." He pointed at the road leading to the city centre and, his voice still lowered, said, " I hear he went back on an order a few days back. Not somethin' I've ever heard happen before. Fancy a wander through the Shambles? Tread old haunts once more? I hear there's a theatre company renovatin' the sunken theatre—it's been derelict since your old friend set fire to it two years ago."

"Old friend? Who—Shirrel?"

"That's the bastard. Never understood why you were friends with the boy but—"

"Why we were friends?" Mayel exclaimed. "I might have been young, but I wasn't so stupid as that. If Shirrel wanted to be your friend, you were his friend. Lest o' course you wanted to wake up on fire."

"Well, that won't happen now. Mad bastard decided to stay inside the theatre as it burnt. Perhaps he was watchin' his own performance?"

"Don't ask me to explain how his mind worked." Mayel was too lost in his memories of poverty and childish spite to notice Shandek's effort at a joke. "Anyway, what about this theatre company?"

"Ah yes. Someone was sent down to collect a little token of their respect to Spider, and it turned out they had none."

"Are they mad?"

"Perhaps. The man sent got a bad beatin'. Apparently they have a few albino boys workin' for them, vicious, hairless shites, who walk around barefoot, jabberin' in some language no one else can understand. They must have come from the Waste or somethin', never seen their like before. Started more than one fight in the taverns too, drink like Chetse, so I'm told. Anyway, they worked the messenger over and dumped 'im in the street. Don't talk so well now, might not walk again, neither."

"So Spider said to burn the place down again?"

"Exactly. Only it didn't happen, for reasons I didn't get told, and Spider called back the order the next day. Said he'd come to an 'accommodation' with them and they were to be left alone." Shandek sounded less than pleased at being kept out of the loop: the theatre bordered his own fiefdom.

"Sounds scared."

"That's what I think. Those albinos must be pretty nasty, to frighten that bastard."

"So why are we going there?"

Mayel's expression must have betrayed what he was feeling, because Shandek took one look at him and burst out laughing. "No, I'm not takin' you to fight them, you fool! Spider said we couldn't lean on them, and I'm not inclined to." Shandek waved an admonishing finger in Mayel's face. "But he didn't say nothin' about talkin' in a friendly manner. We're just going down for a chat—see what we can see. It might be that they're just insane and got lucky, but I doubt it. No, they've got somethin' nasty up their sleeves and I'd be interested to find out what. And of course, there's my golden rule of life—"

"Which is?"

"When someone's got somethin' to hide, there's money to be made. There's somethin' going on there; might be they could find some use of a man with local knowledge, a man who knows how to find things quietly and quickly. Either that, or the authorities might pay to know more about them."

"And if you make a powerful friend in the process?"

"All the better, my lad," Shandek declared with a chuckle. "A new friend warms the heart, that's what I always say."

The Shambles was a place of dark, narrow alleyways. The two proper streets that cut through the district had been crammed with stalls and carts almost as soon as the cobblestones were laid. The smell was just as Mayel remembered: rotting vegetables, sewage, and meat gone bad in the sun. The gutter down the middle of the street was invariably clogged with bloody entrails and what off-cuts were too rancid for even the feral animal population. The area was a warren of tiny houses that brought back a host of memories. This was where Mayel had been born; this place had been his first education. For all the squalor, the sense of community was palpable, and right now he could feel fierce eyes watching him without recognition, resenting the outsider being publicly paraded by the man whose word was law in the shadows of the Shambles.

"Do you want to go by the old house? I rented it to a tanner and his family—eight squealin' brats, all a match for you and your sister."

Mayel shook his head. He didn't trust his voice not to betray the emotion he felt now. The Shambles was smaller to his eyes, ruder and meaner than it had seemed when he'd not known better. Guilt gnawed at him. He'd left with his father, hugging his sister tight so as to not lose her in the crowd of people fleeing the city. Their mother lay on the one bed in the shack they called home, dying of the white plague. With her last breath she urged them to flee. He could still see the blood-flecked foam bubbling from her mouth as she pleaded for them to save themselves.

For some reason his father had decided a life of service to Vellern would save them—and perhaps he'd been right, though Mayel had learned at the monastery that the white plague was nowhere near as contagious as the peasants believed it. Whatever the truth, they had set off on their pilgrimage to the Island of Birds. After a week of tramping dirt roads, his sister had stumbled, and never found the strength to get up again. The memory still left a knot in his stomach. He hadn't had the strength to hate his father then, but he'd made up for it later.

"I understand." Shandek's voice was softer now. He knew the start of the story, and recognised the pain on Mayel's face. "You never told me what happened to your da'."

"He died," Mayel replied flatly. "After a few months he realised a monastery where they didn't make wine wasn't the place for him. Tried to slip away at night in a small boat. The Bitches took him."

"The Bitches?"

"The rocks around the island. The monks always claimed that only people who'd fished the lake their whole life are able to navigate through them. They don't even let men from the village sail alone until they've thirty summers. Everyone else ends up smashed against the Bitches."

"Right." Shandek lapsed into silence. Sympathy was an underused emotion of his. What could a man say? Pity was a woman's province, and he didn't like to intrude. Instead, he let his eyes wander the familiar lines of his home. After thirty-three summers of walking these streets, he could pick up the slightest change, whether it was a rise in fortunes permitting repairs, or the subtle indications that a man or woman were drinking more than they were working nowadays. Shandek kept an eye out for these people. It didn't do to have utter misery and complete poverty. It was like he always said: make sure the sheep are fat before you fleece them.

The sunken theatre occupied a sudden open space on the eastern edge of the Shambles, where the busy thoroughfare of Long Walk was an abrupt border to the district; folk tended to emerge blinking in the newfound light after the narrow alleys of the Shambles. Dodging the carts and sliding through the currents of humanity that flowed back and forth, Shandek led his cousin across to where low stalls and barrows encircled the theatre, unconsciously echoing the barricade of shrines around the Six Temples further north. A pair of willow trees obscured much of the theatre's southern aspect, but Mayel could see building work going on.

"They're adding a tier?"

The sunken theatre was open, with an arched greystone wall running around three sides. At the stage end the ground fell away into a deep pit, within which a building looking like a warehouse had been constructed so its roof was level with the street. It served as both offices and backstage for the theatre. Mayel guessed that was where his so-called friend had died.

The low single-storey wall enclosing this large chunk of ground had flat-roofed rooms all around its interior. It looked small, compared with the space inside, like a child's toy made out of proportion. Mayel had remembered the theatre as more imposing, even without the wooden palisade now being erected to raise the height of the wall.

As he and Shandek got closer, they could see workmen and scaffolds behind the market carts that were trading as usual, ignoring the commotion behind them.

"Another tier," Shandek confirmed eventually.

They had stopped by a butcher's stall. The woman who was running it wore a loose-fitting brown dress, low-cut and sleeveless, and Mayel could make out the tiny dark circles of blood dried into the material. He stared at the woman as her eyes drifted, listless and unfocused, over the street ahead. Her pallid skin was stretched tight over bones that looked too big for her body. "Sign of a nasty habit," he muttered, more to himself than his cousin.

"Eh? Ah, that one." Shandek sniffed, though Mayel couldn't tell whether it was mild disgust or embarrassment—whoever supplied the woman might well be giving Shandek a cut of the proceeds. "Been workin' hard on killin' herself slow, that one. Six weeks since her children died in a fire, and she won't see another six."

As they spoke, the woman jumped at a crash from the scaffold behind. She looked fearfully at the wall a few yards behind her, as if watching it for danger. The wall itself was blank and featureless, yet it was at that she stared, rather than the windows of the new second floor above.

"Folk say she cracked before the fire," Shandek continued, "that it was her fault. It's said she'd been jumpin' at shadows, an' talkin' about daemons being after her girls. She set fire to the house to frighten off the shadows. Now she's got nowhere else to live. Either she sleeps in the temples, where the fires burn all night, or she's in the opium dens before nightfall. Her husband will be somewhere about here; she's only good for leavin' at the stall for a short while."

Shandek fell silent, frowning at the woman for a handful of heartbeats before nudging Mayel into movement, towards the theatre's main entrance. "What with people runnin' from shadows, and these stories of a dark man walking the night streets, there's somethin' up with this city."

Mayel didn't reply, but submitted to his larger cousin's urging. Even as they walked away, he kept his eyes on the woman for as long as he could. There was an echo of something in her face that made him shiver. For a moment, he thought he heard screams, and the crackle of flames. Then they passed around the corner and the spell was broken.

The main entrance was open, and freshly painted—as they turned in to the open gateway Shandek had to check his stride to avoid a man crouching at the right-hand gate, putting the final touches to the elaborate picture.

Mayel stopped and looked, trying to imagine the whole image, while Shandek muttered an apology for his foot clipping the painter's trailing heel. The painting was not what Mayel had expected, not the usual sort of scenes that hinted at the delights awaiting them within.

"*The Broken Spear, Five Wives of the Sea*—even *The Triumph of Gods* would be a more obvious choice than this one," Mayel muttered.

Against a granite sky of roiling cloud, the aftermath of a battle on a bowl-shaped plain. In the background, a huge castle crowned by five massive towers. One of those towers had been shattered and flames, painted with such skill they seemed real to Mayel, licked at the castle wall. Before the walls towered the varied shapes of the Reapers, Death's violent Aspects, who embodied the ways men feared to die: the emaciated face of the Soldier glared down at the slain around his feet, while the Burning Man stood on a hillock behind him with arms outstretched like a martyr. The Great Wolf was a vague shape in the background, stalking its prey in the blurred shadows, and the Headsman reclined on a distant block of stone with his axe propped on his shoulder. Strangely, it was the Wither Queen who was painted in the greatest detail. Mayel felt her cruel gaze, her pale grey eyes, slice into him. Her lips as thin as dagger-blades were slightly parted, as though she was about to speak his name.

He felt her cold touch on his skin. His mother wasn't the only person Mayel had seen dying of disease; he had known some who had endured agonising months of her cruelty. The Wither Queen robbed her victims of everything, of the person they had once been as much as the life her lord demanded. Though she was a God, Mayel hated her for what she was.

The detail of the plain below the Reapers was vague; angular shapes hinted at a carpet of slaughtered men and creatures. Somehow the magnitude of the horror was increased by the remoteness. Framing the entire plain was a high ridge of grim rocks the colour of sand. Mayel looked closer and realised that there was the faintest of detail on the rocks, almost like the grain of wood. He shivered, thinking of the pine boxes wealthier folk used to bury their dead in.

"Gods, man," Shandek exclaimed, "you've quite a skill there. This is better than any I've seen in my life."

"Thank you, sir. It's . . ." The painter's voice tailed off as he looked from Shandek to the painting. A small man with the dark skin that spoke of a western heritage, he wore little more than rags, yet his face was clean and his hair carefully trimmed. His expression was one of dazed bemusement, as if he couldn't believe he had been able to produce it. "It is the best thing I've ever done, by a long way."

"I didn't know you cared anything about art," Mayel said to his cousin, unable to tear his eyes from the painting.

"Ah, I've seen a bit in my time." Shandek grinned.

"When? You're no collector."

"No, but I've been in plenty of places belongin' to men who are. You have my compliments, friend. Can you tell us where the man in charge is?"

The painter gave a wince and jabbed his brush towards the interior. "The minstrel will be in one of the boxes. Sitting in shadow. If you go in they'll find you soon enough."

"They?" wondered Shandek aloud, but the painter had already returned to his work. Shrugging, Shandek stepped through the gates and glanced into the dim, cramped room where the money-collectors would work, counting the copper pieces as folk filed in. It was empty yet, without even a stool or table.

A walkway led off both left and right, to storerooms of no more than two yards' depth on the outer side, and the boxes for the rich folk further in on the inner wall. Ahead was a short flight of steps leading into the theatre itself.

Shandek hopped up these and turned to beckon Mayel to follow. The youth hesitated, still unnerved by the painting on the door. The style reminded him of religious paintings, the ancient and holy images they had been so proud of on the Island of Birds.

Behind him, he felt the presence of Brohm loom close. He'd been shadowing them, and he wasn't going to enter until Mayel had.

"Why did you want me to come here with you?"

"Why?" Shandek puffed his cheeks out in dismissal. "No great reason, cuz. I wanted to speak to you before I came, thought you might be interested. Also, you got more learnin' than me. These artistic types might say somethin' clever and I wouldn't know whether to agree or stab 'em."

Mayel sighed and started up the steps. Something nagged at him. *I don't want to be here at all, but what am I frightened of? Jackdaw won't be here, and what else do I have to be afraid of?*

As if in answer, a figure leapt out behind Shandek and grabbed him by his shoulders in a blur of bone-white. Shandek yelped and tried to turn, but his attacker held him tight, pinning his arms back. Mayel saw a white, hairless head and a savage flash of teeth over Shandek's shoulder. His cousin flailed madly as Brohm shoved Mayel aside and ran for the stairs, but before he reached his employer, the albino had jumped backwards and effortlessly tossed Shandek away.

Brohm raised his massive fist as he charged, but the albino was quicker. Darting forward, he lunged low and crashed a fist into Brohm's stomach, stopping the larger man in his tracks. Brohm gasped and doubled over, sinking to his knees, only to be grabbed by the scruff of the neck and thrown down after his master. Mayel heard the thump of Brohm falling and rolling on the rough paved steps. Then there was silence.

Having dispatched both men from his path, the albino paused, hairless head bright in the sunlight. He was dressed in cropped linen trousers and a laced shirt, sleeves cut well short of the wrist. As Mayel took in the albino's malformed face, he wondered whether this was a human at all. It looked as if some God had formed the albino from white clay, using a detailed description, but without actually seeing the real thing. The features were too smooth, the jaw protruding and thick. Its eyes were over-large, curling almonds of blackness. Meeting the albino's gaze drained the warmth from Mayel's heart, drawing him in to a cold and pitiless place.

He tore his eyes away as the albino continued to inspect him, looking at him as if he were an insect, or a rabbit that had surprised a wolf by not running. He looked down. Its bare feet were split down the middle and Mayel's breath caught when he realised each foot mainly consisted of two great toes, a short talon curled down over the end of each.

"That's enough, I think," called an unseen man. The albino's head snapped round, but soon dropped its glare. It pointed at Mayel, then retreated with alacrity.

"Please, come out into the light. My guard dog won't hurt you."

Mayel stared out into the open auditorium, frozen with fear, until a burst of swearing rang out. He scrambled up the steps.

"Pissin' breath of Karkarn!" his cousin groaned. "I'll shove that painter's brush so far up his arse he'll paint with his tongue from now on."

"Now, now," said the voice, and a man dressed as a minstrel came into sight, lounging in a box with his feet up on the barrier. Around his neck was a golden chain, with strange discs, like coins, decorated with jewels. A peacock feather sprouted from his hat. "I am certain the painter will have told you no lies, so you can hardly blame him for the actions of others."

Shandek hauled himself up. Brohm was sitting upright, clutching his gut. Neither looked badly hurt.

"We jus' came here to talk. Didn't hafta set your wolves on us," Brohm muttered.

The minstrel gave a sniff. "They're dogs, not wolves."

"Look more like wolves to me," Shandek replied, dusting himself down and walking up to Mayel's side. The albino retreated into the shadow of another box. Mayel scanned the theatre, the empty rows of stone steps surrounded by cramped rooms for the rich, all looking down on the pit, a round area of flattened earth. There were deep shadows at the back, where Mayel thought he glimpsed another white face.

"There is a difference. Wolves do not take orders, wolves are not tamed."

"You call these tame?" Shandek wondered, rubbing at his temple, where a bruise was starting to colour the skin.

"Certainly. They obey my commands without question and since I have given them instructions to dissuade trespassers, they are most enthusiastic in the execution of that order. I did not say they were less dangerous than wolves, quite the opposite. Shandek, you should understand that." The minstrel's voice was low and mocking.

Mayel felt somehow sullied.

"Why should I understand that?" Shandek wondered. "Never met one of these bastards before."

"You should understand because you own dog-fighting pits," the minstrel explained. "The savagery in a dogfight surpasses anything a wolf would do. It is men that make them dangerous—men have corrupted the wolf and created a more dangerous creature in his own image."

"You sound like you disapprove of the change," Mayel interjected, "yet you make use of these dogs and all their savagery."

"*I*, disapprove?" The minstrel smiled, showing bright white teeth in his tanned face. "Not at all. Wolves were made into dogs to serve a purpose, and it is those who control the purpose who are to blame for whatever may happen, not the animal. All things change over the course of time. Those who fight it are shouting without air in their lungs."

"You mean silent?" Mayel found himself asking, almost hypnotised by the minstrel's voice.

"Drowned."

Mayel felt himself being drawn into the minstrel's dark, piercing gaze. The minstrel was just a man, from the south somewhere, Mayel guessed, but like his albino, his eyes were devoid of humanity. "But where did your dogs come from?"

"I have travelled far, even into the Waste. It's a stranger place than folk would like us to believe. Change there is a harsh master. Only the strong have survived."

"Wait a moment," Shandek interrupted, "my name—?"

"How could one not have heard of you?" the minstrel broke in smoothly. "You are the man who is lord of this manor."

"Knowin' my name's one thing, recognisin' me's another. As for this bein' my district, that's close enough, and I don't like new folk in it who I don't know."

"Yet you come with only one thug in tow. That young man doesn't look much of a threat."

"Never mind him. Who're you?"

"I'm sure you know what reception we gave the last man who marched in here. You're being a little demanding, don't you think?" The minstrel slipped his feet off the barrier and stood as though to leave the box, but he remained in the shadows.

"I'm not here to break heads until we get tribute, that's the Spider's domain. I'm just lookin' to see that there's no trouble in my district—and per'aps to see whether there's business to be done here."

"Ah, a man of enterprise. Excellent news. Someone who understands the value of things, of people. In that case, this conversation might just be worth continuing." The minstrel tipped his peaked hat. "My name is Rojak. Join me in a drink."

He produced a fired-clay bottle and set it on the barrier. Mayel noticed the paint was worn and cracked—clearly the painter had more menial work to come once he'd finished the magnificent gates. Four small cups, half a finger-length in size, followed the bottle.

Rojak pulled the cork and poured a clear liquid into each cup, then offered one each to Shandek, Brohm and Mayel. Mayel sniffed: it smelled sharp, a rough-edged brandy laced with something, peach, maybe. The taste was sickly, but he swallowed it down as fast as he could and ignored the sting.

"Wonderful. Now we're friends."

"It seems we are," Shandek replied. He cast his eyes around the theatre. "So, you the owner of the company?"

"The leader. Our owner is, well, here only in spirit." Rojak gave a sly smile. "I am the playwright. The actors are engaged in various pursuits in the city until we have prepared the theatre."

"Commissioned by Siala?"

"Why do you think that?"

"She's just taken control o' the city. Don't sound like the White Circle is so popular as she'd like t'believe. Maybe she's tryin' to get the support of the city, in case the Farlan attack, or somethin'."

Rojak raised an eyebrow. "For a man some might describe as a 'local criminal,' you have an astute mind. We have not, in fact, been commissioned, no."

"So why Scree?"

"It was felt that our talents could be well employed here."

"By someone who'd never been here?" snorted Shandek. "I don't mean to be rude, Master Rojak, but I don't think Scree was the best choice. This city ain't rich or cultured, not compared to some. I hear you're taking the theatre for the rest of the year, but few folk'll pay to see your plays. If it does come to war, things will be even harder for you."

"Your concern warms my heart. I, however, keep my faith. We have a number of plays to show. Our work will be tested out and refined as the weeks pass. Once this summer is over, we shall be ready to move on to the rest of the Land." Rojak's eyes gleamed. He stared straight at Mayel, who recognised that look of contained savagery; he'd seen it in the eyes of one of the brothers at the monastery, a man who'd preyed on the youngest novices. But he thought this was worse: this minstrel was no slobbering coward, and his avarice was for the whole Land. His pleasure would be in the pain of nations. Amidst the wreckage of civilisation and cowed peoples, that soft smile would grow ever broader. Mayel tried not to shudder visibly.

"A strange time for showin' plays at all," Shandek said. "These are dark times, accordin' to what I've been hearin' on the street."

"Then they will need diversion from the cares of life."

"Can't see many goin' to the expense. If we war with the Farlan, as I've been hearin', folk'll need every penny just to buy food, and they'll likely get taxed for half of that too. I'd say you'd get better money as soldiers, or bodyguards to a merchant. Your dogs could guard a man as easily as a theatre, and they'd be more willin' to pay."

"My dogs are as devoted to our art as I am." Rojak inclined his head towards the albino, hovering in the shadows like a ghost. "The petty squabbles of the powerful are not our concern. Our place is here, and here we will stay, to spread our message to every man, woman and child of Scree. We will witness the changes that are to come, changes I have foreseen in the fall of coins, when the storm comes to Scree, commissioned by a calling greater than the White Circle."

Mayel took a tentative step back. The minstrel's voice had risen above a whisper for the first time and his hands, once piously clasped, now flew about, gesticulating sharply. He slipped over the rail.

Rojak's words echoed inside Mayel's head, trembling his bones like the crash of falling tombstones. Alarmed by the minstrel's sudden animation, he cast a look at his cousin, who was equally startled.

And then it was over. Suddenly still once more, fingers again interlocked, Rojak peered down at the ground, as though saying a silent prayer, not blinking, hardly breathing. He appeared oblivious to their presence.

Shandek was as confused as Mayel. Had those last few moments been a piece of drama, an indulgence by a playwright, or was it something more? Mayel bit his lip, worried.

Twenty heartbeats passed. Still Rojak didn't move, though his head and shoulders were now bathed in sunlight too bright for Mayel's eyes.

Finally: "Power has come to this city," he murmured abruptly.

Mayel recoiled at the sound of his cruel, velvety lilt.

"Slipping furtive and fearful, it comes in the night. There are games being played here—plots to be acted out, blood to be shed. There will be a spring torrent of cleansing, and those born will emerge in the blood of others." Rojak's head snapped up, the black irises burning like acid into Mayel's skin.

Mayel felt a twist of terror in his bowels, as though that corrosive gaze had seared his gut.

"Take care what games you play, young sparrow. Eagles soar above these streets and vultures watch from the trees. They will prey on you and your like."

Mayel staggered back as though he'd been struck. His mouth opened, but all sound was stolen from him. In the corner of his eye he caught a movement, a dark flutter in the deep wings of the stage. The memory of Prior Corci's tattoos rose unbidden, the stain of feathers on Jackdaw's cheeks and forehead like a painted helm.

Mayel turned to flee. Shandek called his name and reached out, but Mayel, filled with the fear that had been his constant companion for the last few weeks, slipped through his cousin's fingers. Despite the ghastly spectre of pursuit, he couldn't help but look back. There was nothing in the pit beyond empty shadows. The deep steps leading down to it were all in sun, except the very top, which was cut through by the straight line of the roof's shadow.

Something caused Mayel to hesitate. The worn step with a chipped edge. The unbroken line of shadow. The shadow of the building behind Rojak. He looked up again. The minstrel had not moved. His head was still bathed in the clear morning sun that rose behind his head and left his face in shadow.

Seeing Mayel's aghast expression, Rojak smiled coldly, lips parting to show his small, sharp teeth.

"Where's—Where's his shadow?" Mayel whispered, uncomprehending. He looked again at the straight line of shadow cast by the rooftop behind Rojak and felt a chill steal down his spine. He bit back a scream, flapped an arm towards his cousin, then fled as though the denizens of Ghenna were calling his name.

CHAPTER 11

"I THINK I COULD GROW rather used to being the lord of all I survey."

Tila, riding at Isak's side, chuckled. With the summer sun beginning to fade on the eastern horizon, the shadows of the alders that lined one side of the road were reaching deep and long over them. Isak watched the flickers of light and dark washing over the lead riders. He shifted again in his saddle; uncomfortable in the formal riding tunic Tila had all but ordered him to wear that morning. He was making damn sure she noticed his discomfort.

"I think you're already rather used to it, my Lord," Tila replied, flicking her loose hair over her left shoulder, enjoying the touch of the sun on her skin. "You don't look embarrassed when a regiment salutes you any more. I would say you are already more comfortable in your title than Lord Bahl ever was. He commanded a room as few could, but at heart he was too humble a man to want to rule a nation."

"Humble?" Isak mused. "Not the first word I'd use for him, but I suppose you're right. Ruling is a chore. I think he'd have been happier as a general of the armies, one who didn't have to bother with the rest of society. It might not have been my dream, but it's a fair alternative."

"Alternative to what?" Tila laughed.

"Oh, I don't know. I never really dared think about the future. Father would sneer whenever I even mentioned joining the Ghosts, and I suppose I grew up not expecting to amount to anything. I soon learned to keep quiet; a future was for other folk, not me."

"And now you are lord of all you survey." Tila hesitated.

Isak could see there was something on her mind. "What is it?" he asked softly.

"It's been the best part of a year since you last saw your father. I know you didn't part on good terms, but he is your kin, and you are now the greater. Is it not time for you to see him again, to set things right between you?"

Isak sighed, his anger, normally quick to rise, softened by the lovely day.

"You're dead to me," that's what he said the day I arrived at the palace. If he doesn't want to see me, there's not much I can do and I don't intend to mourn it."

"But it was said in haste, after an evening of drinking. How often in your life have you regretted something you've said?"

"Never," Isak insisted.

Tila arched a pretty eyebrow. "Two weeks ago you told me to shift my fat—well, let's not repeat it? But I think we both agree you regretted that pretty quickly."

Isak broke into a grin as he remembered her incandescent reaction. "Well, perhaps once or twice."

"Then wipe that smirk off your face and admit you're wrong," Tila said coldly.

"Fine, I admit it. Gods, has Carel been giving you lessons in how to scold me?" Isak said, exasperated.

"Not at all, but he might have mentioned something about not letting you get too big for those ridiculously large boots." It was Tila's turn to smirk now.

Isak stuck his tongue out.

It had been deliciously warm all day, perhaps a little too hot for riding in formal clothes, but not even Isak complained with any real feeling. This stretch of the South Road was one he knew well, and he was enjoying the beautiful countryside of the Saroc suzerainty. Dominating the western sky-line was the squat bulk of Tayell Mountain—known locally as Greenjacket because of the thick band of trees around its middle. The northern half of the Saroc suzerainty was hilly, and there were plenty of rivers and streams, ensuring fertile alpine meadows and vineyards—it was renowned for the rich crops of wine grapes which proliferated on the sunny slopes. There was excel-lent autumn hunting, and though it was occasionally prone to flooding, when snowmelt swelled the rivers, this lush, vibrant place was a pleasure to travel through most of the year. This was the perfect time to go north.

Isak's party planned on spending the evening at Crosswind Fortress, where the suzerainties of Saroc, Selsetin and Foleh met. By a curiosity of geography and politics, Foleh's boundary bulged out to encompass Cross-wind, and however illogical it might appear, the fortress was the suzerain's traditional seat.

Isak turned in his saddle to look down at Tila. "You know, when I made you my political advisor, I didn't give you licence to run the rest of my life."

"I know," Tila said with her most glittering smile, the one she normally reserved for Count Vesna. "But I'm far better at it than you are."

"Huh!" Isak muttered. "I think that man's having a bad influence on you."

"I'm sure I don't know what you mean," Tila replied, fooling no one. Her so-called chaperone, Mistress Daran, was fully aware that the count was smitten with Tila, but opted for a quiet life, as long as they were discreet. Isak was beginning to realise that behind the rigid veneer of Farlan custom, the rules could be surprisingly flexible at times.

"Count Vesna's the only other person I know who thinks they can get their way just with a smile," Isak said, laughing in spite of himself. "You're becoming quite a match for him; he'd best be careful—he is getting old, after all, and his charms are fading."

"Oh hush, leave him alone. A few grey hairs are distinguished, ask any woman! It's certainly more attractive than a spotty over-sized teenager, no matter what his title is!"

Tila's retort provoked a snort and Isak inclined his head, conceding the point. "The countess certainly seems to agree with you," he said, jabbing a thumb past his dragon-emblazoned guards to the column behind them. Suzerain Saroc, with his hurscals all dressed in red and white, was followed by Countess Saroc and Count Vesna, the countess sitting high and proud in her saddle. Vesna was apparently regaling her with a comic poem, told with every ounce of theatrical flamboyance he could muster.

Tila tilted her nose and pointedly ignored him.

Bringing up the rear of Isak's cavalcade was a column of light cavalry, which included men from Lomin and Tildek, who had surrendered as soon as they could. They had had little choice but to follow Duke Certinse's orders, so instead of sending them home, where they would once again be under the influence of the Certinse family, Isak had decided to keep them close. Just in case their new-found loyalty to the Lord of the Farlan proved weaker than he hoped, a regiment of Saroc troops rode alongside them.

Looking ahead, Isak spotted Crosswind Fortress, coming into view through the trees. The castle, one of several guarding the approach to Tirah, was a compact, square building with a lone tower at the corner nearest to them.

"It's not as big as Nerlos Castle," Tila commented.

"It doesn't have to be. Look at the way it dominates this whole area." Isak waved a hand in a chopping motion, and explained, "This is an open floodplain; the castle has unrestricted views from east to west, and this is the only road good enough for an army to move north through Saroc. It runs so close to the castle you could lose thousands to just a few companies of archers stationed on the wall."

"Thousands? Surely not?"

Isak nodded. "Trust me, and if not me, then Vesna. There would be huge casualties, even if you just tried to go past the castle, and more if you tried to take it. The ground around here is so soft and waterlogged from the flooding rivers that it's useless most of the year round."

Passing the last of the alders they trotted out into the killing ground before the castle, a thousand yards of open space between them and the stone walls. The road took a circuitous route to keep to the highest and driest ground. The road was built up slightly from the ground and studded with stones on each side, while the rest of the plain ground was flat and featureless. The size of the plain made it look like a minor road, though it was as wide and well-made as one might expect of such an important route.

Feeling exposed, Tila shivered and pulled her shawl over her shoulders. She didn't speak as they made their way towards the castle, the evening shadows slowly lengthening behind them.

"Looks like Suzerain Foleh has guests," Isak commented when they were no more than a hundred yards from the castle. Not a scrap of wind stirred the flags on the tower or above the gate. Isak couldn't make out the devices, so he was forced to guess from their colours alone. Foleh's—a raven's wing impaled on a barbed spear, if he could see it—would be the flag on the tower, placed higher than those of his guests. The tradition of bearing flags was introduced to cut down the number of disputes caused by armed noblemen going unannounced through a suzerainty. The Farlan were a proud people, and the sort of men willing to back down from a fight didn't often ascend to the nobility.

"It's strange to think that I've come this way so many times before, and he'll have never known, but today he'll welcome me in like a conquering hero."

"And the others?" Tila asked, squinting up at the limp pennants. One was white with a small black design that Isak couldn't make out, beside it one of green and white, and a white flag speckled with red furthest to the right. "The right-hand one must be Suzerain Lehm's rose petals crest. That means he came as soon as he received your summons. And that means the middle one must be Suzerain Nerlos' thistles and quills—but whose is the one beside it?"

"General Lahk," Isak realised all of a sudden. "He rarely wears it, but I saw his colours once. Lesarl told me that Lahk was made a marshal twenty summers ago, though he prefers 'general,' for obvious reasons. His crest is a black falcon holding a ducal circlet in its claws."

Tila smiled. "It can't have taxed the Keymaster's gifts too much to produce that one."

"And he's come to meet me," Isak mused. "Interesting."

"Hardly surprising though," Tila said. "The new Duke of Tirah should parade into his city, not slip back in the night accompanied only by a dozen guards!"

The drawbridge was down, the gate open. As they approached, Isak saw a handful of men emerge. From their colours he could guess who was who, but it was the oversized figure of General Lahk who advanced to greet Isak first at the lip of the drawbridge. Lahk, dressed as formally as Isak had ever seen him, greeted Isak with open palms, in his own livery and with an empty scabbard swinging from his hip. *Oh Lahk*, Isak thought to himself, *what foolish ancient tradition does that come from?*

"Welcome back, your Grace." The white-eye general leaned to one side and looked down the column of soldiers behind. "I had thought to provide you with an escort, but I see you've already found one."

Isak smiled. From Lahk, that was as close to humour as you could hope for, and he appreciated the effort. He knew full well it would be hard for the general to treat a young man of barely eighteen summers the same way he had the lord he had revered and served for more than half a century. Isak remembered his harsh words to Lahk on the road to Lomin the previous year and felt a pang of shame, but he knew there was no going back. The best he could do was start afresh, and if the man once found unworthy of Isak's previous title could manage it, Isak would too.

"I have," Isak replied in a bright voice, "but I'll never complain about having the Ghosts or you at my side."

Carel raised a hand to signal the halt down the line and Isak slipped from his horse. He returned the general's formal greeting, then stepped closer and grasped Lahk's forearm. Lahk was still a very large man, but Isak was taller now. For a brief moment Isak thought he saw something like gratification in Lahk's eyes, relief that the new Lord of the Farlan might yet measure up.

"This is the first time I've seen you in your own colours."

"It didn't seem appropriate to use any other's, and I did not wait to have a replacement made. I hope you don't take offence that the regiments I brought had no alternatives to wear."

"Replacements?"

"Yes, my Lord." Lahk looked puzzled for a moment. "The Palace Guard will need a new uniform now, in your own colours."

"What? No!" Isak exclaimed in dismay. "Don't change their uniforms!"

"But they are your personal legion, my Lord, not independent; they can't wear another man's colours in your service. It would be unseemly—quite aside from what the rest of our people might think. We must never give the impression that the Ghosts are not completely loyal to you."

"I don't give a damn how it would look. I've spent most of my life dreaming of wearing that uniform. I know the pride they take in it—as does the rest of the tribe—and I don't care what anyone else thinks; I won't insult the men who died for that banner by making it redundant. The Ghosts wear the colours they've had for the last two centuries. Tell them I never got my chance to pass the trials for the Guard and I've got to have something to aspire to. Whenever I need a close guard, then they will have to wear my colours—but that will just be a company of men drawn from the Ghosts."

Lahk's face was a blank mask, but Isak guessed at the conflict going on under the surface. Eventually, he cleared his throat and bowed. "A company, yes, my Lord. I'm sure they will appreciate the gesture."

"The regiments are camped in the meadows behind the castle? Send someone to direct the cavalry there and get them camped."

He turned towards the noblemen waiting patiently behind the general. Their host was a half-pace ahead of the others, a grey-haired man slightly stooped by advancing age. "Suzerain Foleh, would you do me the honour of showing me to your most unpleasant cell? You have an unexpected guest."

Returning from the privy, Isak turned down the brightly lit corridor back to the castle's main hall and stopped. On his left he spotted a small, unassuming arch leading to a spiral stair. Half-covering it was a flag, suspended from a rail fixed at the very top of the stone wall. Isak was sure it hadn't been like that when he'd come this way. His need had been pressing, admittedly, thanks to rather a lot of Suzerain Foleh's excellent ale, but his mind wasn't fuddled yet. One of the servants must have just gone through and forgotten to pull the flag back after him.

Never one to ignore his curiosity once piqued, Isak leaned through the gap and peered upwards. A single torch at the top illuminated the way, but aside from well-worn flagstones and a musty scent there was nothing to see.

With his customary stealth, the Duke of Tirah padded up the stair, which wound round a full circle before opening out on a dim, square room.

The beams in the ceiling were low compared to the rest of the castle, a finger-width from his hair. A banister ran around a wide square hole in the floor that made the room more of a gallery than anything else. Leaning on the banister were two men, one Isak recognised as Suzerain Foleh's steward, and another liveried man. Both were staring intently down to the hall beneath, pointing at the table and the folk below. The steward said something, and his companion nodded and straightened up. He gave a cough of alarm when he saw Isak.

The steward's eyes widened as he followed his companion's gaze, but Isak motioned for them to be calm. The servant hovered uncertainly, glancing to his left, where two pitchers of wine stood on a small table, and Isak suddenly realised where the man had been going. There were no servants in the room below, yet the goblets had remained full the entire evening. Isak stepped away from the stair and gestured for the servant to continue, which he did with a hasty bow. He looked relieved to be leaving.

Isak leaned on the rail as the men had and looked down to see his dinner companions. There were twenty-three people around the table, settled into an easy informality after a decorous start. He could see three or four conversations around the table. Catching the steward's eye, Isak grinned and hunkered down to enjoy the show. The steward visibly relaxed and fetched a goblet of wine, which he pressed it into Isak's hand.

"Thank you," Isak whispered.

The steward bowed and, when Isak gestured at the rail next to him, hesitated for a moment, then resumed his position beside the lord of his people. Isak had to stifle a smile; he'd never seen a man lounge in quite so formal a way, but he was beginning to recognise the effect of his title. He'd have to get used to it.

"What's your name? You've been in Suzerain Foleh's service a long time?" Isak asked, too quietly to be heard by those below.

"Dupres, your Grace, my name is Dupres. I have spent my life working in this castle, and I have been steward to the suzerain for six summers."

Dupres was a man not long past forty, Isak judged, with a widow's peak and worry-lines around his eyes. He had seen the man earlier, constantly at his master's elbow, discreet, but anticipating his every need.

"You serve him well; I have seen few servants so attentive."

"Thank you, my Lord."

From below, the voice of the Countess of Lehm caught Isak's attention. He leaned further over the banister to hear the conversation better.

"Count Vesna, has Lord Isak said what he intends to do with Duke Certinse?"

"He's going to put the man on trial, of course." Vesna's response was curt. He hadn't liked her tone any more than Isak had. She was treading a careful line, for speaking about Isak while he was absent was a discourtesy most nobles wouldn't dare. Isak knew the customs of the nobility were still largely a mystery to him, but he had begun to recognise the formal ways in which a person of noble birth would couch a completely opposite request.

"And you have not counselled him against this?"

"Against it? Let the traitor hang, that's what I say."

Isak couldn't yet work out if the countess was either stupid and insulting, or if she was carefully positioning herself to make some point, that Vesna would later tell him in private.

"But is that wise in the long term?" The other voices around the table had fallen away; every face was watching the exchange as intently as Isak.

"How would it not be wise, my Lady?" enquired Tila. "Duke Certinse is undoubtedly a traitor. He ambushed us and tried to kill the Lord of the Farlan. For that, execution is the only response."

"It's a merciful one," growled Lahk, more to himself than anyone else.

The countess pointedly ignored him. "But Duke Certinse is a man of title, of position in society. It is hardly seemly that he be treated like a common criminal. And Lord Isak has not yet been officially confirmed as Lord of the Farlan, so there could be legalities to complicate and prolong the trial."

"Then he is at least Suzerain Anvee," interjected Suzerain Saroc sharply. "Certinse and his family were not defending their suzerainty against invasion by another. If I had been at their side, then perhaps they would have a case to discuss, but there can be no argument here."

The countess raised her hands in deference. "I am not condoning his actions, merely questioning whether it is a wise course to publicly hang the man. It cannot do the common folk good to see the highest of the nobility executed, especially when others will fall with him. Every tavern gossip across the Land will delight in the particulars of that trial."

"You fear insurrection?" Tila responded, forcing the countess to turn back to her.

Isak thought he saw a flicker of doubt on the woman's face, but she continued without hesitation, "Nothing so dramatic, but the embarrassment and disgrace will be wide-reaching. The more foolish the nobility looks, the closer to the common folk we appear, and that could give rise to dangerous illusions. With General Lahk you have enough of his peers in this room to hold the trial here, and now."

Isak turned to the steward and grimaced. "You hear that, Dupres?" he whispered. "Don't you start thinking yourself the same species as the countess, now."

"I would not dare to, my Lord," Dupres replied dryly.

"Even now that I'm suddenly not a commoner, I fail to see what she fears. The rich are rich, the poor are not. Such are the lives we lead. When I was poor, I wanted to be rich, not because I hated the nobility, but because it's better than being poor. And yet this lot seem to live in terror of the day when their servant turns around and declares himself lord of the manor."

"Such a thing is possible, my Lord," Dupres said. "Revolt has happened countless times in the past, despite the best efforts of the nobility."

"But usually for a reason. When there is famine, and the lord does nothing about it, who can blame a man for trying to feed his family?"

"If it wouldn't be too bold, my Lord . . ."

Isak waved Dupres to continue. He wasn't interested in decorum, he wanted the man's opinion. Dupres looked hesitant for a moment, but he'd seen enough today to realise how informal the white-eye was with his aides.

"Whoever is managing your estates in Anvee while you're away—I'm certain he would blame a man for stealing food, as much as declaring himself lord of the manor."

"Perhaps, but when was life ever equal? When revolts do take hold, there's rarely much that changes in the end: a different man gets rich, or the whole region collapses. Does a more equal way exist? The nobility are convinced it does, and they spend their days fearing it. The commoners they're so frightened of get on with some real work instead."

Dupres had no answer to that.

Isak drained the goblet of wine and the steward immediately took it to refill.

"Will you join me for a cup? It would be good to hear a sensible man's opinion on the state of the Land."

"It, ah, it would be unseemly, my Lord, for the steward to be drinking the wine he serves—"

"I know. It is considered a blurring of boundaries," Isak replied glumly, before clapping a hand on Dupres' shoulder. "Fortunately, as I was commenting on the way here, I happen to be lord of all I survey. And that includes you, my friend, as well as our noble friends down there."

"The suzerain would still be displeased." There was a hint of hope in Dupres' voice, despite his words. It was clear that Isak was not to be dissuaded, and how often would this chance arise, for Dupres to drink and talk as an equal with Nartis' chosen representative? But convention had to be acknowledged.

"Bugger him. I'm his lord too, and we white-eyes are notoriously fickle creatures. You have to put up with a lot from us, and he'd hardly be happy if you refused an order from me." Isak grinned. "Which I have just issued, by the way, so be a good lad and fetch yourself a cup."

Isak guessed that the hunter's moon had to be somewhere near the horizon by now, and midnight not far off. He raised a silent toast with Dupres to Kasi's passing that evening and they resumed their curious vigil.

"So, how lordly do I appear?" Isak muttered to his companion. "No, wait, what I would hear is how folk have taken news of Lord Bahl's death."

"Well, my Lord . . ."

"Do stop doing that every time you speak to me—makes everything you say take twice as long! No true lord would be in a darkened corner getting drunk with his host's steward, therefore it must be a delusion of yours, and one should always call delusions by their proper name."

"But if you do, don't they cease to become delusions? Call something by its proper name and it becomes a true thing."

"Oh, let us hope so," Isak sighed.

Dupres narrowed his eyes at Isak for a moment then nodded. "That you would care about it answers your first question, I think. As for the second, we were frightened—as probably the rest of the tribe were too. Lord Bahl ruled us for two hundred years. Our grandparents knew no other lord. To lose that, and under circumstances that were never fully explained, is to lose the cornerstone of your world. Can you tell me what happened?"

Isak shook his head. "He was doing something that would have made the tribe more secure. I can tell you no more of it."

"Of course. What I can tell you is that we were cheered by news of your exploits arriving with the death notice."

"My exploits? The battle in Narkang?"

"Exactly. Folk are calling you Isak Stormcaller; they say that you wield a power Lord Bahl never did."

"Bahl rode the storm in his own way." Isak grimaced and waggled his pure white fingers in Dupres' face. "But he didn't pay the price I had to."

"So that's true?" Dupres asked in astonishment. "You really were touched by Nartis when you called the storm?"

"Not exactly. That was the day Bahl died—Nartis was close to me that day, his hand on my shoulder. If it hadn't been for that, I wouldn't have survived when I called the storm myself. To call such power requires a bargain of sorts, I'm told. The magic almost killed me, and it stripped all colour from my arm. The mage I spoke to said that if I had died, it would have continued until all colour was lost from my body—or perhaps that it would have continued draining colour until I was dead; the jury was out on that detail."

"Magic," Dupres shivered. "I'm glad I'm not so blessed." He scratched at the red embroidering on his sleeve, a band of grapevines that encircled the left-hand sleeve. The right sleeve bore a variety of fruits hanging from branches. It prompted Isak to wonder whether Dupres had to serve wine with one hand and food with the other. He vaguely remembered Tila saying something like that, but the details were lost to him.

"Magic has its advantages," Isak pointed out, vaguely feeling as though he should defend it, but without knowing quite why. "If you're not giving in to your own base desires, the price you pay is worthwhile."

Dupres grimaced. "Still. Paying prices you cannot guess at, consorting with daemons—I'd rather not. I know its uses, and that you have such power relieves many fears. To know our armies are still led by a powerful man is reassuring in troubling times, but I'm deeply glad it's not me having to do it."

Isak grunted. "But what if my every act seems to make times more troubled?"

Dupres didn't have any answer to that and the pair fell into silence. Isak's gaze drifted the length of the table. There was nothing left of the meal aside from piled platters of fruit. Men were leaning on the table, now, debating the ramifications of executing Duke Certinse. The room was lit mainly by four brass candle-wheels hanging from the balcony where Isak watched. The iron chain holding one was tantalisingly within reach; Isak could see in his mind the white droplets of wax falling, if he only reached out and gave the chain a twist. His hand actually twitched towards it before he remembered himself and stopped.

"Look at my faithful subjects," Isak muttered, swinging his goblet towards them. The remaining wine slopped up, but fell back into the cup rather than dripping down the cleavage of the woman beneath. Isak shared a relieved grin with Dupres and continued, "They all sit there talking happily, despite their master having disappeared from the room. Surely one of them should be wondering if I've fallen into the privy by now."

"Perhaps they give you more credit than that," the steward replied, warming to the irreverent conversation, "or they are secretly concerned, but etiquette restrains them from voicing their concerns."

Isak nodded with mock gloom. "More than once over the last year I've suspected that tradition will be the death of me."

At the table below Tila's voice cut though the wider conversation. "But that encourages Lord Isak to bypass the rule of law. Surely the examples of Lord Atro and Lord Bahl demonstrate the need for constant restraint, rather than encouraging a lord to exercise religious authority."

"Perhaps, my dear," replied the countess, an indulgent tone in her voice. Isak could just imagine Tila's expression. "But I do not feel it is appropriate for dirty laundry to be done in public."

"Dirty laundry, my Lady, is done by servants," Vesna joined, "as I believe you were at pains to point out. But, while he will be surprised by its source, I'm sure Chief Steward Lesarl will be glad of your endorsement that he need not bother with legal technicalities; it does take up such a large proportion of his time."

"Hah, now he is one I would like to see publicly hung!" the countess exclaimed, "and from what I hear, Lord Isak shares that opinion."

"The Chief Steward is loyal to his tribe," Vesna said firmly, stamping firmly on any such rumours. "Lesarl will serve Lord Isak as well as he did Lord Bahl, and he will continue to do the Farlan a great service. Now that Duke Certinse is under guard and his uncle dead, you should be more concerned about enemies from abroad rather than anyone within the tribe."

"And who poses a greater threat than that sadistic megalomaniac, who will no doubt be spending every waking hour devising ways to bypass your noble lord?"

"The White Circle is the most immediate. They proved themselves to be our enemies in Narkang, and while their leader may be dead, the organisation is not. You heard tonight that Siala has been quickest to act; there can be no confusion as to why she has taken direct control over Scree. Without that city under her control she cannot be sure of winning the war in Tor Milist—indeed, resolving that conflict must be her first priority, to free up her troops. With Scree and Tor Milist under her control, she will not be challenged for leadership of the Circle, and that will give her the powerbase to mount a strong resistance against any action we might take."

"Your assessment sounds right," Suzerain Foleh said. The portly old man had always been, by his own admission, more a merchant than a soldier and he was happy to concede authority in the military field to the hero of the tribe, despite Vesna being his social inferior. "But I have heard the Circle is plagued by infighting, lacking any sort of controlling structure. Wouldn't any attempt to create a kingdom from those three city-states just as easily provoke an internal struggle that would become as drawn-out as the war in Tor Milist itself?"

"Surely the first step to defeating your enemy is to know what he wants," the Countess of Lehm interrupted. She directed an enquiring look up and down the table, and asked the assembled men of politics and war, "We still do not know what the White Circle's ultimate goal is. Should we not be directing our efforts towards that, before we go as far as invading Scree?"

She was greeted with silence. The question of the White Circle's motivation was long-standing, and the only people sitting at the table able to answer had kept their own counsel. Isak watched their faces carefully. He knew more than most, and even he still hadn't made up his mind what to do.

"For the moment we should consider Siala's goal to be a three-city state," Vesna said cautiously. "If we prevent that, we block the pursuit of any further ambition, at least for the time being; their position is precarious and their priority is now survival."

"I think that's my cue," Isak muttered as he straightened up and raised his voice. "I'm glad you think that is the priority," he called down to Vesna, "because you're going to be the one to do that."

Everyone looked up in surprise, Suzerain Foleh blanching at hearing a voice echoing down from the servants' station. He peered up past the candles, not quite believing Isak was really standing up there.

"My Lord? What are you doing up there?"

"Enjoying a drink with your excellent steward." Isak raised his goblet and gestured back at the way he'd come. "I found a stairway and wondered where it led, nothing more." He tried not to beam at the astonished faces gaping up at him, but he did find it terribly entertaining to see the Land's finest completely speechless.

"What am I going to be doing, my Lord?" Vesna asked. He knew Isak well enough not to have been too surprised by the white-eye's actions.

"The lull in Tor Milist will not last long, and we need to ensure Priata Leferna does not defeat the duke. The answer should be obvious enough."

"You want to aid Duke Vrerr?" Tila demanded, too infuriated to remember the formal niceties. No one seemed to notice. Isak guessed from their faces that most of them were still trying to work out why a duke would voluntarily share a drink with a steward.

"If the alternative is a coalition of united White Circle cities on our southern border, why not?"

"Duke Vrerr is a cruel despot who has abused his people for years," she protested, "and prolonging the war means more will die of famine. You know they cannot feed themselves as it is."

"Would you prefer me to kill him? We could conquer the city, expand our borders a little?"

"Of course not." Tila faltered briefly. "But you do know how Vrerr governs? By torture, murder, destroying entire villages at the slightest provocation. He doesn't even bother to control his soldiers; half of them are mercenaries, little more than regiments of bandits."

"But there is nothing I can do about him unless I depose him. At the moment the only alternative is the commander of the White Circle forces, Priata Leferna, and she is certainly not acceptable. Thus, esteemed ladies and gentlemen of the jury, we can hope that Duke Vrerr is competent enough to resist the challenge, or we can lend some assistance. I am fully aware that the people of the city would actually be better off under White Circle control, but that would not last if they subsequently find themselves at war with us." *And this is what it is to be Lord of the Farlan,* Isak thought sadly. *I know exactly what sort of man Duke Vrerr is, and I have to ignore it for my own selfish ends.*

"Count Vesna, you will lead a division of cavalry into Tor Milist lands. I don't want Vrerr's troops supplied with horses or weapons, but I do want you to do what you can to damage Leferna's position there. Consider yourself in charge of a mercenary company.

"Anything that results from prolonging the war is, I'm afraid, not our problem. It is a means to an end, and the suffering it causes is necessary. Full intervention in the war will result in a puppet government in Tor Milist under my control, and history shows that whenever we've done something like that in the past, it's been a bad idea in the long run."

"Hardly a comfort to those who'll die," Suzerain Foleh pointed out. There was no accusation in his voice; he knew the realities well enough.

"No comfort at all, but there'll be no gratitude if the Ghosts parade all the way down the Alder March either. We can't solve their problems for them; once the White Circle threat is dealt with, we'll look at the whole situation again, but we need to find a way that doesn't turn unhappy peace into terrible civil war."

Thus speaks a king, came a sudden voice in Isak's head. The white-eye stopped dead; that was as clear as he'd ever heard the dead spirit in his mind.

The normal echo of self-pity and overwhelming loss was absent as Aryn Bwr said, *Compassion and morals have no place in a king's deeds.*

Says the one who rebelled against his own Gods? Isak thought with scorn. *Come then, advise me.*

You are a poor copy of one who was never our equal, snarled the last king. *My war was beyond your comprehension. You beg for advice? Very well, regrets are for fools; action is what makes a king great. Failure to act is cowardice—and that is something history will hate you for.*

The anger in Aryn Bwr's voice was palpable. Isak turned abruptly away from the balcony and headed for the stair. Suddenly the small room above the hall felt enclosed and stifling.

I never wanted to make choices like this, he thought miserably. *A carelessly announced decision and I condemn how many thousands to death? This is no way to live.*

Come now, mocked the dead soul, *a white-eye thirsts for power, does he not? The fire of magic in your veins; the fury of the storm at your snow-white fingertips: it's given to you for a reason.*

Isak looked down at his hand. He was marked forever by what he'd done in Narkang, using the power of his God to slaughter hundreds of Fysthrall soldiers and mercenaries as they breached the wall of King Emin's palace, but the change was only skin-deep.

"That is how I was born to be. It doesn't have to be who I am," he murmured to himself.

You deny your own nature? That is a path to ruin, to pretend you are something you are not. I have seen it a hundred times. It will leave you as empty inside as you fear to become, because of the decisions you are forced to make.

"At least that would be my choice," Isak said. "I would have chosen who I was; what more can anyone ask?"

It is the hard choices that make a king.

"It is the hard choices that make a man. That will do for me."

CHAPTER 12

TRYING TO RESIST THE URGE to loosen the stiff collar of his dress uniform, Major Jachen Ansayl strode off down the corridor with as much dignity as he could muster. The old uniform still fitted, but it had been years since he'd had to put it on, and it had never been comfortable. Today it seemed to catch at every small movement, as though it no longer considered him worthy to wear it. The embossed buttons had scratched his fingertips and the collar squeezed his throat, leaving him breathless whenever he stood less than perfectly straight.

He shouldn't have worn it—half of the men here would take it as an insult—yet he had nothing else. Five years' exile up a mountain didn't do much for a man's wardrobe. Jachen ran his hand through his chestnut hair, tugging at the tangles. The cheap soap at his lodgings had not helped much in making him look something approaching presentable. He couldn't really afford private lodgings, but the alternative was the barracks here at the palace, and he didn't think that would be wise.

Following the servant's directions, he found himself standing before an unassuming door. He had enough sense of direction to recognise that he'd been sent around the back of the Tower of Semar, the remotest part of the palace; it appeared he was being kept out of everyone's way while he waited for Swordmaster Kerin's summons. After the hostile faces in the Great Hall he could see the sense in that.

Jachen sighed. "What am I doing here?" he wondered aloud. "Has Kerin found a new way he can punish me?"

Once they'd seen great potential in him; the Swordmaster himself had recommended his promotion. Personally, Jachen had never been so sure.

He opened the door and stepped inside, sniffing dust and polish, antique wood and lamp oil, the faint mustiness of a room regularly aired but not lived in. It reminded him of the Temple of Amavoq, where he'd gone to pray and consider his choices before being transferred to the rangers—not that there had been much of a choice, in truth, but Jachen had never been one to take the easy road. Obstinacy and stupidity tended to get in the way.

Shutting the door behind him, Jachen hesitated. A single slit window far above head height on the opposite wall cast a shaft of light to the centre of the room, illuminating tall mahogany pews that were so dark they could have served in Death's temples. They also lined the walls on his left and right. On the far side was a massive oak table with a carved top, under which the wood curved inwards and down to thick root-like feet, giving the impression that the table had been hewn from a single great tree. The style was archaically intricate, too overblown for modern tastes—no doubt why it was in here, left only to the admiring eyes of those being kept out of the way.

As his eyes adjusted to the weak light, Jachen stiffened. Peering over the backs of the central pews he saw he was not alone. A bulky figure was squatting on the floor, shrouded by the dark tent of a cape that spread around him.

"Forgive me," Jachen said. "I hadn't realised anyone was in here."

If the man heard, he made no sign. He was crouched between the far end of the table and the pews, head bowed low. His hair, though not particularly long, was tied up in a top-knot. A soldier then, Jachen thought, and from his size, a white-eye, perhaps one of the Guard.

"I've been ordered to wait in here. I'll not disturb whatever you're doing—ah, what *are* you doing?"

"Playing hide-and-seek, of course." The reply was a low rumble, suggesting a massive pair of lungs.

The major licked his lips and gave his uniform another tug before asking, "Hide-and-seek?"

"Hide-and-seek," confirmed the figure, head still stooped as if in prayer. "What of it?"

"I . . . Nothing. It's just a little unusual. I was not expecting you to say that."

"Much of what I do confounds prediction."

"Who are you?"

"Who in damnation are you?"

Jachen bit back his first response. *Just keep your mouth shut. If Kerin's going to give you another chance, don't blow it by starting a fight before you've even reached the man's office.*

"My name is Jachen Ansayl," he replied, adding defensively, "Major Jachen Ansayl."

"Ansayl, eh? Bastard, are you?"

"That's rich, coming from a white-eye." *Damn.* The name Ansayl marked him as a bastard (or grandson of a bastard, in Jachen's case) of the Sayl suzerainty north of Tirah. He'd grown used to the jibes, learning through bitter experience that it was better to meet them with a joke than a scowl. Either was a bad idea here.

The white-eye gave a throaty chuckle that sounded like the grating of a tomb's door to Jachen. He raised his head and looked straight at Jachen, his disconcerting eyes shining out of the gloom like Arian's cruel light on Silvernight. Jachen had never liked white-eyes, despite years of soldiering alongside them; he had never been able to get used to the dark malevolence they all exuded. Even those who weren't violent drunkards unnerved him.

This man was younger than Jachen had first thought. His features were sharp, calculating. A faint prickle of foreboding ran down Jachen's spine. The white-eye emitted a long sigh, as though only now emerging from whatever trance he'd been in, and flicked aside his cloak. A lump appeared in Jachen's throat as he saw the fine clothes. His heart sank further when he saw the naked silver blade that lay across the white-eye's lap, glowing faintly in the shadows.

Damn again. All the way to the Dark Place.

"My Lord, I—"

Jachen's apology was cut short by a raised hand. "I can let it pass."

Lord Isak rose and Jachen found himself edging backwards. The new Lord of the Farlan was almost as big as Lord Bahl, though not yet quite as solid. *Not quite as solid?* Jachen scoffed at himself. *This man could tear you in two with his bare hands and your first thought is that he's not so large as another giant of a man?* He forced himself to stand still as Lord Isak sheathed his sword with a flourish and began to inspect Jachen with unnerving curiosity.

"You were going to take a seat." He indicated the bench on Jachen's right.

"A seat? Oh yes, of course. But that was . . . I didn't—"

"Sit."

Jachen's legs started back and he sank down on the bench, spine straight. His sword had slipped under the arm-rest of the bench and was caught; feeling foolish, Jachen tried to hide his embarrassment as he fumbled with the clasps on his scabbard before finally freeing the weapon and laying it down beside him.

Lord Isak hadn't moved. His head was cocked to one side and he had a slight smile on his lips. Finally he stepped back and eased his weight onto the corner of the oak table, which groaned and creaked alarmingly in protest.

"So, Major Jachen Ansayl, what are you doing here, apart from disturbing vital matters of state and occult importance?"

"Occult importance?" Jachen echoed. "You said you were playing hide-and-seek."

"Do you see a horde of children running around the palace looking for me?"

"Well, no."

"Do you expect your lord to be engaging in such childish games?"

"Of course not."

"I was a few weeks ago."

"Oh. But you're not now?"

He smiled. Jachen felt his shoulders tense at his lord's expression, the predatory smile of a serpent. *Bloody white-eyes, why do they always put me on edge?* He felt his hand start to move up to his neck to tug at the high collar again, but stopped it. No need to make his nervousness even more obvious.

"No, I'm not playing childish games. Do you know what this is?" He held up what looked like a glass sphere, about the size of a normal man's fist and turned it in the rays streaming from the slit window. Where the sunlight caught it, the object burst into a glittering display that reflected on the walls of the room.

"Oh Gods, that's a Crystal Skull, isn't it?"

"Good boy. When someone like me plays hide-and-seek, I've discovered there's rarely any fun involved. A mage called Dermeness Chirialt is wandering the palace, trying to find me, while I use this. I'm told that channelling so much power can make me easy to find, so on the battlefield every enemy mage will immediately have my position fixed in their mind. I'm guessing that won't be much fun either."

"Ah—No, my Lord."

The Duke of Tirah continued to stare at Jachen as though the major were a new toy. "So are you going to tell me why you're here?"

"Of course, my Lord, I'm sorry. I was summoned by Swordmaster Kerin for a meeting."

"About what?"

"I don't really know. I've been working at ranger stations for the last few years now—as far from civilisation as Swordmaster Kerin could find. My current posting is on top of a mountain—it's not that far from the nearest town, but most Farlan don't go beyond the tree line, so I only have ghosts and daemons for company most of the year." Jachen paused, a thoughtful frown turning suddenly into awakening anger. "That bastard—he *ordered* me to come in here—he knows what my temper's like. He must have known you were in here and hoped I'd say something stupid." Jachen half-rose from his seat before a growl froze him midway.

"It looks like he was right."

Jachen sank back down. "But we've history, he and I. My posting wasn't the first punishment I've had since—Well, since things went bad. This is just like Kerin to let me get myself into trouble, but I can't believe he—"

Lord Isak slammed his palm against the tabletop beside him. Jachen blinked. He'd not even seen the white-eye's hand move.

"Despite what you may believe, not every action is solely about you." He slipped from the table and advanced around the central pews. "According to some people, the same cannot be said for me, but that just goes to show the idiocy of some people. However, I am Lord of the Farlan, no matter how young I might be. Kerin is *my* Swordmaster; he answers to me. I am not a tool for punishing rangers with dubious records and ill-fitting uniforms. Do you understand me?"

Jachen nodded dumbly.

"Good. How old are you?"

"I—Thirty-seven summers, my Lord."

"Thirty-seven eh? You share that with Count Vesna at least, though you look older. Still, you're younger than the last, which can't be a bad thing."

"The last what? Count Vesna? My Lord, I doubt many men in this palace would think I had anything in common with Count Vesna."

"Kerin obviously does."

"My Lord, I don't mean to be rude, but I have no idea what you're talking about."

"Clearly not." Lord Isak pointed to Jachen's throat. "Loosen that top button. Perhaps you'll think a little clearer with some blood reaching your head."

Jachen flushed as he followed Isak's instruction.

The white-eye beamed. "See, your colour's returning already. Divinely granted infallibility is a wonderful thing."

"Infallibility?" Jachen said, trying to catch up with the conversation. "Again, my Lord, I don't mean to be rude, but I don't think such a thing has been recognised by the Cult of Nartis."

"Damn. Really? I'm finding it hard to tell whether I'm always right, or whether most people simply have more sense than to argue with a seven-foot giant capable of ripping a man apart with his bare hands and burning whatever is left to ashes." He advanced a couple of paces, close enough to reach out and touch Jachen, and peered down to inspect him.

Jachen couldn't swallow. His throat was suddenly too dry.

"Perhaps you're right after all; your colour seems to have gone again. I must have been wrong." He stepped back and smiled. "Now consider this: over the last day, I have met with four men, all sent to me by Swordmaster Kerin. All of them have excellent service records, proven skills of leadership and useful political connections."

"I—I imagine you need to have a new commander of your guard." Jachen paused. "Oh Gods."

"A new commander!" exclaimed Lord Isak with affected delight. "Correct! I must have been right about the collar after all. Now, what do you think Swordmaster Kerin was doing when he presented men who irritated me beyond measure?" He raised his finger—as white as a bone in moonlight—and began pacing, looking for all the world like a schoolmaster lecturing an errant pupil, rather than one of the most powerful men in the Land.

"Firstly, Scion Cormeh, who will soon be Suzerain Cormeh, from what I hear. I could tell from his expression that the pious little shit disapproved of my cursing; he was lucky to get out of the room without being strangled. Next, a knight from Foleh, who lacked any personality, nodded at everything and managed no more than three words in any given sentence. I can't trust any man who's going to follow every order I give without question—I am a bloody white-eye, after all."

Jachen froze. *Gods, I didn't say it out loud, did I?*

Lord Isak turned like a sergeant on the parade ground and continued his lecture. "Then there was the colonel with the ridiculous moustache. Despite Kerin's recommendation, the man was a complete idiot. He obviously considered my opinions worthless because I was less than half his age. The last one was . . . well, he was ugly. Very ugly. Face like a ten-week-old side of lamb. It annoyed me." He shook his head. "I didn't get close enough to smell the man, but I'm confident he stank—and as you know, I'm never wrong."

Lord Isak glanced towards the door. Jachen followed the movement, but he saw nothing untoward. The door remained steadfastly shut and he could hear nothing beyond it. When he returned his attention to Lord Isak, the white-eye was scrutinising him again.

"Kerin gave me those four, then you. You don't really fit with the rest of the list, so why?"

"I don't know," Jachen said with feeling. "The Swordmaster knows I have done *some* things right in my life, though he's no great admirer. I led a night assault on a castle. I saved the life of the former Suzerain Danva, who showed his gratitude by buying me my commission. I also served as his hurscal for a year."

"Only a year?"

"I have a history of making bad decisions."

"So what do you imagine were Kerin's thoughts on the subject of including you on this list?"

Jachen took a deep breath. He was warming to Isak: the young man had an unnervingly intense air about him, but Jachen was beginning to enjoy the luminary presence of his lord. Either that, or abject terror had made him light-headed. *Probably best not to speculate which.* "A counter-point to the others, no doubt. If you are making a choice, variety is always preferable."

"Does that strike you as like the man?"

"No, not really," Jachen admitted. "Swordmaster Kerin's too clever for that."

"So why send me men likely to annoy me?"

"To direct your choice towards the one he wants."

"And that would be you?"

"I'd say I've managed to annoy you at least as much as the others, so who comes after me?"

Lord Isak grinned. "You might be right there, but there's no one else. Any other thoughts?"

Jachen hesitated. *A history of bad decisions. Oh well, all or nothing here.* "That you're hellish to serve, dismissing perfectly competent officers for no good reason. You want a commander who suits your eccentricity, but is experienced in battle and able to think on his feet."

"How many think when they're on their back?" Lord Isak countered, his grin widening.

"Quite; you also need a commander who understands your puerile sense of humour. Lastly, that a sensible man would have to be desperate to take the post because there's a good chance of being run through or blasted by the wrath of the heavens, or both, even." He dared a breath. Isak was still smiling. In fact, the Duke of Tirah appeared decidedly pleased.

Perhaps Kerin has got this right after all, Jachen thought hesitantly. *With Count Vesna at his side, Lord Isak doesn't need the best tactician in the army, nor a champion as commander of his guard. He needs a man he can stand to speak to every day as much as anything.*

"It's a fair point," the white-eye replied. "Do you know what my last commander did when he thought I was making the wrong decision? He clouted me round the head in public. For that I almost squeezed the life out of him. Do you think you could do the same if you thought it was right? Do you still want this post?"

"I don't ever remember wanting this post, my Lord. Certainly I don't know whether I'd have the guts to face you down from doing something stupid, but I'll take it if you'll have me. Maybe I do want a chance to prove myself again."

"Only maybe?"

"Maybe I just don't care any more." The comment came out with the flippancy of truth before Jachen could bite it back.

Lord Isak's expression fell. He looked grave.

Damn. How much did I really mean that?

"I hope that's not the case. I need a man to temper the flames of my anger, not let them run amok. Don't you have any family to prove yourself to?"

"Don't think there's much hope there," Jachen sighed. "In any case, I've served long enough to know that there's only one person you can prove anything to and that's yourself. Men who look to be heroes are usually the dead ones."

"Good. Tell me one thing: what exactly did you do to get in Kerin's bad books in the first place?"

Jachen grimaced. "In the first place would be going back a ways, but what the men hate me for is leaving my post. I abandoned my regiment for the sake of my wife and daughter."

"Did they survive?"

"Of the regiment? A few."

"I meant your family," said Lord Isak.

"My daughter did. She hates me for a coward, like the rest of the tribe."

"Most men would want to justify what they'd just said."

"It's my tale, and mine to tell as much of it as I want." Jachen couldn't help sounding petulant as he said it. The insinuation in Isak's voice had been obvious, and Jachen had risen to it.

"True. I'm just intrigued when a man makes so little effort to defend his actions, especially when he has been recommended by one of the most respected soldiers in the Land. Kerin's covered himself well, though; he's not formally suggested you, merely arranged a meeting. That way no one can complain about being passed over, and he doesn't get in trouble if I hate you. About which, by the way, Major Jachen Ansayl, I'm still undecided."

"Ah, Lord Isak, might I make a request?" Jachen said, hesitantly. "Could I ask that you call me Major Jachen, or even just Jachen? I realise it's informal, but there'll be enough men reminding me I'm a bastard without you doing so."

"Done—but I still might call you one from time to time."

Before Jachen could think of a suitable reply, there came a sharp rap on the door behind him, and a dazzling young woman strode in without waiting for a response. She spared him a puzzled glance before falling into a graceful but perfunctory curtsey. She looked as if she was about to attend High Reverence at the Temple: her white dress was spotless and a silk scarf was draped over her arm, as if ready to cover three of the four beautiful charms pinned into her lustrous braided hair (after all, no one would go into Nartis' Temple leaving uncovered devices of Triena, Goddess of Fidelity, Ial, an Aspect of Ilit, and Anarie, Goddess of Calm Glades, an Aspect of Amavoq). With a stab of guilt, Jachen realised that Anarie was the only God he had prayed to in the last few years. She'd not answered.

"My Lord, it is time."

He sighed. "Of course—but Tila, first I want you to meet the new commander of my personal guard, Major Jachen Ansayl, who prefers to be called Major Jachen. Jachen, this is Tila Introl, my political advisor. I suggest you keep your temper around her. Lady Tila's tongue is barbed and she lacks my sweet temper."

"Major Jachen." The woman acknowledged him with an incline of her beautiful head. Her long lashes fluttered down, and Jachen felt as if she had recorded every detail of his person in an instant, from the scuff marks on his boots to the missing button on his cuff. His head skipped a beat when her rich brown eyes met his own, then ached at her frosty words as she continued, "Your reputation precedes you." She made no attempt to hide her disapproval as she dismissed Jachen with a flick of the head.

She turned to Lord Isak. "I doubt the men will accept him."

"That's his problem," he replied. "If he can't lead them, then he's no use to me. He told me about abandoning his men, but I think he's worth a second chance."

"Did he tell you everything? That he was a mercenary for years, fighting for Duke Vrerr, and other thugs? That he once slaughtered a castle's entire garrison when it surrendered—"

"Hold on there!" Jachen broke in, suddenly finding his voice. "That's a lie. We wiped them out, yes, but no man of that garrison ever asked for quarter. If they fight to the last, you don't get a choice about taking prisoners."

Tila shrugged. "The truth won't matter in the barracks. As you say, my Lord, it's his problem. The Synod awaits you."

Lord Isak gave an exasperated sigh and gestured for Tila to lead the way. Jachen followed them like a lost child. Every dozen steps they were interrupted by people greeting Isak, most formal, but a few more friendly—at one corner he was set upon by flurry of liveried clerks, warning him Chief Steward Lesarl was searching for him. Jachen was ignored by everyone, lost in his new master's shadow. That suited him fine. From there he could observe the Land as Isak strode through it like a catalyst, affecting everyone he passed. *But if that's true, what have I got myself into? You're a damn fool, Jachen*, he thought. *Next time, first find out what happened to the last man who did the job.*

The Chief Steward came upon them moments after his clerks. His formal clothes indicated Lesarl had important meetings this morning, yet he still managed to retain his customary air of dishevelment and disorder. Beyond a sharp look at Jachen—unsurprising, considering his reputation—he said nothing, but led Isak into a small office. Jachen, with no further orders, followed behind. As he watched the exchange between the two men, he wondered if there was any truth to the rumours that the men detested each other. He could see nothing untoward; Lesarl was a prickly, brusque man as far as Jachen knew, but the Chief Steward's manner was sufficiently deferential. It was widely known that Lesarl treated some suzerains with open contempt, but here gossip appeared to be growing its own fertile ground. He could discern no truth to any of it.

"Since you're calling the nobles to Tirah," Lesarl said, standing close to the white-eye, as if to a long-time confidant, "I've set the investiture ceremony for two months' time. It's a rare event, so we might as well make the most of it and have all the suzerains there. After getting the Synod's approval you have a number of other meetings." Lesarl nodded towards Jachen. "You might want to think about whether you take him in to all of them; you don't trust him as you do Carel."

"It appears I'm the only person who didn't know he was a candidate for the position," Lord Isak said pointedly. "Perhaps I should be asking *you* whether I can trust him."

"My Lord, of course Kerin asked my opinion, and I have no objection— if I had, the Swordmaster would not have put him in front of you. As it is, I always suspect folk who covet a position of influence. Far better to find an unknown man you consider useful." He acknowledged Jachen with a cold smile. "Easier to kill this one too, if he's not up to the job."

Isak snorted. "Let's give him a week or two first. What about these other meetings?"

"Principal ministers, the City Council, the Honourable Association of Merchants, and then later tonight my coterie."

"Coterie?" Isak asked.

Lesarl gave Jachen a warning look as he explained, "My personal—let us call them advisors. They hold no actual position, and you will never see them at meetings, but they are integral to keeping the nation running. You need never speak to them again, but it is right you meet them and know their faces and their skills. That you will do alone, for their identities remain a state secret. Whilst it is rumoured abroad that I have my own network of spies, if I discover Major Jachen has been talking about my coterie, he'll disappear—and not just up a mountain this time."

Lord Isak waved a hand in dismissal. "Fine, it'll probably be the only thing I properly remember. There are so many meetings, so much to sign—it's all starting to blur. No wonder Lord Bahl left so much of this up to you!"

"My Lord, no one man can run a nation. It will take you time to absorb all the details—you were not trained from birth to do this, after all, but your aides were. After a few weeks the legal requirements will all be resolved and government will return to normal. Until then, trust me to ensure that everything is being attended to. Your priority is to establish yourself as Lord of the Farlan, a head of state the people can trust, one who will keep life going as usual. Your position as a warrior has, I think, been adequately affirmed. Now, just remember to conduct yourself in meetings as calmly as possible. We would prefer people forgot about stories of the battle of Chir Plains and saw only the intelligent ruler they now have."

"And begging the favour of the Synod is the first step in that?" Lord Isak sighed.

"The approval of the Synod is an ancient custom," Lesarl said. "It may be a formality now, but that was not always the case. It is a good reminder of how divided the tribe once was."

"So there won't be any political bargaining going on?"

Lesarl's smile sparkled back to life, reminding Lord Isak of King Emin of Narkang. "My Lord, that you could think such a thing of our holiest men . . ."

He sighed. His Chief Steward found his entertainment in the strangest of ways. "Gods, it's going to be that bad? Tila said they'd at least conform to the ritual format."

"I'm sure it will start that way," Lesarl agreed, "but I suspect the sitting cardinals will be keen to get to business soon enough. After all, you intend to execute Cardinal Certinse's sister and nephew. There is one final thing: your father. I don't know if you want to give him a position, or a manor, in Anvee, perh—"

"No. He won't accept anything from me." He sighed. "Just keep an eye on him, keep him out of trouble."

"As you wish, my Lord," Lesarl said with a sniff. For a moment he looked as if he would speak further, then he bowed low and backed away.

"Isak, concentrate. Repeat it back to me." Tila grabbed his deep crimson tunic and tugged it left and right, finally succeeding in straightening the rucked shirt underneath it that was ruining the line.

Isak shooed Tila's hands away. "The sitting cardinals are named Certinse, Veck—Honestly, what sort of a name is Veck?"

"Never mind that now," Tila snapped. Her voice sounded strangely loud in the bare antechamber. They were alone, aside from Jachen, who lingered uncomfortably by the door. Two of Isak's personal guards, clad in full armour, stood outside the room, warning everyone away. This was the administrative side of the palace, part of the main wing given over to governmental use. The high-ceilinged oval hall on the other side of the door was the Synod Chamber. It was intentionally set apart from the main wing. Isak hadn't asked why. No doubt there was symbolism involved, but he had quite enough to remember already.

"Yes, mistress," Isak growled without a trace of contrition, and parroted back to her, "Certinse, Veck and Echer are the sitting cardinals. Echer is High Cardinal, but he's very old now so he'll let the other two speak. The high priests always defer to the three most powerful of their number, and of those Jopel Bern, the High Priest of Death, will take the lead since Voss Aftal will not want to come into direct conflict with the head of his own cult. The only other high priest who might speak is from the Temple of Belarannar, the white-eye Roqinn."

"Good, and your two allies there?"

"The Corlyn, and High Chaplain Mochyd. Satisfied now? Tila, calm down; I remember everything you've told me. Now give me a moment to myself, will you?"

Tila hesitated, then curtsied in acknowledgement and stepped back. Isak stretched his back and shoulders. The suit of thick linen Tila had produced might be striking, but he felt constrained by it. She had a thing about putting him in scarlet and gold. He put his palm against the wall; it was cold, and for a moment he felt like it was drawing the very life out of him. When he withdrew his hand, he could feel the ghost of its touch still, a chill tingle running over his skin. *How much am I going to have to give to this place?*

"Right," he announced, "Major Jachen, if you would lead the way? The Duke of Tirah must be presented by a soldier, demanding entrance by knocking on the chamber door with the pommel of his weapon." He grinned at Tila, who looked pleased he had remembered what she'd been drumming into him.

Jachen bobbed his head and stepped forward, slipping his sword from its scabbard and reversing it. He rapped three times on the brass plate screwed into the heavy wooden door, sheathed his weapon, took a deep breath and placed a hand on each of the handles. He looked at Isak, who nodded, flung open the doors and swept into the room, announcing Isak's new title in a clear voice.

He stepped aside, and Isak walked past, looking at the collection of wizened faces peering up at him from a massive oval table. Jachen and Tila pulled the doors shut, then followed to take up their positions on either side of the Duke of Tirah.

"The Synod welcomes you, Lord Isak, Chosen of Nartis and Duke of Tirah." Isak followed the cracked voice to its owner, High Cardinal Echer. The withered old man raised his arthritis-clawed hands, palms towards Isak, in formal greeting. "May the hand of Nartis guide you."

Isak returned the greeting and bowed low to the assembled men and women, sitting in this dim and dusty chamber, silently awaiting the future. Only two could be called young and relatively healthy: Cardinal Certinse, whose family connections had heretofore advanced his career, and Roqinn, the white-eye High Priest of Belarannar. At nearly one hundred summers, Roqinn, like Lord Bahl at more than twice his age, looked no more than forty. Even the jittery new High Priest of Larat, obviously mindful of his predecessor's violent demise when he had tried to look into Isak's mind, was white-haired, his face a mass of lines.

"My Lord," said someone, Cardinal Veck, he guessed from Tila's description, "in deference to our High Cardinal's frail state of health, it has been agreed that I speak in his place. Do you object to this change of protocol? Would you request another in my place?"

The cardinals wore robes of white and midnight blue, edged in scarlet. They reminded Isak of the Knights of the Temples, but he told himself not to get hostile—there would be time for that later.

Isak nodded his agreement and looked around. There was one wall of long thin windows, but half a dozen torches burned brightly to aid the aged priests' failing sight. The walls were decorated with the flags of each of the Gods represented by the Synod. The two largest, Death's golden bee on a fresh white field and the coils of Nartis' black snake, outlined in white thread, on a deep blue background, hung opposite Isak.

These images, the two banners fluttering side by side atop temples and city gates throughout Farlan lands, were etched into Isak's mind. For a moment he ignored the Synod members squinting up at him and stared at the flags, thinking of the power they represented, and the thrall in which they held mankind. Back in Narkang, on the bloodied floor of the jousting arena, religion had suddenly become something more—not polished artefacts on holy altars, not the sombre drone of voices as incense filled the air. Instead, a primal force had suffused him, raw and savage power setting every nerve on fire. He'd been connected to the ground beneath him, even as the torrent of energy had borne him up into the glittering surge of spring air. That was the God he knew, the God that had claimed him without thought or care for the consequences.

These priests are nothing, whispered a voice in the back of Isak's head. *They care only for worldly matters. Only the white-eye could survive the barest touch of his master. They know nothing of Gods. Such power never flowed through their veins, never shook their bones. Kill them. Even together they could not truly oppose you.*

Quiet, spirit, Isak commanded. *This is not your business.*

You let yourself be commanded by a maid. You tie yourself close to the games of the Gods. Each ceremony and tradition is a string to bind you, each prayer a piece of your soul you offer—

I said, enough! Your babbling bores me. Every word of sense you speak is twisted; I will not be a despot so I must listen to these people.

What difference to the slaves in the field you might send to death on a whim?

Perhaps none, but for me there is. Now be quiet.

"Lord Isak," Cardinal Veck continued hesitantly, looking somewhat puzzled by Isak's vacant expression, "you come before us to claim honour beyond that of kings?"

Isak bowed.

"Before a man can be placed above kings, he must look up to the heavens and know his own place. Sit now, without threat or pride."

Isak unbuckled his swordbelt, letting it fall to the floor for Jachen to sweep up, then approached the table and eased himself onto the stool that had placed ready for him. The Synod members sat in ornately carved chairs, but Isak must sit before them in humility.

"Now, in the presence of the Gods here represented, and the tribe of the Farlan, state your claim."

Isak waited a moment, trying to gauge how loud he should speak, then began, "I claim the title of Lord of all Farlan. I claim acknowledgement of the Synod that I am Chosen of Nartis and worthy of this title; His Will done by my hand, His Majesty upheld by my deeds."

"High Priest of Nartis," called Cardinal Veck. On his left, Voss Aftal flinched. "Do you accept this man's claim to Nartis' favour and blessing?"

Most of the Synod looked keenly interested in the proceedings; Aftal appeared to be as frightened as the High Priest of Larat. He tried to clear his throat and gave a strangled splutter. "I—Yes," he managed finally. "He has been touched by the storm and emerged from its light marked as a brother. The Cult of Nartis so accepts Isak, Duke of Tirah, as Chosen of Nartis and first among His Blessed."

"Then the claim is acknowledged as valid," intoned Cardinal Veck, looking for all the world like he was enjoying himself.

Isak glanced down the line of faces. There were three women on the Synod. The High Priestess of Amavoq was staring so fiercely at him that Isak began to wonder if he'd done anything to offend her.

Have I even met her before? I don't remember it. Isak suddenly smiled as he realised the old woman's eyesight was failing and she was squinting, trying to bring him into focus. *And you suspected the worst. You're a fool. Reasons behind every deed, enemies in every shadow.*

Enemies in the shadows! shrieked Aryn Bwr unexpectedly. *'Ware the shadows, their eyes and claws! 'Ware the terrible webs they weave!*

Isak ignored the voice.

"High Chaplain Mochyd," the High Cardinal called next, turning to his right and looking to the furthest seat. "To be Lord of the Farlan, a warrior is needed to keep us strong. Will you follow this man into battle?"

"I will," came the gruff reply. "He has led our armies and rained righteous fire upon the enemies of our tribe. I will follow him."

Like most chaplains, Mochyd had been a tall man, and powerful. Time and hard living had aged him, not the magic that had so drained the high priests. Though white-haired and wrinkled, there was strength and will in those old bones, Isak thought, and that couldn't be said for the men of magic on the Synod. He could see why Lord Bahl's circle of friends had included a number of chaplains. They tended to be fiercely loyal, so devoted to their calling that it became the essence of their being. They were men Bahl understood.

"Corlyn," called the cardinal next, "to be Lord of the Farlan, a man of piety is needed. Do you trust this man to be an example to the people?"

The old man with gentle eyes on Veck's far left gave Isak a benevolent smile, and said calmly, "I do."

That was it; the Corlyn said nothing more. Isak tried not to smile at the thought of him as a spiritual leader—he'd only remembered to visit the Temple of Nartis after returning to Tirah because Lesarl had reminded him. A less suitable choice he couldn't imagine.

And yet . . . And yet, strangely, he couldn't tear his eyes from the Corlyn's silent smile. The head of the Cult's pastoral branch, a man he'd never met, wasn't asking for anything. Tila had said the Corlyn would support Isak simply because he had no personal agenda to push, and he liked to annoy those members of the Synod who disdained him for exactly that reason. He was, in truth, a simple man of his God, wanting only to guide the people in their faith and rejecting the power that becoming high priest offered.

A hand to guide him on the right path. If one old man still had enough faith left to trust a feckless youth with this, why couldn't he be right? Isak was pondering this when a curious, unpleasantly smug smile crossed Cardinal Veck's lips. Isak's instincts kicked into action as he felt his heart quicken. He catalogued every detail of the cardinal's appearance: the neat clipped beard, the rings on his fingers, a pair of diamonds set in gold, a fat silver band engraved with the badge of the cardinal branch, and a firegem surrounded by sapphires. The cardinal was moistening his lips and twitching his thin eyebrows, the only remaining trace of the dark colouring of his youth. Even the long hair protruding from a mole on his right cheek was white.

"Well, my Lord. We have had assurances of your strength and moral virtue. Now it just falls to us to determine whether you will be a good ruler as well as a good man. The requirements of office go beyond the strength of a leader's arm."

Isak matched the cardinal's gaze impassively. Veck's words were a departure from the ritual, but he had expected nothing less. A rumble of disapproval sounded from the direction of the High Chaplain, but neither man paid him any attention, both refusing to be the one to look away first.

"Lord Bahl's long reign saw many changes," Veck continued. "The strength of our nation was rebuilt by his hand, there can be no doubt. However, there will always be some changes that are for the worse. We certainly do not blame Lord Bahl for such things but it is felt by the Synod that certain figures, the Chief Steward first among them, have pursued an agenda that has diminished the influence of the Gods within this great nation of ours."

"If you wish to accuse Chief Steward Lesarl of something, it should be done in a more formal—more *public*—arena, I believe." Isak's tone was soft and level, without a hint of antagonism. Let them think he was willing to sacrifice the man—maybe they believed the rumours of his dislike for Lesarl. The truth was that while Isak might not count Lesarl as a close friend, he was entirely aware that the Chief Steward was invaluable to the Farlan. If others hoped he might put personal feelings first, they were welcome to think that way. It cost him nothing, and left them running in the wrong direction. Lesarl was as aware of his importance to the nation as Isak was.

"Nothing so dramatic as that, my Lord. The Synod is a little concerned that the government has become too secular, that we are forgetting the guidance from our Gods."

"And you have proposals for me to consider?" A wave of nausea hit Isak. These men could think only of their petty wants; this is what they were reduced to: comparing their own fiefdoms to others and squabbling over the differences. Had they ever been devoted to a cause higher than their own, or was this the measure of their life's work?

"We have certain suggestions, yes."

"Please, name them."

His abruptness caused the cardinal to hesitate momentarily. Tila's voice drifted through his mind. *Don't get angry, that's how mistakes are made.* Isak scowled at the admonishment from his subconscious. He bit his lip and tensed his gut around the building swell of anger. His fist tightened at the effort, but when he released it, Isak found the petulant clouds dissipated.

"First, the treatment of sacred creatures," Veck went on, blithely oblivious to Isak's inner turmoil. "Bear- and wolf-baiting is now a regular occurrence in many regions. Fighting-snakes command prices of up to fifty silver crescents apiece. These activities are grave insults to the Gods. They must be stopped."

Isak smiled inwardly. He was being eased in to the argument.

"As far as I am aware, the only species of snake willing to fight is the ice cobra, and if you'll consult your texts I believe you'll discover ice cobras are not sacred—they're noted for it, in fact. There are no other snakes in these parts that will fight each other. An adder is more likely to curl in a ball than fight."

"Fighting-snakes are being imported from other states."

"Your point is noted. Please, continue."

"The organisation styling itself 'The Brethren of the Sacred Teachings' has been recently active, and you yourself, *my Lord*, have met with them. These 'Brethren,' *my Lord*, are unsanctioned by any cult. They are no better than wild mercenaries. Their secrecy is violently guarded, even against the proper authorities."

"The proper authorities, meaning you? They came to my aid during an attempt on my life. I hardly think that constitutes wild behaviour—good citizenry, perhaps?"

"That there happened to be several hundred of them ready for war in Saroc does not constitute good citizenry to my mind," sniffed Cardinal Veck.

"My Lord," broke in Cardinal Certinse, "I have had word that a company of dark monks even now inhabits my ancestral home, thieving and arresting as they please."

Isak leaned forward, a flash of controlled fury in his white eyes. "Do you really wish to argue with me over the meaning of good citizenry?" he growled. "The Brethren were not the only soldiers riding in Saroc that day. Did you not read that in your reports? The reason they are in your family home, Cardinal Certinse, is because a number of your family have proved themselves traitors, and the Brethren provide escort to those I have charged with rooting out those others also involved. Surely you cannot object, as it is one of your fellow cardinals conducting this investigation?"

"Disten?" spluttered Cardinal Certinse. "The man is a maniac, a delusional monster. His hatred of my family is well known. He is a disgrace to the office. His appointment was nothing more than an indulgence."

Isak breathed deeply, determined his temper would not boil over. He could see beads of sweat on the cardinal's brow, unsurprising, since he himself had been accused of consorting with daemons by that very same Cardinal Disten. Though Disten might find something in Tildek Manor, Cardinal Certinse would have been far more careful than the rest of his family. Even Lesarl was less than confident of finding evidence against him. In his usual style, the Chief Steward was forming alternative plans to deal with the cardinal.

"What I know about Cardinal Disten," Isak replied in a measured voice, "is that he did not strike me as mad in any way, and whatever accusations he has made against your family were revealed to be true that day. I saw the evidence myself, for Suzerain Tildek and Duke Certinse led troops under banner into the Saroc suzerainty without invitation, that a crime in itself, and then attacked my person. They would have succeeded in killing me, had the Brethren of the Sacred Teachings not anticipated the act."

"How can you be sure the Brethren themselves did not engineer this—had my brother attacked you by the time they themselves were under assault?"

"Yes. I had lost one man by then."

"Which could very well have been a mistake, a stray arrow by a nervous scout," urged the cardinal, sensing a thread to pull.

"Perhaps," said Isak, "but unlikely—by the time the Brethren had appeared, the mages in your brother's company had already reached me with sorcery, sorcery with a particular stink about it, unmistakable even to a man like me, not long schooled in the magical arts. Your brother consorted with necromancers, Cardinal Certinse. The Suzerain of Tildek and the Duke of Lomin rode under arms with necromancers. Go consult your laws, if you will, but I made sure of the point myself. The penalty is death and their assets are forfeit." Isak leaned back. "Currently I am disinclined to completely destroy your family, but that may change."

"Necromancers?" said Jopel Bern, the High Priest of Death, sharply. "If that is true, then Duke Certinse has violated religious law and should be turned over to the Synod for trial."

Isak shrugged. "Currently he is not charged with that. If you wish to prepare a case, by all means do so, but I will try Duke Certinse before his peers for the attempted murder of a peer, and for treason."

"Treason? You are not Lord of the Farlan yet," Cardinal Veck said pointedly.

"That is technically true." Isak gave the Synod a cold smile. "We will surely be debating that point. I will be very interested to note all dissenting views from the suzerains assembled." He rose and straightened his tunic with a sharp tug, noting with grim satisfaction that more than just the High Priest of Nartis recoiled at the sudden movement.

He cast a hard look down the length of the table. "Now, honoured members of the Synod, list your other *suggestions*."

The High Priest of Death turned slightly to Veck, raising a hand slightly to dissuade him from speaking further. The cardinal nodded and eased back in his chair, arms flat against the thick armrests.

Bern sat up straighter and cleared his throat. "Lord Isak, our goal here today is not to cast accusations, nor to provoke conflict. We mentioned the dark monks to ask you to declare them unwelcome in Farlan lands, unless they submit to the scrutiny of the proper authorities."

"The matter is in hand. I have already made it clear to them that I will not tolerate unknown armies marching through these lands."

"Your wisdom precedes ours then," Bern replied, bowing slightly. "Furthermore, we ask permission to create a force to work in conjunction with your own men, to root out heretics and daemon-worshippers so past conflicts are not repeated."

Isak took a step forward until his thighs were touching the curved edge of the table. He leant forward slightly and said softly, "My orders to the Brethren were that I would not tolerate any organised bands of soldiers in these lands if they do not answer to me. There will be no exceptions to this law." *And I'm buggered if I'm going to let an army of religious fanatics run around burning anyone they take a dislike to*, he added in the privacy of his own head. For some reason, that struck him as amusing. *The Synod wanted proof of my suitability to rule. I didn't say that aloud—I must have learned something after all.*

"While we're on the subject," Isak continued, "the same can be said for the Devoted—just in case you were about to ask for them to be welcomed back into Farlan lands."

"There is a rumour that you had allied yourself with the Knights of the Temples already," said the high priest.

One of my men has a big mouth, he thought, a little crossly. "I have made such no alliance," he snapped, "and Lord Bahl's edicts on that organisation stand."

He stopped as a prickling sensation ran through his head. The whole room seemed to shudder before his eyes and from the corner of the room, he heard a whisper: *"Isak."*

He whirled around, but saw nothing out of the ordinary except Tila, staring at him, wide-eyed and a little confused.

Isak frowned as the voice came again: *"Isak."* Blinking, he turned back to the Synod, who were watching him uncertainly. He took a moment to steady himself and reached out with his mind to the Skull fused around Eolis' hilt, relieved when he touched the power there to recognise that whatever was going on, he wasn't under attack. He suddenly realised that the voice was Xeliath. For her to reach him like that, awake and defended, it must have cost her dearly. Panic began to stir. Had someone found her before Morghien and Mihn could get to her?

He took a deep breath and looked around the table. "Esteemed members of the Synod, I have urgent matters to attend to. Please send word to Chief Steward Lesarl when you have reached your decision, I have no more time to waste playing games." He put both hands on the table and leaned forward, looking at each of the Synod in turn, then said, quietly, dangerously, "If you intend to oppose me, think very carefully before you act. I am not a naïve boy, however many summers I may lack in your eyes. I know full well that if a majority of court-ranked men declare for me, your own approval is not necessary. My patience is limited, as you will see tomorrow when my men start building a gallows outside Duke Certinse's cell, in case we might find a use for it. Good day to you all."

He didn't wait for a reply but swept out of the chamber, drawing Jachen and Tila in his wake. He left the mighty Synod, a collection of shocked, frail old men and women, silently wondering how their world had changed.

Voss Aftal, the High Priest of Nartis, gripped the armrest of his chair and tried to control the fear he felt. He had lived for sixty-four summers; most of those had been taken up with the gentle routine of ritual at the Temple of Nartis, a majestic building of pillars and sharp-peaked roofs where only the high altar had walls. The wind rushed through constantly, and during storms, as the God brushed his soul, it was a humbling place to be.

The strength of Nartis was beyond Aftal's understanding; it was a force that took away his breath and drained his body of the strength to move. It had always frightened him, this gulf between man and God too palpable to ignore. And yet there was a familiarity in the soaring power of the God of Storms, rooted as it was in the patterns of the Land.

Aftal's heart had grown cold at Isak's mere presence, because there was no familiarity there. The youth's power waxed with every day, cold and wild, tied to nothing, controlled by nothing, and it ruled his entire being. The high priest trembled as he wondered what this snarling youth with wild eyes was not capable of. Folk were whispering a new name in the streets now, even his priests: they were calling him *Isak Stormcaller*. The burgeoning terror in Aftal's heart told him they were wrong.

This boy did not *call* storms. Isak *was* the storm. And they were all caught in his wake.

CHAPTER 13

ISAK STOMPED HIS WAY UP THE STAIR to the ducal personal chambers in the main wing of Tirah Palace, ignoring Tila's questions and storming past the guards who snapped to attention. He smashed his fist against the oak door and felt the latch on the inside give way. The door flew open and crashed against the inside wall, causing the elderly man tending the fire to give a yelp of alarm. He jumped up with poker in hand, knocking a log from the hearth in a cloud of soot and sparks, then turned to apologise for crying out— suddenly realising that he still held the poker as a weapon, and it was pointed at Isak's heart.

"My Lord, I—I do apologise," he stammered, dropping the poker as though it had scalded him.

Isak jabbed a thumb towards the door and growled, "out."

Hard on the servant's heels, he was about to slam the door shut after him when he saw Tila hurrying up the stair, skirts bunched in her fist so she didn't trip.

"No one comes in," Isak announced, and the guard on his right gave a jerk of the head. Not waiting to hear Tila's complaint, he dragged the door closed and roughly twisted the bent latch back into place again, then stalked over to the window, a wide aperture as tall as he was, framed with solid wooden shutters. A balcony ran around that corner of the building, opening onto each of his rooms. He stood looking out at nothing, the breeze ruffling his clothes and calming the angry tangle within his mind. Finally, his tense shoulders dropped a little in relief: Xeliath had only called his name. There had been no fear in her voice. Perhaps he shouldn't have stormed out of the meeting . . . then he shook his head. No, she may not be in danger, but for her to have reached him like that meant it *was* a matter of importance.

Isak lay down on his huge bed and looked up at the painted beams on the ceiling, thick bands of red that ran the length of the room. He closed his eyes and tried to clear his thoughts, but it didn't take long for his fingers to start twitching in irritation at the stillness. With a sigh he sat up again.

"Perhaps I can do this without being asleep," he said out loud. "How about it, spirit?"

Lamentable wretch, spat Aryn Bwr in reply, *blind and ignorant creature!*

"Fine, be like that," Isak said, determined not to let himself get wound up by the dead king's insults. "It can't be so difficult—she said we shared a connection, so I'll find her if she wants me to."

He sat cross-legged and, running his fingers around the Crystal Skull as if he were stroking a woman's cheek, pulled it loose from Eolis. It was warm to the touch, and so silky-smooth he could hardly feel the surface. Isak had discovered from his tentative experiments that the Skull responded better when it was in contact with the flesh that had had its colour burned from it by his God's lightning. He had wondered about asking Dermeness Chirialt, the mage who'd helped him make Carel's sword, but decided he probably didn't want to know the answer. He was afraid of finding out something fundamental had changed, that his mortal flesh had been replaced by something else, something less than human. Isak had never expected frailty to possess its own attractions.

Isak raised the Skull and watched it slowly return to shape. The line of the jaw came first, then the dome, followed swiftly by the angled planes of the cheeks. For a brief moment it was a disconcerting blind face before the sockets sank down. Once the Skull was solid again, Isak cupped it in his hands. It looked oddly bifurcated, bright white on one side and a dull pink on the other.

He raised it to his chest and touched it to the scar there. Burned into his skin on his first night in the palace, the runic form of her name was his closest link to Xeliath. That would be the path he'd follow.

The witch of Llehden waited on a rolling plain of shivering wheat. It was a place of bland nothingness. A handful of trees stood nearby, but there was nothing beyond. Xeliath had not seen the need to go further than that. There was no sunlight, nor sound, and the plain was an uncomfortable, disconcerting place to pass an hour. For someone inextricably woven into the fabric of the Land, the witch felt it a terrible loss to be in this slate-sky place of dead memories. She pulled her shawl tighter as the breeze picked up. It felt like the ghostly wind was able to draw the warmth from the living, despite knowing that the cold wasn't real.

Xeliath was a little way off, delighting in her restored grace and making the most of her time in these dreams, turning cartwheels, letting her skirts fall about shamefully, swinging from the branches of the trees. She knew well that soon she would have to return to her twisted and damaged true body, but until then she sang with pleasure at the sensation of strong limbs being once again fully under her control. At this moment she was hanging upside-down with her legs wrapped around a bough, crooning softly to herself in the strange language of her people.

"Are you sure he heard you?"

"I'm sure." Xeliath didn't turn her head. Her soft chestnut hair hung loose and free. It still struck the witch as strange that the girl's hair was almost exactly the same shade as her skin. It seemed unnatural somehow, in some ways as disturbing as an albino's lack of colour. It made Xeliath's eyes even more striking. A curl of a smile on her lips could be electrifying. Though the girl was normally all youthful innocence, she possessed the arresting presence of a white-eye. "The Gods have chosen this one well," murmured the witch. As Isak's queen, Xeliath would have been able to bewitch men with a glance; those who didn't find themselves hanging off Isak's every word would tremble when his lady spared them the briefest of moments.

Xeliath stretched out her arms as far as they could go, turning her wrists in circles. The witch blinked, and when she opened her eyes again, Isak was standing directly in front of the brown-skinned girl.

Xeliath squealed with delight and wrapped her arms around the massive scarlet- and gold-clad apparition. Isak started, he'd appeared just a few inches from Xeliath's face, and was immediately grabbed, but his struggles ceased almost at once as the girl locked lips with his. Her slender fingers gripped a handful of his thick black hair to hold him close.

His passion reflected hers and the massive white-eye lost no time in swinging Xeliath down from the branch and enveloping her in his arms.

"Where's a bucket of water when I need one?" wondered the witch aloud. Isak jumped and tore himself from Xeliath's arms. Eolis was half drawn before he recognised the speaker.

"You! What are you doing here?"

"Waiting for your raging hormones to calm down."

"Well, if I'd known there was a queue . . ." He smirked.

The witch had no intention of giving him the satisfaction of a reaction, but Xeliath was quick to take offence, and though significantly smaller than Isak, the Yeetatchen girl showed no hesitation in reaching up and jabbing him hard.

The witch managed not to smile at Isak's yelp. The flash of anger faded quickly when he turned back to Xeliath.

The witch made a note of that small detail, tucking it away in a corner of her mind. She would decide later if it was worrying. Xeliath's charms held Isak in thrall, as they would any other man, but she was cut off from a real life. Outside her excursions into dreams, she was nothing more than an imprisoned, frustrated child. The only thing she might be able to control in her life was Isak . . . the witch wondered if he were the one who would end up determining the course of history.

She shook her head to clear her thoughts. "We brought you here for a reason," she said. "There are matters that need your attention."

"Matters that need my attention?" Isak took a step towards her. "I'll tell you what needs my attention: the largest nation in the Land. My investiture ceremony, so that I am legally recognised, and the trial of a daemon-worshipping traitor, and once I've got those out of the way, I have a war to prepare for. You'll forgive me if I don't feel like sorting out anyone else's problems, especially when ordered to by someone I've hardly met—I don't even know your name."

"Her name?" Xeliath walked around him and stood next to the witch, her eyes flashing. "Don't you know anything about witches? They give up their names when they stop being apprentices. To give you her name would be as dangerous as you handing cuttings of your hair to any passing mage. As for giving you orders—she's trying to warn you, that's all. She's an ally. You might at least let her finish speaking before you bite her head off."

"How do I know she's an ally?" Isak said, a little grumpily. He felt like he was being ganged up on.

"You need proof?" the witch cut in. "If I were an enemy, do you think you would so easily have left my domain bearing those gifts from the Knights of the Temples? To be a witch is to be able to feel the heartbeat of the very Land itself, to be part of the patterns and rhythms that bind it. It does not tell me the future, but I can sense something of what that pattern might result in—just as I can sense when there is something wrong in that pattern." She shuddered. "What I feel right now is a danger to us all, and it grows with every day. I know this because of what I am, because of what I have sacrificed to become what I am."

She broke off. There was no easy way to explain what it meant to be a witch. The scent of warm earth and blood, the wind through the trees, the touch of sun and shade upon the skin: these things explained her as much as anything. The people of Llehden knew that. They treated her like a local Aspect, with fearful respect, understanding that she was nothing like them. At times she lived like a noblewoman, with children bringing food and clothes for her, sent to her to see and to know their local witch, to understand what a witch was, as their parents had done, and their parents' parents. They grew up knowing the witch was beyond normal cares, yet still she cared for them. Like the animals of the forest, the deer and the wolves, she watched over the people who were part of Llehden's fabric. If the Coldhand folk stole a baby, it was she who would stride off into the night to fetch it back, no matter what the cost. She would face down vengeful spectres and ease difficult births, whichever way they had to go. In some ways she was more similar to Isak than the young man would ever realise; in others, more opposite than seemed possible for allies.

"What is this danger?" Isak asked quietly. Xeliath's words had calmed him, and the witch's words too had had some effect. He remained silent for a minute, then asked, "Don't you think I have enough troubles to be dealing with?"

"The danger is not just to you but to us all."

"But I'm the one you want to do something about it?"

"You have been given your gifts for a reason. Such blessings are not random. Whether you choose to be deaf to it or not, your destiny is calling." The witch sighed. She could see her manner grated on him, and was reminded briefly of the King of Narkang. King Emin, like white-eyes, had a natural ability to stir emotion in others. Isak and Emin both had a majestic presence that demanded obedience from—or roused antipathy in—those around them. That the witch was obviously immune was clearly nagging at Isak, no matter how hard he tried to ignore it.

"My destiny is calling?" Isak said. "There are quite a few opinions about my destiny, and none of them agree."

"Your opinion is the only one that matters," the witch said. "You have broken away from whatever plan any God or daemon had for you, and now all that remains is to find out whether you have the strength to accept the burden of your remarkable abilities."

Isak looked away from her, silent.

"And your hand?" she asked.

Isak instinctively glanced down, sliding the hand slightly into his sleeve. "The side effect of a spell," he muttered. "I hadn't realised there would be a price."

The witch raised her eyebrows. "There is a price to everything; even in the unnatural world, as any mage will tell you. The only question is what that price is, and for whom it is worth paying that price."

"You want me to judge people's worth?" Isak asked in surprise.

"Absolutely not; help those you can and leave judgment to the Gods."

"And that's why you called me here," Isak guessed.

The witch nodded. "I have felt a shadow over the Land, a shadow that gathers over a city to your south." She saw a bank of wind roll over the wheat behind Isak, as though her words had caused a shiver in Xeliath's mind. They felt nothing, though. The breeze itself passed as if it did not exist.

"Scree?" Isak said, surprised. "That's where Emin—the King of Narkang—has gone."

"How do you know that?" Xeliath demanded, breaking her silence. She walked back to Isak's side and took his hand in hers.

The witch watched, thinking for a moment that the girl really was afraid, but as Xeliath ran her fingers down the inside of Isak's massive palm it was clear that she was just making the most of her restored senses.

"One of his agents told me," Isak admitted. "I think Emin wanted me to hold off a full-scale assault until he's found whatever he's hunting there."

"Do not march your army into Scree at all; there is a scent of madness and pain hanging over that city. Invasion would only worsen it. The shadow hanging over the city—"

"Shadow?" Isak interrupted sharply. "What sort of shadow?"

"I know only that I sense a darkness there." The witch frowned. "Does it mean anything to you?"

Isak looked uncomfortable as both women looked at him. After a moment he admitted, "It's probably nothing, but—Well, I'm sure there's been a shadow watching me in the past. And King Emin is preparing to wage war against some shadow-daemon he calls Azaer. Do you recognise the name?"

They both shook their heads. The witch had heard little enough of Azaer, and if the boy already considered the shadow an enemy, there was nothing more for her to tell him.

"Maybe the shadow *is* watching me, especially since I was sent to Narkang to forge links between our two nations." He stopped and leaned closer to Xeliath. The girl was not the only one to find comfort in their contact, it appeared.

"What would you have me do?" he asked eventually. "Going to Narkang with only a bodyguard when I was Krann was one thing, but I'm the Lord of the Farlan now. King Emin might be able to manage that, but I'm a little more conspicuous. You might need to find someone else to fight your battles this time—or maybe go yourself."

"I am." *That tripped the great lump*, the witch thought with a twitch of satisfaction.

"You're going to Scree? Alone?"

"Not entirely. I have a travelling companion. He is also somewhat conspicuous, but the journey is long and I will need a guardian."

Isak shifted his feet, keeping eye contact, as if he could see some extra truth in her eyes.

The witch saw he was curious, both about her companion, and about what exactly was going on in Scree. She let the questions bubble in his head, then pressed her point. "The shadow over Scree brings a convergence. It draws King Emin in, as it has Siala, and I fear many others." *And if I had any choice you would be kept far away from that place, but I think it's gone too far*, she thought to herself. *It may be that our only chance to stop it is to meet power with power. If that doesn't work, we must hope that at least it will make you understand the gravity of the situation.*

"What is it that you fear?" Isak said softly.

The witch hesitated. "They are men and women of power in Scree, these mercenaries, mages, lords and warriors. The White Circle will have no choice but to recruit mercenaries to protect the city, unnatural mercenaries, like those that call themselves Raylin, after a long-dead Elven warrior cult. The name flatters them, but they are monstrously powerful warriors, with all manner of magical abilities, and they're innately drawn to violence. If they are left to run unchecked, they will fuel the destruction."

"People like you and your travelling companion?" Isak gave a rather forced smile. "Men like me? Is the only difference the fact that I have a title and the mark of a God on my soul?"

"I hope the difference is greater than that. These people are savage and brutal—if you were truly one of them, you would be a plague upon the Land."

"And have you appointed yourself the Land's protector?"

The witch froze. *How dare this swaggering pup accuse me of that?* Her mother had cried the day she told her she was to learn witchcraft. It had sounded exciting then, but years later, the witch understood why her mother had whispered, "I'm sorry it must be so, but a witch is needed here, and a witch there shall be."

She bit her lip. One hot temper was bad enough, and she had two to contend with here. "Take care how you insult those who would be your allies," the witch warned. "You are not the only one appointed to a role in this life, so be thankful you at least are well rewarded." She lifted her shirt, exposing her belly and a mess of scar tissue. "This is my reward for doing what must be done. This scar was from a colprys; its claws opened me up as I killed it. I had to sew myself back together while lying on the forest floor with scavengers sniffing all around."

She remembered the weight of the colprys, the talons puncturing her gut. In the forest twilight its rough grey skin had been hard to distinguish; only the hisses and snorts and the tremble of the branches as it moved from tree to tree gave it away. It had so nearly not been enough. The witch shivered. "Have you ever stitched yourself together, my Lord? It is far from pleasant. I was not asked to drive the colprys away from that village, because they knew I would not need asking. It is the path I have accepted for this life."

The massive white-eye dropped his eyes. "I'm sorry, I shouldn't have said that. I can't help feeling like whatever I do, I'm being forced, guided down paths for someone else's gain. It makes it hard to take any sort of advice at face value." He looked stricken for a moment. "I really am sorry."

"You have good reason to feel that way," the witch said, laying a hand on his arm. "There were powers planning your birth long in advance. The seeds were planted during the Great War." Her anger had subsided; a lifetime of control was not so easily lost, and Isak's face showed true contrition. He hadn't been brought up to understand responsibility, the witch reminded herself. This had been thrust upon him, less than a year ago, and now the entire Land looked to him with both expectation and apprehension.

"Seeds?"

"The noble warriors you have as your aides might not have mentioned it, but most wars resolve little, and the Great War was no exception. The hatred does not die, and the original causes are often refuelled by the pain and suffering inflicted on both sides. The enmities endure, and all look to the day their chance comes again."

The witch reached out to take Isak's white hand in her own. "Before your final rest you will walk many paths of the dead. The aftermath of such conflicts requires this, for there is no easy way to lay those ghosts to rest. Our lives are like paths in a forest, choices made at each fork, and sometimes they will lead you to clearings bathed in sunlight, sometimes into shadow. Your path has been walked before, by all those whose mistakes and failures set the course of your life, whose weaknesses have unbalanced the Land."

"The paths of the dead." Isak nodded to himself, lost in his own thoughts, still gripping Xeliath tightly by the hand. "It has felt that way sometimes, as though I can feel the footprints below me and the ghosts alongside."

"They are there, never forget that, but they do not own you; not Aryn Bwr, not this shadow Azaer, not even the Gods. You cannot change the past, Isak, but perhaps you can free the future of its shackles. In a land under shadow, you can give the hope of dawn."

Isak looked humbled by her words. This was a hard thing to lay on someone so young, she knew that all too well, yet there was no other course: she had to trust him, and hope he was strong enough to bear the strain. The choices were ultimately his alone. For all her wisdom, she couldn't make them for him.

She looked from the hulking lord to the girl intended as his queen. Xeliath had been quiet throughout their exchange, perhaps feeling an echo of Isak's pain.

"I hope to see you in Scree, and show you that you will not have to do this all alone. There are those who care, those who will make sacrifices when it becomes necessary. And now—" she raised an eyebrow in Xeliath's direction, "now I should leave you two alone."

CHAPTER 14

COUNT VESNA LOOKED OUT THROUGH THE TREES at the scrappy tufts of grass that were briefly bathed in sunlight as a break appeared in the cloud. Behind him a horse whickered softly. He saw his own horse's ears twitch, but a reassuring pat on the neck was enough to keep the borrowed animal steady. He shifted his feet slightly, wincing as he accidentally pressed down on his damaged toe, the product of a lucky escape two days past. The little horse turned and inspected the count, nostrils flaring, questing towards his hand in case a treat was on offer. He forced a smile and rubbed its nose affectionately, then sighed and returned to his vigil.

The only sounds came from the river ahead and the small stream to his left that ran into that river. He could hear nothing from the men positioned on the other side of this small wood, something he'd have considered a blessing at any other time this last week. The war had dragged on a long time in Tor Milist and now most of the duke's soldiers were little more than irregular troops, some no more than bandits enjoying the protection of a banner.

Their commanders exerted no control—indeed, many were worse than their troops—and rape and pillage were more common features of the war than actual battle. It had been a blessing to get away from the drunken louts who were his temporary allies, but Vesna couldn't shake the feeling that they might have slipped away instead of sticking to the battle plan.

"You look like a man who's thinking too hard." The speaker, his rough Lomin accent harsh to Vesna's ears, was a bearded veteran he'd promoted to sergeant-at-arms as soon as he'd met the man. Sergeant Tael was a dour forester in the employ of the Duke of Lomin, whoever Isak decided that was now to be, and one of the few old hands in his regiment. "Men who think too hard before a battle don't come back."

"I know that," Vesna replied, "but I've no intention of dying here."

"Do any of us?"

Vesna forced a wry smile. "You're a tight-mouthed bastard, Tael. I don't pretend to know what you intend."

The comment provoked a snort from the sergeant. "Aye, well, it ain't to die here. I've a grandchile on the way and I'm looking forrard to bouncing a rabble of little'uns on m'knee before I go."

Tael squinted at Vesna, then gave the count a calculating look. "From your face, I'd say you're thinking about your own."

"Remember your place, Sergeant," Vesna warned, more out of habit than anger.

"Aye sir, but I don't want to see a hero die in such a Gods-forsaken place either. Might lose m'faith if that happened. More important, it'll be one damn sight harder for me t'get home in one piece if you're dead." He waved a dismissive hand towards the horsemen behind. "These gutless shites won't hold if they see you go down."

"They're not all bad."

"Not all, but enough. The men we got from Saroc are fine troops, but neither captain is worth much. One's new, other's too well-bred for his own good."

"Enough!" Vesna snapped. "They're your superiors, and it is not your place to rate officers, only follow their orders. Clear?"

"Aye, sir," he drawled. From the set of the sergeant's face, Vesna could see it wasn't the first dressing-down the man had had for voicing his opinions. There were scars on his face that he wore proudly—one very obviously an infantryman's spear-cut—but there were probably scars on the man's back that he was less proud of.

Vesna surveyed the rest of his men. Four regiments in total: the two from Lomin and Tildek he'd fought against all too recently, one from Saroc and another from Nerlos—now with a complement of little more than three hundred men. They had all undergone the general training that was their liege's most vital duty, but few had real battle experience. The regiments Duke Certinse had provided contained some veterans, but most had been too young for the patrol rotation of those parts, where most Lomin men gained their experience. Unfortunately for the Farlan, it was the current set that had been wiped out before the battle of Chir Plain, so Certinse had chosen on the basis of the commander's loyalty.

"They're cowed, no more than that," Vesna muttered to himself. "There's little to be proud of in these parts, and a soldier needs that."

The men were hidden in a gentle dip in the ground. The trees, mostly elms, stretched past the stream for another few hundred yards, beyond which, Vesna devoutly hoped, his allies still waited. They were the dregs of six regiments, now fewer than three hundred in number, led by a man with a scar around his neck that was clearly a noose burn. The troops paid lip service to Duke Vrerr's battle orders. They killed the enemy whenever they had the advantage, and terrorised the region in between sorties. A soldier found pride where he could. Only wide-eyed boys thought there was much praiseworthy to be found in war itself, but even the old hands among the Farlan were sickened by some of the things they'd seen here.

Nothing had been prohibited by the duke, and the mercenaries employed by the White Circle were just as bad. Vesna had heard from his new allies that part of the legion they had been tracking were savages recently come from the Waste, bringing with them a host of evil magics and rituals. They'd heard rumours of small battles being fought in the deepest part of the Waste; of a so-called king of the Waste who was fighting all and sundry—the Elves, the Siblis, even the Menin, if the more fanciful tales were to be believed. Vesna believed little of this, but he had to admit it was worrying that they heard *anything* from the Waste.

The Travellers, the wandering tinkers, provided most of their information about those parts, telling tales of huge fertile plains in the areas less affected by the destruction of the Great War where towns had sprung up. Perhaps a king of the Waste had indeed arisen, and it was Isak's destiny to defeat the man. It was a depressing thought. Vesna had always feared the Waste. It was irrational and childish, he knew that, not based on anything in particular, but it awakened a nebulous terror, nightmares of his bones slowly decaying inside his armour while his soul wandered a blasted landscape with only the wind for company.

A burst of voices and clattering weapons broke the peace of the day as a flock of starlings leapt from the trees, startled into flight and heading as one over the river ahead. Vesna raised a hand to signal his sergeants. Tael gave a short whistle that was echoed down the line and the troops swung up into their saddles. Vesna did likewise, and stood high in the saddle to check his men. Spears were raised to signal readiness and the men began to drift towards the edge of the wood. Beyond the tree line the noise grew as shouts of alarm came from the thieves and murderers on the other side. The enemy had been sighted.

The heavy beat of hooves began to rumble closer. Vesna saw the first of the duke's men clear the stream and tear past his position, following the curve of the wood around to the open ground where they were to reform. The stream was small and shallow, no obstacle at all, and the duke's men had foraged these parts for the last two years. Tael jabbed a finger out towards the horsemen tearing up the soft ground Vesna had been musing over.

"Look, that red-haired rapist shite is leading them. Bastard's made sure he's first away."

"The man's a coward, but he's not stupid," Vesna replied. "We need him for the moment. Once we're off home I might think about an accident befalling him."

Tael grinned, showing crooked yellow teeth. "My Lord, I'd be honoured to join you on that if I could. Got daughters, I have—I'd surely like the chance to explain to him the difference between spoils of war and wickedness."

"Then you shall have it," Vesna promised as he tightened his grip on his reins.

A handful of stragglers followed the main group, men who'd fallen, or whose horses had shied from the stream. There were always a few. Soon the ground was clear again, though scarred by the regiment's passage.

The sound of hooves grew louder. Vesna raised a fist in the air and turned to Sergeant Tael. "Sounds like they've taken the bait."

"Aye, sir. Just hope our 'allies' remember to stop running."

"They will," Vesna said with more confidence than he felt. "And if they don't, we'll do it on our own anyway. Mercenaries don't have much stomach for a fight when they're taken unawares."

"And what if they've brought some fell magic from the Waste?"

"Then you're buggered, Sergeant."

"Me?"

"You. This armour's magic." Vesna gave a bleak chuckle. "There's a good chance any mage will sense that and go straight for me."

"And you're the one wi' the armour, so it's hard luck on anyone around you," finished Tael.

"For a sergeant you're not so stupid." Vesna broke off as the first of the enemy came into view. "Here they are. Give the signal on my order."

Tael nodded and raised a horn to his lips.

"Think, man!" Vesna snapped. The sergeant looked back at his commander in surprise, then realisation dawned. Tor Milist troops didn't use the complex horn commands the Farlan had developed. It wouldn't be the end of the Land if the Farlan were seen to be involved in the conflict, but they were trying to keep officially distant.

"Sorry, sir. Old 'abits."

Vesna waved a dismissal and drew his sword, raising it up for the nearby troops to see. Tila's image appeared before his eyes, hands clasped tight together as she'd said goodbye. She was wearing the green dress, his favourite. *I must be getting old. Death has been a constant companion and I don't fear him, only the loss of all I hold dear.* "Gods, which is worse?" he said out loud.

"Sir?" asked Tael anxiously. Vesna gave a start; he'd not intended anyone to hear him.

"I was wondering which was worse, having nothing to lose, or having so much to lose you suddenly fear it," he admitted in a rare display of weakness—he knew as well as anyone the men following him needed him to be a symbol of certainty and decisiveness, even if the experienced among them suspected it to be illusion. Sometimes illusion was enough.

"Tsatach's fiery balls! If you don't know the answer to that, you ain't got much to lose—or maybe you just can't see what's clear in front of you."

Vesna reached behind his back to grab his helm and pull it on, pausing to grin at the gnarled sergeant first. "Perhaps you're right there." He signalled with his sword and spurred his horse, and the beast leapt towards the open ground ahead, his men roaring and following his lead.

Splattered with blood and mud, Vesna picked a path through the dead and the dying. As he lurched over the churned ground of the battlefield, trying to find solid ground in between the piled corpses, he felt as if the field was trying to pull him down, to claim him as another fallen soldier.

He stumbled for a moment and his enchanted sword sank up to a foot into the ground before catching on a buried stone and stopping dead. The count yanked the weapon out and stomped onwards, his face blank. The battle had been swift and frantic, and now all he could hear were the cries of the wounded, and the screams of those too badly damaged to live being given mercy. Forced into a corner, on ground that hampered their every move, some of the mercenaries had still fought to the last, refusing to surrender even with shields in splinters, javelins spent and axes blunt.

Those who hadn't been killed in the fight had been run down and trampled as they tried to re-cross the stream. The Tor Milist soldiers had pursued and killed as many again, more confident when presented with the enemy's back than when faced with the threat of hand-to-hand combat.

Vesna looked grim as he realised this legion of mercenaries had survived the Waste, only to fall victim to the simplest of ambushes.

Something caught his eye and he scrambled forward. Sergeant Tael lay staring up at the sky, propped against the hip of a mercenary face-down in the mud with a hunting knife protruding up from the back of his neck. Vesna felt a moment of hope: the knife was Tael's; the sergeant had at least had enough strength to defend himself. The count sheathed his sword and fell to his knees at Tael's side. At the sound of his metal armour creaking, the sergeant stirred, a groan escaping his lips.

"Tael, open your eyes," Vesna commanded urgently. Slowly the man did as he was ordered, squinting up at the sky in confusion, then focusing on Vesna. The sergeant wore only a leather jerkin covered in steel scales, small protection against puncturing wounds, like the one in his belly, from which protruded an ugly stub of bloodstained wood. A blade of grass was stuck to the splintered end and almost without thinking, Vesna brushed it off, prompting a hiss of pain from the sergeant. The stub was much too big to be an arrow; it must be a spear, and the longer blade was most of the way through Tael's guts, by the looks of it. Vesna had seen enough such wounds to know exactly how bad Tael's chances were.

"How did you get stuck with a spear, you old bastard?" Vesna muttered. "You were in the thick of it, roaring like Tsatach himself. If you'd been struck as we charged, you wouldn't have made it this far." He looked up and around. The point where the stream met the river, marked by a row of willows, was only fifty yards away. The soldiers waiting here had been so tightly packed one man had nearly killed his fellow soldier with his backswing.

The sergeant's eyes fluttered for a moment, then a semblance of strength returned to his face. "Stabbed me," Tael whispered. "Bastard was on the floor an' I was busy with 'is mate. Went right under m'sword—never even saw 'im till I fell on 'im."

Vesna put a hand on Tael's shoulder, that familiar, caustic mix of regret, shame and relief churning in his gut. He'd had a lifetime of death, and he knew well the importance of a familiar face, a friendly touch and a voice talking, however inanely. He squeezed Tael's hand, and was rewarded with some pressure in return. The sergeant's words from earlier came treacherously back to him: *I'm looking forrard to bouncing a rabble of little'uns on m'knee before I go.* What to say to the man now? This wasn't their war, they had no place here. In a Land where life was short and brutal, Vesna had asked good men to die in a place that meant nothing to them—all because a young man who barely understood the blessings he had been given had ordered them to, and because he had sworn an oath to follow that young man, no matter whatever foolish fancy came into Isak's head.

"No, that's not fair on him," Vesna said to himself. "He can't be blamed."

"Fair?" echoed Tael distantly. "What's fair? Fate's a cruel mistress—

nothing fair in all this." He gave a soft wheeze and pawed at the ground as he tried in vain to adjust his position. Vesna helped him shift a little so he was less uncomfortable.

"Thanks," Tael murmured once the pain had subsided a little. "Don't want m'last hours to be watching vultures above."

"Has it done that much damage?"

Tael grimaced in reply. "Oh Gods, yes. I've been stuck before; this one's got me." Another wheeze, then he scowled. "Heard some bugger once say there was no better death than surrounded by your enemies. I wouldn't bother wi'it, was I you. I'm lying on the one as got me, and I can't say it matters much." He twisted his head in a vain effort to look at the man he'd killed.

"Be still," Vesna cautioned.

"Or what?" he said bitterly. "I might die? Bit late for the warning now." Despite his words, Tael gave up his efforts and went limp, defeated by the pain. "It's a good knife, that one. Made by one of the best smiths in Lomin. Think I've had m'last use of it now, so you're welcome to it."

Vesna nodded his thanks and jerked the dagger from the dead man's neck. Tael was right, it was a good knife—the tool of an experienced woodsman rather than a soldier's last resort, nicely balanced with a slight forward curve. He wiped it on the dead soldier and pushed it into his belt, next to the finely finished dagger given to him by an uncle.

"I'm sorry," Vesna blurted out suddenly.

"For what?"

The confusion in Tael's voice increased the weight of guilt bearing down on Count Vesna. "For . . ." His voice tailed off and he gestured down at the jagged stub embedded in Tael's belly, then swept his hand around to encompass the entire battlefield. He could see a raven hopping from one body to the next, hardly bothering to keep clear of those men still walking among the dead. There were enough bodies on which to feast that, when disturbed, the carrion birds moved on with little more than a harsh caw and a desultory flap of a lazy wing.

"The war's your fault?" Tael asked. "No? Well, shut up then and keep me company. I know you lot keep brandy for after battle."

Vesna did as he was told and sat irreverently on the corpse. He pulled out his hunting flask, took a swallow and handed it to Tael. It was expensive liquor, strong enough to scald the back of the throat. Vesna didn't much care for brandy, but anyone who'd smelled the shit and mud and spilled guts of a battlefield understood its use.

"I'm not sure I can keep doing this," Vesna said as he stared off towards the dull horizon. "It steals a part of me every time I go into battle. There's less of me every time—one day either I won't come back, or it'll be just my body that does. How do I ask a girl to marry someone who's fading away, a twilight man?"

"What sort o' girl is she?"

"Pure," Vesna replied after a moment's hesitation. *Gods, we're sitting here talking about my problems? Is that selfishness or mercy?* "She's young and beautiful, but what amazes me most is how pure she is. She has as much faith in the Gods as she did when she was a child. She was brought up to play the great game as well as any, yet I don't see her touched by it. I don't want her to be sullied by the man I am and the things I've done." He spat into the muddy puddle by his boot. "Hah, look at me. This sounds like some pathetic deathbed confession."

"Don't stop," rumbled Tael. The words were an effort now as pain and blood loss took its toll. "I'll not be confessing m'sins here. Don't regret what I done, men I killed. Ain't afraid o' dying; ain't running from what I done. If Lord Death don't like some of it, well, he can look me in the eye and tell me so 'imself."

Vesna gripped Tael's hand, holding hard for the few moments of the sergeant's life remaining to him. "I wish I could be proud too," Vesna said. It didn't matter what he said, just that he keep going as Tael faded.

He poured another slug of brandy down Tael's throat. "Not all the men I've killed have been downed in battle. Some were killed in duels; some I simply murdered. Somehow it doesn't matter that I was ordered to—I still did it. When my judgment comes, if it's true that Death weighs the good against the bad on his golden scales, orders won't matter. When a man realises that, how can he think of marrying so pure a girl?"

"Does she know?"

"Everything? Gods no. Used to be because they were state secrets—things that could do only harm if they ever came to light, and best lost, even after we've gone—but now . . . Now it's because I fear showing her that part of me; the part that took advantage of drunken wives when I was told to, poisoned food and brought about hunting accidents. There's no good in what I've done there, only necessity."

"She won't see that?"

"I don't know what she'll see." Vesna hung his head. "But if it disgusts me, how could she feel any different?"

"Don't know all you did, but—" Tael paused to catch his breath.

Vesna almost told the sergeant to save his strength before wondering what he would be saving it for—a handful more heartbeats? Was that worth giving up on life early?

"Bet lots o' men like me would thank you," Tael wheezed, wincing as he fought for each word. "Whatever you did, bet it gave 'em time t'see their children grow. Give yourself the same time."

Vesna felt his chest tighten in sympathy, breathing becoming a sudden effort, but he couldn't bring himself to leave the sergeant, an ageing forester who had come here with nothing to gain and found only a chunk of steel, driven into his gut, taking everything he had left. The far-off voices of his soldiers washed over him as he felt Tael's life slipping through his grasp. Only the image of Tila's smile remained clear in his mind; the bite of the brandy at the back of his throat and the cold smell of the blood and mud faded into the background as Vesna sat staring at the body in his arms, waiting for answers that failed to come.

CHAPTER 15

THROUGH THE HAZE OF AN ANCIENT MEMORY she saw his face again, fixed on some distant trouble, while she slept. His stern beauty was frightening, almost alien when not smoothed into a smile. She looked down at the hand he was propping himself up on the bed with, so close to her bare belly that she could feel the tiny glow of heat radiating from his skin.

She reached out and ran a finger softly down the back of his hand, watching the emotions wash over his face as contemplation was overcome by surprise and surprise surrendered at last to pleasure. She smiled at him—he was ever wary, alert, when on campaign, constantly listening for the enemy, or reaching out into the air to detect any traces of magic drifting on the winds.

She was young, and smitten with the languid beauty of the shining king, but she was utterly at ease here in his tent, guarded by the cream of the Dragonguard. Their mission was to map in detail the very north of their borders, and trap whatever great beasts they could before they declared all-out war with the remaining tribes of men: an easy mission, little more than an extended springtime hunting trip that afforded them the privilege of distance from the queen and the two princes.

Their eyes met, then their lips. His smooth fingertips on her thigh, circling her kneecap and trickling down towards her toe. A voice came from outside the tent, words too distant for her to hear, but she felt the canvas roll underneath her as her lover rose and left the bed. She watched his stooped, slender frame struggle to pull on his riding clothes and buckle Eolis to his waist.

She reached out to slide her fingers through his, intent on calling him back to bed for one last kiss, but as she tried to call his name her throat dried. Something caught her tongue, and the breath in her lungs faded, leaving the words hovering in her mind. She froze, feeling a sense of horror creep down the nape of her neck, unable to even scream.

The image faded as the tent's close walls turned grey and became a dark and troubled sky. She looked around and saw the spilt blood, the ruined bodies and furrowed earth. She herself was on her knees, her hands manacled behind her back and the fire of open wounds on her body. A sword had scraped down her skull and ruined her helm. A lance of flame had hit her arm and thrown her from her horse. She was flanked by her brothers; one was wheezing through a ruined lung, the other was shivering in fear, trying to shake off the blood running freely over his eye. The bones of his ankle jutted out through the skin. She watched in disbelief as a silver corpse, stiff, cumbersome in death, was dragged to the crest of the hill. It seemed an insult to the hypnotic grace that Aryn Bwr had been so lauded for.

Now he was dead, nothing but a filthy shell. They could visit no further indignities on him—or so she thought until the voices began to echo out over the plain. Up above, the air shimmered, reverberating with each syllable. The eight voices, haunted by the loss of their kin and the exertions of a battle that had weakened them nearly to oblivion, swept down to where she knelt. Her ruined body rocked back at the spoken fury that was building into a crescendo of retribution. There was nothing more they could do, not to the dead—and yet they found a way.

At last the tears came, not for the defeat and humiliation, nor for the hurt done to her, nor fear of whatever judgment was to come. She cried for the king she worshipped, the lover she was devoted to for all time. And yet his name faded from her mind, the letters carved into her heart no longer intelligible. When the Gods were finished with the corpse and had tossed it into a festering pit, his name had vanished, gone from her heart, gone from the minds of those who had accompanied him for a hundred years, rent from history.

A distant knocking broke Zhia's sleep. Her eyes opened to a new Land, one changed in every way to that time before the war. It helped ease the ache in her heart to think of it as a different place, a different world. The loss was a memory she had learned to live with, one for the private moments of her dreams, but rigorously denied even a minute of her waking life. That world was gone, and yearning for its return would do her no good at all.

She yawned and stretched her slim frame, questing down the bed with her toes until they touched the footboard and pushed into the groove cut a few inches from its base. She forced away the later part of the dream by focusing on the happiness of what had gone before, something she had learned to do many years back, the only way to quell the pain enough to be able to carry on. Exercises of the mind soothed and transferred her attention to happier subjects: remembering the feel of his skin on hers, so unlike the touch of a human, the cadence of his voice that had captured her heart the very first moment she heard it, and the feel of his breath on her ear as he whispered to her in the night. She'd almost been frozen with shock when she first saw Lord Isak wearing that armour, killing so smoothly and efficiently. It had felt as if her heart had been torn open for a moment, and all that buried loss flooded back afresh.

She had a few minutes yet before Panro would come to wake her, and Zhia felt a comforted smile creep onto her lips as she recalled the brush of Aryn Bwr's lips on her belly. Despite the intervening years, her mortal life remained bright and clear in her memory and she had no problem remembering that. She slid her palms between the cool linen sheets until her arms were stretched out and her body was spread like a virgin sacrifice.

The room was almost completely dark, the shutters on the windows screwed shut each morning before dawn. It made the room stuffy in the relentless afternoon sun, but Panro aired it well each morning before she went to sleep. It was a small enough inconvenience when compared to the alternative.

A discreet rap on the door heralded Panro's arrival. The tall man entered and walked to the side of the bed. Zhia hadn't bothered to move; he was alone. She listened to his footsteps, trying to detect his mood. Her powerfully built manservant had a peculiarly dainty manner of walking, treading softly, taking great care over each step. Today, detecting nothing unusual in the neat patter, she assumed his mood was as placid as usual.

"Coffins," she declared, rolling over in bed as he placed her chilled tea on the bedside table. In his hand was a candlestick that he used to light the lamp beside her bed. Her smile widened.

"Coffins, Mistress?"

"Coffins," she confirmed, nodding with mock emphasis. A long curl of hair fell over her face. "Why do people think we sleep in them? They're small, and hardly comfortable."

"You told me your spirit would return to your tomb when your body died, that only there would you regenerate," Panro reminded her as he swept the curl away with one deft finger.

Zhia ignored what might be considered impertinence in a servant; her hold over him was magical, so he couldn't be blamed for the love he held for her—and a man's touch, however slight, was delightful, particularly after her dreams of Aryn Bwr. She stretched again, and said, "But that's when I die. Why would I want to spend every damn day in a coffin when this bed is just so deliciously comfortable? Waking up like this is one of the few pleasures I have left." She grimaced and added, "It takes a few foggy moments before the years catch up with me, and for that I am inordinately grateful. I would be utterly miserable if I had to wake in a coffin instead."

"Yes, Mistress."

Zhia gave him a coquettish smile. When one awoke in a mood this good, there really was only one thing to do—but first, she should check on who was waiting downstairs. "Who have we for this evening, then?" she asked.

"Mistress Legana and Mis—the woman Haipar have come, with a nobleman they called Aras." Haipar had made it plain she didn't want the usual honorific, and Panro, a stickler for the correct forms, heartily disapproved.

Zhia gave a groan. "Ah, Count Lurip Aras. A pretty little man, but dear me, he is dull. Unfortunately, he is also rather useful to me, and one of the few decent soldiers this city has, so an enchantment of bonding was well worth the effort. I assigned Teviaq to his command staff, thinking any daughter of that morose bitch Amavoq might teach him the value of silence, but I think it's only encouraged him." She brought her hands up behind her head and looked Panro up and down. Her manservant had an athletic frame and towered over her, but she had always preferred men far larger than herself. *It's probably Aryn Bwr's fault*, she thought with a grin. *After all, most things were.*

She pursed her lips and blew softly at the sheet covering her. Only a shred of magic was needed to make it slither over her body to the foot of the bed, leaving her naked, exposed to the lamplight. She glanced down, admiring her smoothly tinted flesh; the previous night she had succumbed to the latest fashion; bathing in rustroot-infused water had stained her skin the colour of a true Fysthrall woman (though there were few enough of those about in Scree), instead of her normal deathly pallor. The effect greatly amused her.

It obviously had an effect on Panro too, for his rapt gaze was sending a tickle of delight down her spine. He appeared particularly entranced by the curve of her buttocks, so she shifted position a little, the better to enhance his view, and smoothed a slender hand up her thigh. A pert rosy nipple was just visible as she turned towards him.

As a slight gasp escaped his lips, she reached up to take his hand and pull him towards her, whispering, "Well then? I wouldn't want to keep my guests waiting long."

"Ladies, my dear Aras, I do apologise," Zhia called as she swept down the broad staircase that faced the open entrance to her reception room. She was clad in a flowing white dress, with elbow-length gloves, and an evening stole draped over one arm. The house was of the classical design—wide, open rooms, narrow windows running from floor to ceiling—and Zhia thought it suited her perfectly, for she too was "classical": ancient, yet still beautiful, and very desirable.

Her guests rose to their feet as she swept in. She took note of the contrast in clothing: the count was immaculately turned out, his ash-blond hair fashionably loose about his shoulders, while Haipar, her usual linen shirt dirtier than usual, had clearly spent the day in the field. Legana trod the middle ground, for her tunic, though finely tailored, was also stained. She had heeded some of Zhia's advice, for she had obviously attended to her hair and make-up before returning to the city. *Honestly*, Zhia thought, *Lesarl is a fool at times. He sees a beautiful woman and simply assumes she's capable of infiltrating any organisation by blinding them with her looks.*

"Mistress Ostia, you look ravishing as always," Aras oozed, earning a blushing smile from the vampire. Her bonding enchantment ensured slavish devotion, but not mindless thrall, which would have rendered him useless to her.

"You look a different colour, at any rate," Legana commented, trying to stifle a smirk. Zhia had promised to teach her to blush or cry on demand; she claimed few things turned a man's mind like the blush of a beautiful woman.

"I know. I thought I would give the gossips something to wonder about," Zhia said as she held out her hand for Aras to kiss. "I'm hoping Siala will take this as a reminder of the Circle's earliest traditions; she's foolish enough to be distracted by such matters."

"I thought you'd been impressed by her," Legana said. "She appears competent enough whenever I've spoken to her."

"My dear, your benchmark has been set by Farlan spies—perfectly com-

petent at whatever Chief Steward Lesarl sends them off to do, I have no
doubt, but you must agree that they lack sophistication."

Legana scowled. Zhia had several times chastised her lack of education
and her quickness to violence.

"Siala differs from you, Legana," Zhia continued, ignoring the girl's
colouring cheeks, "because she is intelligent and educated, but she is unable
to use that properly. You have not had the correct instruction, but since
you've come under my wing you've responded admirably. By the time you
reach Siala's age, I will have made a queen of you. Siala is what one hopes for
in an opponent, intellect without imagination, but I will not accept that
from my allies."

She bade her visitors be seated again, and settled herself on a chaise
longue, arranging her skirts decorously around her. She nodded for Haipar to
begin her evening report.

The shapeshifter wiped the smile from her face and cleared her throat.
"We have received the weekly reports from the legions, but there's nothing
of particular interest. The training programmes are running well, but they're
far from battle-ready. One colonel has admitted seeing the benefits of
merging mercenary companies with our recruits."

"And the others?"

Haipar grinned. "The others are still bitching about it, of course—I believe
the words 'affront to our honour' have been mentioned several times."

"Madam," Aras interrupted, almost spluttering in indignation, "your
orders are gravely insulting to a military man—you force the city's finest to
stand alongside common mercenaries, men who will hire their swords to the
highest paymaster without considering the wrong or right of it, and you
place savages on the command staff, where they give orders to noblemen!"

"Ah yes, how are the Raylin settling in to their new roles?" As she spoke,
Zhia allowed a trickle of magic to slide over her fingers to be certain the
enchantment on the count still held. There were so many mages and spies
around that she would have been foolish to simply assume he was still hers—
and Zhia Vukotic was not a fool.

Haipar chuckled. "It rather depends on who you're talking about. My
companions are greatly enjoying themselves—Tachos Ironskin was a ranking
soldier in the Chetse army anyway, and my friend Matak Snakefang has
thrown off his usual surliness to become the consummate general. As for the
others, some are less encouraging. Veren's Staff is causing chaos by forcing
every religious observance he can think of onto the men. Apparently he called

a halt to manoeuvres yesterday and made four thousand men perform the devotionals!"

Haipar couldn't stop laughing when she saw Zhia's expression.

Exasperated, Legana broke in, saying, "Bane hasn't yet grasped your orders. He's with the Second Army, but he spends his days wandering the camp in a daze. His single accomplishment has been to execute a soldier he believed to be a vampire. On the training ground. At midday. Under the sun."

"Don't underestimate either of them," said Zhia softly. "They're both quite mad, but their value on the field will be great. Ironskin is happy with the training, I trust?"

"Hah, Ironskin is," Legana scoffed. "The colonel commanding him is less so. Apparently he has restructured the entire army into Chetse battle-order . . . without actually mentioning that fact to his commander. There has been no talk of duels yet, but I have no doubt they're trying to find a way to murder him. Do you want me to step in?" Legana's position in the army structure was indeterminate, but she was a potential Circle member, and Ostia's aide, so the officers assumed she was in effect Siala's voice, and thus obeyed her orders without question.

"No, Tachos Ironskin knows war better than most, in this city or elsewhere, so he can do as he sees fit. A phalanx requires intense training, and if he can provide it in a matter of weeks, I will be delighted." Zhia smiled. "I can't believe they'll manage to kill him, and it does a Raylin good to be kept on his toes; they're a quarrelsome breed and a good conspiracy will stop him starting any other trouble. If you find anyone running a book on the matter, do back him on my behalf."

"The others are happy enough by Raylin standards and causing no real trouble yet. As for the Third Army," Legana said, "I really can't say. We're kept well away from them. Siala has the Fysthrall troops under total control, though she's brought more into the city these past few days."

Zhia was far from surprised. "She knows I have control over the city guards now. I was expecting her to boost her strength within the city. She will want to test her authority, so make sure the guards do nothing to antagonise the Fysthrall—they must back away from any conflict. Have any that don't obey flogged."

"She is paranoid about assassins," Legana added. "For some reason she suspects the city has been overrun with foreign agents, all looking to kill her."

Zhia gave the Farlan assassin a stern look. "In that case we should keep an eye open." She looked thoughtful for a moment. "But this might be a useful distraction. I shall get one of the Jester acolytes to make the threat appear real. They are skilled enough to narrowly fail, and playing the assailed sovereign will keep Siala busy."

The Jesters, the sons of Death, made their home in the deepest part of the Elven Waste where they were worshipped as Gods by the local tribes. They demanded martial excellence from their followers, very like the original Raylin. Zhia had secured the services of six of their acolytes, half-brothers, sons of some chieftain. She spent most evenings walking the night streets with them. They were skilled and loyal warriors, and perfect for the more delicate spying missions.

"Which reminds me," Zhia continued after a pause, "one of our acolytes—I forget which one; it is starting to annoy me that they refuse to give their names, and the white masks make them all look alike—but whichever it was, he said last night that they are noting a number of illegal entries into the city. Since this is not their city, they do not care, but they felt they should inform me."

"So there really are assassins in the city?" Aras asked.

"One would presume so. The interested parties will be augmenting their own households. King Emin won't be able to keep his sticky little paws out, and the Farlan consider this their territory. The only questions are whether the Devoted are going to bring a significant presence to the table, and who else might get involved. Are the Menin also gathering intelligence this far north? If I were in charge in Circle City or Raland I would certainly have put some agents in play."

"Yet with all this going on, still you find time for your little project, this theatre in Six Temples?" Haipar didn't try to hide the snap in her voice.

"Which remains as mysterious as ever," Zhia said pointedly. "There have been rumours of hauntings throughout that district, a number of out-of-the-ordinary murders—"

"Does that mean out-of-the-ordinary by the standards of your own daily routine?" Haipar continued.

Zhia raised an eyebrow and Aras half rose from his seat, hand on his rapier's hilt. "Haipar, do I detect a note of displeasure in your voice?" Zhia asked smoothly, motioning for Aras to sit back down.

He glared at Haipar, but they all knew the threat was empty—though he could best Haipar with a blade, she wouldn't bother with a sword; her own claws would have split him groin to gizzard almost before he'd drawn his weapon. His magic-imposed loyalty to Zhia was not so great that he would test Haipar in her lioness form. He had no false illusions there.

"Well, you did turn the head of the Prefecture—I wouldn't think we have to look too far to explain unusual deaths."

"He is under control, I assure you. As for your personal feelings about vampires—" Zhia started.

"You know I don't give a damn about them—except when they could cause us difficulties," Haipar replied hotly. "You know better than anyone how they can suddenly snap—if they can't withstand the pressure of the change, they explode into murder."

"And I repeat: it is under control," said Zhia, very quietly.

Legana sighed; she couldn't understand why Haipar kept prodding; Zhia's anger was not to be taken lightly but the Raylin was constantly argumentative whenever the subject of the theatre came up.

Zhia rose gracefully and walked to the windows. "These deaths have nothing to do with me or my breed. There is something else afoot. The acolytes have been watching the theatre. This company doesn't spend much time rehearsing, but the players have made some interesting contacts amongst Scree's criminal element. And surely you have heard the tales of the *Dark Man* who walks the streets, snatching children—in the slums, of course, but nonetheless, the result is a state of panic in four districts of this city."

"And you should attend to this personally?" Haipar muttered.

Zhia leaned forward in her seat. "This is a situation I do not understand. I have lived for millennia; I have founded half a dozen cities, and I've lost count of those I have ruled. Believe me when I say it is rare that I do not understand something."

Her companions all subconsciously moved back at the frosty tone of her voice.

"What do you want to do?" Aras asked, hoarsely.

Zhia turned suddenly and beamed. "To do? I want us to go to dinner now, and afterwards, you may accompany me to the theatre's first night for a little culture—I suspect the experience will be illuminating."

"What meat is this, Mayel?" The abbot was looking quizzically at the lump of indeterminate meat in his spoon.

The young man grimaced, his own spoon halfway to his mouth, and tried to avoid the abbot's gaze. "Rabbit, Father. Good rabbit stew."

The abbot took another tentative mouthful. "Are you sure?"

Of course I'm sure it's not rabbit, you stupid old bastard. You should be glad it's actually dog, considering what some folk are eating these days. He shrugged. "The butcher told me it was rabbit, Father, but folk are saying that food's getting scarce. If this heat continues, who knows what we'll be dining on soon."

The abbot didn't press the point. He was too tired. This summer was the hottest anyone could remember, and every day the heat sapped more strength from the abbot's frail body. Whatever magic he was doing in the cellar of their tumbledown house, it was compounding the problem, and if he were not careful, he would run himself into the grave. It was always the old ones who went first, collapsing in the street, never to get up again.

These days they ventured outside only after the sun had gone down, and even so, it was still humid enough to bring on a sweat. Mayel wiped his face on his sleeve again, but it didn't have much effect, for his clothes were sodden with perspiration. That was about the only thing about the monastery he did miss, fresh habits to wear—even if it was the novices who did the cleaning. He took another mouthful of dog stew. Suddenly life in the monastery didn't seem all that awful.

"I did hear some interesting gossip from the butcher though," he piped up, hoping conversation would stop them focusing on the grim stew. "Some madman is saying the prophecy of the Flower of the Waste has been fulfilled; that the tribesmen in the Elven Waste have joined under a king and have marched on the Elves—or the Siblis, the butcher wasn't sure which. Not that he thought it was really true—but he did swear that he'd had it on good authority that the Devoted have started fighting amongst themselves. The Knight-Cardinal ordered troops from Embere to attack their forces in Raland, and Telith Vener was waiting for them. Word is that Vener would have wiped them out if it hadn't been for a third Devoted army that stopped it all and forced the Knight-Cardinal's troops to return to Embere."

"And why is that interesting exactly? The squabblings of soldiers mean nothing to me, and should not to you either."

Mayel suppressed a sigh at the abbot's stern tone of voice; he could feel another lecture about attending to the divine coming on. "But Father, we're not in the monastery at the moment, and these are dangerous times. I heard that the Farlan might invade, that the city might become a battle-ground—"

"Pay no heed to what you might hear in a butcher-shop," the abbot repeated. "You would do better to spend a little more time here in prayer than gossiping in the street or running errands for your cousin."

"We have to pay for his help somehow," Mayel replied hotly. Mayel knew he had proved himself invaluable to the abbot, securing much of what he needed on credit with Shandek. He doubted the abbot would have lasted a week without him; mage or no, you couldn't protect yourself from a knife in the back day and night. "I've been clerking for him to repay him for the use of this house and the protection he's given us."

"You are paying him for this ruin? You almost killed yourself going upstairs," the abbot grumbled, looking at the state of the wall beside him. Mayel had grown to loathe that pinched expression. Since the heat had taken over, the abbot had been impossible to please, despite Mayel's best efforts.

"Everyone pays for their living quarters, Father, and not everyone gets the protection we do. Folk know his men are watching us, so they keep their distance, just as you wanted. The slate's far from clear, even with the work I'm doing for Shandek now."

"Should we be so indebted to anyone?" the abbot asked, querulously.

"I think Shandek's decided we're a safe investment, me being family and you being a high priest. Maybe he thinks that there's money in the monastery, so if he wants a reward he's going to have to get you back there safely."

"But what use have we for money at the monastery?" asked the bewildered abbot. "In any case, the prior is still hunting us, and I do not know if I am strong enough to face him now, not if he has truly allied with a daemon."

"But he won't be prepared against people he's never met." Mayel hesitated, but then—Well, he was sure the abbot had guessed Shandek had some criminal connections. "Shandek's put the word out about Jackdaw, so he won't be able to show his face here—there are more than enough people who'd be glad of the bounty the Temple of Death would pay for a daemon-worshipper."

"Mayel," the abbot said sharply, putting his spoon down with a clatter, "you speak as though you know Prior Corci to be in the city—do you? *Is he?*"

The novice froze, and then muttered, "Well—"

"Mayel!" the abbot shrieked. "Have you seen him? Merciful Vellern protect us, has he seen you? Was it today? Could he have followed you back here?"

"Father Abbot, relax," Mayel interrupted hurriedly, trying to placate the old man, "I haven't seen him."

"Then what is it?" he said, still shaking. "I can tell there is something you're not telling me."

"I did think I saw Jackdaw, when I was at the theatre with Shandek," he admitted. "But I didn't actually *see* anything—there was a movement in the shadows, that's all, and I got frightened." He went on, looking shamefaced, "Since then, I have felt like someone was watching me, but I swear, I've never actually seen him."

"You could have led him back here," the abbot insisted, fear reducing his voice to a whine.

"What choice did I have?" Mayel demanded as the abbot rose, knocking his bowl of stew to the floor in his haste.

"I must prepare," Abbot Doren continued, more to himself than Mayel. "There's so much to do before he finds me," he said, pulling open the battered door that led to the cellar. He was gone before Mayel had moved. A muffled bang from downstairs indicated the abbot had slammed the door behind.

Mayel looked at the mess on the floor and sighed. He scraped up the remains of the stew and the shards of pottery and returned the uneaten portion in his own bowl to the big pot simmering above the fire. He couldn't stomach any more of it tonight.

"Balls to this, I'm going to find something better to do," he growled, and pushed open the kitchen door to reveal the dark city, as caked in sweat and dirt as he was. Scree had never been considered beautiful, and with the unnatural heat drying everything, the streets now stank like a bloated corpse. He kicked the door shut and went out into the night.

Doranei dropped from the wall and crouched in the shadows, holding his breath while he listened for sounds of pursuit, taking in the features of the ten-yard-square walled courtyard as he counted twenty heartbeats. No light filtered in from the house that made up two of the sides. The few terracotta pots with withered stems drooping from them and a half-full stone-edged pond with four stone trout rising from the surface suggested the house had been closed up for the summer months. There was no guard, so there was no one to give him away to the Scree city guards who had been chasing him.

He couldn't hear them any longer. "Damn," he muttered, brushing dust from his hands. Normally escaping a city guard so easily was something to be pleased about, but not tonight. He checked the pack on his back, but everything was secure, including his pair of sheathed swords.

He was ready to start running again. He walked to the pond, dislodged one of the pots on the low wall and watched it shatter on the flagstones. The King's Man didn't bother to listen any longer. He jumped to reach an iron bracket fixed to the house and hauled himself up, using toeholds in the rough-mortared stone wall to reach the roof three storeys up. There he paused, silhouetted against the hunter's moon to wait for his pursuers.

"Bloody wizards." He looked around at the streets. "'You're a good runner, Doranei,' he says. 'You'll be a fine decoy,' he says. Didn't bloody tell me the guards were bloody blind."

Finally he heard confused, urgent voices coming from the winding streets, and spotted torches bobbing here and there as the men of the city guard fanned out down the side streets. The night air was still, and strangely quiet. Doranei could hear the guards distinctly.

He looked about to fix his location. A domed building, the biggest land-mark, that had to be the Temple of Death, half a mile to the south, sur-rounded by the five grand temples to Nartis, Belarannar, Vellern, Karkarn and Vasle. Around them in turn were shrines to every other God and Aspect the good folk of Scree had been able to think of.

In the dark he'd somehow blundered further than he'd intended, and now found himself well into the district north of Six Temples, where some of the oldest and most splendid houses in Scree were to be found. There were regular patrols, but old money too often had little to spare for expenses like maintaining a city staff when they left for the country, as most of Scree's noble families had done.

A shout came from behind him, taken up by other voices a lot closer than Doranei would have liked. "There you go," he said to the night air. "Now keep up, you bastards—for a bit, anyway. I'll give you a much-needed workout."

He'd scanned the streets for the best escape route, but he'd picked badly; there wasn't a lot to choose from here. A wide, empty avenue ran towards the hunter's moon, nicely illuminated—and useless for his purposes, for the torches would round the corner and be onto it before he'd managed to climb down and get away. He ran the length of the slate roof-top and hopped the gap onto the next building, and again, until he reached a tall building that protruded out into the avenue, creating a bottleneck with a smaller house on the other side of the street.

This suited Doranei's purposes nicely, for it was the quickest way to cross the avenue and get away from the guards. People rarely bothered to look up in a city, especially where most streets were narrow, with overhanging buildings.

He crouched in the lee of a chimney, assessing the jump, when a splintered crash came from the first house behind him. The city guards had broken in, assuming he was trapped. He couldn't see any movement in the street; this was probably his best chance.

"I think I might be making a terrible mistake," Doranei muttered as he fumbled in a pocket. He took out two fat leather bands with an iron brace and hook attached to each, slipped the bands over his wrists and pulled the laces tight. He manoeuvred himself onto the dark side of the gently sloping roof as silently as he could.

The hooks nestled in his palms, rough and cold against his skin. They were made of cheap, soft iron, perfect for his need. With luck, he wouldn't have to use them, but this was a long jump and he'd seen what happened to men who were unprepared. It was hard enough to keep your grip when your body slammed into the side of a building, and almost impossible with cut palms from hitting the building's stone edge. There was a low parapet running around the roof edge, so all he needed to do was to get enough of his body over it, then simply fall into the gutter—out of sight, and safe.

He took a deep breath and set off, head low, legs pumping hard. The jump was far enough that he didn't want time to think about it. He kicked off, keeping his eyes fixed on the point he'd chosen, legs and arms wheeling forward. The air whistled past his face as the building lurched up to meet him and almost immediately he realised it was even further than he'd thought. He wasn't going to make it over the wall.

With only a heartbeat to decide, Doranei dropped his left hand to his chest and turned inward, so his forearm would take the force of the blow. In the next instant he hit the stone facing, just below the wall, his left arm numb, his right arm up and clawing at the stone.

The impact jerked his body around as Doranei got the hook over the ledge. The wind had been driven from his lungs and stars burst before his eyes, but he bit down the pain and let the momentum swing him back, then, hanging precariously from his right-hand hook, he kicked up as hard as he could.

He moaned thanks to Cerdin, God of Thieves, as he swung his leg over the parapet, and with one final burst of strength, he heaved the rest of his body over and into the gutter.

He fell onto his side and lay there fighting for breath as his mind caught up. He tried to ignore his own wheezing so he could hear what was going on around him. Voices in the street were raised, but not shouting, and more importantly, there was no sound of running feet. There was no doubt the guards would have heard him hit the rooftop but if they'd not been in time to see him, it would have simply confused them—after all, a man would have to be mad to try that jump. It was a fair bet that they'd not even consider the possibility.

Get moving, Doranei shouted in his own head, letting the training of his youth take over when all his body wanted was to stay there and whimper. *Move now, or soon you will not be able to move enough to get off this damn roof.* He twisted as best he could to inspect the roof. The gutter would take him around the corner of the house, at which point he could risk standing up to find somewhere to break in. There was no way of telling if the house was occupied, but it wouldn't be the first time he'd had to tie up and gag a household before making his escape. He'd certainly distracted the guards for long enough, so now all he had to do was find a dark little hole to hide in. Mistress Siala had posted mages to detect any sort of magic user entering the gates, so King Emin's mages had to be sneaked in over the city wall, but they should be safe now. The Brotherhood would have wasted no time in getting the pair away once the guards were distracted.

As he lay there the pain began to grow in his left arm, a hot, sharp throbbing that was fast spreading up towards his fingertips. Gingerly, Doranei eased himself up and tried to move his fingers. He hissed with pain, but at least he could do it, proving the arm wasn't broken. That'd do. The pain he'd live with for the time being.

He cut the laces with his dagger and stowed the hooks back in his pocket. He crawled to the end of the gutter, eyes focused on his destination and teeth gritted as he fought the fire in his damaged arm, but once he'd made it to the back of the house, he realised Cerdin—to whom every member of the Brotherhood prayed for luck—had not abandoned him. Here was a balcony, with steps leading down to the courtyard below.

Doranei hauled himself upright, took a moment to recover his balance, then trotted down the steps until he could climb onto the wall that encircled the courtyard. The walls were all connected, and while he would be more exposed, he could run along the top much quicker than if he stayed on street level, where he would be forever clambering over these same seven-foot-high walls. He headed towards Six Temples until he spotted an alley that offered the seclusion he was searching for. The only problem was that there were voices up ahead, and the smell of spices hanging in the air—cloves and cinnamon. He sighed and shrugged. He'd be past the diners before any of them could call out.

Doranei glanced down as he passed, catching sight of a private dinner for a handful of well-dressed nobles—and, oddly, a woman dressed more like an infantryman. His momentary lack of attention was his undoing.

Something smashed into his shoulder, knocking him off balance and spinning him around. One foot slipped and he flailed wildly for a moment before the other went from under him and he fell, clipping the wall with his injured arm before crashing onto a thick shrub growing below.

He groaned as pain flared all over his body and fading yellow trails of firelight smeared across his vision. The scuffle of stools scraping over stone heralded a boot landing on his chest. Doranei froze, anticipating a cold blade slicing his throat or sliding into his gut.

Instead, someone chuckled. The boot was removed from his chest and the person stepped back to allow the light to fall on his face.

"A handsome, if somewhat battered, man falling at my feet," declared a woman in a pretty, cultured voice. "This day has been a remarkably pleasant one. Haipar, help my young suitor up so I can see him better."

The dazed Doranei felt strong hands grip him by the shoulders and lift him into a seating position. Very slowly, the Land came back into focus. One of the women was still seated, a goblet in her slender fingers and a smile on her face. Looming over him was the only man in the group and the female soldier, both with their hands on their hilts. A third woman, remarkably pretty, stood on the other side, her dagger drawn.

"Legana, my dear, your aim is impeccable," said the seated woman. "I must remember to give a glowing report of your skills—though not your taste. We now have no wine to offer the gentleman."

"Offer him wine?" exclaimed the man. "He's a common thief! We'll send for the city guard and be done with him."

Bugger, thought Doranei, *I could take one, if I'm lucky, but not both, not with my arm like this.*

The woman rose and approached Doranei, crouching down to look him in the face. The King's Man blinked to clear his sight, and got a jolt of surprise. The woman was stunning, even more arresting than her beautiful companion. Her skin was a dusky red, similar colouring to the Fysthrall soldiers he'd fought in Narkang. Her eyes were shining sapphires in the dim light, and so piercing he could feel her gaze prickle over his skin.

"He's no thief, Aras. This one is much more interesting." She peered closer and Doranei could see her note the tattoo on his ear. "I suspect your *heart* is not in a life of crime?"

The emphasis was not lost on him and Doranei nodded. She was obviously of the White Circle, but he wondered how she knew so much. Only a very select group knew anything of the Brotherhood.

"What would you like me to do, then?" asked the woman soldier, her hand still on her sword. As Doranei's mind cleared, he took in the appearances of the other diners. The man was handsome, and stood like a soldier, despite his frippery. Much the same could be said for the woman whose aim had proved so inconvenient. Legana? A Farlan woman, he now saw. The soldier, Haipar, looked like a savage from the Waste. For a while he wondered whether his brain had been addled by the fall, but no matter how much he tried to blink it away, Haipar's appearance didn't change.

"I want you to see if he's injured, and if so, tend to his wounds," the woman who was so obviously in charge ordered. "If he is whole, fetch him a seat so that he may join me in a glass of wine."

The one she'd named Haipar gripped Doranei's tunic and hauled him to his feet, not bothering to ask how he was feeling. He managed to stay standing, despite the cacophony of complaints from different parts of his body, but he failed to stifle a low moan; his ribs were burning with pain now.

"Legana, if there are any of the city guard out there looking for someone, tell them to stop and return to their posts. I will deal with this one." She looked speculatively at Doranei and appeared to make up her mind about something.

"And then you can all leave us," she added, waving them away.

"Mistress, he's carrying weapons," protested Aras.

"And here I am, a helpless little girl? Go away, and ensure we're not disturbed. If you want to be useful, fetch some more wine."

The nobleman jumped to obey. The two women didn't appear cowed, as Doranei would have expected in a White Circle city, but neither protested. Doranei felt a foreboding curiosity—even injured, he was pretty sure he would be able to overpower so slight and unarmed a woman, though her confidence was disconcerting, and strangely disarming.

Haipar hovered at his elbow as Doranei hobbled unsteadily to the nearest chair and eased himself down, then she left, passing a servant scurrying in with another jug of wine. The girl set it carefully on the table, then fled, pulling the wooden door shut behind her.

The woman now sitting opposite Doranei didn't move. She appeared to be studying his face, noting the dryness of his lips, his eyes darting towards the wine jug, the swelling cheek. It was a full minute before she spoke and by then his throat was burning for a drink.

"My name is Ostia," she said. "May I pour you some wine?"

Doranei's throat tightened. *Bugger again: Ostia.* He knew the name, of course, from the aftermath of the battle in Narkang. Dumbly Doranei nodded his head and accepted the goblet when she passed it. *Oh Gods,* he thought, *Zhia Vukotic herself. What in the name of Ghenna do I do now?*

"We wear symbols of those that are now at war with each other," Zhia continued, oblivious to his stream of thought, "and yet you seem remarkably quiet. What is your name?"

"Doranei, Madam."

"Madam? I think Mistress is the appropriate honorific here, young Doranei."

He blinked for a moment. It was strange to be called young by a woman who appeared less than thirty summers. "I didn't think you were the strictest adherent to the Circle's code, Mistress Vukotic."

"You will refrain from using that name, young man," Zhia snapped before her expression softened into an indulgent smile again. "It would be an inconvenience to me if anyone overheard you, one that would cause me considerable bother."

"My apologies," Doranei said, lowering his eyes briefly. "That was petulant of me."

"Ah, the king has taught you some manners as well. How refreshing. I do prefer assassins to be civilised; those who aren't tend to have something to prove. I can't stand men who are just waiting to be provoked."

"I doubt many of them stand for long." Doranei regretted the words immediately. King Emin encouraged a loose informality within the Brotherhood that sometimes made them speak their minds too easily. Some men, like the Farlan Lord, Isak, enjoyed being taken aback from time to time, but others had found themselves compelled to call the King's Man out—however stupid an idea that invariably was.

"A soldier's flattery, how sweet of you," Zhia purred. "With such a tongue you must have charmed more than your fair share of Narkang's maidens—that is, of course, if your king allows you to mix with ladies who enjoy such compliments. Please tell me he doesn't hide away you pretty young things."

The King's Man felt his cheeks redden slightly. Despite the mocking tone, Mistress Zhia's velvety voice seemed to run like a feather down his spine, making him shiver in curious delight and dread. He wondered if she was using magic on him—she was quite skilled enough—but he'd always been a fool for a pretty face, magic or not.

"Oh, I've embarrassed you now. I do apologise," the vampire twittered on. Doranei, forcing himself to look her in the eye again, saw she was enjoying acting the foolish noblewoman. "I'm sure the king doesn't want your sword to be blunted by such activities; weapons must be kept keen, after all. Still, I must make this embarrassment up, for surely I could not live with myself if I sent you away without redeeming myself."

Oh good, a vampire's playing games with me. This is likely to turn out well.

Zhia stood with a flourish and stepped with a dancer's grace to Doranei's side. She took his elbow and, with no apparent effort, lifted him to his feet. Her thin hands felt as solid as oak underneath him, her strength disconcerting in such a delicate form. Upright, Doranei was a good half-dozen inches taller than Zhia, but he felt as brittle as a fallen leaf in her hands. She deftly slipped the straps from his shoulders and drew his pack off him. The movement was surprisingly tender and Doranei found himself suddenly aware of her delicate perfume. As her lips parted slightly, Doranei felt his breath catch.

Oh Gods.

"So now, will you let me make it up to you?" Zhia leaned closer, unblinking as she stared up at him and he inhaled even more of the sweet scent.

Doranei nodded dumbly.

"Thank you," she whispered. He began to edge towards her lips just as Zhia stepped back. "In that case we should leave," she said firmly.

"Leave?"

"Of course," she said breezily. "You'll be accompanying me to the theatre tonight, and the curtain goes up soon."

"Theatre? But I—" Doranei floundered. "I can't, I've got to—"

"Nonsense," Zhia interrupted. "It will be an education for you; trust me that your king will not begrudge you the trip. Now, if you've found your feet, we should be off."

She didn't wait for a reply but propelled Doranei towards the shuttered door. He tried to protest, but the words wouldn't come. Instead he let Zhia guide him through the dim streets, past the glaring eyes of any number of city guards, until they arrived at a theatre surrounded by chattering citizens of all classes, all bedecked in their finest. Wreaths of henbane cascaded over the walls and scores of torches gave off long trails of scented smoke. As they approached, Doranei looked around with growing trepidation. Flickering shadows reached out around the shuttered barrows that surrounded the theatre.

Whispers skittered around the street, faster than the King's Man could catch to make sense of. The darkness loomed as they approached the gate, where a pair of albinos scowled at the pair of them but stepped back as Zhia met their gaze. When he passed through, Doranei felt a chill hush settle about his shoulders. As he walked into shadow, his only comfort was the firm grip of a vampire on his arm.

Oh Gods.

CHAPTER 16

AS LONG FINGERS OF CLOUD drifted silently past a crescent moon, Doranei made his way to the heart of the Northern district, to the house of King Emin's agent in Scree. It was at least two hours past midnight by his reckoning. His head had been throbbing since the play and he was struggling to be sure he had not been followed. The most likely candidate was Zhia herself, however, and he wouldn't stand a chance pitting his wits against the ancient vampire, not even if he were at the top of his game. The hot night air mixed with pain, wine and bewilderment was making it hard for him to remember the way.

The streets were dead, strange for a man whose training ground had been the never-sleeping criminal dens and murky side streets of Narkang. Doranei turned into a nondescript road and halfway down, after one last check around, slipped a key from around his neck and unlocked an unremarkable door set slightly below street level.

"And which of the six pits of Ghenna did you fall into tonight?" said a soft voice from the darkness within.

"One of the more curious ones, Beyn," Doranei replied. "Did everyone get over safely?"

"All present and correct. We thought you'd been taken."

"I almost was. I certainly wasn't in much state to carry on running."

"So?"

Doranei felt he didn't know Beyn well, despite being in the same unit for the past seven years. Beyond their service to the king, Doranei knew only that Beyn liked to spend his time charming women with his striking looks—usually only for the challenge.

"So I went to the theatre instead."

"The theatre?" Beyn paused for a few heartbeats before he chuckled. The Brothers all developed a rather twisted sense of humour sooner or later, characterised by the ridiculous wagers they were constantly making with each other. Doranei knew his story would amuse them all. "Well, I hope you enjoyed it. Go and make your report to the king now."

Despite his headache and injuries, Doranei smiled. A moment of interest, then he was dismissed. That was the Beyn he knew, aloof, insufferable at times, but always aware of his duty. Doranei crossed the room to the door. A dim glow spilled out from the hallway as he opened it and he looked back to see Beyn sitting with a crossbow cocked and pointing at the street door. They exchanged nods and he left in search of the king.

The nondescript house was large enough for the thirty members of the Brotherhood and the handful of others King Emin had brought along. It was surprisingly well built, for only a quiet murmur reached his ears from the other end of the corridor. Doranei thought of the house's owner, a locally renowned artist called Pirlo Cetess. It would be good to see him again—if he was still alive, of course. There were none of the usual decorations one would expect from a household in mourning, so perhaps their assumptions had been wrong when their messages had gone unanswered. He could only hope so.

"Doranei, so good of you to join us," King Emin commented as Doranei entered the main reception room. The king's head never rose from the papers strewn over a large mahogany table. By the light of a torch Sebe was shaving another's face. That was the way in the Brotherhood: they would trust none but each other to put a blade to their throats. That had been a little harder after Ilumene had gone on his killing spree, slashing some of the king's closest friends to bloody ribbons and carving his name into the queen's belly. But trust there must be, and certainly there could be no mirrors allowed in the house. A reflection lacked substance; it was too close to a shadow to be safe.

The king was dressed in grey tunic and breeches. Black braiding differentiated him from his men, but not from the shadows. "Are you hurt?" he asked.

"Not badly, but it'll be a week before my left arm is useful for much."

"Haven't been trying to feed guard dogs again, have you?" He chuckled grimly.

Veil, the man with the shaving bowl perched precariously on his lap, smirked and Sebe paused in his labours to push back his own tangled hair and grin at Doranei, his scarred cheeks crinkling as he did so. Doranei just blinked at the king and shrugged. When he had been five, Doranei had tried to pat a dog through the bars of a gate. The guard dog has taken half of his little finger and a piece of his childhood innocence, but the lesson had been learned. It hadn't been mentioned in Doranei's presence for years, yet the king remembered.

"I went to the theatre, your Majesty." That made King Emin look up, Doranei noted with satisfaction. "In the company of Zhia Vukotic."

The king went so far as to raise his eyebrows. "Well now, that is an interesting turn of events. I wonder how you managed to hurt yourself at the theatre." The king straightened and gestured towards a small stairway beside the fireplace, normally hidden by a bookcase. "Come and have a look at this."

Doranei followed the king up the narrow stairs into Cetess' private study, where the artist hid those academic interests that coincided with the king's. It was a small, windowless room, carefully removed from the eyes of the city, and Cetess' patrons, when they visited. The room was in complete disorder, papers and books scattered everywhere. A sense of dread twisted in his gut.

"Where is Cetess?"

"A good question," the king replied, gesturing towards the far wall. "So far we've not been able to find out exactly what happened, but there are more than a few worrying details." He pointed at a blank tablet, identical to those overlooking the king's bedroom, hanging on the wall. "Look."

It took Doranei a moment to work out what was wrong. The tablet, a smooth piece of purple Narkang slate cut from the same slab as its pair, was completely blank—and that was the problem; what happened to one happened to the other. They were delicate creations and easily damaged, but this hadn't been hurt. Only a thin wisp of chalk dust marred its dark purple surface.

"I might not know much about magic, but isn't that impossible?"

"I know quite a lot about magic," Emin replied, "as do Endine and Cetarn. We all agree that it *is* impossible. Neither of our learned colleagues have an answer."

"And you?" All the Brotherhood were in awe of King Emin's remarkable ability at problem solving.

"Perhaps the sheer impossibility is reason in itself? Magic is a fickle beast, and the advantage of not being a mage is that I do not pretend to be its master. Mages assume they understand the nature of that beast, but when one observes magic, it squirms through your grip."

"I don't understand, your Majesty."

"Neither do I," Emin said with a smile. "But this thing has been done; a thing we know to be impossible. Therefore what if the only way it could be accomplished is if we could easily recognise it as impossible? That the clandestine deed could only succeed if its secrets were betrayed."

"That was an explanation?"

The king laughed at Doranei's bemused expression. "Hah! Not quite, merely my thoughts on the subject. The message on the tablet in my room was not written by conventional means, else it would still be here. You cannot erase such a message once the tablet is broken. So the message was done by unconventional means, as a way to lure us here. The fickle nature of magic means that it can only be accomplished if the task fails."

"But we are here," Doranei objected.

The king raised a finger. "Here, and yet aware that we have been lured here, and thus forewarned of any ambush in the making; perhaps even protected until we have the opportunity to realise the trap exists." He shrugged, one long finger sweeping away an errant strand of hair. "It is only the makings of a theory, nothing more. I have yet to make sense of the idea."

"I wish you luck. Have you been able to find out what happened to Cetess? Was it—him?" Doranei was hesitant to speak Ilumene's name in King Emin's presence, the Brotherhood's only traitor, and loved as a son by his king.

Emin shook his head. "No, nothing certain. The servants tell of voices in the night, laughter echoing through the walls and shadows in empty rooms. There is little sense to be made of it, yet it is reminiscent of Azaer's deeds in Narkang." Emin bit his lip thoughtfully. "All we know for sure is that every single member of his staff swears that Cetess locked up the house as usual and retired to bed. When they awakened, the house was still locked, but he was gone. He hadn't slept in his bed. There was no sign of violence, no body, no keys."

"So what do we do now?"

Emin raised an eyebrow. "I think I should hear about your evening." He sat at the small desk protruding out into the centre of the room and fixed his piercing blue eyes on Doranei, who eased his pack off his shoulders as gently as his injured arm would allow and let it fall to the floor with a metallic thud. He did likewise with his leather tunic, eager to be rid of its steel-strengthened weight, and dropped into the other chair in the room.

He cradled his left wrist. "My night at the theatre," he muttered with a rueful smile, "came about because of the good aim of a Farlan agent."

"Now you're just teasing me," the king said.

Doranei held up his hands. "We're not the only ones interested in Scree, not by a long way. Here's what happened . . ."

King Emin and Doranei spent more than an hour, going over the faces in the crowd, the actors—and the vampire Zhia Vukotic. Doranei hadn't been able to concentrate much on the play itself—a tragedy of mistaken identity centred around three princes all falsely claiming to be the Saviour—as his pain grew throughout the evening, but he tried to recall every detail. He watched a grim resolve fall over Emin's face as he suggested, a little nervously, that one of the masked actors could have been Ilumene.

"But you could not swear to it?"

"No, his role was small." Doranei grimaced as he tried to clarify his suspicions. "There was something about the man's poise. He overshadowed the lead actors without having to speak a word."

The king didn't reply. His chair creaked alarmingly as he leaned back, scowling into the distance. Doranei began to wonder what state Cetess' wine cellar was in. All he could think about was spending what was left of the night in the loving embrace of a bottle.

"Come," the king said at last, and made for the door. "We should speak to Endine and Cetarn. I think they will have to provide our first lead." He opened the door and stopped, his hand wrapped around the brass handle.

For a moment Doranei saw his king as a weary old man, embittered and burdened. The brilliant blue of Emin's eyes looked dampened by age, and his hair in the weak light looked momentarily grey.

"Don't let me make this about revenge," Emin whispered. Doranei almost reeled in shock at the sudden show of weakness, but the king was lost in his thoughts and did not even notice. "Promise me that when it comes to it, you'll stay my hand."

"I—you don't mean to kill Ilumene?" Doranei asked in confusion.

"That's not what I meant. Ilumene is now a valuable servant for Azaer, there can be no doubt about that, but that was not the only reason he was turned. It was one betrayal I could not stand, the one that would cloud my judgment. When the time comes you might have to remind me that our true goal is not revenge. Azaer grows stronger now—the twilight reign may soon be upon us, especially given that we believe the prophecy mentions this city, and then there will be no time for petty vengeance."

Doranei's eyes widened. "And Coran? He"ll kill me if I get between him and Ilumene."

"Let me worry about Coran; our bond is strong enough to restrain him. We must find Ilumene and the minstrel, and work out what they are doing. Revenge will have to wait."

"In that case, I will be there to remind you."

"Thank you." The king straightened his back and stepped through the doorway. "But first, we have to find them."

The two mages they had smuggled over the wall into Scree while Doranei led most of the guards away were an unusual pair. No doubt there had been a good few jokes about getting Shile Cetarn's bulk over the wall, though they all knew it was Tomal Endine who would cause the most problems—Mage Endine looked like a sickly child, with thin arms and pale, squinting eyes. He barely reached his colleague's chest, but though he looked continually wary of being crushed by Cetarn's bulk, he could usually be found in the larger man's lee. If he had to run more than twenty yards, he would probably expire in a wheezing fit.

As weakness produced a constant nervousness in Endine, so Cetarn was infuriatingly cheerful, and as was often the case with close colleagues, the pair bickered and squabbled like an old married couple. Despite his physical frailties, Endine was also a fair battle-mage, and both had a grasp of the subtleties of magic that made them invaluable.

Doranei and the king found the pair at last in the attic, a dusty corridor running the length of the peaked roof and piled with discarded furniture, where they stood glaring at each other over a sheet-draped table that had been placed in the middle.

"Gentlemen," the king said, a note of warning in his voice, "we will not be having an argument at this time of night. Our presence here is supposed to be secret. There will be no repeat of last year's incident at the queen's birthday celebration."

Cetarn's head snapped up. "If you think I'm going to let him get away with—"

"You fat lying oaf," squeaked Endine furiously, pounding his fist on the table.

"I said *enough!*" the king barked, cutting both men off. "We have more important things to do than dwell on past squabbles. I asked you to discover what magic has been used in this house; have you discovered anything?"

The pair eyed each other warily until, with a shrug, Cetarn stepped away from the table.

"If there was magic done here, it was not recent enough to detect. Considering the time period you mentioned, and the subtlety I would expect from the spell, that is hardly surprising."

"But what we can tell you," Endine joined in, "is that there is a great deal of magic in this city; enough that my ears were fair ringing before we'd even got over the wall. Scree has no College of Magic, so either there just happens to be a lot of mages conducting research here, or something else is going on. There are a number of quite distinct flavours in the air."

"Can you tell them apart, identify their nature?"

"Certainly, given time," Endine said with a nod. "Tonight we will prepare this place and make it secure. I shall give Tremal a list of our needs and the Brotherhood can secure them tomorrow for us." Endine gave a nervy grin; he was a compulsive thief himself, and he was much attached to Harlo Tremal, a man who could steal almost anything. "Then half a day of rituals will ward this house in the normal way, and another half-day will suffice to consult our daemon-guides and begin the process of unravelling the weaves in this city."

"Good. You should know before you start that process that Doranei here spent the evening with Zhia Vukotic."

Endine blanched.

"I do not believe she poses a threat to us," the king continued, "but I hope I don't have to remind you that all vampires tend to be touchy, and Zhia possesses a Crystal Skull. Steer clear of her."

"Yes, your Majesty," Cetarn replied, nudging Endine, who, looking like he was about to be sick, nodded. Suddenly, Cetarn looked thoughtful. "That would explain some things. Are you likely to see her again?"

Doranei felt a prickle run down his neck as they all turned to him with expectant expressions. "I—ah, well, perhaps I could."

"Excellent. Try to find out how much she is using it."

"How do you propose I do that?" Doranei asked, aghast.

"I don't care how." Cetarn's plump lips widened in a smile. "However you can—my point is that the sheer scale of magic being used in the city could be largely explained by her use of the Skull, though I would be disappointed by her inelegance." He paused, lost in his thoughts, and frowned at the floor. "But the situation may have demanded it, I suppose."

"And you should know, your Majesty," Endine continued as his colleague trailed off into silence, "that there is a necromancer in the city."

Emin glanced at Doranei. "Could that be Zhia?"

"Certainly," replied Endine, as Doranei said "no." The King's Man hadn't intended to speak and felt a flush of embarrassment as soon as the word escaped his lips. Emin gave him an inscrutable look that lasted longer than Doranei would have liked, but eventually decided not to comment.

"I would expect an immortal vampire to be more than proficient in necromancy. That is logical. Whether she would bother with it is less certain—the discipline may be beneath a mage of her skill." Endine's tone was one of professional admiration. It reminded Doranei of how the king had spoken of his first meeting with Zhia on the streets of Narkang. "I would not expect her to lower her skills to that level often, and the activity we have felt is on a much larger scale, done by someone with great skill and strength, who does not fear detection.

"Of course," Endine continued with a preening expression, "we would not expect much of Scree's mages, or those left within the White Circle. I doubt they are as accomplished as Cetarn or I, so it might just be that the necromancer has a healthy contempt for the city's mages."

"Let us hope so," said Emin. "Well, Doranei, it looks like we will have to find you something more suitable to wear to the theatre next time. Gentlemen, finding this necromancer is your first priority. I suspect there will be few coincidences over the coming weeks, perhaps even this damned heat is part of it all. Azaer's games are complicated, usually obscure, but never lacking in purpose. That there is a powerful necromancer in the city will be part of that game; I want him or her found. The more of this puzzle we uncover, the better our chances of stopping whatever Azaer intends for Scree. I suspect this will be the shadow's boldest venture yet and I intend to spoil it."

CHAPTER 17

THE EVENING LAY THICK AND HEAVY on the city's streets. Twilight had brought only a slight respite from the fierce warmth and the cobbles radiated heat like cooling hearthstones. Without even a desultory breeze drifting past, Mayel sat slumped against the brick wall of the tavern and swigged warm ale that did little to allay his thirst. Beside him, Shandek was scrutinising every passer-by, occasionally running a hand through his long greasy hair as though he could brush the heat away.

Brohm was not with them. Shandek had sent the large man off with Shyn, one of his other thugs, on some errand that Mayel was not party to. Mayel hadn't pressed the issue: Shandek was keeping that to himself to make the point that Mayel wasn't yet in his inner circle, and wouldn't be until Shandek saw some of the profit he'd been promised. You played it carefully with Shandek, whether he was your blood or not. He could see Shandek's patience thinning.

Scree had settled into a piecemeal kind of existence now that summer had a firm grip on the city. The sun's reign had forced the inhabitants into a twilight lifestyle. They attempted to sleep at night and through the hottest part of the day, leaving dawn and dusk for business. The air was syrupy, draining, sticky on the skin, and Mayel found it an effort even to raise his cup. The last few weeks had seen a cycle of terrific thunderstorms hammering the city, each clearing away only to begin building for another onslaught. The next was now well overdue.

Mayel was finding it an exhausting existence. The strange half-days were wearing at everyone. The stall owners ringing the theatre no longer called in constant banter to each other, instead staring disconsolately out at the near-empty streets. The previous day one had taken a filleting knife to her neighbour, for no reason that Mayel could discover. The only sound now was the rustle of a poorly affixed poster that proclaimed the name of the theatre's previous play. Though the billing had changed today to a comedy called *The King's Mule*, one poster for the dour tragedy *A Lament of Feathers* still remained.

"What I don't understand," Mayel croaked, "is how those damn flowers stay alive."

"Flow'rs?" said Shandek, his voice slurred by torpor as much as alcohol. His head lolled as he fixed Mayel with a glassy look, for all the world like some ghastly animated corpse.

Mayel raised a finger and waved it indistinctly at the theatre. The surrounding walls were covered in long hanging bunches of henbane; its dark-toothed leaves glistened malevolently in the light of the torches that dotted the wall. Within a few days of the henbane being hung, buds had appeared and soon developed into bell-shaped yellow flowers. Despite the heat and the lack of either water or soil, the plants were thriving. During the day they were smothered in a constant hum of bees.

"Those stinking great things. The crops in the fields are withering, so how do those stay alive?"

"What do you know about flow'rs?"

"Not much," Mayel admitted.

"Shut up then. Look, the acrobats are comin' out." Shandek pointed to the theatre gates as they opened for six figures dressed in bright clothes. Three were the albinos Shandek and Mayel had already encountered, still barefoot, but now wearing coats covered in long strips of coloured cloth. Two of the others were men; one was slim and wiry, with diamond-patterned tattoos covering his arms and a bloody teardrop on his face, a mockery of a Harlequin's costume (though he was dressed in black, which no Harlequin would ever wear). The other was a sallow-faced individual who looked more a beggar than an actor. His hair was matted and filthy, his features drawn, his skin unhealthy, as though he had been sleeping rough for months now. That one was certainly no acrobat, but in his hands was a long wooden flute that provided a tune for the tumbling.

The sixth in their group was one of the reasons Mayel and Shandek were there. The woman with long rusty-red hair was a good few inches taller than her male companions, and the centre of the little troupe. Each step was sinuous and elegant; she was too graceful to be humanly natural, Mayel thought. When the woman danced, her hands and feet were so quick he could hardly follow the steps, but it was her precision and deftness that made his breath catch.

"Our friend is back," Shandek commented with a nod towards the theatre. On the second-storey roof of the theatre, almost hidden against the thick blanket of cloud, Mayel could just make out a figure. A cigar end glowed bright for a moment.

"Is it the same one?"

"Aye, I'd put money on it. Ilumene, he called hisself, won't forget him in a hurry. I've seen bully-boys of all sizes on these streets, and that's not one I'd mess with." Shandek gestured up to the roof and grimaced. "Even if he didn't have a crossbow on him."

"Why do you think he's there?"

"They're expectin' trouble," Shandek said. "You've only to walk down the street to see how tight-strung people are. I don't know what's goin' on here, but there's somethin' in the air and it's more than just a storm."

"What do you mean?"

"Have you been to temple recently?"

"Hardly," Mayel scoffed. "It's enough that the abbot makes me perform the devotionals every time I'm at the house without wasting more of the day at the temples."

"If you did, you'd notice you're not alone in thinkin' that. This time of year Belarannar's temple should be near-full, not 'most empty." He went to pour himself another drink and found the jug empty. He squinted hopefully into its open mouth before slumping back against the wall with a sigh.

"These last few weeks have been strange," he continued. "I've heard nothin' from Spider, though I know his boys have been busy, what with fights breakin' out all over the city and the city guard and Siala's troops circlin' each other. They don't even bother with madmen preachin' doom and destruction. I've had word the Devoted are sniffin' past our borders in the east and it won't be long before the Farlan make theirselves known."

"What do you think's going to happen?" Mayel asked anxiously.

Shandek belched, eyes fixed on the female dancer who was beginning to weave her hypnotic dance as the rat-like beggar played a slow, mournful tune.

"I think the Farlan have left it too late; heard this Mistress Ostia has got the mercenaries too well-drilled to break at first sight of the Ghosts ridin' up. Doubt they'll find it easy to take the city. We all know the Farlan have no stomach for a long war." He tried to spit on the floor, but his mouth was too dry and all he managed was a sticky gobbet that flopped out onto his chin.

Mayel's snort of laughter was quickly cut off by a sharp cuff to his head. He rubbed the sore patch and frowned at his cousin, but changed the subject. "So what's this new play they've announced then?"

"Called *The King's Mule*," Shandek muttered, his voice thick with drink. "It's rumoured they're goin' to execute a real criminal in the final act—that's why all these people are here." He gestured around and Mayel gave a start as he realised they were surrounded by a crowd, all chatting and whispering fervently.

So much for death being entertainment for the mob, Mayel thought, with a bitter smile. *The rich seem to have just as much of a taste for it.* "They're all here," he whispered, "noblemen, mages—even priests." He pointed at a man in the unmistakable white-streaked robes of Vasle, God of Rivers, who was haranguing three women, two of them in the robes of the White Circle. "They've all come to see; maybe we'll find a buyer tonight."

"That priest hasn't come to enjoy death. Vasle's a gentle God; he's here to object, I'll wager. And he's a brave one; that's Mistress Ostia he's tearin' strips off."

Mayel peered through the crowd of people. "How can you tell? Her face is covered by a shawl."

"See the one next to her, wearin' a sword with her dress?"

"I've seen a dozen different women from the Circle wear swords like that," Mayel objected, still unable to make out the faces.

"Aye, but you catch that one's face, you won't forget her in a hurry. You'll be dreamin' about kissin' her for a month!" Shandek grinned. "They say she don't like men much, but I don't believe that. Reckon I could put a smile on those sour lips."

"What about that Ostia then? Folk say she's a mage, and getting ready to depose Siala. How about her for a buyer?"

Shandek nodded thoughtfully. "Ostia could be the one; I've heard that too, but for the moment it's Siala givin' all the orders. First I'll watch 'em a bit. You need to find out what your abbot's playin' around with now—no more waitin'. Tellin' me you *think* it's some ancient magical artefact ain't enough—can't negotiate if we don't know what we've got to sell!"

"It's difficult," Mayel insisted. "If he gets suspicious, he'll leave, and take his chances somewhere else."

"You're runnin' out of time, cousin," Shandek growled. "Be bolder, like our friend the priest there."

Mayel turned back to see the priest becoming increasingly animated, shaking his fist at the women, his voice loud enough to make the whole street stop and stare.

"If that's being bold, I think I'll pass on it," he said. "The man's going to get himself thrown into a cell if he carries on that way. If he touches any of them, he'll be in trouble—Oh, there he goes!"

A mutter ran through the crowd as a scuffle broke out. Two guards had stepped in, one receiving a flailing elbow in the face for his troubles. The other grabbed the priest by the scruff of the neck, not even seeing the fist of a young nobleman as it arced towards his face. After that, there were only thrashing limbs and angry shouts for half a minute before the rasp of steel being unsheathed stopped everything dead.

"These nobles," Shandek said under his breath and he began to lever himself upright. "None of the bastards 'ave a sense of humour. Time for another jug."

Zhia stared down at the figure on the floor in distaste. The priest was a large man, but Legana had laid him out with one crisp punch. He was spread-eagled on his back, legs splayed out, one hand groggily reaching for his bruised cheek. Legana stood over him, sword drawn and levelled, holding off the men who had joined in the brawl.

"My dear, my respect for you just continues to grow," Zhia said out of the corner of her mouth, her eyes fixed on Mistress Siala as the ruler of Scree stormed over. The woman was flanked by rusty-skinned Fysthrall soldiers. In the flickering light their glistening armour shone weirdly, as though crude lamp-oil had been spilt on it. Zhia sighed inwardly. No doubt Siala would see it a slight that the priest had chosen Zhia to voice his complaints to. Siala was beginning to realise that Zhia rivalled her for power in the city, and she was taking every opportunity for confrontation. That the vampire gracefully backed down every time seemed only to goad her further.

"Mistress Ostia, what is the meaning of this disturbance?" The ruler of Scree looked drawn and weary. The constant politicking amongst Scree's nobles was clearly taking its toll. Zhia knew Siala was working night and day to maintain her support in the city and keep the opposition from uniting behind anyone else.

"A complaining priest, Mistress Siala, nothing of great consequence," she said soothingly.

"And his complaint?"

"The granting of permission to execute criminals on stage." She kept her tone conciliatory, her eyes low.

"And what do you propose to do about it?"

Zhia shrugged. "He was raving, and you yourself gave the minstrel permission. I have decided to assume he had been drinking, though that cannot excuse laying a hand upon a Sister of the Circle. I'm sure we can find a nice quiet cell for his temper to cool off."

Siala gave a brusque nod. "See to it. I doubt he'll try it again. Legana, whilst I commend your swift action, do remember that as a Sister of the Circle you should try to conduct yourself with a little more grace. We keep dogs for a reason." She waved a dismissive hand at the guards beside her and Legana bowed in acknowledgement, sheathing her sword.

"And now, Legana, you will accompany me to the play. I've hardly seen you since Mistress Ostia took you under her wing, and I think it is time we caught up."

She caught Zhia's eye and the vampire gave a miniscule nod. It was to be expected that Siala would interrogate Legana, so her story was ready prepared. With the briefest of bows to her companions, Legana followed as instructed.

As soon as Siala had moved on, Zhia beckoned Haipar over. "Have him put in a cell, give him a day or so alone to calm down."

"Yes, Mistress," Haipar said with mock solemnity. Zhia guessed Haipar was resenting being forced into respectable clothes to visit the theatre. Once the two battered guardsmen had hoisted the priest up and taken him away, the onlookers, realising this stage of the entertainment was over, began to drift inside. Zhia felt the pull herself, some force gently urging her in.

She stopped and turned to Haipar to see whether the Deneli had noticed the same, but Haipar seemed oblivious. She couldn't be sure the broad-faced woman from the Waste was even registering that people were walking past her. Haipar stared towards the gate, lost in thought, her face blank and empty.

The smell from the food-carts, burnt fat, tamarind and honey, suddenly washed over them. Zhia felt her mouth begin to water at the scent of honeyed meat on the wind, but her attention was focused on Haipar. The effect of the breeze was like someone shaking the shapeshifter awake; startled, Haipar looked around with a confused expression before finally setting off for the theatre entrance, faltering after a few paces when she realised Zhia was not beside her.

Zhia looked up at the roof of the theatre and the clouds beyond. Her nerves were alive with strange sensations, a prickling under her fingernails that she couldn't place: something familiar, yet curiously alien—rare enough in itself for an immortal, but a blend of contradictory strains that had Zhia confused.

There's something I've missed here, but what is it? I can feel magic surrounding this building but its nature eludes me. She stopped; through the gloom of night she suddenly made out a face on the roof of the theatre, looking down at her, apparently grinning at what had gone on below. All she could see was that face, the glow of a cigar end and the outline of what looked like a crossbow. *Who are you, and who's that crossbow for? This square is crawling with soldiers, so you can hardly be here for security.* As though she'd asked the question aloud the gargoyle-like figure disappeared in a flash of movement. Only a wisp of smoke remained behind, which soon disappeared to nothing.

"Perhaps I should be a little more direct in my snooping around here," she said out loud.

"What are you expecting to find?" Haipar asked, returning to Zhia's side.

"Answers, my dear." Before Zhia could say anything else, someone discreetly cleared their throat behind her.

"Your pet is back," Haipar said acidly, "and this time he's got ribbons in his hair."

Zhia turned and beamed at the men now standing before her. King Emin, in the centre, sported a magnificent broad-brimmed hat that kept his face in shadow. Doranei, at his side, looking considerably less at ease than his king, wore a high-collared formal tunic. He stood with eyes lowered and lips pursed, unable—or unwilling—to meet her smile.

Zhia inclined her head; the White Circle ruled here, and that was all the respect any man was offered. "It is delightful to see you again, sir," she said, careful of his title in such a public place.

Emin bowed low, sweeping off his hat. He was smiling. "Mistress, you honour me by remembering your humble servant." Zhia returned the smile. It was hardly a surprise that King Emin knew exactly how to act, and yet she found herself pleased all the same. When she did find the time to lock wits with this man, she suspected she would not be disappointed.

"And Doranei, how handsome you look!"

The King's Man glowered, and continued to scrutinise the cobbles at her feet.

Zhia looked at the remaining men, six members of the Brotherhood, dressed alike in dark tunics and high riding boots, these men were definitely bodyguards. The king looked more like a successful merchant; his lack of fashionable quirks made him almost anonymous.

"But your constant companion? Left behind?" Zhia enquired. There were quite a few white-eyes in the city, many of whom had been drafted into the Third Army to bolster the Fysthrall troops and set them well above the troops Zhia had influence over, so Coran would not have attracted undue notice. His absence surprised Zhia, and left her a little irritated—she had heard all the stories about the two having undertaken some obscure rite to link their minds, or souls, maybe, but she had not yet had the chance to observe them together.

"These are tense times," Emin replied, "and his temper is somewhat short, particularly in this uncivilised weather."

"Tell him I sympathise. Tense times indeed, and thus your presence here is a remarkable risk."

The king's face remained politely blank and inscrutable as he replied, "A necessary one, Mistress. I have taken a few precautions in case I am recognised by the Circle, your good self notwithstanding, but I'm not here to continue that fight. I have business that cannot be delayed."

Zhia looked at him for a moment, her head tilted on one side, as if she were pondering her next remark. Finally she sighed, and said, "I suggest you take care. Something is happening in this city, some sort of convergence. Your presence raises the stakes even higher."

Emin nodded. "That comes as no surprise," he said mysteriously. Then he turned his attention to the ornate theatre gates. "Look—I think the performance is about to start. We should find our seats."

"One of my companions has had to join Siala, and my box will be terribly empty. Doranei, would you give me the pleasure of your company?" Zhia asked, a smile trembling on her lips. "Haipar is no great fan of the theatre, and she does grumble so."

"Haipar? The shapeshifter?" Emin asked sharply, receiving a nod from Haipar in response.

"And she is not the only Raylin in the city," Zhia added as she offered her arm to Doranei. His cheeks flushed as he stepped forward and she beamed at him and patted his solid forearm with girlish affection.

Turning back to the king, she bade him goodbye. "It has been a pleasure, as always—and I hope this happy chance meeting will be but the first of many. It would please me if you would join me for dinner one evening." She grinned suddenly. "The Circle, for all its many talents, is not known for its conversationalists."

"Of course, Mistress," Emin said with alacrity. "And do be careful to return Doranei in one piece, he is somewhat delicate."

Ignoring the amusement of Doranei's fellows, Zhia smiled in reply and swept through the gates, Doranei in tow and Haipar following close behind.

Zhia had retained one of the best boxes, in the newly built second tier. The darkness of the corridor was broken only by thin lines of light that leaked out of the gaps between the thick canvas curtains covering each small doorway. They could hear muffled voices and the scrape of chairs as their fellow theatre patrons made themselves comfortable for the evening's entertainment.

To Zhia's surprise, her private box was already occupied. As Doranei politely held back the curtain for her, the oil lamp within illuminated a person—a man, she quickly realised—sitting with his back to the stage. He looked up and Zhia could see his tattoos, black feathers on both cheeks, and an ugly red scar that cut down one side of his face. Oddly—for the tattoos alone marked him as other—he was dressed in a labourer's shirt and cropped trousers.

"While the boy who served us last night was somewhat lacking in common-sense," Zhia commented as she entered her box, "I confess to being a little surprised that he has been replaced by a monk . . . albeit a monk of unusual habits."

"A former monk," the man replied. His sharp-featured face looked shifty, suspicious. "Vellern and I have parted company."

"And so instead you grant me your company: am I to be placed above the Gods?" She turned to Doranei as he peered past her at the stranger and said quietly, "Could you give us a moment alone?"

The King's Man gave a grunt, looking hard at the former monk before retreating.

"I'm not here to discuss the Gods," the man replied sourly. "The minstrel told me to speak to you. Your interest in us has not gone unnoticed."

"And you're here to warn me off?" Zhia said quietly. There was almost a sneer in her voice.

"I am here to say that we will not tolerate your spies any longer."

Zhia bent down to look the man in the face. "What is your name, little man?"

"My name? Jackdaw. My name is Jackdaw." His eyes betrayed his growing apprehension.

"Well now, Jackdaw," she snarled, ensuring he got a good look at her teeth and enjoying the way his face turned from white to green, "tell your *minstrel* that if he wants to frighten me, he needs to work a little harder than this."

"He—That was not the intention," the monk almost spluttered. "He hoped we could come to an understanding."

"And what exactly is it that you wish me to understand?"

"That we need not be competitors," the monk said, almost pleading, "that we could help each other—be allies."

"And exactly what help would I need from you, little monk?" Her voice was soft, and menacing.

"What do you need? My master has a particular talent for helping the ambitious." He sounded less shaky, back on firm ground. Ambition was something he could understand.

Zhia's hand darted out and she seized the monk around the throat. Jackdaw yelped and scrabbled at her fingers, but for all her apparent delicacy, he was helpless. She felt him reach for magic and the familiar coppery tang filled her mouth as she tore the energies from his grip.

Jackdaw gasped with shock. He began to tremble, as if he had only now recognised what danger he'd been sent to confront.

"My ambitions are my own. What do you think you can give *me*? What can I not take for myself?"

"How can you take something you know nothing about?" Jackdaw croaked. "What is more valuable in an age where the future is not certain than information?"

Zhia looked at him, considering. What else was going on in this city that she didn't know about? She knew spies for the Knights of the Temples were making overtures to Scree's élite, though they were hardly likely to fall for that. A necromancer was performing increasingly complex experiments somewhere in the poorer districts, but necromancers tended to be oblivious to politics. Neither were particularly interesting to her, at least at the moment.

"You presume much, for a failed monk," Zhia said, her voice laced with scorn. The idea that the minstrel might fill in the blanks in this increasingly complex puzzle was horribly tantalising, and so she rejected the offer out of hand—she knew her own weaknesses quite well enough to see when someone was playing on them.

"I am just the messenger," Jackdaw protested, quaking again,

"Well, messenger, get out." She pulled him up from his seat and shoved him towards the curtained doorway. "If your master wants to speak to me, he must do me the courtesy of attending on me in person."

As the monk stumbled through the curtain, she called softly, "And tell him to bring something real to bargain with. If I wanted promises whispered in the night I would find myself a love-struck boy."

Doranei watched the tattooed man retreat, then raised an eyebrow at the vampire.

"Don't give me that indignant face," she snapped, waving the Narkang agent back into the box. Doranei smirked, having at last elicited a reaction from her, but wisely said nothing as he took his seat next to her. Haipar poured them all a drink from the jug of wine conveniently found on the little table in the corner, then took up position behind Zhia. From there she could watch them both.

"So, Doranei," Zhia began conversationally, once she'd arranged her skirts comfortably, "what are you and your king doing here?"

He sighed. "I couldn't tell you even if I did know."

"Even if you did know?" Zhia repeated with a light laugh. "Oh, dear boy, you're a member of the Brotherhood, not some thick-skulled infantryman. It is a certainty that King Emin holds much back, but to believe that he would bring his élite guard to an enemy city and not so much as mention the eventual goal? Please, don't insult us both."

Doranei raised his hands. "What do you want from me? To give up the king's closest secrets? Yes, we're here for a reason, and no, the king hasn't said he wants that reason to be made public."

"I do understand, Doranei, but you need to remember that we are *not* enemies. The situation grows increasingly fraught in Scree, and even Siala must have noticed. Food is becoming scarce, Siala's own restrictions are starting to cause extra shortages, and this sucking heat is making the people restless. Civil order is on the verge of breaking down, and no matter how many soldiers there are on the streets, if the good citizens of Scree go on a rampage, we will not be able to contain them."

She looked back at Haipar, then at Doranei. Taking one of his hands in hers, she said, "Strange as you may find this situation, it might be that we should attempt to trust each other. There are enough hands being dealt into this game that it will take a combined effort to have any effect on the eventual result."

Doranei shrugged. "I will mention it to the king."

Zhia noted his expression and left the matter alone for the moment, but Haipar had no such sensitivity.

"He can't be here for political reasons," she told Zhia. "If the king were here to deal with the White Circle, he'd bring an army. If it were an assassination—of any kind—then why bother coming in person? He's here because he's looking for something, or someone, maybe. If he were a mage, I would guess at some sort of artefact, but as he's not, maybe a weapon?" She closed her eyes for a moment, perhaps to see her own deductions more clearly, and continued as if speaking to herself, "Perhaps, if it was Aenaris, but I can't believe Ostia wouldn't know if that was in the city. So that must leave us with a person—so who is it? A spy? A defector?"

"Interesting logic," said an accented voice from the other side of the curtain, "but still flawed—not even the magnificent Ostia could sense Aenaris if it is not being used."

Haipar jumped up, the scrape of her chair not quite masking the shiver of metal as she started to draw her rapier.

Zhia shook her heard at Haipar as a lithe figure flashed into the box. Almost before anyone had realised, Haipar's hand was stayed, then pale hands rammed her weapon fully back into its sheath.

"Let's not be uncivilised," the man murmured, placing a hand on Haipar's shoulder and guiding her back into her seat. The shapeshifter was white, unable to resist this strange man, though not because of brute force, but through some more subtle compulsion.

Zhia watched Doranei assessing the newcomer. He obviously didn't recognise the style of clothing, but he had noted the man's jet-black hair and his unusual dark blue eyes—few in this part of the world had eyes like those. Doranei glanced at her, then looked back to the man.

Dear Doranei, Zhia thought with a certain amount of satisfaction, *I don't think you'd have noticed his eyes in this light were it not for the fact that you resemble a butterfly watching the pin whenever I look at you.*

"I suggest you keep as still and quiet as a mouse," advised the newcomer.

Zhia was certain Doranei had recognised that however tough he might be, he stood no chance against this man. To survive in these dubious circles was to recognise when you were completely outclassed.

"Well, isn't this a rare honour?" she commented coolly, careful to ignore Doranei's meek acceptance of the order. Koezh, her elder brother, was not one for playing games, but there was no need for her to mark the boy out as anything more than an aide.

Koezh looked closely at Doranei and Haipar, then, deciding neither was a threat to him, relaxed and accepted the goblet Zhia was holding out to him. "You're playing lady of the manor again?" He lifted the goblet in a silent toast.

Zhia smiled. "It is the position I was born to, after all, so *playing* is not entirely the correct word."

"You didn't think so when you were growing up—it was all we could do to drag you out of the stables, or stop you running around after the falconer like a love-sick puppy."

"Ah, but as you see, I am now all grown up," Zhia said, "and a few years have passed since then, and more than a few since you last walked these parts. What brings you to grace our presence, dearest brother?"

Haipar, sitting stiffly, felt her eyes drawn to the black-hilted broadsword at Koezh's hip. This massive weapon was a far cry from the elegant rapiers most men considered the correct choice for a night at the theatre.

She was not alone in noting the sword. Zhia had no need to open her senses to feel how bloated with savage power Bariaeth was. The last king had poured all of his grief and rage into that weapon, and even now it exuded a cloud of choking sadness and hurt. *Oh my dear brother, our God-imposed curses should be enough for any person to bear—but you never could refuse another burden, could you?* She didn't need to voice her fears; her brother knew well the risks he took.

"Events are moving apace," Koezh told her. "Aracnan tells me a Saviour has arisen, so I thought it was time I stepped out onto this stage once more."

Zhia ignored his attempt at a joke; Koezh had always been a serious man, and rather dour; humour did not suit him. "The Farlan boy?" she asked. "How can Aracnan be so sure? It wasn't that long ago that you were convinced Kastan Styrax was the Saviour."

"He believes so." Koezh raised the goblet to his lips, but hardly wet his lips. "I'm sure Aracnan is a Demi-God, so perhaps *his* instincts are to be trusted—certainly more than mine," he added with a bitter smile.

"Is Aracnan here?"

"Somewhere. We made camp outside the city and he disappeared in the night on some business of his own."

"You made camp?" Zhia felt her foreboding grow. "Did you not come alone?"

Her brother frowned. "No; is that a problem?"

"Scree is witnessing some sort of convergence," Zhia said. "Did you bring Joy?"

Koezh nodded abruptly.

Doranei, who had been watching the exchange whilst trying to appear indifferent, tried to cover his inadvertent gasp with a cough—Joy was the Crystal Skull Koezh had inherited from his father.

Zhia gave a small, private smile; few people would expect her brother to come bearing joy; sometimes she felt the name given to that particular Skull had been something of a joke on Aryn Bwr's part. "So the Legion of the Damned is camped outside the city? I suppose I should have expected as much." Her brain was racing.

"What is the Legion of the Damned?" Doranei couldn't help but ask.

Zhia looked at him crossly, trying to warn him to stay out of this, then softened a little, drawn almost against her will to his innocence about such things. For some reason, she found it endearing. There were not many men able to make her forget the centuries between them.

"The Legion of the Damned is well-named," she told him. "It's an army of mercenaries. My younger brother, Vorizh, made the mistake of turning a necromancer to vampirism several hundred years ago. The combination has proved, ah, troublesome." She grimaced delicately. "In this case, the necromancer had hired mercenaries to protect him and his lands, and in one of his most successful experiments he used a spell to take their life-force and replace it with magic. They did not take kindly to this—although they are now extremely powerful, and of course, they're untouched by the effects of time. Think of the Damned as an army of minor Raylin and I am sure you will understand the danger."

She turned back to her brother. "Something is drawing power of all kinds to the city—more than a score of Raylin, the remaining White Circle mages, the King of Narkang, and a necromancer I do not believe is allied to any faction. Now we have added Aracnan, who makes all of the fifteen or more Raylin I've employed pale into insignificance, two of the Vukotic family and at least two Skulls. There is also the immediate prospect of Scree being attacked, either by the Farlan, or by the Knights of the Temples—or maybe even both.

"What other forces remain hidden, that I do not know. The Farlan Lord holds two Skulls, and the minstrel who commands this troop of players wears an Augury Chain around his neck."

Beside her Doranei gave a splutter of alarm and cried, "What? No!" before lowering his voice and whispering, "Oh Gods, are you sure?"

"Certain," she said. "I saw it myself."

"Do you know his name?"

"Rojak."

Doranei cursed under his breath, his fingers clenched into fists. "So it's true then."

"What is true?" Zhia said, surprised. Now here was another piece of the puzzle, perhaps. "You know this minstrel?"

Doranei's eyes drifted past her towards the stage, where a flutist was coaxing slow, mournful notes from his instrument. Zhia reached out and snapped her fingers in front of his face to gain his attention again.

"Doranei, listen to me! Do you know this minstrel? Is this why the king is here?"

Doranei shook his head. "Not exactly; but we had hoped to . . ." His voice tailed off as he found himself turning back to the stage, then he wrenched himself back to his companions. "I must inform the king immediately."

"Not yet," Zhia said firmly. She pointed to a tall man dressed in robes of green and gold emblazoned with a pair of bees flying upside-down who had launched into the narrator's opening speech. The costume was finished off by a jester's cap. "The performance is starting, and if you leave now, you will draw attention to yourself. One of the players was on the roof with a crossbow earlier. Would this Rojak's associates recognise you?" Doranei nodded, glancing towards the curtained entrance with suspicion. Koezh saw the concern and shook his head.

"There is no one out there, not even a servant."

He slumped a little in acquiescence. "I can find the king at the interval, then. They will not kill him here."

"Are you sure? It might be too tempting to ignore."

"As sure as I can be," Doranei said. He looked uncertain, trying to balance his own knowledge with what help Zhia might be able to provide. "Their feud is a long-standing one," he started, "and just assassinating the king lacks . . ."

He floundered for a moment before Zhia interjected, "The personal touch? The need a man has to drive in the knife himself?" She sighed. "The centuries go by and folk do not change. I hope that if the time comes, your king will prove himself the better man and not hesitate. After all, I cannot have an opponent in Heartland who is prone to grandstanding—he will be a sore disappointment to me."

Doranei nodded, but his attention was on the stage again, his face thunderous.

Interesting, Zhia thought, *this Rojak has really got under the king's skin. I wonder what exactly did the minstrel do, and why?* As that thought crossed her mind, she turned to follow Doranei's gaze. Now she acknowledged both the colours and the cut of the narrator's clothes. *So this play is merely to goad King Emin? That means they know he's here already. But what purpose does this all have?*

Zhia forced her own eyes away from the stage and back to the conversation at hand. "I shall have to tighten security in the city. We have so many strangers wandering the streets that it's only a matter of time before people start to die." She looked at the two men facing her. Koezh wore a look of brotherly affection, a welcome change from the drawn, world-weary face he generally sported. Doranei appeared to be gripped with some sort of ghastly fascination as he looked from one sibling to the other.

"Please don't take offence," Doranei began hesitantly. Zhia immediately pouted, causing him to stammer as he continued, "but, since you are only masquerading as a member of the, ah, the White Circle—"

"Why do I care?" Zhia finished for him.

Doranei nodded and bowed his head.

"We are cursed to care, my brother and I. The Gods saw to that in their final judgment. Do you know nothing of our history?"

"Little," Doranei admitted. He looked around to check no one was paying them any attention, and lowered his voice even further. "I know that you were turned into vampires, the undead. To stay alive you are forced to drain the life from others, and the touch of sunlight will set your skin aflame."

"The youth of today, they live only for the moment." Zhia gave a schoolmistressy click of the tongue. "That was not the only curse bestowed that night—foresight I could not have expected from a God, yet one of them did realise that to be such a monster would drive a person mad, so to ensure every drop of horror was wrung from this punishment, the Gods decreed that we would *not* decline into madness, but that our sense would remain, and our wits would be untouched by either the passing of years or guilt over our deeds." She could feel her fingers tighten as she thought of that gnawing guilt; it had been her constant companion down through the uncountable years.

She looked away from Doranei, not wanting to see the horror in his eyes as she continued, "They wanted to make sure we would always understand the fear in a man's eyes as we drain his life, and that we would always be sickened with compassion for others. We will never become inured to this. Our people were punished for following us out of blind loyalty. In turn, we now feel the suffering of innocents, more strongly than you could ever imagine."

"And my presence may only worsen the situation," Koezh surmised.

"Exactly," Zhia said wearily. "Which is why I want you to leave."

"Leave?"

"You and your Legion can do nothing to prevent this city descending into chaos. Anything you do will only fuel the fire."

"So you would have me hang back and do nothing? Let the White Circle and the Knights of the Temples determine the course of the next Age?"

"Our time will come, but not yet." Zhia rubbed her arm, where the tight-fitting silk clung uncomfortably in the heat. "The best thing you could do is march south."

Koezh cocked his head at her. "You think Lord Styrax is that much of a threat, even with such a great distance between him and the Menin homelands?"

"I do," Zhia said with certainty. "In the thousands of years since the

Great War, has there ever been a warrior to match you? I doubt it myself, yet Kastan Styrax cut you down and took your armour as his prize. If there is any man in the entire Land who can conquer the Chetse and win the hearts of their warrior orders, I think it is Kastan Styrax."

"And then he will not need fresh troops from the Ring of Fire," Doranei finished. "If he wins the loyalty of the Chetse, who knows how far his empire might stretch?"

"There might be no limits. If the city-states of the West descend into chaos, as they are threatening to do, they will be unprepared for the Chosen of the War God."

"Narkang is ready, and the Farlan are even more powerful than the Chetse," Doranei objected.

Koezh turned to the young man with an amused expression. "Narkang is ready? Narkang was saved only by a stroke of fortune, so I hear. If the White Circle had taken the king and his city, your precious Three Cities would have quickly followed. As for the Farlan, years of unrest have weakened them, and now their greatest leader in a thousand years is dead. In Lord Bahl's place they have a young man said to have the fury of a storm running through his veins, bearing gifts so laden with power and the weight of history that even his own generals must be nervous." Koezh leaned over Doranei and gave the younger man a cold smile. "I would say your readiness could be improved a shade. At the very least, your king should conclude affairs in these parts and see to his own borders. Complacency is a foolish thing to die for."

Zhia smiled as her brother gave Doranei a condescending pat on the shoulder and gestured towards the stage beyond. "Now be quiet and watch the play. A little culture will do you good."

With the briefest of touches on her gloved fingertips, Koezh left soundlessly. That was their way. Experience had taught them that their encounters should be brief and tender, else arguments break out, with dramatic consequences. Zhia was actually ahead in those stakes, having murdered her brother three times now, but they had long ago agreed that the novelty of killing each other had worn off and it was too much of an irritation to do so merely out of pique.

He would do as she asked; Scree was her affair now and he wouldn't interfere. As the Land edged closer to the brink of ruin and change flickered across the skies, they both knew this might be their best chance.

Zhia smiled.

CHAPTER 18

A WALL OF CLOUD SURROUNDED THE CITY, obscuring the moons and stars. Jackdaw could sense it enveloping the city, drawn by one man's call. The streets simmered in an unnatural humidity, as if the city were festering in its own sour humours. Wherever there was a flat roof he could see bedding laid out, and restless bodies shifting and squirming in the oppressive heat. The citizens of Scree were desperate to escape the stinking closeness of their houses but, in truth, outside was little better.

How long since I felt the breeze? he wondered. *It must be just a few days, yet the memory feels more like a dream.* From their high station, looking down on the dark bulk of the theatre, he could feel the heaviness in the air, a building storm that had refused to break, but instead lingered with sullen obstinacy, prickling the hairs on his neck. The sudden downpours of early summer had stopped, leaving the population panting like dogs and staring up at the sky with pleading eyes.

The taste of blood persisted in his mouth. He'd bitten his tongue in surprise when that bully from Narkang had crept up on him earlier. Ilumene's mocking grin had shone out from the shadows when he had least expected it. He probed the cut, wincing at the sting, but persisting, because in some strange way it reminded him he was still alive. Was it pain to drive away the numb aching in his heart, or just a reminder that he was human, with a human's foibles? But every time he felt the cut, he saw the blood, the man's life spilled out onto the stage, the final bitter act of their latest play.

"Now," Rojak announced from his right. Jackdaw flinched, constantly taut with dread whenever he was in the minstrel's presence. It was some three hours till dawn, and the city was almost silent in its miserable discomfort. Jackdaw had to stifle a yawn. He couldn't remember the last time he'd slept, not properly. He wouldn't tonight either, not with the sight of blood filling his mind.

"We are entertaining Scree with a fine barbed comedy, do you not think?"

Jackdaw said nothing. The play was mildly amusing, in a gross, simplistic way, but the initial humour was soured by the murder at the very end.

Though Jackdaw—like the whole city, it appeared—had known it was coming, the sight of so much blood had sickened him. He'd turned his head away as the criminal plucked from the city gaol had howled and flopped around on the stage, interrupting the play by his refusal to die quickly. Ilumene, eyes glinting with fierce delight, had pointed out the anonymous figure of King Emin as the audience shuffled out in a cowed silence. The king's face had been as dark as thunder. The man from Narkang had not said why he hated his king so deeply, and Jackdaw was afraid to ask. Ilumene constantly hovered on the brink of savagery; the man's handsome features invariably twisted into a cruel scowl at the very mention of this king.

Thinking about Ilumene's hatred brought Jackdaw full circle back to the hateful play. Already the stallholders surrounding the theatre were lost to the spell carved into the timbers of the theatre's wall as it was being constructed. A few continued to work, scarcely even aware of their motions but driven by long-ingrained habit, but the rest had taken to roaming the streets muttering about ghosts, already lost to the madness. They were feeling the bitterness and gloom that echoed from the play's every line and washed out over the city by the minstrel's magic. Just the previous morning he'd listened to a fruit-seller, muttering to himself, hands clasped together, head twitching nervously, staring down at the feet of those passing by. He was terribly afraid that the man had been quoting a line of prophecy, from "The Twilight Reign": *Six temples, empty and crumbling—darkness heralded by song and flame.*

Lost in his thoughts, Jackdaw almost missed Rojak's question, until Ilumene turned slowly to face him, his dagger hanging loose from his fingers as always. The edge was razor-sharp, but somehow Ilumene never nicked himself, even as he spun the blade through his fingers. The cuts and scars covering his hands were all intentionally inflicted; the only time Ilumene seemed to notice the knife in his hands was when he was slicing a new pattern into his own skin.

Quickly Jackdaw muttered something congratulatory, desperate to get Ilumene's eyes off him. Rojak smiled at his words and affected a preening of his clothes. If the man had not filled Jackdaw with such creeping dread, it might have looked comical. The minstrel's clothes were worn and tatty, and he gave off a stench of putrid flesh, for his body was rotting from the inside out. Soon he would be dead, but until then his awful prescience and unnatural powers burgeoned with every passing day. Jackdaw had no desire to know what disease Rojak had contracted, but it would not be coincidental. Their master was too cruel and calculating for that.

"And what is a vital ingredient of all comedic works?"

Jackdaw frowned, trying to find the right answer, but even the words of the script refused to be pinned down.

"A mistaken identity, of course," trilled Rojak, for all the world as if they were having a sparkling conversation, "with the inevitable humorous results."

Humorous? I doubt anyone but Ilumene would find them funny, Jackdaw thought, but he said nothing. The opium Rojak smoked didn't ever cloud his mind; he was always listening, ever ready to pounce on a hesitation or a misjudged word. Jackdaw had made that mistake once, and the thought of doing so again sent shivers down his spine. The shadow watched constantly.

Rojak peered over the edge of the rooftop they were stood on, looking intently down at the empty street below. "And as it happens, we know someone who is desperately seeking a face in the crowd, don't we, Ilumene?"

"We do, and it would be rude to disappoint the man," Ilumene purred in agreement. "Especially when he was like a father to me for so many years."

Whenever Ilumene spoke, it unnerved Jackdaw. The man was powerfully built, and he had hard callused palms that felt like wood when he slapped Jackdaw's face. He looked like a professional soldier, but his accent was cultured, suggesting intelligence behind that brutal façade. He was strangely hypnotic, and he could, when he chose, be as charismatic as a white-eye. At those times, Ilumene frightened Jackdaw even more than usual.

"Surely he'll kill you?" Jackdaw croaked.

"I doubt it," Rojak said. "Ilumene's former comrades would never dare, for the king will want to deal with this personally. I find their keenness to find us positively heart-warming."

"You want to run the risk of them tracking you down as well?"

Rojak raised an admonishing finger. "But then there would be no mistaken identity, thus no humorous unmasking once it's too late."

Jackdaw struggled on. "You want me to make someone appear to be you, or Ilumene?"

"Only a few weeks in the theatre and already you are learning its forms!" Rojak beamed. "They're here to find Ilumene, so let them see what they want to see."

"But who? Who is it you want them to kill?"

"Come now, that would hardly be fair on our poor actor. He is a man who has done nothing wrong, so he shall not be harmed." Rojak waved Jackdaw away dismissively. "Go and begin preparations for the spell. It must be ready by midday."

"Where shall I meet you?"

"Oh, not me, I have other business to attend to. Ilumene, was there a member of the Brotherhood you held in higher regard than the others?"

The big man frowned. "Beyn," he said after a moment's thought. He balanced the dagger on the back of his fingers. "Ignas Beyn is one of the few who is not blind to the king's faults. He's loyal to his master, but he's no fool."

"Then Ignas Beyn shall be our second party, but whether he walks through flame or darkness, he shall see it through untouched." Rojak spoke slowly, as if intoning a spell. The minstrel was not a mage in the classical sense, but he wielded great power, an understanding of magic's nature so profound it contained its own force. Jackdaw, a fair mage in his own right, suspected this was closer to how a witch worked, harnessing the brutal potential of the Land itself. This was an unforgiving talent, and laden with consequences; Jackdaw preferred using magic he could channel, rather than standing between mountains and hoping not to be crushed as he directed them to move.

And both bit players to survive, Jackdaw thought grimly. *Both to witness Azaer's strength; a strength born in weakness. Who could have guessed that embracing what makes it feeble would give the shadow such power? It stands between darkness and light and so directs both. When a man's own strength is turned against him, what defence can he possibly muster—and what are the Gods but power incarnate?*

"I assume you will need Ilumene to accompany you for the spell?" Rojak said, his attention returning to Jackdaw. "Well then, you both must be at the tavern called The Lost Spur at midday, where you will observe a stranger, a Menin."

"Do you know his name?" Jackdaw asked. "There are quite a few who could pass for Menin in the city. How will I know which is the right one?"

"He is also looking for someone," Rojak replied, his eyes distant, fingers running softly across the strings of his lyre. "His name is Mikiss, Koden Mikiss."

From the darkness below, Jackdaw heard a sharp hiss cut through the night.

The others heard it too. Ilumene's free hand moved surreptitiously to his sword and Jackdaw saw a cold smile creep onto Rojak's lips. The sound had come from the alley, too soft to be heard in anything but the dead of night. Jackdaw recognised it immediately: one of the four Hounds, the forest-spirits called gentry, enslaved by Rojak. Now the spirits stood guard, and that noise meant they had seen someone watching their new master.

"Oh Princess," said Rojak, almost apologetically, "we did warn you to keep your nose out of our affairs."

Jackdaw glanced at Ilumene, who looked as confused as he was. Before either could speak a snarl broke the silence in the shadowy alley below. It was swiftly followed by the rasp of swords being drawn. As Jackdaw craned to see, he was rewarded by a sudden flash of movement, a glimpse of metal and a bone-white mask.

The spy slashed behind him as he ran, catching nothing but not waiting to look back as he jumped up onto a wall and crouched to leap again. Before he could move, a pale limb flashed out and pushed him backwards off the wall. The spy rolled as he hit the ground, cutting up again with twin swords. One caught in a wooden ladder and stuck fast; he didn't wait to try to pull it out but immediately abandoned the weapon and darted away, heading for the mouth of the alley. From the shadows one of the Hounds appeared, kicked away the spy's legs and disappeared back into darkness again. The man crashed down, hitting the floor hard and taking a moment to recover before he scrambled to his feet. He'd lost his other sword now and was in the process of drawing a long dagger from his belt when a muscular hand reached out from beyond Jackdaw's sight and dragged the spy away.

The man shrieked, and Jackdaw flinched. The snarling that followed told its own story and he could not help but picture the long, sharp teeth tearing the spy apart—but somehow the spy managed to pull free, and it was the Hound that staggered back, blood running from a long gash across its chest, ripping open both leather coat and flesh. Jackdaw could see blood on the Hound's muzzle, but it was the spy who darted forward to press the advantage, a curved dagger raised high and threatening.

He didn't get more than two steps before a blurring shape hit him in the shoulder and bore him to the ground. Jackdaw saw him turn and try to stab his new attacker, but a third Hound fell upon him at that moment and clamped its jaws around his forearm. The man howled in pain as one slashed down with its claws and lunged forward to snap at his throat. The screams stopped, though the spy fought on for a few more seconds, beating at the Hounds with his free hand, kicking wildly, like a panicked deer.

And then it was over. The Hounds bent low over their kill, rending the spy's flesh from his bones, and Jackdaw could bear to watch no longer.

As he turned away, he realised Rojak hadn't noticed—normally the minstrel took inordinate delight in death, but for some reason he was still looking out over the empty rooftops, a satisfied smile on his face.

"Perhaps you will heed the warning a little better next time, Princess," he said to the night.

Without warning, a great flurry of movement appeared beside Jackdaw, fat trails of shadow suddenly rippling away like leaves caught in a whirlwind. Jackdaw and Ilumene both jumped back, the latter drawing his sword in the same movement. Rojak stayed still, betraying no surprise at the darkness coming to life a foot or two from where Jackdaw had been standing.

"That was a poor lesson, then," snarled Zhia Vukotic as the movement coalesced to reveal the vampire, clad in a white fur-trimmed evening gown that accentuated the rusty stained skin of her neck and shoulders. She stepped forward, sparing a withering look for Ilumene, who had been advancing to meet her until Rojak raised a hand to stop the man.

"I sent the man to gather information and information is what I have gained," she told the minstrel. "Anything else is no great consideration."

For a moment it looked as if she would storm past the three men towards the stair that led to the ground, then something stopped her.

She leaned close to Rojak, her delicate nose screwed up in disgust at the smell, and spoke softly, calmly. "You think to issue me with warnings? Perhaps you don't quite understand the balance of power in this city. Your theatre may have official sanction from Siala and protection from the Spider, but if you are determined to see unfortunate accidents happen to all your players, I will grant that wish. No patron, however powerful they may consider themselves, can protect you from me."

"Of course, Princess," Rojak replied in his usual tone, quite unfazed by the immortal vampire standing close enough to pluck his heart out. Jackdaw shivered at the man's lack of fear, his absence of any real emotions. If Zhia did pluck his heart out right now, what would she find in her hand? A healthy organ, still beating, or a rotten piece of carrion? Was there anything Rojak had left to fear?

Rojak gave a small sigh. "But in the service of my art, what sacrifice would be too great?"

"There's your tavern, sir." Major Amber pointed. "Almost there now."

Mikiss followed the soldier's outstretched finger and tried to summon up a smile, but in the blistering sunshine, labouring under the weight of his pack, he couldn't find the strength for anything more than a grunt. He began to tramp towards the tavern. The crumbling bricks of these buildings seemed to have been burnt red by the unholy summer sun. Everything he'd seen in Scree told of a careless neglect; even the larger buildings looked dirty and battered when they closed on them.

"What a shithole of a city," muttered one of the men behind them. The two soldiers acting as bodyguards were brothers, Keneg and Shart. They didn't look particularly similar, Shart being a few inches taller than his older, broader brother, yet their voices were almost identical. Mikiss could never be sure who was speaking—although Shart was always the more talkative—unless he was looking at them.

"That's saying something," Major Amber replied. He smiled back at the two behind, the strange eyes that gave him his nickname glinting in the light. "Don't you two come from Dorin? I was there in the summer, after the snows had gone; never seen such a festering rat-pit in all my life."

"We can't all be brought up in the lap of luxury, Major."

Amber gave a snort. It was an old joke, repeated interminably during the journey. Mikiss had come to the conclusion that all soldiers sniped and teased each other, however absurd the reason. Whenever the mood fell sombre, there was always a piece of foolishness to fall back on, a welcome distraction to Death's hand forever resting on their shoulders.

Amber had been born into minor nobility and was thus accused of being pampered and indulged, while Shart spoke too much and Keneg not enough. It was as simple as that, but none of them ever tired of the same old jokes. When they had been hiding from a group of soldiers one night, Mikiss had found himself glad of their idiotic levity.

Now the major stopped his small party, stepped into the shadow of a building and let his pack fall to the dusty ground. The others followed him, and Mikiss gave a heartfelt groan as he dropped his pack, already thankful for the ease of his torment, however brief.

"Now boys," Amber said, looking warily at the passers-by, "just because the end's in sight, doesn't mean we're going to relax. Sir, you'll be staying here with Shart and the packs. Keneg and I will go and give some names to the barkeep. I've no reason to think there's going to be a problem, but we don't take risks and I'm buggered if I'm running from the City Watch carrying that pack if I don't have to." He had decided at the start that the timid army messenger would be a clerk to anyone they met, rather than the leader of their group. That left him in charge, at least in public, and mostly Mikiss preferred it that way.

Major Amber took a moment to pull his scimitars from his pack and slide the holster straps over his shoulders. He unwrapped the bleached leather from around the hilts and settled them into their sheaths, giving each a tug to ensure he could draw them without restriction. He straightened his shirt, rubbing a hand distractedly over his belly. He was a professional soldier and disliked being without his armour, but this heat made it impossible to wear even the lightest of mail. All three found themselves unconsciously checking for armour that was no longer there.

Keneg slapped the scabbard of his broadsword, a thick weapon Mikiss thought of as an unholy cross between sword and axe. He nodded at his brother and stepped up beside Major Amber.

"If there's no reception to speak of, I'll send Keneg out and have the beer waiting for you."

Shart whispered urgently, "See if there's anything better than that piss we got in the last place. Bloody westerners and their poor excuse for beer; that stuff was halfway to water!"

"You'll get what you're given," Amber growled goodnaturedly, "but if it'll shut you up for half a minute I'll see what I can do."

The pair strode off, Keneg half a pace behind the major, continually scanning the street as befitted his role of bodyguard—though any local thug would have to be brave to the point of madness to tangle with Major Amber. There was nothing noble or gentle about the tall Menin officer. His weathered face bore a number of scars, one of which was obviously a sword cut, and his shaved head added to the brutal façade. That Amber was dressed in fine clothes was a minor point, and of no importance once one had taken in the size of his scimitars and the brutal lines of his face.

Mikiss watched them walk away, then realised he didn't have to be on his feet any longer. He sat down heavily on his pack and gave a sigh. For a few minutes he just watched his feet, unrecognisable to him without the elegant cavalry boots he normally wore. Eventually his attention wandered to the building sheltering them. The brick looked old. It was crumbling at the edges, and dark streaks showed years of run-off from the neighbouring building. Five yards on, the ground dropped away a little, though Mikiss could see no reason for it; whatever function the drop had served was long-forgotten. Now all it contained was the shrunken corpse of a small dog, little more than a bag of bones and scrappy fur, curled awkwardly in the corner. It was attended by half a dozen lacklustre flies. Mikiss frowned. Something about the corpse looked odd.

He leaned forward to look a little closer. It was the dog's legs—it wasn't the angle of its body that was strange, but the length of the rear legs, which were too short. With a start Mikiss understood and turned away, revolted: the little dog's hind feet had been cut off. "Gods," he muttered, "is that what they do for sport in this city?"

He pulled off a sandal and rubbed the dry, blistered skin on the ball of his foot. The sandal was Chetse Army-issue, with three straps winding around the ankle to hold it secure. He was glad not to be wearing the heavy fur-lined boots reaching halfway up his thigh favoured by the Menin cavalry, but the grit of Scree's baked roads had worked its way between every toe and under every nail.

"Good soldier's foot you've got there," Shart commented, leaning over to look at the underside.

"Filthy, you mean?"

The soldier chuckled, knelt down and grabbed the foot, much to Mikiss' alarm. He twisted it slightly and pointed down at the rough surface underneath. Once Mikiss was paying attention, Shart gave the foot a firm slap with his massively strong sword-arm. Mikiss gave a yelp of surprise and snatched his foot back.

"That's what I meant," Shart said with a knowing glint. "They may be ugly and filthy, but you don't get much tougher than a soldier's foot. Trust me; if I'd done that before we set out, you'd be crying like a girl." He stood up with a satisfied smile, and stuck his thumb into the thick leather belt that held his daggers and the long-handled axe he was so proficient with.

Mikiss stared at his foot, then back at Shart. "I think you meant to say 'crying like a girl, *sir*,' didn't you?"

"That I did, sir. Apologies for the slip, but I hope you'll let me blame it on the weather." Shart grinned. The army messenger was not one to take his rank seriously.

"That I will," Mikiss replied, wiping an already-sodden sleeve over his face. "Gods, I didn't expect it to be so hot here."

"None of us did. Don't feel natural if you ask me, sir. The way folk have been walking past with their eyes glazed over, and how they're dressed, I don't reckon it's normally so hot this far north."

"I think you're right," Mikiss replied, squinting at the handful of people in the street. "Those soldiers on the Gate obviously didn't have the uniform for this sort of weather."

"Not soldiers, sir," Shart said with a reproachful tone. "Those buggers are only city guards, useless bastards who couldn't make it into the army."

"I thought the army took anyone?"

"Aye, it does." Shart broke off to squint towards the tavern. Mikiss turned to look too, but it was only a well-built man leaving the building, not Keneg. "But there are always some who don't have the stomach for it. Watchmen still get weapons, but they have a bed to sleep in every night and they never face real enemies. Give me any twenty regular troops and I'll cut through a hundred city guards like they were made of butter."

He cocked his head at Shart. "But if they've got eighty more weapons than you do—"

"Hah! Don't mean nothing—a hundred men is just a confused crowd till they're trained. If we get in a fight here, you'll see what I mean. The city guards won't know where each other are, so they'll just get in each other's way. Keneg and Amber know where I'm going to be, what I'm going to do next. I don't do things to surprise them, so they're watching my back at every step." Shart smacked a hand against the head of his axe, tied to his belt with leather thongs, and pointed towards the tavern. "There's the little one," he said, reaching for the packs at his feet.

Mikiss sighed and hoisted his own onto his back, then realised he was going to have to carry Amber's as well. "It seems a bit rich to call him 'the little one'—Keneg's twice as broad as you are."

"Ah true, the boy does like his beer." Shart gave Mikiss a comradely slap on the shoulder and chuckled as he bounced against the wall. "But he don't like it when people call him the ugly one."

A wave of mixed odours hit Mikiss as he stepped over the threshold: sweat and straw, mildew and spilt beer. The tavern stank. It might be no dirtier than any other he'd been in, but the unnatural weather had produced a stench that had an almost tangible presence, one that Mikiss could feel even in the back of his throat. It made him gag, and even Shart grimaced.

The main room had a square central bar of oak and stretched a good ten yards. With no fire or lamps, Mikiss struggled to adapt to the gloom after the glare outside, despite every window and door being propped open like a desperate plea for the wind to return. The major leaned on the bar talking to a massive broad-shouldered man with his curling beard tied into a fat bunch that swung wildly, punctuating each nod or shake of his head. Mikiss guessed the man was a former soldier, for though he was taller even than the Menin officer, his deportment was deferential. Old soldiers knew trouble when they saw it, and this man, surely more physically powerful than Major Amber despite his bulging gut, was instinctively acting like a man under orders.

Shart gave a small cheer as he saw the two full tankards of beer at the major's elbow. He had drained half of his before Mikiss had even dropped the packs and picked up his own. Amber and the barkeep were talking quietly. The local language had its roots in Menin, since the original inhabitants were largely Litse and Menin. Mikiss couldn't understand enough for a conversation, but Lord Styrax's preparation for the campaign had been meticulous. Elite troops of Amber's calibre were able to speak all the important dialects in the West, to cover eventualities just such as this.

The major gave the barkeep a nod and laid a silver coin on the bar top, saying something that sounded like, "yes, for all!" before turning to Mikiss.

"All seems fine so far," he commented, casting around the room again and seeing nothing of concern.

"So he will give us directions to find Purn?"

"He was told to expect us—well, you, anyway. Purn's servant left instructions a week ago and has been in each evening since to fetch his master's evening meal."

"Servant?" Mikiss asked dubiously. They all knew the reputation of necromancers.

"Aye," Amber replied grimly while Shart called the barkeep over to refill his tankard. "Don't think he's too popular, but when the money's good, who's going to complain?"

"So is Purn nearby, do you think? It's rather busy for him in this part of town."

"Doubt it, but that doesn't matter. Safer for him to get his meals from further away, and it's not as if he cares whether the food's cold by the time it arrives, not in this weather."

"So what do we do now?" Mikiss asked, eyeing Shart as the man enthusiastically set about his second pint.

"We wait and we eat," Amber said firmly. "The man's not coming until evening and I don't want to be wandering the streets just waiting for some bored patrol to pick a fight." He nodded towards the barkeep, who smiled nervously in response. "He'll bring us food in a while and make sure our tankards are kept full."

"Are you sure you want to let these two drink all afternoon?"

A smile split across Amber's face. "They know their limits. Trust me, even if they start singing and dancing on tables, they'll sober up in an instant if someone draws a sword or throws a punch. That little incident was just them letting off steam."

"Letting off steam?" Mikiss shuddered. The brothers had been bleeding profusely by the end of the vicious fist-fight they'd had a week back.

"Aye, they didn't do any real damage. Shart's got too many words in him; sometimes they just come out too fast and he gets on Keneg's tits. Keneg has to remind his brother which one's the elder, who's in charge."

"They beat each other to a pulp!"

Amber's smile widened. "We got a saying in the army, 'No man's your brother till you spill blood with him.' Those two know there's no grudge to hold; even Shart knows that he's not going to win most of the time, but he don't care. They kick off, get it all out of their system and forget about it before the bruises fade." The major gave Mikiss a friendly thump on the arm, which was still smarting from where Shart had accidentally slammed him into the wall. "Anyone else spills their brother's blood, and not even the worst fiend of the Dark Place will stop them."

Mikiss looked at the pair. Shart was chatting animatedly with the bar-keep, clearly enjoying the chance to practise his language skills. Keneg was staring at the floor, happy in his own world of silence. They couldn't be more different. *Most likely half of their arguments start when Shart accidentally hits Keneg while he's talking*, Mikiss thought, watching the younger waving his hands wildly to demonstrate a point.

Presently something resembling food was brought out by a greasy-haired girl. Her eyes were dark with fatigue, betraying a lack of sleep that left her movements weary and sluggish. Even Keneg's glare when she slopped a little of the brackish stew elicited no response.

Mikiss watched Major Amber hunker down over a tough crust of bread, though his eyes were firmly fixed on the right-hand corner of the room. Mikiss could barely see the men sitting there, a broad-shouldered man roughly Amber's size and a smaller companion. They had been anxiously watching the new arrivals, which had prickled Amber's instincts. Now the mismatched pair were huddled together over their table, examining something.

"Strange," Amber whispered to Mikiss when he realised they were watching the same pair. "An odd pair of labourers: one damned pale and skinny, the other as much a soldier as I am, and from those scars on his hands I'd say one who's seen the wrong end of a torturer in his days."

Mikiss half expected Shart to make a joke, but the brothers were busy with their food. The only sign they gave of having heard Amber was a surreptitious loosening of weapon ties. "Do you think they're here for us?" he asked.

"I doubt it; General Gaur said there were bad things brewing in this place. Knowing what Isherin Purn's sort are like, I'd expect his favourite taverns to be at the centre of whatever is going on. Whatever those two are about, it might not be anywhere near legal, but as long as it's nothing to do with us I don't care."

They lapsed into silence, concentrating on the food, grateful at least that the poor excuse for stew had softened the bread a touch. An hour crept past, then another. The day grew hotter as the afternoon wore on. Through the open shutters and doors they could hear the sounds of city life dwindle to almost nothing under the oppressive weight of the heat.

Major Amber advised Mikiss to try to get some sleep, and did likewise himself. Mikiss lay on a bench, trying to summon the strength to move, but even that was beyond him. He had never experienced weather like this before; even in Thotel the air moved, and during the hottest part of the day you could retire deep within a stonedun. Here, there was no scrap of breeze to offer even the smallest respite, just an overpowering helplessness that weakened both spirit and limbs. Sleep was elusive; his body jerked itself awake every time his eyes drifted closed because of the day's stultifying oppression.

"I hate this city," he muttered feverishly. "With my eyes closed, it feels more like the Dark Place."

"Don't close your eyes, then," Amber growled beside him.

Mikiss gave a disconsolate sigh and stared at the dirty beams in the ceiling until he realised something. With a grunt he sat abruptly up, feeling his damp back peel away from the bench below. His head swam and he had to rub his face to restore some life to it. "Our friends have left," he said.

"Went about an hour ago," Shart replied shortly. Even his natural garrulousness was defeated by the heat.

"I didn't hear them."

"Who cares?" Amber asked, still lying on the bench with his eyes closed.

"It's just strange they left when it was still so hot."

"It's cooling," Keneg said unexpectedly.

"How can you tell?"

"The sounds outside. Folk are getting ready to start the day again. The farmers are probably bringing their produce to sell."

The sound of footsteps in the doorway stopped their speculation. The major raised his head, and blinked hard.

A comical figure with sweat-plastered sandy hair and a rounded belly stood at the doorway peering into the gloom at them. His arms were over-large, out of proportion with the rest of his body, hanging loose at his side. He wore the simple shirt and cropped breeches of a servant, looking out of place in this city of dust and sweat because they were scrupulously free from both—even if they did bear traces of his last meal. He wore nothing on his feet—then Mikiss realised the strange man's feet were completely different sizes and shapes—one would have been relatively normal, were it not for the neatly webbed toes, but the other was chubby and child-sized, a squat lump with fat little toes curling into the floor. Despite the oddness of his feet, they didn't seem to slow the man down as he lurched towards the bar, his thick arms swaying from side to side.

The barkeep gave the newcomer a reserved nod and pointed towards the major before leaving for the kitchen. The strange man turned to regard them all for a moment, then frowned at Amber. Mikiss realised the major must have claimed to be Mikiss himself, just in case there was a nasty surprise waiting for them.

"Master Mikiss?" the man enquired, taking a few steps towards them, his voice surprisingly welcoming, considering his evident wariness.

"And you are?" said Amber.

"You are Master Mikiss?"

"Depends on who you are."

The strange man didn't reply for a moment. Eventually he shrugged. "My name is Nai, and I am servant to Isherin Purn. Are you Master Mikiss?"

Mikiss stood up. "I'm Koden Mikiss," he said.

A broad smile flourished on his face. "But of course you are." His Menin was impeccable, with no trace of any foreign inflection. As Nai grinned, Mikiss realised they were actually of similar ages, although the servant's weather-beaten face made him look older. "Gentlemen, we have been expecting you," Nai continued smoothly. "I hope your journey was enjoyable enough?"

"It was long, dirty and exhausting," Amber cut in, "so enough of the pleasantries."

"Very well, sir," Nai replied, completely unflustered by the major's brusque tone. "If you would all be so good as to accompany me?"

The barkeep brought out a covered bowl which Nai swept up with one hand, then scuttled back to the door. Mikiss groaned as he heaved his pack back up onto his shoulder and followed the soldiers out of the tavern into the blindingly bright afternoon. The sun, though lower in the sky, cast a white carpet over the paving stones and it was still hot enough to make the air in his lungs feel thin and inadequate. His knees began to tremble after only a few steps.

"Here, let me take that," Shart offered. Mikiss looked up at the man's outstretched hand and shook his head. Shart was certainly stronger and fitter, but the sodden state of the man's shirt was testimony to how hard the journey had been on all of them. However much he hurt, Mikiss had been determined from the start not to be a burden, and he had no intention of starting now, so close to their goal. Shart gave a brief snort; of approval or scorn Mikiss couldn't tell.

Mikiss was vaguely aware they were moving away from the heart of the city as they struggled on, first over uneven cobbles, then smooth packed-dirt roads lined with tall limes with wilting leaves of green and yellow and a type of hawthorn Mikiss had never seen before, its twisted branches covered in thin leaves and sharp spines.

It took them more than half an hour of walking at Mikiss' erratic pace before they reached an area within sight of the city wall that was largely derelict. A handful of roughly mended buildings bore signs of life, but it struck Mikiss that there were no birds to be heard, not even where the trees had shrivelled fruit still hanging from their higher branches. A few people idly watched them from the shadows of doorways and windows, curious only at who might be fool enough to be out under the still-fierce sun.

This far out, past the old South Barbican that had once protected Scree, the houses stood well apart from their neighbours. Nai led them to a large, gloomy place that looked as if it had once been a country manor house until it was swallowed up by the expanding city, then abandoned to the ravages of wind and rain.

"This is where Purn lives?" asked Amber sceptically. It had once been a fine building, but now, surrounded by a high, rusted iron fence with wild undergrowth encroaching on it, the house looked neither inhabited nor habitable. Its nearest neighbour was in even worse condition, bearing the unmistakable black smears of fire-damage.

Mikiss sniffed the air. Here, more than elsewhere in the city, there was a smell of decay. Most of it was the house, he suspected, but there was something beyond the stink of unwashed bodies and rotting vegetation: a sharp smell of decayed meat. Perhaps this was just a hint of the horrors one might find in the home of a necromancer.

"This is where my master lives," Nai confirmed. "Much of his work is conducted in the cellars, so we do not need all of the rooms. You are welcome to make use of whatever space you find above ground, and the house is reasonably sound, but I do suggest you keep clear of the attic. The floor is especially bad up there."

Shart craned his head up to the roof, noting the large gaps in the tiles. "I see what you mean about the attic," he muttered, "but your idea of 'reasonably sound' might be a little different to mine."

"It serves our purposes," Nai replied, "and of course we would not want anyone passing by to think there might be value in investigating the building."

"Don't you have guards?"

"Most certainly," the servant said with a small smile that filled Mikiss with foreboding, "but they lack both subtlety and the sense to make distinctions between children playing and enemy agents."

"As well as a heartbeat, no doubt," Shart muttered.

"As well as a heartbeat," Nai echoed with strange enthusiasm. "And we prefer to keep a low profile, especially as tempers in the city are running somewhat high."

"Have there been riots?" Major Amber asked.

"Nothing overly dramatic, but the mood in the city has changed. There is no desperate scarcity of food yet, but that hasn't stopped fights breaking out most nights." Nai gestured up at the pale blue sky and said gravely, "Since the weather turned, the people of Scree have been acting like animals. They rut and fight and scream in the street. Before long the city will begin to tear itself apart."

He turned back to the house and gave a heavy sigh that seemed to begin in his feet and rise all the way up to his strange sweat-flattened hair. Then he shook himself abruptly and pushed aside the gate for the soldiers to enter.

"Welcome," he intoned as each passed him. Mikiss felt a shiver run down his spine, as though some malevolent spirit had stroked the hairs on his neck and then fled. The fact that Nai carefully replaced the broken, rusting gate just confirmed to Mikiss that something unholy prowled the grounds.

A weed-infested gravel path led from the gate up to a tall studded door flanked by a pair of columns covered in rusty lichen and a vibrant green creeper that covered part of the building, obscuring several windows.

The rubbish and broken planks piled up on the doorstep led Shart to assume there was no way in from the front. He led the way round to the right, following patches of gravel that were all that remained of the original drive to the rear of the building. The fence was fifty paces or so from the house, yet somehow Mikiss felt crossing that distance would be a harder trek than it might at first appear. Buried in the undergrowth, partly swallowed by an untended rhododendron bush, he spotted a small stone housing, some two feet high, with some sort of metal grille at its entrance. Mikiss wondered how the people of Scree buried their dead and shuddered.

Around the back of the house was the first sign of habitation, a neatly swept courtyard surrounded by a low wall. The rest of the grounds remained wild and untended. One enormous pine overshadowed the area. Next to it were three smaller trees, just shy of twenty feet tall, spreading their spiky-leaved branches in a dome that reached almost to the ground.

"Gentlemen, leave your packs here," Nai said, gesturing at the courtyard floor. He had barely finished speaking before four thumps indicated they had acted immediately. Nai smiled, noting that the soldiers might have shed their packs, but they had not cast off their weapons.

He crossed the courtyard and walked past the sun-blistered door to a large iron panel, almost five feet square, set at an angle on the floor. He gripped the thick iron ring, grunted in effort and hauled the panel up and open.

Mikiss noticed that the panel was more than an inch thick. He was impressed. Nai was neither tall nor particularly solid, yet he hadn't been hugely taxed by the fortified cellar door. Clearly there was more than just strange feet to this servant; he would bear close watching.

Nai stepped back, a lopsided smile on his face and a triumphant edge to his voice as he announced, "Gentlemen, allow me to present my master, Isherin Purn."

Looking into the cellar, Mikiss could see nothing at first, then outlines started to suggest themselves. The faintest of lights grew out of the darkness, not lamplight, but a strange green glow with no visible source. He made out steps leading down to a wide room, with a table, or maybe a bench further back, with smooth curved shapes upon it. He didn't look too hard because at the foot of the steps was the silhouette of a man, quite still and silent, with that strange green light playing around his head and shoulders. Mikiss could not suppress a shiver.

CHAPTER 19

FIRES DANCED IN THE TWILIGHT, the heat prickling his skin. Fragments of stone and brick under his feet made his footing treacherous as he picked his way down the street. Somewhere behind him he heard a scream, a voice he knew as well as his own—wife, lover, friend? He couldn't tell. His memories were filled with clamouring voices, mingling in his ears, drowning each other out before he could identify any of them. Each one triggered a new wave of guilt, but faded before he could attach a name or deed.

In the distance came other sounds: people shouting, the splinter of wood, the groan of disintegrating walls, the high ring of steel meeting steel. The voice behind him screamed again and this time he turned to face a misshapen creature with blood on its claws and bodies lying at its feet.

Gripped with fury, he left his shining sword in its scabbard and leapt forward, mailed fists outstretched and reaching for the creature's throat. They slammed together and spun off into the wall of a building that crumbled under the impact. They collapsed with it in a cloud of dust, still holding hard to each other. He felt the clouds massing above, growing in intensity and power; their strength filled his arms and he twisted his fingers around the creature's wrists, feeling something snap. His thumb drove deep into the desiccated flesh of his foe.

The creature howled and broke its grip on him, scrabbling to escape but unable to evade his swinging fists. He connected, watched its chest crack and crumple like dried plaster struck by a hammer. He kicked out, smashing it to the ground, then used his own great weight to pin it down.

He roared with triumph as his fingers surrounded the paper-like skin of its throat and began to squeeze, harder and harder. It scrabbled ineffectually, beating at his huge shoulders to no effect, emitting a stifled whimper of fear.

His hands tightened, breaking bones and crushing its windpipe until the creature moved no more—and only then did he see the fear in its eyes. Only then did he look at its face and realise that during the struggle it had become his own face, haunted and afraid, even in death. He released his grip, stumbling backwards in horror from the armoured corpse that lay beneath him. As he retreated he fell, but there was no ground beneath him to stop him, only high banks of earth rising up on either side as he fell deeper and deeper. The light from the fires grew distant as he descended into the darkness of the grave.

Isak flinched, suddenly realising how fast his heart was beating. The dream that afternoon was a new one, wrecking his sleep as he hid from the relent-less sunshine in the cellar of the house they had taken. It lingered in his memory even now, several hours after nightfall. He recognised the taste of fear in his mouth, the vivid images in his mind and the ghosts of sensation on his fingertips. This was no ordinary dream; the similarities to his long-standing nightmare about Lord Bahl's death were all too apparent. Even in the hot night air he could feel Death's cold touch on his skin. He wondered if this too was prophetic.

"But what does it mean?" he whispered to the night. "How could I have been fighting myself? I died, but the black knight wasn't there. Is anything set, or has my corrupted destiny now turned me away even from that?"

He wiped a hand across his brow, feeling a slick sheen of sweat under his fingers. They had been in this city less than a day and already he was hating it. Even on the Chetse plains he'd never felt such heat. He didn't need his Crystal Skulls to tell him that this was far from natural; every fibre of his being told him so. There was magic in the air; a bitter, dirty pall hanging over the city that made his head throb. He felt both light-headed and disem-bodied, and yet burdened by the weight of the Land. He found himself unable to separate one confused thought from the next and his foul mood only deepened.

He'd snarled at Tila for the crime of asking what was wrong, then found himself unable to say sorry—what started as an apology sent her away in tears, Vesna following swiftly behind, his expression thunderous. Only the forlorn look on Major Jachen's face had spurred him to fix things.

The sound of shuffling feet pierced the miasma of thoughts: someone shifting in the shadows, just below his own vantage point on a stone walkway that had probably once been part of the old city wall. Isak's hand went to his side and he wrapped his fingers around the unfamiliar handle of the mace he now carried. Eolis was wrapped in a bundle of cloth and tied securely to his back; they couldn't risk it being recognised and the sort of mercenary Isak was pretending to be wouldn't own such a fine weapon.

He eased himself forward and leaned out over the edge of the wall. There was a tense silence in the area tonight. Unless it was just a product of Isak's own anticipation, the locals appeared to be aware that something was going to happen. Whoever was standing below him was the only person Isak had seen all night, other than his own soldiers and the two Brotherhood men who'd told him of King Emin's plans.

He edged his way out, ready to leap back and strike, when he saw it was just a young man standing there alone. Strangely, he appeared to be looking at the same crumbling old house Isak was. *What part do you have to play in this?* Isak wondered. *Are you working for Emin? If not, what in the name of the Dark Place are you doing watching that house?*

Doranei and his companion, introduced as Sebe, had told him the king had personal business with one of the men seen entering that house. Isak had joked at the time that he was attracting trouble again—after all, he'd been in the city but a few hours when he saw Doranei, hurrying back to his master with the news—but neither Brother had even smiled, and that spoke volumes. Doranei and Isak had spent more than a week together; Isak considered him a friend. But that afternoon he had been too preoccupied for anything but business, and their sharing of news had been brief, and it had ended almost as soon as Ilumene had been mentioned.

Isak studied the boy leaning against the wall: young, skinny, average height for a youth of fifteen-odd summers. No weapons.

"A strange night to be taking the air," Isak said softly. The boy spun around in alarm, for a moment not seeing Isak's face and then gasping when he did. "Getting a moment's peace away from your family?" Isak's command of the language was not perfect, but it was good enough to be understood.

"No sir," came the sullen reply. *Sir,* Isak thought with interest, *an odd way for a local to speak to a foreigner unless I look older than I think I do.*

"Then what are you doing? It's a bad night to be out."

"Every night is a bad night in Scree," the youth said, "but I think I'm safe on the streets around here. Safer than you, anyway."

Isak gave a grin. "Really? I'd heard this was one of the worst districts for criminals."

"They're just poor round here, not criminal—unless you think being poor is a crime." The youth gave him a defiant look. "But there are criminals out tonight, and they're the ones I'm waiting for. They don't much like white-eyes, so if I were you I'd go somewhere else."

Isak thought for a moment. The youth had definitely been watching the house, but as far as Isak could tell, it was a derelict building—certainly nothing to interest normal criminals.

"What's your name?"

"What's yours?" the youth snapped.

"My name? Ah, Horman," Isak replied. *Now why did I say that? That's not the name I'd agreed with Vesna. What made me think of my father?*

"Fine, if you say so. I'm Mayel."

Isak reached out a hand. "Well, Mayel, how about you come up here and tell me all about these criminals." Mayel took a half-pace back as Isak's massive arm loomed forward. "Come on; share a pipe with me."

The promise of tobacco seemed to clinch it for the young man, who took a step forward and grasped Isak's hand. The white-eye hauled Mayel up without effort and deposited him on the walkway.

"Gods, you're a big bastard," Mayel exclaimed when he saw Isak straighten up.

"Easy there, you were calling me 'sir' a moment ago."

"Sorry, bad habit," Mayel apologised, not mentioning which was the bad habit. "Just hadn't expected it; you're bigger than any white-eye I've ever seen."

Isak ignored the point. "What's that accent I can hear? Are you a local? It sounds like you've been educated, but you're hardly dressed like a merchant's son."

Mayel plucked at the ragged clothes he had on. "I was a novice at a monastery, I got some learning there. What's it to you?"

"Just working out who I'm dealing with," Isak replied breezily. "Always best to find out beforehand. Here, help yourself." He offered his pipe and tobacco pouch and Mayel took them with delight.

"So what are you doing out here?" Mayel asked once he'd filled the pipe and lit it. "Have you enlisted with Mistress Ostia's army?"

"No, we're escorting someone, some lord's mistress." Tila had insisted on accompanying them and Isak hadn't been able to dissuade her. He knew he wouldn't hear the end of forbidding it outright, so in the end, he'd agreed that the White Circle would likely not harm a woman, and accepted her suggestion that she play the lordly whore being escorted by mercenaries in these troubled times.

"One of those White Circle bitches?"

"Probably," Isak grinned. "You should be careful what you say about them in strange company though."

"Ah, you're not tied to them. I hear the only white-eyes the Circle have are ones they trot around on leashes. They don't speak or piss without permission from their mistress."

That drove the smile from Isak's face. He'd come close to becoming little more than a pet of the Queen of the Fysthrall. Wondering how his life would have turned out if she'd succeeded was a sobering thought. As far as they could tell, he'd have been made to march his armies all the way to Tir Duria and lay siege to that fortress city, costing tens of thousands of lives. It would probably have been the ruin of the Farlan nation in the process.

"So who does your mistress belong to? Someone powerful?" Mayel asked, enjoying the pipe enough not to have noticed Isak's changed mood.

"Don't know. Why do you ask?"

Mayel suddenly looked apprehensive. "I've been away for a few years," he said, hunching his shoulder. "I'm still working out who the people with power are."

"I don't think he's anyone very powerful, just a man who's very fond of his pretty mistress." Isak pictured Count Vesna and almost smiled again. The man had looked constantly anxious since they had met up again on the border. He and his band of soldiers were bloodied and grim, drained by the weeks fighting Duke Vrerr's cause. The reunion had been muted, and since then Vesna had rarely left Tila's side.

Isak gestured towards the unlit house. "So why don't you tell me why your criminal friends are interested in that house?"

"Why should I? What are you doing here?"

"Watching out for a friend. He has business with someone in that house."

Mayel frowned. "What sort of business?"

"A personal dispute."

"And you're just sitting here watching?"

"It's personal," Isak replied gravely. "If he wanted my help he would ask, but he won't need it."

"He will once my cousin's men arrive," Mayel blurted out. "They've also got business there, and you don't want to get in their way."

Isak cocked his head to one side. "Now what sort of business could they have with that house?"

"People have been disappearing in the city; we hear it's got something to do with the man who lives in that house. My cousin runs this district and he doesn't like madmen preying on his people; he's going to have a look around that house and see what's there."

Isak stared at the house. It was completely dark, and silent; he couldn't even see any movement within the grounds. That struck him as a little odd; while Doranei hadn't explained fully what was going on, Isak would have expected anyone the king was interested in to have posted guards, or at least to inspect the grounds once or twice. He'd been watching a good while now, and he'd have guessed the house was deserted.

Emin would soon be making his move, then they would see just how dead it was around here.

To be on the safe side, Isak reached down and picked up a couple of small stones lying near his foot. Ignoring Mayel's curious expression, he tossed them over his shoulder and they pattered away into the darkness. Within a matter of heartbeats, Major Jachen was crouched down at Isak's side, betraying no surprise at the presence of the young stranger.

"Where are the others?"

"I sent most back to the house with the tart," Jachen replied, keeping in role. "I know what you're like for getting into trouble, so I kept Leshi, Tiniq and Jeil with me."

Isak grinned. Lesarl had added the rangers Leshi and Tiniq to his party. They were Ascetites, men whose latent talent for magic had never developed, but instead they had natural and learned skills pushed beyond normal limits. The pair were as stealthy as Mihn and almost as quick and strong as the white-eyes of the Palace Guard. Tiniq was the twin of a white-eye, General Lahk, which was apparently impossible, while Leshi had the remarkable ability to be able to stand so perfectly still that he faded into the shadows. In a forest, even another ranger could walk within a few yards of the man and never see him.

With the losses to Isak's personal guard and the great danger posed by entering Scree with so few soldiers, it had been prudent to fill the gaps with more unnatural troops. In addition to a squat, bearded battle-mage who'd introduced himself as Mariq and said nothing else since to Isak, there was a knight from Torl whose remarkable skill with a bow meant he too had to be an Ascetite, and Shinir, one of Lesarl's female agents, who had only a loose relationship with gravity whenever climbing was necessary—she was also the most spiteful and unforgiving woman Isak had ever met.

Their addition had already provided one unexpected bonus. As they were trying to work out how Mariq and Isak would get past the White Circle mage attending the gate, their Ascetites had gone through, and their strange abilities had so thoroughly confused the mage that she'd developed a migraine and abandoned her post, leaving Isak free to walk straight in.

"Tell them to keep their eyes open," Isak said, pointing down the empty road leading towards the heart of the city. "I have a bad feeling about all this; tell them to be ready to raise the alarm."

Mikiss sat in the broken chair and sank slowly into its cushioned back. They were in the cellars of the house, a damp, cramped network of rooms that served as home for Isherin Purn and his servant Nai. The smell of mould and stone was overlaid by the scent of dead vegetation and dank earth which crept in through a grille near the ceiling. There was no one else around as far as Mikiss could tell, but he couldn't shake off the feeling that they were not entirely alone. A presence seemed to linger in the dim corridors and gently creaking rooms above; Mikiss knew nothing about necromancers and had no wish to, but his imagination was producing any number of alarming ideas.

"What you thinking about, sir?" Shart asked from opposite Mikiss. "You're looking kinda spooked over there."

"Aren't you? You do remember what our host's calling entails?"

"Sure," Shart chuckled.

"And you don't find it at all unnerving?"

The soldier grinned, chiefly out of amusement at Mikiss' discomfort. "Of course all this daemon crap is weird, but you serve in the Cheme Third and you get used to it after a while."

Mikiss had guessed as much from the stories they had told him on the journey north. The Cheme Third Legion was Lord Styrax's favourite, made up of men he trusted above even the Bloodsworn and the Reavers.

"Also," Major Amber growled from the corner of the room, a brown earthenware bottle clamped firmly in his lap, "the whole stench-of-death thing becomes familiar enough when you serve in the Third. Us three have holed up together with a nice pile of corpses keeping us warm before; had to, else we'd have been caught and spitted." His eyes were fixed on the bottle in front of him; from the way the man had been pulling on it, Mikiss guessed it was almost empty. "You watch a man you know go through various stages of decomposition and death becomes just another comrade."

Mikiss watched the oil lamps flicker. They were turned low, just enough for him to make out the lines and corners of the room. The door to the room was open, in the vain hope of a breeze; from where Mikiss was sitting he could see the dim light from the cramped kitchen where Nai was preparing something for his master. Somewhere beyond that, sheathed in shadow, was the door to Isherin Purn's study, a room Mikiss never wanted to see inside.

"Karkarn's horn," Shart exclaimed, "you're being miserable tonight—if you don't mind me saying so, sir. Stench of death and presence of daemons aside, we've got food I can recognise bits of, drink so we don't care what the rest of the food is, and we can make Keneg sleep in a different room to us. In my book, that puts us well ahead of where we were yesterday."

"Ah, this house puts me on edge; this whole damn city puts me on edge." The major grimaced. "Don't any of you feel it?"

"Feel what? All I feel is this heat."

"The . . ." Amber's voice tailed off as he gestured vaguely in the air. "I don't know what it is exactly but there's something—"

He didn't get any further as a scream pierced the night air. They all jumped up, scrambling for the weapons they'd left propped against the wall. Mikiss caught himself on the arm of the chair he'd been sitting in and careened into Shart, who ploughed through Mikiss, knocking him out of the way and not missing a step as he went for his axe. From outside they heard men shouting, more than a few, and deeper sounds Mikiss could not place; sounds that reached down into his gut.

"Shart, keep with Mikiss," Amber snapped. His yellowy eyes glowed in the weak light.

"Prefer to be outside, sir," Shart commented, his eyes not leaving the doorway where Keneg was standing ready with both hands wrapped around the hilt of his brutal sword. "No room to swing in here." Shart hefted his axe, raising it so the head banged against the cellar's low ceiling. The commotion outside continued, more screams, more shouts. A great hissing began from near the grille, a sibilant rustle of dry leaves and withered skin.

"Fair enough, just keep tight," Major Amber said. "Sounds like Purn's got some tricks, so don't go looking for trouble because it might not understand friend or foe. The trapdoor is barred so we go up into the house. You two lead and get to the outside door, see what you can see. We'll go up a floor and look out over the back. Keep your ears open and don't stray into the grounds."

The brothers led out into the corridor, past Nai, who was busy murmuring and making strange gestures over a blank wall. With a start, Mikiss realised that the wall had been the door to Purn's study only a few moments ago.

The spell completed, Nai turned to face them, a purposeful expression on his face and an iron-tipped club in his hands. "I doubt they will make it to the house," he said with grim certainty, stalking past the soldiers and heading for the stairway that led up into the house. A great yawning groan suddenly cut through the clamour from outside, followed by a pair of heavy thumps, then the shouting came back with renewed intensity.

"That might prove unfortunate," Nai said to no one in particular. The soldiers exchanged glances, but kept silent as they followed him into the old kitchen. The only reminder of the room's former role was a great iron stove, rusted into uselessness by years of rain sweeping in through the shattered window. Someone had nailed up a few boards so there was no gap large enough for a person to climb through, but there were gaps to see a little of outside. As Mikiss trailed in he pulled out his own sword, as much for comfort as anything else.

Nai, peering between boards, said, "Looks like locals. My master's pets will soon see them off—ah, they're running in all directions. Some are making for the courtyard."

"Pitchforks and flaming brands?" Shart asked. Nai gave the soldier a deeply unfriendly look as the brothers shared a snigger and barrelled out of the rear door.

Mikiss heard a cry of alarm break off as Keneg roared, then the clash of steel, followed by shrieks.

Major Amber grabbed Mikiss by the shoulder and gave him a shove towards the door. "Come on, then, sir, just your average angry mob. You've been trained, they haven't. Stick close to me and you'll be fine." There wasn't time to argue even if Mikiss had dared, as he found himself swept along into the courtyard where Keneg and Shart were facing down half a dozen men. Two more were already down, lying there clutching their wounds and screaming.

Mikiss realised that Amber was right, so he raised his sword and ran at the nearest enemy. Swords took training, clubs didn't; the man raised his weapon preparing to smash it down on Mikiss, only to find Mikiss' blade buried in his gut. On the right, Amber was wielding his two blades with lethal efficiency, catching a club on one and hacking into his assailant's knee with the other, then following that up with a blow to the man's neck when he fell to the ground, wailing like a child.

Suddenly there was a bright burst of flame. Everyone hesitated, turning to see what had happened.

Mikiss looked around the illuminated grounds and saw men standing in groups wherever there were gaps in the vegetation, wildly fighting off the strange figures assailing them. One such group was being attacked by three bony, bloody figures dressed in rags. They had no weapons that Mikiss could see, but one stopped a club in mid-swing, then swiped a palm across the man's face with such force the man spun around and collapsed in a heap on top of one of his comrades.

But the weirdness of that little group paled into insignificance next to what was going on in the centre of the grounds, where a creature something like a massive hairless bear stood hacking at anyone within reach of the double-headed axes it brandished in each hand. When it had cleared a circle, it leapt, a clear ten yards in one stride, and began again.

Mikiss started shuddering uncontrollably when he caught sight of a man just hanging in the air, flailing madly as unseen claws shredded his flesh and droplets of fresh blood sprayed all around him from severed arteries.

The Menin soldiers ignored the horrific scene, but took advantage of their enemies' momentary distraction to dispatch the last of the men in the courtyard.

"Where has that light come from?" asked Amber angrily, scanning the grounds.

Shart reached out a hand, pointing off to the right. "There, there's a mage in that bunch."

A large group of men had formed a circle just inside the grounds, and were hewing a path through the injured and dead towards the house. One of the walking corpses burst into flames and blundered away.

"They're not locals; they're fighting as a unit," Major Amber suddenly announced. The foreigners were now providing the only serious assault on the grounds; everyone else was dead or dying.

When Mikiss saw someone point towards them, he opened his mouth, ready to shout. But he closed his mouth in horror as a nearby bush started shaking violently, then lashed out with supernaturally long branches to envelop the man who'd pointed. A shadow crossed the still-hovering light and the branches slewed sideways and grabbed the man beside him instead, tugging the helpless figure into the body of the bush. Three of the attackers ran forward to help their comrade, but branches whipped at their faces and drove them back.

"The master will be pleased," Nai commented brightly as the attackers struggled in vain to save the man, but all too soon it was over as, with one last shuddering moan, the man fell silent and the bush stopped shaking. Someone called out something, and in the next instant the bush burst into purple flames and an unholy howl echoed through the air.

"What the hell was that?" Shart asked.

"Just one of the master's pet projects," Nai said airily. "We hadn't had a chance to test it properly before."

"They're a determined lot, I must say," the major remarked, "and as it doesn't look like your defences are going to stop them, and we don't have the numbers, we should get back inside."

The foreign unit was inching its way towards the house, hampered at every turn by the new horrors springing up. The giant creature had killed every man in its vicinity, and now it turned towards the remaining group. The bright flare left Mikiss' eyes watering as he tried to make it out, but all he could be sure of was the dark skin, a mass of criss-crossing scars and tattoos, a low-hanging jaw with unusually sharp canine teeth, and horns that curled forward past its eyes.

"Come on, you bastard," Amber growled, grabbing Mikiss by the arm and dragging him back inside. "Shart, check the other side of the house; let me know if there's anyone out there as well. Nai, your master had better get more involved or we're in trouble. There must be more than one mage out there."

Shart ran into one of the front rooms. There was a clatter as something broke under the soldier's weight. Then he called back, "Soldiers at the gate, pikemen of some sort—maybe the city guard. There are women in white standing before them. They've not come through yet."

"Damn, White Circle mages? How in the name of the Lowest Pit did they get here so fast?" Amber looked at his men, assessing his options, then ordered, "Nai, go and tell your master we need a diversion."

"That won't be necessary," said a calm voice from the cellar stair, making them all jump. Isherin Purn loomed suddenly from the kitchen shadows and stepped into the hallway, a smile of quiet pleasure on his face and a red flicker in his eyes. "Nai, please fetch my books from the study table."

"We've got at least three separate parties surrounding us, two with mages. You have an escape route planned?" Amber snapped.

Purn glared at him, and both the major and the messenger recoiled. The necromancer was a thin man, and hairless, no taller than Mikiss. He was believed to be around sixty winters, but his face remained unlined. Mikiss guessed that was some dark pact. It gave the necromancer an air of unearthly, timeless cruelty.

"Major, you will modify your tone of voice with me." Purn's voice sounded distracted, as though the physical world were only part of what he had to concentrate on at any one moment. "I have released the wards on the boundary and triggered all the invocations within the grounds."

"They hadn't all been triggered already?" the major asked, a little taken aback.

"The magic is complicated; you will not understand it," Purn said. "All you need to know is that there will be more appearing as we speak, drawn by the murder already done. They are free to leave the grounds now, and you will be just as great a target as any other mortal nearby."

"Isn't that going to make this even harder?" Amber asked, trying to control his temper.

"Not at all, as long as you stay close to me. In the general chaos they will cause it will be simple enough to go unnoticed." Purn turned at the sound of his servant returning, laden with a bulky canvas bag slung over his left shoulder. "Ah, excellent, Nai; you are sure you have them all?"

"Yes, master," Nai replied, "and you had missed Chalem's *Experiments with Fire* so I took the liberty of bringing that as well."

Purn sniffed. "The loss of any book is a waste, I suppose." He pointed past Amber and through the high empty reception rooms. "Come then, Major, that way, please. Get ready to go through one of the windows, but don't leave the building until I have joined you."

Purn's smile faded as he touched his fingers against the splintered door frame, concentrating. He began to whisper under his breath. As Amber grabbed Mikiss by the collar and hauled him off after the brothers, they caught sight of a thin finger of flame that darted up to the ceiling and spread in all directions. By the time they had crossed the two rooms to reach the tall shuttered windows on the far side, a deep orange light outlined the doorway and Mikiss could hear the flames hungrily consuming the building.

Shart and Mikiss set to clearing away the debris below the window and forcing the warped shutters open. From outside came the sounds of magic; the fierce crackle of lightning and, suddenly, a raging wind, all overlaid with panicked cries. Despite the noise, Mikiss heard Purn's footfalls as the necromancer marched in after them, silhouetted against the rising flames.

"Well now, chaos reigns in my wake," Purn declared, "so let us be off."

He pushed past the soldiers and peered out of the window, then hopped through with remarkable agility. As Keneg and Shart followed, a great chattering began in the low undergrowth nearby.

"Tsatach's balls, what's that?" Shart demanded, looking anxiously at Purn.

The necromancer tugged his cloak straight. "That? A local spirit I recruited to the cause." Any further explanation was cut short as a shape burst from under a bush and leaped at Purn. It passed straight through the necromancer's body, skidded on the ground and slammed into the side of the house.

Mikiss stared down at it as the spirit scrabbled to right itself. It looked somewhat like a spider, only with four short, powerful legs, each one ending in a pair of large claws. He couldn't see the face, which was set deep into the body, but the hiss of fury it directed towards Purn was all too obvious.

The necromancer stared down at the creature, an expression of mild curiosity on his face. He said nothing, but continued to inspect the creature, until Shart took matters into his own hands and slammed his axe down onto it, cutting it nearly in two. "It didn't seem to like you so much," he said, hauling his axe free. "It looked at me for a moment, then went back to working out how it was going to gut you." He stopped talking as a black man-like shape rose up behind Purn, claws outstretched.

The necromancer disappeared entirely as the phantom touched him. It surged forward and raked its claws down Shart's face, and he howled and collapsed in a heap. The phantom ignored Keneg, who jumped over his prone brother and attacked, but it was like trying to cut through fog. His sword was useless against the strange being.

Major Amber shoved Mikiss out the way and vaulted through the window, but before he could join the attack, a shaft of white light lanced out from inside the room and pierced the shadowy form assailing Shart. The phantom reeled, shrieking, and rose up in the air, writhing and screeching, then fled over the tree tops until it dissipated in the sky.

Mikiss turned to see who had cast the spell, and was shocked at the sight of Isherin Purn, standing placidly beside his encumbered servant. He looked back: there was no trace of the necromancer on the ground.

"But? I saw it—"

"What you saw was an illusion," Purn said.

"My master abhors the prospect of physical injury," Nai explained, rather contemptuously. "He sent an illusion of himself on ahead to see what was out there."

"They are now released from my control," Purn protested, "and obviously some will try to kill me for imprisoning them in the first place." He looked flustered now, as if Nai's unspoken reprimand had struck a nerve.

Nai gave a snort that seemed to indicate sympathy for the daemons outside and clambered out of the window. Mikiss gave Purn a puzzled look, but the necromancer had regained his composure and his dark glower returned. Mikiss didn't wait to see the red glow return to Purn's eyes. He almost fell out of the window in his hurry to escape.

Shart lay on the floor, the major kneeling over him, pressing hard on his chest. Mikiss could see blood all around him.

The major's face was grim when he looked up. "Purn, can your magic help him?"

The necromancer laid a hand on Shart's bloodied face. He shook his head. "Your man is dead. I could have him up and walking in half a minute, but I doubt you would appreciate it." He didn't have to go into detail.

Before anyone could move, a group of men rounded the corner of the house, weapons held low against whatever they were likely to meet. They stopped dead when they saw the Menin soldiers. The sight of six men, one probably dead, rather than a horde of daemons, left them momentarily confused.

One man said something and the rest closed ranks, in anticipation of attack. Keneg obliged with a roar and Major Amber ran to his side, followed by Nai, who abandoned his bag of books and snatched up Shart's axe from the ground. Keneg battered aside one pike-head and decapitated its owner without a pause. The major followed suit before anyone else had the chance to attack.

Then Mikiss found himself screaming a warning—a woman was sprinting around the corner after the soldiers. He couldn't work out what she thought she could achieve, for she carried no weapons . . . She was making straight for Keneg, who raised his sword and stood ready. The woman didn't slow her charge, but her body blurred and dropped low to all fours with astonishing speed and Keneg's blade met nothing as a huge lioness came up under his guard and slapped one razor-sharp clawed paw into his gut. The lioness buried its teeth into Keneg's forearm and used its great weight to bear him to the ground.

Major Amber rushed to join the attack, but the lioness pulled Keneg, howling in pain, out of reach, dragging him by the arm as if he were a rag-doll. Amber raised his sword, preparing to rush the lioness, when another group of soldiers rounded the corner, led by a second woman brandishing two swords.

"Put up your weapons," the woman shouted, the men behind her spreading out. On her left was a nobleman, dressed as if for a state banquet but clearly able to use the needle-sharp rapier in his hand.

"Fucking animal," Keneg bellowed, swinging his free arm around to punch the lioness in the throat with all the strength of a desperate man.

Major Amber stood ready against the oncoming soldiers as Keneg struggled to his feet, trying to buy them some space, all thoughts of his own safety long vanished. Once upright, Keneg charged forward, swinging wildly at the lioness, who growled at him and retreated, leaving him facing the other woman. He screamed a challenge at her and rushed in, but she parried his blows with ease, her twin blades moving in perfect unison.

Finally Keneg gasped and sank to his knees, his fury gone in a shudder of pain. The woman hardly broke her stride as she spun around and pierced his body, heart and lung. He heaved one great hacking cough, gouts of blood erupting from his mouth, and sank to the ground.

"Gentlemen." Yet another woman stepped forward from behind the attackers, dressed as a member of the White Circle. She carried no weapons and wore no armour, but there was a grim promise in her voice as she said, "I suggest you drop your weapons immediately; I am in no mood to play games."

Purn stepped forward. "And I suggest you get out of our way or I will summon the daemons walking this place to destroy you." Mikiss saw the deep red glow radiating from the necromancer's eyes again.

"Oh, spare me," the woman growled, pushing her shawl back to reveal lustrous black hair and elegant features. "They might be daemons, but they're not stupid."

Purn gave a yelp and staggered back, one hand raised as though to ward off a blow. The woman, bristling with barely restrained anger, stepped towards them, apparently completely unafraid of the weapons they still carried.

Purn gave an unintelligible cry and turned to flee, diving for the bag of books Nai had dropped and hunkering low over them as shadows from all sides appeared up to envelop him.

When the shadows faded away, the necromancer Isherin Purn was nowhere to be seen.

The woman with the short swords started to move forward but stopped at a raised finger from the White Circle mage.

"No, forget him; he'll not have gone far, and with luck he'll deal with some of the creatures he released here so I won't have to bother." She bestowed a glittering smile on Major Amber, Mikiss and Nai.

Mikiss felt himself shy away from her look as a sense of horror flooded his mind and the fingers holding his sword went numb.

"Now, gentlemen; please be good boys and come quietly."

Not far away, Abbot Dorn sat in his study behind locked and barred doors, fearfully watching the wildly flickering light cast by an oil lamp on the wall beyond. His hands shook as he felt the heavy footfalls of daemons walking the Land and heard their voices echo out on the rushing streams of magic. Despite the unnatural heat, he felt the room grow cold and the shadows deepen. There was no breeze in the cellar, but the lamp suddenly guttered down to almost nothing, leaving only a trembling finger of light. The abbot reached under the table that served as his desk and slipped open the box there. He withdrew the Crystal Skull and cupped it in both hands, as afraid of the power it contained as he was of the shadows drawing closer.

As soon as he touched the Skull, he realised his mistake: every one of the horrors walking Scree's festering streets noticed the change in the magic-laden atmosphere and turned to find him.

"*We see you.*" The words whispered around the cellar.

Abbot Doren whimpered and turned around wildly, trying to see who-ever was speaking, but there was nothing there. The room was locked and secure; he was alone, except for the shadows.

"*We will come for you.*"

The abbot crashed into his desk, spilling books and dirty crockery onto the floor. The Skull, its surface slick against his skin, almost slipped from his hands. Pulling it close to his chest, he tentatively drew on its power. The shadows withdrew, but not far. He could feel them lingering at the edges of his mind, and around his dilapidated home.

"*We can wait,*" the voice assured him with a malevolent chuckle. "*You are all alone now, and you cannot stay strong for ever.*"

"Alone? No, I have Mayel," Abbot Doren muttered.

"*Alone,*" the voice continued, cold and assured, "*in a city of enemies, hunted, and all alone . . . all we need do is wait.*"

All through the night the abbot wept silently, hearing that soft laughter in his head. When dawn at last arrived and Mayel had still not returned, he realised the voice had been correct. He was all alone, and the darkness was waiting.

CHAPTER 20

WAKEFULNESS CREPT UNEASILY OVER MIKISS, beginning with an ache behind his eyes and growing into a dull pain that reached through his skull and down his spine. Though his eyes were closed, he still tried to recoil from the light that pierced his eyelids and sparked a strange sense of fear. He tried to move, and discovered that his hands were bound behind his back and his muscles almost cried with fatigue, as though he had been running through the night. His lips were crusted and he moaned with the effort needed to breathe in the dusty sweat-laced air. Exhausted beyond belief, he slumped back down.

He felt something touch his brow. Whatever it was, it felt hot and rasping on his skin, and as he flinched away from it he smelled a man near him, a scent of dirt and grease. Then a waft of perfume, near-imperceptible, reached him from further away. As he tried to recognise it, Mikiss realised how parched his throat was. From somewhere on the other side of the room a chair scraped. He felt it through the stone floor on which he was lying as much as heard it, then sandpaper hands cradled his head and raised him up.

"Awake at last. You must be thirsty." A woman's voice plucked a string inside him.

Mikiss tried to reply, but nothing came out except a wheeze. He recognised Nai as the person holding him when the necromancer's servant said crossly, "Damn you, woman, after all you've done to him, you tease him about it?"

"Oh, quiet now," the strange woman replied tartly. "Just because your hands are untied doesn't mean your tongue can run loose; if it happens again, Legana will cut it out."

Mikiss heard the swish of her skirts as the woman walked closer. "Here, give him some wine to drink. It won't satisfy him, but I need him to speak a little more coherently."

A goblet was held to his lips and Mikiss slurped greedily. When he finally managed to force his encrusted eyes open, the room was nothing more than a blur for a moment, then the outlines of people started to take shape. After a few moments he could make out Major Amber, bound as he was, lying in a corner, and two women standing before a covered window. Groggily, he sat up and tried to focus on the speaker, the woman who'd faced down Isherin Purn.

"What have you done to me?" Mikiss croaked. "Feels like I've been drugged. How long did I sleep?"

"You slept most of the day, the sun is on its way down now."

Mikiss winced as he looked at the light behind her. "Then why is it so bright?"

"Because what I did to you was rather more permanent than drugging," she said, shrugging. "You are my prisoners, but I don't care much for interrogation; it's messy, noisy and unreliable."

He looked up at Nai for answers and saw the strange manservant had a thunderous look on his face. Whatever she'd done, it was bad enough that even the prospect of mutilation would not cow the man.

"I don't understand," he rasped. "Why the light? And who are you?"

She sighed. "How discourteous of me. My name is Zhia Vukotic, and I hope you enjoyed the dawn yesterday, because it is the last you'll ever see."

"What?" Mikiss tried to rise, but was betrayed by exhaustion. He fell back against Nai, and as he did so, he felt something around his neck, a bandage of some kind. He stayed silent for a few moments, then almost sobbed, "You've—"

"I've shared my curse with you, yes," Zhia Vukotic told him impatiently. "Nai, please check the wound."

The servant growled, but deftly unwrapped the length of material around Mikiss' neck. As he peered down, Mikiss saw his eyes widen and he mouthed a curse before releasing Mikiss and letting him fall to the floor.

"It's almost healed," Nai said as Mikiss groaned.

"Excellent. Now, Messenger—Mikiss—you can fight this, or you can accept what has happened and get on with it," the woman said, almost preening. "It doesn't really matter, because my power over you is now absolute. You *will* answer my questions, so the only matter for debate is how much discomfort you wish to endure before you do so. Do you understand?"

Mikiss stared at her with a glazed expression. When he turned to Nai, the servant looked both horrified and disgusted, a look echoed on Major Amber's face.

"While we're on the subject of the current state of play, you will all do better if you accept that I own you now. You have committed capital offences in Scree—spying and necromancy—so your lives are forfeit. I offer you clemency, in the form of servitude." She looked at the woman beside her. "As Legana knows, I share my secrets only with those who have secrets of their own, but since I can hardly trust any of you yet, I have taken the precaution of placing a small enchantment on you, to prevent you repeating anything said in my presence. Do you understand?"

Mikiss looked at his companions. Nai, still defiant, said nothing; the major just shrugged his shoulders, as though a change of master meant little.

"What do you want with us?" Mikiss asked.

"You will tell me about your mission in Scree," she said. "After that, I'm sure I will find a use for you."

"And if we don't tell you?"

"You no longer have the choice," she said apologetically, "not now the wound on your neck has healed."

Mikiss' hand flew to his neck. The skin was a little tender, but he could feel no injury.

"My curse has you fully in its grip now," she went on, watching his exploration, "and it is now a small matter to compel you to speak, or to do exactly as I wish. So let us start. Tell me about your mission in Scree."

As Zhia spoke those last words, Mikiss felt as though his head had been seized in a vice and wrenched upwards. The blood fizzed and boiled as he fought to keep his mouth closed; black and purple stars burst in front of his eyes until, through no volition of his own, he felt his mouth open and words began to pour out.

It didn't take long, for Lord Styrax had told Mikiss little more than his immediate task: to find the necromancer Isherin Purn in Scree and either secure an artefact of great power from him, or through him, on Lord Styrax's behalf, obviously, or report back on how to acquire it. The necromancer had told him little more in the brief time they were together, for he was intent on hearing all about the Menin conquest of Thotel.

When Mikiss had finished his uncontrolled babbling, the vampire looked far from satisfied.

"So the necromancer said nothing more, other than that he was sure there was a Crystal Skull in the city?"

"He was not so foolish as to go hunting for the bearer of such a weapon," Nai interjected. "Either it would be in the hands of a practised user, in which case his strength would not be enough, or not, in which case the wielder would most likely use it with abandon, and be unable to control the energies released."

"He could not tell which?" Zhia pressed.

"He suspected a novice, since he had detected experiments performed with the Skull."

"So when the opportunity came," mused Zhia, "he asked his former lord for help, no doubt hoping Styrax would send someone foolish enough to do the confrontation for him. The most likely outcome would be the death of all those involved, leaving Isherin Purn to skip through the ashes and claim his prize."

For reasons Mikiss could not fathom, this cheered the woman immensely. She announced breezily, "So, we have someone running around the city with a Crystal Skull. Legana, why am I not surprised?"

The pretty dark-haired woman looked taken aback at being addressed, but she said at once, "Because it confirms some things and explains others. If you'll forgive my presumption, I'm rather more interested in Purn's original mission in the West." She looked at Mikiss. "Did you say he was Malich's apprentice?"

Mikiss didn't reply until Zhia turned back to him, whereupon the words spilled out unbidden. "His apprentice, yes, sent to stir up trouble within the Farlan. I don't know any more."

"Who does?"

"Nai."

Legana turned to the necromancer's apprentice, who remained sullenly silent. Zhia gave a hiss of irritation. "Perhaps I turned the wrong one? It can be rectified easily enough if you don't start to speak now, and I will know if you lie."

Nai hesitated a moment, then shrugged. "Isherin Purn was once an acolyte of Lord Salen's at the Hidden Tower. He used his position with Malich to torment Lord Bahl with dreams of his dead bride."

"To what end?" Legana broke in, taking a step towards Nai.

"To gain control over him," Nai said bleakly. "They made him believe he could resurrect her. It was the only way Lord Styrax could draw Lord Bahl away from his armies and kill him."

"Oh Gods, of course!" the woman breathed. Mikiss looked at her, surprised at the emotional response, and suddenly realised she was most likely Farlan. Yet another spy caught up in Zhia's games? "He used the Chetse Krann to remove Lord Chalat, but when Styrax planned it all, the Farlan had no Krann and he had only Lord Bahl's own weaknesses to use against him."

Nai gave a snort, unable to restrain a proud smile. "And a remarkable feat of magic it was too, to confound someone so old and powerful," he said.

"You helped him do this?" Legana demanded.

"Certainly. I helped my master in a—"

Before Nai could finish, Legana had grabbed him by the throat and slammed him against the wall. He gasped in pain and grabbed for her arm, but she whipped a dagger from her belt and clubbed him with the pommel.

Nai howled and clouted her around the head with his other hand, but she retaliated by kicking him in the crotch and, when he doubled over in pain, a knee to the face sent him crashing down.

"Enough!" Zhia shouted, the word echoing through the room with such force that Mikiss winced and strained against his bonds in an attempt to cover his ears. "Children, children," the vampire continued, her voice a caress, "this is no playground, and you will not fight unless I say so. Is that quite clear? There are rather more—" She stopped at a crash from elsewhere in the building; a door was being smashed open, and there were angry voices.

"I fear the subtle hand of our fair ruler," Zhia sighed. "I'm surprised it has taken Siala so long to decide that I must be to blame for the events of last night. On the subject of Lord Styrax's conquest, I understood the tunnel under the mountains had been destroyed, and who else but Lord Styrax in those parts has the power to do such a thing? So if he was aware of the tunnel, he was also aware of the Fysthrall; could it be coincidence that Lord Styrax dealt so effectively with the two most powerful lords of the West, while King Emin, the other great ruler in these parts, was attacked by the White Circle over some obscure prophecy? Is he really so adept, I wonder?" A mixture of admiration and puzzlement crossed Zhia's face.

The noises resolved themselves into voices arguing outside the room. "A discussion for another time, I think. Legana, open the doors so Siala can glide straight in, or the drama of her entrance will be lost while she waits for a servant to do it for her."

The Farlan woman obeyed, and Mikiss heard another woman barking orders, followed by the clatter of footsteps coming towards them.

"Mistress Ostia, I hope you are not overly taxed by relaxing at home while my city collapses into a Gods-cursed wasteland!" Siala cried as she swept into the centre of the room, ignoring Legana, bowing rather inelegantly, and the bound prisoners sprawled across the floor.

"On the contrary, Mistress Siala, I have spent the entire night restoring order to large parts of the city," Zhia said. "This wretched necromancer had an inordinate number of daemons and local spirits bound to him, and tracking them all down was not an easy task."

"I hope you have an explanation for all this," Siala demanded, not in the least mollified.

"An explanation?" Zhia said coldly. "For what, precisely?"

"For why a necromancer was able to set up residence in my city without you or your agents finding out about it; how you managed to get there so quickly with a detachment of troops and how you nevertheless allowed the entire situation to spiral out of control, letting daemons run wild through my city." Siala's face was scarlet with fury; any trace of the calm control she'd once possessed was gone. "There are still mobs roaming the streets, attacking people at random, accusing normal people of being daemons and setting fire to them!"

"None of which is my fault," Zhia replied softly, dangerously. "I have the entire city guard out trying to regain order. There is very little more I can do without troops, and the only soldiers in the city are not under my command."

"Don't you think soldiers would merely exacerbate the situation?" Siala growled, stalking up and down the room, neatly avoiding Zhia's prisoners.

"It depends how they are handled," Zhia said. "Without strong control, there will be massive loss of life, but they are still the best way to keep order on the streets."

Siala paused for a moment in her pacing, then the ghost of a smile appeared. "I am glad we are of the same mind. As of this moment, martial law is declared. There will be a strict curfew after nightfall, and I have ordered the Third Army into the city to enforce it."

"The entire Third Army? The Fysthrall soldiers will panic the populace even more," Zhia said quietly.

"I doubt that," Siala said. "It might shock them into thinking twice before they riot again. I believe the appearance and superior discipline of my Fysthrall troops will quieten the city in a way you have proved unable to manage."

"And my city guard?" Zhia asked, refusing to rise.

"Shall be posted at the Greengate, where all city supplies will now enter the city. That will be the only open gate to the city. Your aides will be based there, in charge of keeping us all fed. These are your prisoners from last night?" she said, rounding on Mikiss abruptly.

"They are. I was in the middle of interrogating them, to discover where the necromancer had escaped to."

Siala made a dismissive gesture. "Don't worry about him; I have him."

"What? How did you catch him?" Zhia's usual calm slipped momentarily, much to Siala's apparent pleasure.

"He made his way to the Red Palace last night, looking for my protection—specifically, for protection from you. He tells me that your skills as a mage are rather more advanced than you led me to believe—and that you and he have crossed paths before . . . which prompts me to ask what else you have kept from me." Siala gave Mikiss a cursory inspection as she waited, then appeared to lose interest. She turned back to Zhia.

The vampire was thinking quickly. The necromancer wouldn't have disclosed her true identity yet; he'd keep that for when he really needed it, so it made sense to say he had come into conflict with her before. Now she needed to know exactly what he had told Siala, and exactly what threat the wretched woman thought she was.

"He must have mistaken me for someone else then; perhaps I overestimated the man," she said after a few moments. "I was going to suggest we bind him to your service, but if he is so weak as to be afraid of me, then it might not be worthwhile."

"Perhaps," Siala acknowledged, refusing the bait, "but I think I may find some use for a man capable of raising daemons; we are preparing for attack, after all." Siala turned to leave. At the door she stopped and ran a fingernail down the lacquered surface, tapping it thoughtfully. "The sun is setting soon, Mistress Ostia. Recall your guard—and do be careful not to wander the streets at night. I have instructed the Fysthrall troops to be most rigorous in the execution of their orders."

She didn't wait for a response but walked out through the crowd of clerks and Fysthrall bodyguards she'd left in the corridor. Legana was quick to pull the doors closed behind her, anticipating a furious outburst, but Zhia did nothing more than walk to a side table, above which hung a tall rectangular mirror in a frame of gilt leaves.

"So, she thinks to put me under house arrest?" she said softly.

"That's hardly going to be a problem," Legana said. "Running rings around her soldiers isn't going to cause us many difficulties."

"I'm not so sure," Zhia said. "She's testing me; she wants to see the true extent of my powers. It wouldn't surprise me if Purn himself offered to help her."

"Is she going to try to kill you?"

"No, not yet," Zhia said, "not while the Farlan are getting ready to attack. She cannot afford to lose any mage yet, and I've been careful to give her no cause to see me as a definite threat."

She smiled, and Mikiss felt it through the hairs on his neck. An echo of her hunger caused his chest to tighten. As the evening light faded, he found his eyes growing sharper; the gloom of the unlit room began to suit him well. Being this close to Zhia let him sense something of her unnatural vitality . . .

The smell of blood wafted tantalisingly past his nose: Nai had picked at a scabbed-over cut. Mikiss shivered at the feelings the smell provoked. As he tried to block it out, his gaze kept returning to Zhia, marking every small detail, from the curve of her lips to the trailing thread hanging from the hem of her skirt, from the raised toe of her slipper—

The latch on the door clicked open and jerked Mikiss from his scrutiny as a muscular woman with grey hair entered, a soldier at her heel. The man walked uncomfortably, as though he'd just come from a good kicking. Mikiss felt his nostrils flare; no fresh blood on this man; the injuries were not new.

"Mistress Ostia," the woman said, looking carefully around the room as though anticipating an ambush of some sort, "you have a visitor."

The soldier faltered when Zhia called out in honeyed tones, "My dear Doranei, can you not bear to be apart from me?"

The man stopped when he saw the bound men and carefully inspected their faces before he allowed himself to look at Zhia's shining eyes. "I come on official business; we heard you took prisoners last night."

"Indeed I did. Were you looking for someone in particular?"

"A man seen entering that house," he replied grimly, taking a hopeful step towards Amber for a closer look.

"An old friend of yours?" Zhia asked in a rather more business-like tone. Doranei gave a curt nod. "Then you are mistaken; none of the men in that house could have been known to you."

"You're certain?"

"Absolutely. It appears you have been misled." The emphasis was not lost on Doranei, and he didn't argue further. "The occupant of the house was a Menin necromancer," she went on. "These were the men seen entering the house, along with two more acting as their guards."

"A necromancer who won't last long once Lord Isak reaches the city," Legana interjected darkly.

Mikiss blinked. Were Zhia Vukotic and the Farlan allies or not?

"Lord Isak? But he's here already," Doranei said. "He arrived yesterday, with a small bodyguard."

"Lord Isak is in the city?" Zhia looked taken aback. "That confirms all my suspicions: there is some force drawing the powerful into Scree. I am surprised the Chosen of Karkarn are not also here."

That last was directed at Mikiss, who ducked his head to avoid Zhia's eyes, yet still couldn't stop himself saying, "Lord Styrax is busy in Thotel, his son has been the victim of some sort of magical attack and Lord Cytt has been dead for months now—it's rumoured that your brother killed him."

Zhia raised an eyebrow. "A magical attack? How interesting; I think we shall have to discuss that at greater length—but for the moment we have Scree to deal with. Siala is becoming an irritation to me. I lack the patience for her games, and now I see an opportunity. Killing Siala myself might leave me having to vie with the other sisters of the White Circle for control of the city, so better that someone else kills her so they have no recourse but to come running to me to take over the leadership."

"And you think to use my lord to do that?" Legana asked, anger rising in her voice.

"My dear, it would hardly be using him against his will," Zhia promised. "Once you make your report, I am sure Lord Isak will be hard to dissuade— and that I anticipate his reaction and profit by it is hardly using the man to my own ends."

"Why would Lord Isak want to kill Siala?" Doranei asked, looking lost.

"Because Siala has the necromancer; no doubt she believes him to be a useful weapon for protection, rather than the means of her own destruction." Zhia smiled at the irony. "Try not to kill anyone if you break the curfew, Legana."

"You won't need to," said Doranei. "He'll be at the theatre tonight. Only the southern districts are under curfew from nightfall; for the rest of the city the curfew ends half an hour after final curtain so the show can continue."

"Under the circumstances, that shouldn't really surprise me," mused Zhia. "You are a fount of useful information tonight, aren't you?" She stroked the man's cheek, a predatory smile on her lips. "And I see you're recovering your strength swiftly. I look forward to seeing you in complete health."

As Doranei blushed and struggled to find the words to reply, she turned again to the mirror. She cradled a small bag that hung at her waist and whis- pered what to Mikiss sounded like an incantation, though he could not make out the actual words. He felt the air thicken and a curtain of shadow descended over her reflection, growing darker with every moment, until he could hardly make out any detail. She ended her chanting and leaned forward to stare into the murkiness.

For a few heartbeats, nothing happened. Mikiss frowned, trying to work out what was happening to the mirror when he started to recognise a shape, the lines tracing a different pattern, overlaying the images of Zhia and

Legana that he'd originally been able to see. Now the sweep of Zhia's hair had become the curve of a man's neck and the line of her shawl was the edge of a swordbelt running across his chest.

The man, wreathed in shadows, peered forward with a puzzled expression, then stepped up out of the mirror onto the little table.

Mikiss recoiled as the man entered the room. The newcomer was dressed in dark but expensive clothes: a nobleman on campaign. The enormous sword strapped to his back radiated a brutal ugliness. It felt like a fire had flared up into a blaze and Mikiss felt his hands begin to tremble at the sudden aura of malevolence that filled the room, almost drowning out the electric tinge in his head. That, and the clear family resemblance, told Mikiss the newcomer was one of Zhia's brothers. The effect of both in the room together meant Mikiss could suddenly hear his own heartbeat drum loud in his ears. His head swam and he struggled to keep sitting upright.

The man had the dark blue eyes prevalent amongst the Vukotic; Mikiss had seen traders visiting Menin lands with the same distinctive look. Even in the gloaming, Mikiss could make out that strange cobalt colour that seemed to glow with a faint inner light. *Oh Gods, is it Koezh or Vorizh?* Mikiss thought to himself as his fear subsided on a note of black humour. *The Land has truly fallen into madness when a sensible man hopes it is Koezh Vukotic standing in front of him.*

He stared at the man, racking his brain until he remembered Vorizh was rumoured to be the greatest of spies; no man ever saw him enter a room, and none could track him down. Would that extend to his sister?

"More pets?" the man asked, looking intently at Mikiss. "You're collecting quite a menagerie: shapeshifters, Farlan beauties, Menin spies—" He frowned as he saw Nai and added, "Curiously battered mages with odd-sized feet." The necromancer's assistant scowled and shifted uncomfortably, still suffering from Legana's kick.

"Considering Scree's residents, it's a modest selection," Zhia said. "Now, I have need of you, o brother mine."

"I thought you didn't want me in the city?"

"I didn't, Koezh, but the situation has changed."

"Changed? How?" Koezh walked into the centre of the room, inspecting Legana and Doranei. Mikiss had no idea what he was looking for, but after a while Koezh gave Doranei a slight nod of greeting. The soldier blanched, but returned the nod, despite his obvious apprehension.

"I have yet to understand quite what is happening here," Zhia admitted.

"I'm certain I'm missing a vital detail, but I think it's now clear that whatever is happening in Scree is going to happen. There is nothing I can do to prevent it. The stakes are being raised daily."

"So you want me on hand for when you need me?"

"Exactly. I can't be sure how many of the city guard and mercenaries will follow me; I believe there is a spell being worked on the whole city, centred about the sunken theatre, that is slowly affecting the people of Scree," Zhia said.

"Affecting them? In what way?" To Mikiss, Koezh sounded like a well-spoken academic analysing a problem—hardly what he'd expected.

"The city guard reports that violence is rife throughout the city, and it's increasing. Siala has brought in troops to try to control it but the rioting is getting worse. While she hopes that a show of force will intimidate the mob, if things continue this way, no one in this city will have reason to do anything but fight to the death."

"You believe that will happen to the entire city? No wonder you want the Legion of the Damned waiting for your call."

"Exactly; there has to be a purpose to all of this, and I intend to be there at the end to do something about it."

Koezh laughed at the determination in his sister's voice, though his was a voice permanently tinged with sadness. "I think that runs in the family. How many endings have we witnessed between us?"

"Enough," Zhia said firmly, "but I prefer to keep to the present. Siala has pulled the majority of her Fysthrall troops into the city. They were camped south of the city, just off the main road to Helrect, to keep the links between the cities secure. Usefully for you, she has kept the camp restricted. Only a select number of White Circle members were allowed to approach it."

"So when we clear out the remaining troops in the camp, we'll be left alone." Koezh gave a nod of acquiescence. "I understand; we will take the camp tonight."

Zhia raised a finger to her brother and went to take Doranei by the arm. "No need to be hasty about it. First I think you should join us for the evening, enjoy a little society while some yet remains in Scree."

When the evening's light had faded to nothing more than a faint brightness on the eastern horizon, two figures left the cover of the trees to the west of Scree and looked out on the houses beyond, clumps of buildings on dirt streets before the city walls. These rough homes had been erected by those too poor to afford the security of the city walls.

One of the figures crouched and ran her fingers through the dust on the ground. The stubble of what was once long grass came up easily when she tugged at it, the desiccated stalks crackling and breaking as she rubbed them through her fingers.

"This place is dying," the witch of Llehden said, shaking her head sadly. For one bound so closely to the Land, it was exhausting to be here where the natural life was fading. Even in a desert, there was a balance and flow, but in Scree that balance had simply collapsed.

"So what can we do here?" her companion asked. He would have looked massive compared to the witch's slender frame, had there been anyone nearby to see them. His long cloak, torn and stained by years of living in the wilds, hid a body as powerfully muscled as a Chetse white-eye. Long, tangled hair covered a strangely proportioned brow and jutting jaw, but it was the midnight blue colour of his skin that would have attracted the crossbows had they tried to enter the city openly, instead of merely watching others do so.

"You don't have the power to redress the balance; what is it you hope to achieve here?"

"Understanding." She looked around.

"Of what?"

"Of a threat your father and his ilk cannot understand, Fernal."

Fernal nodded and scratched his cheek with a cruelly hooked talon that explained why he carried no weapons on his belt. The colour of his skin marked him as a Demi-God, an unclaimed child of Nartis. His kind were less common than they had been in previous ages, now there were just a handful walking the Land. Fernal was one who had accepted his lot and lived a quiet, relatively peaceful life away from normal men.

"Azaer has finally shown its hand?"

The witch straightened up and brushed the remaining dust from her hand. "The shadow's stench hangs over this city; the people are turning against each other. I know of no other mind that turns men inwards and against themselves like this."

"To what end?"

"I have no idea," she replied sadly. "I have never had any contact with

Azaer's followers; I have tried only to heal the victims of the shadow's machinations. I feel the shadow is anathema to all I hold dear, and I fear it."

She used her walking staff to drag a path through the dust. Fernal peered down at the shape she was drawing, his bony brow looking even more crumpled than usual as he tried to make out the symbols.

"Will you try to stop it?"

"Of course. Whether I can or not, I will not stand idly by." The witch stopped drawing in the dirt and stared at what she had done for a while before she erased it with her toe. She looked up at Fernal, a rare display of concern showing on her face. "I've seen enough of Azaer's deeds to know that it goes against the balance of the Land; that in itself is enough for me to choose a side. In the last town we passed, they swore priests were being beaten in the street, temples were being burned. Tell me, Fernal, without people to worship them, without temples and priests to glorify them, what are the Gods?"

The blue-skinned figure was looking out over the city. Somewhere behind the walls a lambent glow indicated that the riots had begun early that night. "Just a voice on the wind," he replied.

"Well this is an evening for the unexpected," Koezh commented coolly, walking with Legana on his arm, the perfect nobleman. "I almost feel like introducing myself to Lord Isak, just to crown the peculiarity of it all."

At Koezh's side, the young Farlan woman, still trying to hide her discomfort, followed his pointing finger to where a tall figure in a cape stood at the head of a squad of guards.

"I suspect he would not react well to it. Everyone here is somewhat tense; understandable perhaps, after that repulsive travesty we've just sat through."

I shouldn't tease her by suggesting such things, Zhia thought as she observed Legana, rather surprised at how fond she was of the prickly Farlan agent, *but it is fun to watch her stepping out like a countess. I suspect she cares less that my brother is a vampire than that he's a male one!*

"The boy was sufficiently respectful when I last met him," Zhia replied. They were taking a turn around the theatre, ostensibly to avoid the confusion of coaches and sedans crowding around its exit. At her side, rather more comfortable than Legana, Doranei stifled a snort. She gave his hand a squeeze and leaned close to his ear. "You disagree?"

They stopped at the head of the main street leading into the Shambles. A burning cart illuminated half a dozen Fysthrall soldiers who stood in a nervous knot two hundred yards down the road, flinching behind their shields as stones clattered down on them from every side. Zhia was pleased to notice Doranei couldn't stop himself breathing in her scent before replying.

"Having spent a few weeks in Lord Isak's company, respectful isn't the first word I'd have used for him," Doranei said with a faint grin.

"Really? I rather believed you thought highly of the man," Zhia said. Behind them a handful of guardsmen, Major Amber, Nai and Haipar, shuffled to a halt. She watched the Fysthrall troops huddling under their shields while they tried to edge away, and briefly wondered if she'd brought enough men with her.

"Oh I do," Doranei answered hurriedly, "and I wish I could have gone to greet him tonight—if it had been under other circumstances—but he's a white-eye, and one of the Chosen. I don't think he feels any great need to be respectful to anyone—and it doesn't come naturally to him anyway." He shot a cautious look at Legana, not wishing to start trouble, but she didn't appear to take umbrage.

"Do you know why he is here," Koezh asked, "pretending to be a mercenary bodyguard instead of at the head of an army? From what you told me of Narkang and the White Circle prophecies, he would have justification enough."

"He was lured here by one of Azaer's agents," Doranei said.

"Azaer?" said Koezh, a little taken aback. "The false daemon-cult?"

"Azaer exists," Doranei confirmed. "It may not be a true daemon, but it's certainly some sort of immortal, albeit an unusual one—Azaer has no form or physical power, unlike normal daemons, but it does have guile. It exists as a shadow only, teasing out the cruelty and arrogance in men for its own purposes. I doubt you'll have come into contact with it, or its followers; the shadow is too weak to risk going near either of you." He hesitated. "Well, so King Emin believes, and he's come into conflict with Azaer's followers more than once. Azaer prefers to steal its followers, to use words and magic to turn them against what they once believed in."

"Which brings us back to this minstrel of yours," Zhia said. "I doubt you would have been able to see the wings but he was there tonight, watching the crowd." She felt Doranei's body tense as she spoke, but pressure on his arm stopped the man from turning around to look at the building. She knew they would be watching her closely now.

"My late arrival has left me without all the facts," Koezh interrupted, "and if I'm to play, I need to know everything. We have an immortal that is neither God nor daemon, and you tell me the criminal executed on stage tonight was no wrongdoer but a priest?"

"Exactly so," Zhia said, remembering with distaste the final scene of the play they had just watched. It was surely no simple mistake that the theatre troupe had taken the wrong prisoner from the gaol for that night's performance. "The entire play was a bitter mockery of the Gods, and then instead of using a condemned man as they were supposed to, they killed a priest, one I had put in gaol to cool his temper," she said bitterly. "Fate's eyes, the priest had been complaining about the execution of men on stage!"

"And the crowd laughed," Koezh finished, dismissing the irony with a shake of his black hair. "Azaer wants to turn the people of the city against the Gods? You said the temples have been all but abandoned in recent weeks, and you've had to post guards to stop people throwing things at the priests—"

He was interrupted by a terrific crash from somewhere up ahead, followed by the sound of splintering timber and crumpling walls. Screams and shouts were interspersed with cheers and laughter. The orange flicker in the night sky fell away as the burning building collapsed in on itself, but Zhia could hear a low growl swell menacingly, and she knew the light would soon return.

Footsteps echoed from the dark side streets: men skulking in the shadows, looking for easy prey. They must have decided Zhia's party was not for them, thanks to her guards, and because she was wearing her white shawl, marking her as a woman of the White Circle. They weren't all mages—only a few had any real ability—but rumour was a powerful tool, and many believed all who wore the shawl had magical powers.

"But *what* is the goal here?" she wondered aloud. "There is a very patient mind at work behind all this."

"It's pretty obvious the actors are no simple band of travelling players," Koezh said. "Those albino siblings look like gentry to me, and if they're here, in a city, they must have been stolen away from the woods they belonged to—and that, to me, is more remarkable than the presence of mages or Raylin."

The clump of boots made them turn; two columns of soldiers trotted towards them. Seeing Zhia's shawl, the man leading the troops barked an order in their jagged language and the men clattered to a halt. Some were injured and their scaled armour and fat shields looked rather battered.

Zhia recognised the leader's facial tattoos marking him as an officer bonded by a Fysthrall woman. There were gaps in the ranks, so they must have seen some fighting already tonight. Zhia was intrigued and worried: a mob would have to be in a frenzy to take on real soldiers, especially troops as uncompromisingly efficient as the Fysthrall.

"Calling Falcon," Zhia called, reading his name from his cheek. She was always a little disappointed that the Fysthrall's methods of subduing a man's spirit were so effective—when a soldier was bonded, he was given an animal's name, for he was no longer a man, but a woman's property, and his new name, his owner's and his army unit were then tattooed onto his face. *Crude*, Zhia thought to herself, *that it worked only confirmed their opinion of their menfolk.*

The man bobbed his head in acknowledgement and hurried to her, kneeling immediately. "Yes, Mistress."

"You have lost men already tonight?"

"Yes, Mistress; two died in an ambush. We killed many before they were driven off." His command of the local dialect was excellent, but his accent was thick. He kept his eyes on her feet; this one had been well trained, Zhia realised. He looked about fifty summers—forty parades, in Fysthrall, from the annual ceremony all males performed from the age of ten. She didn't recognise his face or the owner's name so she guessed the woman was either dead or of very low family status.

"Are they attacking anyone, or just soldiers enforcing the curfew?"

"Anyone, Mistress—several of your Sisters have already disappeared this night, I have heard."

"Well then, you will escort us home," Zhia said.

"Mistress, I have orders—"

"No longer." She pointed. "It's that way."

CHAPTER 21

FORDAN LESARL, CHIEF STEWARD OF THE FARLAN, had spent his entire life in the service of his lord. He had been educated from birth to take his father's place, taught how to use men like disposable tools. His foresight had led to the creation of a network within each city-state that was unrivalled throughout the Land. It was run by Whisper, one of Lesarl's coterie of unofficial ministers, and based on a web of local agents well-used to dark-eyed men and women looming out of the shadows with a list of requirements.

The Farlan agent in Scree was a corpulent merchant, Shuel Kenn, who had done well to hide his surprise when Lord Isak himself had appeared and demanded a base for his operations. Despite the glitter in his eyes that suggested Kenn was already calculating the profit he might make from playing the dutiful host, he had spared no expense to fulfil his employer's wishes. The house he provided for Isak was not his principal residence, but it was large and luxurious, and well situated in a quiet street a short distance from the homes of the truly wealthy, so they could enjoy the city guard's protection whilst maintaining their privacy. A walled courtyard surrounded three sides of the house, and a large old chestnut tree in the middle obscured the view should anyone consider watching the rear, while the street-door was fortified against anything less than a full-on battering ram.

Tila and Vesna sat on a covered balcony at the rear of the house, facing the morning sun and drinking warm tea flavoured with lime and honey. After the horror of the two previous evenings, Scree was peculiarly silent.

"All night, whenever I closed my eyes, I saw that stage covered in blood," Tila whispered, clutching her cup. The shadows around her eyes betrayed her disturbed sleep, and Vesna was worried that what few hours' rest she had managed had left her even more troubled.

"I know," he told her. "I've seen prisoners executed in public before, and never found anything in it to entertain me. To execute prisoners on stage, as part of a play—that's abominable, but to murder a priest, before the whole city? It beggars belief. I haven't the words." Vesna pinched the bridge of his nose against the tired ache building behind his eyes. He was a seasoned campaigner, and his own uneasy rest had taken him by surprise. "There was a time when death didn't move me," he said, reflectively. "I wonder what happened?"

"You grew up," Tila said, squeezing his hand affectionately. "I've decided that to survive as a soldier, you have to live like a child—to see everything through the eyes of an adult would be too much to bear."

Vesna looked down at her fondly. "Perhaps you're right. In Tor Milist, a sergeant told me I was thinking too much. Doing that'll get you killed, but all I could think about was you. What a pathetic place to die; furthering the cause of a man I'd happily kill. All those who died there . . . for the first time I felt guilty. I'd dragged them somewhere they had no need to be." He paused, his voice dropping low. "What a pathetic way it would have been to lose you."

"Don't think like that," Tila said. "Duty took you there. I might not agree with Lord Isak, but he believes it was in the best interests of the tribe, and that decision is now his to make. We must obey our lord."

Despite his despondency, Vesna smiled at Tila's sudden vehemence. He frequently forgot the twenty summers between them, until some tiny detail brought him up short, and when that happened, the years sat heavier on his shoulders, even as Tila's bright smile lifted him up.

"Aye, we'll follow his will, though he's little more than a lad and you're not much better! Gods, to be that young again." He pointed at the chestnut tree that dominated the courtyard. "That reminds me of when I was a lad; we had one at Narole Hall and I'd climb it every time I did something wrong." Vesna laughed suddenly. "It happened so often my father threatened to cut the damned thing down."

"And did he?"

"No, it was an empty threat—he did exactly the same when he was a boy." He shook his head. "I've started missing that house recently, though I've not lived there in years."

"What happened?" Tila asked. "It's your family home, isn't it?"

Vesna gave a weary shrug. "I inherited my father's debts. He was a good father, but a poor manager of estates, and I ran up a few more myself after he died. Don't think I appreciated the place when I was young; parts of Anvee are beautiful, which is why a lot of old soldiers go there to find a peaceful retirement. Of course, they still need to eat, so they train boys like me, whose parents want them to last beyond their first battle. It's only now I realise those old veterans found something genuine there. When I was a lad, all I could think about was getting to the city and joining the army."

"So you had to sell your home?"

"Almost. The local magistrate was an old friend of my father's and he found a merchant who liked the idea of living in an ancestral home. The merchant was a good man: he gave me a fair price, and agreed that if ever I could repay that money, with remarkably modest interest, I'd get my house back."

"But you haven't?"

Her question provoked a flush of embarrassment. "Somehow I never managed to save the money—first of all I had a lot of debts to pay off, but since I had inherited an Elven blade from my father, and I was my swordmaster's finest student, I decided paying debts wouldn't get my home back, so I commissioned my armour from the College of Magic and decided to win honours on the battlefield instead. I knew nothing of trade, so where else was the money to come from?"

"And the money you've made on the field has gone to servicing the remaining debts?" Tila finished his sentence. This was a common story; those who held a debt could sell it or pass it on. It was a cruel system, for one missed payment, maybe because of illness, or an emergency, was often enough to start the descent into bankruptcy. Once they were caught in this trap, few found a way to escape.

"Mostly," Vesna admitted. "When I was knighted I was given land, of course, but it's not worth enough to pay more than a third of the debt. Perhaps I should give trade a go, now I feel too old for battle."

"Nonsense," Tila said. "There's no one in the tribe Lord Isak trusts more than you; the sensible money's on him appointing you as General Elierl's replacement in Lomin. There's no duke there, so the eastern border needs an experienced commander more than ever."

"But what if that's not what I want?" Vesna asked sadly. "What if my nerve's gone, and all I've left is an unsavoury reputation, and not even a child to pass my weapons on to?"

"But that's not true," Tila insisted fiercely. "Your nerve isn't gone or you wouldn't have made it here; you'd have died outside Tor Milist. Doubting yourself is only human, but I know you'd not even pause to think before stepping between danger and your lord—and while we're on the subject, do you think Lord Isak has never doubted himself? He's only a little older than I am and he grew up on a wagon train, yet we now expect him to make decisions that affect nations! Suzerains, dukes and high priests defer to him on theology and prophecy; Isak must be horrified at the life he's found himself living." Her voice softened. "He'll need you to understand a sane man's doubts, otherwise you'll not be there when he no longer knows which way to turn."

They heard footsteps ascending the stairs from the unused study below and turned to see Major Jachen's face bobbing up into view. Isak's Commander of Guards always looked sheepish when he was forced to disturb them. Clearly he'd come straight from his bed and hadn't passed a mirror on the way, for his hair was plastered down over his scalp on one side and sticking up on the other. He wore a loose linen shirt and, bizarrely, despite the hot weather, a Chetse warrior's kilt.

It was the first time Vesna had ever seen a Farlan in Chetse dress. It had clearly been made for Jachen, for he was taller than most Chetse and the kilt still reached his scarred knees—yet another sign of how far Jachen had gone to evade his past?

Vesna smiled inwardly and breathed in the faint aroma of Tila's skin. He had been forgiven his own reputation once he joined Isak's inner circle; perhaps redemption was also within Jachen's reach.

"Count Vesna, Lady Tila; Lord Isak requests your presence." Jachen sounded awkward, as though the formality of his position still did not come easily to him. "We have a visitor," he added, "a woman, apparently one of the Chief Steward's agents."

Vesna hauled himself to his feet and offered a hand to Tila.

"Major, have you managed much sleep recently?" he asked suddenly. Jachen's reddened eyes and sickly complexion made him look like he'd spent the last two days drinking. "For a man who's just woken up, you don't look very well rested."

"I find it hard to sleep in this heat, and my head's been aching ever since we arrived here," he admitted.

"Surely you're used to the heat?" Vesna pointed at the kilt; the Chetse lived far to the south and much of their territory was little more than desert. Jachen must have served there to get into the habit of wearing a warrior's kilt.

"This heat's not natural," Jachen said, "but you're right, it shouldn't be enough to stop me sleeping. Feels like there's something in the air, like a song just out of hearing. I'll be glad to see the back of this city."

"How about your dreams?"

A hunted look flashed over Jachen's face. "What about them?"

"You don't look like you've been having normal dreams recently."

The commander lowered his eyes and said quietly, "Recently? Not for years now." He coughed and turned to leave. "Lord Isak is waiting downstairs."

"We're coming, but . . . Commander?" Jachen stopped and Vesna caught up with him and gave him a firm pat on the shoulder. "Get properly dressed first. You're not a mercenary any longer."

There was a sparkle of defiance in Jachen's eye, quickly checked. He nodded, and excused himself.

The open reception room that served as the heart of the house was ringed by enough pillars for a temple to Nartis. There was a mezzanine balcony, and above, it was open to the sky. Lord Isak circled a young woman, who was sitting comfortably on a cushion, watching her lord. Gone were the trappings of state and title; instead, Lord Isak, clad in a loose sleeveless shirt and cropped breeches, looked more like the suspicious, bare-footed youth he had been a year ago. Only the sheathed sword that he kept switching from one hand to the other and the whitened skin of his left arm that bore the kiss of a hundred searing lightning bolts marked him as someone different.

Two of Isak's guards stood at the main door, armed with the short-handled glaives favoured by the Ghosts of Tirah. On the balcony Sir Kelet prowled, his beautiful silver-inlaid bow at the ready. Perched on the edge of the balcony, her bare toes hanging over the empty space below, was Shinir, Lesarl's sour-faced agent. She was balancing her sickle-like khopesh, a brutal single-edged weapon, on her finger, and her long chain-link flail was draped around her shoulders. She never bothered hiding her dislike of Vesna, but he ignored her as he passed. Shinir could be a useful asset, but she was unstable, too close to being a Raylin for his liking. He knew that if he did get into an argument with her, he'd have to be ready to end it.

In contrast to Lord Isak, who fidgeted like a boy before his first battle, the young woman sitting cross-legged in the centre of the room was still and calm. Her hair was tinted red, like one of the White Circle, but she was undoubtedly a pure-blood Farlan.

Vesna felt a jolt as he realised he'd met her before . . . it took him a moment to place that beautiful face, then he had it: she'd been at a meeting in Lord Bahl's tent, after the battle of the Chir Plains. She'd been standing silently at the side and he had dismissed her as an assassin. It looked like she was rather more than that.

"Vesna, Tila, this is Legana," Lord Isak announced. "She is here to infiltrate the White Circle. Lesarl's orders." He gave a sour laugh. "And although we've discovered their plans the hard way, she's unearthed even darker secrets."

"My Lord?" Vesna stopped. There was obviously more to Isak's agitated state than just the sweltering nights and the magic unleashed throughout the city the previous night.

"The death of Lord Bahl, or so she claims." Isak finally settled, leaning back against the pillar in front of Legana.

"My Lord, I thought you would want to hear that part of my report first," Legana said.

Vesna thought he detected a slight northern drawl. "First the context," he said. "I want to know how you have heard such things; how such secrets were brought into the open."

Legana bobbed her head, a wisp of rusty hair falling across her face. "Mistress Siala assigned me as an aide to Mistress Ostia—the name assumed here by the vampire Zhia Vukotic, as you know; Siala remains ignorant of her true identity. The night before last, Mistress Ostia—Zhia—captured the necromancer's associates during the assault on his house. One was his assistant, who told us that his master was Menin by birth, and had been trained in his arts by Lord Salen himself. He was sent west to stir up trouble in these parts, and became acquainted with Cordein Malich, later becoming his apprentice."

"Malich?" Vesna gasped. "The Menin have been planning their invasion for that long?"

"But how did this necromancer's apprentice bring about Lord Bahl's death?" Isak interjected.

"Did Lord Bahl ever mention his dreams?"

"Not that I remember. Why is that important?"

"Because they used his dreams, his memories of his lost love, against him. Lord Styrax has been planning this invasion for years—how else could anyone have brought an army across the Waste intact? The one thing he had not anticipated is you, Lord Isak."

"Of course not," Vesna said, pacing the room himself. "How could he, when he was working so many years ahead? We knew some form of necromantic power was involved when Lord Charr usurped Lord Chalat. The Chetse were defeated because of this. Lord Styrax has used our own weakness against us: the Farlan had only one Chosen, and we have a history of insurrection, while the Chetse are prone to over-obedience. Thotel fell because no one challenged Lord Charr's orders, even though any seasoned soldier could have seen the danger."

"And Mistress Zhia believes Lord Styrax may have influenced the actions of the White Circle as well," Legana added.

Vesna stopped his pacing and swung around to examine Legana. "Thus directing their efforts towards eliminating the other great leader of the West?" he asked.

"So she believes."

"I can think of no one more able to unravel deviousness, and at this point there is little I could not believe of Lord Styrax. I suspect he would even put our own dear Chief Steward to shame."

"Impressed, Vesna?" Lord Isak asked.

"Enough to respect him as an enemy," the count replied. He put his hand on the hilt of his sword as he continued, "Rather more importantly, it means we cannot forget the threat to Lord Isak. We will have to watch for assassins and instruct Mariq—"

"No." Lord Isak's soft interruption stopped the count. A prickle went down Vesna's spine as he saw a hunted look in his master's eye. As he looked around the room, he saw they too had felt the change, a sudden cloud crossing the sun.

"My Lord?"

"He will not send assassins."

"How can you tell?"

"I know, leave it at that."

Vesna checked his urge to question further. Isak had told them about his dreams, the Yeetatchen girl Xeliath, the soul of Aryn Bwr kept prisoner in his head, even what the dead Elf had claimed about Kastan Styrax being born the Saviour, until he chose his own route. Isak had mentioned a connection between the two of them, but not wanted to go into detail—and only a handful of people had been told that much. Obviously he would explain no further in the presence of Jachen or Legana, no matter how loyal they professed themselves.

Vesna did his duty and changed the subject back. "Legana, what did this necromancer do to Lord Bahl's dreams?"

"He used them to torment Lord Bahl with visions of his lost love, driving him to a certain place on the White Isle, where Lord Styrax could ambush him."

"Are we to assume that Zhia is aware of your true allegiance?" Tila asked suddenly, stepping forward from the foot of the stair where she had been observing the conversation.

Legana nodded.

"So she is aware that you are reporting to Lord Isak?"

Legana smiled. "It is her hope that Lord Isak will kill the necromancer, because he has made some sort of bargain with Mistress Siala and currently resides under her protection."

"So this could be nothing more than some artifice of Zhia's, to have us do her bidding?"

"I don't believe so," Legana said plainly, turning to look at the younger woman. "Mistress Zhia had already come to the conclusion that Mistress Siala was more an obstacle than a help, even before we learned of Lord Isak's presence in the city."

Vesna watched the two of them. It was rare to see a woman more arrestingly beautiful than Tila. Legana managed to command the room almost as much as Isak, who was a white-eye, and stood a foot and a half taller. To Vesna's experienced eye, Legana was not happy with the attention her beauty brought. White-eyes, he knew, were born to demand attention as entirely natural, and Isak had quickly shaken off the habits of his isolated upbringing, but Legana had obviously never grown too comfortable with the effect she had on a roomful of men.

"You keep saying 'Mistress,'" Tila observed, as though sharing Vesna's thought and taking it a step further. "That's the form of address demanded by those of the White Circle. Have you grown attached to the Sisterhood?"

Legana looked startled at the suggestion. "It has become a habit out of necessity; it would be too easy to make a mistake if I wasn't careful to always keep to the forms—and the future of the Circle is hardly one I would want to tie myself to. The White Circle suffered grievous losses in Narkang. They have no expansionist plans at present. Shoring up their defences before they are slaughtered by Narkang and the Farlan is their only goal, and it's Zhia who is effectively in charge of four of Scree's five armies. They are finished as a power in the Land."

Tila didn't respond, but her expression was cool and her eyes fixed on Legana. When the agent turned away, Tila gave Isak a small nod and stepped back out of the conversation again.

"So we have an associate of Malich's in the city, one who was also involved in the death of Lord Bahl and remains an agent of the Menin." Isak shrugged. "It's a simple decision then; we kill him first."

"My Lord, he is under Siala's protection, and a necromancer is constantly on guard; the attack on his house will have made him doubly watchful."

Isak's eyes flashed. "I don't care. This necromancer is an enemy of the Farlan and a threat to us all." He pointed a finger towards Tila. "Those of you who lack any defence against magic will be the ones hurt in the crossfire when he comes after me."

A furious hammering on the front door broke off the discussion. They could hear angry voices in the street outside, growing louder, then the person beating at the barred door yelled out above the racket, "For Vellern's sake, let me in; they're going to kill me!"

"It's Mayel," Isak said, surprised, "the kid we brought back here the other night. Let him in."

The guardsmen raised their glaives and one used the butt of his weapon to knock the bolt open and raise the latch. The former novice barrelled through, barging the doors wide open as he rushed in, and Isak caught sight of the figures following him: half a dozen townsfolk, armed with clubs and sticks and what looked like meat cleavers. Clearly the madness that had gripped the population was worsening.

One guardsman drove his door shut, but the other had moved outside to see what was happening. Seeing the onrushing mob, he stepped away and raised his weapon; Vesna shouted for Tila to get up the stairs and pulled out his longsword. Isak had already drawn his, and when the first of the invaders hurtled in, the white-eye spun around as gracefully as a dancer and beheaded him neatly. Blood fountained from the attacker's neck as the body crashed to the marble floor.

As others followed, still shouting and screeching incoherently, they found themselves set upon from all sides. The guardsmen slammed the door and bolted it against further incursions. By the time they joined the fight, it was almost all over: Lord Kelet's arrows had taken two down, and a third was gaping down at Legana's knife buried in his chest. Count Vesna had battered aside a club and impaled the owner, while Shinir, leaping down from the balcony and swinging around a pillar into the fray, had used her flail and khopesh to good account, trapping a fat man who looked like a butcher and hacking through his collarbone. She left the khopesh there as she tossed her chain flail around one of the remaining two people and yanked hard; the chain caught the astonished invader under the chin and slammed her against the pillar with a sickening snap.

The last man standing, his bloodstained cleaver raised uncertainly, took a step back. He never even saw the guardsmen behind him, swinging their glaives in unison. The room fell silent as they listened for more voices outside. Vesna looked up to Kelet, who had another arrow nocked and ready.

He made his way around the balcony to a window and peered up and down the street outside for a few seconds. Finally the knight from Torl called, "Looks clear, my Lord."

"Shinir, get out to the back and check there," Jachen said, his voice husky. He had drawn his sword, but he'd not had to fight—Lord Isak had made it clear that he had some very effective killers in his personal guard now, and that was not *his* job. *He* was to watch for what was going on beyond and around any fight, and to guard Tila from any threat.

"Karkarn's black teeth," breathed Mayel, eyes widening as he watched Shinir scamper up a pillar and vault onto the balcony with consummate ease. "You're like no mercenaries I've ever met."

"You were a novice in a monastery; exactly how many mercenaries *have* you met in your life?" Jachen snapped, advancing on the youth.

"Being a novice doesn't make me brainless," the boy said. He pointed at Shinir. "No normal woman does that. Maybe a Harlequin could manage it, but no damned soldier."

"Congratulations, you've just seen a damned soldier do it," he said sarcastically.

"I say you're not normal mercenaries. No lord's tart—ah, begging your pardon, Miss," he added hurriedly as he caught Vesna's expression, "but no lord's mistress is so valuable she's protected by a white-eye his size—" he jabbed a grubby finger in Isak's direction, "and a woman touched by magic, not both. Not when the city's terrified the entire Farlan Army's going to appear at the walls at any moment."

"Why are you here?" Lord Isak interjected. "I thought you were going to see if your cousin survived the other night?" After the chaos of the night at the necromancer's house, Isak had beaten a hasty retreat rather than get entangled in a fight with the city guard. He'd seen some of the creatures crashing through the fence and decided on the spur of the minute that it would be too cruel to leave the boy to fend for himself, so he'd dragged Mayel along with him. Mayel had spent half of the next day in shock, huddled in a corner of the room, before he regained some semblance of his normal insouciance. He'd shaken himself all over, like a dog, and announcing he had to find his cousin, he grabbed some food and disappeared before anyone could talk him out of leaving the safety of the house.

"I did, but I hadn't realised the state the city's in. I'd never have made it back here if I'd not known the streets as well as I do. As it was—" Mayel gestured towards the corpses in the middle of the room. "They came after me because I was alone. No other reason."

"And your cousin?"

"Dead." His shoulders fell. "Dead, with most of his men, when the Dark Place spat out its creatures at them."

"And he's the only person you know in the city?" Vesna asked, recalling what Ilumene, the supposed King's Man, had said to Isak: *a priest on the run.* He was beginning to think it was no coincidence that Mayel had been a novice at a monastery. The city was spiralling into chaos with breathtaking speed, and Vesna was increasingly fearful that it was not by chance. Doranei had already told them Ilumene was now an enemy of Narkang and Morghien had hinted at a shadowy hand behind much to do with Isak too. *What if this is only the next step?* Vesna thought.

"Who else could there be?" Mayel replied hotly. "I've been in a monastery for the last few years."

"Perhaps someone from that monastery, then?" Vesna pressed. He hadn't sheathed his sword. Now he began to advance on the youth. There was something not right about this boy.

Mayel took a pace back.

"Perhaps someone who needed to hide in the city, someone who needed a native to help them?"

"I don't know what you mean," Mayel blustered—but his eyes had already betrayed him.

"Balls you don't; you know exactly what I'm on about," Vesna said angrily. Very deliberately, he tore a strip of clothing from one of the dead men and used it to wipe his blade clean before sheathing it. Then, before Mayel realised what was happening, he'd stepped forward and grabbed the boy by the throat.

"You've been lying to us," he said, "so how about you spill what you know or I'll beat seven shades of shit out of you?"

Mayel struggled against Vesna's grip. "I've not—"

He stopped abruptly as the count punched a fist into his gut, driving the wind from him.

"Not what?" he roared, shaking the youth like a terrier holding a rat. "You're not going to tell me the truth?"

"I don't—!"

Mayel's gasping protests were cut off as Vesna slammed him into the wall. Terrified, he cowered, hands held out like a pleading supplicant.

Everyone else in the room kept silent and watched. They had all seen far worse; so far Vesna had been remarkably restrained. Mayel was obviously no trained liar; it wouldn't take much longer to get the truth they so desperately needed to hear.

"Trust me, boy; I can keep this up all day," Vesna threatened, his voice silky. "You'll want to give it up long before I do." He snarled, and punched Mayel sharply.

The boy howled and flopped to the floor, and Vesna picked him up again and pinned him against the wall.

"Ready to tell me yet?"

"All right!" he gasped. "Please, stop it, and I'll tell you."

Vesna held him there for a few heartbeats, then let Mayel sink to his knees. He left the boy there as Isak beckoned and led him to a corner of the room where they could speak without being overheard.

Taking that as his cue, Jachen began removing the bodies as noisily as he could.

"Feeling better?" Isak asked softly. "You've been boiling inside for days, my friend, something I recognise only too well. Now you've hurt someone, does that help?"

Vesna sighed. "The boy's no good at lying. It looked worse than it really was; I pulled most of my blows. He's not really hurt much. I apologise if I went too far."

"You were serving me as you should," Isak said, laying a hand on the count's shoulder. "It's just novel that I'm the composed one. Is there anything I should know? Not as your lord, but as your friend. What really happened in Tor Milist? Something there shook you up."

"It's—" Vesna shook his head. "Now is not the time, but I would like to speak of it. Let us deal with the boy first."

Isak led the way back to Mayel, who was sitting with his back to the wall, grimacing.

He lifted the youth to his feet and inspected the damage. "You'll have a fine bruise or two, but I don't think he's done much more than rattle your teeth. I'll be glad if I get no more than that before I get out of this city."

Mayel touched a finger to his rapidly swelling cheek. The man who'd hit him was a strong man, and a fair bit taller. "You'll be telling me he pulled his punches next," he muttered, glaring at Vesna around Isak's massive body.

"And that shows it's just your pride that's hurt. A wise man once told me that was easily given up to save your life."

"I'm sure the old sod would feel smug if he saw this then," Mayel spat.

"I'm sure he would, but *you* don't get to call him an old sod," Isak replied, and slapped him sharply on his bruised cheek.

The youth yelped and recoiled.

"Enough of the games. I'm losing patience," Isak growled, looming over the youth and glowering until he thought Mayel looked frightened enough to tell the truth. "You had something to tell me."

Mayel started shaking. Rubbing his cheek, he looked up at the huge white-eye towering over him. He had suddenly realised he was in over his head, and these men were not going to take it easy on him because he was just a scrawny ex-novice. "Why do you even care about the monastery?" he whispered.

"Call it professional interest," Isak said, watching expressions dance across Mayel's face. Vesna was right; the boy was no accomplished liar. "A priest was murdered last night, on stage, in front of a cheering crowd. From what I hear that's not the only priest who's been treated with something less than respect by the good citizens of Scree, and I'm curious as to why."

"I don't know much about that," Mayel said quickly. "I came to Scree with the abbot of my monastery. We were hiding from a rogue monk; the prior of our order."

"Who's called?"

"Prior Corci, but everyone called him Jackdaw. We brought some holy relics with us and Jackdaw wants them." Mayel shuddered visibly as he said quietly, "He killed someone trying to get at them, so the abbot decided to flee." By now all the bluster had disappeared and he was just a frightened boy.

Isak stepped back a pace to give him a bit of space. "Do you know what the relics are?" he asked, his voice less angry now.

Mayel shook his head. "No, the abbot was careful never to let me see them."

"But you have your suspicions?" Isak pressed.

"I can't be sure, but both Abbot Doren and Jackdaw are mages. When I went looking for news of my cousin, I also tried to visit the abbot, but I was driven off as soon as I entered the grounds. I got a splitting headache—no, more than that, it was a pain in my head, but not like anything I've ever felt before. It was as if I could feel his presence all around me, but suddenly he was terrifying, not the sickly old man I know. It felt—" He paused. "It felt like he'd gone mad, and I could feel his fear." Mayel scowled at the floor and rubbed his cheek. "I know that sounds ridiculous but I could taste it on the air before I even reached the house. He was a mage, I suppose."

"Driven mad by fear?" Isak looked fascinated and worried at the same time, a look that was echoed around the room.

Mayel shrugged. "The house was quite close to your necromancer's; perhaps the relic attracted one of the daemons when they escaped the grounds. The abbot was really paranoid, right from the moment we left the monastery, so a daemon attacking the house could have pushed him the rest of the way."

"And what is your plan now?"

Mayel didn't answer at first. Nervously, he looked around at the others in the room and tried in vain to read their expressions.

Isak did the same. The only person showing any emotion was Tila, and she was doing a fair job of hiding her anxiety over Vesna's sudden show of fury. Only the set of her lips and poise betrayed her. He wasn't surprised at the other blank faces; it was second nature for spies and career soldiers to hide their feelings.

"I don't have a plan now," Mayel said reluctantly. "My cousin's dead, and I can't go back to the abbot. With the city the way it is, I don't know what I'm going to do. No one's going to be hiring while mobs are roaming the streets. Even my cousin's house has been ransacked—by his own men." There was a trace of indignation in his voice now, and he raised his chin a little defiantly.

"Have you ever considered the life of a fighting man?" said Isak with a grin.

"Not really," Mayel admitted as he weakly returned the smile. "People trying to kill me has never appealed; even a monastery sounds better than that."

"As soon as you go out of that door, people will try to kill you," Isak said baldly. "My way, you've at least got a sword in your hand and comrades to keep you alive."

Relief and suspicion clashed on Mayel's face. "You mean a sword like that one?" he said hopefully, pointing to Eolis.

"Hah, perhaps not quite like mine," Isak said with a laugh, instinctively jerking the blade away from Mayel's attention, "but I'm sure we can find you something to suit your abilities. One of the men will show you how to avoid sticking yourself with it."

"Why would you want me?"

"The same reason your abbot did; we're not locals here. We've good trackers, but none of us are from Scree, so that probably makes you worth feeding."

He turned to Jachen. "Take him to whatever dark corner Tiniq and Leshi are lurking in. Our newest recruit is going to tell them exactly how to get to his abbot, so they can go and investigate."

"Of course." Jachen remembered not to salute, and beckoned for Mayel to follow him.

"My Lord," Legana said, once Mayel was out of earshot, "what are my orders?"

Isak cocked his head, trying to decide whether he should send her back to Zhia Vukotic's side. *And what is* our *next step?* he wondered to himself. *Is there anything more to do in this city beyond finding a safe way out? I think we've come too late for much else.*

"Does the vampire know what is happening in Scree?" he said finally.

"She has her suspicions," Legana answered. "She believes the ones running the sunken theatre are casting some sort of spell that is affecting the whole city. They're followers of Azaer, if King Emin's men are to be believed."

"Looking at what's going on outside, there's not going to be a city left for much longer, so their plan must be nearing completion."

Legana inclined her head in agreement.

Isak scratched his neck. "No doubt the theatre will be exempt from the curfew tonight. Perhaps we'll find our answers there." He beamed and raised his left hand. Curls of orange flame began to twirl around his white fingers. "If not, let's burn the bastard down instead."

CHAPTER 22

FROM THE TOP OF ANHEM'S TOWER, the tallest building in Scree's north-eastern corner, Rojak watched the first shadows of evening steal over the Land, catching men and beasts unawares, wrapping them in deepening threads of twilight. He looked back at the city, where he could see a squad of brutal Fysthrall soldiers chopping their way though a crowd of locals. The rusty-skinned foreigners were worried these people were working themselves up into a frenzy, as had happened half a dozen times over the last few days, but in truth this lot were crying out for food, not slaughter. The Fysthrall didn't understand their language.

The minstrel smiled. "Misunderstandings cause such misery, more than ill will could ever manage."

"*Is that a challenge?*"

Rojak gave a strange, girlish laugh. "Perhaps not tonight," he told his master.

Beside him, Ilumene pointed out over the fields, at a towering column of dust they'd been watching as it drew closer. "It'll be a close-run thing. Who will bother to ask why we have a Devoted army outside the walls? How many in this city would believe that they're here only to protect the sanctity of Scree's temples, as they claim, and not in fact waiting like jackals to feed on the spoils of a failing leader?" He jabbed a thumb to the north. There were parallel thin red scabs running down the thumb from nail to wrist, and he curled it to ensure the cuts remained open. Against the clear pale blue above the horizon a dirty smear indicated the presence of another army. North, where every road led to Farlan lands.

"If those Farlan come any closer, the Devoted's commander will be forced to turn and face them; he'll have to dig in, or risk being raided by the Farlan cavalry every hour. The Farlan will interpret digging in as a gesture of intent and act accordingly."

"*And now it is time for us to give a helping hand. Ilumene, our favourite son; find us another priest for tonight's entertainment.*"

"The show must go on, eh?" Ilumene's weathered face lit up with malicious mirth.

"There will be an audience. The good folk of Scree are consumed by their hatred of everything around them; they have passed the point of no return now," said the minstrel, dismissing him with a gesture.

Ilumene ran lightly down the thick stone steps to the street below, past the Hound that Rojak now needed to help him get about. It was obvious to all concerned that what they sardonically called *their theatrics* was taking its toll on the minstrel, who was becoming increasingly brittle with every passing day.

Rojak looked down at the little finger of his left hand, inspecting his most recent injury. He'd scraped his hand when he'd lost his balance on the steps, and a good inch of papery skin had been shredded, revealing desiccated grey tissue that did not belong in a living man. As Scree failed, so did he— but the knowledge that this was one more victory he would steal from King Emin elicited a chuckle from his wasted throat. He winced and fumbled for the flask of brandy he carried at all times.

"Now for the ill will I promised you," said Azaer, an icy breeze sliding gently over Rojak's ear. *"Send Flitter and Venn to the camp of the Second Army; tell its commanders who their mistress truly is."*

"Will they be believed?"

"Belief is a fickle creature. Those who believe do so because they wish to. Bane and Veren's Staff could no more restrain themselves than King Emin could when he heard Ilumene had been seen. Ironskin is the voice of reason in that camp. His unique affliction was punishment for offending Karkan. I'm sure he will be keen to follow his comrades to please the Gods."

"Should we not wait until we see Siala's reaction to the Devoted?"

"The Devoted are in no rush to fight; they have yet to decide who their enemy is. When they see the Circle's mercenaries fighting each other, they will stand back and watch; as Ilumene so aptly said, their nature is that of jackals. The Second Army will march on the Greengate, as that is where the vampire's troops are. Every other gate is already barricaded, so this will bottle them all up together. Let them squabble amongst themselves, and turn on each other just as their Gods do."

"Their weakness is our power," intoned Rojak.

"Certainly, but let no one claim we are cruel; they shall be warned that their own flaws betray them."

"A new play for tonight?"

"The last play. After tonight we will retire to the wings and the theatre will be no more. We shall have nothing more for them but our final curtain call."

"So which is it to be for our last performance, my Master?"

"*Twilight reigns, the gates are locked and within, the city burns. What could it be but* The Shadow Crucible*?*"

"Tell me again why we're here?" asked Morghien through gritted teeth. He strained to pull himself up to the next branch. The trip had been an arduous one, despite Mihn's many talents, and for once Morghien was feeling his age.

"The answer to that hasn't changed," Mihn said softly from the branch above. His attention was occupied by the earthwork ramparts surrounding a hill less than a mile away. The smooth sweeps of dark slope were illuminated by paper lanterns of yellow and red.

Morghien gave a grunt and finally pulled himself up. Once he'd found his balance, the man of many spirits turned his head up to see Mihn, who was standing nonchalantly on a slim bough, his staff resting across his shoulders and his arms hooked over it.

Morghien knew better than try to keep up with a former Harlequin when it came to acrobatics so he made sure of his grip before speaking again.

"I actually meant, why are we climbing this bloody tree?"

"Ah, I apologise," said Mihn. "I'd assumed you were continuing the litany that started as we crossed the Green Sea, but now I realise it was a whole new complaint."

"Tsatach's balls, I'm here as a favour to your master. I've got every right to complain if I want to," Morghien muttered.

"I'm sure the magnanimous Lord Isak will be pleased you're taking every opportunity to exercise your rights," Mihn said cheerily.

Morghien scowled at him. "Now we're here, what can you see?"

"Much of the estate, all nicely lit up for our benefit. It is Meqao's Day today. Of all of Amavoq's Aspects, Meqao—Hunter of the Silent Wood, as he's known in these parts—is the most beloved by the Yeetatchen."

"He's the one with the antlers and the huge—"

"No, that's Bohreq, the Herdfather. I thought you'd had an education?" Mihn scratched at his ankle absentmindedly for a moment, before feeling the bandage on it and withdrawing his hand. Two days back he'd been bitten by a hunting hound on the loose, and though the wound was minor, he'd bound it to keep it clean. "Meqao has the head of a silver-furred wolf and carries a spear in one hand, a brass bell in the other."

"Brass bell? What damned use is that to a hunter?"

Mihn looked down and Morghien thought he could see the man's eyes glint in the gloom. "I would be happy to recount the full saga of 'Meqao and the Lady of the Bluebells'—of course, it will require a gong, a bell and a jug of water, and three hours of your close attention." He smiled.

"Perhaps later then?" Morghien sighed. "Wouldn't it be easier to get in to Lord Ajel's home if we dressed you as a Harlequin and got you to recite the saga?" He'd not meant it seriously, but he realised he'd overstepped the mark when Mihn tensed. The cool evening grew frosty.

"Don't suggest that again," Mihn said eventually, his voice tight and quiet.

"I am truly sorry," Morghien began. "I didn't mean—"

"I know, but best the conversation goes no further." After a moment of quiet, Mihn pointed. "That is how we'll get in: if we run along the ditch bounding the meadow until we reach that dip, we'll come up behind those trees hung with lanterns."

"Lanterns? Can you see if it's a sacred grove dedicated to Amavoq, or an Aspect that lives on the hill?"

"Not from here, no. You think an Aspect would notice you?"

Morghien gave a low whistle. "Hard to tell, but last night Xeliath told me Lord Ajel has made a local Aspect of the hill protector of the compound."

"So it will probably object when we take Lord Ajel's daughter from her bed chamber?" Mihn wondered.

"I hope not. She doesn't know the details of the bargain her father made. I'm hoping the Aspect will only notice if Xeliath is being taken against her will; she's determined to leave on her own two feet. Her father wants her present at the feast, but she's sure if she misbehaves she'll be taken back to her room and given something to make her sleep."

"So we'll have to carry her out?" Mihn said.

"No, Xeliath's a cunning little minx, even touched by the Gods as she is in the waking world. She's been behaving herself of late and they've been letting her take her own medicine. She says they know now she's not a prophet, so they're not afraid she'll get loose and hurt someone. Tonight she'll be awake enough for our purposes. She says the festival's important to the Yee-tatchen, so security should be lax, and that's good for us."

"Assuming we even get there."

"Have faith, my friend," Morghien said with a snort of amusement. "As long as I keep out of that sacred grove I doubt we'll be noticed."

Mihn peered down, eyebrows raised. "No complaint? Well in that case, let us join in the festivities."

The compound occupied a small hill, the highest ground in the area. It stood at the southern end of the Silent Wood, the expanse of forest that belted the island, and a sheer-edged gorge made it virtually impenetrable for potential invaders from the east. It had been hard enough for Mihn and Morghien, and they had neither horses to lead nor an army to feed, and they had Xeliath to give them the lie of the land. All Yeetatchen, noble-born or not, were taught to scout, so her description had been far better than Mihn had expected.

The Yeetatchen compound was not defended by walls, but by earthen channels. There was little stone; the buildings set into the hillside were built of wood, and several had trees jutting through their roofs.

The only problem they encountered making their way down the ditches was the eight inches of water at the bottom, which constantly threatened to betray them to the patrolling guards, no matter how adept they were at travelling quietly.

At the end of the first of the long, dark ditches, Morghien touched his companion on the arm, stopping him from starting on the ten yards of open ground between them and the next bit of cover.

"I have a better idea," Morghien whispered. He mouthed something Mihn didn't catch and, as he finished speaking, he gave a deep sigh and closed his eyes, quietly expelling the air from his lungs. Mihn watched as a tiny wisp of fog escaped Morghien's pursed lips and quested out a little, as though tasting the wind—then a figure stepped out from Morghien's body and turned its head to Mihn, who gasped in shock and backed up to the side of the ditch.

The figure was female; he could see that in the smoky lines of her face and the long, flowing hair that merged with the curve of her back. From her waist down she was less distinct, though the tendrils of fog that connected her to Morghien were almost tangible. Mihn felt the colour rise to his face as he realised the figure was entirely naked, but she appeared not to notice his embarrassment. He recognised her now: Seliasei, an Aspect of Vasle, the first and strongest of Morghien's spirits.

Seliasei scrutinised Mihn for a few moments, her expression blank, then stepped forward and bent down to place her hand in the ditch water.

"Vasle is God of Rivers," Mihn murmured to himself. He began to see Morghien's plan. *These ditches are connected*, he thought, *and if they all have water in, Seliasei will be able to lead us safely past any guards.*

Morghien was still standing with his eyes closed, as if in a trance. Mihn hoped he'd be able to wake Morghien if anyone did come.

Apparently satisfied with whatever she felt in the water, Seliasei straightened and drifted forward. Mihn saw the hint of legs walking, but her movement was too graceful and ethereal to be human. As Seliasei moved out from the darkness and into the faint light, she dissipated until she was little more than a suggestion in the air. Mihn thought the guards, whose night sight had probably been ruined by the lanterns that adorned the whole compound—and who would probably have sneaked a drink or two to celebrate Meqao's Day—would dismiss anything they saw as fancy. Even if they didn't, were they really going to run to their commander claiming they had seen a ghost?

Mihn watched Seliasei as the Aspect, followed closely by Morghien, made her way around the earthwork and disappeared from view, then he shook himself and followed them until they reached a corner of the compound that was, according to Xeliath's description, in easy reach of her bedroom.

Less than a hundred yards away stood a great circle of tents where the household were celebrating Meqao's Day. Mihn could hear voices raised, haunting and beautiful in the cool summer air. He smiled slightly, remembering how much he had enjoyed feast days as a child. Without thinking, his lips began to move and silently join in. The song the Yeetatchen were singing was one of the oldest known, written before the Great War, when Amavoq and her Aspects regularly walked among the Yeetatchen people. The rapturous silence that greeted the singers at its close tugged at his heart.

"Well, lad," Morghien said at last, "up you climb." He gestured to the fat creeper entwined around the oak-bough wall.

Mihn gave the creeper an experimental tug. It seemed sound. "I hope she's right about being able to make it out of here by herself," he whispered. "I don't fancy having to lower a white-eye down on my rope." He checked again for servants or guards, then began to climb. There were plenty of handholds and within half a minute he'd slipped a knife up between the shutters and opened the catch.

He looked down at Morghien, barely seen in the shadow of the wall, who nodded. Mihn pushed open the window and slid over the window sill onto a large rug. He looked around, cataloguing the spartan room. There was an ornately carved bed, with posts carved like bent branches, leading up to a canopy of leaves above, and a massive chest along the wall opposite the bed.

The only personal details Mihn could see were a silver-backed hairbrush on the chest and a stuffed horse, a child's toy, on the foot of the bed. Mihn took a step towards it; the small horse looked old and well loved. No doubt Xeliath kept it still because she could no longer ride in real life, something any Yeetatchen would mourn.

A sound came from the bed, hoarse and strained, as if the voice was rarely used. Mihn thought perhaps it was his name being spoken, but he couldn't be sure. He took a step closer, still not able to make out who was under the dark blankets. He was afraid to speak in case they had made a mistake and he was in the wrong room.

The person in the bed moved and suddenly a soft light spread out over the blanket. Mihn froze; he'd spent enough time around Isak to know this wasn't lamplight.

"Xeliath?" he whispered. The light grew, mapping out the lines of her body under the blanket.

"You are Mihn?" she croaked, her hand twitching as she struggled to prop herself up. He strained to hear the musical notes of the Yeetatchen dialect, but she sounded more like a withered old woman than a girl in her prime. He tried to reply, but the words caught in his throat for a moment as he studied the ruin of her face in the magical light. Her short-cropped hair exposed her left side, and the damaged flesh, the slack muscles underneath trembling occasionally, on the brink of spasm. The eyelid drooping over her left eye hid the tiny pupil, and made the bright white iris of her right eye all the more startling.

"I—yes, I'm Mihn," he said before realising that he'd spoken in his original tongue, a language he'd not used aloud in years. He repeated the words in Yeetatchen and saw the beginnings of a smile.

"He didn't say you'd be handsome."

Mihn looked down, caught between embarrassment and amusement. "Somehow that doesn't surprise me." A floorboard outside the room creaked and the latch clicked, and Mihn covered the ground in two quick steps to reach the person entering. He smashed an elbow into the person's head, a boy, he saw, who dropped like a stone. Mihn caught him just before he clattered to the floor and eased him quietly to the ground, then closed and bolted the door against further interruptions.

Xeliath grunted in effort as she tried to get up, but Mihn ignored her while he checked out the servant boy. He was out cold, but hadn't suffered any lasting damage. Mihn pulled a length of rope from around his waist and a cloth from around his arm and soon had the youth bound and gagged. Then he took the boy's small knife from his belt and shoved him under the bed.

"Are you finished now?" Xeliath asked.

"Not quite." He worked the chest onto the rug, then dragged it to the door. Like that it wouldn't be enough to stop a determined man, but Mihn was inventive: he jammed the servant's knife and one of his own spare blades between the floorboards right up against the chest so it was wedged tight up against the door—it wouldn't hold forever, but it would give them a few precious minutes. He chuckled to himself. Close inspection of his knife would show its local origin, courtesy of the merchant who had unwittingly provided it a few days before. A little bit of luck and a few hot tempers should send the chase in entirely the wrong direction.

Xeliath had succeeded in pushing back the blankets. Laid out next to her was a man's riding jerkin and trousers. "You'll have to help me dress myself," she said, her voice a little stronger than it had been at first. She pulled feebly at the cotton shift she wore. "I can't manage alone."

"My Lady—" he began, before his heart melted. *She's a white-eye who's been crippled*, he reminded himself. *She'll have been stronger than any normal man under her father's command until her destiny was linked with Isak's; this must be doubly painful.* "I understand, my Lady."

He went about the task as gently as time permitted, and Xeliath never made a sound, even though her pain was written on her face. Her right side looked perfect, but her left arm was curled in on itself, the tight fist bent around something hard and smooth, pushing the knuckles against her bony hip. The arm was the most damaged part of her body, as if whatever had happened had started in her fist, then spread. Her leg was not badly affected, but it was wasted from under-use, the veins showing clearly through the dry, flaky skin. She stared intently at the pattern of oak and elm leaves carved into the canopy, enduring the manhandling with her lips pinched together.

When Mihn had finished, he sat her up to slip on her boots and lace them up.

At last she looked Mihn directly in the eye. "What is he like?" she asked softly.

"Lord Isak?" Mihn was surprised by the question. "Don't you know?"

"I know what he looks like in his dreams," she whispered, "but sadly, dreams are only that. They tell me nothing of who he is."

Mihn helped her upright and let her take her weight. After a little unsteadiness, she looked able to walk. "Lord Isak is a young man trying to be a good lord," he said after a moment. "He's trying to understand what's been done to his life."

"He fights it, though."

"That's only natural, isn't it? As a white-eye?"

"It is in his blood to do so, but it is not always the answer. He may need others to show him that."

Mihn hesitated, disturbed by the direction of her thoughts. "Let's get you out of here so you can tell him yourself." He guided her towards the window, opened the shutter a little and peered out. The area around looked empty of armed men. "Can you climb?"

"I'll manage."

"Are you sure?" Mihn looked at her sceptically until Xeliath took his hand with her good one. Her fingers, shaking a little as he had helped her out of bed, now clamped around his wrist and began to crush it. After a few moments, Mihn gave a gasp of pain and she released him.

"I get the point," he said dryly. "You're still a white-eye."

"Good boy."

"But without meaning to offend you, my Lady, you are going to find it hard to climb with only one arm. Your left is completely useless, isn't it?"

She grimaced as her shoulder spasmed, as though responding to Mihn's question of its own volition. With her teeth gritted against the pain, Xeliath brought her left arm up to chest height, visibly shaking. With what looked like great difficulty, she turned her wrist so Mihn could see what she held.

"I think we should bring it with us nonetheless," she whispered.

Mihn hadn't been able to identify it as he'd struggled to fit Xeliath's ruined arm into the shirt sleeve, though it felt smooth, and as warm as her own skin, for all its solidity. Now, in the dull moonlight, he saw a glassy surface and his heart went cold. The last time he had seen something like that, it had been fused to Eolis, Lord Isak's sword . . .

The Crystal Skull given to Xeliath had done the same thing, only this one had fused itself to the hand with which she'd first gripped it. It had probably attached itself to the bones within as well. To take the Skull of Dreams from Xeliath would require more than theft: it would need mutilation.

Mihn suddenly realised Lord Isak had been right to send him here. Sooner or later someone would try to take the Skull from her, and Xeliath would most likely die in the process.

"May I be allowed to tie a rope around you, in case you slip? I promised my Lord I would bring you safely to him."

The young woman shook her head. "I have been imprisoned here for the best part of a year; I will escape it by my own strength or die trying. The wishes of the man whose fault this is do not concern me." With no small amount of difficulty, she fought her way down the wall, clinging fast to the creeper as she searched for secure footholds. Her gritted determination paid off and she half-fell into Morghien's waiting arms.

They set off by fits and starts as rainclouds began to gather above. With Seliasei's ghostly assistance, they got to the edge of the forest as the first fat drops began to clatter through the leaves. Morghien led the way, a throwing axe ready in his hand, while Xeliath allowed Mihn to walk at her side, a secure arm around her waist in case her underused leg muscles failed her.

"Thieves, are they?" said a woman's voice behind them.

Mihn stumbled in shock, almost knocking Xeliath to the floor, while Morghien whirled around with his axe raised. Mihn could do little to help his companion beyond turning Xeliath so she could see who had spoken, but Morghien did nothing once he'd raised his weapon.

Standing a few yards behind them were three young women in long dresses. They had hair curling to their waists. The middle one had skin the same shade as Xeliath's. The girl on the left was a rich ebony, and the one on the right had a silvery sheen to her patterned coffee skin that caught the moonlight.

"Thieves they must be, sisters," answered the right, smiling like a cat at Morghien as he put himself between Xeliath and the strange women. "Thieves stealing the jewel of our household, I think."

"And on our father's day as well," continued the ebony-skinned woman. Her flesh was so dark Mihn could see little of her face beyond sharp little teeth and eyes that flashed green. "Shall we permit it?"

"How could we permit it?" purred the middle sister. "Stolen from our domain, when we are bound to protect her family? No, they must be punished."

"We've stolen nothing," Morghien said, prompting all three women to turn their hungry attentions solely on him.

"Strangers come and creep in through windows, hurrying away before the alarm is sounded, with a noble child under their cloaks. Thieves, we think," she spat, with undisguised venom. "Avoiding the guards is easy, but us? Not so; we can sense all that goes on in these parts, and how could we not notice a foreign spirit walking our fields?"

Out of the corner of his eye, Mihn saw a brief white flicker around Morghien's head. *Seliasei*, he thought. *If she's worried, perhaps we should be too.*

"They steal nothing, wolf-cubs," Xeliath replied firmly. "Leave and let us pass."

The middle sister spared her a pitying look, all the time flexing her long fingers impatiently. "You do not order us, we grant that boon only to your father."

"Wolf-cubs," Mihn blurted out. "You must be the Daughters of Meqao, the Aspects of Amavoq bound to this place."

"We are," said the sister with ash-bark skin, "and we do not care who you are, so be careful of how you speak to us."

"He'll speak to you however he wishes," Xeliath snapped, "and you will run back to your trees and hide there until we are far away. In the morning, when you eventually appear before my father, you will say I have run off to be married to a soldier I met when he presented me at court, and he should not follow. He will hear from me soon enough."

The sisters took a step forwards, hungry expressions showing long teeth and hanging tongues. "And why should we do that, little one?"

"Because otherwise you are my enemies."

As Xeliath spoke, Mihn felt a sudden warmth in the arm held close to him. He could feel a fire building inside her, one that sent a surge of prickling energy rushing through his body as well. He could see the sisters felt it too, and suddenly they were nervous.

"What do you have in your hand, little one?" the middle sister asked, rather more uncertain now. A burst of white light came from Xeliath's side, shining from the Skull through the ruined hand. The sisters howled and staggered back, shielding their eyes from the light. The lightest-skinned of the three dropped to her knees with a wail that stopped only when Xeliath halted the surge of magic. Thinking quickly, Mihn was ready to take her weight when the effects of the coursing energy hit Xeliath and she sagged onto his shoulder.

"I am blessed by your mistress, Lady Amavoq herself. Be content you are doing her will in helping me."

The three sisters stared at her fearfully, then turned and ran as one. They had gone just a few paces when their bodies became insubstantial and vanished to nothing.

Xeliath panted furiously and forced herself fully upright again.

Morghien gave her a curious look and laughed. "Lady Amavoq, that great romantic," he said and laughed again.

Xeliath gave him an angry glare and he kept his mouth shut as he sauntered past her and back into the forest. An obscure little smile played across his face for the first time in weeks.

Mihn sighed inwardly and hoped Morghien wouldn't infuriate Lady Xeliath as much as he did Lord Isak. Even the beautiful half of her face was presently twisted into a scowl.

"Are you going to follow him, or stand there looking like an idiot?" she muttered. "Come on, move."

Mihn sighed again. It was going to be a long journey home.

"Now isn't that strange?" Isak said under his breath. Keeping a safe distance from the squads of Fysthrall soldiers that ringed the sunken theatre and the surrounding streets, Isak and two of his guards were crouched behind a parapet that edged the flat roof of a nearby building. It gave an excellent view of the crowd outside the theatre's gate, and Isak recognised several people. A rough wooden frame covered in sailcloth above them kept them in shadow. The owners of the building cowered and stayed safely indoors, content to leave Scree's madmen outside.

"Bloody mad, I'd call it," Tiniq said beside him.

That was the longest sentence Isak had heard from General Lahk's brother all evening. For a ranger who was at least twenty years older than he looked, Tiniq was as jumpy as a raw recruit, and had been ever since they arrived in Scree, constantly looking over his shoulder and twitching fearfully, as though he could hear the mournful bell of Death's gates somewhere nearby.

"That they're putting on a play I can understand, if what Legana said about a spell is true, but for folk to walk these streets to see it is nothing more than madness."

"It must be part of the spell," Leshi replied from Isak's other side. The two unnatural men were Isak's only guards that evening, to help them go unnoticed, though the ranger, Jeil, was keeping watch in the street. Mayel, who was their guide, was huddled in the far corner of the rooftop, keen to see, but desperate not to be seen. After nightfall, his city was given over to flame and fury, and he had no wish to be drawn further into the madness.

"Look at the rioting, the meaningless violence; at least this place is protected. Coming here probably looks like the sensible option to them, even though they have to brave the streets to get here."

"Forsaken!" howled a voice behind them. Tiniq was a blur as he jumped up, sword drawn and raised, ready to protect Isak. In the street behind them where Jeil lurked, an old man staggered down the street, dressed in rags, a bloody wound on his balding head leaking blood down his face. He appeared oblivious of the men watching him. His voice fell to a mutter, jumbled syllables that made no sense, then rose again to a roar as he proclaimed: "Failing city bound to a failing heart! She brings ashes; words and ashes from the darkness underground."

"Jeil," Isak hissed, "shut the old bastard up before he attracts attention."

Hearing a voice, the old man stopped and peered up at Isak. He brandished a rusty dagger in the white-eye's general direction. "What Gods abandon, so fire shall purge!" he screamed. "They have cursed us; their servants cast spells upon us and must be sacrificed to the flame!"

Jeil stepped out of a nearby doorway, a short crescent-headed axe in one hand. Tiniq scampered across the roof towards his comrade, sensing trouble as Jeil said, "Bugger off, old man, or I'll kill you and you can see what Lord Death thinks of your words."

The old man stared at Jeil for a moment, incomprehension fading to fury in a heartbeat. "Servant of the Gods!" the man yelled. He raised his battered dagger and lunged forward at Jeil, shrieking. The ranger fell back to give himself room, only to hit the wall behind him. He swung the axe up and caught the old man in the armpit, pulling his own knife from his belt to catch the old man's blade.

The wound didn't look like it had any effect on the man as he slashed down, his blade glancing off Jeil's dagger and into the ranger's arm. Jeil kicked out in desperation, and succeeded in driving the old man within reach of Tiniq's broadsword.

They watched his head tumble off and roll a little way down the street.

Isak and Leshi were close behind, their weapons at the ready, but the street beyond was empty.

"Well, wasn't he nice?" Isak commented grimly as Tiniq wiped his blade clean on the old man's rags and set about binding Jeil's arm.

The Shambles was strangely silent around them. Mayel said most people had barricaded themselves in their homes, those who weren't out trying to find food, to buy or steal. A crowd had built up at the Greengate, where all the city's supplies came in. A mob had already demolished and set alight a market to the west.

Mayel came to the top of the stair. "How are we going to get out of this?" he whispered, his panic barely kept in check. "Almost the whole city's like this—so we either burn with the madmen or get slaughtered by the armies outside the walls."

Isak realised the boy was so terrified he was close to breaking down; he needed a little hope if he were to survive the next few hours. Isak unwrapped the leather covering that kept curious eyes from the sparkling hilt. He drew Eolis and held it up in front of Mayel's face to catch what light there was.

"You probably didn't notice when you saw it the first time," he said, "but this is no ordinary sword, and I am no ordinary mercenary." Mayel stared at Eolis, wonder showing on his face, but still no understanding. Isak continued, "One of those armies out there is mine."

"Oh Gods, you're—"

"*Walking blindly in shadows,*" interrupted a female voice in Isak's head, drowning out Mayel's words. He whirled to see a cowled figure step into the open from an alley on the right. Isak's guards cursed and drew their weapons, but he raised his hand to stop them.

"And you are?" Isak said.

"*As ever; a light in the darkness.*"

Isak thought for a moment, her words forcing a memory to stir. "Witch?"

She laughed, prompting his guards to exchange curious looks. "*I've been greeted in more friendly ways, but yes, you are correct.*"

"I don't know how else to address you."

"Ah, my Lord," Tiniq began in an uncertain voice. Isak cut him off with a chopping motion. The ranger looked completely confused at the one-sided conversation—as Isak's guards had the first time he met the Witch of Llehden—but he didn't have time to explain.

"*And it is how you will continue. You already know that a witch should never reveal her name to anyone.*"

"*Can you not give me some other name to use?*" Isak said in his mind.

She advanced towards him, her face catching the moonlight. She looked more tired and worn than she had been in his dreams, as if the journey to Scree had aged her. Perhaps it was the effort of leaving Llehden?

"*Call me Ehla, then; it is the Elvish rune for 'light.'*"

"Well, Ehla, now you're here do you think you'll be able to stop the spell?"

"Unfortunately not; it will soon be completed. Events are out of our control, I saw armies marching on the city as I crossed the wall."

"You crossed the wall tonight?"

"I would be a poor witch if I could not fool a few city guards," Ehla scoffed before gesturing towards the theatre. *"You were watching the audience?"*

"It seems safer than watching the play itself."

"Shall we, then?" She pointed up the stairs where Mayel was watching them. He misinterpreted her intent and shrank back, but Isak ignored him as he led the way back up to their vantage point, the witch close behind.

"Who can you see?" she asked as she sat on the low wall the men had been crouching behind, her back resting against the wooden roof support.

Isak pointed towards a group of women surrounded by city militia and said, "Over there is Mistress Ostia, with her various agents and mercenaries." He said the words aloud, realising that his men would be more confused by no conversation than half of one, but he wasn't sure he wanted Mayel to know about the vampire, so in the privacy of his mind, he added, *"Ostia's the name Zhia Vukotic has taken within the White Circle."* He continued, "One of them is also my agent. By the theatre's gate, Mistress Siala is doing the same as us, except I'm told she's more interested in the members of the White Circle, reasserting her control over them."

"Who is it you're watching for?"

"The powerful. I think Siala is deluded, thinking that the White Circle remains a power in the Land. Scree is tearing itself apart, and the people here believe there are six armies outside the walls, all waiting to pick their bones. I'm looking to see who Mistress Ostia has with her, who King Emin has brought with him, and what Raylin are walking the streets of Scree."

"And what good will that do you?"

"You said yourself events are out of our control," Isak said, struggling to keep his temper in check when the very air he was breathing felt hot and agitated. He could feel the stifling waves of magic being exuded from somewhere around the theatre, like a scent of rotting flesh, and he could almost feel the pervading miasma of effluent stink, the result of the unnatural heat and the riots, that crawled like a pestilence on his skin. The combination of the two had him constantly on the verge of gagging.

"I just want to know who's going to cause me a problem if I have to fight my way out of here. Why did you come over the wall if you don't believe you can do anything?"

"That we may not win here is no reason to simply submit. Scree is an unimportant city; none of the great powers control it, so there must be another reason why this is happening. There must be more to this spell than what we can see."

Isak paused. "Legana said the Menin were searching for a Crystal Skull. Could this be a way to find it?"

"You with your two Skulls have been lured here; why go to so much effort to find only one?" The witch hesitated, a flash of doubt in her eyes. *"I could only see that being worthwhile if it were the Skull of Ruling, the most powerful of them all, so the legend goes."*

Isak nodded, that made sense. Ruling, the last of the Skulls to be forged by Aryn Bwr, had been given to his eldest son and heir, Velere Nostil, to help him rule after the Great War—Velere's mother, Valije, had foreseen Aryn Bwr's death at the Last Battle. He knew that rebuilding after the destruction of the Great War would require genius, and his heir would need help. Neither Valije nor Aryn Bwr had foreseen their son's assassination by Aracnan two years into the war, and no one knew what had happened to the Skull until it reappeared during the Age of Darkness, in the hands of a Litse warlord.

"Mistress Ostia has one also," Isak added, "and Legana tells me her brother has arrived in the city, so he will no doubt be carrying his own."

"There are at least five Crystal Skulls in the city?" The witch sounded aghast. *"That does not bode well. Power attracts power. What do you plan to do?"*

"Now? Watch the faces, and once the crowds have left the theatre, burn it down." Isak broke off and peered at the people waiting outside the theatre. "What's happening now?" He pointed towards Mistress Ostia's group. Some soldiers had joined her and they could hear urgent voices arguing, some calling over to Mistress Siala's troops. As they watched, a nearby company of Fysthrall soldiers hefted their weapons and started at a trot down a side street. After a little more discussion, Ostia's group followed them, weapons drawn.

"It looks like one of those armies outside has lost patience and attacked the city."

"It must be the Greengate that's been attacked if it's Ostia who's going to deal with it," Isak reasoned aloud, "but who's doing it? The Farlan wouldn't, and I doubt the Knights of the Temples are so driven by their dogma that they've abandoned all reason and attacked when they're so outnumbered by the White Circle armies."

"The spell on this city promotes chaos and madness; most likely the mercenary armies and Raylin have decided they no longer need to take orders from the White Circle."

"Then we're in more danger than ever before." He turned to his men. "Tiniq, can you contact your brother? We need to send a message to General Lahk."

The ranger shook his head as the witch interrupted Isak. *"My companion can do that. What message shall I give him?"*

Isak turned to the witch. "Will your companion make it through the picket lines alive?"

Ehla smiled. *"I should hope so; he is a Demi-God, a son of Nartis."*

"Well then, tell them to dig in and hold their position. They are not to attack the city until your companion passes on my particular order. When I am ready to break our way out, we will head for Autumn's Arch—Mayel, that's the gate, right?"

The young man flinched at being addressed unexpectedly and nodded hard.

"Good," Isak continued, "Autumn's Arch is the least defended, and we'll take them by surprise while Lahk marches in. If the Greengate's being attacked, Autumn's Arch is their only option—the New Barbican in the north is the best defended, the Princess Gate to the east is closest to Siala's palace and has the Dawn Barracks nearby, and going for the Foxport in the south would leave them far too exposed to the mercenary armies stationed there."

"And how will these orders be believed? Fernal is not Farlan; your general may think him nothing but a Raylin employed by the Fysthrall."

"Tiniq, how do we get your brother to believe the messenger?" Isak asked.

The ranger looked bemused for a moment. "I suppose, ah, something about our childhood? He has a scar on his knee from stabbing himself, the first time we went hunting."

Isak couldn't help laughing, remembering when he'd done something similarly stupid and Carel's expression when he'd had to admit it. He repeated it for the witch's benefit, and she gave a curt nod.

"My Lord," Jeil interrupted. Blood was seeping through the bandage Tiniq had wrapped around his forearm. "If there is fighting at the Greengate, should we not retreat to the house?"

"No," Isak said firmly, "I'm sure Zhia will be able to handle them. We're in no greater danger yet. I want this theatre destroyed before the night is out, then we'll make our way back and work out how to avenge Lord Bahl."

"You're here for vengeance?" the witch asked in a disapproving tone.

"No," Isak replied grimly, "but vengeance I'll have all the same."

The witch gave him a stony look and Isak could feel the reproach in it. *"There's an old saying in Llehden: your greatest desires are always accompanied by your worst fears. What is it you fear, my Lord?"*

Isak looked away, unable to answer.

CHAPTER 23

THE LIGHT OF DAWN was no more than an icy gleam beneath the receding clouds when four groups of men appeared at the head of the huge ancient steps leading down to Thotel's Temple Plain. The ground was still soaked after the night's deluge and all around was the rush and clatter of falling water, pouring down from rocky clefts in the cliff, feeding the lake at its southern end where most of the city's water came from.

The two oldest men embraced and shared a questioning look, but the remainder were careful not to catch each other's attention as they assembled at the top of the massive stairway and waited as the western horizon brightened and the clouds parted before the light.

General Dev breathed in the damp scent of the plain. He remembered the last time he'd gone there, the night Lord Chalat had abandoned them—or been murdered, he still wasn't entirely sure. Dev had had his skull cracked that night, leaving him bedridden and unable to oppose Lord Charr's insanity which had ensured the Menin victory over them. Whether he would have been able to stop Charr was open for debate, but as Commander of the Ten Thousand, he would have been the only one in a position to try. The enormous guilt he felt was only compounded by his current collaboration with the Menin and, until he found a way out of this impossible position, it would continue to gnaw at his insides.

The fading gloom unveiled an ochre landscape streaked with long trails of rusty red clay and sandy seams. The cliffs surrounding the plain were dotted with straggly plants that clung to tiny ledges, and bats and flying lizards filled the air, returning to the caves in which they roosted. The heart of the plain was dominated by the gigantic pyramidal shape of the Temple of the Sun, where their patron God Tsatach heard the prayers of thousands around the Eternal Flame. Its copper peak was as bright and gleaming as the day the temple had been raised.

A sound came from their right. The general turned to see a man standing before the Temple of Nartis, one of three temples not standing on the plain itself. Dev, peering through the pillars, could see it was empty.

Odd, he thought, *shouldn't the priests of Nartis be performing the final ritual of the night?*

The man walked towards them and offered a respectful bow that was not returned. General Dev glanced at his companions. Each group consisted of a tachrenn, commander of a thousand axemen, and a few of their command staff—like General Dev, they had been instructed to bring only their closest advisors, and no guards. No doubt they feared they were to be slaughtered before the city awakened, but General Dev suspected something else. Killing them quietly, even in guarded stoneduns, was easy enough to arrange. They wouldn't have been invited to the Temple Plain if Lord Styrax wanted them all dead. To bring together the commanders of the legions that comprised the Ten Thousand—or at least, those who remained after the Menin's comprehensive victory—with neither ceremony nor great secrecy: that spoke of respect, rather than a knife in the back.

The man, a Menin servant, he assumed, wore a nondescript grey robe tied at the waist, and loose grey trousers. He beamed at the eight groups of men. "Good morning, General Dev, and Tachrenn of the Ten Thousand; my Lord requests your presence for a small Menin tradition down on the Temple Plain."

"Do we look like we care about Menin traditions?" spat Tachrenn Lecha, a tall Chetse with his arm still in a sling from a spear-wound he'd received in the battle.

"Lecha," General Dev rumbled, unwilling to let the younger tachrenn stir trouble already, "it's a little early for incivility."

"Incivility? General, you do recall that they have occupied our capital city—or has your new creature-friend made you forget that?" said Lecha, appalled at what he viewed as his commander's collaboration. Tachrenn Lecha had organised much of the city's resistance; General Gaur had said as much in his last meeting with Dev, and he had made it clear they were losing patience with the man. Dev was far from happy with the situation himself; he was getting pressure from both sides, and life grew more complicated with every day. Very few Chetse approved of his current understanding with Lord Styrax and he had yet to decide himself whether he'd done the right thing.

"I remember," Dev said, ignoring the tachrenn's disrespectful tone, "and I also remember that our legions lack the weapons to stop Lord Styrax slaughtering any part of the population he pleases—and I also remember that most conquering armies would have executed us all after our city fell. I remember hearing only yesterday that a Chetse army marching to our aid from Cholos was crushed. So until the time has come when we are in a position to throw off our oppressors, please try not to antagonise the white-eye currently ruling us."

Not waiting for a response, the ageing Chetse started off down the massive stair. He could feel the resentment behind him, but he knew there was nothing to do other than ignore it. Beside him hovered his nephew, a young infantryman acting as his aide since he was still none too steady on his feet after the recent injury. As he neared the Temple of the Sun and once again saw a white-eye waiting for him, General Dev felt his head start to throb again. His vision swam for a moment, causing him to hesitate enough for his nephew to notice and take his arm.

"Gods," Dev muttered, loud enough only for his nephew to hear, "I was too old for this even before I got my skull cracked."

After more than two hundred steps, set in a zigzag of three straight sections, he found himself on the plain, approaching the looming bulk of the Temple of the Sun, which was lit faintly from within by the eternal flame. The white shaft of light that ran from altar to apex shone only inside the temple's boundary line. The pale stone of the temple glowed, and grew even larger in the dim of dawning morn.

Once they reached the temple, Dev realised that none of the figures waiting for them beside the small fire was in fact Lord Styrax, though the lord's son, Kohrad, was there, slumped in a campaign chair and wrapped in what looked like white ceremonial robes. He looked drawn and sickly still, and the skin of his face and hands was blistered and scarred.

Curious: removing that burning armour from his body weakened the boy more than anyone could have expected, Dev thought. The man hovering at Kohrad's elbow looked like a doctor—he didn't envy the man if his charge died.

Predictably, General Gaur was amongst those awaiting them. The bestial warrior nodded to the group, but had the good sense not to greet Dev personally. The apparent leader was Duke Vrill. He was the exception to the white-eye rule, for not only was he smaller than most of his kind, he was little more than half-decent as a warrior. Even stranger, he made up for that in other ways, for he was renowned as a cunning and patient strategist.

Dev guessed the duke must have recently returned to the city. He had been overseeing the ongoing campaign against the last two Chetse cities defying the Menin. Tachrenn Lecha insisted the continuing resistance was a sign that they could still drive the Menin out of Thotel, but Dev knew he was not alone in believing the only reason Cholos and Lenei remained free was because neither city was important enough for Lord Styrax to bother with yet.

"Honoured guests," Duke Vrill declared with a broad grin, his arms spread theatrically, "it is a Menin tradition to take tea at the breaking of dawn, in a place of quiet reflection. I do hope you will join us in saluting the day's first light."

One of the assorted soldiers gave a snort of amusement. Lecha voiced the collective thought. "What tradition is this?" he asked. "Just to drink tea as dawn breaks?" He didn't bother to hide the contempt in his voice, but Duke Vrill ignored it, as few white-eyes would have.

The Menin duke stepped forward, his eyes on the tachrenn, and said softly, "Just to drink tea, and to consider the beauty of the Land as it is revealed."

"No particular ceremony with the tea, then?"

"None; I've always thought that ritual tends to get in the way of enjoyment—but it is tea brought from our home in the Ring of Fire. You could consider it symbolic tea, if you like." Somehow, the duke managed to keep any mocking tone from his voice.

Dev stepped in before Lecha refused the tea on symbolic grounds—this was obviously a face-saving pretext so both sides could come together in relative peace. He could smell business needing to be discussed.

"I would be glad for tea," he said loudly, "and like all old men, I have learned that one should take any opportunity to appreciate the beauty of our Land."

"One must always take the time to pay attention to what's around," boomed a deep voice from the temple, and they turned to see Kastan Styrax step out from the lee of a pillar. The massive white-eye lord was swathed in a long grey cloak, but Dev's schooled eye detected the full suit of armour underneath the enveloping material.

"Strange, none of the others are dressed for battle," Dev muttered to himself, looking around discreetly. The two soldiers tending the fire had sheathed swords on their hips, of course, as did Kohrad Styrax and Duke Vrill, but no one else was armoured.

What is playing out here? Dev wondered. *Styrax's helm is lying on the temple floor, and he surely knows no crowd of old soldiers is going to miss his gear—he wants to make it very clear that he's the only one ready for battle, but why? I really am too old for this.*

Once the two soldiers had served tall cups of pale green tea to each man they retired to a respectful distance.

Dev realised Lord Styrax was watching him fixedly and with a curt nod, he ordered his aides to do likewise. One by one, the tachrenns copied him. Although some looked less than happy, it would have been a gross insult not to follow their commander's lead. Even Tachrenn Lecha wouldn't defy his general quite so openly.

"Gentlemen," Kastan Styrax said, once the staff were out of earshot, "now we are no longer lords and commanders, merely old soldiers sharing tea and grumbling about the state of the Land, as old soldiers are supposed to."

Old men grumbling about the Land? What do you have to grumble about, O lord of all you survey? Dev wondered, then: *Gods! Are you asking a favour of us?*

Lord Styrax walked through the group to face the War God's temple, second on the plain only to Tsatach's own Temple of the Sun. A stylised image of Karkarn in his berserker aspect, with long wild hair and savage canines, had been carved above the entrance. When the Menin lord turned back to the men, there was a satisfied expression on his face.

"Tachrenn Echat," he said suddenly, "I hear condolences are in order."

The tachrenn looked alarmed for a moment at having been singled out. Echat's darker skin and delicate features marked him as from the easternmost part of the Chetse territory, one of the desert clans who lived on the fringes of the Waste. It was a harsh and unforgiving place that bred the finest Chetse warriors; many of the Ten Thousand were recruited from those wild parts. Echat shook his head, as if to clear it, then said, "The raids, you mean?"

"Certainly," Lord Styrax said. "I hear your own clan took heavy losses—though not without giving a good account of themselves."

Echat looked stunned for a moment, as much at *who* was offering him condolences as the fact that the lord even knew of the action. "I thank you for those words," he stammered a little, "but every child of the desert is well used to the danger. It is just another aspect of life for us."

"No doubt—but I hear there is more activity in that part of the Waste this year. A number of my own troops have also been lost."

Just what are you saying? Dev wondered as he watched the exchange closely. *Echat has played it down, but they've been hurt badly, and not just by the Siblis. There is word of Elven raiding parties too.*

"These things are rarely predictable," Dev said out loud, ignoring the grateful look on Tachrenn Echat's face. When Lord Styrax turned to face him, Dev was filled with the certainty that this was no idle chatter. "The nature of the Waste has always been chaotic," he added.

"True enough, but news of the recent upheaval can only embolden raiders," Lord Styrax said. "Jackals are quick to exploit any weaknesses they see."

General Dev spread his hands in a gesture of helplessness. "There is little we can do to aid them; the desert clans will have to fend for themselves for the moment."

Lord Styrax sipped his tea with a thoughtful expression that didn't fool

Dev for a moment. The white-eye looked past the men as the first rays of dawn crept over the cliffs surrounding the Temple Plain.

The cynic in General Dev saw Lord Styrax had positioned himself carefully. A very old shrine to the sun's first light, a minor Aspect of Tsatach called Kehla, stood on the cliffs directly west from Tsatach's main temple. It consisted mainly of an archway, through which the rising sun now appeared, bathing the Menin lord in golden rays while the surrounding ground remained in shadow.

Styrax raised his cup to the sunrise and downed the liquid. The Chetse soldiers all sank to one knee as their patron God appeared. They bowed their heads and, lips moving in unison, said the dawn prayer together.

"I'm sure most of you are wondering exactly what I have to grumble about," Styrax began suddenly.

Dev flinched at the unexpected sound. He looked quickly at the tachrenns to see if anyone had noticed—his position was tenuous enough without them seeing him jumping at shadows—but their attention was fixed on the white-eye.

"Well, to answer that," Styrax continued after a moment, "the breaking of the curfew vexes me."

There was a pause.

"The curfew?" Dev asked eventually, feeling a little confused. Since Lord Salen's death and the massacre of his troops, the streets of Thotel had been relatively quiet. Other than a few hundred youths throwing stones at patrols, there had been no trouble at all. "A handful of children throwing stones shouldn't be causing you many problems."

"It doesn't cause me problems," Styrax said, closing on Dev, "but it does sadden me. My men are forced to retaliate against children and that breeds hatred—a hatred that could last generations." The big white-eye swung around to glare at the Chetse soldiers. "Old men send out children to be killed on the streets so the hatred stays alive," he growled. "Unrest is to be expected, but to fuel it with the blood of innocents: that is shameful."

"My Lord, I am sure it is not being organised," Dev said after a tense pause.

"As am I," Styrax replied in a level tone, "but neither is it being dissuaded by the men they look up to, men like you, soldiers, and the men of the priesthood. I would not be surprised if there are some who are actively encouraging it. That I call cowardice, and it shames you, leaders of cowards."

Is he offering to help stop the raids in the east in return for order to be restored in the city? Before Dev could think of how best to reply, the ground shuddered—once, then again, and again, like the heavy footfalls of an approaching giant. Dev looked around in alarm. The sound was coming from the Temple of the Sun itself, but all he could see was the Menin lord's helm and the great altar with the eternal flame whispering insistently above it. For an instant, Dev thought he saw a shadow moving across the furthest pillar, as though something massive had stepped between it and the eternal flame.

"What in the name of Tsatach's balls was that?" Tachrenn Lecha breathed, his hand feeling in vain for an axe that was not strapped to his back.

"That," said Lord Styrax, staring fixedly at the temple, "is the demand for a price to be paid."

"My Lord?" asked Duke Vrill, a slightly anxious look on his face. Clearly he was as much in the dark as any of them.

"A little personal business," rumbled Lord Styrax. "Gentlemen, I suggest you stay very still, no matter what happens. You might have heard the rumour that a creature of the Dark Place thought itself clever enough to enslave my son's soul through a suit of magical armour." As he spoke, he unfastened the cloak he'd been wearing and let it fall to the floor, revealing the armour he'd stripped from the vampire lord Koezh Vukotic after beating him in single combat. Hanging down his back was the great twin-fanged broadsword he'd won from his predecessor.

This is no coincidence, Dev thought. *You wouldn't be wearing a full suit of armour if you hadn't expected this. You've summoned it!*

"General Dev, if I remember my scripture correctly, Tsatach is a God with exceedingly strict views on honour and oath-breaking; am I correct?"

"You are—but surely your son has made no oath to this daemon?" the general answered. "I thought daemons could only incarnate if they were given a means to do so." *Oh Gods*, he thought to himself, *is a daemon about to incarnate and take its prize? You think that Tsatach will allow this to happen inside his own temple because of bonds of honour?*

"I believe that is correct," Styrax said as he gestured towards his sickly-looking son, "and so I have given it that means. To free my son from his enslavement I had to give the daemon something in return. I gave it a pledge of service."

A gasp ran around the assembled Chetse. None of them were mages, and despite their positions they had very little to do with the supernatural side of the Land, but any sane man knew the price of such a pledge.

"You are making pacts with daemons?" Dev spluttered.

Lord Styrax gave a growl as he tore Kobra from its bindings. "I will not stand by and let a daemon play its games unhindered, whether it is a prince among its kind or not. Now my son is free and I have been able to choose what comes next."

"What have you chosen?" Dev murmured, hardly able to believe what he was hearing.

"What do you think?" the white-eye laughed, sparks flashing in his eyes. "The creature can pluck my soul from my cold, dead body, but it won't get it without a fight."

Flexing his massive shoulders under that unnatural black armour, detailed with beaded whorls, he loomed large and terrifying in the early morning light. The cruel fanged tip of his sword glowed with savage power and the Crystal Skull fused to his cuirass caught the weak dawn rays to momentarily dazzle General Dev.

The old man took an involuntary pace back, shrinking away from the palpable sense of furious strength. In the distance, he felt a shudder through the rock beneath his feet, closer this time. The daemon was near.

The white-eye turned and stalked into the temple, heading for the helm he'd left there. The Chetse soldiers exchanged glances, unsure what to do. Dev gathered his senses and looked to the Menin for answers, but Duke Vrill and General Gaur showed no emotion. Either they knew exactly what was going on, or they had the presence of mind not to show their own confusion.

More worryingly, Kohrad Styrax suddenly looked animated. There was a new gleam in his eye, an alertness to his poise, as if he were anticipating what was about to come.

Inside the temple, Lord Styrax had donned his helm and was going through a complex weapon drill as though this were nothing more than morning exercises. Again Dev felt a tremble run through the ground, but this time it was a constant shudder, like the footfalls of an army of souls. Dark shapes began to flit around the inside, but Lord Styrax paid no attention to the amorphous forms, intent instead on the slow, smooth movements of his drills.

Behind him, Dev felt a sudden wind whip up from the ground, dragging trails of dust around his heels and swirling in tight spirals towards the massive pillars of stone that supported the temple's apex, growing in intensity until it shrieked across the carved stone, the sound so piercing that the watching men all flinched and clamped their hands over their ears. Inside the temple, the air darkened.

"What's happening?" whispered one of the tachrenns.

"The Dark Place," croaked Kohrad gleefully, "the boundary between their land and ours thins as the daemon tries to cross over. Listen hard; those are the voices of the damned!"

Dev listened. As the shrieking wind grew it was all too easy to imagine a chorus of wailing voices ringing out as the air inside the temple shuddered and wrenched, as if under some invisible assault. Only the dark knight, calmly moving through his drills, was unaffected, standing impervious to the fraying boundaries of the Land, apparently untouched by the storm swirling all around them. Something skittered away from the stone at his feet and was picked up by the wind and dashed against the underside of one of the walkways that skirted the temple.

Dev followed the sound and went white as he realised shadowy figures had assembled there, drifting in and out of existence as the howling ebbed and flowed. He narrowed his eyes, but he couldn't fix his attention: the figures faded when he looked directly at them, it was only in his peripheral vision that he could make out that they were all staring intently down at the temple floor. A finger of dread crept down his spine and he lowered his eyes.

There, standing just before the altar and towering over even the massive Menin white-eye, was the daemon.

Kastan Styrax didn't react as the daemon flickered into existence, though, distantly, he heard both the Chetse soldiers' alarm, and his son's hoarse cry of anticipation. Kohrad was still weak after the exhausting rituals, spells and surgery that had removed the armour from his body, but the young white-eye had every intention of witnessing his father's vengeance.

He stepped forward, sizing up his enemy. He couldn't remember the last time he'd faced someone larger than he, for the Menin were the tallest of the Seven Tribes. The daemon was twelve feet tall, far bigger than he, and its head was half-obscured by a black cowl which cast a shadow over a face covered in a criss-cross pattern of dark, deep scars. The daemon turned its head towards Kohrad, and the boy started spouting a stream of invective.

Styrax smiled; Kohrad must have complete confidence in him to be hurling obscene abuse at a daemon-prince when he could hardly swing the sword at his side. He had no idea just how powerful it was—not that it mattered; Styrax knew he had to fight it now. The daemon haunted his dreams nightly, looking for a way to gain his soul. He knew it would come as soon as it was called.

How many birds will I take with this one stone? he thought. *To be free of the daemon would be enough, but if these tachrenns see me defeat it—a feat Lord Chalat could never have managed—they'll follow me across the entire Land. If in the process the temple is unfortunately destroyed—well, we shall see if a Crystal Skull does indeed feed the eternal flame.*

Yellow eyes shone bright in the darkness and the daemon opened its mouth to reveal a double set of thin, pointed teeth. Lord Styrax was more concerned with the double-headed flail the daemon had in one hand and the cleaver-like weapon in its other. Its tri-toed feet sported massive hooked talons. Through the ripped and tattered cloak it wore he could glimpse plates of bone and slabs of muscle, all overlaid by scarred skin and, in parts, bony protrusions that looked almost like a scrappy pelt of curved fangs. Even in the warm air, the daemon's breath was clouds of vapour.

"Your promises are empty, your word is broken," it snarled. *"This temple yet stands; my name is unspoken and unworshipped in this place."*

"Do you think I ever had any intention of serving you?" Styrax replied calmly, walking around the daemon, forcing it to turn awkwardly to remain facing him. Those powerful legs were impressive, but as Styrax had guessed, they weren't designed for turning in a circle. "Do you think I would defile this place by speaking your name?"

"You are nothing compared to me, little mortal, and your arrogance has earned you a place in Ghenna. My realm waits to welcome you."

Styrax stopped circling. He didn't want to give the creature time to get comfortable. It came from a place where magic dictated everything, and now it would have to adapt to the requirements of the physical world and its physical laws. "You don't own my soul, daemon; you never did." Drawing on the Skull he carried, Styrax wove a protective web about himself. His magical skills were proficient, and with the Skull he was probably more powerful than the daemon, but it was an ancient being, and he didn't want to risk getting into a magical struggle. He was banking on the fact that it would be unused to single combat with weapons alone. With a shell of raw energy from the Skull around him he would be safe from the subtle spells that would come so naturally to such an entity. *Now all I've got to contend with is the strength and speed of a daemon-prince,* Styrax thought to himself wryly.

The daemon, feeling the white-eye's protective energy, gave a bestial roar and glared, jerking its flail, ready to strike.

Keeping one eye on the daemon's feet as its talons clacked on the stone floor, Styrax moved fast across the centre of the temple, and the twin mace-like heads whistled harmlessly past as, predictably, the daemon swung the flail at his head.

It wasted no time in following up the attack, spinning gracelessly around and attacking with the cleaver, forcing Styrax to back up and shift his balance.

He was on the alert now, careful to keep his broadsword from being snagged by the flail's chain-links. He slashed at the daemon's left hand; Kobra glanced harmlessly off the daemon's wrist as Styrax side-stepped the flail as it came back around. He hacked down at the elbow joint, but missed, shuddering in pain as the cleaver came down onto his own shoulder-plate.

He was forced into a crouch by the power of the blow, but the armour held and, roaring his defiance, Styrax drove upwards towards the daemon, slamming the scored shoulder-plate into its gut and putting his full weight into pushing it back. He swung Kobra, smashing aside the cleaver as it came down again and following that with two deep cuts across the daemon's midriff. As it fell back under the force of his attack, Styrax caused a greyish slab to appear at an angle under its feet. Unbalanced, it staggered sideways and he dropped to the ground, lashing out with one tree-trunk of a leg and connected with the daemon's knee.

Propelling himself upright, Styrax slashed with all his prodigious strength, a straight cut up that would have split a normal man from groin to scalp, but the daemon jumped back with unnatural speed. Styrax readied himself for the counter-attack, but it never came.

Instead, the daemon gave a deep, cold laugh. "*Your skills are impressive, but you are still just a mortal, little man,*" it mocked.

Styrax didn't reply, beyond shifting to a more comfortable grip on the hilt of his broadsword. The exchange had lasted only a few seconds, but it had been long enough to tell him what he wanted to know about the daemon. When it struck, it moved with blurring speed, and not even a white-eye of Styrax's ability could match that. But the daemon had revealed its greatest weakness. It had no imagination.

He leapt forward, slashing from first one side, then the other. The daemon gave a little ground but it parried each blow with ease. It could not see the satisfied little smile on Kastan Styrax's lips, for his mouth was hidden by the black helm he'd won from Koezh Vukotic, his greatest test so far. Koezh was a superb swordsman, his skill had been considered supernatural even when he had been a normal man marching under his father's banner during the Great War. Against Koezh the ancient vampire, Styrax had needed every ounce of guile he possessed, blended with the unnatural speed and skill granted by his patron, Karkarn, the God of War himself. Against this daemon-prince, all he needed was a brain. It mocked him for being a mortal, yet it was exactly this that would prove its undoing.

Styrax flourished his sword, noting the daemon's eyes following the tip until it came to rest again. He spoke loudly, so even the watching Chetse could hear. "Daemon, you're a fool." He took a step forward, moving out of the way when it thrashed the air with its flail and tore up a chunk of stone from the temple floor. Sending a surge of magic beneath his feet, Styrax swept up through the air above the daemon's head, easily deflecting the surprised swipe it aimed at him, then dropped down and scored a glancing blow on its shoulder.

Again, the daemon reacted, but Styrax had already shifted position and as its enormous arm lifted, he lunged, stabbing Kobra's fangs into the armpit, pushing deep as the daemon howled in pain and fury.

Styrax retreated and gave a roar of adrenalin-fuelled satisfaction. "Do you see this, daemon?" He brought the sword closer to its face as dull greenish ichor dripped from its fangs. "You bleed, daemon, like any mortal; can you feel it now?"

He drew a heady surge of energy into his body and felt flames rise from the armour encasing his body, an echo of the armour used to ensnare his son. In the distance he heard Kohrad's strained bellow, hoarse defiance that sent a thirst for revenge shuddering through his body.

"And that feeling is fear—can you feel it now?" he asked. "Have you been a prince among daemons for so long you've forgotten fear?" He was happy to take his time now, to put on a show for the watching commanders.

Try to take my son's soul? For that, I'll make you hurt. "I'll show you what fear is again, daemon, and when I send you back broken and ruined to your pestilent burrow in the deepest pit of Ghenna, before you are consumed by the scavengers there you will tell them. You will spread the word and teach them to fear me. I will destroy and leave for the vultures any daemon that thinks it can own or control me or mine."

He charged forward and smashed aside the daemon's sword, stepping inside the reach of the flail and grabbing its wrist. As it tried to get an arm around his neck, Styrax reversed his sword and stabbed backwards into the daemon's gut, then snapped his head back to smash the reinforced peak of his helm into the daemon's jaw. Before it had time to recover, Styrax wrapped his free hand with white coils of fire and punched into the daemon's right arm. The fire exploded on impact in a shower of burning glassy shards that buried deep into its flesh.

With Kobra still reversed he slashed it up across the inside of the daemon's right knee, halting the backswing almost immediately as he grabbed the hilt with both hands and drove the tip back down into the open wound. The fangs went deep and the daemon screamed.

Now Styrax could hear its fear. For perhaps the first time in ten thousand years the daemon-prince was afraid.

"Fear me," Styrax growled, ripping his sword from the wound and drawing another great swell of magic into his gut. White sparks burst at the edges of his vision as he drew as much as he could, resolving to change the manner of attack before the daemon could adapt. Around him the temple swam and he heard a shrieking chitter run around the walkway. The flames rose on his body, growing fierce and hot on his skin, but the pain was both exhilarating and intoxicating. At that moment he knew how his son had developed the addiction to the daemon's armour.

He punched forward with both fists, hammering them into the daemon's scarred midriff and releasing the magic inside at the same moment. The flames rushed through him and surged over the daemon as it was slammed backwards into one of the temple's great pillars. It crashed with the sound of mountains colliding, and the great blocks of stone creaked and wavered under the impact.

"Do you fear me yet, daemon?" Styrax roared.

A howl of rage preceded a torrent of black energy that flew towards him. Styrax dived out of the way and it hit the stone floor where he'd been standing an instant before, cracking the stone with a crash. His shield wouldn't stop raw power, but at least the daemon would be fighting on a white-eye's terms rather than its own.

Styrax retaliated with a wildly thrown spear of fire that lanced into the pillar above the daemon. It scorched a ten-foot segment black and tore another great hole in the stone.

The daemon jumped up in the air, cleaver ready to cut down into Styrax's body. The white-eye rose to meet it, using his body like a huge armoured fist, knocking the daemon off-balance and driving it into the white shaft of the eternal flame. A bright burst of fire flashed out across the temple as the daemon passed through Tsatach's holy light and it screamed in pain. Styrax gave it no chance to recover. He dived through the flame himself and stabbed down into the torso of the daemon, putting all his weight behind the blow. It howled and punched up at him, launching the Menin lord up into the air to smash one of the walkways between the pillars. The stone slabs exploded in a shower of stone shards and blistering sparks and the entire temple shuddered as the magic holding it up started to fail.

Styrax crashed to the ground, the shock of the impact sending a stab of pain through his body. For a moment the Land seemed to stop around him—

The scent of grass appeared in his mind. Styrax smiled inwardly as he remembered his father; the mornings out in the meadow when he'd first learned how to use a sword. Caution and calm had been his father's constant mantra; "Lure them into rashness, never do so yourself." Styrax nodded and felt his lips twitch in echo as his father, now centuries deceased, repeated that advice to his son: "Pride, my son, pride is a reaper."

—and the Land rushed back with noise and fire and pain and light assaulting every sense. His instincts retook control and drove him forward. Not even stopping to catch his breath, Styrax ran to the temple altar as purple bands of magic lashed down, carving great rents in the paved floor where he'd crouched just a few moments earlier.

Bracing his good foot against the altar, he pushed off into the air, feeling the muscles in his back strain as he readied another blow. Kobra was covered in ichor now, and it left a trail of deep crimson light through the air as it smashed into the daemon's own cruelly curved weapon, which exploded into a thousand tiny shards. Styrax let the force of the blow spin him back around, giving him a moment to recover his wits.

A fountain of magic erupted from the broken stub of the cleaver, green trails whipping around like enraged snakes. The daemon hissed and threw it away. It skittered across the floor for ten yards before coming to an abrupt halt. Out of the corner of his eye Styrax saw the lashing snakes slam down into the ground and begin to worm their way under the stone paving slabs, driving them up.

The daemon now held its flail with both hands, keeping the mace-heads moving, swinging them up threateningly whenever Styrax took a step closer. *So fear has taught you something then,* he thought with a grim smile. *Try to keep me at bay while you work out what to do.*

He feinted forward and was rewarded by the flail being whipped across where his knees would have been. As soon as the heads had passed Styrax leaped forward for real, following the swinging chains back to the source and chopping down to sever the daemon's right wrist. Burning green ichor spurted out over the temple floor and it reeled back, trying desperately to ward him off.

The white-eye ignored the flail as it clattered weakly off his armour and lashed out at the daemon's already damaged knee-joint. The force of the blow sent a judder along the blade that numbed Styrax's hands, but his ferocious resolve drove him on and he turned to smash an elbow into the daemon's gut. The handle of the flail crashed against the side of his head, sending black stars bursting across his eyes, but the daemon was weak now, and the battering, though painful, was too weak to stop him.

He rained down blows until at last he had the daemon-prince on the end of his fanged sword. Kobra pierced its chest and pinned it against a great marble column.

Styrax staggered for a moment. The air was alive with colours and magic rampaging uncontrolled; the air shuddered under the assault and he could hear the screams and hollers of the inhabitants of the Dark Place all around him. On the edge of his sight he saw flames against a looming darkness, the border between realms weakening further. His eyes were blurred and fiery pain flared in his gut, but he had enough strength left for the killing blow. With a roar he yanked Kobra free then hewed savagely at the daemon's neck and deep into the pillar behind. The impact almost lifted him off his feet as the black sword cleaved through stone; for a terrible heartbeat the darkness descended and the heat of Ghenna's sulphurous fires washed over his skin, then he tore the blade clear and staggered out beyond the temple's boundary line into the cool morning light.

He staggered forward, a groan escaping his lips as he fought to find the ground under each step. It took a few moments for the Land to steady underneath him and the fire behind his eyes to fade enough for him to see again. He sank to his knees and tore his helm off, gasping at the touch of the morning air on his skin.

Somewhere behind the blur he heard someone—Kohrad?—shout, "Father!" Then someone tried to slip his fingers around Kobra's hilt . . . with an effort he made out Kohrad's face and forced open his fist so his son could take the sword from his hand.

Drawing Kohrad close, Styrax put his lips to his ear and whispered fiercely, "Find it."

As he spoke, a symphony of shattering stone filled the air and a tremble ran through the ground like a massive earthquake. The pillar Styrax had hacked into was buckling as the magic was drawn into Ghenna with the daemon-prince's broken spirit. A thunderous crash split the air as the pillar collapsed onto the ruined temple floor, followed by the relentless sound of thousands of tons of stone imploding as the Temple of the Sun became a daemon's cairn.

Eventually the devastation slowed to a halt and the echoes of the temple's death faded away, leaving nothing more than a memory ringing in their ears. After that, there was only a ragged sound that Styrax could not place for a while until he realised it was his own laboured breath. Around him, everything was perfectly still, the hush of a temple at prayer.

He blinked as the Land crept back into focus. It was covered by a haze;

for a moment Styrax wondered what had happened to his eyes until he realised it was a cloud of dust. He let Kohrad help him to his unsteady feet and bear his weight for a moment longer, then a voice in the back of his mind reminded him that the young warrior still had a task to perform.

He straightened and gave Kohrad a light shove towards the ruin of the temple, then made his way waveringly to the group of Chetse commanders who were standing some twenty yards off. They looked aghast, too stunned to even move. One had sunk to his knees in prayer; the others just gaped at the collapse of Tsatach's greatest temple in the Land—and the eternal flame, the burning heart of the Chetse tribe.

He had just snuffed it out.

The dust swirled out to cover the Temple Plain, fading into nothing in the clear air above them. Somewhere behind him a loose piece of stone thumped heavily onto the packed earth of the temple floor.

"Gentlemen," Styrax said hoarsely to the assembled Chetse, staggering sideways for a moment before he reasserted control over his body, "gentlemen, you are dismissed."

They stared at him, shocked and uncomprehending. He took another step and his lip twisted into a snarl as the ever-present bloodlust screamed to take charge once more. He heard one start a horrified prayer, but it was only fleeting as they turned and fled like a herd of spooked deer.

Kastan Styrax, Lord of the Menin, grinned drunkenly. He felt a trickle of blood fall from his lip; maybe he'd bitten it. He swung around and saw that Duke Vrill had also backed off to a safe distance. That amused him; this was Vrill's best chance to kill him and become Lord of the Menin himself . . . but no, Vrill had more sense than that. Kohrad carried Styrax's own sword after all, and he was not as weak as he looked.

Styrax looked out at where the low morning sun shone from just above the western cliffs. In his chest he could feel his heart hammering away, reminding him with every thump that he was still alive. At each beat he wanted to call out, to shout with laughter. He wiped the blood from his mouth, never once taking his eyes from the horizon beyond which the Gods lived in splendid isolation away from their mortal subjects. The legend was that they had retired there to recover after the Great War and the horrors they had inflicted upon the defeated, and there they would stay, apart from the affairs of mortals, content to sit and play with strands of destiny, as long as they never again had to see any of their own dying at the hands of mortals.

Were you watching, you bastards? Do you fear me yet?

CHAPTER 24

BREYTECH EASED THE DOOR OF HIS ROOM open far enough to peer out at the street beyond. It looked quiet now, but he still had to be wary. He'd barricaded himself in the cramped room for days now, and from the shouts and screams outside, he knew the city was falling further and further into chaos. Over the last month the Chetse trader had seen the character of the city change completely as the locals descended into savagery. Though he was a frequent visitor to the city, Breytech had never seen anything like this before. Passers-by had turned on him, or attacked their fellow citizens, without provocation or intimidation, as abruptly and unexpectedly as a sentinel lizard guarding its nest: timid one moment; savage the next. He grimaced; at least with a sentinel you had a chance of escaping. In Scree the people didn't have the sense of animals; they wouldn't content themselves with just chasing you off.

He fought the urge to close the door and push the table back against it. Eyes that had grown used to the gloom of shuttered windows squinted in the painful light. It was the hottest part of the day; the sun was fierce enough to kill the old and sick. He was a Chetse and knew perfectly well the dangers of Tsatach's ferocious glare, but he had to gamble that even the insane would not venture out at midday. As much as he wanted to stay and hide, he knew he had to get out before his tired limbs grew too weary to carry him out of this place to replenish his water skin. He looked back at the cramped and airless room that had been his prison for the past week, since things had become really bad, and felt revulsion crawling over his skin as he realised he hated that space with a passion he couldn't explain. The weather had been merely warm when he rented the room, and what reason had there been for anyone to think he would spend much time there beyond sleeping? But worse it had become, and the four square yards of grime-encrusted floorboards had started to stink like a festering gaol.

Beyond a table and bed, and the chamber-pot that had forced him to unblock the door each day and risk being seen, much of the room was taken up with Breytech's remaining wares, stacked against one wall. He'd removed the canvas sacks filled with bolts of cloth from the warehouse he usually used after watching the owner, a man he'd known for five years, go crazy. Two nights ago the man had burned his own building down, screaming frantically all the while about shadows with claws.

He found his own mind wandering now as the waves of heat radiating from the streets made him drift feverishly away. Images of his children appeared in his mind; their skin untouched by the smallpox that had taken them from him. When he'd rolled over on the straw-packed bed this morning he'd felt his wife's soft breath on his ear and had turned with a smile to greet her, though she'd been gone these past three winters now. And all the while, there were sounds on the edge of hearing: distant shouts and howls that a part of him wanted to join in with, the quiet hum of a priest's incantation, the groan and ache of the building as it suffered through another blistering day. On occasion, a faint scent of tainted sweetness found him, like overripe peaches left out in the sun. The stink of waste and decay was all he smelled in Scree now. He'd even forgotten what a breeze felt like . . .

With a real effort of will, Breytech drove the confused thoughts from his mind and muttered an old mantra his grandmother had taught him, a prayer of sorts against the maddening effect of the sun that could drive men from the road and out into the desert. It had no effect on the pounding behind his eyes but the words were comforting and kept his mind focused. He edged out into the street, eyes flickering nervously around at the baked empty road.

Scree was as still and silent as only a dead thing could be; the diseased city streets looked on the verge of crumbling to dust, all the life sucked from them. Breytech crept forward, mouthing the mantra and keeping in the shadows as best he could, though in truth there was no hiding from the relentless sun. He wore a shapeless white desert robe and a scarf of the same material draped over his head to protect him from the sun. Hidden in one voluminous sleeve was an ancient long-knife, its edge battered and scarred with use, but still dangerous enough to afford him a small shred of comfort.

The main street before him was empty of all life. With the bright sun reflecting off bleached stone and the air shimmering uneasily under its assault, he found it hard to make out details—until he realised with a start that the largest building around, a merchant's office, he thought, was now just a charred ruin.

Without warning a whisper reached his ear as it raced around the confines of the street. Breytech flinched and looked behind him, pushing his scarf back a little to afford a better view—but it was still empty: no people, nothing alive to move, or speak. Despite the beads of sweat running down his throat, Breytech felt a chill pass through him, as though a ghost had laid its pale hand on his neck.

For a few moments he was frozen to the spot, until a drop of sweat from his brow ran down his nose like a tear and it jerked him into action, sending him stumbling off towards the spot where he thought he'd seen a well. If that looked unsafe, he would have to go further south, to the Temple District, maybe. He'd seen a shrine to Vasle—surely the God of Rivers would not fail him? For a moment he wondered whether he should have brought an offering, but then he thought that Vasle was unlikely to be listening to prayers from Scree. Perhaps only Death walked these streets, with his more awful Aspects, like the Reapers, at his heel. Or perhaps even they had deserted the city and turned their back in judgment. What curse on men, when even the final blessing of Death is denied them?

As he scampered from shadow to shadow he saw bodies. A whimper of fear escaped his parched mouth. Some were burned, limbs curled up in their final moment of pain. Some were missing limbs, even heads; others lay with the weapons that had killed them still in the wounds, eyes staring up to the sky as though pleading for help from Gods that had abandoned them.

He was beginning to feel like the sole survivor of some atrocious cataclysm. He peered into shattered doorways, but with the sun so high, there were only impenetrable shadows within. Slumped against one half-burned door was the torso of a child, missing its limbs. Breytech looked around, but they were nowhere to be seen. He tried not to dwell on why they might have been taken away. The fearful voices in the distant corners of his mind shrieked more urgently, and it was all he could do not to wail uncontrollably himself.

His sandal caught a stone and sent it clattering over the open ground. He gave a whimper of terror and crouched down beside the remains of a barrel, the closest thing to cover he could see. The horror of being found gripped like a vice around his stomach and he clamped his lips together to stop himself crying out in fear. At last the stone came to rest and silence descended once more. He didn't dare even breathe for a few more moments.

Finally he opened his mouth to gulp air down and felt the cracked skin on his top lip tug and tear, followed by the luscious taste of liquid on his tongue. His finger was halfway to his mouth when another sound came and he froze.

A moan, as soft as the absent breeze, but too abrupt. With shaky hands Breytech pulled his dagger out and gripped it tightly. Hunched low, like a nervous rabbit, he looked over to where the sound had come from—there! Across the street, behind a brutalised façade of a shop. It came again, and Breytech felt a tiny trickle of terror.

As he watched, a pale, hairless head rose slowly up from behind the shop's counter. His whole body trembled as he saw the head turn and cast about the street, searching for him, like a wolf that has caught the scent of a deer. In his fear he hardly noticed that his teeth were buried hungrily in his split lip until the taste of blood flooded his tongue.

The tang of blood made him swallow eagerly, but as he did so, the strange head flicked around like it was on a spring, and a loud, hoarse moan broke the silence. A second head appeared and the sound grew.

Breytech could stand no more. He tried to run, but his stiff muscles refused to comply. He forced himself into a stagger, and lurched forward a few steps, until he tripped on a broken piece of brick and fell to his knees. There was a crash from the shop and he heard the clatter of feet behind him, and voices, now loud and insistent, rather than in the corners of his mind but still furious, still awful.

"Priest! Servant of Gods!" someone howled.

A choir of rabid shrieks took up the call. "Priest! Prayer!"

Breytech looked down at his robe and a finger of dread crept down his spine. His robe—because of that, they thought he was a priest? Before he'd barricaded himself in his room—before the city had fallen completely to madness and ruin—he'd heard whispers that people had turned on the priests. Children had thrown stones at the temple acolytes, a priest had been murdered on stage, and the city guard had done nothing.

He ran, and when he picked out the curve of a dome up ahead and he recognised it, he was filled with a sudden surge of energy. Six Temples. The Gods. If there were still soldiers in the city—if the streets had not been entirely given over to howling lunatics—then surely they would be defending the temples? It wasn't close, but he had no choice. He prayed that the monsters pursuing him were as starved and thirsty as he.

As he ran, more guttural voices broke the stultified afternoon air, ringing out from all over as wrecked doors and broken shutters were flung open. Breytech kept his head low, his eyes on the ground ahead of him, trying to pick a path through the rubble. He didn't look back, but after a hundred yards he realised they weren't gaining on him and a flicker of hope sparked in his heart. Ragged figures swarmed out of gutters and through archways, but while the voices grew in number, they came no closer.

His grandmother's mantra returned to him and he muttered it with every heaving breath until he turned the corner and realised he was almost there. A square building surrounded by shattered benches and tables and a screen of withered vines on the far side was all that stood between him and the Temple Plaza.

He barrelled around the building and—

A pain exploded in his chest—

The sky flashed black and pink as the great temple dome ahead of him vanished from sight—

Breytech felt himself spinning as the air was driven from his lungs. He crashed to the floor in a confused heap. The howls of daemons battered at his ears, but he could see nothing except a fierce brightness that burned at his eyes. Instinctively he raised his arms to cover his face and felt a stab of pain. He blinked and tried to focus on the arm, eyes widening when he saw the livid red gash. He flinched as a man's laughter cut through the monstrous barks and yelps from his pursuers.

"Taken a wrong turning?" said the man, from somewhere nearby.

"Please," Breytech babbled, tussling with the local dialect, "you've got to help me!" He struggled up to his knees and looked back at the rabble that had been chasing him. They had stopped well short of the Temple Plaza and were pacing back and forth nervously. Only now could he make them out: emaciated figures, half-naked and blistered under the afternoon sun. They were covered with grazes and scrapes from head to foot, with numerous fat, dark scabs that looked like plague pustules. Their unwashed, unkempt hair was matted and patchy, and many had great patches of scalp exposed where clumps had been torn out. Breytech realised he would have pitied them, had their faces not been so deformed with rage.

"Help you?"

The man's accent sounded strange until Breytech placed it as from Narkang. He looked up and saw a face tanned enough for a Chetse—and no offer of help.

"Why would I want to do that?" the man said, shifting his shoulders under his armour, which shone in the sun. Thick trails of sweat ran from under the battered skullcap. Slung on his back was a steel-rimmed round shield and a bastard sword hung from his hip, gems glittering on the hilt.

"But you're a soldier. You're protecting the temples."

The soldier cocked his head.

Breytech heard shuffling footsteps behind the man and looked around him into the Temple Plaza. Past the ring of shrines that encircled the six huge temples were two figures dragging a third towards the Temple of Death. Three figures, no more, and none apart from this one looked like a soldier. Other than them, the plaza was completely deserted.

"Where are the others? Where are your men?"

The man gave an evil chuckle and looked back towards the three near the temple. "My men are there, but I wouldn't say we're protecting the temples."

Breytech whirled around to look at his pursuers. They had remained on the edge of the plaza, loitering uneasily, but when they realised he was staring at them they began to hiss and stamp their feet. One or two took a hesitant pace forward and Breytech quickly averted his gaze.

The men by the temple caught his eye once again as the dark-haired captive shook himself free and made a feeble bid to escape. He was hampered by a stiff leg and his hands were bound behind his back, and he was caught easily by a small man bizarrely dressed head to foot in black who scythed the other's legs from under him with a sweeping kick.

Breytech felt himself sway and his knees threatened to buckle as the sun's heat became a physical force pressing on his shoulders, but he steeled himself and stood firm. He checked his own pursuers again. They were slowly creeping closer, like nervous children. He took a step back and turned to the soldier, but the man was already walking away, tossing a thin-bladed dagger up into the air and catching it, again and again.

"Wait, they're coming this way," Breytech croaked, catching the man up.

The soldier stopped. "Of course they are," he said. "They're not frightened of the temples. The Gods have left this place; they have no need to fear it."

"Then why did they stop?" Breytech asked, bewildered, his head spinning. He slipped and fell to one knee, his palms flat pressed against the grit and dirt on the ground. Breathing in, Breytech tasted the dust on the air, as dry and dead as a tomb, and realised he could go no further.

"They stopped," said the soldier, "because while they do not fear the Gods, they know to fear me." With that, he started off towards the temple again, cheerfully calling over his shoulder, "But I'm leaving now, and all they have left is a man dressed like a priest."

Breytech gaped at the steel-bound shield on the soldier's back, flinching as it caught the sun and reflected into his eyes. Then he heard the slap of feet on stone behind him and turned to see the pack descend. He opened his mouth to scream but the words died in his throat as he stared into the fevered eyes of the one leading them, a young boy of no more than fifteen winters whose chest was stained with dried blood. Teeth bared, the boy howled like a creature of the Dark Place and raised his thin hands ready to strike, fingers bent like eagle claws. They tore towards him and at last he found his voice again.

Breytech screamed and his terror echoed over the plaza. Their voices added to his until their high shrieks of rage and triumph swamped his lone voice.

Soon all was silent again.

At the Temple of Death, Ilumene stopped and looked back to watch. The creatures that owned Scree's streets battered the Chetse's body long after he was dead. They were quiet now; intent on their task, barging each other aside in their struggle to obliterate the remaining vestiges of the man.

He smiled and entered the temple, spitting on the fresco of Death's cowled image that faced the open doorway as he passed. "Run away and hide, you festering relic," he said out loud. "Your time is over. Scree is a pyre to your failed glory and from its ashes will be born something greater than you could ever comprehend."

CHAPTER 25

DORANEI STARED AT THE SPEAKING-HOLE set into the door, which shuddered with the force of being slammed shut. He resisted the urge to turn around. It was bad enough that he was standing flat up against a closed door, like an errant child made to stand in the corner and unable to see the mocking eyes on his back; it was worse that those eyes belonged to the Brotherhood. He'd been the butt of every joke since first going to the theatre, when Zhia Vukotic had treated him like a favourite plaything. Now, though his command of the local dialect was not perfect, he was pretty sure that the stream of invective that had come through the speaking-hole before it had been slammed hadn't included her best wishes and a warm welcome.

"Maybe she's eating," said a helpful voice behind him. Doranei tried to resist the urge to turn and clout Sebe around his scarred ears; it would only start the others off again. Instead, he continued to stare at the door as though force of will alone could open it.

"Don't say that," rumbled Coran, "you might make him jealous."

"Ah, neck envy," Sebe snickered. "Don't worry, my friend, I'm sure you're the only one to her taste!"

He endured it in silence, eyes fixed on the polished grain in front of him. Dusk was drawing in and a lull had fallen over the city. The streets had been largely deserted on the brief journey here, with only a few pockets of private militia protecting the houses of those rich folk still in the city, but he couldn't have risked coming alone. Zhia's men guarded the end of the street and they'd only been let through because the officer in charge had recognised Doranei from the theatre.

"Try knocking again," Sebe suggested. "You got such a warm welcome the first time."

A spark of childish antagonism flared in him and he felt words rise in his throat. The king had warned them to keep their tempers in check; whatever magic was being done in the city, it was designed to turn folk against each other. Instead of replying, he reached out with his right hand and rapped smartly.

"At least he takes direction well nowadays," Beyn said from a little further away. "She's had a good effect there."

Doranei's three companions had found places of concealment to watch the street in both directions; they had to assume the streets would not stay deserted for long. The officer Doranei had spoken to had made it clear he was getting his men indoors before nightfall, to avoid attracting trouble. Outside the city, armies waited like restless storm clouds, gathering in an ever-tightening funnel. The fighting at the Greengate was only a minor squall, but it heralded something far worse.

"He's a polite boy," Sebe answered, "always had a lot of respect for his elders."

"True, but I hadn't realised he went for women *that* much older than he is."

"You don't meet many that are so old; let's face it they're somewhat scarce."

"My money's on him getting a crossbow bolt in the face," Beyn contributed in a chirpy tone. Doranei almost smiled; the Brotherhood would bet on anything amongst themselves and once the subject had been brought up there was nothing that could distract them from their ridiculous wagers.

"I'll take him being ignored no matter how long he knocks," said Sebe quickly.

"Nah; spat in the face and told to piss off," said Coran.

"What's the wager then?" Doranei asked.

"You're joining in?"

"Absolutely." Doranei did smile this time, confident he knew better than they how Zhia or her companions were likely to react. At any rate, he'd not have to pay the bet if it did turn out to be a crossbow bolt in the face. "What's the wager? Anyone got one in mind?"

"I hear," Sebe began, "there's a Raylin called Mistress leading one of the mercenary armies, and that she's got two pet wyverns. A claw or a tooth of one of them from anyone who loses; that's the wager."

"Agreed. Well then, I say I'll be dragged inside by a beautiful woman," Doranei said.

Beyn spluttered. "The boy's confident, I'll give him that."

"Don't think it's confidence," Coran said, "I reckon he's just got good ears."

On cue, the speaking-hole popped open again. Instead of the unshaven face of the man who'd answered it last, Doranei found himself beaming at Legana, though from the Farlan woman's expression, he could have been a cockroach crawling on the doorstep. Touching him didn't appear to be on her current list of options, let alone dragging him inside.

"Can't keep away?" she said, turning her head to see who else was standing out in the street. "Or did you think today was a good day to take in the evening air?"

"Men from Narkang laugh in the face of danger," Doranei replied, his Brothers chuckling in the background.

Legana gave him an unfriendly grin. "Well then, you'll enjoy your journey home. It's after sunset that the lunatics come out, in case you hadn't noticed."

With that, she slammed the speaking-hole in his face. Doranei's mouth hung open, frozen in the act of replying. After a few moments he shut it again. Nothing happened on the other side of the door. He turned to look at Sebe, who was crouched two yards away on his right, behind an iron railing that was choked by withered brown weeds.

The man gave a noncommittal shrug and scratched at his newly shorn scalp. Sebe, like many in Scree, had decided his long black hair was too great a nuisance in this oppressive heat. The King's Man had seen a lot of violence in his years of service and the jagged scars on his face and scalp attested to that. Without his ragged curls he looked like a battered, grinning monkey— which hadn't escaped mention.

Doranei was about to step back from the door when he heard the bolts slam back and it jerked open to reveal a scowling Legana, her sword drawn. Four burly guards waited a respectful distance down the dim corridor. Legana wore a thin white cape over her clothes; the trappings of the White Circle still had a powerful hold over many of Scree's citizens.

"What do you want? We don't exactly have time for social calls right now."

"Intelligence, Legana. We've business to finish before we leave the city."

Legana gaped. "Have you not been paying attention to what's happening in Scree? There's not going to be a city left in three days; it's a miracle that the fires haven't already levelled it. The Second Army has turned on us and is killing anyone they find, and your king is running around with less than a company of men as his only guards. I think you should forget about your business and start worrying about how you're going to survive. Whether you men from Narkang fear danger or not, you're fools if you have any goal now beyond saving your own skins."

Doranei bristled at the comment. "We understand the situation perfectly well." He paused and lowered his voice so the guards wouldn't hear. "Your lord has promised us help."

"The Farlan are going to march on the city?" Legana whispered furiously. "Does he really want to get embroiled in this mess?"

"That's not our decision to make, but I do know he wants you to report for orders as soon as you can."

"Damn, how does he expect me to serve a master and a mistress at the same time?" she muttered with a scowl. "I can't keep running off for orders if he wants me to remain as Zhia's aide."

Doranei let her fume for a little longer before coughing obviously. "Could you let us in? As you pointed out, the lunatics will be on the streets again soon."

"I thought you laughed in the face of danger?" She wrinkled her nose at him. "Frankly, you stink like a month-dead hog; I don't really want you to come any closer."

"You try smelling like roses when you've been wearing mail for days."

She pulled open her cape to reveal a Fysthrall breastplate underneath. "Some of us have been doing more than skulking in the shadows over the last few days, and we still manage to avoid having our own personal flies circling us."

"So are we coming in?"

Legana sighed. "She's just woken up." She grabbed Doranei by the tunic and pulled him inside, waving a hand graciously to indicate that his comrades should follow. They didn't waste any time, trotting past Legana and watching the guards warily.

"I'll take you up to her study; your Brothers can wait down here." She pointed to the formal reception room, hardly the place for soldiers in stinking leather and armour, but it was clear they had been using it as a barracks over the last few days.

Doranei grinned at his companions and followed Legana upstairs towards Zhia's study. The last time he'd been there, Koezh Vukotic had stepped out of a mirror and joined them for an evening at the theatre. That felt like a lifetime ago. He gave a slight shake of the head as he trudged behind the Farlan agent. Even considering the strange existence that had been Doranei's life for many winters now, he felt frighteningly out of his depth. In the service of his king, Doranei had murdered, stolen, lied and kidnapped. His loyalty had always been unquestionable; he might not have been the shining light that Ilumene had been, but he knew King Emin trusted him as much as he did Coran. Rarely had he felt so adrift.

Now, in this city that shimmered uncertainly under a midday sun fierce enough to kill, the real world of loyalty and service felt a distant memory. With the day split in half by a savage and sapping afternoon, Doranei had found himself drifting through the streets as though it were all a dream—a dream in which he was terrified what would happen if his lord and the enigmatic enemy of the Gods living here ever ended up on opposing sides on the battlefield. They hunted a traitor, and he knew the king would be watching him closely.

Opening the door to the study, Legana stepped to one side to let him past into the empty room. Thick curtains covered the tall window and the room was lit only by a pair of candles on the table and the oil lamps flanking the door.

"Zhia is speaking to Mikiss. These first few days of being turned are difficult, she tells me. She'll be with you soon."

"Mikiss? The Menin soldier she bit last time I was here? Does she really have time to nursemaid a fledgling vampire? I'd have thought she would be off to the fighting at the Greengate as quickly as possible."

"A few more minutes won't matter," Legana said. "Fledgling he might be, but Mikiss will still be a dangerous presence on the streets once his head has cleared. The Greengate is in good hands; Haipar commands there and now her companions have come through the Foxport with some of their troops, the Greengate won't fall." She cocked her head at him, looking curious. "If you're so worried about wasting time, what are you doing here? What intelligence do you need from us before you make your escape?"

"I told you, we have business to conclude," Doranei said firmly.

He strode into the centre of the room and faltered. The table on his right had been laid as though Zhia was about to sit down to dinner, half a dozen shallow wooden bowls piled with food in the centre of the table alongside a lead-chased decanter of what he hoped was just a rich, dark red wine. The table was laid for two. Had she been expecting him—or someone else?

"Have I interrupted your dinner?" he asked cautiously.

Legana gave him a sly smile. "Not mine, but Mistress Zhia hasn't eaten yet."

Without giving him time to reply she left, closing the door. Doranei stared after her, but once her footsteps had receded there was no sound from the other side. Sniffing gingerly at the decanter he satisfied his own curiosity: wine, and the rich scent of an old vintage at that. He'd have to be careful not to let this cloud his mind. Five chairs stood at the table, a strange long-handled sword hanging in its scabbard from the back of one. Words he couldn't read were detailed on the surface of the scabbard, the letters interwoven with trails of ivy and bluebells. The leather-wrapped hilt of the sword took up almost half of its entire length and lacked any decoration while the guard was nothing more than a ridge following the line of the hilt. It wasn't the sort of weapon he'd expect a lady to use.

Stop being a fool, Doranei chided himself. *She's not a lady, she's a bloody vampire; strong enough to rip your arms off. That's probably as light as a twig to her.*

He turned his attention to the mirror that Koezh Vukotic had walked through during his previous visit. Lifting it up to look behind, pressing his hand against the surface to be sure it was solid, he could find nothing unusual about it now. The only result was a greasy smear on the surface, and with a muttered curse Doranei tried to wipe them off with his sleeve. The resultant smudge was marginally worse than the finger marks. He looked around for a cloth, but other than the curtains he could see nothing.

He stopped and gave his reflection a grim smile. *People are tearing each other apart outside and you're worried about getting the furniture dirty? Just what is happening to you?*

Behind him, the latch clicked open. His eyes shifted from himself to the reflection of the door as it opened and Zhia came into the room. Like Legana she was dressed in ornate armour, a white patterned skirt reaching to her knee, with tall boots underneath and greaves strapped over those. It was the first time he'd seen her in anything but elegant silk. At her hip was a sheathed dagger that matched the curious sword hanging from the chair. What really caught his attention was her hair, dyed rusty brown again, pre-sumably to reassert her links with the Circle now that there was an army at the Greengate claiming she was a vampire.

Doranei felt his gut tighten; he'd not thought about it the last time he was here, but weren't vampires supposed to have no reflection? Hadn't the Gods cursed their vanity as they cursed their betrayal? His mind raced as he tried to recall the scriptures he'd so studiously ignored as a child.

"Are you going to just stand there instead of greeting me? Normally I'd be pleased I could make a man stop and stare, but your expression is not that of the enamoured," Zhia purred. Doranei didn't miss the slight edge to her voice.

"I can see you; how is it that I can see you?" he said, turning at last to face her.

"Because you're a clever boy," she replied, "and I shall give you a prize for it later."

"You know what I mean." His stern tone provoked a coquettish smile that froze him like a rabbit in an eagle's shadow.

"So serious all of a sudden, my dear? I rather like that commanding glare of yours; you really should use it more often. If you're going to pout until you get your answer, it is this; others can see us, we cannot see ourselves. The Gods said something about pride when they cursed us, but I must confess to being in a little discomfort at the time so I didn't pay as much attention as I should have."

She raised an eyebrow at his expression. "Oh, don't look like that; however majestic your Gods might be, they had spiked both of my heels and I was missing more skin than I care to remember." She walked up to him and rose slightly on her toes to place a soft kiss on his lips. Doranei felt his hands tremble at the touch; his whole body ached at her scent. It took him a moment to regain enough control to slide his hands around her waist to bring her closer, but when he at last did so Zhia gave a contented murmur and linked her own hands around the nape of his neck.

When they broke from the kiss, Zhia kept a tight hold on him as she looked him in the eye, an enigmatic smile on her face. Despite feeling intoxicated by her presence, Doranei was still disconcerted by the sudden closeness. The fingers of just one of those hands on his neck could snap it without appreciable effort, and the inner light of those deep blue eyes was like none he'd ever seen. The closest equivalent he knew was the bust of Nartis that stood in the royal baths in Narkang: each eye was a flawless sapphire. It was a blasphemous comparison, he knew, but undeniable. Not even King Emin's cold, glittering eyes shone so brightly.

"Now; as pleasant a diversion as you are, I suspect that was not the only reason for your visit?"

"The king asks for your help."

"And what do you ask for?" she said unexpectedly. Doranei blinked, distracted by both the question and the sensation of Zhia's finger stroking the line of his spine.

"I—I would like you to help my king."

"Nothing else?" The stroking stopped as she pushed her sculpted fingernail into his skin, not hard enough to break the skin, but just enough that he could feel the prickle of pain there.

He made a show of thinking for a moment. "Another kiss would also be nice."

"Only nice? I must be losing my touch," Zhia said, brushing his lips with hers before she pushed out of his grip and went to the table. "Sit, have you eaten?"

He nodded, but still joined her at the table. She plucked a fat olive from one of the bowls and popped it in her mouth. A trail of oil ran down one of her fingers until she caught it with her tongue and meticulously licked it off.

"I thought vampires didn't eat normal food," he said.

Zhia gave him a derisive look. "Oh sweetness, and you were doing so well too. Blood gives me something of the person's life essence, that vitality that separates them from rock or water. It is that vitality that I lost all those years ago, but there would be a lot of hollow space inside me if it was merely magic keeping my body together. Far better to just build bones and muscles the same way a normal person does, even if the magic inside then makes them stronger." She took another olive and sat in one of the white painted chairs there, indicating for Doranei to do the same. "But I don't think the favour your king is asking for is an essay on the habits and physiology of vampires."

"It isn't. We know you have had agents watching the theatre—"

"There's not a lot left of it now," Zhia interrupted, "and as for the spell carved all around the outer wall, I have only a vague grasp of how it worked. They managed to prevent my agents from discovering too much. Legana tells me it was Lord Isak who burned it down. There is nothing to be learned from the shell that remains."

"But the players didn't die in the fire," Doranei said. "We don't care about the spell cast on this city, only the ones casting it."

"The minstrel?"

"Amongst others."

"Are they really so important to you?"

She offered him one of the bowls and instinctively he reached to take what was inside. Once he'd inspected the contents of his hand, Doranei's stomach sank. He couldn't even make a guess as to what it was, but the slimy texture and ridged green skin didn't inspire much confidence. Trying not to think any more about it, Doranei popped the object into his mouth and chewed quickly before swallowing it.

He cleared his palate with a mouthful of wine, then said, "They are followers of Azaer; it's worth the risk if we can kill even some of them."

"You fear this happening in Narkang?" Zhia said, offering the same bowl again with the twist of a smile on her face.

"No," he said as he declined the slimy ridged thing politely, "but it shows that Azaer is no longer content living in the shadows. How much do you know of it, even now? I doubt you've ever encountered any of its followers in the past. The shadow wouldn't have risked going anywhere near you, considering how powerful you are. Now it appears that has changed, and the shadow's confidence grows. It has made a grand promise of the horror it is capable of bringing; and it has taken great care in the slaughter of priests." He leaned forward in his seat. "Azaer wants the Gods themselves to witness what it has done in Scree, he wants them to watch, and to fear for their very existence."

"You think it so powerful?"

"Powerful?" He shook his head. "No, not powerful, otherwise it wouldn't have maintained such a low profile. But perhaps that is the danger; if few recognise it, then it can run unchecked for years—like the Malich affair, but on a global scale, and spanning centuries, perhaps even millennia." Doranei frowned. "Malich is dead and gone, yet now Lord Isak has learned the man's apprentice is in the city, he will not leave until that necromancer is dead. The echoes of Malich's deeds return to haunt us—and he was just a man from Embere. What if he had been an immortal, with limitless patience and guile that we cannot even guess at?" He stopped, seeing she was not fully convinced. "Have you ever heard of Thistledell?"

His question seemed to catch Zhia off-guard. After a while, she nodded uncertainly. "In passing—was it something horrible, done the day before Silvernight? I don't believe I have ever heard the full story."

Doranei shook his head. "I'm not surprised; you won't find anyone willing to speak of Thistledell these days. This was the coronation festival—always the most popular of our summer festivals because the king is extremely generous. It's almost impossible to believe such a thing could have happened in such a quiet little village, and over the years people have worked hard to forget—there aren't even any signposts pointing to Thistledell now." Doranei hesitated, disquieted himself. "I accompanied Ilumene there soon after I joined the Brotherhood, and what I saw scarred my soul. We stood there and watched the men from the neighbouring villages sift the ashes to unearth the bones. I still remember his words: '*There are traces of darkness in our every deed. Whatever weakness was inside these people, were they any different to us?*'"

"How to see the shadow within a shadow?" Zhia said with weary understanding.

Doranei looked into her eyes and remembered she and her brothers had been touched by a greater horror than he'd ever known.

"Azaer turned them against each other?" she asked.

"We don't know what happened exactly, only that they thought they had been blessed when a talented minstrel arrived for the celebrations . . . and then they tore each other apart."

Zhia nodded slowly. "And now your minstrel has come to Scree, to spread his traces of darkness here. I will give you one of my agents to guide you; Rojak and his companions have gone to hide in the slums to the south."

She closed her eyes and took a steadying breath, then began to whisper in some flowing arcane tongue Doranei could not recognise. He sat still until Zhia looked at him again, her earlier joviality gone. With a sigh the vampire pushed herself to her feet.

"My agent is waiting for you downstairs; he will follow your commands without question." She took Doranei's hand and held his fingers up to her cheek a moment. "Once you have your revenge, leave this place before it consumes you, or the minstrel will have won after all."

Zhia gave him a delicate kiss, hardly more than a brush on the lips, for all the tenderness in her eyes. "Be careful; revenge is a wild beast and more often than not it isn't just the intended who are hurt as it rampages. I wouldn't like to see you hurt, not when you're such a sweet diversion. Tell your king he's lost this round, it's time to salvage what is left and prepare for the next."

Doranei nodded dumbly and yielded to her gentle urging towards the door, but something stayed his hand as he opened it. Turning, he looked back at Zhia who was standing perfectly still in the centre of the room, her hands clasped together.

"What horrified the king about Thistledell was not that such a thing could happen, but what it meant. It isn't Azaer's way to force others, only to urge them. If we are all capable of such things, if that evil lives within every one of us, how can we hope to fight it?"

With that he turned to go, but before he could shut the door behind him Zhia called out, her voice as vulnerable as a child's, "It's choice that makes you human; never forget that, just as it is fear that makes you less than human. Fear the darkness inside you and it will consume you—accepting that it is there is the only way to conquer it. Remember, Doranei, that you will always have a choice. However hard it might be, there is always choice."

Zhia sat and watched the candles burn slowly down. Outside, the city was strangely silent, but it remained as hot as ever. She'd hoped the destruction of the theatre would lessen that at least, but the sun had burned down as fiercely as it had the previous day. She sighed and reached for the wine, filling the goblets on the table. As she set the decanter down, the latch on the door clicked open again. The man who entered wore a studded leather surcoat and had crossed scimitars sheathed on his back. He was bloodied and bruised, but he hadn't bothered to clean the filth and gore from his skin or clothes; only the linen bandage around his neck was fresh.

Oh, honestly, Zhia thought to herself as she indicated the other seat. "Is that bandage entirely necessary, Major? It will stand out a bit when you return to the Greengate."

He grunted and walked behind the chair, resting his elbows on the back as he cast an unfriendly look over the food at her. She could see in his eyes that the gesture was intended exactly as she'd seen it. "Not exactly my problem. You wanted to see me?"

"A little civility wouldn't hurt, Major. I doubt the rations for the garrison are quite so good, and you must be hungry."

"True," Amber growled, "but I don't see you offering it to the rest of them as well. Let me make this clear for you; this is not my cause and it isn't my city, but I bleed in battle alongside the men still out there. I don't particularly enjoy abandoning them to go and have dinner with the woman who holds the purse strings."

"Your sense of honour is admirable," Zhia said, careful not to rise to his antagonistic tone, "but I expect your sense of duty to your lord supercedes it."

"Of course it does."

"Then sit."

When she didn't say any more, Amber's frustration eventually subsided. He slipped off his baldric and hung his scimitars on the back of the chair and slumped down at the table.

"Good boy. Now, your mission in Scree is over. The Skull you were sent here to find is doubtless out of your reach, your companions are dead or lost to you and the necromancer—if he ever was a true ally of yours—isn't going to be healthy company soon. Perhaps I can offer you an alternative to returning home empty-handed."

"I'm not for sale." Amber's fingers tightened into a fist.

"I'm not proposing you become a mercenary; merely that I help you get home."

"I don't understand," Amber said.

Zhia offered him one of the goblets of wine and he took it, his expression one of puzzlement. "The White Circle is finished," she said. "The remnants of their power are in Scree, and soon Scree will be no more. I shall have to revise my position in the Land to be a little less obvious, perhaps, but I will certainly outlast the Circle and its members."

"What's this got to do with me?"

"Well, Major, you might have assumed I've made an alliance with the King of Narkang, but I assure you it is nothing more than an understanding. I have enough enemies that I see no reason to make more. Their goals are not mine, but as long as their plans don't conflict with my own, there's no need for trouble—and it's always sensible to be owed a favour when you're the enemy of the Gods."

"And you want to offer the same to Lord Styrax?"

"In a fashion. I have no plans for empire-building, so I see no reason to get in the way of his. I've spent many years among your people; I've seen them at their weakest and at their strongest. Right now, they are led by a man whose footsteps echo across the entire Land. I think he would be a good man to come to an understanding with before our paths cross."

"You don't care that he invaded your homeland and killed your brother?" Amber asked incredulously.

"Did you expect a desire for revenge?" Zhia gave him an indulgent smile. "My brother is immortal; as you've seen, he has recovered entirely from the incident and will bear no grudge. Do you know how many mortals have managed that throughout history?" She leaned across the table and held out her hand. "Koezh was an exceptional warrior when he was mortal; from the age of sixteen he was bested in single combat only three times, the first time by a celebrated Elven duellist who had offered to train him." She raised one finger. "The second time, by Eperal, Ilit's most violent Aspect, who took a wound that would have killed a man, in order to disarm Koezh." The second finger went up, then the third. "Lastly, of course, Karkarn, the God of War himself. Since then, only one mortal other than your lord has managed the feat and that was largely down to luck. Koezh tells me your lord was not lucky; he was astonishing."

Amber nodded. "I've seen Lord Styrax fight; you have good reason to be worried."

Zhia almost choked on her wine. "Worried? My dear boy, your lord is a great warrior, but Koezh and I are not children. To take on both of us would show a severe lack of judgment, and I would think considerably less of Kastan Styrax if he tried it."

Amber drained his cup and stood up again. "So what is your message?"

"That if he speaks, I will listen. I know he has not crossed the Waste solely to conquer the Chetse, so don't even try to deny it."

"You will listen? That's the entire message?" Amber pulled his scimitars back on and grabbed a handful of flatbread from the table.

"Small steps, Major, small steps. When the Menin armies move north and near wherever I decide to settle, I'm sure the Cheme Legion will be at the fore. When that happens, you might have a visitor in the night."

"What about Mikiss?"

Zhia raised her eyebrows. "Don't worry yourself about him; Mikiss is better off at my side. All I ask of you is to be at the Greengate when the city guard needs you; they're not soldiers and they'll need one to lead them. My intention is to destroy the Second Army and use the Greengate to evacuate those we can."

"Evacuate them? Why do you care about the people of Scree?"

"That is not your concern," Zhia snapped. "Just be ready when I give the order. I walked the city last night; the mobs have been working themselves up into a frenzy, and they will boil over very soon, tonight maybe, or tomorrow at the latest. When that happens, even the soldiers in this city will be in great danger, and I would save anyone I can. Once we are away, you will be free to leave, understand?"

Amber stared for a while, trying to see in her face why the vampire had been stirred to compassion, but eventually he gave up and just nodded. "I understand."

"Good, now return to your post," she ordered. "I have murder to assist."

CHAPTER 26

"GENERAL, THE SCOUTS HAVE RETURNED," Second Lieutenant Mehar reported.

General Jebehl Gort looked up from the map into the anxious face of his aide, hovering at a respectful distance. Behind the lieutenant, Gort could see the dark outline of Scree, crowned by torches that burned unhindered by any evening breeze. From all around him came the sounds of an army camp going about its business, but to his experienced ear it was worryingly quiet. Soldiers preparing for battle tended to act in certain ways, and this wasn't normal. His men were subdued and apprehensive; they gathered in small knots, talking quietly in shaky voices that betrayed their fear. They had heard what was happening in Scree, and now they were asking themselves how there could be any victory over a city of madmen.

There was another worrying detail: the absence of background noise in fields that should have some life—most creatures fled before an army, but it was disconcerting to hear absolutely nothing, not even the wind. They were an island adrift in unearthly seas.

The shadows of twilight thickened steadily beyond the pickets, reminding Gort of a rhyme he'd heard as a child, spying on his father as he sat drinking with old comrades late into the night. Those powerful, proud men were the reason he'd followed in his father's footsteps and joined the Knights of the Temples, but that night there had been no drunken singing or horseplay; that night they'd behaved like they were in mourning. One of them, a bear of a man from Embere, had repeated again and again a sad little rhyme in his own language.

Gort's father had whispered a few lines:

Shadows rise and faithful fall,
The reapers sing and the lady comes
With ashes in her hair and secrets in her hand . . .

Those words had echoed through Gort's dreams for many years, not just because of the strange atmosphere that night, but also because of the ghastly look on his father's face as he spoke. He had never seen that side of his father again.

He shook the mood from him; this wasn't the time to indulge in childish fears. He needed to look strong for his men, both noble and common-born alike. His aide had the right idea: despite the sweltering conditions, Lieutenant Mehar looked positively resplendent in his formal armour. As an aide to a general of the Knights of the Temples, he had to stand out among the soldiery, so his brass-plated cuirass, vambraces and greaves were all spotless and shining.

Look at him, the general thought, *another sign of how the order has lost its way. He must dress that exact same way every day he is on duty, while I go into battle wearing antiquated scale-mail because the Codex of Ordinance dictates it.* He shook his head. *And my second-in-command could order me flogged if I decided to wear a cuirass. We really have lost our way in this Land; I hope Lord Isak can restore us to the true path.* He sighed and turned back to the young man.

"What do the scouts say, Lieutenant?"

"The remaining mercenary armies are marching on the southern gate of the city, General."

Gort caught the attention of his second-in-command, General Chotech, and beckoned. The Chetse dismissed the men he'd been talking to and hurried over.

"General, you should hear this; the mercenaries are on their way to the Foxport. Lieutenant, what was their order?"

"I'm not sure, sir." The lieutenant coughed nervously. "The scouts were vague; they said the mercenaries had no order. I presume they meant both armies were attacking."

"They're attacking?" General Chotech spluttered. "Has everyone in this damned place gone insane?"

"It appears that way," Gort said levelly, "but I would remind you, Lieutenant, not to interpret what you expect men of the line to mean from what they say; soldiers may be an excitable breed, but scouts tend to be veterans and most of 'em have a modicum of sense." He sighed as the chastised aide nodded dumbly. "However, you could be correct; if they were marching as reinforcements for the city garrisons, one would expect a little more order. What the locals have told us appears to be true; the people of Scree have forsaken sanity and the Gods. They turn on each other like animals."

"What are we going to do about it?" General Chotech asked.

Gort turned to his aide. "Lieutenant, you are dismissed. If Major Ortof-Greyl has returned, please send him to us."

The lieutenant gave a curt bow and left, looking unhappy at being ordered away.

Gort leaned closer to the Chetse. "I believe we must also march on the city."

"If we become embroiled in that mess there'll be no escaping until it's finished," Chotech hissed.

"I know." He scratched at his armpit as best he could through his scale-mail. Campaigning and an unremitting summer sun were not the best combination for an old man's hygiene, but the bath he yearned for would be a disgraceful waste of water. "I don't believe we have a choice. We are the Knights of the Temples and we have a clear duty."

"General, I understand your point," Chotech insisted, "but we have only six thousand soldiers here; Siala must have at least fifteen thousand to defend the walls, while we do not even know who's commanding those two armies marching on the south. They might not be taking their orders from anyone!"

"I agree. Whoever is leading them—and no matter what we've heard, I can't believe the White Circle would be quite so foolish as to put Raylin in charge of whole legions—they must have decided it is time to salvage what booty they can, while something of Scree still remains. I can't believe any mercenary would agree to march into a burning city to defend it."

"A move driven by desperation, then. Their supplies must have run out and their commander has realised to keep them together he must give a reason."

"Exactly, a move that could prove disastrous once they're inside the city." General Gort broke off as he saw a man labouring through the gloom towards them: Major Ortof-Greyl was struggling to reach them with the aid of a crutch under his right shoulder. As he neared, they could see that his face was bloodied and his mail torn.

"Gods, what happened, man?" Gort exclaimed. "Did you speak to Lord Isak?"

"No, sir," Ortof-Greyl replied, panting heavily. Lieutenant Mehar trailed behind the major, plainly confused. The aide, not privy to the secrets of their group, had no idea why the major had been sent to the Farlan Army camp in the first place. "I only got as far as the outriders."

"And they did this to you?" Gort said, gesturing to the younger man's head wound.

"They did. I asked for an audience with Lord Isak and they refused outright; they wouldn't even take me to their commanding officer. I'd gone ahead of my two guards and before they could make up the ground, the scouts had given me a kicking and ridden off."

"Do you know why?"

"No sir, but I suspect Lord Isak is not with them," the major said, casting an uncomfortable glance at the lieutenant. "Their bluster was hiding something, I'm certain of it."

"Major, the scouts say the full complement of Palace Guard is with that army, and a large number of nobles and hurscals; surely the core of the Farlan Army would not be here without their lord? No, it must be a miscommunication; Lord Isak would not want his nobles to think that any sort of agreement had been made until he understands our motivations." He gave a dry laugh. "And it's not as though any Farlan noble would believe what had really taken place was a selfless act; they probably wouldn't even understand the concept."

"Yes sir," the major replied with a short bow. The man clearly disagreed, but he knew when not to argue. "What are your orders?"

Gort looked at Chotech. "As I was saying, we must not forget we are Knights of the Temples. Whether we succeed in bringing order to Scree or not, we cannot stand back and do nothing; you took the same oath as I did: 'Defenders of the faith, a bond greater than blood or nation.' It is our duty to the Gods, and whether the citizens of Scree have abandoned the Gods or not, I will die before I do so."

His second-in-command gave a heavy sigh and leaned over the map laid out in front of them. "You're right, of course. Priests murdered on stage for the entertainment of the mob, and hunted down on the streets like dogs? We cannot allow this to continue. It's only a matter of time before the Six Temples District is razed. Whatever evil is fuelling this madness, we cannot stand aside."

"Good; prepare the men. We will secure a section of the city and hold it. The New Barbican, I think—that's the closest, according to our intelligence, and we don't want to be moving any further through that city than we have to. Then a second area surrounding and protecting the Six Temples District. General Chotech, I doubt the garrison of the New Barbican is large, but it's the strongest gate. I need you to prepare an assault that can take it before reinforcements arrive—"

Gort broke off suddenly as a dull clang rang out. The three men looked up as a second sonorous peal echoed through the camp.

"Call to stations?" he wondered aloud as nearby groups of soldiers split up and marched off to their assembly grounds. From either side of his tent, half a dozen soldiers dressed in white-lacquered heavy armour rushed up with their swords drawn and fanned out around the general. They were his bodyguards, and they were reacting to the ponderous ringing of *call to stations* exactly as specified in the Codex of Ordinance. If it had been the furious clatter of the attack alarm, everyone in the camp would be reaching for their weapons.

"Lieutenant, find out what's going on," Gort called.

The lieutenant bobbed his head in acknowledgement and marched away, but before he could reach the line of tents ringing the command tent, a young soldier—scarcely more than a boy, swamped in his studded jerkin—burst through.

"General Gort, message from the advance scouts!" the soldier yelled at the top of his voice. "The Farlan are advancing!"

Gort instinctively turned towards where the Farlan had been camped, but the fall of night concealed any dust trail or movement he might be able to see. He motioned for his bodyguards to let the boy through and forced himself to stand straight and calm while the youth fought to regain his breath.

"Sir, the Farlan are moving towards the city in advance formation."

"Not towards us?" Chotech blurted in surprise.

"No, sir, towards the Autumn's Arch gate." Once the young soldier had regained his composure he seemed to remember who he was now talking to. "The foot legion of the Ghosts are in front, ready to assault the gate, but the remainder are lined up in columns."

"Columns? They're not expecting serious resistance then," Gort said. "But why are they attacking at all?" He paused, then suddenly slammed his fist down onto the map-table. "Damn it, of course! Ortof-Greyl, you were absolutely right; Lord Isak isn't with his troops, he's already in the city. That's why they're not worried about assaulting the city, Lord Isak is waiting inside with a few élite squads to take them by surprise; it's the only explanation."

"Your orders, sir?" Chotech asked.

Gort was silent for a while, his face twisted into a scowl. "It makes no difference. We have no choice; we must march on the New Barbican and try once again to make it clear we are not Lord Isak's enemies. General Chotech, take a party—and the major, if you're up to riding, young man—and approach the Farlan. They won't dare beat up a general. If they won't take you to their commander, send them back with a message and return."

"And the message?"

"That we are Knights of the Temples, sworn to protect holy ground from desecration. That we intend to march on the city and protect the temples. Our men will have orders to consider the Farlan allies against the common foe unless attacked and I ask that they send a deputation to us at their convenience."

"Yes sir." Chotech strode off towards his own tent where his horse was waiting, already saddled. Major Ortof-Greyl struggled along behind.

"Lieutenant Mehar," General Gort snapped. The lieutenant jumped, wary of further rebuke, but the general was looking out over the heads of his army, towards the walls of Scree. "Get the men ready to attack."

Set apart from the clank of steel and the urgent calling of men, he sat in the dark peace of an empty room, alone with thoughts that echoed the chaos outside. His head throbbed with the surging energies in the air: magic and the voices of the dying, the shrieks of the mad and their brutal desire to kill. He could smell it all; that desire he knew as well as the rage coursing through his body that left his hands quivering. He'd sought this place out in desperation, fleeing from the animal stirring inside as the badgering questions broke in a tidal wave over him. As the army had marched in through the gate, the nobles and officers had all crowded around him as soon as they could with a thousand questions and requests, all completely unaware of the effect Scree had had on him, or the news he'd just received.

Here there were only bare floorboards, split and warped with age. A shutter clung grimly to the window frame by one last rusty hinge. A curtain hanging over the doorway was the same grey as the walls in the weak light. There was nothing to disturb or distract as he sat on the floor with his silver blade across his lap, listening to the ragged movement of breath through his tight throat. He closed his eyes and listened to his own heart beating, counting out the pauses between inhaling and exhaling, bringing the wild gasping once more under control, just as Carel had taught him all those years ago.

Slowly his hand began to uncurl from a fist and the great hammering of his heart calmed to a steady thump. The pressure behind his eyes subsided a little and he felt a flush of relief. For all the monstrous side of his soul raged and blustered, it could still be reined in by the human side. The comfort was meagre, but in darkness, any tiny thread of light was to be embraced.

Isak opened his eyes and ran a finger down the smooth blade of the sword in his lap. The whispery echo of magic tingled on his fingertips as he brushed the invisible runes that had been beaten into the silver, but he hardly noticed. His thoughts were fixed on the events of the last half-hour.

Grave news, my Lord. The voice echoed through his head like an accusation. Had he known that it would come one day? Had he been wilfully negligent?

It had been a simple enough thing to cow the defenders of the Autumn's Arch gate into surrendering; half were nothing more than frightened city guard, suddenly facing a straight assault from the Ghosts of Tirah. The poorly trained men from Scree had grown up with the threat of the Farlan on their border, and they'd all heard stories of the prowess of the Ghosts, a professional legion the city could not hope to match. When Isak had appeared in the street behind them with a spitting corona of raw magic blazing about him, Mariq adding to the display before being joined by King Emin's pair of mages, most had simply broken and run. Those who surrendered he'd sent south to the Greengate to join Zhia Vukotic's motley army—by the time General Lahk had ridden up to the gate, it had been cleared of defenders and unbarred.

Isak gritted his teeth and took another moment to will his hand to unclench from around Eolis' hilt. It had been a strange meeting, that one: General Lahk at the head of a column of soldiers who roared a greeting to their lord, while a small party of liveried suzerains followed on the general's heels, all looking buoyed and elated at the taste of battle in the air. By contrast, the witch's companion, Fernal, had been disturbingly silent. Fernal's monstrous bulk made the mounted men beside him look small and fragile, and even the Ghosts greeting their comrades in Isak's guard had fallen silent when Isak and Fernal stood face to face. The contrasts and parallels made every man present catch his breath and wonder what would happen.

Fernal was of a size with Isak but, unlike Isak, he looked far from human—it wasn't just the deep blue of his skin, which faded into the evening gloom; the thick mane of hair that fell from his head and neck, framed a fierce lupine face with blackness and highlighted the white gleam of his eyes and curved fangs. Where Isak was clad in his armour and long white cape, Fernal wore no clothes, save for the tattered cloak that hung loose on his shoulders and served as a reminder to anyone watching—or perhaps to himself—that he was not some mindless creature from the Waste. He carried no weapons, and kept his taloned fingers turned inward, away from Isak.

For a few precious moments the two had regarded each other as proud equals, then they had exchanged a respectful nod. Fernal had bowed low and introduced himself in a smooth, deep voice that had sent a wave of relief rippling out through the watching rank and file. The sound had clearly unnerved Fernal; he straightened quickly with a hunted look in his eye that made the nearest soldiers freeze, as though they had heard the hiss of an ice cobra.

Isak stepping forward to clasp Fernal by the arm had broken the tense moment, but the son of Nartis had been clearly relieved when Isak turned to the other men and he was able to slip back into a dark corner where the witch awaited him.

It had been with relief and a welcome smile that Isak had finally taken General Lahk by the wrist after the strange formalities with Fernal. Only then had he seen the troubled look in Lahk's eye, anxiety in the face of a man legendary for his lack of emotion.

Grave news, my Lord.

In that moment he'd felt the air change around him, suddenly laden with boiling energy.

This should have been foreseen and prevented. Chief Steward Lesarl apologises for not pressing the matter further with you.

His throat had dried. Any feeble attempt at a reply went as the general ploughed on, almost as if afraid to pause for breath before he'd finished.

Your father, my Lord, he had said quietly. *Your father is missing. Taken.*

Isak could feel it bubbling under his skin: that restless nag of guilt and anger, made worse by the fact it had no outlet. The only person he could find to blame was himself. He was the one with the power—he was the one who'd failed to recognise there could be a threat. His father Horman was as wilful and proud as he was. The antagonism between them had been constant, but it hadn't really mattered before Isak had become one of the Chosen. Now their relationship was a matter of state: a tool for insurrection, or for another nation's use against him.

But that wasn't what haunted Isak; it was the damage that followed in his wake. First Carel, lying sick and enfeebled in a bed, missing an arm; and Vesna with that broken look in his eyes—both men were seasoned campaigners, but they had been indelibly scarred by Isak's company. Now his father, who'd not even wanted to be a part of Isak's new life, was paying the price for his association. He was Chosen, and cursed. Would the rare gift of his friendship exact a similar toll on everyone?

Isak winced as the fire behind his eyes threatened again and the insistent spark of magic swelled in his palms. This almost primaeval feeling welled out from his gut, begging to wreak havoc, to tear the house apart, to do anything—just to distract him from the guilt which threatened to drown him.

"Do not blame yourself for the actions of others," said a voice inside his head. Isak's eyes flew open in alarm. The witch of Llehden was standing in the doorway, motionless. Even the rise and fall of her breath was imperceptible. Ehla reminded him of the statues from his dreams of the White Isle: timeless and forbidding, yet calming, still.

The dreams of the White Isle, and Bahl's death there . . . they hadn't returned since they had come true. Nowadays his nights were more fragmented, jagged shapes in his mind, scraps of Aryn Bwr's brutalised memories, mingled with his own fears for the future. Apart from when Xeliath chose to visit him, Isak dreaded his dreams. The familiar trepidation of the White Isle was almost preferable now.

"Who else am I to blame?" he said aloud.

"What use is blame?"

Isak's hand tightened, but he kept his anger contained. "What in the name of Ghenna do you mean by that?"

"Blame serves no purpose other than to fuel the fire inside you." Ehla's face softened somewhat. *"Don't focus on who is to blame, or who should bear guilt for what has happened. Care about rectifying the matter, not stumbling over it."*

"I'm Lord of the Farlan," Isak said in a controlled voice. "Despite what some think of me I've learned a little of what that means. I know my duty to the tribe is more important, but such things cannot go unanswered or we will appear—"

"Duty to the tribe?" the witch scoffed. *"No wonder there are so few warlocks in the Land if all men are so blind. A man thinks he is a great lord if he sacrifices himself to duty to the tribe, never once thinking that the tribe is better served if he recognises the duty he has to himself."* She squatted down suddenly to be on Isak's level, her fierce gaze seeking his. *"Blind faith in duty will drain you as surely as a vampire, and leave you nothing more than a dead husk. Your lord knew that, did he not? Lord Bahl knew that it would use him up and spit him out, suck the very marrow of his being and leave only dry, broken bones."*

"Your blood, your pain, shed for those who neither know of it nor care," Isak mumbled, remembering Bahl's warning when Isak had first strapped on the last king's armour. *The taste of magic buzzing through that underground chamber, the rasp of a dragon's scales running over the stone floor.* The old lord had warned him that those close to him were in danger, so why had he not listened?

Ehla cocked her head. *"He said that to you? So he knew what it was doing to him, and he warned you against it. Xeliath tells me he died in the Palace on the White Isle, searching for a Crystal Skull."*

"He was driven to it," Isak said, suddenly desperate to defend Bahl's decision though he knew it had been foolish. "A necromancer drove him there so that Kastan Styrax could kill him."

"And before he went, he warned you not to become the same as he, not to make the mistakes he could not help but make. He gave himself to guilt and grief; lost himself in duty until there was nothing left of the man he'd once been, only the lord. He didn't want you to fail in that duty as he had."

Isak leapt up, Eolis flashing through the twilight as he cried out angrily. Ehla did not back out of range of his sword's terrible gleam but faced him down with an expression of calm determination, raising a hand to stop whoever was behind her in the corridor. Isak felt a flood of magic course through his body as he realised it was Fernal there, watching over the one he'd sworn to protect.

"There is no need for anger; you do not curse him by accepting that as a man he had faults. They are as much a part of a man as his qualities and they tell far more about his character." She took a step forward, close enough to reach out and put a comforting hand on Isak's arm.

For a moment he thought she was going to touch him, to pass on her serenity, perhaps, but she made no more movement towards him. He lowered the sword, ashamed of his temper.

"Accepting one's own faults is vital for any man, even more so for a lord. Without understanding what is inside you, it is impossible to understand the Land outside your mind; it is the filter through which you see everything." She turned and walked away, so smoothly that she glided like a ghost, the tattered hem of her dress silently brushing the cracked floorboards.

Before she turned to go down the corridor, she paused to give Isak one last considered look. *"Look inside yourself, my Lord. Understand what lies within you first, and then you will look upon the Land with fresh eyes."*

Isak found himself unable to move as the witch departed. He heard the creak of the stairs as Fernal walked down them, and finally the bang of the door as they left the house and he was again alone in a silent oasis, separated from the others by the walls he'd placed within himself. It took him a while to realise his anger had all but vanished, like smoke on the breeze. The guilt remained; that could not be so easily erased, but now he was not consumed by the desire to destroy everything within reach he could think clearly. He unclipped Eolis' leather scabbard from his belt and sheathed his sword before sitting down, this time with his back resting against the wall.

"Look inside? What would I find there?" he wondered aloud. "A boy, pretending to be a king? A king, pretending to be a boy?" He grimaced. "A beast straining at its shackles? Or all of them?"

He thought on Ehla's words. *Fresh eyes. He needed to look upon the Land with fresh eyes.* "What I need fresh eyes for is this damned city, for a way to understand the madness here," he said aloud.

And finally he realised the witch, intentionally or not, had been teaching him a lesson sorely needed, *and* guiding him towards the answers they had all been seeking, answers neither Zhia Vukotic nor King Emin could provide, but that might spell salvation for them all in the years to come.

Look within yourself.

Isak smiled and did so. There, he found fresh eyes.

So now, my chained dragon, he thought, *before I go to kill Isherin Purn, I need your eyes. You've been hiding yourself away inside me ever since we arrived in Scree, as quiet as a mouse—or as a child hiding under the blankets. Like a king pretending to be a boy. Something here frightens you, doesn't it? Something on the air, something you recognise.*

He stretched out his legs and placed Eolis between them.

So, tell me about Azaer.

Like flowing swathes of grey in the darkness, the mercenary armies surged over the shattered remains of the Foxport gates and into the city. Rojak watched them through failing eyes, sensing the frothing tide of hatred and petty jealousies, now inflated to monstrous proportions by the theatre's spell, more than seeing the men themselves. He was propped against a cracked column, part of the once-grand entrance to the Merchants' Forum, and the building's prominent position gave him a fine view of his handiwork. The inrush of soldiers swept up the maddened flotsam of the city's population and drove it on through the channels of Scree's streets. He felt them in his veins, their energy forcing his weary heart to beat on, the violent movement rocking his dying body as viscous, sludgy blood filled his arteries and powered his muscles.

The Forum towered over the neighbouring buildings. The fire that had ravaged the fretwork roofs around the central courtyard and devoured the beams holding them up could do nothing about the fat stone platform the Forum stood on. On one of the steps, where blood had pooled in the worn-away centre and dried to form a cracked lake-bed, a figure lounged contentedly. She watched her own handiwork with a girlish self-satisfaction, looking back at Rojak every minute or so to ensure he was appreciating how prettily her blazes were lighting a path through the city. Flitter had cast off her delicate theatre clothes in favour of a stained tunic and hauberk, but there was still an intangible femininity about her carriage that Rojak recognised as something that would have stirred him in those years before Azaer called him to service.

He did not give her the satisfaction of appreciating the fires, instead forcing his face into a mask that hid his approval. He could feel her annoyance growing at his lack of reaction. Through the pain in his chest, a flicker of pleasure still shone. At one stage they had all assumed they could manipulate him. One by one, Rojak had dismissed their efforts. Flitter was simply slow in realising that she was nothing compared to him, her fires were paltry in comparison to the conflagrations he had wrought. Only by the light of the coming dawn would Scree be seen as the sculptured masterpiece over which he alone had laboured.

"It is time," Rojak croaked. His throat was a ruin; speaking was a rapturous agony that sparked every nerve in his body, one that would soon culminate in the final pain of his demise. *Not death, never death*, he thought with the twist of a smile. The loss of his body was inevitable, even necessary, considering the runes cut into his festering flesh that echoed those once painted on the theatre's walls, and the ultimate goal of that spell. But he would not die.

I will be spared the gross indignity of that empty being's final judgment.

He gave a cough and saw Flitter looking up at him. Clearly the ruin in his throat had made him difficult to understand. No matter. As he tried to push away from the pillar, one of the Hounds saw his intent and scampered to help. The creature's arms were like polished oak under his body and he submitted gratefully, letting it bear most of his weight down the two dozen steps to the street below.

"Where are you going?" Flitter asked, appearing in a blur on the cobbled road before him. Rojak kept his eyes on the street. She had always moved faster than he could see, even when he was healthy.

"We go to finish our task."

"But surely it's done?" she said.

The remaining Hounds joined them, stepping out from the shadows to surround Flitter. The woman paled and instinctively slipped her fingers around the hilts of her hooked knives as the Hounds stared inscrutably at her with their large black eyes. Her eyes flickered between the two she could see and strained to focus on the one just on the periphery of her vision. When at last her nerve broke and she turned to face it, the movement prompted all the Hounds to grin wolfishly and lope off down the street.

Only the one assisting Rojak remained, and the minstrel knew which of them, dog or master, Flitter was most frightened of. He could feel her eyes on him as he watched the Hounds trotting through the dark and snuffling at the air, as though there were horrors worse than them in Scree.

"What else would you have me do?" Flitter asked, looking cowed. "I thought driving the people towards the abbot was all you intended."

"Merely a means to an end," Rojak whispered, "as is everything in this city." He took a tentative step forward, his helper as gentle and tender as a nursemaid. "They will not hurt the abbot, only frighten him into doing something foolish."

"They will tear him apart!" Flitter said. "The Skull will not protect him against thousands who are so lost to madness they do not understand fear."

"They will not harm him," Rojak asserted, wincing at having to repeat his words. "I have another plan for the abbot, and when it comes to fruition I must be there."

"To do what?"

Rojak stopped and looked deep into her eyes. They widened in horror as he looked deep into her soul. Her mouth fell open to shriek but no sound came, only a tremble of air from her shuddering lungs.

"To do our lord's will," he hissed.

Leaving Flitter shaking and gasping, Rojak and his Hound started off down the street again. In the distance he heard hollering voices, discordant sounds of no meaning against the background of the growing crackle of flames. On his cheek he felt a breath of wind as Ilit's zephyrs tentatively crossed the boundaries he'd raised and once more explored the avenues of Scree.

He smiled. His strength had been too meagre to maintain that blockade any longer, but the wind's return would serve him as well as its absence had. Flitter's fires were burning quickly now. The newly returned breezes brought him a taste of their soot and he knew it wouldn't be long before it carried sparks and heat as well. The placement had been careful, sending the throngs of people east towards the abbot and the soldiers of the Greengate; now they would spread the flames throughout Scree as well.

He heard footsteps behind him, Flitter hurrying to catch up, calling out as she did, "Rojak, they've seen us! Not all went that way, there are some behind us."

He could hear the panic in her voice, which was understandable; they'd watched the common folk of Scree tear each other apart with a frenzy even Rojak could scarcely believe. *The cruelty in the hearts of men,* he thought to himself. *How we underestimate it. Master, you are the only one who sees them for what they truly are.*

"Do not be afraid," he said as clearly as he could. "I am the herald of their saviour; they will not harm us."

Flitter appeared in front of him again, forcing Rojak to stop abruptly. "Are you sure? They're coming after us," she said anxiously, looking over his shoulder.

"Foolish girl," Rojak said, "why are you afraid? None of them could catch you, and I have already told you that I am safe."

With difficulty he turned. Twenty yards down the street a pack of a dozen or so people were scrabbling towards them with savage intent, some on all fours, like the animals they had become. They closed the distance quickly. Rojak could see the twisted face of the leader, a large man with a gross hanging belly, criss-crossed with scratches, rattling a long club on the ground before him as though it was a blind man's cane. Part of his lip was torn away to expose the bloodied teeth underneath, but his eyes never left Rojak as he advanced. The minstrel recognised avarice there. Greed and envy were his favourite of man's weaknesses.

Even after all this, Rojak marvelled, *even after the curses I have placed upon these people, the vestiges of humanity remain; the arrogance, the envy, the foolish desires—curses of the Gods that they do not recognise in the faces of all those around them. Oh, how their weaknesses rule them.*

As the group neared, they faltered. The Hound supporting Rojak snarled furiously; not yet letting go of the minstrel's arm but tensing under him, readying for the fight. Rojak stared at the big man, daring the mad-eyed wretch to come closer—and astonishingly, he did, shuffling nearer until Rojak could smell his foetid breath.

The man's eyes darted between Rojak's face and his chest—the augury chain, Rojak realised. He was careful not to break the man's gaze. His body was too frail to chance anything. One hasty swipe could pitch him to the ground, never to rise again. Soon, soon he could allow that, but to come so close and be undone by nothing more than a bold animal—He took a calming breath. That could not be permitted.

The leader of the pack sniffed nervously, as if unnerved by the odour of decay that overlaid his own base stench, and reached out a tentative hand. The fingernails were torn and bloody, one ripped off entirely, and the man's fingers twitched and trembled uncertainly. The minstrel summoned enough strength to squeeze the Hound's arm, keeping the creature still.

At last he broke eye contact and looked down. The man was brushing a wondering finger against Death's coin, then his hand began to close about it. He didn't even notice the shadow falling over them, the deepening dark of night that enveloped Rojak. He chuckled and the man froze, arm poised to grip the coin and wrench the chain off him.

"If it is death you want," he began.

"*Then death you shall have*," finished a cruel voice from all about them.

The man let the coin fall from his fingers and staggered back, falling fearfully to his knees.

"*To touch my herald is to ask to share in his blessings*," the shadow continued, and a note of pleasure crept in to its voice. "*So you shall.*"

The man gave a distressed wheeze and fell down, his legs sprawled out before him and a look of horror on his face. He raised his hand and a desperate keening rose in his throat. Rojak smelled the familiar corruption on the air as he watched the man's finger start to fester. Fat blisters of pus grew and burst all over his hand. The man howled and swatted frantically at his hand as the pustules swiftly worked their way down towards his blackening elbow, but he succeeded only in spreading the contagion onto his left hand.

He fell onto his back, limbs spasming as the blisters popped and hissed on his skin, spattering a foul paste of blood-streaked pus over his belly that began to distend and strain at the skin. His companions were almost yelping in fear; screaming, they fled into the side streets, leaving the man to his unnatural fate.

Rojak hardly noticed, for his bright eyes were fixed on the crumbling figure before him. Fingers curled and fell to the floor like fat maggots tossed into a fire; the man gurgled in terror as he writhed at Rojak's feet. Distantly, he heard Flitter spewing onto the street and the sound sparked a laugh in his belly.

At last, the decaying shape before him stopped squirming as what remained of the man's life fled under Azaer's touch. He watched the remains a little longer, then, with a fastidious sniff, he turned and let the Hound support him as he set off once more on his final mission.

Up ahead, somewhere in the streets where they were heading, Rojak felt the pulse of a colossal surge of magic arc through the air. It shook the very ground under his feet, and was followed by a bright white flash, then a crash of thunder, like a raging giant—then a sudden, terrible silence.

Rojak shuffled on, eyes half closed as he felt the enormous swell of suffering ring out through the city that was so closely linked to his own body.

"Abbot Doren, little black-winged bird snug in your nest, so glad you could make your presence felt," he said softly, as though whispering into the ear of a beloved child. Against the dark swathe of sky lit by bloody flickering spots, the first screams began. Rojak's tongue flashed out to taste the air, as though he found some lascivious delight in the mingled corruption and rising stench of fear.

In the distance, coal-black clouds obeyed his summons and drew closer.

"Our sheep have gone to fold and the night has no more need of its herald; let the final act begin," he murmured.

"So tell me about Azaer."

"*Azaer.*" The word came back no louder than a whisper, fomenting a buzz of fear that rippled from Aryn Bwr, through Isak's body and out into the city beyond.

"*You do not know what you ask.*"

"I'm asking for knowledge—and surely I need not remind you that I'm all that stands between you and Death's final judgment."

"*Threats, from a whelp?*" the last king replied with scorn. "*I had legions burning under my hand, Gods screaming their last at my feet.*"

"And for that, the deepest pit of the Dark Place has your name carved above its entrance," Isak said. He had heard there were daemons that restlessly walked the Land searching for the soul of Aryn Bwr, trailing the chains with which they would bind him, if ever they found the enemy of the Gods. He hoped that was just a myth—his own enemies were plentiful enough without vengeful daemons joining their ranks.

"*I hear them,*" Aryn Bwr said, as if in answer to Isak's thought, until Isak realised he meant only the creatures of the Dark Place. "*I hear them singing my name in the twilight.*"

"Even here? Amidst all this?"

"*They are with me always, and still I fear to know more of Azaer.*"

"And yet you won't tell me what you do know about Azaer—what does the shadow hold over you?" Isak asked in amazement.

"*Morghien knows. That scarred wanderer was broken when his soul fell under the shadow. To look Azaer in the face is to allow the shadow to see your soul, to look right through you. Your threats are merely of pain and the emptiness of death.*"

Suddenly Isak understood. His breath caught as the heat of Scree fell away from his awareness. "Not just to be faced with the void, but to have the void stare back at you."

"*Azaer is no daemon, no God, no mortal. Look Azaer in the face and you see a horror no daemon could imagine, the part of you that exists in the void.*"

"But what *is* Azaer?" Isak insisted, disturbed as much by the horrific reverence in Aryn Bwr's voice as his words. The most accomplished, the most highly blessed—no matter what he had done with those blessings—of mortals, and Aryn Bwr was in awe of a shadow?

"*I have no answers for you there.*"

"You must know something. You've stayed hidden all the time I've been in Scree; you're afraid of something in this city. I think your paths have crossed before."

For a moment there was complete silence. Then—

"*Whispers . . . Shadows speaking to me from a cloudless sky while the stars watched and the moons hid. Long in the night, deep in the night, in the height of summer during the Wars of the Houses, and I, barely adult, yet leading my House's armies, I walked the pickets when I could not sleep and found I was alone in that. Even the sentries were beyond rousing, though they stood still at their posts. I could see dawn lightening the sky on the horizon, but the Land was still dark, so dark that even the shadows had voices.*"

"Azaer spoke to you?" Isak spoke softly, hesitating to interrupt.

"*Perhaps it was a dream, but what figment of the living mind would reveal such truths? These were terrible truths, truths that would change the face of the Land for ever, leading me down paths I had feared to tread, and showing me my own soul, its true shape and shine.*"

"Paths within you, or hidden places?" Isak asked. "Why did the shadow come to you? What made you special?"

"*Why do shadows do what they do, go where they go? Shadows follow the living, witness to our deepest secrets. The shadow found me because I was the one to be found— even so young, my genius was lauded by all. What use to tell secrets to fools? Even in darkness, the shadows will follow.*

"*The blinkers were taken from my eyes. Azaer does not lie—Azaer cannot lie, for if you draw the shadows back, you reveal what is hidden. The shadows illuminate the path, they do not force one to take it, and certainly not one such as I, born to change all and leave Gods broken in my wake. Fools forge weapons to their own devices, I learned that before my tenth season, when my uncle showed me the mysteries of fire and metal. This you already know to be true: iron and stone have their shapes within them, and those shapes should never be denied. Not all steel should become a sword.*"

Sudden laughter rang through Isak's head, so fleeting that he wondered if the last vestiges of sanity Aryn Bwr had retained were gone forever.

Then the voice returned with a chilling clarity. *"You above all know this to be true: you, the weapon both men and Gods tried to forge to their own ends, resulting in—well, not what was wanted. Azaer does not forge, but Azaer can see the shape within, because it itself lacks mortal flesh."*

"Where did the shadow lead you?" Isak asked.

"Deep, deep into darkness, down paths that had not been there under Tsatach's fiery eye."

"Where?" Isak insisted, desperate for concrete information. This mystical litany was beginning to try his patience.

"No place mere mortals could find," the dead spirit said, oblivious now to everything except his memories, *"no place to be found, except at twilight, where one world meets the next; between the edges of what we know and what we fear. We were three days' ride from where I would build Keriabral, on lands my House controlled, though I never found that barrow again. It was outside of time, the link between this life and what lies past Death's final judgment."*

"A barrow," Isak said, sensing they were getting somewhere useful, "so you were underground?"

"Down into darkness, into the bowels of the Land, the heart of the Land, a point of balance, a place of harmony and standing stones. Deep; so deep I feared going further would bring me to the six ivory gates of Ghenna itself."

"And what did you find?"

"Gifts, links in a chain, twelve means to a thousand ends."

"Twelve gifts . . . and there was no price for these gifts?" Isak asked hoarsely. He could guess what they were now, for this was a scrap of history that made sense at last. Aryn Bwr had been a mage-smith of great power, but weapons that struck fear in the Gods themselves? The ballads and stories of that age told how Aryn Bwr had forged the twelve Crystal Skulls and made gifts of them to his allies. Nowhere did it say how he had managed this, nor from what he had forged them.

"A fool's price, a fool's soul. I paid nothing, but I knew I would not witness the Land I re-forged. I strove for a legacy and it was that they tore from me. I was never driven down the path, only shown the one I would choose. My actions were predicted, anticipated, by hateful shadows that whisper and laugh in the night . . . they knew they would have me one day. They were always watching, always waiting, ever-patient for their prize." He broke off suddenly and Isak felt a chill breeze run through his head.

"*In a moment of desperation, I gave it, in return for petty revenge,*" Aryn Bwr said at last.

"Revenge?"

A memory stirred, one Isak recognised from his dreams. A great fortress crowned by towers as massive as the one he had come to know so well in Tirah: Castle Keriabral, Aryn Bwr's fortress, where he should have died—until, in a last desperate act, he'd called out a name and secured a completely different fate.

"I remember," Isak said, subdued. Pain and grief flowed from the dead king's spirit now. It took Isak a moment to shake off the anguish and pursue his original line of questioning.

"What does Azaer want? What links the Skulls to the destruction of Scree?"

"*Deeds done openly betray little; done in the shadows, they speak the truth.*"

Isak hesitated. "All this could be misdirection? Thousands of people are going to die—have already died. It cannot be so simple. If Azaer has had only a light hand in events, then it most likely hasn't the strength to become more involved—this change in tactics means either it's growing stronger, or it's taking a risk."

He tailed off as he tried to understand it all. For the hundredth time since his elevation, first to Krann and then to Lord of the Farlan, he cursed his own ignorance. He'd stolen time whenever he could to struggle his way through impenetrable scrolls and ancient books. He was not one who found pleasure in reading, but he knew the worth of knowledge. He had begun to associate the scent of leather bindings with a yearning for the breeze in his hair, and the feel of the rough parchment under his fingers brought on a sense of dread, a precursor to the stilted, ritualistic style of writing that invariably fogged his mind.

"It can't be," Isak muttered, more to himself than Aryn Bwr.

"*All deeds serve a purpose,*" the dead king replied solemnly, "*but what use can shadows have of grand gestures?*"

In short, careful phases they came within sight of the barricade. They were all listening hard for voices: signs of panic, sudden shouts, anything that might signal the order to attack. Doranei looked at the half-dozen wooden houses blazing away on his left, casting long shadows over King Emin's painfully small company. The men made their way down the middle of the street in three neat columns. They marched smartly, keeping in formation, their best defence against the barricade's defenders. Even so, every one of the Brotherhood had an ear cocked for that first whistle of an arrow shaft.

"Your Majesty."

Doranei didn't need to turn his head to know it was Beyn, on their right flank, who'd spoken. The street was silent aside from their quiet footsteps and his voice carried easily.

"Something in the shadows," Beyn said.

"Something?" the king echoed.

"Figure; too quick to see properly, but tall, not a citizen."

"Hooded and cloaked in white? Watching us?"

"Yes, all in white. Looking towards the barricade, but he saw us too. Moving alone, not frightened to be seen."

"Tell me if it gets any closer," King Emin said. "We don't want to get caught up in someone else's problem."

"What is it?" Endine whispered, unable to keep quiet.

Doranei looked at his king, who looked perturbed by the news, however calm he sounded.

"Scree's end is near, then," he said quietly, sadly. "When the Saljin Man ventures inside a city's boundary, it's because it is no longer a city."

"The Saljin Man?" Now Endine sounded afraid. "The curse of the Vukotic?"

"The very same. The daemon can follow any member of that tribe. No doubt it can sense the death hanging around Zhia. We should move faster."

They picked up their pace, no one needing to be told twice. They'd all heard about the daemon that plagued the Vukotic tribe, and not even Coran wanted to try his arm against it.

The ground by the barricade was littered with corpses, most unarmed and many painfully thin, and those arrows the defenders had not bothered to recover after beating off however many assaults they'd endured. Doranei tried not to look at any of the bodies too closely as he carefully stabbed every one within range, in case one of the rabid creatures was only injured. They'd been lucky so far, encountering no more than a dozen stragglers between Autumn's Arch, where they'd left the Farlan Army, and the Greengate.

Lord Isak hadn't bothered trying to talk King Emin out of the expedition—he was busy organising his own fool's errand, though Lord Isak had more soldiers to accompany him to the Red Palace, where they believed the necromancer was holed up. The white-eye had grasped the king's wrist in friendship and saluted the rest of the small band, just as any Farlan soldier would, kissing his bow-fingers and touching them to his forehead. The other Farlan had followed suit, and Doranei felt a flush of foolish pride that Lord Isak had spared them the moment of respect, before the Brotherhood had dropped over the barricade and marched south, heading for the spot where their mages, Endine and Cetarn, had sensed a Crystal Skull being used.

"That's far enough," called a voice from the barricade. Doranei froze as he tried to see who'd spoken; it was the local dialect, but not spoken by a local. As if bidden, a man clambered up the barricade and removed his steel helm to reveal a cropped mess of black hair and a mass of cuts and bruises.

Doranei had seen that battered head watching him from the floor of Zhia's study: the Menin soldier who had so reminded him of Ilumene for a moment, though there was hardly a passing likeness. *Amber?* he thought Zhia had called him when they'd attended the theatre with Koezh. *Was it a proper nickname or one she'd bestowed that night on a whim?* In the flickering firelight, the Menin hooked the spike of his axe into his belt, though Doranei could clearly see the crossbow in the man's other hand.

"I wish to speak to your mistress; does she still live?" Doranei called after hurriedly clearly his throat. He told himself it was the heat and dust in the air that had dried his throat, nothing more, and certainly not the fear of attracting attention to himself when they were so exposed out on the street.

"Does she still live?" The Menin gave a cough that Doranei realised was a surprised laugh. "Aye, she lives," Amber said in a wry tone, "and I'm sure she'll be glad to see another of her pets is still alive. Is that the whole of your company?"

Doranei looked back at his companions. All but five were men of the Brotherhood. With King Emin were his white-eye bodyguard Coran, the mages, Endine and Cetarn, and the Jester acolyte Zhia had given them to guide them to where Rojak and Ilumene were hiding. They didn't need the masked man now, but Zhia had assured the king that the acolyte would remain loyal, and an extra sword was always welcome, even if Coran kept between the king and the acolyte at all times. They were less than a full company, though every man there was too valuable for the regiments. "This is all," Doranei called.

Amber waved them over. "Shift yourselves, then; our friends are coming back for another try."

Doranei didn't even bother to look back. He and his Brothers raced for the rough barricade surrounding the Greengate and scrambled up it, Amber helping by grabbing the scruff of Doranei's collar and hauling him up while the raggedly armoured mercenaries beside him reached out hands to help the others. The Menin officer turned to do the same for the next man, and hesitated when he looked King Emin in the eyes and was caught by his icy-blue glittery stare.

"Gods, if your eyes were darker I'd have thought you one of her brothers," Amber said gruffly to cover his hesitation.

"There would be worse companions to have this night," Emin replied as he climbed the barricade of overturned carts, barrels and broken furniture as nimbly as a goat.

"Bloody hope so," Amber said with a slight grin, wrapping his thick fingers around Torl Endine's arm and lifting the scrawny mage up onto the top of the barricade. "Otherwise my night's only going to get worse."

Endine gave a small squawk, but the constant state of terror and the effort of running through the city had drained any real feeling from it. As Amber put him down, Endine sagged into a small heap of bones and worn rags, like a horse recognising the knacker's yard. Amber gave the mage a jab with his toe that almost sent him sprawling backwards. "Don't see why you're sitting down for a breather! I know a mage when I see one, and you lot are a damn sight better at scaring off those poor bastards behind you than arrows are."

Endine started to riposte, but all that came out was a weak wheeze.

"You'll have to excuse my feeble colleague," Cetarn declaimed. He didn't look hampered by his paunch as he set about clambering up the barricade with all the gusto of a schoolboy. None of Scree's dangers seemed to have affected the oversized mage in the slightest, something Doranei put down to a noble upbringing, and the blind determination of the noble-born that every danger was nothing more than a game to be enjoyed with almost childish enthusiasm. What really annoyed him was that most of the time the approach worked.

"Endine cannot help himself," Cetarn continued when he reached Amber.

Doranei could tell that the Menin soldier got a surprise when he realised the mage was both taller and wider than he was. *There you go, bet you've not seen that from a normal so often*, he thought in a moment of petulance.

"I have grown used to carrying him under my wing. Once he's recovered his breath, Endine will find some clever way to prove his worth."

Amber looked from one mage to the other as the rest of the Brotherhood slipped past him. "It's not a wing, it's a paw, if you ask me," he muttered under his breath, then, louder, "If that's how you want it, then fine; just do something about that lot." He pointed towards a small crowd behind them, skirting the edges of the buildings as they approached, as though the light from the fires further down the street might burn them.

"Certainly, what would you like?" Cetarn replied brightly, pointlessly pushing the wide sleeves of his robe up to reveal pale skin marked with delicate tattoos and neat scars. Any high-ranking soldier would recognise the summary of Cetarn's skill and experience; the Menin battle-mages would have something similar. Major Amber looked sharp enough to understand what the scars and tattoos signified.

"Makes no difference to me," Amber said, reaching down to retrieve his crossbow. "Zhia says there's no chance for them, their minds are broken. Best you can do is make it quick."

He ignored the windlass mechanism and cocked it in Chetse fashion, leather pads protecting his fingers as he pulled the string back by hand; a crude attempt to impress, but no doubt worthwhile if Major Amber was trying to keep a disparate band of militiamen, city guards and mercenaries together.

"My dear boy, I'm not a white-eye," Cetarn said, ignoring the look he received from Coran. "Mass slaughter isn't really my speciality; it requires too much raw magic and not enough subtlety. If you could use those bows to buy us a little time? Thank you." The fat mage gave an extravagant flourish of the hands, like a street conjuror. "Now, I've always said a good mage must adapt to his surroundings—"

"No you don't," Endine coughed from near their feet, determined to find his voice if it meant an opportunity to annoy his colleague. "You always say, 'What's the point of having all this power if I can't bend the very fabric of the Land to my will?'" He gave a very poor imitation of Cetarn's deep voice.

"Oh honestly, I say that once—"

"Gentlemen," growled King Emin, "not the time."

"Of course, your Majesty," Cetarn said with a quick bow, "I have let myself be distracted." He dropped to one knee, his head bowed as though in prayer and his right hand outstretched with his fingers splayed. "This city has an overabundance of shadows. I'm sure it can spare some for us to employ."

Doranei turned to see the king's reaction, but he could read nothing. Emin's face was as blank as a Harlequin's mask, lit with daemonic light as he held the wick of a bottle up to a torch and handed that to Coran to hurl at the approaching figures. Doranei followed the path of the bottle until it reached the ground and shattered to spread a pool of flame across the centre of the street. More guards arrived on the barricade, muttering to each other in grim, low tones, but the only sounds Doranei focused on were the hiss of fire and the hushed drone of Cetarn's voice.

Doranei was glad he could not understand Cetarn's spell when he saw the shadows all along the street twist and writhe. The mage's hand jerked in response to the movements, until he gained control over the dark shapes littering the floor and began to move and shape them, the deft strokes of a conductor leading his orchestra, coaxing them up, tugging them out of their hollows and cracks until they rose up through the air.

Doranei could see figures through the shadows, as if looking at them through a wall of smoky glass across the entire street. They moved backwards and forwards, peering at the dark curtain but clearly not seeing through it as Doranei could.

They paced with frustration as their prey was swallowed by the night, before giving up and turning back down the road the Narkang men had used, heading north towards the Farlan. The spell took less than a minute to complete, but by the end, Cetarn was sweating with the effort, and the soldiers were shivering at what he'd accomplished. Endine hammered his palms against Cetarn's fat bicep, a strange look of jubilation on his face.

"How long will that hold?" King Emin asked coolly.

"I wouldn't like to estimate," Cetarn replied breathlessly.

The king nodded; he knew his mages well enough to recognise "*You should be impressed I managed it at all.*"

"Will you be able to continue with us?"

Cetarn summoned the strength to look offended at the suggestion. "I am not the feeble one here, your Majesty. I shall continue as far as these hired thugs you keep as bodyguard." He clapped Doranei on the shoulder and managed to look defiant once the younger warrior had stiffened his back to take some of Cetarn's weight.

"Ah, sweetness; not war nor famine can raise mountains between us," purred a voice that sent a prickle down Doranei's spine. Beside him, Cetarn's cheerful expression collapsed. Doranei's nostrils flared automatically, craving the scent of Zhia's heady perfume as though it were a drug. He flinched at the sudden touch of soft fingers on his cheek, but his alarm melted under the force of her smile.

"This is hardly the time for quoting poetry at the boy," said King Emin as he inclined his head respectfully to Zhia. He was wearing his favourite wide-brimmed hat, instead of the steel helm hanging from his belt. Strangely, he had pushed a tawny owl's feather into the band, rather than something grander, but the significance was lost on Doranei. "And I've always rather thought Galasara was a self-important bore, except for his last laments."

Zhia raised an eyebrow. "'Poets and kings raise monuments to their own glory,'" she said.

Doranei recognised the quotation by Verliq, the most skilled human mage in history, whose only record was scores of treatises on magic and the nature of the Land.

The king conceded the point with a small smile. "But for some reason I find myself footing the bill for both."

Now they were behind the barricade and safe for the moment at least, Doranei took a moment to take in details. The barricade was longer than they had expected, encompassing a large area around the Greengate, including an entire street of houses, the contents doubtless stripped out to be used as building material. The reason for the size became obvious when he looked over towards the Greengate itself, where a great crowd of people huddled, thousands of terrified faces turning to watch the newcomers.

"Refugees?" the king asked, pointing towards the mass.

"Certainly, you didn't think the entire city had gone insane, did you?" Zhia said. "These are what's left of Scree's population, the ones untouched by madness. Many are not natives, which tells us something of the spell used, but not all of them, and I've not exactly had the time to work out the fine detail. Once my brother wipes out the remaining armies outside the gate, we can get these people away. They are innocents in this game, and I intend to deny Azaer as many of their lives as possible."

She was dressed as Doranei had seen her last, that strange combination of white patterned skirts and armour. Doubtless the White Circle had strict views on women fighting with the men, but he remembered Lord Isak saying that their queen had been a white-eye, and, as King Emin delighted in proving, folk imitated their monarch's habits as closely as they could. Strangely, Zhia still wore the shawl of the White Circle clasped about her neck and hanging down over her pearl-detailed cuirass.

Slung across her back was her oddly proportioned sword, a favourite weapon among the Vukotic, he finally recalled his swordmaster saying. Lessons felt like a lifetime ago. Like most of the Brotherhood, Doranei was a soldier's orphan. They were taught basic weapons-skills at the orphanage, and those who showed promise were handed over to the street-gang King Emin had adopted as a training ground for his young bodyguards. It was a strange double-life, mornings of petty theft and running errands in the gambling dens followed by afternoons with noble-born fencing masters or heroes from the army.

Doranei smiled. *How much has really changed? Consorting with thieves and murderers one day, kings and princesses the next. The trick is to be able to tell the difference.*

"I assume you're chasing the Skull," Zhia said suddenly, "but why? You have no ability yourself; why risk so much for a trinket that can, at best, only act as an unpredictable shield for you."

The king didn't bother to deny the reason he was going south; he knew every mage in the city would have felt the artefact being used in such a reckless manner. "Others will be seeking it out, others I would deny ownership of such a weapon. I suspect the minstrel will want it for himself, and right now there are few men in the Land I would like to kill more, quite aside from the power that Skull would give him."

"You know which it is?" Zhia's expression grew sharp.

"Lord Isak suspects it is Ruling, and I'm inclined to agree; it is the greatest of them and if the shadow desires any, it would be that one."

"And it is worth the risk? Holding a barricade against the mobs is one thing. If they catch you out in the open they'll tear you apart." Zhia pointed to the south, where an orange glow lit the sky. "They're being driven by those fires, and however skilled your bodyguards are, they cannot hope to survive against maddened hordes of thousands."

"Then come with us," King Emin said plainly. "You could see us there safely and stop Rojak, whether he has found the Skull or not. Doranei tells me you're determined to see these people to safety?"

Zhia nodded, her shining sapphire eyes briefly finding Doranei, who found himself unable to meet them. "I see no reason why they should all die just because some malevolent shadow intends to use their deaths to announce its presence in the Land. I've seen the ones wandering out there; they have lost all sense of reason or safety, and when fire spreads throughout the city it will take them all. Azaer will have the blood it craves, but my soldiers are protecting thousands who do not have to die."

"And then what? What do you intend at dawn, when you're in a makeshift camp somewhere out there? These people won't follow you then."

"Perhaps I overestimated you," Zhia said scornfully. "I am not like you; I do not yearn for the adoring crowds. Once they are out of the city and safe, my role in this play is over. I will go my own way. Haipar is a more caring woman than I, so I'm sure they will reach Helrect unmolested."

"So you will not come with us after the Skull?"

"I already possess one, remember?" Zhia's eyes flashed, but she kept any sign of irritation out of her voice. For all the emotion she betrayed, she could have been discussing the price of fish at a dockside market. "Ruling does not interest me in the slightest. The longer Velere Nostil owned that Skull, the more I disliked and feared him."

"What do you mean?"

Zhia gave a cold laugh. "Be careful what you wish for," she said, staring King Emin directly in the eye. "It may not prove the blessing you think."

"The Skull is not what I seek."

Doranei felt a flicker of pride in his king, a man who had created a nation and commissioned his own state crown. What leader, conqueror or king by birth, would be able to resist the lure of the Skull of Ruling? It was said that it would confer an aura of power on even those without the ability to wield it as a weapon. There was only one thing stopping King Emin becoming a tyrant: he knew perfectly well which desires drove him.

"Of course it is." There was the hint of a smile on Zhia's face now. "Whoever you want to kill—whoever's plans you intend to frustrate—don't pretend it has no lure for you."

She turned to survey her own men, nervously gathered at the barricade, staring into the darkness. The vampire wore no helm and her long hair was loose, and every time she moved her head, locks of gleaming black hair danced in the growing breeze.

"I don't think I'll really be needed here," she said after a moment. "I've been keeping myself in check to avoid the inevitable irritations that would otherwise follow. You need me more than you're willing to admit." She closed her eyes for a moment and placed her palm flat against her chest; Doranei saw her mouth what looked like *Come* before she looked up at the king again.

"Amber," she called to the big Menin soldier who'd stood far enough to one side for courtesy, though close enough to watch everything that had been going on. He gave a grunt in reply and straightened up.

"Major Amber, I think it's time I took my leave," Zhia told him. "You've no real need of me now, and as a man I knew once said, 'When companions appear, a journey should begin.' Stay with Haipar and you'll be safe enough. I'll be visiting her once this business is concluded, so I will find out if anything unfortunate happens to you." She fixed King Emin with a grim look as she said this.

Doranei saw that had cheered Amber up greatly. No doubt he had been taking bets with himself on which Brother would be sent after him. Denying Kastan Styrax, Lord of the Menin, any intelligence might prove crucial over the next few years. Doranei knew they'd still try, but if they had to wait until the mercenary army was well clear of Scree, it would be far harder.

A fearful keening rose from the huddled masses at the foot of the city wall as the ragged refugees shifted like the parting seas to form a corridor down which marched the other Menin soldier currently in the city. Mikiss as a vampire looked completely different from the confused and bloodied messenger Doranei had first seen on the floor of Zhia's study. He stalked towards them, his face in shadow, as though the flames refused to light it. He wore a long, richly embroidered cerulean-blue coat, and pushed through his crimson belt were two long axes, the handle-butts a whisker from dragging along the floor and the spike tips brushing his ribs. Mikiss wore no armour except for the thick brass vambraces strapped on over the sleeves of his coat. Doranei had no idea why. He was keeping a careful eye on Mikiss; the change affected people in different ways. Sometimes a mild spirit could be corrupted overnight into a deranged monster, and there was no way of knowing until it was too late.

"Ah, my protégé arrives," Zhia said brightly. "I think Mikiss is starting to enjoy my gift."

A growl escaped Amber's throat. His face darkened, and Doranei realised that Amber, the only one of them who knew Mikiss before, was less than happy with the change. Doranei had to sympathise: if one of the Brotherhood had been turned, Doranei would have killed him in an instant, to spare him from the horrors to come. The juxtaposition of that fact and his reaction to Zhia's perfume grew more troubling every day. It was true that the Vukotic family were apart from most vampires, but there was still a monster inside every one—even if Doranei could think of her only as the victim, caught on the losing side in a war.

More figures drifted towards them. Two Jester acolytes trotted from the far end of the barricade, their white masks bobbing like ghosts through the gloom, and four shapes detached themselves from a knot of soldiers standing in the lee of the largest building, resolving into Haipar the shapeshifter, the Farlan woman Legana, still in her White Circle armour, the necromancer's assistant Nai and a tall, bulky figure Doranei remembered glowering from darkened doorways at Zhia's home.

When her small entourage had gathered, Zhia began to speak. "I've played the stateswoman long enough, and events have taken a strange turn these past few weeks. Haipar, every soldier here will follow either you or Amber; take these people to Helrect and decide what you want there. There's no army to protect it, so you can take control, or you can take what pay you're owed and get out—"

"I'll be coming with you," Haipar growled, "Erizol and Matak are both dead; I'm going to see this through to the end."

Zhia paused for a moment, on the point of speaking before she abruptly shrugged. "As you wish." She gave an almost wistful sigh. "You Raylin are a curious breed. Legana, you should come with us too. Panro, collect my personal belongings and meet me at the far side of the barricade."

King Emin coughed. "Lady, we cannot be encumbered by baggage; it will slow us down."

The vampire, a small smile on her face, said, "Your Majesty, they are only a few personal items, nothing that will get in your way." Her hand went to her neck and from underneath her cuirass she pulled three chains. She smiled, her long teeth shining bright. Each chain was strung with cut gems, a fortune in fat, glittering stones. "When you live as I have, you learn the value of travelling light, but there are certain little luxuries no lady in my condition should be without, and gems are good currency wherever one finds oneself. Now, shall we be off?"

CHAPTER 27

Isak kept his eyes on the ground to avoid the shattered bricks that littered the road as he ran to the street corner where Major Jachen and the ranger Jeil were crouching. Above them the end wall on the first floor of the building had been smashed through and he glanced up into the black tear in the wall. The building had been converted into a barracks for the Fysthrall soldiers, which must have pleased the rich folk living all around. This part of the city was still dark, for the moment protected from the conflagration they could see consuming south Scree.

"How does it look?" he asked softly.

Jachen looked up. Only his eyes were visible through the helm, but they were enough to betray the man's anxiety. "It looks quiet, my Lord. The scouts have not seen any mobs following the decoy troops."

"They're there," Isak said with certainty. He shone in the darkness with an intensity that made him feel all the more vulnerable. The moons were high and bright, free from the cloud that hung in a wreath around the horizon, and casting their light down to catch the exposed armour of the Farlan soldiers. "They're probably keeping clear of the Fysthrall soldiers and whatever mages they have left."

"The good news is that one of the scouts saw troops leaving the Red Palace compound for the Princess Gate, presumably to secure it for when they escape the city."

Isak nodded. "Pride; without Scree the Circle is finished. Siala won't abandon the city until the last moment; she won't want to leave unless she has to, and she certainly won't want to walk out into the welcoming arms of the Devoted, or the Farlan. No doubt the news that we'd entered the city put a smile on the woman's face."

"We've sent the decoy troops to the south side of the palace, close enough to dissuade Siala from trying to escape."

The advance troops consisted of a division of light cavalry led by Suzerain Torl. The clattering of hooves on cobbles was sure to attract attention from the mobs, which was the intention, and Isak was confident the soldiers would be able to ride through all but the most crowded streets.

He looked back at the troops behind him. Those who'd been with him from the beginning in Scree had been bolstered by a regiment of Ghosts and the suzerains from Saroc, Nelbove and Fordan, the first to beg to accompany him. The others had quickly followed, but he'd refused them, allowing those three only after Tila had whispered in his ear that they were men desperate to prove their loyalty. For the first time in what felt like a long time, Isak had laughed out loud. Here and now, these men still played their games, thinking about allegiance, respect, even dynasty. Only the look on Suzerain Fordan's face had stopped his laughter: the man was willing to risk his life just to show he was as true as his father had been—though there had been no breath of suspicion otherwise, still Fordan felt compelled to do this before he could walk proudly in his belligerent father's shoes.

"How far to the palace?" he asked.

"Five hundred yards, my Lord," Jeil said softly. "I counted ten guards on the nearest stretch of wall; the rest moved off when they saw the Ghosts to the south. There are no foot patrols beyond the wall."

"Good." He beckoned and a handful of figures started to converge upon him. "I'm taking Leshi, Tiniq, Shinir and Vesna; that's all. Jachen, watch our backs, and get ready to wade in if we get into trouble."

"Only five of you?"

"It has to be quiet. I don't know how many Fysthrall are still in the palace, but probably more than we can handle. Vesna, are you ready?"

The count gave a curt nod. He looked strange in full armour, especially when on foot and standing next to the more lightly armoured rangers. He had the face-plate of his helm up, the lion mask staring up into the sky. His face was tight, fixed in an expression of concentration, as though he could will his doubts away.

"Let's seek our revenge," Isak said softly.

They kept to the shadows as best they could, but they were still painfully obvious on Scree's dead streets. The silence was disturbing. A city without people was a body without a beating heart. The stench of corruption filled the air. Soon the conflagration in the south would burn everything away, leaving only ash in its wake.

When the wall was almost upon them, Isak pulled off his silver helm and edged his head around the corner of the building, his blue hood blending into the shadows.

What if they did see it? Isak wondered privately. *In this place the Gods have abandoned, would they be glad to see the face of Nartis?*

There were half a dozen torches burning on the wall, just enough to illuminate the oil-coloured scale pattern of Fysthrall helms, and the white scarves around the soldiers' necks. Every one was shifting uncomfortably or pacing the wall. The ground before the wall was a stretch of formal gardens, with lines of low bushes that might act as shallow trenches for the attack party. Dotted around the gardens were several dozen crumpled shapes. After a few moments Isak could see there were arrows sticking up from some of the bodies.

"Now we need a diversion," he whispered, "something to get us close enough to kill them all quickly."

"And your plan?" Vesna asked.

Isak could hear a strain of hope in the man's voice. "Worried that I might be making it up as I go along, my devoted bondsman?"

"I'm not your bondsman any more," the count reminded him, "but I remain a loyal servant of the tribe, so obviously I'm eager to find out what you want me to do."

"Excellent." Isak smiled. "Now I need to find some bats."

"Bats?" Vesna and Jachen spluttered together.

"Bats. Night's heralds, Death's winged attendants. Look at the men on the wall; they're all shuffling about, or pacing, or twitching: no one's standing still. That tells me they're nervous. I think we should borrow the majesty of the Gods as we're going to punish a heretic; there's symbolism and *everything* there."

Isak grinned at the count, who shook his head wearily. "You're an example to us all, my Lord," Vesna said darkly.

Isak reached over and patted the man on the slight peak of his helm. "That's what I thought. Now shut up and let me concentrate."

He pulled off one of his gauntlets and closed his eyes as he ran his fingertips over the Crystal Skull fused to his cuirass. It was unusually warm to the touch, as ever, but now the Skull felt as slippery and elusive as a wet icicle. His fingers slid almost without resistance over its surface as he reached out with his senses to the Land beyond. The air was thick and heavy in his throat;

he could almost taste the putrefying wounds of the dying city. Scree was expiring, almost on its last breath. He felt the empty streets all around him, the stony dust of its broken bones and the hot stink of its bloating flesh.

In his mind Isak kicked away from the ground and surged up into the cooling night sky, letting the oppressive street-level air drop away like a shed skin. He sensed the reviving kiss of the wind high above and felt a gasp of pleasure escape his body as the gusts lovingly wrapped him in their chill arms. The cold bright moons prickled his skin and drove the remaining vestiges of Scree's choking oppression from his body, purging the poison from his veins.

Isak sighed. He hadn't realised how much he'd missed using magic, feeling the energies thrumming through his bones, but he'd had no choice— with the vast power available through his two Skulls, one small lapse of concentration would have announced his presence to the rest of the city. He couldn't risk it before, but now . . . now it was like returning to the embrace of a lover.

The witch said to accept what was inside me, he thought with a smile, *so why should that not include magic? It's been with me my whole life, shaped me from womb to throne. Either I embrace it and keep control over it, or I risk letting it control me.*

He cast his mind back to the battlefield outside Lomin, that winter landscape feeling an age away during this brutal summer heat, and he recalled that scary moment when he literally lost himself in the rampant tides of magic flowing through his body. *I refuse to let that happen again*, he told himself sternly.

Soothed by the bright night sky, with only the moons for company, he found a moment of contentment—and then, at last, Isak could feel the distant presence of Nartis once more, beyond the western horizon, watching between one moment and the next as the Land continued unaware of the scrutiny. It was nothing like the raging torrent Isak had felt upon Bahl's death—when the looming storm had rushed in to crash over his fragile body and raise him up to where the Gods stood—but something altogether more gentle and comforting. Isak's connection to his God was a delicate thing, too weak to be noticed, until times such as this.

If the God of Storms took note of such a small thing, he did nothing about it. Isak sensed a vigil of sorts, one centred on the black pit of Scree beneath him. Below he felt his body almost swallowed in the darkness. The weight of the city beneath him was a black stain on the Land; a hole through which the normal order was draining away.

He reached his arms out wide, towards the distant clouds that had been kept at bay for too long. Isak gasped at the vastness of it all, for a moment terribly afraid for the thin shadow of his own soul, spread out over so many miles as the clouds started massing, closing a jealous embrace on the city.

And then here they were: flickering wings and sharp clicks in the darkness, shapes that darted and dodged after insects, flying in long, graceful spirals, drawn ever closer to his light.

He hadn't known what would happen once he was here, but he trusted the witch of Llehden. He remembered when first they met, when the gentry of Llehden had welcomed him as a brother—these creatures that cared nothing for the squabbles of man had recognised in Isak something he didn't quite understand himself. He was no prophesied Saviour—Isak needed no further proof of that, whatever any fool prophecy foretold—but the wilds had always been where he was welcome, and the mark of the Gods had deepened that connection; now he felt bound, and now he had to learn to understand.

The bats eagerly clustered around him, their sharp hunter minds curious at what they could sense in the air, though they couldn't trace an outline of him against the clouds. They followed him down, spiralling towards Scree and the street where Isak's body still crouched, before jinking away at the last moment towards the walls of the Red Palace. He opened his eyes just in time to see the swirling cloud of shadows descend upon the terrified soldiers, a darting funnel whipping around them as they ducked down fearfully.

Isak took a few steps forward, out into the moonlight where his armour shone brightly, and slid his helm over his head. No warning voices came from the wall; the Fysthrall guards were too intent on hiding from the column of bats that was spinning tighter and tighter. Isak felt magic billow through the night air, blossoming on the wall like flames bursting into being. He slid the shield from his back and onto his arm, anticipating an attack, before realising it was coming from the bats themselves.

"What have you done?" moaned the usually reticent Tiniq.

Isak tore his eyes away from the bats for a moment; General Lahk's twin looked like he was about to be sick. He felt a shudder echo through the air from the wall and looked back to see the bats had vanished, to be replaced by a tall figure holding aloft a tall silver standard topped by a stylised sculpted shape.

"What is that?" Vesna asked grimly, loosening his sword. "Have you woken another elemental?" His tone wasn't accusatory, just determined.

"Piss and blood," Tiniq replied, dazed, "look at the standard."

They all did so, then Vesna hissed with trepidation, "Merciful Death, Isak, it's the Gatekeeper."

"Gatekeeper?" Isak said. He thought he recognised the standard from somewhere—a circle open on one side with a fist pushed in—but the memory was old, indistinct. Suddenly his heart chilled. "The Herald of Death?" he gasped.

"It must be," Vesna said, though he sounded scarcely able to believe what he was saying. "The Herald takes the dead through his hallway, 'where only bats and Gods may linger,' and on to Death's final judgment. He holds the keys to the throne room of Death."

"And he's here to help us," Isak finished. "Perhaps the Gods have not entirely abandoned this city." He pointed to the soldiers on the wall. Those that hadn't fled were silent, staring in horror at the motionless figure, completely oblivious to what might be happening in the streets of the city.

"My Lord, you don't understand!" Vesna sounded aghast. "The Herald of Death does not leave his halls, he does not appear before the living. He isn't a Bringer of the Slain, he's not one of the Reapers—he should not be here!"

"Well he is," Isak snapped firmly, "and whatever portent you intend to read into his presence, it helps our cause. This is a city of the dead and we hunt a necromancer, so I think the rules are changed. Now move yourselves!"

Not waiting for the other four, Isak broke into a run towards the wall. There was a deeply set postern gate to the right but he ignored that, instead heading directly for the nearest part of the wall. From the corner of his eye Isak could see the others making for the gate, Shinir first, ready to scramble up and over to unbar it from the inside, as planned. It was Isak's task to leap straight onto the wall and kill the guards before they could raise the alarm.

He let energy flood his body, infusing his limbs with a burst of new strength. The wall was ten feet of fat grey bricks, but he vaulted up onto the walkway effortlessly. The nearest guard turned at the sound of metal on stone and died before his eyes could focus on the massive white-eye. A second died in the next heartbeat, still staring at the black skin and crimson robes of the Herald of Death. Only the fourth managed to raise a weapon in his defence and Eolis sheared through the spear-shaft and into the heart with ease.

Isak caught a glimpse of the Herald as two more Fysthrall, shaken out of their trance, ran down the walkway towards him with spears lowered. The Aspect of Death was taller than he, and had perfectly black skin. There were no eyes nor mouth, only slight indentations in an androgynous face. The smooth curve of its skull was broken only by its ears—and at that, Isak's memory stirred: the Herald could not see the dead and had no words for them, though Death himself saw all in those halls, and His words were as tangible as the pale grey stone walls.

Isak dragged his mind back to the present in time to deflect the two Fysthrall soldiers, turning into one spear with his shield while felling the other with his sword. The rusty-skinned soldier didn't check his stride in time and Eolis flicked out to pierce his chest. The other tried to pull back, but Isak was faster. He drove his sword across the man's throat. Both fell silently.

He looked towards the postern; the two corpses above it told him Shinir was already at the gate. That moment of distraction almost cost him dearly as a blow to his shoulder spun him around and almost knocked him off his feet. Looking past the motionless Herald, Isak saw a soldier desperately trying to reload his crossbow, and another spearman on the wall, looking bewildered and terrified. Isak, realising he couldn't risk being hit by another bolt, flung Eolis overhand twenty yards. The sword buried itself into the crossbowman's chest, as easily as a knife sliding into butter.

Seeing Isak unarmed, the spearman found his courage and rushed forward wildly. Isak didn't bother drawing the dagger at his belt. Balling his hand, he drew a fistful of warm night air and punched it forwards. The soldier was two yards away when the blow hit him and rocked him back on his heels. He stopped dead, confused by what had happened, and took a moment to look down and check for injuries. The Fysthrall was still bewildered when Isak smashed his shield into his head and dropped him for good.

A hush descended, cut only by a low string of curses from Isak. The line of wall was broken by fat square towers; Jeil had described them on the way, and he had been sure there that there would be no one in them—a major design fault meant the arrow-slit windows had no real views of the approaching streets. As a result, each section of the wall was isolated. They had gained the wall furthest from the main part of the palace and, thus far, they hadn't been seen.

The Herald hadn't moved. It stood and stared straight at Isak, its lack of eyes apparently no hindrance to knowing exactly where he was. Something about its stance spoke of a readiness, of impending movement. Isak suddenly began to feel vulnerable without his sword, but Eolis lay behind the nightmarish Aspect of Death, catching the moonlight as it stood out from the soldier's impaled chest like a parody of the Herald's standard.

He fought the urge to step back. The minor deity had helped them in some small way, but he had this strange feeling that the Herald was on the point of attacking him. In that expressionless face Isak sensed rage, a boiling anger that was hardly contained.

"*You see me,*" whispered a voice in Isak's mind. "*You can smell your prey, but still I am beyond your grip.*" He gave a slight start—then realised it was not the Herald, but Aryn Bwr, the spirit of the dead Elf king he held prisoner in his mind, on the threshold of Death's domain. Suddenly it all made sense.

Isak pulled his helm from his head, revealing the blue mask that echoed Nartis' face. As he did so, he felt the building tension break like a wave on the shore. Relief washed over him, but Isak was careful to bow deeply to the Aspect, ignoring the sharp flare of pain in his shoulder as the arrow-tip twisted in the shallow wound it had made.

"Thank you, my Lord," he said formally. He had no idea if that was the correct way to address a minor God.

The Herald gave no indication of being either angered or flattered. The scarlet-robed figure inclined its own head and turned away. Isak caught a glimpse of an elongated ear on the side of its head before the night air blurred and the Herald seemed to collapse inward on itself, disintegrating into a fluttering mass of black shapes that exploded in all directions and then faded into the night.

"Lord Isak," Vesna hissed, from the open doorway in the nearby tower housing the steps.

Isak blinked at the night, suddenly aware that he was staring into noth-ingness, exposed in the torchlight. "Give me a hand here," he said, dropping to one knee and fumbling at Siulents' hidden clasps. His armour of flowing silver was remarkable to behold, mesmerising opponents and giving him a presence that no mere king could ever attain, but being unable to see joins and clasps until they were open presented problems sometimes.

"How deep is it? Can we dress it and go on?" Count Vesna sounded calmer, more assured. The distraction of battle had caused years of instinct to kick in. Isak was glad to hear the change in his voice, even though he was certain his most loyal of allies would never fail him.

"Sliced the skin, I think, no more. Just help me get this damn shoulder-plate off and the bloody thing out of me—anything more can wait; I'll not bleed to death from a scratch."

Vesna did so, experienced hands sliding under the plate and bringing it up off Isak's shoulder. The white-eye grimaced as the arrow jagged in the wound again, but Siulents had taken most of the force and the barb had hooked just inside the plate. Vesna quickly snapped the shaft and withdrew the crude iron head.

He checked the wound and, some of his old humour back, announced, "It's bleeding happily enough, but you'll live." Once Isak's armour was restored and the reflective helm was back in place, Vesna pointed towards the doorway. "The others are waiting below there. Are you sure you know where we're going?"

Isak nodded and began walking briskly, calling Eolis to him as he did so. "Purn is in there," he said, pointing to a circular tower that rose from the end of a large hall on the eastern side of the palace. "I can feel the magic."

"Can you be sure it's him? I thought the Circle still had a number of mages left."

"It's him. I can feel powerful wards there, and I think the vampire is the only other person here with the strength for that. He's not tried to be subtle; they're a warning as much as anything."

"But you can break them?"

"One way or another," Isak said firmly, "but it won't be neat, so let's get there quickly and quietly. I'm betting every servant left in the palace is holed up in a wine cellar somewhere, drowning their terror, so we move fast and we kill whoever is in our way, understand?"

There was the slightest of pauses from Vesna, and Isak felt the man's weariness like the glow of a flaring ember before the count agreed.

They walked through darkened corridors with weapons drawn. The palace had the air of the recently abandoned; tasks were left unfinished, storerooms left open. There were no servants anywhere to be seen, no footsteps or voices echoing down the stone passageways, until they reached the inner parts of the palace, where the walls shook off their martial air and the redpainted plaster gave a more elegant look.

The first hall they came to housed a pair of soldiers, and Tiniq and Leshi ghosted forward to kill them both, with nothing more than a cut-off cough of surprise from one. The rangers dragged the bodies out of immediate sight, leaving nothing but a red smear on the flanks of the stag painted on the tiled floor.

Isak looked around to gain his bearings, looking like a hunting dog sniffing the air. "He's that way, still in his tower."

"Surely he can sense you?"

Isak shrugged. "He probably felt something happen on the walls, but I suspect he feels secure behind those wards. No point looking for a fight. He'll be wanting to save his strength."

"So what do you want us to do?"

"A diversion of some sort," Isak said. "Set fire to a flour store or something, I don't really care what. Just draw whatever guards he might have away so I can get a clear run at him."

"You're going alone?"

"Not quite," replied a deep, booming voice behind them. As one the Farlan turned, ready to attack, faltering when they recognised the two figures standing in the shadows of the corridor.

"Ehla?" Isak gasped, "Fernal? When—How did you get here?"

"*With rather more subtlety than you*," the witch of Llehden replied, sounding like an exasperated older sister. At her side, Fernal flexed his massive taloned hands, staring fixedly at the weapons still levelled towards him.

Isak gestured and the blades were put up. Fernal stilled.

"*Calling up an Aspect of Death to help you get over a wall? That smacks of showmanship, if you ask me.*"

"It was hardly intentional," Isak said hotly, not in the mood to be chastised by anyone.

"*You can manage something like that by accident?*" She sounded horrified at the suggestion. "*I don't know which would be worse; that your actions could have such consequences, or that a man with your power would want to show it off so badly.*"

"My Lord?" Vesna interrupted uncertainly, shifting his armoured body from one foot to the other. Isak nodded; they were rather too exposed for his liking as well.

"Go. Lord Fernal, they could use your help."

The Demi-God shook his mane of midnight-blue hair and gave a soft growl, until Ehla laid a thin hand upon his arm. Vesna hesitated, looking from his lord to the newcomers before realising it would be better for them to leave. He strode away, the others close on his heels.

Ehla spoke a few words of her own language, soft and soothing, and Fernal fired a brief volley of thick sounds back. Their voices were so different Isak couldn't even tell if they had spoken the same language, but Fernal gave a curt nod and stepped forward to look Isak directly in the eye.

"We have a form of kinship, you and I," Fernal said hesitantly, taking care over the words that fitted uneasily around his thick fleshy tongue and great incisors. The words were clear and easily recognisable, but Isak could see Fernal was determined to get them absolutely correct. He felt a pang of sympathy for the strange beast-man; Fernal must know better than Isak how appearance could be a hindrance to every other aspect of life. The care he took said very obviously *I am not the beast I appear*, in a way Isak had rarely bothered with. "I ask you to keep her safe, as I promised back in Llehden."

"I will," Isak acknowledged with a respectful nod, ignoring Fernal's unspoken words of warning. *Two large men in a cramped room*, he thought, *neither of us wanting to jostle the elbow of the other.*

Fernal loped off after the soldiers with long strides, his thick mane billowing as he caught them up.

Isak turned back to Ehla and immediately felt uncomfortable as he saw he was being scrutinised. There was something about her poise that set Isak on edge, making him horribly aware of every idle movement and pointless gesture, especially when compared to her disturbingly still presence. She was a handsome woman—he guessed her at close to forty summers—but her aura of utter self-assurance unsettled him. It was a mask even more effective than his own, and it ensured he remained a shade off-balance around her.

"Well, shall we go, or continue to watch each other like the last couple left at the village dance?"

Isak sighed. "For a village crone you sound an awful lot like King Emin," he commented sourly, pointing the way.

Ehla cocked her head at him. *"Even isolated as we are, we're still reminded of the man's greatness from time to time, so I shall take that as a compliment."*

"He has his faults," Isak said darkly, and walked on ahead, hand on the hilt of his sword. Behind him, Ehla breathed a word he couldn't recognise, though it sounded like a curse. Perhaps the crone comment had got past the mask after all; he smiled and filed that thought away for later.

After two corridors and another empty hall they found a small storeroom that had obviously not been used recently. It was only six foot square, with a roughly hewn hexagonal pillar rising from near its centre and piercing the ceiling. It looked like an architectural after-thought, but it was perfect for Isak's needs and he said an awkward prayer in his mind to whichever of the Gods were looking down upon him. They were legendarily fickle creatures, the Gods, and he knew he'd be in greatest need of their help once the deed was done.

They only had to wait five minutes. Whatever Count Vesna had set ablaze, it had gone up like a sacrifice to Tsatach and Isak could smell the bitter scent of smoke faintly even before a unit of soldiers clattered past in the direction of the fire.

"How did you get into the palace?" Isak whispered as they waited to see whether any more men were coming from that direction.

"A witch can always find a way in; few have the strength of mind to deny us."

"And in this case?" he replied testily at her elusive answer.

Ehla shrugged. *"I knocked on one of the doors. It took them a little by surprise because they hadn't seen us reach the door, but I persuaded them to let us in and then used a little spell to send them to sleep."*

"Sleep?" Isak said in surprise. A vision of Fernal's great talons and bough-like arms rose in his mind.

"*Certainly. Death should always be a last resort,*" Ehla chided. "*You would do well to remember that; it might come in useful one of these days.*"

Isak suppressed a shiver; her tone had been just a little too prophetic for his liking. He scowled and turned away. "Come on, I can't hear anyone else nearby—unless you're about to complain about me killing Purn?"

"*Not at all; necromancers harm the balance of the Land, so I have no sympathy for them. Let him explain himself to Lord Death and whatever daemons he's made his bargains with. The Land will be better without him.*"

Isak didn't reply. That the Chief of the Gods would be pleased had little to do with why he was here. The worm of guilt over Lord Bahl's death continued to gnaw at him. He'd tried to shake it off—he knew Bahl had been a driven man, not one to pay heed to incoherent dreams—but when you couldn't persuade yourself, what chance was there? The necromancer Isherin Purn was to blame; that was undeniable, and part of Isak clung to the hope that his own guilt would die with Purn's.

They left the storeroom and followed the corridor to a long hall, which was lined on both sides with large sculptures on plinths, some taller even than Isak. They represented the Gods in various poses: Death sitting in judgment over some prostrate sinner; Nartis hunting, his spear raised high over a lumbering bear. Between the statues were smaller dioramas—stilt houses on a river bank, salmon leaping over rocks—made of stone, inlaid with ivory, silver and jet.

The witch inspected one and made a face of disgust. "*They call this art? Dead things cut to resemble the living, while they sit in their lifeless cities.*"

At the end of the hall they passed two enormous blood-red pillars, with grand wooden staircases leading off in both directions, curling around to meet up on the next floor. Isak eased his way onto the first of the polished mahogany steps, trying to gauge how much they would creak under his weight. When he was satisfied, he glanced at the witch, but she was already past him and heading to another doorway on the right, through which he could see a spiral staircase.

"You might want to let me go first," Isak said softly.

"*Feeling the hero at last?*"

He smiled. "No, but for all your tricks, I don't think you can match a necromancer's power."

With his senses, Isak caressed the Crystal Skull fused to his cuirass. The ready power within sent a warm glow through his body, prickling on his skin under the armour and running around the shape of the scar Xeliath had burned onto his chest. *A different tower*, he thought wryly, *a different age. Would even my father or Carel back then have recognised me like this?*

Ehla's hand closed around his wrist. *"Won't he be expecting that?"*

"What do you mean?"

"His wards are obvious to any mage, almost a challenge to a contest of power for anyone such as you. Would it not be safer to be circumspect, in case this is a trap?"

Isak almost laughed. "Circumspect? I'm a white-eye who knew nothing about magic a year ago. How in the name of the Dark Place do you expect me to out-think a mage of his experience? If you have any suggestions, please don't hold back."

"I do."

Isak froze. That wasn't Ehla's voice; he realised after a moment that it was Aryn Bwr who spoke. Gone was the usual sour note of regret and loss in the dead Elf's voice. There was a sudden clarity, and for once Isak was eager to hear what he had to say.

"The spells are simple and direct," Aryn Bwr continued after a pause, as though having taken a moment to study the problem. *"They are set to detect anyone walking up the staircase; such a thing can be easily circumvented."*

"How?" Isak said hesitantly. He looked within himself to check his hold over Aryn Bwr was absolute, but nothing had changed; his captive appeared honestly willing to help. Could the last king have found a way around his bonds? Isak's mind raced, but he couldn't think of anything Aryn Bwr could do. His hold was too complete, too fundamental to be subverted.

"A spell that will turn them in on each other, allow them to negate each other. My tutor called it the grave-robber's spell. It will take more skill to cast than you have. I will have to do it myself."

Isak didn't answer. The witch just stared at him, her expression indecipherable. He assumed Ehla must have heard Aryn Bwr's words, but she gave no sign of it, nor any further advice. The white-eye checked again his hold over the dead king, mistrust and fear delaying any decision. The spirit sensed his indecision, and the familiar sour taste of contempt appeared at the back of Isak's throat, but Aryn Bwr said nothing, nor did he retract his offer.

Quickly Isak took the Crystal Skulls from their places and slid them onto the shield he carried, the only part of the armour not forged by Aryn Bwr. "Fine, do it."

Without hesitation the dead king drifted forward through Isak's consciousness, overlaying and sliding past his mind like a gliding mist. It was done with great care, gently enough that Isak felt only a disconcerted tremble as his hands and lips began to move without his volition. Isak stood still, ready to fight back at the slightest provocation, but the dead Elf was careful not to do anything to antagonise him as he drew a sliver of magic and began to weave it.

The actions were hesitant at first, like a man playing a long neglected instrument, but they grew in confidence as past skills returned. Isak watched in fascination as he felt the syllables of the spell slither over his mind. He couldn't work out the literal meanings, but he was able to discern the shape of the spell. The scar on his chest glowed hot and sharp, as though the part of Xeliath imprinted into his skin railed against Elven touch, but Isak ignored the pain and continued to watch, drinking it all in.

With increasing assurance, Aryn Bwr drew strands of energy, weaving the words of the spell so they shaped the energy and bent it to the task at hand. It required a deftness of touch and instinct beyond anything Isak had seen before; he recognised a true mastery, beyond anything he'd witnessed before.

As soon as it was completed, Aryn Bwr sent the spell forward into the stones of the walls that lined the tight spiral stair.

Isak felt the words lodge and bite like a crowbar, testing and probing at the cracks between stones as more power was fed to them. Within moments, the wall began to groan and a shudder ran through the flagstones underfoot. His eyes widened as the foot-thick stones juddered and shook in the surge of magic like sheets of paper hung up in the breeze.

Thin trails of dust fell from between the stones as first one and then another began to twist within the wall. Isak's gasp of astonishment was drowned out by the grind of others following suit as the walls on each side of the spiral stair suddenly came alive with movement. The great blocks squirmed and fought to escape as Aryn Bwr's incantation droned on, growing in intensity as the stones shook in rhythm with each syllable, the grating sound getting more insidious—

Until, suddenly, it was finished.

The last word hung tantalisingly in the air as each stone in the stairwell hesitated, teetering on the brink for an instant . . . until a soft, unbidden breath escaped Isak's pursed lips. He felt it drift forward, but instead of dissipating, it continued on to the stairway and as it reached the stones, it gave one final spasm before spinning neatly around, that movement rippling away to the next and the next, leading away up the staircase. Wherever a spell had been left in wait for anyone ascending, a bright flash of white or green burst from nothing as the magic was torn apart, leaving angry sparks crackling in the air. The sounds continued up the stairs, out of sight, then there was a great yawning of timber, the scrape of dagger-points on stone, one final snap and a flash of light . . .

The echo of the spell raced away behind them to other parts of the palace as a stunned silence fell over Isak and Ehla.

"*Now it is safe for you to walk,*" said the last king in Isak's head, leaving a sense of satisfaction lingering as he receded unbidden back into the depths of Isak's soul. The white-eye cast a sideways look at Ehla; her face remained inscrutable and she paid him no attention as she stared ahead.

As though in response to that final crash echoing away, a gust of wind came up from behind him, bringing another taste of smoke on the air. That stirred Isak into action and he replaced the Skulls before advancing to the foot of the spiral staircase.

After a slight hesitation he began to walk up the stairs cautiously, his shield raised above him. The warm glow of raw energy enveloped his body. Ehla followed him, two paces behind. After half a dozen steps, the stairs remained still and quiet, the stones of the wall sat neatly in line. The only trace of magic was a dwindling metallic scent and a sooty scorch-mark near the top.

Isak moved softly when he reached the scorched bit, but nothing happened and before he was really prepared he found himself before a narrow iron-studded door. He was inspecting it as Ehla caught him up, but he could detect no magic bound into it, and Aryn Bwr kept silent in his mind. With a shrug, Isak lowered his shoulder, ready to smash the door down, when the gnarled head of the witch's staff appeared in front of him.

She slid into his field of vision, careful to keep from touching the wall. "*That door is reinforced,*" she said into his thoughts.

"*You don't think I can break it down?*" Isak replied. The energy shuddering through his limbs was crying out to be used.

"*I'm quite sure you can, but using power for power's sake? Don't kill when it is not necessary; don't destroy when a little elegance will suffice.*" She pressed a pale hand against the iron lock and closed her eyes.

Abashed, Isak released his grip on the magic raging over his armour and pushed it back into the Skull. He eased himself back to allow Ehla a little more room, but she didn't seem to notice as she concentrated. A click came from inside the door, then the grind and clunk of bolts sliding back. A slight tremble ran through her body as each one shot open, but her voice rang strong in his head as she opened her eyes and smiled at him. *"There, now all it needs is a little push."*

Isak reached out the emerald pommel of Eolis and nudged the door with it, but instead of just swinging open, as he'd expected, the scrape of metal heralded the entire door crashing down onto the floor of the room beyond it. Under his helm, Isak raised his eyebrows in surprise, and a pleased sound came from Ehla's direction, almost as if she could see his face.

"I certainly didn't expect you." The voice was unexpected.

Isak peered inside; the room was dimly lit by a single large candle on a bracket to the right of the doorway. The objects at the far end were nothing more than shadows. Ahead of him, still seated at a long desk supported by four thin legs, was the Menin necromancer, Isherin Purn.

Isak ducked through the doorway, his sword and shield ready. "Who did you expect?" he asked cautiously.

"Someone else." Purn's command of the Farlan dialect was flawless, better than Isak's, despite the fact that he was Menin by birth. "Aracnan, to be precise."

"Aracnan? Is he in the city?" Isak was getting a little confused.

Purn shrugged. "Not that I've seen, but I asked myself who would not mind the mobs roaming the city, *and* be able to break through my defences so adeptly. I once—*ahem*—borrowed something that belonged to Aracnan. He claimed it back without resorting to unpleasantness, but I've always suspected he was just biding his time." The necromancer tilted his head a little to the side. "Perhaps he wouldn't have made quite so much noise getting in here, but the question remains why you've bothered to make the journey when we've never even met."

"Can't you guess?"

Purn thought for a moment. "That damned vampire gave you my servant? The wretch; Nai never could stop his chattering. I doubt you even had to torture him."

Isak said nothing. If the necromancer was in the mood to talk, perhaps just to prolong his life another few minutes, there was always the chance he would say something of interest.

"So you're aware of my orders," Purn continued, his hands starting to slowly move.

Isak reached out an armoured hand and the necromancer's arms were stretched out and held fast, bonds of magic looped around them. Isak narrowed his eyes. An object hung from Purn's belt, a slim shard of glass encasing a raven's feather, or something similar, and glinting in the weak light. With a thought, Isak tore it away from the mage and across the room for Ehla to snatch out of the air.

"An escape plan?" Isak asked. The witch nodded, cradling the object in both hands as she inspected it.

"A useful little toy, I think I'll keep this for myself."

"Try anything else like that and I'll pull your arms off," he said conversationally.

"You're going to kill me anyway," Purn pointed out. There was no panic in the Menin mage's voice; he sounded as calm as a monk after prayers.

"But I had intended to do it cleanly," Isak said. "I promise you, it can hurt a lot more if you annoy me, whether I should be leaving as quickly as possible or not."

"A fair observation," Purn said with infuriating acceptance. "I've recently learned not to underestimate a white-eye's determination."

"Explain," Isak commanded, causing the strands of magic to tighten by way of encouragement.

"You're here to kill me; at any other time I'd be fighting tooth and nail to stay alive. Today, however, the sun dawned with a blessing for me."

"I asked you to explain," Isak warned.

Purn gave a thin smile that grew wider as he spoke. "Men of my profession often find themselves party to bargains with the creatures of the dark. Upon my death a number of debts were set to be collected, but the Lord of the Menin has done me a great service. My slate is wiped clean."

"You still have Death to answer to," Isak said.

The necromancer dismissed the comment with a wave of the hand. "Every man must answer to Death; that I am in a position to worry about it is more than satisfactory, a boon I could not have hoped for." Since his hands were restrained, he dipped his head towards Isak. "Lord Styrax faced down one of the greatest of daemons this day—I advise you to remember that when he reaches your lands."

"Is he all they say?" Isak asked, trying to control the trepidation in his voice. Kastan Styrax had defeated a daemon? First Lord Bahl, then a creature of the Dark Place; was there anything that could stop the man? Images from his dreams filled Isak's mind: a fanged blade driving into his gut, a black-armoured knight who would mean his death. *I know I can't stop him, I've always known that.*

Purn laughed. "All they say? I have heard soldiers and courtiers sing his praises, but how could they really understand? There is a prophecy that says his standard will fly above every city in the Land, but that does not interest me, and I suspect neither does it interest Lord Styrax. Empty men strive for glory or power, for flags and gold and nations on bended knee. The great care only for the stars and the heavens above."

Isak glanced at his left hand. Encased in silver, the skin underneath remained a perfect snow-white, unchanged since he'd called the storm down onto him on the palace walls in Narkang. The memory of soldiers fighting on the wall reminded him that time was not on his side.

He stepped forward with grim resolve, Eolis raised. "Then when I see your lord, I'll warn him that those who reach too high end up burned. Give my compliments to Lord Death."

CHAPTER 28

A T GENERAL GORT'S SIGNAL, the columns of light infantry advanced with flaming torches held high against the darkness, marching down the Bearwalk, the wide avenue that ran almost directly south from the New Barbican. It would take them most of the way to Six Temples. They were exposed and vulnerable on that wide avenue, but Gort was determined to keep a tight grip on his growing fears. That he wasn't exactly sure what was frightening him was making his imagination run riot.

The Knights of the Temples had taken the New Barbican with a minimum of fuss, and since then they had seen none of the mobs the New Barbican's defenders had spoken of with such terror—in fact, they hadn't seen *anyone* at all. They marched through abandoned streets, watching the shadows nervously and feeling increasingly disconcerted.

General Gort felt horribly alone, the only man on horseback at the head of the column and a prime target for even a mediocre archer. Behind him rumbled a dozen carts, guarded by sappers, then General Chotech, his long, curved axe resting on his shoulder, led his ranks of heavy infantry. His men were armed with heavy shields and thrusting spears: at the first sign of the mobs roving the city, they would lock shields and present a spiked wall that even disciplined troops found hard to break through.

The general turned and inspected the troops with him. A legion of infantry and two hundred lancers stretched out along the Bearwalk. The major of the lancers saw him and gave a theatrical salute, prompting a smile. Major Derl was an excellent officer, from Canar Thrit, a city well known for producing fine soldiers. He was experienced enough to know any idle gesture would be noticed by the nervous troops, so Gort suppressed his own fears and gave a cheery wave in return, noting a few smiles before he turned his attention back to the road ahead.

"What have I got us into?" he muttered to himself. "Will a legion be enough?"

His horse twitched its ears at the sound of his voice and he tightened his grip on the reins. The horses were as skittish as the men. Perhaps they too sensed that this was not a place for the living. It was obvious, and not just in the smashed windows of abandoned buildings, or the shadows lurking at the base of every shattered wall, or even the brutalised corpses strewn across the city. He couldn't decide which was worse, the hellish sight of fire raging unchecked through entire streets and consuming everything in its path, or the broken ruins wrapped in unnatural dark. He felt the sweat trickle freely down his spine. The heat was still a palpable weight on his shoulders, despite the stiff wind that had recently picked up.

General Gort caught Lieutenant Mehar's eye and the aide obediently stepped closer.

"What do you make of this place, Mehar?" he asked. "It's so hot at night you can hardly bear to wear a shirt, let alone armour. You're a scholar, what are your thoughts?"

Relief flushed Mehar's face for a moment. Gort suppressed a smile; the young man had been worrying that he was being punished for some failure; unusually, he'd been excluded from most of the general's meetings over the last few weeks. Mehar was a good aide, and he had a fine intellect, but his devotion to the order made it hard to tell what he would make of discussions about a deal with the Farlan, or the developing quarrel with the Knight-Cardinal. Right now they couldn't risk finding out.

"It feels like the Land has been turned on its head," Mehar said hesitantly. He was a shy young man of twenty-five winters whose temperament didn't fit with his large, athletic frame. His father had been barely bright enough to swing an axe, but he had been keen to ensure his eldest son spent as much time studying as trying to fill his father's over-sized shoes. It had paid off: Mehar loved his books.

"A natural order has been upset here, sir. I think that's why the horses were reluctant to pass through the New Barbican gates. What we need to know is whether this discord is the result, or the purpose."

"And we'd need a mage to work that one out?"

Mehar nodded unhappily. Their order vehemently disapproved of magic, of any description. It was their greatest weakness in battle, but it was a belief they all held to: magic was an unnatural art, and the province of Gods, not men. Individuals who had the talent were not blamed for it, but they were encouraged to forsake the magic inside them. The order considered magic to be an addiction, one that could be controlled through faith.

"I just hope we don't find it out the hard way, sir." He took a breath and looked around at the gutted shells of building that lined the avenue. "The natural order of things is that of the Gods on high and mankind, their servants. If that has been reversed, what are we going to find at Six Temples?"

Gort paused. "Not a comforting thought, Mehar. Not comforting at all."

Neither man spoke again until they reached the far end of the Bearwalk.

Parties of light infantrymen flanked the main column, half carrying torches, the other half with weapons at the ready. The wavering light illuminated the rubble of an old marketplace, the remnants of broken stalls and shattered awnings.

Gort started at a dark shape that flitted behind the furthest stalls, tall and flowing, with a bone-white face—but in a blink it was gone, and the soldiers marched on unhindered. *The light from the torches*, the general assured himself, *the moon catching a pane of glass*. To the flicker of doubt in his heart he said nothing.

At the end of the Bearwalk stood a large, ornate fountain, and beyond that six smaller streets fanned out, leading to different parts of the city. The fountain itself was old, though its stone looked scrubbed clean; those statues that remained whole—a scattering of cherubic bodies reaching up from the lower bowl, three pike rising out from corners of a central plinth, and a pair of legs that were all that remained of whatever Aspect had fed the fountain—had been scoured by centuries of wind and rain. The broken fragments in the now-dry bottom of the lower bowl made it clear that someone had vented their rage upon the fountain, stopping when the Aspect's statue had been destroyed.

Gort rode closer to the fountain as his troops spread around it and locked shields, waiting for the light infantry to regroup. His height afforded him a good view: there were not only smashed limbs of stone, but human remains too. The people of this thirsty city had refused whatever succour this Aspect of Vasle might have offered, fouling both fountain and water so no one could drink from it.

Gort lowered his eyes and whispered a short prayer, a lament for the passing. Aspects might be nothing more than local spirits subsumed by a God of the Pantheon, but they remained part of the divine. The waters no longer ran here, so this part of the divine had died.

Mehar appeared at his side, looked inside the fountain then carefully stepped away. He swallowed, and said, "Your fears were justified then, sir."

"Thank you for your approval," Gort snapped, irritated by the young man's tone. "I will be sure to check every other decision I make with you."

Mehar's mouth dropped open. For a moment Gort thought he was going to retort, then he shut it again with a snap of teeth.

The general looked away; he didn't have to explain himself to his aide, and certainly not when they were in the field, surrounded by enlisted men. He waited in brooding silence for the ranks to form up into companies, tight blocks of fifty soldiers ringed by smaller knots of flickering torches held high in the gloom. He shifted in his saddle. The hot night air was responsible for an infuriating itch that had worked its way under his skin, even to the back of his throat, while the stink of rot from the fountain grew heavier.

The clatter of hooves preceded Major Derl as he led his lancers into the plaza and joined General Gort at the fountain.

"Blood and piss," the major growled as he looked over the lip, "let's hope they've treated the temples with more reverence."

"There's no reason to suppose they have," Gort said. He gestured at the roads leading off the plaza, all dark bar one, where a burning building had collapsed halfway down the street. "Which of these takes us to Six Temples?"

Derl looked up at the pedestal where the statue of the Aspect had been. "We were told the fountain pointed directly towards Six Temples. Could they have torn it down intentionally?"

"They tore it down because they're godless wretches who have forsaken their sanity," Gort growled. "They are animals, not men. They act as their instincts tell them—they do not have the forethought to lead us into a trap."

"Animals can still possess cunning, sir," Derl said, before he caught sight of Gort's furious expression and added quickly, "but only the insane desecrate a shrine, of course. Mehar, why have those damned skirmishers not come to report to the general yet?"

Mehar jumped. "I will summon them at once, sir."

"Don't bother," Major Derl said dismissively. "I wouldn't trust them anyway." He stood up in his stirrups and turned to look back up the Bear-walk. Gort did likewise. Halfway up they could see the torches of the cavalry company he'd ordered to follow behind, to protect their line of retreat. They would hold there, with another positioned here, within eyeshot: no great defence, but enough to summon help if required.

One lancer broke off and made his way over, offering a sloppy salute to the general. Gort glared at the insolent cavalryman, but said nothing. The man was so pale, his face drained of energy and slack with fatigue that he looked about ready to fall from his saddle. The dark rings around his eyes were a strange contrast to the feverish glow within.

"Woren, which road takes us to Six Temples?" Derl asked.

The lancer looked around at his surroundings as though astonished at being there. Slowly, he raised a finger and indicated two of the streets, wavering between the two. He opened his mouth to speak, but managed nothing more than an exhausted sigh.

Strange, thought Gort, *the man must be a native of Scree, but is he the only one we could find? He looks touched by fever, or madness, maybe—is this what has happened to the rest of the city?*

"Well?" Derl demanded.

"That way curves round to the east," Woren said dully, indicating the left-hand road. "The other goes straight, leave it at the Corn House and past that to the north edge."

"Right." Derl turned to his commander. "Sir, I suggest we head for the east, since the road is better; we don't want to be confined if we are attacked."

Gort nodded. "Send the skirmishers off, lancers behind." He leaned forward in his saddle, staring intently at the street they were about to take. Did he see a movement in the darkness there, a flash of skin even whiter than Woren's? Or was that just his own fear?

"Mehar, as soon as we're within the outer ring of Six Temples, block as much of the south and west as you can so our backs aren't exposed; use everything you can find, unless it's been blessed, and everything we've brought in the carts." He didn't notice his left hand going to the hilt of his sword and tightening around the grip.

He spoke up so all the men nearby could hear, hoping conviction would swell into courage. "This whole city may have turned against the Gods, but while there are still temples here, our oath to defend them binds us."

Isak took the lead as they ran back through the corridors of the palace. The handful of soldiers they met were dispatched without breaking stride. The sounds of destruction echoed in their wake: men dying, the distant crashes of the fire Vesna had set raging out of control. Isak didn't care how much noise they made now.

When they reached the postern gate there were no guards waiting, and when they checked, they could see the remaining guards on the wall were leaving their posts and fleeing for the far side of the palace. They could hear the roar of flames echoing through the passageways they had run through. Outside, orange shards were leaping higher and higher into the night sky.

Without further delay, Isak charged through the open gate and down the stepped gardens until he was once again in the lee of the building where he'd left Major Jachen and the ranger, Jeil.

The troops he'd left behind were already mounted and formed up, ready to leave at a moment's notice. Only Jachen, Jeil and Suzerain Saroc were on foot, and as soon as Isak rounded the corner they ran forward, leading their horses.

"My Lord, we have to hurry," Saroc said, his voice muffled by a black-iron helm with a red chalice painted on the left cheek. The plate armour accentuated his short stature; he would have appeared comical had it not been for the massive axe resting easily in the crook of his arm.

"What's happened?" Isak asked, sheathing his sword and swinging up into Toramin's saddle. His huge charger danced on the spot, the emerald dragons on its flanks rippling as he did so.

"Jeil went to check on the decoy troops. The mobs have found them. We need to get you away to safety before they move further this way."

Isak didn't move. "And what about the decoy troops?"

Jachen stepped forward. "They're surrounded, my Lord. There's nothing we can do for them."

"And that's it?" Isak asked in astonishment. "You're happy to leave them to it?"

"There is nothing we can do, my Lord," Jachen repeated. "There are thousands attacking them. We're not enough to help—and the sight of you will drive them into a greater frenzy."

"So you suggest we abandon them? Leave men you've fought alongside to be torn apart by a mob?" Isak roared. "Or is it simply that you're as much a coward as I've been told?"

"My Lord," exclaimed Suzerain Saroc, "it is not a question of cowardice; Major Jachen has a duty to the tribe, and that must come first."

"Come before the lives of five hundred men and the most loyal suzerain in the tribe?" Isak turned to Count Vesna, but he remained silent. "Vesna, have you got nothing to say about this?"

"My Lord . . ." His voice tailed off.

His face-plate was up, and Isak could see the helplessness on his face. At last he realised what the count had been talking about in Tor Milist: good men were dying when they shouldn't have had to. To Isak's surprise, Count Vesna said nothing more. "You can't agree with them," Isak gasped, almost pleading. He felt a clammy horror sweeping over him. He'd had a change of heart in Tor Milist; was he now going to leave these men to die, without even a word?

"I—Lord Isak, duty must come first," Vesna said eventually.

"Duty? Will even you not follow my orders?" Isak growled, his shock turning now to anger.

The other suzerains, Nelbove and Fordan, had dismounted and come to add their voices to the argument, but Isak's obvious fury kept them silent.

"Well? What about it, my loyal subjects? Are you going to follow me, or does one of you want to be the first to try to force me to run?" Isak's voice was tight with fury. Eolis remained in its scabbard, but that meant little; they all knew he could draw it in the blink of an eye.

"My Lord," said Major Jachen, moving a half-step forward.

Isak whirled to meet the man and saw naked fear in Jachen's eyes, yet the former mercenary refused to buckle. A spark of defiance remained and he forced himself to stand tall and match Isak's relentless gaze. "My Lord, they are loyal to death. They will follow you."

"Well, what are we waiting for then?" Isak snapped.

"You'll have to cut me down first, my Lord."

Isak faltered, surprise overriding anger momentarily. "What?"

"They'll follow you to death if you ask them to—"

"And you won't?" Isak cut in angrily. "Last time I looked, you were also under my command."

"Do you remember the first time we met?" Jachen said with fatalistic calm. "You asked me if I'd have the guts to face you down if I thought you were wrong."

Isak thought for a moment. "So this is you clouting me round the head, is it? You've picked a bloody stupid time to grow a spine, Major Ansayl."

Jachen ignored the jibe. "I am in command of your personal guard. My first duty is to the tribe—and that is to keep you safe. You said it yourself: you're a white-eye, and you don't always make the best decisions, and you need a commander who'll tell you when you're plain wrong."

Jachen could see the men behind Isak standing open-mouthed, but he didn't dare change tack now. The massive white-eye was as surprised as any of them, but at least it had deflected Lord Isak's anger for a moment, and made him think. *Oh Gods, am I putting my life on a white-eye thinking rationally?* he thought, surprised at how calm he felt.

"You think it's wrong to think our comrades worth saving?"

"Right now, yes," Jachen said firmly, sensing his lord was wavering. "The mobs number in their thousands, many thousands. Whether those men are torn apart or not, my duty is to keep you safe. Their loss would be a tragedy, something to pray over when the time is appropriate. Your loss would be a catastrophe, for the entire Farlan nation, maybe even the entire Land. The loss of five hundred soldiers means almost nothing to the future of the tribe, while the loss of the Lord of the Farlan is a disaster that puts us all in danger. There is no Krann to replace you. We would be adrift and at each other's throats before winter."

"Do you think I don't know that?" Isak said, more reasonable now. "But what use is a lord who runs from danger and leaves his men to die?"

"One that knows his own value to the tribe," Jachen said softly. "Most of those men are going to die, and only the Gods could change that, but as soon as the rabid folk of Scree see you, they'll want your blood first. You're a white-eye lord, and Chosen of Gods they have come suddenly to hate. For all your strength, my Lord, you cannot kill them all."

Isak stared at the major, mouth half-open to retort, but unable to find anything to say. He couldn't fault anything Jachen had said . . . but to so lightly condemn a division of men to death? What did that make him?

Is this what it is to be lord? To carelessly choose who lives and who dies? He felt sick at the thought.

"*It is,*" rang out a powerful voice in his head. Isak jumped at the unexpected contribution from Aryn Bwr. "*To be mortal is to be afraid of what comes after; to be afraid of consequences. They make kings as they worship Gods, because they are too weak to make choices themselves. Offer them a shining figure they can pretend is better than they are and they will embrace you as their saviour.*"

Isak kept silent, trying to come to terms with what he had to do. An image of Lord Bahl appeared in his mind, the blunt lines of his face and his usual grim, inscrutable expression: a face to trust, a man to rely upon, no matter what. *And inside he was wracked with loss and guilt, but as long as his people didn't know that, they would have stormed the gates of the Dark Place at his side.*

Slowly, Isak nodded; Lord Bahl would have made this decision. It would have pained him, and their deaths would have weighed on his soul, but only his closest friends would have ever seen that pain. The needs of the tribe would always come first. Isak hated himself for it, but he had to do the right thing.

"Fine," he said in a muted voice. "We make for the rest of the army." He didn't look at anyone.

From the streets south of the Red Palace came the clamour of voices, and the sound of hundreds of feet thumping on the cobbled ground. Without delay Isak remounted, gesturing to everyone to do likewise.

"And we go quickly," he said in a louder voice as he drew his sword.

"Is there anything else I can get for you, my Lady?" the soldier asked, hovering in the guardroom doorway.

Tila looked up, her face blank for a moment until she returned to the present. "No, thank you," she said eventually.

"Are you sure?" The guard's face was half concealed by shadow, but he looked concerned. "Lady Tila, when did you last eat?"

"A while ago," she said, not really sure when that had been.

"Shall I fetch you something? You're not looking your best."

Tila sighed, her fingers twisting the citrine ring on her left hand. "I'm not hungry, and I'm not ill, I'm just worried."

He tried to look relieved, but Tila couldn't tell if it was genuine. "Lady Tila, I don't care how mad the people of Scree are, they couldn't hurt Lord Isak. All he needs to fear are the Gods themselves!"

"I'm afraid you are wrong, Cavalryman," Tila said wearily. "Lord Isak is stronger and faster than any man, but he is flesh and blood. After the battle in Narkang I bound his wounds. He has as much to fear from battle as you or I. Is there any news from the city at all? Do we not have scouts or mages reporting back?"

"Of course," he said, wondering how much he should say. "There's no word of Lord Isak. I heard one of the mages tell General Lahk that some of the Knights of the Temples were on the move. There's talk they're going to ambush Lord Isak, but the general says he was expecting them to move."

"General Lahk is correct," Tila said firmly. "The Devoted will not harm Lord Isak—they will head straight for Six Temples and protect it against the mobs, nothing more."

The soldier nodded and Tila thought she saw a fleeting glimpse of surprise on his face, though it was obvious enough to anyone who knew anything of the Devoted.

Behind her the narrow guardroom window was open to the city. Bars made it secure against intruders but they did nothing against the ebb and flow of sounds from outside, voices, the clatter of hooves, and behind them, further away, noises she couldn't identify. The newly returned wind rustled through, bringing no relief from the sticky heat within.

The soldier bobbed his head, trying to catch Tila's attention as she stared pensively at nothing. "Are you sure there's nothing I can get you?" he repeated doggedly.

Tila nodded. "I'm sure. I left my books in Tirah and that's all I want right now."

"Your books?"

"Oh, everything: history and diplomacy, journals, treatises on prophecy —in times such as these, who knows what scrap of information—a past allegiance, a war long-past—might prove crucial to us now. I feel so useless sitting here; surrounded by people moving with a purpose, while I have none. If I had my books, I could at least pretend to be something more than a liability." She sighed again.

The soldier shifted his weight, deeply uncomfortable. He was there to bring the lady a pot of tea, not to tell a noblewoman how to make herself useful. He knew men who'd been flogged for expressing opinions on the subject, so he kept his mouth firmly shut. As expected, she didn't seem to be looking for a contribution from his corner anyway.

"If you change your mind," he ventured after what he thought was an appropriate pause, "if you do need anything, just call. I'll be down the corridor."

Tila looked up, bleary-eyed. "I'm sorry; I didn't mean to keep you. Thank you for the tea; please tell me when Lord Isak returns."

The soldier bobbed his head and ducked out of the room, leaving the door ajar.

Tila listened to the half-dozen heavy footsteps that took him to his station at the entrance to the guard tower, then returned to her thoughts, and a creeping fatigue. She tried to count the hours since she'd slept properly and gave up. The heat had reduced a full night's sleep to restless hours punctuated by snatched moments of rest.

She looked around the guardroom. She'd come in here because there was a pair of massive armchairs in the centre of the room, presumably liberated from some officers' mess, and each one was easily large enough to contain her small, exhausted frame. Between them was a battered leather-bound chest held shut by mouldering buckles that she was using as a footstool. She curled up again and let her thoughts blur and drift. The clatter outside began to slowly recede into the background.

Tila's eyelids sank inexorably down as her head filled with the stuffy air of the guardroom that smelled of dust, dried mud and old wood shavings. There was an empty grate beside her, where shadows danced over the cold ashes. She tried to focus on the blackened hearthstone, attempting to pick out the worn, sooty lines of the image cut into it. She expected to see Grepel of the Hearths, Tsatach's most domesticated Aspect, with her burning tongue hanging out like a dog's, but Tila's brow contracted into a frown as she realised the undulating lines bore no relation to Grepel. Her mind tried to frame the shapes around other Aspects of Tsatach, but the effort proved too much as her thoughts floundered like a deer in a tar-pit. A sense of weight built relentlessly, dragging on limbs already weakened by fatigue. Her breath grew shallower. All the while the flame of the oil lamp guttered, flickered and grew ever dimmer.

Unable to resist, Tila submitted and felt herself drift down into the shadowy embrace of sleep. Sliding up the walls of the guardroom, the darkness rose until the feeble light from the oil lamp was nothing more than a distant glimmer, subsumed by creeping fingers of darkness that flowed over her skin, soothing and lulling away the weariness. Enveloped in that comforting touch, Tila skirted the boundaries of sleep for a time, her awareness dulled as she listened only to the sound of her own breath, in and out, in and out . . . until that too was lost to the quiet of the night.

Then there was only the darkness.

A sudden breath surged through her body, forcing her eyelids open a crack and rushing with a tingle from her lungs out to her fingers and toes. Tila stared ahead in surprise at the unfamiliar room smelling of dust and mould, and the oil lamp in front of her faded almost to nothing, down to vapours. The guardroom, the Autumn's Arch gate. Images and faces returned: the door left ajar, the small cylindrical cup in her hands coming back into focus.

A chair where she sat so snug and warm, another opposite her, facing away from the lamp. The shadows looked longer now, lying thick within the other chair, so it looked almost like a man sat there, the worn, scratched leather supporting a shoulder there, and an arm . . .

What am I doing here? she thought bitterly. *Why did I make sure they brought me, when all I could do was to slow them down?*

"Because they are men without families," the shadow answered her. *"You bring order to their lives, and a balance, that reminds them of who they are."*

Is balance what they really need? she found herself thinking, as if the shadow had actually spoken to her. *A good soldier is one who can cast off who he is, put aside everything of him except instinct and training.*

"*And you remind them of their fears,*" the darkness in the empty chair continued. "*By your vulnerability you demonstrate what price they might have to pay, you wear the faces of those they might lose. What use are you now to your lord?*"

I am his advisor, she told herself. *I have taught him about history and prophecy—*

The shadowy figure laughed. "*And yet you cannot even see when it is on the cusp of being fulfilled. You failed to recognise the danger of the last king on Silvernight, you ignored all the signs while you pursued your own desires.*"

How was I to know? I couldn't have known—

"*You failed him when his life was in the greatest of dangers and now once more your inadequacies prove a burden.*"

A burden? Tila asked herself. *What now? What have I done so wrong?* She felt tears welling in her eyes as dread stole over her.

"*This task you appointed to yourself, yet cannot fulfil. The role so crucial to the fortunes of your lord given to a foolish slip of a girl with a head full of gossip and some childish notions of scholarly work, playing the minister and guardian of her lord's person.*"

She could not control her deep, juddering sobs now. *What have I missed?*

"'*Twilight heralded by theatre and flame, the scion and sire kill in the place of death—*'"

"'*Treasure and loss from the darkness, from holy hands to a lady of ashes. A shadow rising from the faithful,*'" she continued with mounting horror, "'*his twilight reign to begin amid the slain.*'" *Oh merciful Nartis—his father!* His father is missing!

"*And he meets his allies at the Temple of Death,*" the voice in her head finished triumphantly. "*And thus once more you fail him.*"

Swathed in a cloak of night, Aracnan watched the Farlan soldiers below, raising their barricades ever higher as they prepared for assault. Three legions were camped outside the city gate, lines of tents and cooking fires huddled close to the wall. A rampart of earth studded with sharpened stakes had been thrown up in a crescent around them. Pickets lined the rampart and most of the soldiers had been formed into regiments, ready for the general's command—but still dozens of men were preparing food, irrespective of what violence might be occurring soon.

"*A statement to those of us watching*," said a voice beside him. He knew better than to turn. Shadows were best seen out of the corner of an eye.

"I don't think we need take note of any such statement. Leave that to the cattle out there."

Their voices were strangely similar; more than once Aracnan had wondered whether there was anything to read into that.

"*I prefer to observe it all nonetheless*," the shadow said with the breath of a chuckle.

Despite himself, Aracnan felt a chill run down his spine. Laden with malevolence, the shadow's laughter cut to the bone in a way Aracnan had never experienced before. Having trembled at the rage of Gods and lived more years than he cared to count, he had never been so unsettled by so simple a noise. *And that is why I've joined him*, Aracnan thought. *All my life I've been forced to adapt and survive. I recognise my better here, and in turn he knows I'm no mere mortal plaything.*

He shifted the bow and quiver over his shoulder to a more comfortable position as he looked out into the dark streets of the city. In the south an awful orange glow consumed the air. The bow was one he'd taken from Koezh Vukotic's armoury. It epitomised the quality of the methodical Vukotic craftsmen. It wasn't yet time for him to take a hand in events—he wasn't yet past the point of no return, however much he could taste it on the coming wind—but there was something refreshingly direct about a well-placed arrow, and events might yet need a helping hand. Magic would leave no trace, while craftsmanship could be identified and hasty conclusions drawn. Aracnan had learned over the centuries that a little misdirection was often worth the effort.

Aracnan saw the vast destruction already inflicted on the southern districts, filtered through swirling sooty clouds. The slum districts were the worst affected; some were already obliterated because of the close wooden houses—and the inferno was growing. It had driven the maddened, mindless people further north, and they lingered on the fringes of the light from the Farlan lines inside the city. Had they noticed the soldiers there, they would have attacked without a moment's thought, blind to their own lack of weapons and driven by a compulsion that was all-consuming.

He felt little towards them; certainly he took no pleasure in the senselessness forced on them by Rojak, but they were not his kind and the life of an immortal was ruled by pragmatism. If Azaer could give him what he wanted, then he would follow the shadow's orders. Neither of them was so foolish as to ask for trust. He was not even worried by the thought that Azaer might use him to lure Isak to the right place—such was life. As it was, Aracnan had only to guide the wandering mobs to where they were required, currently held back from the Farlan lines by a simple enchantment of his.

Aracnan had found himself impressed at the magic wrought by Rojak. Rarely had he seen such accomplished magic worked by a mortal, let alone such devotion. Few believed so fervently as to bind their own soul to a spell, but Rojak had done that at his master's bidding. While the minstrel was failing fast, Aracnan had a suspicion tonight wouldn't be the last time he suddenly smelled peach-blossom on the breeze and turned to see that mocking smile. Death might only be the beginning for Azaer's greatest servant.

"Have you delivered your message?" he asked, letting his gaze wander slowly from the wavering figures hiding in dark corners to the barred guard-room window where the girl dozed.

"It is done."

"Will you now explain it? I assume declaring your intention through prophecy is not merely conceit."

"Forewarned is forearmed."

Aracnan thought for a moment, the skin of his gaunt, hairless head contorting strangely until realisation dawned. "Ah, I understand; the hidden face of covenant theory, the perversity of magic. To achieve grand deeds you must first sow the seeds of your own destruction."

"Now that would be a little foolish," said the shadow, *"but it is nonetheless necessary to allow for the possibility of those seeds to exist. No magic is unstoppable, no spell irreversible. Without that element of the unknown, nothing could be achieved, but perhaps it is possible to guide the unknown in a certain direction."*

"The girl has been warned that her lord is just a player in your game so you can predict their reaction?"

"Exactly so. Even now she is trying to find General Lahk to explain the danger. Better that than to gamble on what someone is thinking and leave it to chance."

Aracnan made a sweeping gesture, as though gathering up the threads of a fishing net and drawing them towards him. "Well then, let us make sure we know what General Lahk will be thinking about."

The movement ended as his hand reached a pouch sewn onto his black stiffened-leather armour. He pushed one bony finger inside and smiled as the energies comprising his spell danced up his arm, prickling the skin as they dissipated into the black clouds above him and vanished.

Almost immediately the first howls of animal rage rang out from the streets below. They were joined by hundreds more, merging into a great roar of wordless voices and running feet that drowned out the warning shouts from the Farlan pickets.

CHAPTER 29

ojak watched the scene playing out before him and felt a flicker of satisfaction break through the pain wracking his body. The dead were scattered all around. Men, women and children lay curled up in tidy bundles, or sprawled in almost comic poses. Others were little more than lumps of flesh rendered unrecognisable by the brutality done them. He sat in a broken chair scavenged from somewhere by one of the Hounds. It was far from comfortable, but he was in no position to complain—he was in no position to do anything but sit and watch the final death-throes of Scree.

"It is done," he whispered, to himself or his master, Rojak was not sure now. *I am done*, he added to himself. Azaer's shadows, so close for all these years, felt like they had penetrated him, flesh and bone. As the corruption inside him raged unchecked, his soul faded faster, merging with the intangible essence of his master.

"*Not done, not quite.*" The susurrus reply echoed in ghostly fashion all around the broken building. Rojak couldn't move, his strength having failed on the steps below. When they had arrived at this place, it had been a scene of fresh devastation, the air tasting abused, and scorched by the rampant energies unleashed by the abbot. The buildings were aflame, or smashed and scattered over the packed-dirt streets.

"It cannot be stopped now, it is too far gone," Rojak said, compelling his thoughts to order. His master, whispering in his ear, had told him some of what was going on in the rest of the city, and Rojak could feel a prickling map of hurt on his skin that echoed the destruction, hot stinging fires that consumed whole streets, the slender needles of Crystal Skulls and divine-touched people scraping a path through the flesh as they moved.

"Lord Isak will soon reach Six Temples and there he will be forced to make a stand with the Devoted." He paused and struggled to breathe. A shriek from somewhere below marked some deranged citizen straying too close to Mistress' remaining pet. "King Emin is so very close now, and soon he will have all that he desires."

"Then let it play out. Make your final moves on the board before you fall."

Rojak tried to nod, but the effort defeated him. Death was so close he could almost reach out and touch the robe, as they said in Embere—

But no, not Death; the Chief of the Gods would not claim him. It was not a black robe he felt all around him, merely shadows. Death would not have him. There was no word for what would happen when Rojak's body failed finally. It would be an ending, but not death.

Rojak's vision whirled, flames blurring for a brief while before the details of the street ahead returned. He could just see the rotting corpse of a wyvern, one of the pair kept by the Raylin called Mistress. The beast had had its fill of the clamour and stink of dead meat all around. It had snapped at what it thought was a corpse, but the moment a canine caught Rojak's sleeve, the minstrel's plague had caught it, passing through its razor-sharp teeth to its tongue and down its throat. Its scales, once glittering in myriad shades of green and gold, had sloughed off as its body erupted in viscous pus-filled boils and thick, black blood had seeped from all its orifices. In a few moments the wyvern was just another rotting pile on the ground.

Rojak sat upstairs in a small house now exposed to the elements after the abbot's magic had torn roof and walls away. It was the closest remaining building to where the abbot himself lay gibbering, curled in a foetal position, in what was left of his cellar. The furious incarnation of Erwillen, the abbot's Aspect-Guide, fuelled by the Skull's power and random blasts of raw energy, had blown up the building.

Much of what remained was still burning fiercely; the protective ring of fire kept the boldest of Scree's citizens away for the time being. There was little of the house left intact now, only the thick stones of the kitchen hearth and the wall opposite it, almost to the height of a man. The rest was broken stumps of wood and heaps of stained brick. Amid the rubble lurked the soot-blackened feathers and claws of the High Hunter. Rojak could hear the beast's laboured breathing, no doubt echoing Abbot Doren's own exertions.

"Venn," he croaked. The slim man came to his side as though gliding on ice, his tattooed face completely unreadable. Diamond-shapes ran down his left cheek, running around his ear and down the side of his throat, disappearing under the frayed neckline of his tunic. "It is time for you to leave."

"Leave?" Venn said in surprise. He spoke in the thick, rolling vowels of Embere. It was an affectation of his, to speak to everyone in the accent of their home, even those like Rojak, who had lost all trace of their past.

"You must leave now," Rojak repeated. "You cannot be caught up in the death of the city."

"You're going to need me here," Venn insisted, pointing towards Flitter, who was crouched in the furthest corner and looking out at the abbot's ruined house. If Rojak had been able to turn his head and see through the fog of shadows that thickened in his eyes, he would have spotted the three tight knots of soldiers that were advancing steadily. "Flitter has said that King Emin outnumbers us. He has the vampire with him."

Rojak beckoned Venn closer and without hesitating he leaned closer, though Rojak could see his nostrils twitch. "What must come to pass here is for me to decide. I have plans for you, so do as I tell you."

Venn didn't argue further. He knew well that Rojak's foresight was unnatural. "What do you wish me to do?"

"Find Ilumene. You and he shall prepare the way, ready the Land for your master's twilight reign."

"How? Ilumene is the general, the conqueror, not I."

Rojak reached out a clawed hand, one hooked finger brushing Venn's diamond patchwork sleeve. In this light it looked pitch-black; only under the sun was it apparent that the tunic was composed of varying shades of cloth that had been roughly dyed. "You are no general, but you must conquer. You were the greatest of your people, until you realised the truth behind the holy words given to the clans. Now you must return to them and spread the word of the twilight herald."

"Will they follow me?"

"The Harlequins have been servants for too long. You must give them a banner of their own. No more are they the children of Death, so fearful of their father they will not wear his colour. Remove their pottery masks and give them black-iron to wear. Give them a banner. Give them a king."

If Rojak had wanted to say any more, it was lost. His body could sustain the effort no longer. He appeared to fold inward on himself, sinking further down into his seat.

Venn bent further down, careful not to touch Rojak's skin as he looked the minstrel in the eye, checking that a spark of life still remained before relaxing. He stepped back and gave a short bow, saying, "As you command, Herald." He was about to turn away, then he hesitated and bent down to Rojak so he could look the dying minstrel in the eye. "Your prophecy, the one you put into the dreams of that stable-boy in Embere; it speaks of a woman emerging from the remains of Scree."

"Treasure and loss in the darkness, from holy hands to a lady of ashes. It is the heart of the 'Twilight Reign' prophecy."

"If you cannot hold them here, how will it come about? They will take the Skull and break the chain of prophecy—if the prophecy is broken, how will Azaer ever walk the Land and become the Saviour?"

"Have faith," Rojak said, gritting his teeth against the pain. "They will take no more than I let them take; our lord's reign is coming. Ilumene knows what is to be done; trust him. Now go."

This time, Venn didn't linger.

The minstrel listened hard for the sound of Venn picking his way out through the broken debris and into the darkness, but the effort defeated him. What sounds he could detect were muted and confusing, as though the bridge between his ears and mind had been washed away. The angry crackle of flames and the uneasy shuffle of the Hounds behind him were all he could make out above the indistinct murmur surrounding him. He could feel the pitiful, maddened figures that could no longer be called human lingering in groups, though a great rolling tide of them had gone north, driven by the firestorms that were even now encircling this place. Those who remained stared with bewildered resentment past the corpses of a hundred of their own at the indistinct form of a God they couldn't manage to hurt.

"What are your orders, minstrel?" To Rojak's weary ears Mistress sounded petulant, and he knew she was trying to conceal her fear. He allowed himself a moment of contempt for mercenaries: when there were glory and riches to be had, they were full of vigour, but put them in a hole and the complaints never ceased. A tiny smile crept onto his lips; soon they wouldn't be able to complain. Soon it wouldn't matter if they did, because there would be no one left to hear.

"Wait," Rojak whispered, "wait until they are closer. They must first kill the abbot, and then when his blood is shed, you will fall on them."

"They've split up," warned Flitter from her post. "One group is circling around behind us."

"Slow them down then," Rojak sighed, his eyelids sliding shut for a few heartbeats. The lure of whatever lay beyond the sleep of utter exhaustion was almost too great to resist; only the touch of his master's ancient breath gently skimming the grazes on his earlobe kept him awake. Azaer was still with him, ever-patient and unrelenting.

He could not rest yet, not quite. There was still his duty to do and he would see it through with his very last breath. It would kill him, but what was life when compared with changing the face of the Land itself? The price would be paid with a smile on his face, Rojak was certain of that. "Take two of the Jesters' acolytes and lead the king's men a merry dance."

"We don't have the numbers to stop them," said one of the Jesters from somewhere behind him. Rojak summoned the image of the tall grey-skinned man who spoke for all of his brothers, his lips hidden behind the white leather mask that concealed everything beneath the eyes.

"You don't have to." Rojak could hardly hear the sound of his own voice now; he was not sure if it was a weakness of tongue or ear, or both. "Draw them in; stall them for as long as you can. It is nearly time."

Head down and riding low in the saddle, Isak watched the cobbles flash past as Toramin's hooves crashed down beneath him. The huge horse charged at breakneck speed, the emerald dragons on its flanks slashing and snapping at the air as he began to outstrip his men. The street was a straight run to the south side of Six Temples, where the ground was more open. It was the quickest way for them to get to the Autumn's Arch.

On the right were orderly lines of torches burning around pickets still under construction, and a tall banner above them all bearing the white sword of the Devoted. There were a lot of soldiers formed up into ranks, more than he could count in the few moments he had. They watched him keenly, but he heard no zip of loosed arrows.

Up ahead he saw sudden movement in the darkness that abruptly resolved into Jeil and Tiniq on horseback, riding hard towards him, keeping clear of the rough curve of shrines ringing Six Temples. Both rangers were waving frantically.

Isak swore and wrenched on the reins to pull Toramin up, turning him towards the temples. The way was blocked on the other side; either the Farlan tried to circle around, or they stopped here to fight. Neither option sounded good. He knew many streets were blocked by collapsing buildings, but the closer he got to the Devoted soldiers, the more of them he saw.

Lahk had told him General Gort was leading them, the same man who had so reverently handed Isak his two Crystal Skulls and pledged his allegiance. They were safe enough; any sane man had to be a welcome ally in

Scree, and hopefully there were more around, enough to ward off even a swollen mob of lunatics.

Toramin resisted as Isak tried to slow him down. They were pounding towards the rubble-lined channels created by the Devoted. Looking back, he saw the others were close behind, spurred on by the sound of pursuit that had been outstripped, but not lost. From behind the Devoted pickets Isak saw units of spearmen spurred into action and realised they weren't sure whether to attack him or not.

Something Carel had told him once suddenly came to Isak: *Soldiers are there to obey orders. Half the time they don't know who they're obeying, so when any rich bastard on a horse shouts, you jump to it. In battle you'll find yourself too scared to argue.*

"They're coming," Isak bellowed, standing up in his stirrups, holding Eolis up high for the men to see, "get to your positions!"

His words had the desired effect. Those who understood Farlan quickly relayed the words to their fellows and the lines became a riot of sergeants and corporals, all bellowing at once as the work parties ran for their weapons.

Isak lowered his sword and slowed to a canter as he reached the furthest picket. The soldiers watched him suspiciously, but none attacked. He looked around quickly; there were groups of soldiers scattered around the Temple Plaza. They must have decided it was too large to fully defend, so they were choosing their ground instead. There was no guiding intelligence behind the mobs, so when the attack came, it would be in the places of the Devoted's choosing.

"Where's your commander?" Isak snapped at the first Farlan-looking soldier he saw. The man's eyes widened and he turned and shouted for his lieutenant, who was already hurrying up.

"General Gort is over there, Lord Isak." The lieutenant pointed towards the Temple of Nartis, where the Devoted's slender banner hung from a long lance. At its base was a group of men all looking towards them. "He's with his command staff, my Lord."

Isak started off towards the general as Suzerain Saroc forced his way to Isak's side.

"My Lord, is this quite safe?" Saroc asked quietly.

"I've met Gort before; we can trust him," Isak said, not looking at the suzerain but past him to where Count Vesna was. "Vesna, get the men ready to fight."

"Your Grace," Saroc insisted, "we might still be able to punch through to the north and work our way round."

"Would you bet your life on it?" Isak shook his head. "I wouldn't. Given the choice between an uncertain run through city streets and a defended position, I've got to take this one. Look at them—" He waved his arm towards the squads of infantry standing ready at the outer ring of shrines and the lancers waiting patiently in the centre of the Temple Plaza. "There's the best part of a legion here, plus us. And when the mobs went after us, they probably gave Torl his best chance of breaking out with whatever troops he has left."

"My Lord, we cannot make a stand here out of guilt—"

"That's not what I'm doing," Isak said sharply. His eyes flashed a warning. "Take care how far you question my decisions. Young I might be, but Lord of the Farlan I certainly am. I've had enough of running away for one night; here we make our stand."

He dug his spurs into Toramin's flanks and the huge beast jumped forward ahead of the suzerain. Saroc didn't bother to try and make up the ground. The conversation had been ended. Behind them Count Vesna was already shouting out orders, to the Farlan and Devoted alike. The Temple Plaza was some three hundred yards across. Many of the shrines that ringed the six massive temples in the centre were large enough to provide a physical obstacle; others weren't, standing like the broken crenellations of a buried castle wall.

General Gort had put his men to good use. They had salvaged anything they could carry or drag from the surrounding ruins. Shattered carts and wagons, scorched roof timbers and even rubble from every non-consecrated structure on the plaza had been used to plug the gaps in the wall. It was certainly too long to defend entirely, but this meant they could pick which fronts to fight on. The heavy infantry would act as mobile barricades where required. With a few ranks behind and shields locked together, they would be able to resist a poorly armed attacker, despite being vastly outnumbered. The smaller shrines were clustered together, and much of the work had been to patch the holes to create long walls that the crazed mobs would just go around, meeting armed soldiers at either end.

"Lord Isak," called General Gort as soon at the distance permitted, "I'm glad to see you again so soon."

He hurried over to meet the Farlan lord, his command staff close on his heels. Isak recognised only one of them from his encounter in Llehden, the Chetse general rather predictably carrying an enormous curved axe, but they all followed General Gort's lead and bowed low to the white-eye.

"Let's forget the pleasantries, shall we?" Isak said curtly, even as he slid from his saddle and went to greet the general with palms upturned all the same. "You're about to be attacked on two sides—more than a legion of the screaming bastards were chasing us this way and, according to my scouts, there are more round the other side of the plaza."

Isak turned to the soldiers behind him as he spoke and saw the two rangers had caught him up. Tiniq offered Isak a quick bow. Both wore only hauberks and skullcaps, but their bows were held ready as usual. Compared to the heavy scales, reinforced oval shields and long spears of the Devoted infantry, they looked under-prepared for the battle ahead.

"My Lord, we couldn't see any safe way through the streets beyond," Tiniq said. "A few hundred followed us back here." He pointed to the eastern edge of the plaza; there were only two real points of access along that stretch and in the faint torch light they could see the lines of infantry strung across the gaps. A company of lancers was already heading over to support them.

Isak nodded. "Tiniq, can any of you make it alone back to our army lines?" He was thinking of the unnatural members of his personal guard.

The ranger shrugged. "Perhaps; Shinir's got the best chance, I'd guess."

"Ask her if she's confident of getting there. I don't want to throw your lives away if there's no chance, not if I might manage to contact them myself." His hand went instinctively to the Crystal Skull on his chest. He'd never yet been able to speak into anyone's mind using it, but Carel always said desperation was the best tutor.

The rangers sped off to consult with their comrades.

"Well, General Gort—" Isak started, then stopped suddenly as his brain managed to catch up and take in the magnificent sight of the six temples that gave the area its name. The nearest was Vasle's, all smooth lines and curves, with five interwoven raised stone channels encircling the main structure like miniature aqueducts. He could just see a trickle of movement in the channels; the holy waters hadn't quite dried up. Perhaps the Gods hadn't been entirely driven from the city.

Beyond Vasle's temple were even more impressive structures, vast buildings designed to house many hundreds of worshippers. Looking around at the other temples he could see clearly—the forest of pillars around Nartis' high altar covered by a jagged series of sloping roofs, and the enormous domed Temple of Death—Isak realised that none of them had been damaged at all. He'd seen quite a few fresh scars on the surrounding shrines and minor temples that formed the outer ring, but the painted frescos and walls of the five temples ringing the Temple of Death all looked pristine.

Oh Gods, he thought wryly, unable to stop himself from smiling. *The Devoted are here to protect the temples; any fool could have predicted that, and perhaps Azaer did. The temples haven't been touched, but now we're here, who knows?*

"He's got a sense of humour at least," Isak muttered, prompting a curious look from the general, which he waved away. "No, it's not important right now. Staying alive is all I care about at the moment."

Gort nodded quickly and something resembling relief crossed the man's face. Isak only vaguely remembered how they had parted the first time they had met, at the old temple of standing stones in Llehden. He'd been exhausted by his struggle with Aryn Bwr and driven to distraction by the bright moonlight of Silvernight, in no condition to hold a conversation, let alone consider the role of the Devoted in what had happened. He had been barely able to stay on his feet, and had to be escorted from the shelter of the trees by Count Vesna. There had been a sudden rush of movement and the sudden wash of moonlight illuminating his silver armour had brought him to his senses barely in time to prevent the milling Devoted soldiers being massacred by the gentry. There'd been no time for farewells, only a hurried escape for both parties and a distant look of what Isak suspected was satisfaction from Ehla, the witch of Llehden, as they clattered past her mouldering home.

Isak shook the images from his mind for now and added, "So let's not waste time. Most of them will be coming from the east, following us. I'll take charge there, and you keep those lancers watching the rest of the perimeter so we're not taken unawares."

To his surprise, no one objected to Isak commandeering what was roughly half of their troops, but there wasn't time to wonder whether Gort's past assertion of allegiance held true for them all, or if they just recognised that here and now, Isak was the best man to lead the defence.

Isak remounted and headed back towards the soldiers on the perimeter. A slow, distant murmur from the dark streets beyond their positions swelled into the growl of a thousand twisted, enraged creatures, no longer human.

Poor bastards; driven mad and driven to their deaths, Isak thought, picking up his pace a little. *But for what? Just so Azaer can demonstrate his power?*

When he reached the tight knots of soldiers he saw relief on the faces of Devoted and Farlan alike. By now they would have all heard stories about him, some true, others not, no doubt. Isak could smell their fear rolling off them in great stinking waves, as obvious as the sweat and leather stench of soldiers campaigning in summer heat. But they saw salvation in his unnatural shining image.

Count Vesna, seasoned campaigner that he was, felt the change too and raised his voice to exploit it. "Now listen, you bastards!" Vesna roared. "What's coming isn't going to be pretty. It'll scare you shitless when you see them, but you're not going to move an inch, do you hear me?"

Isak could see that a good proportion of the Devoted understood Farlan from those who nodded agreement. More joined in as whispering voices translated Vesna's words, many looking at Isak, as if for reassurance. He'd known Lord Bahl for long enough to know his place in this performance. Sitting tall and unknowable atop his enormous warhorse, presenting the impassive front of a divinely blessed warrior, Isak slowly and deliberately hefted Eolis and flicked the glittering sword through a few practice sweeps while his friend spoke. Rogue fingers of lightning danced over his unearthly silver armour.

"Remember," Vesna continued, dragging their attention back to him, "all the enemy has is weight of numbers—you've all been in battle before; you *know* how bloody useless a crowd of untrained troops is. Few of them have weapons, and there's no one leading them, so they'll come straight at us and break themselves on the shield wall."

He levelled his sword at the main line of defenders, where three ranks were already formed up and set at an angle to deflect the onrush of the enemy into a bottleneck studded with spears. "Keep the line and trust the men beside you and behind you. The only thing that'll keep us alive tonight is discipline."

The count forced a small laugh and gestured towards Isak. "And if you don't believe in discipline, believe in the fact that Isak Stormcaller is standing here with you, and there's no daemon of the Dark Place that would dare cross *him*!"

There was no time for anything more. With a great roar, the mob broke from the darkness, spilling left and right around black empty buildings into the faint light cast by the torches of the barricades, a thousand screaming figures rushing towards them. Isak felt the soldiers near him waver, then, grimly determined, face forward. He filled himself with raw energy from the Skulls, then jumped down from Toramin to stand with the infantry, his teardrop shield snug on his arm and sparks crackling furiously over his silver-clad body. It reassured him as much as those around him.

The rush of power flowing through his body drove away the city's oppressive atmosphere. He stepped forward with a feeling of elation, his sword raised and ready, eager to disperse the ragged masses.

Archers went into action, picking off the quickest. Sir Kelet, taking his job as one of Isak's personal guard deeply seriously, claimed his first three kills before anyone else had fired their first shaft. But the maddened hordes appeared oblivious to the flailing bodies and crushed them underfoot.

There were not enough archers among Isak's troops to have any real effect, but the ranks were heartened to see the enemy take the first losses. The Devoted soldiers cheered and began to shout and bellow, working themselves up into a killing frenzy. Isak smiled inside his blank helm. That was what they would need, for this would be grim butchery soon enough. The screaming hordes were close now, barely thirty yards way, arms waving wildly, most clad in rags that could no longer be called clothes, charging on regardless of those who tripped and fell, to be stomped to death under their own comrades' feet.

The skirmishers were next to join the fray, sending a skyful of javelins from the ranks. The onrushing crowd was too tightly bunched for any of them to miss.

The front ranks tensed and drew themselves up, bracing themselves for the impact. Buoyed by the wild, surging magic quivering inside his bones, Isak moved to the head of the bottleneck. *Turn weakness to strength*, he chanted to himself, the mantra of every successful general. His weakness was that he was a white-eye, vicious, and capable of brutality that would shock most normal men. Here it became a strength, a boost to the troops' morale. The enemy were unarmed and pitiful, but the beast inside him didn't care, it wanted only to kill. The chains of reason were gone.

With a crash, the mob drove into the phalanx. The frontrunners found themselves impaled on lowered spear points, while others rebounded and collided with their fellow citizens. More fell, tripping on corpses or unable to keep upright as the angled shields shifted their direction right, towards Isak.

The ranks of Devoted were backed onto a fat pillar three times as high as a man. It had a ledge running around it at shoulder height. As the mob hit the shields, Mariq, Isak's battle-mage, hopped up onto that ledge, a white ball of flame wrapped around his fist, screaming with furious delight.

Isak took his cue and slashed forward with Eolis, letting the energy contained in the Skull fused onto the guard burst out and lash forwards into the onrushing figure. The burst of white flames tore the first man in half and continued on into the woman behind. Flickering tongues flashed out to those around her, blackening their skin and throwing them underneath those pushing up behind. The woman managed to keep upright somehow, but she was shrieking with pain as she was pushed forwards into the bottleneck by the reaching hands behind her. A spear jabbed out and tore through her neck. As she fell, a fine mist of blood hung in the air above her for a fraction of a second then dissipated, spattering those around her.

With Vesna's words still ringing in his head, Isak kept himself in check, cutting down any within reach with brutal ease, but keeping his place in the line. Some wielded long knives or hatchets, but they couldn't get close enough to the line of soldiers to use them; swords or spears cut them down like wheat before a sickle.

The fighting raged on relentlessly. As Isak took down yet another—he'd lost count within minutes—he looked around to see the whole phalanx had each impaled an enemy citizen; there was a moment of strange impasse as neither side could get past the standing wall of dead between them.

Then that moment of hiatus fell apart as one soldier remembered his training and used his shield to bludgeon the dying man off his un-barbed spear. He ran through the next and battle was resumed.

Aside from Mariq, who screamed curses and spells as he threw down ruinous fire to slow the press of bodies, the defenders were near-silent. After the initial attack, the men worked almost as one, like a methodical killing unit, beating forward with their shields, lunging at the next target, disengaging, beating forward again . . . countless hours of training drills paid off as they stood elbow to elbow in tight formation, ranks closed. Very few were yet injured; those few caught with lucky blows were quickly passed to the back and men from the second rank moved forward into any breach, leaving no gaps for the gibbering wretches to exploit.

Again and again Isak felt sprays of blood patter over his armour, and the air was ripe with the stink of loosened bowels and exposed guts, but they couldn't stop to take stock for even a moment. It was just mindless, mechanical slaughter, but their lives depended on their ability to keep stabbing and slashing and smiting their attackers.

"Press forward on my command," Vesna bellowed suddenly from somewhere nearby.

Isak felt the infantry tense once more. He felt a surge of pride in these men, strangers drawn from all over the Land to a place none of them cared about, yet they remained disciplined and focused, and when Vesna called "Forward!" they stepped out as one man.

The mob reeled a little, surprised at the sudden movement, but there were still too many of them pushing onto the troops and the only real effect it had was to crowd those at the front even further. Vesna called again, and once more the infantry shoved forward, using their tall iron-bound shields to bludgeon their way through, while the second and third ranks of the line dipped their shoulders and added their weight to the movement.

In the next few moments the front line of the mob, now too restricted by their fellows to do much beyond wail, shuddered as spears stabbed forward into their bellies, but as they crumpled, they were replaced by yet more keen fighters who were crushed against the shieldwall. Isak heard one soldier cry out as the pressure on him from front and back grew too much to bear, but as the man's voice broke the night air he seemed to find extra strength from somewhere and it became a roar of frustration, anger and pain. His comrades took up the call and a great howl ran down the line. In response Vesna demanded another foot of ground, then another, to drive the enemy to the ground where they could be slaughtered like the beasts they were.

"Lord Isak!" cried a voice from somewhere behind him. Isak let the man behind him take his place, yelling wordless sounds of bloodlust and eagerly closing the gap. It gave Isak a moment of space in which to turn and look at the large shrine forty yards from Mariq's perch that marked the other end of their defensive line. The shrine had dozens of narrow archways, piled one on top of another in what had probably been a carefully devised pattern until the people of Scree had defaced it sometime recently.

Perched on top of the shrine, oblivious (or uncaring) of the impiety to whichever God was worshipped there, was Shinir. She pointed to the ground behind the mob with the handle of her lash, then lowered it and with a savage flick wrapped the chain around the neck of a woman who'd been trying to scramble up the side of the shrine towards her. With a practised movement, Shinir tugged the lash away and the woman's entire body spasmed before falling limp. That done, Shinir returned her attention to Isak, trying to direct his attention to something behind the mob.

She shouted, "Cavalry, sir, a good regiment of Farlan!"

Isak grinned and raised his sword high. "I knew Torl wouldn't die so easily!" he shouted back. The soldiers nearby gave a cheer and pushed forward with renewed vigour as the drum of hooves rose from behind the flailing scrum of crazed citizens.

Isak forced his way to the front of the rank and waded out into the bewildered throng, which had at last recognised the danger. Using both shield and sword to kill anyone near him, Isak began to force his way through the hundreds still left alive. In his wake were the heavily armoured Ghosts of his personal guard, closely followed by the whole line of heavy infantry, driving a bloody path through the mob to the horsemen beyond.

Isak felt a breeze that sent the shadows cavorting all around as the ground grew sticky with blood.

CHAPTER 30

DORANEI FROZE AND SHRANK DOWN beside the splintered trunk of a cherry tree that had fallen into the street. Up ahead he could see Mikiss, the Menin vampire, had stopped and was turning his head from left to right as though searching for a scent. Theirs was the smallest group, with only a handful of the Brotherhood to accompany Zhia, and they were trying to keep as far as possible from their supernatural allies.

The three remaining white-masked acolytes that Zhia had bought from the Jesters padded along nearby. She claimed they would remain completely loyal to her, even if she were fighting the Jesters themselves. Zhia's disparate army was completed by Haipar, Legana, the necromancer's servant Nai, and her own man, Panro, who carried a long canvas bag over one shoulder. Doranei guessed that the bag contained a tent, a last resort should dawn catch them still in the open. Both Nai and Panro were armed with brutal steel-tipped clubs, which they had already had occasion to use on the journey here. Despite the fires that had destroyed large tracts of southern Scree, driving the mobs north, there were still packs holed up all over the city.

Doranei thought the people they were encountering now were different to the mobs. They were still frenzied, but tonight he saw human emotions creeping back in. He recognised terror, because of a Land they no longer understood, a fear that was strong enough to drive them to terrible deeds. This horror had a human soul again, and that frightened Doranei more.

He knew roughly where his comrades were, but they were out of sight now. King Emin was circling around behind their target, while the remaining King's Men had broken off to approach from the east.

The banks of cloud above were obscuring the stars, sliding over the city like a coffin lid. He kept his eyes on Mikiss, who'd been told to lead the way. He wondered whether he had sensed a threat, or just some tasty morsel on the breeze. These days either was possible.

A hand came from nowhere to touch him on the arm and Doranei flinched with shock, his sword rising of its own volition until the hand closed about his wrist and held it tight. He twisted to bring the axe in his left hand around, stopping dead when he saw Zhia's sapphire eyes glittering in the darkness.

"Do calm down," she said. "Are you always this jumpy before battle?"

"Yes," Doranei hissed angrily. "I'm following a maniac through a city of madmen, hunting down a mage with a Crystal Skull. I'm bloody terrified. I bleed a lot more easily than you do, remember?"

Zhia was silent at first as she stared at him. "I'm sorry," she said eventually. "It is easy for me to forget that life is a precious thing. What you fear is the one thing I crave."

Doranei felt a flush of shame as he saw the truth in Zhia's expression, but he knew it wasn't pity she was hoping for. As she released his wrist, Doranei leaned his sword against the fallen tree trunk and took her cold fingers in his hand. "I can't even imagine it, but I don't want to be the one who reminds you of that, not if it causes so much hurt."

She gave his hand a gentle squeeze. "For all of my little problems, there's still a part of me that remains human, and people need to be reminded of pain sometimes. Without it there cannot be joy."

Doranei instinctively checked his companions. They were similarly crouched a short way away, carefully watching for dangers in the other direction. "Perhaps now is not the best time—"

"And when would be better?" Zhia asked sharply before her expression softened. Doranei realised how unused to letting her guard down Zhia was. *And how could she live any other way?*

"We're safe enough at the moment, and once this is over it may be years before our paths cross again."

"I hope it will be sooner," Doranei said quietly.

"So do I, sweetness," she replied with a soft laugh, patting the steel-covered back of his hand fondly, "but such things are not always so simple."

"I know. Whatever my feelings, there's a war to fight here, and we may not always be on the same side."

"And that I know only too well," she said sadly. "It is when sides are taken that the greatest hurt is done."

She leaned closer to him and lifted his helm from his head, then kissed him with surprising force, her desire almost palpable. She held him tight for half a dozen heartbeats, one hand entwined in his hair to bring him hard against her, the other pressed against his chest, as though touching his heart.

"That's why the present should always be savoured," she whispered when their lips parted. "Never forget to enjoy something special when it's in front of you."

Doranei nodded, unable to find the right words. As he looked at Zhia, he felt something on his lower lip. Raising a finger to it, he saw a single droplet of blood. His eyes widened.

Zhia gave him a coquettish smile. "Just a little reminder of me, and something for me to remember, too." Before he could say anything, she added, "Don't worry, sweetness; a scar will be the only gift you get from that." She gestured. "I think someone is getting impatient to be off."

Doranei saw Mikiss glaring at them. "Are we sure we can trust him?" he asked.

Zhia waved a hand dismissively. "They're always a little excitable in the first few days. Mikiss will be close to his old self soon enough." She pointed to his sword, still resting against the tree trunk. "Come on, sweetness, we're not finished tonight yet."

They set off again as a brisker pace, moving as silently as possible, Mikiss still in the lead. The vampires were the only ones with their weapons still sheathed. Doranei had yet to see Zhia draw her long-handled sword. The only person who'd managed to slip past the acolytes to reach her had received a casual backhand slap for his trouble. Afterwards, when none of the attackers had been left standing, Doranei had knelt with his knife to finish the boy off. He guessed his age at fifteen summers, but it was hard to tell as he flailed weakly on the ground, the left side of his face smashed beyond recognition.

The fires had raged unchecked, and Doranei could still feel heat stinging his exposed cheeks whenever the gusty air switched direction, which it did with treacherous frequency. King Emin had travelled in a wide circle to avoid still-blazing areas, and no doubt the ground he was moving over was as hot and cracked as the earth under Doranei's own boots. He didn't know how long it had been since the fires had burned out here, but there were still puffs of smoke here and there, and the stones scattered all around were blistering to touch, as Sebe discovered. He'd shared a nervous grin with Doranei at that, wryly acknowledging that his foolishness had been observed.

Sebe had kept his distance from Doranei since Zhia had joined them. Usually the two were to be found side by side; they'd grown up together, from the orphanage to the Brotherhood. They were brothers, in both senses. Now Sebe watched the lovers, trying to fathom exactly what was between them, and what it meant for the rest of the Brotherhood.

Doranei wasn't worried; Sebe had instinctively moved into his lee at the last attack. They fought well as a pair, and whatever private thoughts Sebe had, they would be shared only with the king, and only if he asked.

Not even Beyn would take action, not unless evidence was produced, and Doranei knew he'd not be alive now if that had been the case. Usually a corrupt or traitor Brother was left thinking himself safe, until the day Coran appeared behind them in some deserted street . . . at which point the king's justice would be done.

Only Ilumene had expected that moment, and only Ilumene had survived. Doranei sighed. Ilumene, the son King Emin had never had. He had been friends with Ilumene from before he first became a true member of the Brotherhood. The man had been easy to like; almost from the outset it had been clear to all that he was first among equals, yet even the veterans had not begrudged Ilumene that. With his easy smile and sharp mind, Ilumene had quickly become the heartbeat of the Brotherhood, the one man untouched by the requirements of his job. *Perhaps we should have thought harder about that.* Doranei grimaced; those had been Sebe's words when Ilumene had betrayed them and gone on his killing spree, taking out the king's allies in Narkang.

Charisma been replaced with contempt as Ilumene grew more and more resentful that he would only ever be a member of the Brotherhood. He'd never spoken it aloud, but there'd been no need: everyone knew he wanted the king to name him as his heir. He had refused to recognise that it was too late for such a thing. By the time the relationship between Ilumene and the king had collapsed, Ilumene had been twisted by his own anger. As king he would have been a despot; desperate to surpass his adopted father's successes and uncaring of the suffering others would have to endure to achieve it.

A stone caught under his boot and he stumbled, earning reproachful looks from his companions for being so careless. The clatter had echoed as loud as a whip crack in the unnatural quiet of the empty street. Zhia gestured and they all stopped where they were.

"Our goal is just down there," she said to Doranei softly, pointing to some burning remains about a hundred yards away.

"Are you certain?"

"No doubt. If you had any magical ability at all your head would be buzzing with the energy around that place."

"It looks like the building exploded."

"I suspect it did. Your king's mages both felt the Skull's use so clearly, and at such a distance that indicates a vast amount of magic unleashed in one moment."

"Enough to kill you?" Doranei asked anxiously.

Zhia nodded. "With ease. Our biggest problem is that this abbot of yours has lost his mind. He was lucky not to burn up that first time, and as it is he will have only hours left to live. A human body cannot survive such recklessness, but if he does not care for his own survival, he can negate my own skill through sheer raw power."

"But you have a plan?"

She smiled, one long canine hooking her lip for a moment. "Of course, sweetness—"

Zhia stopped as a pile of rubble exploded on Doranei's right and a figure burst out towards them. Axe raised, Doranei caught the impact before he'd even turned, but the force of the impact was enough to drive him back as he twisted his body to deflect the person. Something solid, a rock, maybe, caught him a blow on the back of the head, but it glanced off the steel band of his helm and in the next moment he'd come around to hammer the pommel of his sword into his attacker's skull. There was a dull crack and his attacker crashed face-first to the ground and went still.

Doranei's heart was still racing at the unexpected attack, but he straightened up and kicked the prone figure onto its back.

"Damn, a woman," he muttered.

"She's still alive," Zhia said, staring intently.

"How can you—" Doranei began, then, "no, no I don't think I want to know."

He put the tip of his sword to her throat, but the sight of her face stayed his hand. She was tall, as tall as Doranei, with strong healthy limbs, but even covered in the grime of weeks living as an animal he could tell she was young. "Gods, she's hardly more than a child," he muttered.

"Hardly surprising. The young will be the strongest," Zhia commented, walking around him to look down at the woman. "But they're mindless creatures now, however young they are." She looked up at him. "Shall I finish her off? It's a kindness."

Doranei stared back for a moment. "Can you be certain of that? No, she's already unconscious. We'll be gone by the time she comes around, and who knows? Perhaps after tonight her mind will return."

"She has lost her mind," Zhia said gently. "She has lost everything that made her a person. I'm certain of that."

"You said yourself that you have never seen this spell's effects before," he said heatedly. "You can't be sure. They're innocents, all of them—as long as she's no danger to us, what harm is there in a little hope?"

Zhia opened her mouth to argue, but the words died unsaid. She looked around at the blasted landscape. She could see no hope here; it was as ghastly as the battlefields she remembered from her youth. It had a dead air about it: this was a desolate twilight world halfway between the Land and the Dark Place.

But perhaps hope is all that remains? Without the hope burning still so fiercely in his eyes, perhaps he would be just like them, an empty vessel. I have been so long without my humanity it shocks me to see it undiluted in those around me. Suddenly Zhia felt a stirring at the back of her mind, streams of magic shifting like some great beast lifting its head and testing the wind.

"Oh Gods," she breathed, turning back to the fiery ruin up ahead just in time to see a sprawl of energy rise up in the air like tentacles spreading out from a nest in search of prey. "He's discovered us," she shouted.

Without waiting for her companions, Zhia ran for the house.

Doranei stared after her for a moment and felt a fierce glow of heat as she drew deeply on the reserves within her own Crystal Skull. With a cry he set off after her, Haipar at his side and Sebe behind, headed for the rapidly growing storm up ahead. The light from the fires shrank back as whipping cords of spitting energy flooded the area with a greenish glare that made Doranei's eyes water. He stumbled on, almost not seeing one of the bodies littering the ground lurch unexpectedly upwards, slashing wildly with a dagger. He checked his stride and fell sideways, out of the dagger's reach, and caught a glimpse of Sebe at his back, axe raised.

Scrabbling to his feet, Doranei looked for Zhia. She was heading for the burning light of magic, running headlong into the centre of the wrecked house. She flashed from sight and something else caught Doranei's attention, a creature of some sort, indistinct through the haze, although he could tell it was massive.

A blind fear rose inside Doranei, but from somewhere he found new reserves of strength. With a howl he too dived over the barrier of flames and surging magic, trusting Zhia to have chosen the safest path. He rolled as he landed and jumped up, swinging both weapons. From the corner of one eye he glimpsed a long limb snapping out at him and something connected with his axe shaft. He caught sight of a hooked talon snagged on the axe before it was driven back into his chest and he was swept off his feet.

As he fell backwards, one of the Jester acolytes breached the fire and flew past him towards the creature. Bone rang on steel as the acolyte parried with greater finesse than Doranei had shown, but in the next instant he heard the wet slap of flesh being cut open. All his senses were screaming out in panic, but Doranei forced himself upright and away from where he'd landed, just as Mikiss cleared the flames, closely followed by Sebe and another acolyte. The vampire had a savage look of glee on his face, and both axes held out wide. With a swift blow he severed an arm reaching out towards him.

Doranei cried out in alarm as an enormous lioness flashed past him, only realising when it tore a great chunk of flesh from the creature that it was Haipar, rather than some new enemy. As the shapeshifter darted back out of range, Doranei slashed at the creature again, then flung himself to one side as a trident nearly impaled him. Sebe hacked at the shaft to try to break it, but was rewarded only with clang of metal as a feathered wing swept him off his feet.

Doranei jumped forward to defend his friend, fighting with reckless desperation, hitting out at the only part of the creature that was in reach. He was rewarded with a screech of pain, but the wound didn't slow it a fraction; he turned in time to catch a taloned limb just before it eviscerated him, turned again and hacked wildly up behind him to save Sebe from the stabbing trident.

The impact knocked the sword from Doranei's hand, but the moment of distraction proved enough. Through the flurry of feathered limbs, Doranei saw Mikiss attacking the creature from the other side, just before Legana jumped smoothly into the arena, throwing one of her swords straight at the body of the creature. As it struck home, the beast reared back, and Legana pressed forward fearlessly, slashing with all her strength into the creature's body. Mikiss joined her and Haipar buried her huge canines into one reaching arm, using her weight to pin the limb down and create an opening for the vampire. Doranei felt the splatter of gore on his face.

At last they stopped, each one of them gasping for breath and the massive lioness shaking ichor from her muzzle. In the next moment the raging streams of magic swirling and dancing all around them winked out of existence. They blinked at each other, half-blind in the sudden darkness. Doranei began to cough, but felt down for Sebe's arm to help him up. They stood for a moment, supporting themselves on each other as the glare slowly faded from their eyes.

"Congratulations, children," came Zhia's voice from the darkness. "You've killed your first God."

They looked up blearily, searching in vain for the vampire until she used her Skull to cast a pale light. Doranei looked at his fellow victors. Legana looked unruffled, almost pristine, barely breathing hard, while Mikiss beamed with pleasure at the corpse at his feet. In the blink of an eye Haipar appeared as her more usual self, fully dressed, with a blade on her hip. She glared at Doranei when she saw him staring and he quickly turned away.

"God?" gasped Sebe, "that was a *God?*"

Even dead and motionless at last, the creature was so unnatural, so bizarre, that it took him a while to identify the beak and face within the mess of feathers and angular limbs. It looked like nothing he'd ever seen, not even on a temple wall. In the weak light what he could make out of the mess looked daemonic more than divine.

"Erwillen the High Hunter. His Aspect-Guide," Legana answered. "The novice, what was his name? Mayel, yes, he told us about that. I should have realised it would have incarnated, given so great a source of magic."

"We've just killed a God?" Sebe moaned as Doranei retrieved his sword, trying not to look at the sticky mess coating the blade.

"An insane one, if that makes it any better," Zhia said soothingly, looking around for any further dangers. Her strange sword was dripping blood onto the remains of the minor God: rich, red blood that certainly was not ichor. "The High Hunter was as crazed as the abbot." She gave him a wolfish grin. "Don't worry; the first one is always the hardest."

Doranei ignored that last statement. "You killed the abbot." It wasn't a question; the evidence was dripping onto her toes.

"Oh yes, I know a few little tricks, and once he realised I had a Skull too he simply raised his shields against me." She shook as much of the blood off her sword as possible. "He forgot that shields to stop magic cannot stop steel, and his reactions were as slow as one might expect of an elderly monk."

"It was really that easy?" Doranei asked in disbelief.

"Not entirely," Zhia admitted, "but it was always going to be very quick, or slow and completely awful for everyone within half a mile." She gave a cold laugh. "And, of course, he wasn't my first."

The conversation ended as they saw one of the acolytes still on the ground, a huge gash pouring blood just below his ribs. Mikiss stood a yard away from the injured man, his attention alternating between a bloodied tear in his sleeve and the widening pool on the ground, as though he couldn't decide which fascinated him the most. Another acolyte, almost identical in both dress and build, was kneeling at the injured man's side. He had drawn a long dagger and for a moment Doranei wasn't sure if it was to threaten Mikiss.

Then the kneeling man put the dagger at his friend's throat, wrapped his hands around his friend's and drove forwards. He watched as the legs spasmed once, then went still, waited a moment longer, then let go of the dagger, still buried in his friend's neck, and slid the mask up over the pale cropped stubble of his head, revealing a young face, still with puppy-fat cheeks, and a flattened nose that looked like it had been more than just badly broken. The tribesmen from the Waste didn't resemble any of the original seven tribes; the dead acolyte's skin was grey, as though dusted with ash. Doranei thought this no tribal custom, but a sign of how the Waste changed its inhabitants. They had been luckier than many; Doranei had spent a little time in the Waste, long enough to know that humans didn't survive there unchanged. It was for good reason that there were no cities on those verdant plains where once the ancient Elves had built their civilisation.

"Zhia," he said suddenly, dragging his eyes away from the dead. The vampire was crouched down in front of the dead Aspect of Vellern; she turned her head and gave him a quizzical look. "Can you sense the minstrel? He must be here somewhere."

"Why are you so certain?" She finished cleaning her sword on what looked like a wing and sheathed it, then stood up.

"Because he will not—" Doranei stopped dead. "Where's the Skull?"

She nodded towards what was left of a cellar entrance. "Down there, with the abbot."

"You didn't bring it with you?"

Zhia scowled. "I told you, I do not care for it, and frankly, I'm disappointed in your king for wanting it so badly. Aryn Bwr gave it to his son because he knew Velere lacked the strength and majesty to rule after the war. It is a gift for the weak."

"And what if it falls into the hands of the powerful?" Doranei asked angrily. The kneeling acolyte jerked his head at his tone, but Doranei ignored him.

"I hadn't thought you such a fool," Zhia snapped in return. "Your friend Rojak has orchestrated all this destruction, and still you don't see?" She swept her arm out wide to take in the ruins of the city in the distance.

"You think he's lured us here?" Doranei almost shouted his reply as he felt the smoulder of frustration and anger inside him suddenly ignite. "Do you honestly think he would sacrifice the Skull of Ruling and hand it to his greatest enemy before an ambush?"

"I think we have all been blundering in the dark," Zhia spat, shooting a warning look at Mikiss, who'd begun to edge towards Doranei. "I think Rojak has been ten steps ahead for months, perhaps years, and underestimating him will get you killed. And yes, I think you have walked into an ambush."

"Then what in the name of Ghenna's deepest pit are you doing here?" Doranei yelled, his temper boiling over.

Zhia's face softened and, quite unexpectedly, she smiled at him. "Your simple-mindedness is rather endearing," she said. "I'm here because I knew you'll follow your king wherever he goes, and he will not be dissuaded in his pursuit." She reached out and tenderly ran a gloved finger over the exposed skin of his cheek. "And because I seem not to have learned from past mistakes I find myself trailing along after you." Zhia paused and gave a sad smile. "Still, I doubt there's much left for me in the way of punishment this time round."

She stepped away and pointed out over the wreckage to the south. Doranei followed her finger and looked through the waning flames to see a group of figures advancing on them. "Here come your Brothers," she said breezily, drawing her sword once more. "I presume Rojak will consider that his cue."

Doranei's anger had been supplanted by dread as the truth of her words sank in. Rojak had been the architect of this horror, and who could say how far his plans had run?

He staggered back, his ankle catching a splintered beam with enough force to drive a long splinter through the leather before breaking off. Doranei stared down at it as though he'd never seen such a thing before, his mind momentarily fogged. Inside his boot he could feel the sharp scratch of wood against his skin. The splinter—as long as his little finger and almost as thick—hadn't pushed into his flesh, but he could distinctly feel it scrape over his unbroken skin.

He broke out in a manic grin as he bent down to tug the piece of wood from his boot. He inspected the hole it had made. "And I bleed so easily," he muttered to himself, "far too easily, in most cases." Holding the splinter up to his face, Doranei examined it. "But you, my friend, somehow you couldn't manage that," he said, flicking the piece away into the crackling pyre.

He watched the curling flames dance as it was consumed, the heat making the air above waver indistinctly and stinging his eyes. He blinked furiously as he tried to clear his sight. He'd seen something beyond the flames, but what? A random shadow the heat had shaped into something more? Or—

"Oh Gods," he breathed as his eyes focused again. Through the flames, staring back at him, was a massive eye. Gleaming gold in the firelight, the eye bobbed and wove through the darkness as it watched him. *Oh vengeful Death*, Doranei thought, hypnotised by the movement, *that's a long way to move a head. That's a long bloody neck.*

Haipar saw it too and immediately leaped forward over the flames, her body morphing into her animal self, and disappeared into the darkness beyond. Without warning the eye snapped sideways and lunged forwards, the shine of another appearing as the creature turned to face Doranei. His hand tightened around his weapons as the head came close enough to the fire to be visible. A tapering muzzle opened to reveal long dagger-like fangs and rows of smaller teeth. Its head was crowned by fat, stubby horns.

Oh piss and daemons. Doranei scrambled backwards, almost falling over the fallen acolyte behind him. "Wyvern!" he yelled, finding his voice at last.

The moment balanced on a knife-edge, the air charged with expectation as Doranei readied himself for the creature to leap through the flames. Distantly he heard Zhia spit harsh syllables he couldn't understand and the air shuddered with the impact of the spell. The fires ahead of him suddenly surged up bright and fierce into the night air, the heat striking him like a mailed fist. He raised an arm to protect his face as a reptilian shriek rang out.

"Haipar's out there," Doranei yelled, but the only response was laughter from behind him—Mikiss—and he turned to see the vampire raise his axes expectantly. He gave the King's Man a comradely nod, his canines now elongated and gleaming in his smile. Doranei felt a small shiver; Mikiss had looked about to turn on him as he argued with Zhia, but now they were friends again? A soldier who couldn't depend on those beside him never lasted long.

"I can't help Haipar if she wants to fight on her own," Zhia said calmly, her hands tracing shapes in the air as she continued to weave her magic. "A wyvern means Mistress is working for Rojak now; I wonder how many of the Raylin I employed are now against us." She shrugged. "I don't suppose that will make much difference, even if they were all here."

"Zhia!" Doranei had to shout to get her attention. "However many are out there, so is King Emin and my Brothers. We have to help them."

"And so we shall," she replied almost dismissively, "but I don't want to act prematurely."

"What are you talking about?" he asked, but his voice was drowned out by an ear-splitting crack echoing around the street. Doranei turned back, unable to see anything through the flames but certain he recognised the sound of one of Cetarn's favourite spells. "Do you hear?" he cried in dismay. "They're being attacked. Zhia, please!"

A greenish glow pulsing with energy surrounded Zhia as she put her hand to the Skull she carried. "Yes, I think you're right," she said softly, before raising her voice to a shout that made Doranei's bones tremble. "Koezh!"

The wall of fire winked out in an instant. Doranei blinked at the darkness, blind and afraid as he sensed movement all around him. Another whip-crack sound rang out from somewhere to his right and as he took an involuntary step forward, something flashed towards him. Without thought he stepped aside and lashed out with his sword, which caught something, though his night-blindness obscured all detail. An inhuman snarl came from behind him—one of the vampires he guessed, but the sound was so savagely animal he could not tell whether it was Mikiss or Zhia—and a figure darted forwards, striking out at whatever he'd found.

Doranei didn't hesitate to follow; he'd done his share of sewer-fighting, combat in the dark where blows were guided by sound, following shadows moving in darkness. Something scraped down his chest and Doranei wheeled and struck again. He was rewarded with the splash of blood, or something like, on his face. He hacked upwards with his axe to catch any downward blow, and felt the blade bite. It was the opening he needed; stepping forward he thrust the point of his sword forward at chest height. Wherever on the enemy it had struck, it went in deep and was wrenched out of his grip.

Doranei let it go and sank silently to a crouch, chopping down at some movement at his feet in case it wasn't just the kick of a dying man's leg, but the edge only clattered against stone and made him gasp at the impact running through his hands. Nearby he heard a short laugh, someone who was enjoying this as much as Doranei wasn't.

"Not bad," Mikiss said in his heavy Menin accent, stepping out of the gloom to look Doranei in the face. All around the darkness began to resolve into shapes as detail returned, figures running past, paying them no heed. He looked down at where he thought the corpse would be, but had to adjust his gaze to several yards further away.

"Not bad at all," Mikiss continued, "you couldn't even see it like I could, and you're the one that dealt the final blow."

Doranei's eyes widened as he saw the twitching body of the wyvern on the ground, the hilt of his sword protruding from its mouth. *Gods, I drove my hand in there?* The head was at an angle, and the hilt rested against the wicked curved tip of its upper fang. *Someone was looking down on me with a kind heart; a few inches to either side and all I'd have caught would have been one of those teeth in the back of my hand.*

Mikiss was clearly thinking the same thing as he tugged the sword from the wyvern's head and offered it to the King's Man. "A perfect strike," he said. An uncertain expression crossed his face, wavering between fearful and awestruck.

For a moment Doranei caught a glimpse of the man Mikiss must have once been. He gave a brusque nod in reply and turned his attention to the figures streaming past. Over the thump of boots on the ground he heard weapons clashing and screams of the dying, but he could see little other than the flood of soldiers filling the street, charging towards the sounds of battle with grim intent. Haipar was nowhere to be seen.

They were a ragged bunch, looking more like heavily armed savages. Doranei turned to look at Mikiss, about to ask why they were being ignored by the newcomers, when one slowed to look at them standing over the body of the wyvern, his jaw hanging open in a lopsided grin. His tattered leathers and rusting mail hung loose on his body. His baldric was drawn tight, as if that was all that was holding him together. His tightly stretched skin was filthy—no spare meat on this one . . . or any of them, Doranei now saw as he looked more closely.

These men were all lean, verging on withered; they looked fragile, but they carried their massive swords and axes with ease. It was their faces that made the King's Man blanch. Doranei looked closer at the man who had slowed to look at the wyvern and saw one side of his face had been brutally shattered at some point, his ear was a mangled mess and there was an unnatural indentation in his neck. No man could still be standing with an injury like that. No living man.

What was it Zhia had called her brother's troops? The Legion of the Damned? A soft groan escaped Doranei's lips. "Gods, is there anyone actually alive in this city?"

Mikiss broke out into a fit of laughter, dropping one of his axes and reaching for Doranei's shoulder for support as his body shook. The fingers dug hard into his shoulder, pushing through the stiffened leather and mail as though they were not even there. Doranei winced as he was driven down onto one knee and his sword slipped from his hand as his fingers opened of their own accord.

"Be careful, pet," the vampire hissed in his ear, his laughter ending suddenly. "Your life is in our hands."

"Ahem," said Zhia, behind them. Doranei felt Mikiss flinch at the sound of her voice, but the grip did not lessen. "*My* hands, I believe, not yours."

The fingers dug harder for a moment as a scowl passed over Mikiss' face, but he released the King's Man and stepped away, not about to try facing Zhia down. Doranei felt her hands under his arm, but he shook them off and rose of his own volition.

"What's happening here?" he said in a daze. "I thought you said they would make matters worse?"

"Worse?" Zhia repeated. "This place is dead; there is no *worse* to be found here." She pointed towards where Doranei had seen men fighting a few moments earlier. Someone was lying on the ground, surrounded by Koezh's men. Doranei took a long look before he realised the white face he saw was a mask identical to that worn by the Jester acolyte who stood not more than three yards away. Looking around, he saw more, half a dozen dead in a circle where they'd tried to defend themselves against overwhelming odds. Doranei looked around. The acolyte he had been fighting alongside a minute ago was nowhere to be seen, vanished into the night.

"Rojak cannot have been expecting this," Zhia said. "His ambushers were horribly outnumbered. I'm sure the Jesters will have retreated immediately, but any of Azaer's other followers who failed to leave at once are most certainly now dead." Her face took on the cold expression of a woman who'd lived to see every horror the Land could conjure. "This ends, here and now."

"What do you mean?"

"Come with me." Zhia turned away.

Doranei retrieved his sword again and ran after Zhia as she walked through the smoking devastation, entirely at her ease, moving swiftly, though without haste or urgency. The crowds of soldiers parted before her, though Zhia showed no sign of even registering their presence as she headed for a tight ring for soldiers who stood with weapons raised defensively, eyeing the mercenaries, who were looking at them with ambiguous intent.

This cannot be normal, even for her, Doranei thought as he trotted along behind.

In the dim light Doranei had to get closer before he recognised faces in the crowd, though he had already spotted the slumped shapes at their feet that indicated casualties. Clearly the damned had not been the only ones fighting, even if they had ended it swiftly.

Zhia changed direction before she reached King Emin's group to approach a man fully suited in black armour, her brother. His longsword was still sheathed; whatever resistance Rojak had been able to muster, it had not taxed Koezh enough to draw his weapons, not even the dagger at his hip. Doranei had felt Zhia's unnatural strength, so he knew the vampire was far from defenceless. *Black-iron gauntlets and a punch to shatter stone— would even Coran force this famous swordsman to draw?* He took a moment to study the armour. If they ever faced the Menin in battle, that would be how Kastan Styrax appeared because he had stripped an identical suit from Koezh's corpse.

As Zhia reached him, Koezh stopped his silent inspection of the

Narkang soldiers and turned to greet his sister, removing his helm to reveal his smooth face, untouched by years, and the glittering sapphire eyes, so like and yet unlike Zhia's. Neither spoke, but Koezh gave his sister the briefest of nods. What was more surprising was the grunt of acknowledgement Koezh favoured him with. This was still the stuff of uncomfortable dreams; that he could be on nodding terms with such a man—such a *monster.* He recalled the last time they'd met—was it really just a handful of nights ago?—when he had sat just a couple of feet from Koezh, unable to pay any attention to the repellent play on stage because his attention was fixed so firmly on the terrifying siblings. He found Zhia Vukotic completely captivating, to be sure, but Koezh Vukotic was said to be the closest a man had ever come to the greatness that was Aryn Bwr, and it was those similarities that had condemned the Vukotic tribe to rebellion and heresy. That remarkable ruling family had been closer to the Elves than to their own people. He shivered.

"King Emin," Zhia called, "I have a gift for you."

Doranei saw the surrounding King's Men tense and ready their weapons. He could only see one member of the Brotherhood amongst the dead, but he was face-down. The others looked to be Jester acolytes, and he spotted one of the gentry Rojak had used as guards at the theatre. As he approached, Doranei saw the gentry had not gone down easily. It wore only ragged trousers, and its exposed skin was bright white in the darkness, criss-crossed with long gashes. The Brotherhood were trained to be efficient fighters; so many deep cuts meant the creature could endure far more than any man.

Coran, the king's white-eye bodyguard, stepped to one side to reveal his liege. The king was still wearing his ridiculous brimmed hat, a feather stuck in the band, but the look on his face was far from cheerful.

"A gift? You have the Skull?"

"Something far more precious to you."

The king looked momentarily disarmed. "You have the minstrel? Where?"

Doranei felt a jump in his chest. He'd not seen the minstrel anywhere—he had never seen the man himself, though he was sure he would recognise the emptiness in Rojak's eyes. How could Zhia be so certain she had him?

As if in answer, she pointed down the street to a dark husk of a building a hundred yards off, one that had fared better than most in the area. There were a hundred or more of Koezh's undead ringing the building, keeping a careful distance, but with their weapons at the ready.

"You will find him within," she said calmly. "You might want to hurry, even though he's not going anywhere."

"And what do I owe you for this gift?" King Emin hadn't moved, despite the hunger Doranei could see in his face, a hunger echoed in his own heart.

"A favour," she said. Doranei recognised her tone of voice now; Zhia intended to give away nothing more. "I believe it is now time to leave the city, I suggest you do the same once your business with the minstrel is complete."

"I have more business in this city than just the minstrel."

Zhia gave an empty laugh. "There will be no city come the morning, only ash and rubble. The Legion of the Damned has driven off all of your minstrel's remaining guards. There is no one else here." She didn't give the king time to reply, but turned sharply and started walking back the way she had come, Koezh falling in behind her and the undead warriors breaking into a run to stream ahead of the pair as if to clear a path for them.

Doranei held his ground, unable to go anywhere without colliding with one of the mercenaries. He sensed rather than saw Mikiss join the flow, but of those he'd fought beside, it was only Zhia who recognised he was still there.

She paused at his side, while her brother walked straight past, apparently oblivious, and looked at him. A cruel breath of wind brought her perfume to his nose, a faint, sweet scent of flowers, enough to make him catch his breath, before he was caught in the piercing blue of her eyes.

"Look after yourself, Doranei," she whispered. He blinked. He couldn't remember her ever addressing him by name before.

"I don't suppose I need to say the same to you," he croaked.

She reached out a finger and touched him on the cheek. "Perhaps not, but I am glad it crossed your mind. Now go, you should be there when your king finishes this. You will see me again, when you least expect it, once twilight darkens the sky."

"Twilight has come for all of us," Doranei replied without thinking.

"Then it will be soon," she said softly, placing a tender kiss on his cheek before following her brother. Unable to stop himself, Doranei turned to watch her go. Her loose black hair billowed in the wind. She looked a ghostly figure against the night sky.

He jerked awake from his reverie as Coran's deep growl broke the air and the Brotherhood rushed to secure the house Zhia had indicated. One last, fruitless, look around to see if he could work out what had happened to Haipar and he returned to his obligations, sprinting to his king's side.

CHAPTER 31

KING EMIN STOPPED AT THE FOOT OF THE STAIR inside the wrecked building, seeming to notice his surroundings for the first time. After the Vukotic siblings and Koezh's army of undead warriors had left, the king had been in a daze, seeing everything and nothing while his mind was focused entirely on the encounter ahead. His eyes were cold. Now he looked around at the house itself.

As though prompted by his hesitation, Coran loomed out of a darkened doorway, the steel ridge of his helm almost wedged against the low lintel and a look of murder in his face.

He stood erect, every muscle in his body tight with barely controlled rage as he struggled to contain every natural instinct the Gods had given him. His hands were gripping his long mace so tightly that the weapon shook. He'd sprinted here, along with half a dozen King's Men, but he wouldn't go up the stairs, not until the king had arrived. He didn't trust himself.

From the street they had seen someone staring at them, though the angle was such that only from a distance had Doranei been able to make out that it was Rojak, apparently sitting there waiting for them.

Coran's eyes were fixed on his king, silently begging for the order to kill. The white-eye had a particular loathing for Ilumene. Even before Ilumene had nearly crippled him, they had hated each other. But it was impossible for any member of the Brotherhood not to hate Rojak, not after the sick little games he'd played for his master, the horrors he had orchestrated.

"You found no one alive in the house?"

Coran shook his head slowly.

"Well then," the king said to the room in general, though only Coran, Doranei and the mage, Cetarn, were inside. Sebe lingered on the doorstep, his customary grin absent. They were all looking anxiously at the staircase leading to Rojak, and at the king they served.

King Emin slid his axe through a belt loop and kept his sword drawn as he started up the stairs. They creaked ominously under his feet, and he caught his balance as one gave way.

Doranei watched his back as he ascended, his sword tip leading the way. He knew the king would expect him to follow; Doranei had by no means replaced Ilumene as first of the King's Men, but he was certainly a favourite, and his relationship with Zhia had strangely advanced that. The Brotherhood were more than just grey men in the shadows; they were the bloody hands of their king when necessary. Now Doranei had stepped away from that; he stood half in the light. The king had taken this as a sign that he was not simply a blade to be wielded, he might have a greater purpose. Without being given the choice, Doranei found himself halfway into Ilumene's shoes. Already they chafed.

King Emin stopped at the top of the stair. Nothing moved. Perhaps Koezh had killed everyone, leaving the corpse of the minstrel as an object lesson in humility.

Doranei peered past his king at a dead acolyte lying across the top step, looking straight at him with one visible, vacant eye. The battered mask was pushed askew, revealing half a face, but a deep cut to the side of the head had made such a mess that it was impossible to make out whether the corpse was male or female. Silvery-grey hair lay in a tangle, a similar colour to that of the dead man still lying in the ruins of the abbot's house, but luxuriant and flowing where the other's had been hacked short.

He tested the air again, fighting down the soldier's instinct to just block out the stink. The sharp smell of faeces filled the house, overlaying everything with its gag-inducing stench, and over that he could make out the softer scent of ash and embers, adding a dry bitterness to the mix. But beneath them all was another, one hardly noticeable, unless you knew to expect it.

Morghien had first described it as overripe peaches left to fester. This was the smell that accompanied Rojak wherever he went, the reminder of where he had come from. On the fateful expedition to Castle Keriabral, survived at the end by only Cordein Malich and Morghien, one other figure had walked away from the ruined fortress after the horror had played out, one that was no longer a man. The minstrel who had begged to accompany them so he could see the famous castle. He had spent his days there walking with wonder through the wild peach tree woods outside the castle walls, singing childhood songs to himself. He had been a gentle spirit, and a generous man—until a shadow spoke to him one night when the moons were high and the scent of peach blossom was thick on the breeze.

Doranei shifted his weight onto his front foot, anticipating the king moving on, but King Emin remained motionless, leaving Doranei trying not to topple into him. Coran loomed close behind them, and the scrape of his boots echoed in the confined space. Unable to move without colliding with one or the other, Doranei wavered between one step and the next until the king finally moved.

At the top he saw four bodies, two more acolytes, the last of the displaced gentry, and a woman wearing leather armour. Doranei recognised her from the theatre, a dancer of remarkable speed and grace. It was strange to see her lying broken and ruined alongside the ivory-skinned gentry. Both were horribly wounded, and even the acolytes, who were only human in the end, had been brutalised. Doranei knew what it took to kill a man, and this went far beyond that.

Rojak's doomed guards had been hacked apart while the minstrel sat in his chair and looked out over the destruction he had wrought. All Doranei could yet make out of the minstrel was his sweat-plastered black hair that had been pushed to one side, making his skull appear misshapen. Perhaps he was dead after all.

Doranei shook his head, as though that would clear the horror before his eyes. He'd seen this before, this callousness of a man who knew no remorse. Rojak had probably laughed as his followers were cut down, even if he knew his death would swiftly follow. Doranei had seen the tragic remains of Thistledell, the village where the survivors had tried to erase its very existence, out of shame for what Rojak had made them do, and he knew there was nothing sweeter than misery to the minstrel. He doubted even Azaer's purpose mattered to Rojak now; there was only the joy of inflicting fresh horrors upon the Land, for no reason other than his own amusement.

"Won't you come in?" The breathy whisper from the figure in the chair was followed by a rattling wheeze: the laughter of a sickly old man enjoying his final pleasure.

The king didn't reply, but the voice stirred him into action and he stalked across the room while Doranei worked his way around from the other side. Coran went to the top of the stair and stopped, not trusting himself to get any closer unless he was needed. There was a soft hiss and a thud as he allowed his mace to slide through his fingers until the steel-shod butt rested on the floor.

The armchair was damaged, grimy grey stuffing spilling from tears in the ancient fabric. Rojak was angled so his right arm rested on the length of the padded rest, his fingers hanging limp over the end. His other hand sat in his lap. He made no effort to turn, but the set of his body was such that the king would appear in his view first.

Remembering himself, Doranei took a moment to check their surroundings again. There were no obvious places for an ambusher to hide, but he made doubly sure, leaning out over the broken stubs of wood that were all that remained of the wall. There were no ledges or crevices to hide on—the wall dropped straight down to where half of the Brotherhood stood or squatted in a rough semi-circle around the three steps of the front door, guarding against any surprise attack. As Doranei looked down, both Endine and Beyn glanced nervously up. The blond soldier gave Doranei a coolly professional nod, in contrast to the small mage, who almost fell over with the shock of seeing a face appear.

"Please allow me to introduce myself," Rojak said abruptly.

Doranei in turn almost pitched forward in surprise but caught himself in time to step around so he could at last see the minstrel's face.

"That will not be necessary," growled King Emin quietly. He stopped directly in front of Rojak and, after a moment's appraisal, sheathed his sword.

"No? Well you have put your weapon away at least, that will have to suffice as a politeness."

"I see no need to be polite," the king said as he reached into his pocket, "but I don't need my sword with him there, and a cigar would be welcome to mask your stink." Emin nodded towards Doranei as he reached into the neck of his tunic and withdrew a stiffened leather packet. The King's Man gestured down to his comrades on the ground and by the time King Emin had withdrawn a cigar and stowed the packet away, Beyn had tossed up a piece of wood, alight at one end thanks to Endine's magic.

"How delightful, your dogs do tricks," Rojak said hoarsely. Doranei kept his eyes on the minstrel as he reached out so the king could light his cigar. Rojak's body was rigid, and only his eyes and jaw moved, but Doranei kept his axe ready anyway.

Caution rarely gets men killed, said a memory, the voice of a criminal he'd been apprenticed to as a child.

The firelight brought out more detail, even as it deepened the shadows around Rojak. The skin on his face hung limp and loose, speckled by age and ugly wheals, indicating he was riddled with disease. Doranei held the torch up to illuminate the filthy state of Rojak's clothes. The minstrel had soiled himself, more than once, he thought, and great patches of sweat had stained the once-green tunic, but his eyes still gleamed with ferocious malice. He was both repulsive and pitiable.

"And you must be Doranei," Rojak croaked. "Ilumene told me you would be at your king's side; the new favourite, one who could be trusted to be docile and obedient."

"That Ilumene thinks himself merely disobedient," the king interjected, "tells you all anyone needs to know about the man."

"Undoubtedly true."

The wheezing chuckle took Doranei by surprise, but he saw no change in his king's expression, which remained fixed and intent.

"I believe Ilumene still harbours a little jealousy towards his replacement for possessing some quality he never had." Rojak paused for breath, his jaw falling slack, displaying his raw, blistered tongue. "But what characterises each of us better than our own small faults?"

"Many things," King Emin replied without hesitation. "You surround yourself with the broken and the weak, and that is a fault of your own. The weak have nothing but their own failings. Spare us your poisonous, hollow words. They hold no interest for us."

"Hollow? They are anything but." Again Rojak laughed, the effort shaking his brittle, rancid frame. "After all you have seen in this place of death, and yet still you do not see. You ask me to spare you lies, but all I have is truth, and that is all spoken now. Spoken and recorded; copied, catalogued, translated and analysed; I am the twilight herald and my words for you were done a long time ago."

"You waited here and let your guards be slaughtered just so you could taunt me one last time?"

"They are unimportant; the service they rendered was at an end." The whisper was faint now, and Doranei found himself craning forward to catch the words. "I am here because my quest brings me here, and it amuses me to see the look on your faces. I have passed you by a dozen times and more, so close I could reach out and touch your noble brow; it fills me with mirth to reveal myself only here, when any vengeance you may inflict will only do me a service."

He tried to lift the hand from his lap, but his clawed fingers failed to move. He gave a gasp of pain. "Do you see?" he asked through gritted teeth. "My agony is complete. Your retribution only ends my pain. Ilumene kept nothing private, so I know how that little village's demise affected you both . . . and now you stand there, powerless." With a great force of will Rojak managed to raise his hands for a moment. He upturned his palms, like a priest giving thanks. "Was this how you imagined this moment, with your enemy broken and helpless before you?"

Doranei's throat was dry. He was forced to swallow hard and moisten his lips before starting again. "I have thought of this moment often enough, and I told Ilumene of it when the memory of Thistledell was still fresh. My mother's family came from there, though I never saw the place until my first mission as a King's Man; my homecoming was to gnawed bones and trails of blood, to the spirits of the trees bloated on the souls of children, and wearing their faces as Ilumene and I killed them.

"Yes, I have thought of this moment, but one thing my king has taught me is that hatred poisons us. I have seen what hatred does to a man, and I do not want to end up that way. The day I arrived in this city, my king told me to ensure that when this day came, it would be about more than vengeance. You say Ilumene is jealous of my qualities. That doesn't surprise me, for though I haven't the strength of body or mind that he has, that is my advantage over him." He cleared his throat again, aware that the eyes of the two men who had affected his life most were focused on him. "I understand what it is to be human, and what it is to be lacking. Ilumene has only ever lacked understanding, and that is what makes him less than I, and as empty as you. It didn't take me long to realise that when this day came I would have no words for you because there is nothing to say. There is no justification for what you have done, and no fury of mine, however righteous, could give justice to the innocents you've destroyed."

"I agree," said King Emin abruptly. He reached for the dagger at his belt and drew it, looking at the engraved hilt for a moment before tossing it to Doranei. "It is enough that the end is now."

Doranei looked at the dagger. Engraved into the pommel were the king's initials and emblem, the worker bee that symbolised both piety and endeavour.

And when we do not recognise the weaknesses in ourselves, let us hope we have friends to save us from them. He tossed the blade back. A flash of surprise crossed the king's face, but instead of arguing, he nodded in acceptance.

"It is enough that it ends now," Doranei said, as he and the king began to walk back towards the stair where Coran was waiting.

As he passed Rojak's chair, Doranei let the burning length of timber fall into the minstrel's lap. The flame gave a crackle as it caught on the stained material.

"Send our regards to the shadow," he called over his shoulder, certain that Azaer was watching them only too closely. "When the time comes we will be there to end that too."

CHAPTER 32

I SAK GAVE HIS HEAD A VIOLENT SHAKE, almost dislodging his helm in the process, but failing to remove the sweat dripping into his eye. He blinked again, and hissed in irritation, which did even less.

"My Lord," called Vesna as he barged his way past a pair of Devoted lancers, "we can't hold out much longer. We don't have the numbers."

The mob stood some fifty yards away, and whilst they were hardly human any more, showing no sign of noticing the defending soldiers using their last few arrows, some basic instincts remained and they had retreated momentarily from the slaughter. The central phalanx of heavy infantry faced them, ready to return to the killing at a moment's notice, while the remainder were heaping the enemy corpses high, retrieving what arrows and javelins they could and expanding the barricades protecting them.

Still, Isak knew that Vesna was right. There were simply too many of them, and they wouldn't give up, no matter how many died in the process. The weight of armour and weapons was wearing his men down, and they weren't able to kill the mob fast enough to make enough of a difference.

Isak watched an impatient Sir Kelet wrenching arrows out the hands of every man he could reach, not trusting anyone but himself to make every shot count. The white-eye turned to the loitering mob and saw the arrow slam neatly into the chest of a tall bearded man. At that range the knight had his pick of targets and Isak realised he was killing the loudest and most animated; anything to give them a few moments' rest, no matter that it would never be enough. Anything to slow the frenzied return.

"Pull back to the temples?" Isak suggested quietly. "We'll only have Torl's cavalry to cover our backs."

The Temple Plaza was quiet enough that he could hear the zip of Sir Kelet's arrows cutting the air, and the sounds of fighting in other areas, but it was strangely quiet. There were no cries of pain or pleas for help. When a soldier was pulled out of the line or hamstrung by a rusty knife and brought to the ground, he was set upon by the mob like rabid jackals. They didn't stop, even when any sane person could see their victim was dead. Those few soldiers who had been dragged back away from the line and managed to struggle free had still found themselves surrounded, and though they'd killed several of their attackers, they'd all been brought down in the end.

"Could you manage a diversion?" Vesna was as out of breath as the men he now commanded. His helm was scored and battered from rocks and the wild blows that had evaded his shield.

"I'm going to have to, aren't I? There's no sign of General Lahk and we're not going to last much longer. I can't think of anything that'll do us much good right now, and our friend isn't saying anything."

Vesna looked confused for a moment before he remembered Aryn Bwr. "Is there no way you can tell if the other troops are coming? I can't believe the general hasn't ordered a pursuit. That they're not here means they must have met opposition on the way."

Isak nodded. "I've tried to reach them, but I can't sense anyone. I don't have the skill to scry for them, but I think I would be able to find Ehla or Fernal if they were anywhere close. There's just this huge black cloud covering the entire city."

"They must be on their way," Vesna said confidently, "so we need to buy ourselves time. If we pull back to the Temple of Death we'll need a few units in place there first. The only thing that's keeping us alive here is a strong line, and we won't have time to reform that before they catch us up."

"So we need that distraction." Isak looked over to what he could see of the other pockets of defence. The ring of shrines and rough barricades had held better than they could have expected, but the numbers at each picket were thinning fast.

"You," he shouted to the nearest of a squad of Farlan cavalry who were positioned ready to ride down any unexpected intruders, "go to Suzerain Torl and tell the other troops we're pulling back to the temples. He's to cover their retreat and then join us." Isak saw that the torches set as markers down the line to illuminate the weaker points were burning low. The last thing they needed was a breach to go unseen.

He turned back to the count. "You're right, Vesna, we can't delay. Take as many as we can spare from here and get ready at the temple for when I come running with the rest."

Vesna raised a hand to cut Isak off and slammed down the visor on his helm. "Not yet, they're coming again."

Isak turned, sword already rising as the soldiers began to shout to each other and the clatter of steel rang out. Those men still shifting bodies dropped them and scrambled back. Isak's eyes ran along the main rank; a slanted line of thirty men pressed tight against each other with spears held above their shoulders, with two more ranks behind them, ready to brace and drive. Tight knots of soldiers with spears and axes flanked them, ready to chop at the edges of the charging mob. They didn't have the numbers to hold line all the way across the gap, but this was the widest break in the ring of shrines.

This time the onrushing mob was tighter, and came on at a slower pace, not getting in each other's way so much. Vesna saw the change and barked an order, relayed by sergeants at the tops of their voices. Immediately the rear ranks of the phalanx stepped forward and turned their shoulders into the back of the man in front, ready to take the impact. From his higher elevation Isak saw the leading attacker brandishing a cleaver above his head. He opened his mouth, ready to shout, when an arrow caught him in the throat and spun him around into the man beside him. They both crashed down and were trampled by their fellows, but it didn't slow the rest. Isak guessed they still numbered well over a thousand, even with the many hundreds his men had cut down, and now he saw determination in their eyes instead of the previous wild and all-consuming fury. There was a new focus that chilled him.

A bright light flared in the middle of the crowd. Isak looked over towards Mariq, still perched up on his pillar, and saw the mage with one arm outstretched, his face a picture of concentration. On the ground someone burst into flames, and all those nearby fell away, their hands held up to protect their eyes from the sudden heat.

Isak listened to the mage's laughter echoing over the plaza as he dropped to one knee and placed his hand flat on the stony ground. He knew fire wasn't what they needed here; there were too many attackers to kill each one individually and he was wearing himself out.

Closing his eyes, Isak took a long slow breath to clear his mind of the sounds of battle. He felt as much as heard the impact of the mob crashing into the phalanx, followed by a collective groan, drowned out by the sounds of sergeants roaring at their men. The ground seemed to react to his touch, a faint tremble rising up from deep below him. A familiar thrill raced through Isak as his senses were absorbed by the immensity of the Land, dulling the aches and cares of his mortal body. For a brief instant he felt his limbs made of rock and earth until his senses reasserted themselves.

He withdrew with a smile on his lips, a faint memory of that greater mass lurking at the back of his mind, reminding him of the battle in

Narkang. He'd killed a mage there by doing just that, tearing open a grave under the woman's feet. It took little skill, nothing that needed formal schooling, only an instinctive understanding of the flows of energy running through the Land. What they needed was an obstacle to protect themselves against pursuit—and where a wall would serve, so would a ditch.

Isak reminded himself to breathe again, the needs of the body temporarily forgotten. As his lungs filled, so there was a surge of magic from his Crystal Skulls. Mariq gave a cry of alarm as raw power flooded the area, but Isak ignored him and pushed the surging energy down into the earth. It bucked and kicked like a stubborn colt against his palm as he drove it underneath the straining soldiers. Once he was sure it was under his control, Isak opened his eyes to check on their desperate defence. The mob had spilled over on the right of the line and met Isak's guards, who opened to allow some past before a squad of spearmen plugged the gap. Cut off, the intruders lost their advantage of numbers and were swiftly cut to pieces. The Devoted troops were professional soldiers, but every one of Isak's men had been picked for individual skill as well. A poorly armed and untrained mob was nothing without numbers, and even Major Jachen, no more than a fair swordsman, tore his way through the three men who went for him.

A ripple of movement caught Isak's eye. The line was weakening; they just didn't have the troops to resist that weight bearing down on their shield-wall and the fighting was so close that many of the front rank couldn't clear the bodies off their spears and had abandoned the weapons completely, keeping their heads low while the second rank hacked and stabbed furiously over them. Some of the attackers were quite obviously dead, but there was no place for them to fall. One survivor shrieked up at the grim clouds above, his face obscured by blood after a sword cut had sliced open his brow and by a discarded spear in his shoulder. The soldiers ignored him, preferring the noise if it meant he impeded his fellows.

Isak didn't have much time. One by one his exhausted men were falling, and though the damage they were doing would have broken any normal enemy, something unnatural was spurring the mob on. He reached out for the coiled streams of power under their feet and pushed them on towards the heart of the mob. His hand balled into a fist, as though reeling the power out, and he needed his whole enormous bodyweight to anchor it.

The magic fought him every inch of the way, as though desperate to flee from this hallowed ground, but he was too powerful. Once he was sure of the distance, Isak readied himself, visualising what he was about to do. The oversized muscles in his shoulder bunched, driving his fist down harder, before he managed to wrench it sideways. Stones rasped against the silver plates of his gauntlet, then there was an infernal creak that reverberated around the plaza, followed by a sound of rock splitting.

Isak felt the shock run up his arm an instant before the plaza under his knees shook and the ground tore itself apart.

The cries were distant, dim sounds; all he could focus on were the groaning earth and the rampant energies. Though his eyes were closed, yet Isak had a clear picture of what he'd done in his head. His fist had mapped out the long tear in the ground with the skill of a blind man reading a face. He could sense falling bodies and screaming voices, and the roar of soldiers as they staggered forward to the edge of the trench, driven by their own momentum now the weight of the mob had been jerked away.

Isak forced himself to let go of the magic and stood as it fled away from him and up into the night sky. The rush of departing power made him light-headed and he staggered a few steps before the strength in his legs returned.

"My Lord," yelled Vesna, "can you run?" The roaring lion visor gave his friend a chilling look; the gold leaf detail on his black armour melted into the evening dark and only the golden helm stood out. He looked insubstantial, almost ghostly. Not quite a man, that was how Vesna had described how he felt nowadays? Isak's aches and fatigue rushed back all in one go as a pang of guilt brought him back to earth.

Before he could impose order on his thoughts a fresh wave of screams cut through the air as the front rank of soldiers almost collapsed to the ground on the edge of the trench he'd created. The men behind them were quick to drag their comrades back while the third rank set about dispatching the attackers who remained. Isak couldn't see into the trench, but he guessed from the cries that not all of the infantry had made it.

"More blood on my hands," he muttered dismally to himself before he remembered that they were all waiting for his orders. "Enough of that, you bastard," he growled at himself. He couldn't afford guilt now. "They're *all* dead if you don't keep going."

He raised his sword up above his head.

Vesna took that as enough of a reply to his question and roared an order that was echoed by the sergeants nearest him. He ran to Isak's side. "Isak, what about the others?" he panted, his chest heaving with effort. As he spoke, another order was bellowed and the remains of two regiments of infantry broke, running as fast as they could for the temples.

Isak shook his head. "They'll have to take their chances; I can't reach that far with any hope of control. I'd only kill the lot of them if I tried."

More troops broke as the sergeant shouted again and they set off after their comrades towards the heart of the plaza. Only about a company's worth remained besides Isak's guards; the rest were dead on the ground. He could see the writhing mess of bodies inside the trench now. One or two had already begun to clamber up the side of the trench, but Tiniq and Leshi were running along the edge, slashing at the exposed heads as they popped up.

Isak looked at his trench and felt a flicker of satisfaction. It wasn't deep enough to stop them completely, but it ran the length of the ground they had been defending, and the sudden fall would have broken more than a few ankles. It would serve their purpose well. He just hoped the other pockets of defenders had heard the sound and understood what they had to do.

"Mariq," Vesna called out to the mage still perched on the shrine. He was still staring down at the chaos on the ground as the deranged citizens stamped down on each other to get towards their prey. "Mariq, get down here," he called again.

He turned to Isak. "If you give him one of the Skulls, perhaps he can do something. His skill is much greater than yours. It might mean sacrificing himself to save the rest of us."

Isak opened his mouth to reply, then saw Mariq turn. "Shit," he growled, "he's not going to make it."

"What do you mean?" Vesna said, looking back. Mariq had stopped, precariously balanced on a statue. The black fletching of an arrow protruded from just above Mariq's hip and his lips were drawn back in a grimace of pain. The mage looked straight at them, about to call out, when a second arrow flashed out of the darkness and struck him between the shoulders, driving into his flesh with so much force that the head reappeared on his back. The mage gave a tortured gasp and flopped forward, a sudden wild burst of crackling energy appearing all around him before it winked out again and he collapsed on the ground.

"Bloody hands of Death," Isak cried, raising his shield instinctively to cover his face, "where the hell's that archer? I thought they didn't have any!"

"I don't think they do," said Vesna, also raising his shield as he went around to Isak's exposed side and shoved the white-eye as hard as he could towards the Temple of Death. "That's someone else getting involved. Shift yourself."

Vesna raised his voice, trying to be heard above the clamouring howls of

Scree's citizens. "All of you, go! Form up at the temple entrance and hold the line until you're dead!"

Vesna didn't wait for the men to react; Major Jachen had appeared at his side and together they drove Isak on. He stumbled for a few steps but they were relentless and kept pushing him until he managed to break into a run and they found themselves struggling to keep up.

"Can you make another trench at the temple?" Vesna shouted between great gulps of air.

"I think so," Isak replied, slowing his pace so he didn't outstrip them both, "if you don't care about it being pretty."

"If there's a priest around, he'd have to have real balls to complain," Vesna laughed.

That sounded strange to Isak, as if the count's laughter had no place here. That was a sound from times past, from quiet, dull days, when he would growl at his companions out of boredom. Only now did Isak realise how much he'd missed it, and how much he'd come to rely on Vesna and Tila to keep him sane in this strange life of privilege. Their laughter provoked his, and that kept the anger at bay. In Scree there had been no place for laughter.

"A trench you'll have, then," Isak called with a grin neither could see. His pace quickened as though a weight had been lifted, but that didn't stop half of his guards overtaking them a dozen yards later. He glanced back. Still only a handful of people had managed to get out of his trench and were limping after them. The rest of the infantry were close behind him, none as hampered by full armour as Count Vesna. He began to be confident that they'd make it to the temple in time to turn and prepare for the next attack. In the darkness it was hard to see across the plaza but a bobbing torch indicated that at least one of the other defending units had got the message.

Time for a little faith, he thought. *Here's as good a place as any, I suppose.*

The Temple of Death dominated the plaza, and this whole district of the city. Unlike the one in Tirah, which was larger and more impressive, thanks to all those wealthy citizens trying to buy a favourable final judgment, this was not arranged in a cross-shape around the central dome. Here they had foregone the wings tipped with prayer-towers completely, instead building a vast square edifice, with twenty or so slender stained-glass windows occupying the top two-thirds of each side. The temple had to be fifty yards in any direction.

Could they run in and defend it? Isak assumed so, but the temple wasn't entirely made of stone and the walls were still decorated with the summer festival's long yellow drapes. He couldn't remember whether it was in Scree or Helrect that a group of knights had famously been martyred after they sought refuge in a temple, only to perish when their enemies burned the whole place down around their ears. The image haunted him, but they had no choice: they had to fight. The rogue archer who'd killed Mariq had made that decision easier: there was at least one person out there with his wits about him, and plenty of torches had been abandoned at the pickets.

He reached the temple and turned the corner to the western side and the wide entrance—another reason not to hide inside: Death's house had no door, for no one was to be kept out.

They would have to fight, no matter what.

"Where in the Dark Place are the rest?" Isak yelled as he reached the temple entrance. He saw far too few troops for his liking. His heart sank as he saw only the wide frame of General Chotech among the Devoted, still with his massive axe resting on his shoulder, but now as tattered and blood-stained as a Chetse warrior was supposed to look. There was no sign of General Gort or the three hundred soldiers he'd had with him. Suzerain Fordan took care to salute his lord with the warhammer he carried, the same weapon his father had been renowned for using. Isak returned the gesture and muttered a quick prayer that he wouldn't watch this Suzerain Fordan die as he had the last.

"Anyone not here is dead, or as good as," said Vesna as he hurried up beside Isak.

Jachen was with him, looking considerably less fatigued in his hauberk and open-faced helm. He looked around. "No more than a division here," he commented grimly.

Vesna slid up his face-plate and did his own assessment, nodding agreement after a few heartbeats.

"So we've lost two-thirds of our men," Isak said, running to the corner of the temple where an empty waist-high pedestal stood. He pushed a soldier out of his path so he could hop up onto the pedestal and look down on the paved ground in front of the Temple of Death. The entrance faced due east, to catch the dawn light. Isak raised an arm towards Nartis' pillared temple to the north-east. If he could drive a trench in that direction it would cut down the ground they had to defend, without trapping them inside the temple.

"Vesna, get these fucking men ordered and out of my way," he roared.

The sudden bellow caused most of the soldiers to jump and hurry out of the line he was drawing in his head, but some went the wrong way and Vesna had to shout himself hoarse to draw them back. Rapid orders followed, so quickly that Isak hardly made out the words, but these men were professional soldiers; they recognised an order to form ranks, no matter what language it was given in. A good number had already congregated by Count Vesna and their comrades rushed to follow.

Around the corner, their pursuers were only fifty yards behind, once again in a big, formless mass, though they weren't running but advancing by fits and starts, the leading figures casting glances back at those behind and waiting to be overtaken, as though unsure about what they were doing. The imposing presence of the temples had slowed them, but he doubted anything would stop the mob. Isak set the closest alight and saw the man's ragged clothes burst into a bright flare of light, but he didn't wait to see whether it impeded the rest.

As the last of the infantry took up their positions and the cavalry abandoned their horses at the Temple of Nartis, Isak ran down the line he'd pictured in his mind until he was almost thirty yards along. He knelt again and reached out to the Skull fused to his cuirass. This time the magic was eager to serve as it coursed through his body and into the ground. He hardly had to command it before the vast energy running through him started to shake and twist the flagstones there.

A gigantic crash rang out across the plaza as the earth was ripped open, this time with terrifying ease. It drowned out all other sounds, and as a black gulf appeared in the ground, Isak was thrown backwards by the power. He lay sprawled on his back for a few moments while the ground continued to shake. Blinking, he looked up at the night sky. Up above, the clouds glowed red as they reflected the fires raging through the city, but in a break Isak saw half a dozen stars, shining bravely.

"I hope you really are my bloody ancestors looking down on me," he muttered with a manic chuckle as the magic receded from his tingling limbs. He looked out over his feet at the jagged rip in the ground. It was wide; they'd have a problem jumping it, but it wasn't impossible. The paving slab by his right heel upended suddenly, pitching down into the trench to crash onto the stony floor. It was followed by the patter of loose soil.

Isak jumped up and flexed his shoulders. He raised Eolis to the skies, his eyes still fixed on the faint pinpricks high above. "Now's the time to do something more than watch, you bastards," he called as the mob rounded the corner of the temple. Behind him he heard soldiers run up alongside and saw Jachen appear with the remaining Farlan troops. Suzerain Torl took up a position on his left-hand side and Shinir appeared on his right, sparing the time to scowl at the big white-eye. She had looped her flail around her body to keep it out of the way and now brandished a plain round shield taken from a fallen lancer. She had perfected a very simple technique now taken up by many others: she stepped straight into an attacker and smashed the steel boss of her shield into their face, then chopped into their neck with her khopesh.

He looked again at his trench. It was deeper than the last, a good ten feet down, so those who failed to bridge the gap were likely to fall and break bones. Getting out would be a damn sight more difficult too. The defenders were formed into a rough triangle, their backs to the entrance, the three wide arches that spanned the front of the temple.

Isak's trench cut across the plaza towards the Temple of Nartis; the Farlan defended that while the Devoted had strung their shield-wall across the remaining ground. General Chotech had taken a position at the very tip of the triangle, towards the end of the trench, standing over a burly infantryman who knelt with his shield braced on the ground to act as an obstacle while the general swung the axe over him. It would be tiring work, even for a Chetse, but this was what they were reduced to.

He watched Vesna overseeing the shield-wall as the first few citizens loitered in the gloom.

"What are they waiting for?" shouted General Chotech.

"Who cares?" Vesna replied. "Perhaps they're nervous of the temples— whatever it is, it's slowed them down and buys us more time."

The crowd began to thicken, ragged figures massing with whatever weapons they had found. Some had only discarded shields from the fallen infantry, but that didn't matter much. Weapons blunted quickly in battle and a drawn-out fight invariably ended up as a bludgeoning match, where steel-reinforced shields were almost as good as swords. A drawn-out bellow dragged Isak's attention back to the side he was defending and a few score of the swifter members of the mob led the charge towards him. Some carried the torches the defenders had abandoned at the pickets and Isak felt a chill at how close he'd come to ordering his men inside.

Leading the way was a young man with long gangly arms flailing wildly. He wore only a torn pair of trousers and waved a long cook's knife wildly above his head. His face was grossly contorted by hatred, and so focused was he on Isak that he didn't even notice the trench on the ground. Even as he pitched downwards, he was slashing for the white-eye. Isak heard the sickening crunch as the youth's face hit the far side of the trench and snapped his neck back, but he was watching those still coming on.

The first misjudged his jump. He got one knee onto firm ground, then Jachen slashed open his face and sent him falling back. After that they came en masse, and the soldiers found themselves brutally repelling the leaping attackers any way they could. Isak had it easier than most, for he had the weight to stand almost on the very edge of the trench and use his shield to swat away those that jumped towards him. One by one they fell into the trench, and the rush towards the defenders slowed.

"This ditch isn't deep enough," Jachen yelled, crouching down to stab a man in the throat as his fingertips reached up to try and pull himself up.

"If you think you could do any better, feel free to try," Isak shouted, hacking inelegantly down into a woman's shoulder as she leapt empty-handed, clawed hands reaching for him. The magical edge sheared through her torso with horrific ease and as the two halves fell into the trench a great spray of blood spattered over Isak and the soldiers on either side.

"Piss on you," roared Shinir, blinking hard through the blood covering her face, "that's in my damned eyes!"

"Private!" Jachen shouted. "Keep that mouth shut! My Lord, this trench isn't going to be enough; look at them."

Isak had to agree. Now too many were slowing their pace and willingly dropping into the trench, clambering over their fallen and scrabbling at the crumbling edge for enough purchase to pull themselves up. The number of corpses down there would soon start to count in their favour.

From the noise he realised they were fighting on both fronts now. The mob had grown again, and fatigue hadn't robbed them of any ferocity; his soldiers had been fighting for hours against enemies who didn't care about their own safety.

"This isn't warfare," he said aloud. "In battle you know the enemy's got some sort of sense left."

"Bugger that," Jachen said, "this is a race of numbers, and we're going to lose unless we get help. The damn trench is filling up with dead and that's got to be more than a legion queuing up to walk across."

Isak took a moment to watch the crowd of spitting and wailing citizens only half a dozen yards away. This was the first time he'd stopped to look at them closely. They were starved and filthy, some trembling and unsteady as they tumbled into the trench towards him. They looked like the sort of people a duke should be protecting, not desperately thinking of ways to slaughter them.

"There's more of them," Jachen continued, "the fighting must have drawn others." Isak realised the commander of his guard was right as he looked over the heads of the nearest. The plaza was filling up, a bobbing carpet of heads spreading back to the break in the ring of shrines they had been defending only minutes before.

"Then we really do need help," he admitted. "Whoever shot Mariq must have realised that as this became more desperate, I'd likely give him one of the Skulls. The effort would have killed him pretty quickly, but Mariq had more skill than I ever will; perhaps enough to burn us a path through this lot."

"What help are we going to get out here?" Jachen puffed, his sword strokes laboured as he smashed away yet another salvaged spear and stabbed his attacker in the neck.

Isak stopped still for a moment, leaving Suzerain Torl to chop through the wrist of man with a cleaver at Isak's feet. The suzerain was puffing hard too, sounding like he was feeling his age at last, but he didn't hesitate to redouble his efforts to give Isak a moment to think. Torl had fought along-side Lord Bahl often enough to know there was good cause.

Help? Not from the ancestors above us, he thought with a growing sense that an idea was looming. "Of course, bloody ancestors," Isak cried suddenly.

"What are you talking about?" Jachen said.

"What do we have here?" Isak asked before answering his own question. "Nothing, that's what; only the souls of ancestors in the sky and six empty temples."

"I hope you've got a point here." Jachen sounded more than a little concerned that Isak had gone insane.

"More than that," Isak laughed. He saw the ranger, Jeil, on Jachen's other side and raised his voice. "Jeil, do you remember when we got to Saroc and I had a look around to see if I could find something to help us?"

"I—" The ranger looked confused for a moment before understanding dawned. "That water elemental you woke? My Lord, you do remember that it attacked us, don't you?"

"A minor detail," Isak said cheerfully.

"Lord Isak," interjected Jachen, "I recognise that tone of voice by now; it means you're going to do something to worry me."

Isak clapped him on the shoulder, causing Jachen to wince at the unintended force, then paused to drive back two attackers scrambling over the edge of the trench. "It looks like I chose right, then," he said in a more serious tone. "What I need from a commander is for him to worry when I forget to."

Isak reached into both of his Crystal Skulls and his smile broadened as sizzling trails of energy began to snake over the surface of his armour. The air around him shimmered. "What you get in temples is Gods," he explained, as though to a room of schoolchildren. "Every temple and shrine is touched by the God when it's consecrated—that's what consecrated ground *is*. While the Gods might have been driven out of the city, some trace of that spirit *must* remain."

He took a step back from the line and let two men fill his space. Behind him, Vesna ordered a company of Devoted troops to join the Farlan. The trench was filling fast, though blood and gore had made the edge treacherous. The stink of loosed bowels and perforated intestines filled the air, which shook to the sound of wordless shrieks.

Isak tried to clear his mind, ignoring the fearful shrieks echoing up from the writhing mass below him. He tried to black out the glee on the faces of those jumping deliberately down as the screams intensified, closing his eyes and focusing on the magic surrounding him, finding a selfish refuge there. He wasn't sure exactly what he was doing now, but he didn't want to see what would happen if he made a mistake.

"My Lord, what are you doing?" cried Jachen, butting an attacker with his steel helm as the man grabbed his sword arm. They were holding the line, but it was starting to get desperate. The losses at the other pickets had been too great.

"I've woken one God here this evening by mistake," Isak muttered, trying to gain a grip over the magic flooding his body: he needed the energies to be settled, not raging. "Here, in their own temples, no minstrel's magic will stop them incarnating."

"Them?" Jachen almost shrieked. "You're summoning Death and Nartis? Oh Gods, you're going to summon Karkarn?"

"Let's see what we can see," Isak murmured and turned the magic inward to seep into his soul, drawing his senses out into the hot night air. He found his bearings as the confusion of battle and pain cut through him, stirring strange eddies in the drifting currents above. He could feel the warmth of latent power coming from the temples, the familiar call from Nartis' house only a few-score yards away, though overshadowed by the looming shadow of Death, so close behind. After a moment he heard quiet voices echoing through the dark, then the scraping of knives and a low, bestial pant, just on the edge of hearing.

A moment of doubt made him pause as he recalled waking the Malviebrat in Saroc. Adding to their troubles really would be the final nail in their coffin. If, somehow, he brought something other than his intended target into being, there would be no going back.

He held his breath and listened, reaching out as far as he could with his mind to whatever lingered on that plain. A dark cloud hung over everything, and he had to push at every step, trying to find a way around the dulling effect of the minstrel's now-visible magic. After another few dozen heartbeats, Isak made out a number of indistinct presences nearby. He couldn't distinguish them, though he knew they were separate entities. Five stood closest to him. He felt their eyes on him as, lingering at the edges of his perception, they became aware of his questing tendrils of power.

Now they all turned towards him, and there was a taste to the air that sent a shiver through his body, a strange mix of anticipation and bloodlust that felt far from divine. Isak didn't know what else there was to be found here—on sanctified ground they surely couldn't be daemons . . . but he could sense a gratified ache coming from the beings watching over the slaughter. He wasn't reassured, but now there was no going back.

As he hesitated, pondering the consequences, he got more from his surroundings: the all-consuming hatred radiating out from the horde about to overrun the dwindling lines of soldiers, and a growing terror even closer to hand. Screams cut through the fog of his mind and reverberated in his very bones as the fear of his comrades—his *friends*—sliced into his skin like hot knives.

He could no longer delay. Whatever the result, he had to try and save them.

Consequences mean nothing if you're dead, said a soldier whose face he couldn't remember, a memory from years back. Carel? It was the sort of thing the veteran would have said in a maudlin moment before stomping away to his bed, but when had it been? A second wave of screams, louder and more insistent, forced Isak to put the matter from his mind. There would be time to remember, if he lived through the next hour, and to do that he needed whatever fell creatures remained in this place, watching and waiting.

He reached out to the shadowy figures and touched them with his mind. At first they recoiled, rising up towards the clouds, then he opened the Skulls and directed their vast power towards the spirits.

Dear Gods, let my ignorance not prove the death of others, he prayed silently.

The entities drew closer, grasping fingers reaching greedily for the roaring streams of power. Isak gasped and shuddered at the searing pain of so much magic rushing through his body, suddenly fearful as lines of heat ran down his arms and legs. Like claws cutting to the bone, the energies from both Skulls took a savage grip and Isak felt a distant cry ring out in the night. The scar on his chest burned like a flame and he realised Xeliath, wherever she was, was pained by what he'd done. Isak's fear deepened.

His lips were cracked and blistered; they tore open, spilling blood down his chin. Only then did he realise he'd commingled Xeliath's scream with his own. Somewhere he heard Aryn Bwr cry out, and felt his hand tighten around the hilt of Eolis. The twitch of movement was enough to awaken him to what was happening, reminding him of his struggle on Silvernight, when the last king tried to take his soul.

Isak drew in a huge gulp of air, and as his lungs filled, he felt energised. There was no time now for elegance, so instead he used every ounce of strength in his body to wrench the fat, pulsating streams of magic away from the suckling entities, slowing the flow of power. His mind fell back into his body in time to feel himself collapsing back onto the unyielding stone, but in that moment he felt a wash of relief as the burning pain of rampant magic fled from his body.

His eyes flashed open, but for a moment all Isak could see was a dark blur up above and faint bursts of light as his head smashed back against the ground. Lungs burning, he took a raspy gulp of air and flailed wildly until he was sitting upright again. He tried to focus his vision until he could blurrily make out soldiers jumping back from trench.

"Piss and daemons, what in the name of Death are those?" yelled a voice nearby. A name, *Jachen*? It hovered at the back of Isak's mind as his fingers tightened around the hilt of his sword. Jachen, Major Jachen: as awareness flooded back, he scrambled to his feet, coughing and heaving and blinking away the tears that were obscuring his sight.

More voices took up the call and a fresh wave of horror struck Isak, who reeled until he was steadied by an outstretched hand: the ranger, Tiniq, bloodied and battered, yet strangely more alive and potent than Isak had ever seen him before.

"What have you done?" the ranger snapped, his white teeth flashing in the dark. Before Isak could answer, a second shout rose above the clamouring voices of the soldiers.

"Merciful Death, that's the Burning Man!" cried one man in terror. Isak and Tiniq could see the reason for the man's fear: in the heart of the attacking mob stood a figure twice the height of a normal man, wreathed in flame with his hands outstretched, as though blessing the scrabbling citizens around him. Isak remembered a shrine they had passed with the Burning Man's face painted on one of the frescos. He wore an expression of sheer agony as fire curled around his head. Isak could see nothing of the figure before him beyond the dancing yellow flames that soon began to spread out to the people around it.

"Look, with the sword," Jachen called, pointing with his own blade at another newcomer to the mob. This one was as tall as the Burning Man, but wearing armour and carrying an enormous sword, skin shining with an inner white light, illuminating gaunt features and grey matted hair falling about the shoulders.

Isak froze; this one too he recognised from the walls of a shrine—probably depicted in the temple behind him as well, standing guard to one side of the entrance.

Jachen found his voice again, almost sobbing with fear as he named the newcomers. "The Soldier—And oh Gods, the Wither Queen! Look, they're all here—*all* of them, the Headsman and Great Wolf . . . the Reapers have come for us!"

Isak grabbed Tiniq by the shoulder and hauled himself upright, almost driving the ranger to the ground as he did so. Forcing his parched lips apart, he shouted at the top of his voice, "Hold your positions; keep the line!"

"My Lord?" said Jachen in disbelief, staring at Isak as though he too was a monstrous figure from the Land's darkest myths. "You summoned the Reapers?"

Isak hesitated. *I think so—it must have been me, but how was I meant to know?* "I summoned help," he replied flatly.

"The Reapers?" Jachen yelled. "The five most violent of Death's Aspects?"

Isak turned back the mob where a panic-stricken howl of fear was spreading through their disordered number. *The Reapers; you should have known. Of all the Aspects of the Gods likely to be in attendance as the last people in this city prepare to die, which did you expect to be close enough to incarnate?* "We're defending the temples; they are Aspects of Death," he said calmly.

"They're the Reapers," Jachen wailed, almost incoherent in his fear. "They kill any*thing* and any*one*! The Wither Queen doesn't stop to check whether her victims *prayed* to her that morning!"

Isak took a step towards him, Eolis raised and blazing with a fierce light as crackling cords of energy flashed into existence, sizzling from his wrist to the tip of the blade. "Hold your ground," he repeated, fighting to raise his voice above the frantic screams ringing out all around them. "If they want to take one of mine, they'll have to put me down first."

"You're going to fight the Reapers?"

Isak felt the familiar growl of anger rising inside. "I'll not bloody stand aside and watch if they turn on us. Aspects of Death or not, they'll fear the Skulls I carry, or I'll make them do so quickly enough."

The mobs were in disarray; some were still trying to attack, oblivious in their ferocity, while others were trying to flee the Temple Plaza. Most just stood and stared.

Isak found himself doing the same as a prickling sensation of awe washed over him. Stalking like daemons through a field of wheat, the five Aspects of Death tore a swift and bloody swathe through Scree's remaining citizens. The Soldier and Headsman were cutting and hacking with a quiet, grim purpose. The Burning Man and the Wither Queen annihilated with a touch of their long, skeletal fingers. The Great Wolf bounded to and fro, its back strangely hunched, more like a jackal's, and lacking the languid grace of a real wolf. Despite the clamour, Isak could still hear its excited snorts as it chased down those who tried to flee.

The air was filled with people shrieking, screaming, crying, wailing, and there, somewhere on the edge of hearing, Isak thought he heard an echoing laughter. For a moment he thought it had come from inside the temple, as though Death himself was revelling in the most unpleasant sides of himself, but everyone knew Death was impassive. Pleasure didn't come into this, it was just the act itself.

Isak chided himself at being distracted and returned his attention to the terrible slaughter taking place. Within minutes the Reapers had killed more than his men had managed to take down all evening, but in this Gods-inflicted chaos it was even less of a battle than it had originally been. This wasn't a desperate fight for survival, it wasn't the grim repetition of deflect, strike, kill, each soldier trying to control the growing fear inside him as they faced an unstoppable horde. This was different, this was murder, out-and-out butchery, and Isak couldn't quite believe it of Gods. He could see his own revulsion mirrored in the faces of the men around him.

And in an instant, the folk of Scree returned to their senses and a great wave of pleas and prayers emanated from the mob.

An icy hand gripped Isak's heart. The minstrel's magic had been undone, and the savage desires of Gods still gorged upon the minstrel's victims, thanks to the power *he* gave them.

The old men of the wagon train, where Isak had grown up, always said the Reapers taught a man what he was truly afraid of. Take anyone into a Temple of Death and look at the painted images: everyone, man, woman and child, would be able to pick out that one they feared more than the others. Isak had always believed the Burning Man was his; the idea of a man aflame made his skin crawl, but as he looked into the pitiless face of the Wither

Queen, even his powerful limbs trembled. The other Reapers destroyed indiscriminately, but she seemed to take more than just life. As she caressed each terrified face with her long jagged fingernails, she looked into their eyes, and it was as if her dead-grey eyes tore the souls from each mortal body, as her loathsome diseases ravaged their flesh in a heartbeat. She bestowed upon her chosen pain of years in an instant, condensed and refined into the purest agony, and it was that pain that killed her victims as much as the diseases themselves.

Isak's hand shook as the Wither Queen cast her gaze on a crowd of petrified, whimpering civilians. He wanted to howl with fear and guilt. He staggered a few steps back and turned to look at the temple. It was still and silent, the only light within coming from the two torches they had set by the arched entrance that now cast deep shadows over the interior. The high altar at the centre of the building was a solid block of darkness, untouched by the torchlight.

But I never meant this, he thought through a daze as the surging energies from the Skulls howled in his ears and begged to be used. *How has this happened? These men have given their lives to defend what, a grand shrine to these daemons? They will have been told it was their duty to defend the glory of their Gods, and now they see the monsters their Gods really are—Or was this truly my fault? Did I do something to make them this way? Did they take something from me when they took the strength to incarnate?*

"Stop them," said a voice in his head. The scar blazed hot on his chest as he felt Xeliath's presence on his shoulder. "*They are here at your invitation, they are yours to command.*"

"Xeliath?" Isak said aloud, before realising he had no need. "*Where are you? Can you see them?*"

"*I see them*," she said, her voice all grim purpose in his head. Her resolve calmed Isak and helped clear his mind. "*They are feeding off your strength, the power in the Skulls and the fear of your men.*" She gave a small gasp. "*Isak, there's so much energy flowing through you—they're feeding off you like leeches, and as it flowed over your scar, that was enough to drag me here too.*"

"*Can you help me?*"

"*I am miles away; we're guests in a monastery outside your city of Perlir. This fight is yours alone; Gods do not dream, I cannot touch them.*"

"*How do I fight them?*"

"*Face them down and cut the flow of strength. I can sense some strange flavour in the air around you. Whatever it is, it is anathema to them, I think. Without your help they will run like whipped dogs."* A sudden note of urgency entered her voice and jerked Isak back to action. In the distance the screams continued.

Isak grabbed Eolis and used the sword to hold himself upright as the strength left his legs. He was intoxicated by the taste of magic filling his head.

"My Lord," cried Count Vesna, seeing Isak totter. He ran over and grabbed an arm.

Isak looked up drunkenly into his friend's face. Vesna had removed his helm and Isak could see the tracks of tears on his cheeks. Tears of what, fear? Exhaustion? Or maybe loss for the man he'd once been . . .

And yet still he runs to you, still he is there to hold you before you fall, this man who thinks he's failed you. He casts off his own fear before he lets you fall, so who is it who has failed his friend?

"Hold the line," Isak whispered, clutching Vesna's shoulder for support, willing his strength to return. Vesna, there for him despite his own troubles, and so many others: they needed a strong lord, or they were all dead.

Get up, you bastard, Isak screamed in his own mind, *get up and face them, or it won't just be these men here who die. What about the rest of your troops in the city? What about the rest of the Farlan? Do you think Azaer will stop here? No, he'll continue until Tirah is as much of a husk as Scree.*

"Hold the line?" Vesna said, looking up to check the wedge of surviving soldiers. Some had sunk to their knees, all were too tired to speak. Only then did the count see the men wavering—fear of what was happening ruling them rather than mere exhaustion—and he immediately started to bellow orders.

Isak looked around. The mobs had stopped attacking them now, and the exhausted troops looked ready to collapse. Only the sight of the Reapers, still wreaking havoc amongst the people of Scree, stopped them from all crumpling to the ground. Vesna's orders raised heads and steadied a few, and as the remaining sergeants took up the shout, Isak watched their resolve return. He knew it was crucial they stayed in line, for if they ran, the Reapers would slaughter them too. Their only chance was to remain apart from the fleeing mob, separate and in control.

"They're running," Jachen said dully. His sword hung limp in his hand, tip trailing along the ground. It didn't look like he'd have the strength to swing it again this night; Isak was ready to pray that none of them would have to.

"Wouldn't you?"

"Shouldn't we?" Jachen asked. "No Aspect of Death is noted for its pity, but these—"

"If you run, you'll die," Isak said with certainty.

"Then what? We stand here and let them slaughter us?" Vesna was as tired as the rest, and hadn't the strength to protest with vehemence. He sounded resigned, as though he knew this was what Fate had in store for him.

"Not if I've got anything to say about it."

"You can't fight the Reapers."

"Why not?" Isak stood straight again, no longer needing the man's shoulder for support. "There was a war once, remember? Aryn Bwr proved Gods could be killed, and he gave the Land the means to do so. They'll remember; they fought at the Last Battle."

A collective gasp from the men behind them interrupted them and Isak wheeled around to see the Soldier, sword low and head dipped, advancing towards them. His face was veiled by his lank grey hair, but Isak could see the Aspect was carefully scrutinising the mixed Farlan and Devoted soldiers.

The Aspect wore a patchwork of armour, mismatched steel plates and scraps of chain mail hanging off his emaciated frame. His sword arm—the left, which struck Isak as strange, since most left-handed soldiers were forced to use their right—was bare, apart from a steel band around the wrist. The Soldier's skin looked as pale as a corpse's, and as wasted as one of the Wither Queen's victims, hardly strong enough to wield the long leaf-bladed sword with which he had helped to massacre the mob.

The other Reapers were still dispatching those citizens left in the plaza, chasing them down with unexpected swiftness. The Soldier was oblivious to this as he approached the temple over a carpet of carnage, the bones of the slain snapping under his weight.

"Keep your positions," Isak said calmly. He didn't bother to raise his voice; an unnatural hush had fallen over the soldiers and every man could hear his words.

"*It feeds on the fear they feel,*" Xeliath reminded him, "*but remember, you look like a God to them; show no fear and you weaken it.*"

With a deliberately unhurried movement, Isak pushed his way past his Farlan guards and jumped over the trench he'd carved in the Temple Plaza. He kept his eyes on the Soldier, like a sane man does on a dangerous dog. Break eye contact and you lose what little control you might have; despite centuries of breeding, it remembers that it was once a wolf.

"My Lord," said Vesna quietly. Isak raised his shield hand in warning and the count fell silent. Whatever Vesna's objection, it was past the point of making. He'd only intervene now if he thought Isak was in danger—and damn him, he would, as well: Isak had no doubt that Vesna, broken spirit or not, would charge headlong to attack the Aspect of Death if his lord was threatened.

Is this what you do to men? Isak thought as he approached the Soldier. He could feel the pull of its presence now, the aura that Lord Bahl had worn like a mantle of authority, the glamour that Morghien had spoken of, enough to cow men into obedience. Even as he forced himself to face up to the minor God, Isak found himself having to fight the urge to kneel, to lower his gaze and make obeisance, despite the horror he felt in his heart.

Is this how the rest of them see you? Isak asked himself, remembering the battle outside Lomin, calling the storm down onto himself in Narkang, and the images seared into his memory.

This close, he could see that the Soldier was covered with blood; his boots were soaked through and the battered blade he dragged over the ground, careless of its edge, was covered in filth and gore. Isak almost gave up when he realised how much taller than he the Soldier was, but pride kept him going. He wouldn't falter now; he would meet these consequences head-on.

"Give him to me," the Soldier growled to Isak when they were no more than four yards apart. The white-eye looked confused for a moment, then noted the Soldier's intent expression, as though the Aspect was looking straight through his flesh and into Isak's soul. As if to confirm Isak's suspicion, the Soldier sniffed the air cautiously, savouring the scent on the breeze that drifted towards him past Isak's shoulder. At the back of his mind, something stirred.

"He's mine," Isak said simply. He watched the Aspect's dead eyes for any sign of emotion, but there was nothing.

"Give him to me," the Soldier repeated. "His soul is forfeit to Lord Death. We have hunted him for millennia, and no whelp will deny me this prize." The Aspect looked past Isak, at the terrified soldiers behind him. A thin smile appeared on its lips. "Give him to me or they will all die."

Isak felt a rising surge of anger, and a sudden contempt. *Showing your hand so easily? Threatening them just shows me you're afraid, otherwise why would you bother? You really are nothing more than Death's cruel shadow, and you're frightened of me.*

"They will not die and nor will I give you my chained dragon. You have done my bidding here, and just as I summoned you, I now dismiss you. Your services are no longer needed."

"I am your God," the Aspect hissed, "and you do not dismiss me."

"My God?" Isak echoed.

He took a step forward and carefully removed his helm and hood. There was nothing he needed to hide. The Soldier stayed still.

"Nartis is my God, and like the one you serve, he does not command me. He made me; he gave me my strength and my gifts, but that doesn't mean he owns me. With these gifts I act as I see fit, and that includes wielding weapons against enemies, of which the Reapers were not the first."

"Do you think you can deny me?" The Soldier's fury was obvious now, which only confirmed Isak's hunch. "I am a part of you; I am the incarnation of a white-eye's anger—"

"Then you are a part of me," Isak snapped, "but you are not all that I am, and I command the anger inside me. My soul may be stained, I may have been born a creature of anger, but I will not let that make me a monster like you and yours."

Carefully, deliberately, Isak sheathed Eolis and touched his fingers to his chest. "I gave you the power to be here," he said in a controlled voice. His fingers warmed as they rested on the Skull, the magic within a living thing. "And that power is mine to retrieve when I choose."

With a thought Isak took hold of the energy gushing out from the Skulls into the plaza beyond. The magic kicked and writhed under his grip, desperate to keep flowing, and for a moment he wondered if he was strong enough to control that vast stream of power. Could he dam it so that these monsters could no longer feed from it? His self-doubt disappeared in a flash as he realised Aryn Bwr was there, guiding his movements. He could feel the last king's desperation to escape that cruel, hungry gaze and allowed the dead spirit to steer his thoughts and cut the flow as easily as drawing a curtain.

To his immense satisfaction, Isak saw a flicker of surprise cross the Soldier's face, then the Aspect vanished, leaving only a set of bloody boot prints on the stone ground. In the distance he sensed the other Reapers also disappearing from the city. A smile almost crossed his face, but he caught it in time and made sure he was expressionless when he turned back to the living soldiers outside the temple.

He could see no personal consequence of summoning the Reapers; it hadn't marked his skin, like calling the storm had . . . but the dead lay in every direction. This was neither the place nor the time to feel pleased with himself.

Crossing the trench once more, he was greeted with awe-struck relief. Vesna and Jachen wore smiles, but Isak didn't need to hear them speak to know the smiles were forced. They'd just watched him face down the Reapers; it was too early for either to feel anything more than astonishment that they were still alive.

"My Lord," Vesna croaked, "you continue to amaze me."

"Didn't expect that, eh?" Isak coughed, the exhaustion of the evening's fighting catching up with him.

"Could *anyone* have expected that?" Jachen wondered. He had already removed his helm and now he started on his hauberk. His face was covered with sweat, his hair plastered flat.

"You'll get used to it," Isak said with a smile, and made his way to the temple steps where he sank gratefully down.

"Are you well?" Vesna asked cautiously.

"Just tired—and thirsty, now that I think of it."

The words were hardly out of his mouth before Vesna was shouting orders and what remained of the Farlan cavalry staggered for the horses still cowering in the forest of pillars of the Temple of Nartis. The animals had been ignored by both the mobs and the Reapers and though they were still unsettled by the stench of blood and guts, they were unharmed. It wasn't long before the first of the cavalry were heading towards the Temple of Vasle, where the waters still ran. If any of the Devoted objected to the sacrilege, they had the good sense to keep quiet.

The rest of the soldiers had dropped to the ground too, following their lord's lead. Vesna opened his mouth to bawl them upright again, but found himself sinking down almost without thought. Soon all the survivors were sprawled on the ground where just a short time before they'd expected to be ripped to pieces by the ravening hordes. None of them had the strength to speak. Those with pipes intact fumbled with tobacco pouches, sharing with those who had none. A scar-faced man with greying hair found it too much effort to walk the few paces back after lighting his pipe from the torch at the entrance of the temple, slumping instead on the steps a few feet from Isak. He started to puff away, then, almost shyly, offered the pipe to Isak.

The tobacco was typical soldier's rubbish; foul, black and bitter, and under normal circumstances Isak would have cursed at the evil taste, but these were not normal circumstances and he found himself almost moaning with pleasure. If it took away the stench of the dead, of blood and shit and his own rank sweat, even for a few brief moments, then it was a blessing worthy of the temples they had defended.

For these few hundred souls sitting before the Temple of Death, amidst a slaughter the like of which none had ever seen before, the scent of bitter tobacco on the breeze would, for the rest of their lives, remain with them as something blessed.

After a few minutes, they heard a sound in the distance. Heads all around were raised as they recognised shod hooves on cobbles. Somehow, after all the chaos surrounding them, it contrived to sound neat and ordered.

"That'll be General Lahk, then," Isak muttered. He looked around; no one else seemed to be interested in getting up either. Vesna grunted in acknowledgement, but beyond that, none of them cared. Isak reached for the pipe again, nodding his thanks at the soldier, and looked out over the devastation of The Temple Plaza. So many dead—and he wasn't even sure why. He'd been lured to this city for what, for this? Was he merely a complication while Azaer settled a score with King Emin? But no, that couldn't be right, because the traitorous King's Man, Ilumene, had tried to lure him there . . . unless that had been a bluff? Isak put his head in his hands; the effort of thinking was beyond him. All he knew was that any scores of his own had been settled, one way or another, and now he wanted to go home. There were problems enough there and he wanted no more of Scree.

Someone called his name and he forced his head up to see General Chotech walking unsteadily towards him. The general was bloodied and bruised, but his great axe rested still across his shoulders and in true Chetse fashion he paid no mind to his obvious injuries as he advanced.

"Before your army gets here, I would beg an indulgence," he said when he reached Isak.

Isak frowned at the man. "If you want to ask me something, I warn you I'm not in a charitable mood."

That produced a few half-hearted laughs from the watching soldiers, but the general gravely took him at his word. "I ask nothing more than for you to join me in prayer."

For once, Isak was thankful he was too tired to burst out laughing, for the general would have taken it sorely amiss. Instead he gave the man a level look. "Pray? To . . . to Death? After what we've just witnessed?"

"We have survived," Chotech replied. "We have survived when the odds were against us. Death's warlike Aspects saved us, and I intend to give thanks."

Isak opened his mouth to argue, but could think of no valid reason not to. On the face of it, the general was right and, like it or not, Isak was a lord in the service of the Gods. The notion alternately sickened and amused the white-eye, whose lack of piety had always been obvious, but it was not his intention to lead the Farlan away from the Gods. Those who did such things invariably suffered for their presumption.

He nodded dumbly to General Chotech and struggled to his feet, raising a hand to stop Major Jachen jumping up to help him. Side by side with the ageing Knight of the Temples, Isak ascended the remaining two steps and began to walk down the main aisle towards the obsidian block of the high altar.

Their footsteps echoed around the empty building, the sound rising up to the thick black rafters above where more drapes hung undisturbed by the breeze outside. The floor was uneven and Isak, looking down to avoid missing his step, realised each huge flagstone was actually a tombstone, carved to record the names and final prayers of those whose ashes were contained in urns buried underneath the floor.

Isak suddenly remembered the time he'd been taken to the Temple of Death as a child, when the notion of walking over the dead had terrified him. Now he found it strangely comforting that their presence remained for eternity in this place of calm and reflection. The hoofbeats became louder behind him, making Isak smile in the darkness. His friends had reached the Temple Plaza; they would surround him soon enough.

As they reached the altar and Isak slid his shield from his arm, he caught a blur of movement out the corner of his eyes. He had half-turned when something smashed across his chest and glanced off his breastplate. The impact drove him back against the altar, and his arms were momentarily pinned. Unable to reach for Eolis, he kicked out at a dark shape, which roared and fell against the general, twisting as it did so to punch hard into Chotech's gut. The general gave a sharp gasp and doubled over.

The attacker pulled away and in the faint light Isak saw a long blade, and felt a hot line of blood spurt across his cheek. Chotech collapsed, his legs twitching weakly, and Isak knew the man was dead.

In the darkness he couldn't make out much of their attacker, but what detail he could see was enough: a blade in each hand, a deformed, bony head, a single horn extending backwards. No human looked like that . . . the memory of Lord Chalat appeared in his mind. Hadn't the Chetse white-eye fought something like this when he'd interrogated Mihn in the Temple of the Sun? A soldier possessed by a daemon.

He launched himself forward and smashed an armoured elbow into its face before bringing his knee up to its groin. He was much larger than his foe, which stood no taller than a normal Farlan, but as it hit the ground and bounced up, Isak realised it was just as fast as he was, and it was unnaturally strong.

The attacker flew forward again; Isak caught the creature by the wrists and spun around to throw it, but somehow the creature whipped around and slammed both heels into his stomach. Isak felt a sharp pain and realised it had spiked feet. He winced as he flung the creature against the high stone altar, and as it bounced straight back at him he brought down his fist, as hard as he could, on the side of its head. The blow slowed it down enough for Isak to draw Eolis. He let it come; he had its range and speed now.

The creature snarled and shook its mane of black fur, as if clearing its wits. It had bony growths instead of hands, the length of a long dagger; that was what had killed General Chotech.

There were footsteps, and voices behind them, but Isak knew help had come too late. The creature seemed to know it too, for it wasted no time in springing forward, daggers reaching for him. Isak stepped smartly to one side and caught its left arm. Eolis cut its wrist with ease and the creature fell to the tombstone floor, howling in pain. Isak lunged forward, intending to run it through and finish this, but somehow it sensed the blow coming and rolled aside, slashing wildly up towards his face. He dodged the dagger-hand and caught the creature's forearm with his left hand, twisting it upwards and back, feeling the elbow crunch and snap. It gave a shriek of pain, but Isak knew that as long as it was still standing, it was still dangerous.

He forced it around and slammed it against the altar again, then pulled his sword back to deal the final blow. The creature pushed itself upright, the arm Isak had just broken hanging crooked and useless.

"Isak, no!" screamed a voice behind him and he caught a glimpse of Tila sprinting towards him, Jachen and Vesna on her heels. She looked terrified, but before she could say any more Isak turned back and lashed out with a foot, kicking its legs away again. The blow spun the creature off-balance and it smashed the bony ridges of its head on the altar steps as the ring of metal on metal pealed out through the temple.

The Land went quiet; the running feet behind him were dulled. Isak hesitated. *Metal?* He levelled his blade and took another look. He'd kicked the creature in the side of its knee, where he now saw a rough steel brace had been fitted over its trouser. His sword wavered as the creature writhed in agony and he caught sight of its twisted face. Inside his mind, Aryn Bwr spoke words he didn't recognise, and the Crystal Skull on his chest pulsed briefly.

Another blur of movement as an indistinct shadow was torn away from the creature, and a howl of fury rang out to the black-stained rafters. Isak ignored it. The creature howled, but this time it was a human sound, of fear and pain. Eolis fell from Isak's hand as he took a closer look at the man at his feet.

"Father?"

ENDGAME

A RELUCTANT SUN ROSE ABOVE THE HORIZON and began its slow climb through the cloudless skies above what had once been known as the city of Scree. The dawn light illuminated a dead place, scarred by the hand of man and now almost bereft of life. Here there was no rich warble of birds, just the occasional *zip* of jewel-winged beetles and darting dragonflies, and the sharp hum of less harmless insects. The city was once a warren of cramped houses with ramshackle eateries on every corner, a place where extended families lived and ate together, gossiping and arguing all the while. Now there was an unnatural quiet, broken only by the faint sigh of ash shifted by a listless breeze, and the occasional crack or crash as one of the few remaining walls fell.

The firestorm had scoured the city of anything larger, consuming the southern part with a quick and savage hunger, and burning out to leave this devastated wasteland of smoking pyres and vast mounds of rubble. In the north, a few isolated fires smouldered on. Throughout Scree the stones on the ground were still hot enough to cook on, radiating heat like a thousand ovens.

When two silent figures set out through this desolate landscape, it was the blistered ground that scorched their skin, rather than Tsatach's yellow eye. They covered the ground quickly, even the bulkier of the two, who was clad in armour. His companion wore only a black patchwork tunic and trousers, and would have looked like an ordinary traveller, were it not for the swords sheathed across his back. His face was smooth and pale where the skin wasn't tattooed, while his larger companion displayed a lifetime's accumulation of scars on his weathered skin. The strange pair walked silently, with purpose, though no casual watcher would have been able to fathom what that purpose might be. They appeared to know their route, despite the lack of discernible landmarks, almost as if a voice were whispering directions in their ear.

Once in a while Ilumene, the larger man, would pause and turn to look back. Trailing a hundred yards or so behind, like an errant child, was another figure, obviously suffering greatly from the growing heat of day. He had a sheet loosely wrapped around his head and body in a feeble attempt to protect himself from the sun. Dark, bloody scabs had formed on his exposed face, and his hands were a mass of red blisters. He held them turned inwards, trying to protect his palms, but when he tripped instinct caught him off-guard and using his hands to break his fall left him whimpering in agony. Neither Ilumene nor his companion, Venn, waited to help him. Ilumene contented himself with ensuring their follower was still within sight; beyond that they appeared not to care about him in the slightest, keeping a good distance away so they were not bothered by the sounds of his laboured breathing or cries of pain.

Almost half an hour after the first rays of dawn had touched the treetops, Ilumene decided they had arrived at their destination. The only difference to the rest of the city that anyone might have noticed was the increase in the number of charred bodies lying around. He and Venn stopped and watched the progress of the tattered man.

Jackdaw, panting hard, stopped before he reached them, pushing the now-filthy sheet back from his head for a moment to mop the sweat from his face. His pale face was emaciated; even the midnight-black feather tattoos on his cheek contrived to look ragged and crumpled after his time in Scree.

Jackdaw hesitated when he reached them, looking fearfully from one to the other as though worried about how they would react to his presence. Ilumene gave a snort and tossed the man a half-full waterskin. Jackdaw took it gratefully, sucking down long gulps until he caught the scarred soldier's stare. He handed it back quickly.

Ilumene allowed himself a mouthful and hung the waterskin back around his neck, then made his way into the wreckage of a building. Jackdaw looked past him at the bodies, many burned beyond recognition. He paused as he stared at the nearest corpse, a man lying at rest, his hands folded at his throat as though laid out for burial. It was a strangely peaceful sight, especially when compared with the charred heap of long, strangely distorted limbs and hooked talons a few feet away. Ilumene walked up to it and gave the massive body a kick, knocking off some blackened lumps of some unidentifiable material. Whatever it might have been, it wasn't human.

"Was that his Aspect-Guide?" asked Jackdaw breathlessly as Ilumene cursed and tried to shake the mess from his boot.

"Unless you think it likely some other beast this size wandered into the city last night," growled Venn.

Jackdaw didn't reply, afraid of saying anything that might antagonise either of the other two men. They kicked and beat him whenever they pleased, and the mage had been too frightened to do anything in return to Rojak's favoured sons. He stood now with his eyes on the ground, shoulders slumped, looking for all the world like a skeleton hung on a peg.

Ilumene moved through the rubble where the house had once stood, dragged aside a long, blackened timber and kicked chipped slate tiles and other debris out of the way until he found what he was looking for. Jackdaw surreptitiously leaned to one side to get a better look until something snapped under his heel, drawing furious looks that made him scramble back, biting his lip to stop the gabbling apologies that so infuriated them.

Illumine finished glaring at Jackdaw and descended the handful of steps he'd uncovered. A battered wooden door at the bottom wouldn't budge until he kicked it hard, splitting it enough for him to be able to smash through the rusted iron hinges with a lump of stone. Jackdaw didn't need to see Ilumene's face to know how much he was enjoying himself; the former King's Man took an almost childish pleasure in destruction, anything that could break, anything that could bruise.

"What are we looking for?" Jackdaw muttered.

Ilumene said nothing as he ducked his head under the sagging lintel and disappeared from view. Jackdaw allowed a few minutes to pass before he sighed, cleared a space on the nearest flat piece of ground and eased himself down. Venn stared at him for a moment, then stepped up onto the broken door and positioned himself so he could see both Jackdaw and the steps.

They waited in silence. Venn looked off to the northern horizon where he'd once said his home was located, then, murmuring something under his breath, he balanced himself on one foot, keeping remarkably still without any apparent effort. He glared disdainfully at the twitching figure in a ragged sheet.

Jackdaw ignored him, staring morosely at the patch of dirt at his feet.

After a while Ilumene's voice echoed out through the doorway and Jackdaw, grimacing, clambered to his feet. Astonishingly, Ilumene was guiding out a large woman with long, straggly grey hair and a bewildered look in her eyes. Jackdaw could see she had a powerful body underneath her torn and damaged leather armour, and a younger face than her hair-colour indicated. Her solid frame surprised Jackdaw, most people in the city had become gaunt and emaciated after the weeks of chaos. This woman showed no ill-effects of the minstrel's magic, but he could see a dozen more mundane injuries, both recent and half-healed. One eye was half-closed by a long grazed bruise down the side of her head. She was hugging something close, a book, maybe, wrapped in cloth.

"It's all over now, you're safe," Ilumene was saying soothingly. Jackdaw almost convulsed in surprise, at the man's tone as much as anything. Ilumene sounded as kind and reassuring as the monks in Vellern's monastery—until now he'd never known the man from Narkang to be even civil to anyone but the minstrel. He wanted to warn the woman to not be such a fool, to scream at her to run, not to trust whatever poisonous schemes Ilumene had in mind, but instead he looked down and said nothing, paralysed by his own cowardice. All he could do was bite his lip and hate himself a fraction more, if that were even possible.

"What happened here?" she murmured through cracked lips. She looked startled, blinking against the light and wary of the ruined Land she'd awakened to. Jackdaw saw incomprehension in her eyes and realised she didn't even know where she was.

"War, and the cruelty of Gods," Venn answered distantly, not even bothering to look at her. The woman shrank towards Ilumene when she heard the coldness in Venn's voice and he immediately put a comforting arm around her shoulders. She leaned gratefully into his body, bigger even than hers, not noticing the bloody lattice that covered the back of his hand.

"What happened here is nothing for you to worry about," Ilumene repeated. "It's all over now. A new dawn has come."

"Who are you?" she whispered. "How did you find me?"

"All that matters is that you're safe now," he said, stroking her hair.

The woman's face twisted. Jackdaw realised she was trying to smile at her rescuer. *Breath of Vellern, she's forgotten how to smile.*

"Can you tell me your name?"

The woman thought for a moment then blanched and shook her head.

"You've forgotten it?" Ilumene asked, adding comfortingly, "That's of no matter. We'll find you a new name; the most beautiful name there is." Ilumene sounded so benevolent Jackdaw could scarcely believe this was the same man who'd awakened him just before dawn by punching him in the face. He probed a tooth with his tongue; yes, it was still broken; it hadn't been a dream.

"Are you going to take me with you?" she asked uncertainly. It was strange to see such vulnerability from someone who looked as if she was a mercenary, but if she could not remember her own name, she doubtless had no memory of her years of fighting too. It looked to Jackdaw like Ilumene's brutal appearance was causing her to hesitate—*as it damn well should; run, you fool, run from him!*—but there was a hopeful innocence to her weathered and battered face. He could see she was desperate to believe any promise of protection against this blasted world in which she found herself.

"Of course we are," Ilumene replied, and then gestured towards the object she was still clutching to her stomach. "Come now, you have had a terrible time and you will be weak for a while yet. Would it not be easier if my friend carried your burden?"

The former Harlequin hadn't moved towards her, but he was watching her with rapacious intent.

She pulled the book closer to her chest and shook her head. The movement created a faint cloud of dust and Jackdaw realised her hair was not actually grey, just covered in ash. "It is mine," she whispered hoarsely.

"As you wish," Ilumene said gently, "but can you tell me what it is? So I know best how to help?"

"I—" The woman looked up at him for a moment then hunched protectively over the book. The wrapping had slipped a little, but still Jackdaw couldn't make out the words on it. He thought it looked unremarkable, just a plain leatherbound work like the dozens in the monastery library. "It's my treasure," the woman said finally.

"Treasure and ashes," Venn said suddenly.

She looked up fearfully as Ilumene chuckled beside her and brushed her sleeve, raising another cloud of dust. She coughed and spluttered, but never let go of the book.

The phrase banged around the inside of Jackdaw's head; had he heard it before? It sounded like the sort of hateful pronouncements Rojak had come out with from time to time; was this all still part of the minstrel's final plan?

"They were burned," she replied, holding out her fist. Jackdaw saw she was gripping a piece of scorched paper in it and he frowned: the cellar hadn't been touched by fire, so why had a book been burned? "All burned except this one," she went on, "all but my treasure."

Jackdaw's stomach tightened into a knot. Abbot Doren had fled with the monastery's books, as well as the Crystal Skull entrusted to their care. It looked as if the senile old bastard had tried to burn the books, as if they had been part of what they were after when the Skull of Ruling sat in his possession. He stopped. Had they?

Ilumene nodded as the woman opened her hand and let the remains inside flutter down to join the other ash at her feet. He cocked his head sideways so he could see the book's cover and made a small sound of approval.

Jackdaw couldn't stop himself this time. "This was all about a book?" he asked, incredulous. He squinted at the cover himself, and this time made out an embossed symbol, partly obscured by the girl's hand. There was a pair of entwined initials above it, a pair of Vs, maybe, indicating the book had belonged to a nobleman once.

"This is no mere book," Ilumene said, answering the question, much to Jackdaw's amazement. "This contains the writings of a madman."

"I betrayed my God for a book?" he asked in a daze.

"Indeed," Ilumene said with satisfaction, taking the lady's hand and starting to lead her away from the cellar steps, "a book—or a journal, to be precise: the journal of Vorizh Vukotic."

Now Ilumene was finally talking, Jackdaw was determined to find out as much as he could. "The vampire? But he's insane."

"Among other things," Ilumene conceded, "but does that not strike you as strange? He is a man cursed with sanity by Death himself, like his siblings, and yet, unlike his siblings, he goes insane. As a mage, tell me, what sort of power could overcome Death's own curse?"

Jackdaw looked blank. "What power? I know none, bar Death's own."

"There was a time," Venn said softly, "when creator and destroyer walked across the Land hand-in-hand, when they commanded the dust at their feet and the air above."

"Creator—you mean Life, Death's bride? But she died at the Last Battle, and Aenaris was buried with her. Not even with her sword could the Queen of the Go—" Jackdaw stopped abruptly, a look of horror sweeping across his face. He gaped at Ilumene, who gave him a broad smile in return.

Clutching his hands to his chest, Jackdaw wheezed, "*Death's* magic? *Death's own weapon?* But Termin Mystt was broken during the battle, it was destroyed . . ."

"Not exactly," Venn said, nodding towards the book as the woman, her eyes wide, clutched it even tighter. "Not at all, in fact, but history is written by the victors, who tell what they choose to tell."

"How can you, of all people, say that?" Jackdaw asked, still shaking. "You were a *Harlequin*, a teller of the past—a teller of the truth!"

"Exactly so," Venn replied, a nasty gleam in his eye, "and I tell you truthfully: Termin Mystt drove a Yeetatchen maid insane when she touched the hilt during a feast in Lord Death's honour. The Key of Magic is so powerful that it will twist the mind of anyone who touches it—and that was what drove Vorizh Vukotic mad. He stole the sword in desperation, trying to undo the curse on his family."

"You're hunting Termin Mystt," Jackdaw said dully, overwhelmed. "And this book will tell you where he hid it?" A small spark of anger flared inside him and he pointed at the woman holding the book. "What about her? Are you going to kill her to take the book from her?"

The woman gave a whimper of fear and shrank from Ilumene.

Jackdaw waited, shivering, for Ilumene to smash his fist into the woman's face, but the man from Narkang only laughed.

"But of course not," Ilumene said gently to the woman, "not when you're with child. I was sent to protect you both."

"A child? But how do you know?"

"It has been foreseen," Venn intoned, "and when your child is born, you will gift him your treasure."

"Him? It's a boy?" she asked. "I wanted a girl . . . I think I had a little girl, once—"

"A boy," Ilumene said with certainty, "and one who will grow to be a prince. He will build you a palace of ivory." He smiled at her, his arm around her shoulder, and urged her to start walking.

Her steps hesitant, she passed Jackdaw, who was still frozen with shock.

"A boy?" he echoed hoarsely. "A prince?"

"A new dawn, a new Land," Ilumene called cheerfully over his shoulder.

"Oh Gods," Jackdaw breathed as a cold presence swept over him.

"*Gods*," said the shadow softly, "*will soon have no place in this Land.*"

ACKNOWLEDGMENTS

HAVING HAD MORE THAN A FEW PEOPLE to thank regarding *Stormcaller*, I was determined here to simply write "screw everyone else; this was all down to me."

However, while that might apply for most of the text there's also the bigger picture of keeping me if not normal, then as close to it as is feasible— and that's been a collective effort worthy of recognition. My family can never be appreciated enough, and several others I must mention: Ian of the legendary feet, who put up with my evil side for longer than a normal person could; Liv, the honorary little sister who keeps me sane and amused at work; and Fi, who is simply unique in so many lovely and hilarious ways. The Davies boys do sterling work getting smacked around a court and then dragging me to the pub, while Phil, Vik and Vince all further encourage my bad habits. My readers also deserve thanks: Robin "I see dark things" Morero, my favourite brother Richard, and champion cynic-cum-proofreader, Heidi.

Lastly, there's one contribution that could only be described as above and beyond. I'm not sure anyone could be paying Jo Fletcher, editor extraordinaire, enough to spend so long reining in my fractured thought-processes and imposing some discipline on a deeply childish mind. It would certainly have broken the spirit of a lesser person and she must be racking up the good karma as a result.

ABOUT THE AUTHOR

TOM LLOYD was born in 1979 in Berkshire. After a degree in International Relations he went straight into publishing where he still works. He never received the memo about suitable jobs for writers and consequently has never been a kitchen-hand, hospital porter, pigeon hunter or secret agent. He lives in South London, isn't one of those authors who gives a damn about the history of the font used in his books and only believes in forms of exercise that allow him to hit something. Visit him online at www.tomlloyd.co.uk.